A BALLAD OF BELIEFS

John McCormick

ISBN 978-1-7398783-8-2

First Published 2022

Cover Art by RebelSqueak

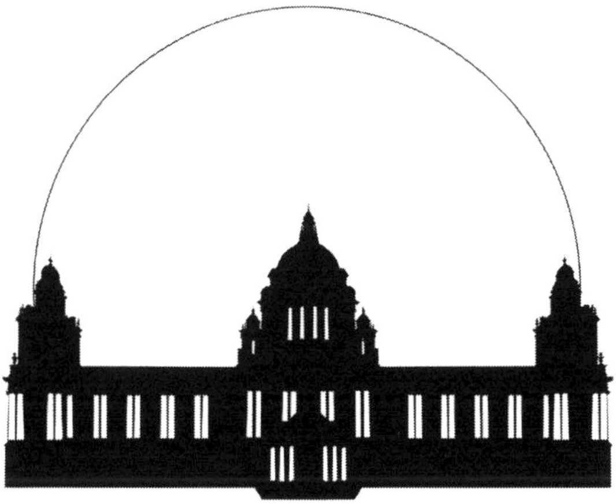

THE COMPLETE TRILOGY

In Memory of Justy

CONTENTS

INTRODUCTION

In May of 2010, the Ulster Museum in Belfast received a curious request from the then Minister for Culture, Arts and Leisure in the Northern Ireland Assembly - the Democratic Unionist Party's Nelson McCausland.

The Ulster Museum, though modest in comparison to many national museums around the world, was and remains one of Northern Ireland's most highly regarded educational institutions, with important collections in, amongst other things, archaeology, geology, art and natural history. It was with the natural history section, in particular, that Mr McCausland voiced his concerns.

If, as McCausland maintained, the majority of his constituents did not accept the scientific explanation for the diversity of life on Earth, then, he insisted, it was the responsibility of the museum to reflect this position by adjusting its exhibits accordingly. In place of the evolutionary theories that the museum promoted, McCausland suggested that the old Hebrew creation story, as depicted in Genesis, the first book of the Old Testament, should be adopted instead.

After a brief consideration, the museum decided to both respectfully deny the request, and to continue providing an explanation for the natural world's variety that was supported by evidence that had, after all, been accumulating for well over a century.

The Hebrew creation story is not unique. There exist, or have existed, from cultures all over the world, many hundreds of attempts to explain the universe; and many of these offer much more richly detailed and imaginative accounts than the story in Genesis. Presumably, then, the Ulster Museum would have felt on safer ground by simply sticking with the one account that enjoyed an overwhelming scientific consensus. The whole incident, though, provoked some questions.

The fact that someone in the DUP was showing an adherence to biblical literalism did not come as any great surprise - many DUP members were, and are, openly proud of their Christian fundamentalism - but the thing that struck me was McCausland's blithe assertion that most of his constituents shared his beliefs. Could this be true?

McCausland's constituency at the time was North Belfast, so his claim seemed to be that a large proportion of the people in north Belfast believed in the historical authenticity of the Adam and Eve story, and that it had taken place in the not very distant past. If this were true, then it must reflect rather badly, it seemed to me, on the education system of Northern Ireland. It seemed the tales that people were listening to in their church services were winning out over the formal education that they, hopefully, were receiving at school. Having grown up in north Belfast, I was a little sceptical of this view, although, to be fair to Mr

McCausland, the overwhelming variety of life on Earth, in my younger days, was not very often, if ever, discussed. It was feasible, then, that McCausland's claims were true.

An idea began to form. An idea for a story. A love story. The novel *Crawl* was born.

Although initially conceived as a one-off tale of star-crossed lovers, *Crawl* started sloping off into realms unintended, and, as supporting characters began demanding more of a voice, it became apparent that one book might not be enough. I know that sounds pretentious, and I squirm writing it, but it happens to be true; few of the characters in the narrative went the way I had originally planned, and on many occasions I reluctantly had to follow where they led. Therefore, for many people, *Crawl* ends just as the main plot is beginning, and so, when *Crawl* was completed, I had every intention of going back to the story in order to bring it to a satisfactory conclusion. At some point.

That point turned out to be almost ten years later. Going back to *Crawl* after so long, allowed me to see it as a rough early draft, and I felt it needed some polishing before I could fully commit to the second novel, which I had entitled *Rise*. A rewrite also gave me the opportunity to get a clear idea of where the story should go, and I was able to get straight into writing *Rise* as a direct continuation of *Crawl*. It didn't take long for me to realise the story would have to be a trilogy, and so, not long after I had completed *Rise*, I made a start on the third and final instalment: *Race*.

There have been many fictional works set in 'Troubles-era' Northern Ireland, but, in my experience at least, they tend to be sombre and serious and relentlessly bleak. They portray a shell-shocked population cowering under a blanket of fear and dank misery. A population afraid to smile. To laugh. To fall in love. They describe an environment where even sex is soulless and mechanical, where every hooded glance is pregnant with dark meaning and mistrust, and where every soul is tainted and warped by the *situation* that has seeped into all aspects of daily life. This may make for a more intense dramatic narrative - and the thirty years of the so-called Troubles were undeniably dark times - but I wanted to portray life as it was for the vast majority who had lived through those times. I wanted to show people just living their lives. Their stupid, funny and unpredictable lives.

One question I often get asked is *What are the books about?* and I am genuinely unsure as to what the answer should be. The nature of faith is certainly a main theme throughout the trilogy, while there are those who would cite the idea of friendship as a central topic - and, of course, it is, at heart, a simple love story - but perhaps if I had to give a one-word response then I would have to say *hope*. It is a story about hope. The fact that that *hope* may be misplaced and a little misguided at times, doesn't matter.

It is still hope.

John McCormick 2022

CRAWL

PROLOGUE

24th December 1989

A line of tall, craggy peaks looks south to see a line of high, green hills rolling back into the distance. In the valley, in between, a river opens up into a broad, salty estuary.

Clinging to the riverbanks and nestled snugly up against the hillsides, a city lies safe and protected, shielded on all sides by the mountains and by the sea.

A cosy place. A happy place.

Belfast.

"Their balls! Do you hear me, Michael? I want their balls!"

"Yes, love," he mumbled automatically as he slipped the pistol into his overcoat pocket.

"It could be one of my Christmas presents," she suggested, and then giggled at the thought.

"Yes, love," he repeated, only half-listening. He could do without this today, he thought. Today of all days. Walking to the front door he suddenly stopped and turned his head.

"I'm sorry," he said, "but what did you just say?"

"Four wee testicles on a plate," she answered, pouring herself another gin and tonic. "That's what I want for Christmas."

"Jesus!" he muttered to himself as he opened the front door and stepped out into the cold. "That'll look fucking lovely under the tree."

ONE

The pretty girls from the perfume counter at Boots were over in the corner, murdering the *Little Drummer Boy.* Behind the bar, a single strand of tinsel danced in the updraft of a microwave oven.

Pressed tight against the counter, Jamesy placed his first order of the day.

"A pint of Bass and a cheeseburger, please."

The barmaid – a slight, dark-haired girl – paused briefly before stepping back a few feet to shout through the open door of the kitchen for a cheeseburger. She then walked over to the pumps to pour the pint of Bass, all the while casting surreptitious glances in Jamesy's direction. Jamesy appeared to be unaware of her covert attention as he fought to keep his place at the crowded bar.

It was busier than a normal lunchtime and a lot noisier. The perfume-counter girls had just begun to grapple with *Frosty the Snowman* when Jamesy's pint was placed in front of him.

"Your food's on its way," the barmaid told him while staring into his eyes. Jamesy nodded and handed over a five-pound note. Taking it, the barmaid loudly informed the clamouring faces around the bar that they all needed to hold their effing horses. She then turned and, giving Jamesy a coy smile, walked over to the till. Jamesy took a sip of his beer as he waited for his change and his cheeseburger to arrive.

He was in the Tudor Lounge, the upstairs bar of Hannigan's, in the city centre. This was the place where it had begun all those years ago and the place that had been the traditional starting point ever since.

Despite the noise and the constant jostling of the boisterous clientele, Jamesy could feel himself start to relax as anticipation for the day ahead began to take hold.

He straightened up when his food arrived. The barmaid held out his change and, dropping the coins into his open palm, fixed Jamesy with what she felt was her most wanton gaze. Seemingly oblivious, Jamesy pocketed the money, picked up his beer and food, and pushed his way backwards through the crowd.

Men! the barmaid fumed before turning her attention to an elderly gentleman who was wearing a pointed red hat with a white fur trim.

"Okay, you!" she shouted. "Santa bloody Claus! What do *you* want?"

Jamesy made his way to where Sean and Joker were sitting. They had arrived earlier and had managed to acquire one end of a table by the door at the top of the stairs. A stern-faced woman, who was nursing an almost empty glass of stout, occupied the other end.

There was no room for Jamesy to sit, so he placed his drink on the table and stood beside Sean as he ate. Joker, having just finished his own cheeseburger, was raising his arms in a leisurely stretch.

"All right there, Jamesy?" he said. "All set to go, are you?"

Jamesy swallowed a mouthful of food and took a sip of beer to wash it down. "Of course," he replied. "I've been looking forward to it."

A tiny silver-haired man appeared and began gushing apologies to the stern-faced woman who simply nodded to the glass on the table before her. Getting the message, the man disappeared into the crowd in an attempt to force his way to the bar.

Joker lit a cigarette and, picking up his drink, took a casual glance around the bar. He could see, in the middle of the room, and just behind Jamesy, some smartly-dressed young men standing in a tight little group, riding the natural sway of the crowd. Joker watched them with some amusement as he could tell – from their awkward little looks and gestures – that they were building up the beer-fuelled confidence to make an approach on the perfume-counter girls. The girls, meanwhile, were trying to pin down *Rudolph the Red-Nosed Reindeer,* although Rudolph, gamely, was having none of it.

"Is Ding-a-Ling not with you?" Jamesy asked Joker who looked up and shook his head.

"Nah," he answered. "He stayed up at his ma's last night, but I'm sure he's on his way." He then knocked back the remainder of his drink and stood up.

"I'm going to the bar, are you two okay?" He gestured to Sean and Jamesy's glasses. Jamesy held up three-quarters of a pint in reply and Sean regarded his own half-filled glass.

"You never heard of pacing yourself?" Sean asked, looking up at Joker. "It's early days, you know."

"Pace myself?" Joker rubbed his hands and grinned at Sean. "What sort of talk is that?" He then turned and pushed his way into the throng, which set in motion little ripples through the crowd that spread out in all directions around the room.

"Joker's in good form, then?" Jamesy said as he took Joker's place at the table.

"Funny, isn't it?" Sean replied. "The prospect of a day-long drinking session really seems to perk him up."

The tiny, silver-haired man returned from the bar with a drink in either hand. He set the drinks on the table and manoeuvred himself into the empty chair that his wife had been saving. They both picked up their drinks and sipped silently, steeling themselves for a trip around the shops on the busiest day of the year.

Joker's height and physique made it easy for him to force his way through to the bar where the barmaid, unimpressed, made a cool appraisal.

"Right, Baldy!" She announced. "You can just wait your turn!"

Joker smiled. He loved Christmas Eve.

Back at the table, Jamesy had finished his food and was wiping ketchup from his mouth with a napkin. Glancing down he spotted a plastic carrier bag at Sean's feet.

"Have you all your shopping done already?" he asked.

"Not all of it, no," said Sean, "but I'm going to need a few drinks inside me before I hit the shops again."

"Yeah, I know what you mean," said Jamesy smiling. "It's already mental out there."

After a while, Joker reappeared with a pint in his hand. "Hard luck, lads!" he shouted over to the small group of smartly-dressed young men who were shuffling back to their original position in the middle of the room, having just received some caustic and unseasonal advice from the perfume-counter girls in the corner.

As Joker reached the table, he motioned for Jamesy to stay seated. "I'm alright standing, Jamesy," he said.

"We're going now, anyway, son," said the stern-faced woman as she and her husband got to their feet. "So there's a wee bit more room for you there."

Joker raised his glass in salute. "Cheers," he said, taking a seat. He gave his beer a long appreciative slurp before making an obvious show of looking at his watch.

"Right, then," he said, glowering around the table. "Where the fuck *is* everybody?"

TWO

A few miles north of the city centre lay a sprawling housing estate, made up mainly of small, terraced houses that ran in parallel rows down one side of a hill that rolled lazily towards the northern bank of the lough that Belfast embraced.

A large portion of the housing estate had been cordoned off, many years before, from the surrounding areas by high, ugly fences of corrugated iron which had been hastily erected by an exasperated British Army trying to keep the population of north Belfast from tearing itself apart.

These fences had sprouted up all over Northern Ireland and the 'Peace Lines', as they were christened, were deemed to be a temporary necessity as the differences between the nationalist and unionist communities became seemingly irreconcilable.

The housing estate in question was called Ardoyne, and its residents were mostly of the opinion that Ireland had been illegally split in two by the British Empire, and the sooner the two parts were reunited as an independent Irish Republic, the better.

The areas immediately surrounding Ardoyne were populated, to a large extent, by people who held a political outlook that differed from this opinion in a variety of ways – the main one being that Northern Ireland was part of the United Kingdom and any attempt to drag it out of the UK and into a united Ireland would be met with a stiff and spirited resistance.

The story of this small part of north Belfast was played out all over Northern Ireland, as communities of British Unionists jostled uncomfortably with communities of Irish Nationalists, leading occasionally – and inevitably – to disagreements that could often be quite heated.

None of this, however, was of any real concern to one resident of Ardoyne as he stood, shivering slightly in the cold, outside the Crumlin Star Social Club.

Snatter had his own problems to worry about but, for today at least, he would try to dwell on them as little as possible. Today was not a day for indulging in any form of self-pity, although, he noted grimly, not dwelling on his troubles was proving more difficult than he had thought.

Still, he decided, a few beers and a lively bit of craic should help matters. He looked at his watch which told him that his ride to a slender distraction from reality was but moments away.

The previous day, Ding-a-Ling had phoned Snatter to tell him that he had arranged a lift for them both with Harry, Ding-a-Ling's brother-in-law, and they would pick him up from outside the Star at eleven. As Snatter watched the second hand tick past the hour, he looked back on the few occasions he had met Harry and realised that, apart from the obvious physical aspect of the man, he did not know him very well at all.

He knew Harry to see, of course, and would always nod or say hello whenever he saw him around the district, but they never mixed in any social way, so, for Snatter, Harry was something of an unknown quantity.

He had heard some unsettling stories about Harry, but in an insular community like Ardoyne, rumours, gossip and Chinese whispers were rife and so Snatter had put the more outlandish tales down to exaggeration.

There were the nicknames as well, though; things like 'Scary Harry' or 'Mad Dog', but Snatter reckoned they were nothing more than a knee-jerk reaction to Harry's size.

For Harry was enormous.

He was not overweight or anything like that; just enormous. Enormous both up and down and from side to side. Brick shithouses, mused Snatter, could only aspire to be built like Harry.

Still, he thought, once you got past the intimidating physical presence, then Harry seemed to be fairly quiet and unassuming.

Just people judging books by covers he decided as an old white Transit van pulled up in front of him.

Ding-a-Ling jumped down from the passenger seat and held the door open.

"You jump on up into the middle there, Snatter," he said. Snatter did so and, as Ding-a-Ling climbed in beside him, they drove off.

"Cheers for the lift, Harry," said Snatter as he realised that Harry was even bigger than he had remembered. Harry simply turned to him and nodded.

A man of few words, Snatter thought quietly. *Or indeed*, he thought much more quietly, *a man of fuck-all words*.

"Should be a good one this year, eh Snatter?" said Ding-a-Ling, making Snatter jump.

"Um, yeah, I can't wait. Been a while since we've all been out together. Have you spoken to Tone lately?"

"Yeah, he phoned the flat last week, making sure we're all still up for it." Ding-a-Ling grinned. "Tone does make me laugh when he's had a few."

Snatter smiled. "He can be overly verbose, I suppose."

"Nah," said Ding-a-Ling, "he just comes across as a wee bit gay, you know? All that fancy, lah-di-dah … what's the word?"

"Verbosity?"

Ding-a-Ling laughed. "Aye, okay," he said. "For want of a smaller word."

"What about Joker? How's *he* doing?"

"Oh, you know what he's like," said Ding-a-Ling, "absolutely hyper as fuck the last couple of days."

"Mmm …" Snatter was barely listening.

"Did you hear he wants me to go over to Ibrox with him in the New Year?"

Snatter turned to face his friend. "Really?" he said. "That should be an experience."

The van turned onto Ardoyne Road which led down to one of the main arteries into the city centre. Harry frowned as he looked ahead at the frenzy of traffic rushing past, and readied himself for a blend of some aggression and blind hope to force his van into the unceasing flow.

Ding-a-Ling was unusually quiet as if suddenly unsure of his next words.

"You know … um … Rosie was …" he seemed hesitant. Snatter's head snapped round to face him.

"Rosie was *what*?" he asked, the pitch of his voice rising slightly.

"Well, apparently, she was round our Karen's last night and –"

"Why?" Snatter almost shouted.

"What the fuck do you mean *why*?" Ding-a-Ling was taken aback. "You know they're old mates, don't you? They went to Holy Cross together and they –"

"I know, I know, okay! Jesus! I just meant … well … what's your point, anyway?"

"Well," said Ding-a-Ling, no longer tongue-tied, "from what our Karen was saying, it seems that Rosie is expecting you to be round at her sister's all day today. Some sort of family thing … I don't know, I was just wondering if anybody had bothered to tell you, that's all."

Karen was Ding-a-Ling's sister and Harry's wife; a fact which caught the attention of Snatter's sudden flood of thoughts.

So different was Karen, he pondered, from Harry. Where one was huge and lumbering, the other was petite and delicate. Where one was quiet and undemonstrative, the other was a loud and shrieking harridan … Snatter realised his mind was deliberately trying to ignore the matter in hand. He turned to Ding-a-Ling.

"What did Karen say to her?"

Ding-a-Ling looked through the window at the passing shops as he considered his reply. This, he reckoned, was one of those rare occasions when the truth could be used as an acceptable answer.

"I think she might have said that she thought you were going into town with me today"

"Shit!" said Snatter unhappily. "What do you mean, you *think*?"

Ding-a-Ling thought about this. "Actually, not so much *think* as *know* because she told me that's what she said. Although, to be fair, she did tell Rosie that she may have got it wrong. Fuck, it wouldn't be the first time, eh Harry?

"How did Rosie take it? Did Karen say?"

Right, thought Ding-a-Ling, *that's quite enough of this truth nonsense for one day.*

"Aye, she was dead on about it," he said. "Absolutely dead on."

As Harry gunned the van into the main traffic flow, a smaller van with *Royal Mail* emblazoned along the side was pulling into a lay-by a little way down the road. The lay-by was cut into a wide pedestrian area that fronted a variety of local shops – one of which was the Ardoyne Post Office.

On this occasion – and despite the traditional IRA Christmas cease-fire – the Royal Mail was being escorted by the British Army. A dark green army Land Rover pulled in behind the mail van and four soldiers jumped from the back to secure the area.

The shopping precinct was busy with crowds of people doing some last-minute Christmas shopping, chatting with friends and neighbours, exchanging festive greetings and ignoring the soldiers who were keeping the Royal Mail safe from harm.

One of the soldiers, keen to do his duty to its full extent, had spotted a potential threat to his current mission. Moving traffic, it seemed, posed an unacceptable security risk. A risk that the soldier took upon himself to neutralise. He stepped into the road and, with calm authority, raised his hand.

The driver of a small blue Vauxhall, directly in front of Harry's van, braked hard and managed to skid to a halt just a few feet from the, now slightly nervous, soldier.

Harry also slammed on his brakes but was a fraction too late. The van slid with sickening force into the back of the Vauxhall, causing several people who were milling around the shops to turn and look, alerted by the particular sounds of an automotive collision.

There was the bang and crunch of crumpling metal, the pop of a headlight bursting, the tinkling of broken glass dropping onto tarmac, and the soft crack of Snatter's forehead striking the inside of the van's windscreen.

Ding-a-Ling, sitting on the outside seat, which was fitted with a seatbelt, had felt no more than a violent jolt and was able, therefore, to observe the subsequent sequence of events.

He watched the Vauxhall driver, a balding, middle-aged man, leap angrily from his vehicle to confront the stupid asshole who had gone into the back of him. He watched the driver's face drain suddenly of colour as Harry stepped calmly from the van. He watched the driver turn in a panic and point furiously at the soldier who still stood in the middle of the road.

"It was him, mister!" the driver shouted, "It was his fault!"

Ding-a-Ling was then able to observe Harry stride purposely past the cowering driver towards the horrified soldier and, with barely a pause, smash his forehead into the soldier's nose, which erupted in a spray of blood.

"Fuck!" said Ding-a-Ling, stating the obvious.

"What's happening?" a dazed Snatter, folded over in the passenger footwell, managed to mumble.

"Shit, Snatter, are you okay?"

"I don't know… I can't fucking see!"

Probably not a bad thing, thought Ding-a-Ling, looking through the windscreen.

"I think you'll be all right," he said reassuringly. "Try lifting your face off the floor, see if that helps."

Ding-a-Ling turned his attention to what was going on outside on the road and saw that events had moved on. The traffic-directing soldier was now rolling on the ground, clutching not only his nose, but also his groin which, Ding-a-Ling assumed, had received some attention from Harry following the brutal head-butt.

Harry himself now appeared to be spinning groggily around in the road with two soldiers hanging desperately from his neck, while the fourth soldier was pointing his rifle at the Vauxhall driver and yelling something that Ding-a-Ling couldn't quite make out. The terrified driver, with tears in his eyes, had his arms at full stretch above his head, but seemed to be trying to get his hands to go even higher.

A crowd had gathered.

Snatter managed to pull himself back into his seat, though he didn't feel entirely conscious, with his vision blurring in interesting and alarming ways.

"You all right?" asked Ding-a-Ling.

"Not sure. I … um … what's happening? Where's Harry?"

"I think we may as well go and get the bus," Ding-a-Ling told him. "Harry's busy."

By now the driver of the blue Vauxhall, still facing the scary end of an automatic rifle being held by a panicked British soldier, was almost sobbing.

"Don't shoot!" he cried. "I'm just a caretaker, I'm a school caretaker!"

This did not help matters much, as the soldier, who was called Bert, and hailed from Gateshead in the north of England, was suffering from the same problem that afflicted most soldiers when they first arrived in Northern Ireland: a feeling of complete bafflement.

The problem was that the average soldier is not designed to process nuanced concepts or subtle geo-political complexities. In fact, the job of a soldier, when stripped down to its bare essentials, is straightforward: kill the enemy.

Of course, a soldier will have a multitude of other tasks to perform during a military career and, more often than not, will never once arrive at a situation where he is required to fulfil his primary function. But that is not to deny the fact that the principal motivation for the basic soldier is a simple one: kill the enemy.

For this reason, the people who are responsible for running the army have little interest in recruiting those who see themselves as free spirits or independent thinkers.

The private soldier throughout history has been dismissed as anything from *cannon-fodder* to a simple *grunt*, and is considered to operate most effectively in situations that are starkly and recognisably black and white.

Bert was, by no means, a stupid person but no one would ever accuse him of being encumbered with a vibrant imagination. He was perfectly content to follow orders from dawn till dusk and then pour fifteen pints of lager down his throat when he was off duty with his mates. It was a simple life, but that, for Bert, was its appeal. Simplicity was security. It was undemanding, it was worry-free and familiar, comforting and safe, and Bert was happy in its cosy embrace.

And then there was Northern Ireland.

How could there be so many factions in such a tiny place? There were factions within factions within factions. There were factions that split from factions only to merge and be absorbed into other factions. It was like a constantly writhing, twisting, morphing, crazed octopus with an endless supply of titles, subtitles, headings, slang, nicknames, pen-names, acronyms, codenames and buzzwords.

You had the INLA, the UVF, the IRA, the PIRA, the UFF and the UDA. There was the Third Force, the Stickies, the ODCs, Sinn Fein, the DUP, the OUP, the United Republican Apprentice Freedom Boys of Ulster and the Popular People's Front of Judea. It was a fucking nightmare.

From one day to the next, Bert could never quite work out just who he was supposed to shoot, so when someone started yelling the word *caretaker* at him, he frantically tried to remember some of his daily briefings, and whether *caretaker* had been mentioned as some sort of codeword.

He had just about convinced himself that he had single-handedly captured the IRA's commander in north Belfast when he spotted movement from the corner of his eye.

As Ding-a-Ling was trying to force open the passenger door of the van, a fifth soldier pushed open the door of the army Land Rover and stepped nervously into the road.

Having radioed for back-up, he had been debating with himself whether he should join the fray, or whether he should just sit, nice and safe and quiet, and wait for reinforcements. Eventually, though, he was forced to admit he had little choice but to get involved and so, reluctantly, and cursing his life, he approached the frenetic little whirlwind that had Harry at its heart. He had chosen exactly the wrong moment.

Harry, still mourning the loss of his van and raging against the two soldiers who were grappling in desperation with his bulk and seething energy, managed to free his left arm just as the Land Rover driver cleared his throat to issue commands that, he hoped, would be delivered in a loud, clear and authoritative voice.

A voice that would demand attention and would brook absolutely no insubordin… Harry's fist caught him on the side of his jaw – which dislocated with a loud pop – and sent him, in a horizontal fashion, into the moving traffic on the other side of the road.

There was a ripple of appreciative applause from those in the crowd who could recognise a perfectly executed left hook, and there was a collective *oooh* from those who followed the trajectory of the unconscious soldier as he sailed through the air.

Jim 'Jimbo' Evans was feeling pleased with himself. He had dragged himself out of bed at an unheard-of early hour and had driven into town just as the shops were opening.

He had thus been able to complete all of his last-minute shopping tasks in a leisurely and organised manner and was now driving home to Ligoniel, in the far north of the city, smugly anticipating the rest of his Christmas Eve to be relaxing and stress-free.

As he approached the parade of shops at Ardoyne, Jimbo could see some sort of commotion happening up ahead.

Typical, he mumbled to himself. *Those head-the-balls from Ardoyne are always getting up to some sort of mischief. Shocking, so it is. Just shocking!* He slowed to a crawl in order to get a better look, when, suddenly, a large green object landed heavily on the bonnet of his car. Jimbo screamed and braked as his windscreen burst in on itself and the large green object slid slowly forward onto the road.

"Harry?" Ding-A-Ling called out. "Me and Snatter are just going to go and get the bus, if that's okay." He was having trouble attracting Harry's attention, but Bert, his nerves stretched, was alert to this new development and swivelled his weapon around to meet it.

"Hands up!" he shouted. "Get your hands up!"

"What?" said Ding-a-Ling. With Snatter swaying gently by his side, he seemed genuinely affronted. "What are you talking about?"

Ever since Bert had been deployed to Northern Ireland, he had been hearing all kinds of conflicting messages. He had even been told on a number of occasions that he wasn't *technically* allowed to shoot *anyone*.

It's not as if we're at war, he was told by those who were supposed to know about these things, but that, in Bert's mind, did not clear things up at all. He was certainly dressed for a war – albeit a war that was set in a forest – and he had all the equipment that was deemed necessary for carrying out a war type of situation but, for some reason, it seemed that his role was to keep the peace.

Peace? That was the exact opposite of war and something that, so far as Bert understood things, no self-respecting soldier should have anything to do with. It was all too confusing, and Bert was not a man who enjoyed conundrums. How much more straightforward it would be, he bemoaned, if he could just shoot someone. How much easier it would be if his superiors could just point to someone and say, *There you go, lad, there's your enemy. Now go fill your boots!*

Not shooting someone, after all the training he had received, seemed to Bert, a terrible waste of the army's time and resources. Not that Bert was the bloodthirsty type, but if the army had gone to all that trouble to turn him into a killing machine, then it would be churlish to appear coy when it mattered. So, Bert had no innate desire to shoot anyone, but if he had to – if he absolutely *had* to – then the condescending arsehole standing in front of him would be the first to go.

The condescending arsehole in question was trying to explain.

"No, it's okay," said Ding-a-Ling. He gestured to Snatter who was swaying from side to side and didn't appear to know where he was.

"Me and him," Ding-a-Ling continued, "were just getting a lift. We're just a couple of passengers and we –"

Now Bert had never been entirely convinced about his theory on the word *caretaker,* but he was sure that *passenger* was a codeword.

Passengers? Weren't they the baby-killing bastards who planted bombs on trains and buses?

"Fucking hands up now!" he yelled.

In a moment of clarity Snatter realised he was staring down the barrel of a rifle and instinctively threw his hands into the air. This turned out to be a cure for his semi-consciousness.

He fainted.

THREE

Bobby's face was arranged in such a way as to make him appear cheerful all of the time. His eyes had a constant sparkle while the corners of his mouth were naturally upturned, even in repose. It was a face that was open and honest and happy. A smiley face. A face that stood in stark contrast to the face that suddenly appeared behind his left shoulder.

This face was a lot more sinister. With sunken cheeks and hooded eyes, and with a scarf covering its lower half, this was a face of menace, the face of a predator.

Bobby felt something hard dig into his ribs as a voice hissed in his ear.

"Just keep walking, you Orange bastard!"

Bobby kept walking. He was in Queen's Arcade, in the city centre, making his way along the enclosed alleyway of shops, and heading for the Tudor Lounge. His pace didn't change and his face remained impassively cheerful. He turned his head, very slightly, to the left.

"All right there, Tone?" he said. "I hope those fingers aren't loaded."

Tone took his hand away from Bobby's back and plunged it into his coat pocket.

"Yeah, Bobby," he said, "you can act as cool as you want, but you can't fool me. The shite was flying out of you there, wasn't it?"

"Okay," Bobby sighed, "you really had me going there."

The Arcade was packed with shoppers making it difficult for the two friends to walk abreast so Tone remained a step behind, and to Bobby's left.

"We're running a wee bit late, aren't we?" Tone remarked. "I thought you would have travelled in with Sean."

"Sean was up and out a bit too early for me."

"Shopping?"

"Yeah," said Bobby. "I could do with doing some as well a bit later on. If I remember, that is."

"Makes two of us."

They reached the end of Queen's Arcade, and Tone was able to fall into step beside Bobby.

"I'd say we're the last to arrive," he said, looking at his watch. "Joker and Ding-a-Ling have probably started a sing-along by now."

Bobby laughed. "We're not that late," he said. They came to a door that opened onto a tiny hall that had a door immediately on the left and a stairway straight ahead. The door led to Hannigan's Bar, but Tone and Bobby climbed the stairs to the Tudor Lounge.

"And just what time do you call this?" Joker shouted as Bobby and Tone came through the door at the top of the stairs. Tone unwound the scarf from around his neck, placed it over the back of a chair and sat down.

"Merry Christmas to you, too, Joker," he said as Bobby went off to find an extra chair. Jamesy stood up, an empty pint glass in his hand. "I'll get this round," he said and looked down at Tone. "The usual, I take it?"

"Good man yourself," said Tone as Jamesy set off for the bar.

Joker stood up. "I suppose I should go and give him a hand," he said, and went off in pursuit of Jamesy. Bobby returned and, having established to his satisfaction that alcohol was imminent, he sat down. Tone leaned back in his chair and looked across the table at Sean and Bobby.

"Well, how have you two been?" he asked. "Still a couple of parasitic drains on society?"

Sean sighed and rolled his eyes, but Bobby replied cheerfully.

"Not for much longer, Tone," he said. "Big year coming up."

Tone nodded but said nothing. Sean was expecting the usual bitter diatribe about lazy and feckless university students, but Tone simply lit a cigarette and stayed silent. He was looking around the room at the diverse Christmas Eve clientele when a thought seemed to strike him. He turned to face Bobby.

"Oh yeah, Bobby," he said. "Who was that you were talking to earlier?"

Bobby looked at him. "What do you mean? When?"

"At the City Hall," said Tone. "I was going past on the bus, and I saw you gabbing away to some happy-looking buggers."

"Oh right!" said Bobby. He was smiling but Tone thought he shifted a little uncomfortably. "They wanted to tell me all about this Jesus fella," Bobby went on. "Apparently he forgives all our sins."

"That's nice of him," said Tone. Sean could smell a rant and tried to deflect Tone by lightening the mood.

"Damn Christians, eh Tone?" he said. "Trying to ruin Christmas for everybody else."

Tone eyed Sean coolly. "I know you're being flippant, Sean, but essentially, you're right. Christianity has absolutely no –"

"Oh, for fuck's sake, Tone, give it a rest!" Joker had returned from the bar, his hands clasped around three pints. He carefully placed the drinks on the table and turned to face Tone. "Or at least wait till we're all too pissed to give a shit."

Tone feigned offence. "Where's the bloody food, Joker?" he said.

"It's coming, don't panic!" Joker headed back to the bar and Tone leaned forward to stub out his cigarette in the ashtray that occupied the middle of the table. Sean turned to Bobby.

"Made your mind up yet about going to Solitude?" he asked.

Bobby took a sip of beer and then shook his head. "I don't think I'll bother," he said. "I've never had much desire to have my head shoved up my own arse."

"Well, obviously, you don't wear your bloody scarf!" Sean protested. "Just try not to smell like a Prod and you'll be okay."

"Are the Glens playing Cliftonville, then?" Tone asked Sean.

"Yeah, next month," said Sean. "Me and Ding-a-Ling were thinking of going. What about you, Tone, do you fancy it?"

Tone thought about it. "Yeah maybe," he said. "You going, Joker?"

Joker was setting down the last two drinks on the table.

"Wise up, Tone!" he answered as he took his seat. "The only ground in Belfast worth going to is Windsor Park, you should know that."

Jamesy arrived with two cheeseburgers. He handed one to Tone and one to Bobby and sat down.

"Seems to get busier every year," he said, mainly to himself.

As Tone chewed his first mouthful, he looked over at Sean. "What's this I hear about Snatter getting engaged?"

Sean considered this and then shrugged. "Nothing official, as far as I know."

"He hasn't been going out with her that long, has he?" Tone went on. "Has anyone even met her?"

"Yeah, I know her from way back," said Sean. "She's … well, she's …" he tailed off and took a swig from his pint.

"I've met her," Joker piped up.

"Excellent!" said Tone. "So at least we know what her tits look like."

"Hey, that's not fair!"

"What colour hair has she got?"

"She's got hair?"

Tone took another bite of his cheeseburger and looked around the table. "Well," he said after a pause, "I think young Snatter has got some explaining to do. And what about you, Joker? I heard you and Carol split up. What happened? She sober up?"

"Yeah, very funny, Tone," said Joker. "No, she started getting all sleepy and weird, you know? I can't be doing with all that crap."

Tone looked at him. "Sleepy and weird?"

Sean interjected. "Carol was having some problems with her blood pressure," he told Tone. "Nothing serious, like, but she started having dizzy spells, you know? Fainting and stuff."

Tone turned to Joker. "You broke up with because she was sick?"

"Well, don't put it like that," said Joker. "You make me sound like a right prick."

"On the contrary!" said Tone as he finished his lunch and put his hands up in protest. "You could be a candidate for sainthood. Has anyone notified the Pope, or whoever it is that deals with the creepy cult that you belong to?"

"I don't think we have saints," said Joker thoughtfully.

"You could start a trend." Tone took out three cigarettes, passed one each to Bobby and Joker, and lit one for himself. "Seriously, Joker," he went on, "you're a prince, you know that? A real bloody prince."

"You been reading Salinger lately, Tone?" asked Jamesy.

Tone blew a smoke ring into the air and looked across the table at Jamesy.

"You always were a smart lad, Jamesy," he said. "And yes, actually, as a matter of fact I've been –"

"Look, Tone," said Joker, keen to plead his case, "there was more to it than Carol not being well. I've never really been into all that couples' shit, you know? It's just not me."

"What exactly *is* you, Joker?" asked Bobby.

"Well, Bobby," said Joker as he leaned back in his chair, "I'm glad you asked. I'm more of your *Lone Wolf* type, you know what I mean? A free spirit. A wandering star. You might as well try and lasso the –"

"In other words," Jamesy said, "she was far too good for you."

"Well, fuck!" said Joker, taking a sip of his pint. "We all knew that!"

The lunchtime crowd had started to thin, leaving a few groups dotted here and there around the room. The barmaid, glancing now and then in Jamesy's direction, was ferrying stacks of glasses back to the bar.

"Anyway," said Joker, addressing Tone, "what's this I hear about you screwing some bird down south?"

"You know what, Joker?" Tone replied. "Have you ever considered that maybe your expressive turn of phrase is contributing to your *Lone Wolf* status?"

"As I have already stated," Joker said, with an air of pomposity, "my current status is self-imposed. Now if you could only –"

"What's the plan here?" Sean broke in. "Do you think we should hold on and get another round in?"

Joker voiced his wholehearted approval of the idea and looked around the table for support. Jamesy shrugged, not minding one way or the other, and Bobby raised his empty glass as an answer. Tone glanced at his watch and appeared to weigh up their options.

"I suppose we could hang around for another one," he said. "See if these two dickheads manage to show up."

Sean went off to the bar, and Bobby followed to give him a hand. Tone motioned for Joker to lean forward.

"Is Ding-a-Ling okay?" he asked.

Joker and Jamesy both looked puzzled.

"Yeah," said Joker, "as far as I know. Why?"

"Oh, I don't know," Tone replied. "He just sounded a bit weird on the phone the other day."

"Don't know what you mean," said Joker, "although he did have a bit of a funny phase a while back."

"Like what?"

"Well, he was trying to get his hands on some videos and –"

"Yes, okay, Joker!" laughed Tone. "I don't think we need to hear any –"

"No," said Joker, "it's not like that. It was an old kids' TV show, you know, *The Banana Splits*?"

"Oh yeah, that's right!" Jamesy said suddenly. "He asked me about it too."

Tone frowned. "*The Banana Splits*?" he asked. "What the hell for?"

"Well, that's the funny thing," Joker replied, "he seemed a wee bit cagey about it. Who knows, though? Maybe it was just a bit of nostalgia, like. I mean it was a bloody good show, wasn't it?"

Tone and Jamesy both nodded, smiling at the memories of Saturday mornings in childhood; sitting cross-legged in pyjamas, on the floor in front of the television, watching a long parade of cartoons.

"Not like the shite kids have to watch these days!" Tone said ruefully.

Standing side by side at the bar, Bobby turned to Sean. "It's not like Snatter to be late," he said. "You can usually set your watch by him."

"True," Sean agreed.

"Of course, Ding-a-Ling on the other hand …"

"Oh, I'm sure there's nothing to worry about," said Sean. "Probably just got held up in traffic."

"You heard about Sticky Mickey, didn't you?"

"What?" Sean looked at Bobby. "That was ages ago," he said, "and anyway, it's …" he seemed pensive for a second and then shook his head.

"Wise up, Bobby! It's Christmas Eve. Not even Ding-a-Ling can get into trouble on Christmas Eve."

FOUR

Reality was all well and good, Ding-a-Ling had often thought, but there were times when it simply got in the way of a good narrative.

"You shot him, you Brit bastard!" he cried dramatically.

Ding-a-Ling liked nothing more than playing to a crowd, and the crowd obliged him by turning towards the little pageant he was presenting.

No one believed for a second that Snatter had been shot, but Ding-a-Ling was well known in the area for his strident and vocal opinions or, in other words, he was a bit of a *slabber*, and so the crowd was lured by the prospect of further entertainment from what was shaping up to be an interesting morning.

Bert, who had just been accused of shooting an unarmed bystander, was not as convinced as the crowd was that he was completely innocent. *Had* he shot someone?

He couldn't remember actually pulling the trigger of his rifle, but the thought had, only very recently, been taking a rather vigorous stroll through the forefront of his mind, and he also had some vague notion of the *fog of war,* where memories can become distorted in the heat of battle.

He began to wave his rifle around in confused desperation and almost pleaded with Ding-a-Ling to put his hands up.

Ding-a-Ling ignored Bert and continued his performance while, behind him, the driver of the Vauxhall was now jumping up and down in the middle of the road trying to demonstrate just how much his hands were, in fact, up.

Approaching sirens could be heard in the background.

Elsewhere, things were beginning to calm down. Harry, his anger having run its course, raised his hands in quiet resignation.

"Okay, okay," he said, and then walked to the back of the Land Rover where he calmly took a seat in the open doorway. He reached down and patted the shoulder of his first victim who was sitting on the kerb nursing his nose and aching testicles.

"You'll be all right there, mate. Nothing too serious," Harry told the soldier consolingly, but the soldier did not appear to be consoled at all and, still holding his nose, told Harry to go *fugg* himself.

Harry shrugged as the other soldiers crowded around him, a little unsure about how to proceed. The sirens in the background were becoming louder.

Snatter was now beginning to come around but, once his present circumstances had established themselves, he began to reminisce fondly about his previous condition.

Ding-a-Ling was in full flow. Having settled on a theme, he was now embellishing a long list of crimes and atrocities, both historical and contemporary, which had been, he insisted, committed by the Imperial British War Machine, and which he now laid squarely at the feet of a bewildered Bert.

"You!" Ding-a-Ling cried passionately, as he gestured to Bert. "Yes, you!" he went on. "You are the very personification of this evil Imperialism. The very face of a thousand years of murder and theft and torture and rape!" Ding-a-Ling, inspired by his audience, pursued his lecture with some gusto. With impassioned and, he imagined, unimpeachable logic, he explained the cold immorality of Britain pillaging the world for wealth and power.

He outlined Bert's part in all of this with such insight and clarity that Ding-a-Ling could see the eyes of this poor, guileless drone open wide with sudden understanding. The unassailable logic, delivered with dazzling articulation, was enough to crush the very soul of this unwitting cog as the scale of his sins was arrayed before him.

Ding-a-Ling was feeling quite moved by the thought of lifting this witless boob from murky ignorance into the warming light of comprehension.

What the blind, bloody fuck is this dickhead yapping about? Bert was frantically thinking, while the familiar undulating rattle of a helicopter could be heard whisking the dull, grey sky overhead. The sirens in the background reached a crescendo, and Snatter, his vision clearing, could see one, and then another, grey Land Rover pull up.

The police had arrived.

Despite Ding-a-Ling's best efforts, most of the people in the crowd, having decided that the entertainment value of the day had diminished since Harry had stopped hitting people, were beginning to drift away.

Several police officers were now spreading out to put a stop to any further shenanigans and some sort of order began to be restored. Ding-a-Ling, however, was unperturbed and continued to play to what remained of the crowd while Snatter groaned at his feet.

Harry was approached by a slightly overweight policeman with a thick moustache who took a notebook from his pocket. A smile spread across his face.

"All right there, Harry?" he said. "Been in the wars a bit, have you?"

"Hiya, John," Harry replied, looking up. "You could say that. Not the best start to the day."

"So I see, so I see," said John, not writing anything down and having no intention of doing so. "So, what's the butcher's bill, then?"

At that moment an ambulance arrived, and the crew busily began to treat whatever injuries they could find. Harry nodded to the soldier lying on the road in front of Jimbo's car.

"He'll be okay," Harry told John as Jimbo stood and stared in disbelief at how much damage could be caused by a single flying soldier.

"Should've bloody stayed in bed," he mumbled. "Bloody Ardoyne animals!"

"Your man here?" Harry gestured to the soldier who, in Harry's mind, had started it all. "His nose is broken, but, to be honest, it didn't look like it was the first time."

"No harm done, then," said John cheerfully.

"What the fu–?" the soldier began but John waved him down.

"All right, all right there!" he said, imposing his authority. "Everybody just calm down. I don't think it's very helpful to go around pointing fingers at this stage of the game. Now what's the –"

"All right there, Harry?" Another policeman had appeared behind John. "I bloody knew it was you when we got the call. You're a desperate man, so you are," he said with a grin. "Just shocking!"

"All right there, Stephen," said Harry, feeling a little distracted. Stephen gestured towards Ding-a-Ling, still in mid-rant.

"So, who's your man there?" he asked, and they all turned to watch Ding-a-Ling's performance.

Harry sighed. "That's Gary," he said, "he's my brother-in-law."

"Your brother-in-law?" asked John. "Karen's brother, you mean?" He watched as Ding-a-Ling, now fully immersed in his role, became more animated, gesturing to his stricken comrade while dramatically draping the back of his hand across his forehead. It was, thought Ding-a-Ling, bloody good stuff.

"Bit of a wanker, isn't he?" said John.

Harry simply nodded. "Harmless enough, though," he said.

"Is there any way to shut him up?" asked Stephen.

"You could shoot him," Harry suggested helpfully.

John and Stephen seemed to consider this, but then John shook his head. "Wise up, Harry!" he said. "It's Christmas Eve. Think of the paperwork!"

"Oh, here we go!" Ding-a-Ling went on, "Here we have the lapdogs of the RUC coming to make sure the forces of –"

"Gary!" Harry growled in a voice that, Snatter imagined, could cure the chronically constipated. "Shut it!"

Ding-a-Ling was instantly contrite. "No problem, Harry," he said. "No sweat at all there, mate."

"Is your mate okay there?" John asked, nodding to Snatter. The paramedic tending to Snatter's forehead turned around.

"We could do with taking him in," he said, "and get it looked at properly."

Ding-a-Ling was appalled. He knew exactly what that would mean. They would end up waiting around for hours at the hospital, before some doctor appeared to tell Snatter to take an aspirin and to go and have a lie down.

"No, don't worry about it," he said quickly. "He'll be okay, won't you, Snatter? It's just that we have to be somewhere and we're already a bit late. And we're going to have to –" A scowl from Harry served to convince Ding-a-Ling that he should stop talking. Harry looked to John and Stephen.

"You'll be taking me in, I suppose?" he asked.

"You know the score, Harry. Damage to Her Majesty's property and all that." John said, regarding the injured soldiers. "We'll be as quick as we can, though, you'll be out in no time at all. Do you want us to let Karen know what's happening?"

Harry glanced at the people who were still milling around. He knew most of them, to one degree or another.

"She already knows," he said in reply.

John followed his gaze and chuckled. "Yeah, I see what you mean," he said, "no secrets in Ardoyne, is there? Well, anyway, let's get a move on."

As John and Stephen helped Harry into the back of one of the police Land Rovers, the other policemen took statements from witnesses and went about the process of clearing up the carnage.

Jimbo had to be dissuaded from driving his car, as it was no longer deemed to be road legal, and he set off in search of a tow-truck – his plans for a stress-free Christmas Eve now in ruins.

The Vauxhall, despite some broken lights and some damage to the bodywork, was considered to be drivable and so the driver, grumbling under his breath, was able to take off.

Bert helped to push Harry's van into the lay-by at the side of the road before clambering into the back of the army Land Rover. He was still unsure as to whether or not he had shot anyone.

"Harry fairly lost the bap there, didn't he?" Snatter said to Ding-a-ling when calm had finally descended.

"Yeah, he's got a bit of a short fuse."

"A short fuse?" Snatter cried in disbelief. "I didn't see any fucking fuse at all!"

"Yeah, well, that's why the cops know him so well. In fact, there's even a –"

"Ding-a-Ling?"

"What?"

"I could do with a drink."

"Yeah, you're right. Come on, then."

Snatter gently felt the bump on his forehead as they made their way to the nearby bus stop.

FIVE

The Tudor Lounge had been an unusual choice, and no one could ever quite remember who had suggested it. There had been so many of them, after all, that first year when a group of sixth-formers from a Catholic grammar school in the city had arranged to meet in town for a Christmas drink. For many it was to be the first date on a long-term relationship with alcohol, and the occasion was considered by all to be a success.

The meeting place, however, was something of a surprise. In a city that boasted many famous drinking establishments, the Tudor Lounge was drab and unfashionable and, perversely in a country known for its bars, aspired to be an English-style country pub.

Dull horse-brasses and dark wood panelling, combined with furnishings of red velvet, gave the interior a gloomy appearance. The heavily leaded glass in the windows prevented much light from penetrating the darkness, which may well have been a blessing, for on rare days in high summer when the cheery rays of the sun could force their way into the dark recesses, the unloved tawdriness of the interior would be exposed. Summer was no friend to the Tudor Lounge, but when the days shivered and shortened and the world was reclaimed by winter's grasp, it was a different story altogether.

It took the bleak and bitter chill of winter to transform the tawdriness of the Tudor Lounge into a warm cosiness. The little coal fire, risible in summer, was suddenly welcoming; a place by which to sit in snug comfort as the freezing winds clawed uselessly at the heavy windows.

The glow from the Tudor Lounge may have been dim but, in a world of frozen gloom, dim was enough, and on Christmas Eve the glow from the Tudor Lounge was perfect.

It just lacked one thing. There was no public payphone anywhere in the building.

Jamesy stamped his feet and watched his breath steam up the little rectangular windows of the phone box that stood in the pedestrian courtyard, just outside the bar.

He listened to Snatter's phone ring for a few more seconds and then replaced the receiver in its cradle. Glancing at his watch, he was beginning to think there might be some cause for concern. He had just spoken to Ding-a-Ling's father and had been informed that Ding-a-Ling had been picked up by his brother-in-law earlier that morning with a plan to meet up with Snatter and then head straight into town.

Jamesy was reassured by the knowledge that Ding-a-Ling was being accompanied by Snatter, who could be relied upon to exert a steadying influence on some of Ding-a-Ling's more capricious tendencies.

Even so, Jamesy had to admit, there was no sign of either of them. Stepping out of the phone box, he caught the eye of an attractive girl who was passing. She smiled at him and glanced back a few times before melting into the crowd. This happened a lot to Jamesy. He was not entirely unaware of the admiring attention he received on a regular basis from women, and, indeed, it was not uncommon even for men to have a vague sense of unease when first meeting Jamesy. And the reason for this was simple.

Jamesy was good-looking only in a conventional way, and his personality, while being earnest and often charming, could be considered, by some, to be distant. He was not someone who would normally stand out in a crowd if it weren't for the one feature that most people found bewitching. His eyes.

Junkie's eyes, Joker called them, even though Jamesy's one experiment with marijuana – which Joker had provided – had ended abruptly with some explosive vomiting and a vow from Jamesy to stick to alcohol in the future.

Joker, however, was not to be dissuaded. It was indecent, he argued, for such eyes to come about without some industrial quantities of psychotropic substances being involved somewhere along the line.

And so, to anyone expressing an interest, Joker would solemnly explain that, although Jamesy was a nice enough guy, he had more chemicals in him than a packet of Spangles.

Joker was more content this way, more at peace with the world, for Joker, much like Ding-a-Ling in this regard, preferred to create his own reality than the one in which he often found himself. That reality, he believed, seldom lived up to his own expectations, and so, in Joker's reality there was an explanation for Jamesy's eyes that sat more happily with his view of how things should be.

Jamesy's eyes were a pale, almost opaque, milky-blue, which, coupled with his dark hair and naturally swarthy complexion, created an exotic look that was instantly striking.

"Any woman could easily fall in love with Jamesy's eyes," an old girlfriend of Sean's had once remarked, "but once you get past that, then what else is there?"

Sean had split up with her shortly afterwards but, despite the casual cruelty of the remark, there were those who felt she had a point.

Not those who knew him well, of course, but even Jamesy would not deny a certain trait he possessed that, to some, would make him appear disinterested or aloof. He struggled with something that, to most people, would come naturally and was partly to blame for his lack of success in maintaining a relationship with a girlfriend: he found it hard to make small talk.

The tiny droplets of meaningless chat employed to cover over any uncomfortable lulls in a conversation seemed to be beyond Jamesy and could lead one to assume he was simply ill-mannered. But he just couldn't think of anything to say.

This may have been a part of the reason for his modest success with the opposite sex, but it was only a very small part. He knew he was physically attracted to women, and they were certainly attracted to him, but in any relationships that he had embarked upon up to now he had inevitably become exasperated.

It wasn't even that he could put a finger on what the exact problem was, but he would often find himself looking for something more than the shallow interactions that companionship demanded. He hoped that this inability to operate on what he felt was a trivial level of communication did not make him an intellectual snob. Maybe he was just confused by women, but they generally seemed to be obsessed by things which, as far as Jamesy could see, were of no importance.

Not that Jamesy was overly concerned by this because, at this moment in time, the great love of his life was the acquisition of knowledge. He was born to study. He was currently working towards an MA in ancient history while also studying for qualifications in geology and anthropology. His eventual goal, after acquiring a PhD, was to become a field archaeologist.

Tone had accused him of wanting to be Indiana Jones, but Jamesy had dismissed the movie *Raiders of the Lost Ark* as glossy Hollywood nonsense. In Jamesy's mind, archaeology meant spending time on a scorched and isolated hilltop in East Africa or the windswept plains of the Euphrates River valley, painstakingly brushing little specks of earth from artefacts that had remained hidden for millennia.

He was passionate about uncovering the secrets of humanity's infancy. He yearned to discover how civilisations, now long forgotten, arose and flourished in the distant past, and then, by pooling together a wide range of disciplines, he could gently tease this hidden knowledge into the light, and so, in his own humble way, add to the great store of human understanding.

Jamesy wasn't popular at parties.

He could imagine a partner in his life at some point, but he felt no need to dwell on it just now. The future, he felt, would see a relationship blossom and develop in its own time and when the time was right. And, at this stage in Jamesy's life, the time simply wasn't right.

As he walked back to the bar, watching the passers-by pull their coats tightly around themselves as the wind began to bite a little more, he smiled to himself. Winter was his favourite season.

Jamesy's idea of the perfect weekend was to wake early on a Saturday morning to discover a cold rain drenching the little terraced streets around the university. A day that no one would ever consider venturing into unless they absolutely had to. A day when Jamesy could happily light the fire, put on the kettle and settle down for many pleasant hours surrounded by textbooks and reference books and not feel the least bit guilty.

Unlike the summer, when a harsh brightness would glare accusingly at him through his window, taunting him for lurking in the gloom while the rest of the world was outside, frolicking in glorious sunshine.

A few times, in summer, he had strolled the short distance to Botanic Gardens with a selection of books in order to sit on the grass and study *al fresco*, but it wasn't the same. The sun would reflect too brightly off the page, making it difficult to concentrate, or a breeze would unhelpfully turn the pages for him, or the ground would become uncomfortable, or a stray football would occasionally hit him in the face. The summer didn't suit Jamesy, but in winter he could hibernate to his heart's content.

He made his way up the stairs to the bar and, after suffering some sexual harassment from the perfume-counter girls who passed him on their way down, he walked through the door to see Bobby with his nose buried in the crook of his elbow.

"For fuck's sake, Joker!" Bobby was saying. "I mean, Jesus Christ, even the IRA have called a truce!"

"That's certainly a feisty wee odour you made there," added Tone.

"Thank you, Tone," said Joker defiantly. "It's nice to know that some people can still appreciate craftsmanship."

Sean looked up as Jamesy approached the table. "Any news?"

"No answer at Snatter's house," said Jamesy, "but Ding-a-Ling's da said Ding-a-Ling left earlier to meet up with him."

"So, where the hell are they?" Tone asked as he lit a cigarette. "We're going to have to make a decision here."

Joker drained his pint and stood up. "I'm going to the bogs," he said. "Let me know what's happening when I get back."

"Snatter and Ding-a-Ling were meant to be getting a lift from Ding-a-Ling's brother-in-law." Jamesy sat down and picked up his drink. "If that's any help."

"We could try ringing Ding-a-Ling's sister," Bobby suggested. "Would Joker have her number?"

"Anyway," Tone had reached a decision, "I say we move on. There's no point hanging around here. They won't expect us to still be here at this time."

Everyone agreed. "I need to do a bit of shopping," said Bobby, "so where will I meet you?"

The itinerary for the pub-crawl each year was fluid, with no fixed route, though there were a few annual stalwarts like the Tudor Lounge at the start and the Botanic Inn at the end.

Sean got up as Joker returned. "I'll go with you, Bobby," he said. "I need to get a couple of things. Joker, do you have Ding-a-Ling's sister's number? Me and Bobby could give her a bell on the way."

Joker took out a small black diary, shuffled through it, then handed it to Sean. Sean copied the number and handed the book back to Joker. "Where to next, then?" he asked Tone.

Tone thought for a minute. "What about Kelly's?"

"Sounds good," Sean and Bobby both agreed. "We'll see you there shortly."

As they headed for the door, Joker picked up his cigarettes and sat down. "I suppose we'll just have to sit and wait for Jamesy to finish his bloody pint, then," he grumbled with a grin.

"Well, I'm going for a piss," said Tone. "Be ready to go when I get back."

Bobby and Sean stepped out into the cold.

"Jesus!" Bobby exclaimed. "Bit bloody nippy, isn't it?"

"Yeah," said Sean, "I think it has something to do with the weather."

Bobby was used to Sean's dry humour and ignored it.

"So, what do you think the deal is with Snatter getting engaged?" he asked. They were walking along with teeth gritted against the wind.

"I don't know," Sean replied. "None of my business really"

"Tone reckons it's the beginning of the end."

"The end of what?"

"Well … the pub-crawl for one thing."

Sean stopped and looked at Bobby. "Did Tone actually say that?" he asked.

"Well, no, but think about it. I mean, it's inevitable, isn't it?"

They reached the phone box and bundled inside, relieved to be out of the wind.

"Inevitable?" asked Sean. "Why do you say that?"

"We're all going to settle down eventually," Bobby said. "I mean, you and me don't even know where we're going to be this time next year. Haven't you thought about it?"

Sean fumbled for the piece of paper that had Karen's number on it. "Not as much as you, obviously," he said.

Bobby hesitated for a second. "I've been looking at engagement rings," he finally admitted.

"What?" Sean was surprised. "Seriously?"

Bobby became a little defensive. "It's just the next step, isn't it? I mean, that's how it goes."

"Not necessarily," said Sean. "Jesus, Bobby, are you saying you have your whole life mapped out, one bloody step at a time?"

Bobby shrugged. "Nothing wrong with having a plan," he mumbled.

Sean stared at him as he dialled the number. He shook his head as he listened for the call to be answered.

"Hello," he said, after a while, "is that Karen? Yeah, it's Sean here … Sean Thompson. I was wondering if you'd seen Gary at all today. What? Yeah, with Seamus, they were supp… What? Lifted? Who? Shit … I mean, what happened to … shit … no, we were just … Look, don't worry! I'm sure there's no problem … I'm sure Harry will be okay …

Look I'll get Gary to ring you or your ma when he shows up. What? What about Rosie? No, I don't know anything about it … Look, I have to go, the money's running out and … No, don't worry about it!"

Sean hastily replaced the receiver and turned to face Bobby.

"Fuck!" he said.

SIX

Born within a few months of each other, Seamus and Gary grew up on the same Ardoyne street and were friends for as long as either of them could remember. Their friendship blossomed not because they were so similar but because they were so different.

Physically, Seamus was stocky and solid with a serious face that bordered on solemn. He approached life with a natural caution, contrasting with Gary who threw himself at life with a reckless abandon. The differences that appeared so stark in their natures proved complementary in a way that gave their relationship a perfect balance.

As they journeyed through their lives together there were times when Gary's hunger for life's experiences would drag them into agreeable situations where Seamus, alone, would never have dared to intrude, while the steadying hand of Seamus would hold them back on the many occasions when Gary was prepared to hurl them both into the abyss. In this way they pushed and pulled and tumbled through their formative years.

When they first started school, at the age of four, Seamus' mother had accompanied them for the first few weeks, and then they were allowed to walk the short distance on their own. Northern Ireland's nascent troubles had yet to mar their boyish outlook and so they would walk past the smouldering carcasses of burnt-out vehicles, past the silent soldiers and the menacing bulk of armoured cars, past the hooded men with milk crates filled with petrol bombs, past the screaming graffiti and the rubble and the broken glass and the barbed wire and the bullet casings, and they would gaze at the chaos of a fracturing society with a mix of fascination and wonder.

Their childish nicknames were forged in childhood during their first year in school, where they met Sean Thompson, a smiling, confident boy who they instantly christened Tommy Gun.

One day Tommy Gun told Snatter and Ding-a-Ling of a pond he had found that contained frogspawn. The idea of Ardoyne harbouring any kind of wildlife was so ridiculous that Tommy Gun was told to wise up and was branded a dirty, filthy liar. Proof would be needed.

And so, after school, they set off on safari into the tarmac wasteland behind Etna Drive that led to the Bone hills.

There were a few pools of filthy water scattered in between the bushes and the mounds of rubbish, between the broken bricks and the patches of tarmac and moss-covered earth, but Tommy Gun led them further into the waste ground until he came to a large, untidy hedge.

There was a rusted, rectangular bed frame off to one side that still contained many of its V-shaped wire springs.

These springs, the boys knowledgeably told each other, made excellent catapults, although that would have to wait for another time as Tommy Gun pushed aside a low branch and crawled inside the hedge. Snatter and Ding-a-Ling followed, and, to their astonishment, there it was. Just as Tommy Gun had described. A small overgrown pond that, indeed, harboured some blobs of clear jelly containing tiny, dark specks of tadpole. To a couple of scruffy, working-class city kids this was beyond miraculous. It was nature unveiled in all her glorious majesty.

Tommy Gun beamed in triumph as Snatter and Ding-a-Ling looked upon him with new respect, and at that moment the two became three.

Plans were made to race home and scavenge for jam-jars, to collect the precious frogspawn, to watch the tiny specks grow into frogs, to have the best pets ever. These plans, however, would never come to fruition, for a million other plans would just get in the way.

They lived in and out of each other's houses and they lived life at frantic boyhood speeds, racing chaotically from football to play-fights and cycling trips, to expeditions into the unknown and building sledges in the winter and *guiders* in the summer. And, occasionally, girls.

There were childish stolen kisses and crushes that came and went, with one memorable occasion when Ding-a-Ling became inconsolable after his *one true love* moved away from the area. Tommy Gun and Snatter coaxed him out his torpor and then teased him for days afterwards.

There were sunny Sunday afternoons when the three boys would sit on empty beer crates outside the Saunders' club and sip from bottles of Coke and gossip like old women while, inside, their fathers would sip from bottles of Red Heart and talk of football and treason. Or wet weekends when they would visit Toby's Hall in Butler Street to watch old Hammer horror movies and to flirt with girls.

On weekdays, as well, they would spend almost all of their time together, both in and out of school. They would explore the burnt-out and deserted houses of 'old' Ardoyne, with ancient, cobbled streets that seemed to have been abandoned for a hundred years or more. Once, in a narrow alleyway, they discovered a wall that was pock-marked with bullet holes, and they had convinced themselves it was the very spot where the British had executed James Connolly; their knowledge of Irish history being a little hazy.

They would roam far and wide and would find adventure everywhere. They would venture as far as the sprawling parkland, known locally as the Waterworks, where they climbed trees and fished and swam and were kids.

Snatter got up and switched off the television. He wasn't really watching it, anyway. *You're living in the past, Seamus, my old mate*, he muttered to himself.

He took a swig from his can of beer, then lit a cigarette. Standing in the middle of the room, looking through the window, he could see the Christmas tree lights blinking in the windows of the houses across the street as the memories played around in his head. He was aware of how much he had relied upon his friends in the past and how much he would rely on them again. They had always been there, he thought, through the sorrows and the joys and the unspeakable agonies. Agonies, he believed, that would have broken him apart, had his friends not been standing by his side.

He thought back to his first day of grammar school, waiting, in the very spot where he now stood, for Tommy Gun and Ding-a-Ling to call for him. Standing uncomfortably in his smart new uniform while his da leant on the mantelpiece with a stupid grin on his face and the tears tripping him. Snatter had felt fearful at what his friends would make of such an unmanly display of emotion, but he needn't have worried, for they never said a word, not then, not ever.

A few years later, his friends, Tone and Jamesy now included, had helped to carry his father's coffin up to the chapel on the hill and, later on, had dragged him away from the suffocating crowd of relatives to go and sit in the local park with a few bottles of illicit cider. They had talked away the evening, both joyful and morose, jeering, cajoling and tipsy. *Doing what they have always done*, thought Snatter grimly, *keeping me from falling apart.*

Was it fair, he wondered, to need their support so much? Maybe he had been through more troubles than most, or maybe he was just more pathetic than most. More needy.

He took a final draw from his cigarette and dropped the butt into his empty beer can. He went into the kitchen and took another can from the fridge. He was feeling restless and uneasy. *Just bloody typical!* he told himself. *Life! Bloody life!* Just when things were beginning to look up, he thought. Just when he was starting to get things straight in his head, then along comes life to fuck everything up. He shook his head as if to clear away the unwelcome thoughts of the present and to allow the warm memories to seep back in. Before long, he found himself in the dreary surroundings of the Department of Health and Social Services.

It had been a strange summer, after their school days had all come to an end. As expected, Jamesy and Sean – who had now shed his boyhood nickname – had achieved the required exam results and were preparing for their fresher year at Belfast's Queen's University. Tone, with typical contrariness, had applied to, and been accepted by Southampton University and had left for the south of England soon after the exam results had been released. Snatter and Ding-a-Ling had signed on the dole.

It had been no great surprise that they had both underachieved in their final exams, for neither had expressed any appetite for further education. Snatter, in particular, had become weary of constant study and of revision of things that held no interest for him. He felt a strange impatience to get on with life after school, though he had no idea what direction that life was going to take.

For a while both Snatter and Ding-a-Ling had enjoyed being unemployed. After seven years in the strict confines of a Catholic grammar school the unrestricted freedom now on offer was almost daunting.

Soon, however, the days began to merge into one and time lost all meaning. Occasionally, usually on Friday afternoons, they would make their way across town to meet up with Sean and Jamesy in the student union bar at Queen's. These afternoons would, inevitably, lead into long drunken nights as the four friends careered around the bars of south Belfast, with the occasional stop at the University Café for some stodgy food to soak up the alcohol.

Such interludes, though enjoyable, only served to highlight the emptiness of the rest of the long days on the dole. Snatter, especially, was becoming increasingly despondent, which only deepened as winter approached.

Jesus Christ! thought Snatter, as he stubbed out another cigarette. *Have I always been such a miserable bastard?* He got up again and went to the fridge. He wasn't even enjoying having a drink, but he thought he should take out another can of beer in case that situation changed.

Was I ever bloody happy? he wondered. *Was I even happy when the cheque came?*

Snatter and Ding-a-Ling had both been half-heartedly applying for various jobs since signing on the dole, although Ding-a-Ling was by far the more half-hearted of the two. Snatter had once watched in horror as Ding-a-Ling casually put down in his list of hobbies, on a job application form, 'not giving a shit', but the lack of any real opportunities was beginning to wear them both down.

Then, in December, the cheque came.

Snatter had forgotten all about his claim. It was his uncle, after all, who had pushed him into applying for it, and it was his uncle who had dealt with any subsequent paperwork.

It was a compensation claim for his father's death from the British government, and it was a sizeable amount; sizeable enough for Snatter to generously thank his aunt and uncle for everything they had done for him. "Ach, we didn't do it for the money," said his uncle, taking the money, and it was sizeable enough for him to purchase his parents' old house. It was the only home he had known, growing up, and it didn't seem right for strangers to be living there. So much had happened to him in that house. Too much, perhaps.

He then had enough left over to acquire the lease to a small newsagent's shop in the centre of town, close to a busy bus stop and with excellent potential.

On the first day that he took over the shop, both he and Ding-a-Ling were excited about this new direction their lives had taken. In theory, Ding-a-Ling was Snatter's employee, though neither of them saw it that way. They were just two friends being paid to hang out together.

At first, things went smoothly. The shop thrived and Snatter and Ding-a-Ling enjoyed the busy routine, joking throughout the day and generally being comfortable in each other's company. Eventually, though, it became impossible for Snatter to ignore the fact that his friend was becoming restless as the routine became monotonous and, although Snatter loved working in his little shop, he pretended to sympathise.

"Yeah, I know what you mean," he would say, "now that we can actually afford to go out on the sauce, we don't have the time, or else we're too bloody knackered!"

"I know, for fuck's sake. It's doing my head in!"

They moaned about it to each other for a while until Snatter came to a decision that would have certain repercussions.

"We'll just have to take somebody else on," he declared, "take a bit of the strain off."

"Can you afford it?" Ding-a-Ling asked, intrigued.

"Yeah, I don't see why not. We're doing okay, aren't we? What do you reckon?"

"Yeah, fuck it, go for it!"

They were both energised by this new project and once an advertisement was placed in the *Belfast Telegraph*, they sat back and discussed the sort of qualities they would like to see in their new colleague.

"Seventeen-year-old girl, mini-skirt, dubious morals ... oh, and a good sense of humour," Ding-a-Ling would suggest and Snatter would try to match it with an equally childish fantasy. Eventually they had drawn up a list of ideal candidates, at the top of which was a seventeen-year-old, mini-skirt-wearing girl with dubious morals, and they eagerly awaited the response to their ad.

Had they taken their list to its logical conclusion then hovering around somewhere near the bottom would have been a six-foot-four skinhead from Sandy Row.

Joseph Anderson was a six-foot-four skinhead from Sandy Row who also happened to be, unforgivably, a Linfield supporter. As soon as he walked into the shop, both Snatter and Ding-a-Ling had dismissed him as a suitable contender for the position, but they also felt obliged to go through the motions of an interview.

They felt very professional as they each held a clipboard and pen, although Snatter was not sure what he was meant to write on the blank sheet that was clipped to his board, while, on *his* sheet, Ding-a-Ling had drawn a little horse.

As the interview progressed, Snatter and Ding-a-Ling's initial feeling that they were in the presence of a potential nutcase had, in no way, abated, but it also became increasingly clear that they had found a soul mate.

"Call me Joker," said Joker, on being offered the job and, so pleased were they all at such a satisfactory conclusion to the interview, it was decided to close the shop early and to go and have a drink to properly welcome their new colleague.

Snatter woke up later that evening on a public bench. In a train station. In Larne.

He was, at first, a little confused. Larne was a busy port about thirty miles from Belfast and was not normally the sort of place where Snatter could expect to wake up. In the background he could hear a strange noise that, in his addled state, he imagined sounded like someone kicking a pig.

"...king eejits?"

Vaguely remembering that he was in Larne, Snatter, with the typical condescension of a city dweller, thought that maybe kicking a pig was considered top-flight entertainment around these parts.

"... okay, son?"

As his senses came more into focus, Snatter became aware of a reddish blur just inches from his face. It appeared to be asking him a question. Also, it was wearing a policeman's cap.

"All right there, son? You with these eejits?"

Snatter looked past the ruddy-faced police officer and could then discern the source of the awful noise. Ding-a-Ling and Joker were standing, or rather swaying, on the station platform, each with an arm around the other's shoulder. They seemed to have discovered a mutual love of the music of The Beach Boys and were treating the good people of Larne to a rousing rendition of *The Sloop John B* while several bemused police officers looked on.

Snatter couldn't help smiling at the memory. It was the first time he had spent the night in a police cell, though it wouldn't be the last.

That first day with Joker set the tone for how things would proceed from then on. It would require only the flimsiest excuse for the shop to be closed early and a drinking session to be instigated. It was after one especially boisterous occasion – a celebration for Joker being nominated salesman of the month, having sold a KitKat, twenty Regal and a can of Coke in one transaction – that Snatter realised if things were to carry on as they were, then he would very soon be bankrupt. He arrived at an inevitable conclusion and the next morning he explained the situation to Joker and Ding-a-Ling.

"Look, I hate to say it, but things are looking bad here. I can see myself going out of business if I don't do something drastic."

"This sounds ominous," said Joker.

"To be honest, I don't think I can afford to keep either of you on. I really need to cut costs and the best way to do that is for me to just run the shop on my own for a while. I'm sorry but I'm going –"

"Well, it's about fucking time!" Ding-a-Ling interrupted.

"What?" said Snatter, startled.

"We were wondering how long it was going to take you to wise up," said Joker. "We thought we were going to have to say something ourselves."

"But –"

"Don't sweat it," said Ding-a-Ling, "we've already got something sorted. I mean, you can't expect us to stay in this dump forever, now can you?"

"What?"

"Look," Joker explained, "we're not fucking stupid." He glanced at Ding-a-Ling. "Well, *I'm* not, anyway. We knew things couldn't go on the way they were. It was obvious. Anyway, me and Ding-a-Ling have been offered jobs in that new electrical place in Royal Avenue. Decent money, too. It certainly covers the old rent, that's for sure."

Joker and Ding-a-Ling had recently moved into a flat together on the Ormeau Road after Joker's girlfriend had kicked him out for being a 'drunken shit' and they were currently enjoying the bachelor life together.

"Electrical place?" Snatter asked dumbly. "Doing what?"

"Trainee salesmen," Ding-a-Ling replied. "We start in a couple of weeks."

Snatter didn't know what to say. A part of him felt disappointed that his friends seemed to be deserting him, but mostly he felt a sense of relief. Everything appeared to be working out perfectly for everyone. So perfectly, in fact, that it was decided to close the shop early and go out to celebrate.

As they established themselves in the first bar of the day, it was proposed that such a momentous occasion should, in some way, be recorded for posterity, and so they agreed to collaborate on a poem that would serve as a fitting commemoration of the event.

The Sacking of the Lads was a rambling and increasingly incoherent epic, casting Snatter as a villainous landlord who heaps a series of torments and some inventive depravities upon the two plucky heroes of the piece. It was genuinely believed that it would go on to stand alongside the works of Homer and Virgil in the pantheon of epic poems – although Joker felt obliged to point out to an unconvinced Ding-a-Ling that *The Aeneid* did not have the word 'tits' inserted at random intervals throughout its length.

Snatter gleefully added some of the more colourful accounts of his debauchery as the beer flowed and the day slipped quietly into the mists of his memory.

This isn't helping, Snatter thought, as he finished another beer. *Maybe I should go to bed.* He remained in his seat. *Maybe it was just that things were starting to go too well.*

After Joker and Ding-a-Ling had left to begin their new careers, life for Snatter had settled into a comfortable regime. It wasn't long before his business improved and, eventually, he was able to employ a woman, called Moira, to help out.

Moira brought such professionalism to the role that Snatter felt slightly embarrassed by the ease with which she was able to increase his takings. Everything, for Snatter, now seemed to be plain sailing.

There remained just one issue that needed to be addressed, but Snatter, if he was being honest with himself, was looking forward to exploring that issue with a mixture of trepidation and excitement.

And then Rosie happened.

Jesus! Snatter got up and debated whether to go to bed or go to the fridge. He did neither and just stood, trapped by his thoughts. *How the fuck did I end up here?* he wondered.

To Snatter, the last few months had been a blur. Rosie had burst into his life and had swept him along before he had even understood what was going on. There was no denying Rosie's beauty, but there was something about the woman that Snatter found terrifying and now, as he stood bewildered by the tornado that had suddenly engulfed him, he was worried. What was he going to do?

Still, he thought, *tomorrow is Christmas Eve. Tomorrow is the pub-crawl!*

He was cheered by the thought. He would forget about his worries for one day at least. Maybe he would even seek some advice. Tone could be pretty level-headed, or Jamesy, with his easy-going wisdom, or Bobby, perhaps. Snatter was aware that, even now, he was relying on his friends, but he didn't care because tomorrow was Christmas Eve. Tomorrow was the pub-crawl. Tomorrow everything would be better.

Tomorrow.

SEVEN

"No, it doesn't make you look like a gargoyle! Stop fucking whinging!"

Snatter took his hand away from the bump on his forehead and took the cigarette that Ding-a-Ling was offering.

"Are you sure?" he asked. "It feels massive."

Ding-a-Ling shook his head dismissively as he lit, first Snatter's cigarette, and then his own. They both took a long draw as they waited for the bus to arrive.

"Saw your da up in the Star the other night," Snatter said. "He was telling me about Sticky Mickey, among other things."

"Yeah, well, it's not something I'm really bothered about," Ding-a-Ling shrugged. "No point worrying about it, is there?"

"So, what about this new job, then?" Snatter went on. "What's the deal there?"

"Joker's uncle got us in," Ding-a-Ling replied. "We start in the New Year."

"Printing firm, is it?"

Ding-a-Ling nodded. "It's not far from the city centre," he said. "They're having some big expansion at the minute and they're looking for trainees."

"Doing what, exactly?"

"Well, me and Joker will be in the die-cutting department. Whatever the fuck that is. Anyway, I suppose it's about time." Ding-a-Ling seemed a little more pensive than usual. In fact, if Snatter didn't know better, he would have said Ding-a-Ling seemed almost morose.

"What do you mean, *about time*?"

"Oh, well," Ding-a-Ling, to Snatter's surprise, actually sighed, "maybe it's time I got things sorted out. Just move on with my life, you know what I mean?"

Snatter nodded, although he had no idea what Ding-a-Ling was talking about.

"There's the bus," Ding-a-Ling said as he dropped his cigarette butt and stamped it out.

Snatter looked at the number on the bus and groaned. "It's a Shankill bus."

"So what?" said Ding-a-Ling. "Doesn't matter, does it?"

"No, I suppose not." Snatter was always nervous about boarding a Shankill Road bus at a bus stop in such a notoriously republican area. He worried about who might be watching, taking notes, making plans, as the bus took him into the heart of loyalist Ulster. Today, however, the bus was almost empty.

As Snatter and Ding-a-Ling climbed on board and moved down the aisle, Ding-a-Ling spotted someone he knew. A small, greasy-haired man was sitting by himself near the back of the bus. On the seat beside him was a large holdall that seemed to be empty.

"All right, there, Macker?" Ding-a-Ling asked as he and Snatter pulled themselves into the seats behind. Snatter was always amazed by the number of people that Ding-a-Ling seemed to know. It didn't matter where in the city they went, there would always be someone who Ding-a-Ling would nod to, or wave to, or stop and chat to. *He certainly gets about*, thought Snatter.

"Taking your bag for a walk?" Ding-a-Ling asked Macker, nodding to the holdall.

Macker looked all around him in a shifty manner that Snatter thought was a bit over-dramatic, given that the only other people on the bus were an old woman, sitting near the front, and the driver, who had his hands full. Of course, there was always the possibility that Special Branch was hiding under the seats. *You can never rule that out*, thought Snatter with a smile. He was beginning to feel in a better mood. His head still hurt a bit, but what mattered was that it was Christmas Eve and he was on his way to the pub-crawl. He could almost taste the first pint.

"No," Macker answered. He then tapped the side of his nose with his forefinger, which almost made Snatter burst out laughing.

"I'm on a wee score," Macker said in a low whisper.

"Really?" asked Ding-a-Ling, suddenly interested. Snatter rolled his eyes and looked out of the window as the bus pulled onto the top of the Shankill Road.

"Aye," said Macker, "I was talking to this fella in town the other day. I sort of know him to see, you know? We drink in the same pubs. So, anyway, we'd both had a few jars and were a wee bit the worse for wear, when he tells me this wee secret."

Ding-a-Ling moved a little closer to hear better. Snatter, who was not remotely interested in Macker's 'wee score', was wondering if they had stopped serving lunch in the Tudor Lounge by this time. He had a horrible feeling that they probably had, but he thought that he and Ding-a-Ling should still be able to grab something to eat in town before they started on the beer.

"And you know where this key is?" Ding-a-Ling was asking Macker.

"Oh aye," replied Macker, "he told me exactly where it is, so as long as I put it back where it was then nobody will be any the wiser."

"And there's really that much gear?"

"Tons of it," said Macker, "straight from the docks, you know? So what do you reckon? You in?"

Ding-a-Ling rubbed his chin as he thought about the offer. He was certainly tempted. He turned to Snatter, who was staring out the window. "What do you think?" he asked.

"What?" said Snatter, his reverie interrupted. "What do I think about what?"

"Macker, here, knows where we can get a load of free cigarettes, cartons of them, just there for the taking, just off the Shankill."

"Free? What do you mean *free*? You mean steal them?"

"No, no, you don't understand," said Macker, "they've already been stolen, and you can't steal something twice, now can you? And it's not just smokes either, there's booze, clothes, electrical stuff, anything."

If Macker was expecting this explanation to reassure Snatter, he was disappointed.

"Oh, I see," said Snatter, "they've already been stolen? Well, that's okay, then. For a minute there I was worried. So, we're talking about a safe house, are we?" He looked at Macker, who nodded enthusiastically. "We're talking about a safe house," Snatter went on, "full of stolen goods, just off the Shankill Road. Is that right? Now, I wonder why the letters U, V and fucking F have just popped into my head, eh? Do you have any idea why that would be?"

"Look, it's no sweat," said Ding-a-Ling, suddenly an expert on the whole matter. "It's Christmas Eve, isn't it? Nobody's going to be there today, isn't that right, Macker?"

"Aye, that's right," agreed Macker, "that's what I've been told."

"Don't do this to me," Snatter said. He could feel his panic levels begin to rise and looked imploringly at Ding-a-Ling. "Do not fucking do this to –"

"What's the big deal?" Ding-a-Ling said soothingly. "It's only a couple of stops away. We jump off, find the house, load up with smokes and jump on the next bus. Wee buns! Think of the look on the lads' faces when we start handing out packets of cigarettes. They'll think it's Christmas."

Snatter groaned. "I sell cigarettes for a living," he said.

"I know, and who the fuck can afford those prices? Remember, I'm still technically on the dole."

For a brief moment, Snatter was tempted to let Ding-a-Ling go off on his own while he stayed on the bus and continued into town, but he knew he couldn't do that.

It wasn't just that he would never forgive himself if anything happened to Ding-a-Ling, but how would he explain to the lads that he'd let Ding-a-Ling go wandering around UVF territory with nothing but a greasy stranger and an empty bag for company? Of course, he knew that Ding-a-Ling was more than capable of looking after himself, but still, there was no way he could let him go on his own. That was just the way it was. Fuck it.

Ten minutes later the three of them were trying not to look conspicuous as they made their way through the maze of little streets that were clustered behind the shops of the Shankill Road. Ding-a-Ling's mood seemed to have improved, Snatter thought, though he couldn't say the same for himself. He was hungry and cold and miserable, and he was following one of Ding-a-Ling's unsavoury acquaintances around the streets of the Shankill.

On Christmas Eve.

EIGHT

They shivered as they acclimatised to the cold, then Tone, Jamesy and Joker strode off in search of the next beer.

"Well, something must have happened," Joker was saying. "Ding-a-Ling was looking forward to today and Snatter's never bloody late for anything, is he?"

"I'm sure they'll turn up," said Jamesy.

"Yeah," Tone agreed, "they're bound to show up at some point of the day.

They walked through the crowds towards Royal Avenue, the main thoroughfare in the heart of the city centre, and then turned in the direction of Kelly's Cellars. As they approached the entrance to the alley where Kelly's was situated, Joker spotted a potential problem up ahead.

A small crowd was standing outside one of Royal Avenue's many clothing stores. It was a crowd of young people who were smiling and chatting and handing out leaflets, while a few at the back were singing carols. What was it about born-again Christians, Joker wondered, that made them stand out? Was it that they looked as though they had all been buffed and polished until they shone? Was it the creepy exuberance? The insincere smiles? Joker shuddered and looked at Tone.

"Easy, Tiger," he said.

"They're the ones who were hassling Bobby at the City Hall earlier," Tone said in reply.

"So what?" Joker protested. "What the fuck has that got to do with us?"

"I just want to hear what they have to say."

"*Bahleeks!*" said Joker. He had been looking forward to his next beer in the warm, inviting atmosphere of Kelly's Cellars. Now, it looked like that pleasure would have to wait.

Tone marched up to the little group with Jamesy and Joker shuffling, reluctantly, along behind him. There was a young man and woman at the front who appeared to be the main point of contact. They were both impeccably dressed and, as Joker had earlier noted, so clean they seemed to shine.

The young man wore a fixed, unwavering smile and acted pleasant and approachable. Tone despised him instantly. The woman, in comparison, was more subdued, happy to let her companion do most of the talking. As she saw the three friends approach, however, she gave a warm smile.

"Merry Christmas!" said the man, whose name turned out to be Greg. Tone would have bet money on it being Greg, or Nigel, or Cuthbert, or bloody Samuel.

"Afternoon," said Tone gruffly. "So, what is it you're selling here?"

"What?" said Greg, still smiling. "Selling? We aren't selling anything. We're here to celebrate the birth, and to spread the word, of our Lord and Saviour, Jesus Christ."

"Born around this time, was he?"

Greg's smile remained unchanged. "Well, no one can say for sure when Christ was born, but the 25th of December is as good a day as any. You have to remember we celebrate the birth, not the date."

"You're aware of the significance of that particular date, are you?"

"Of course," Greg replied, "it's an old pagan festival, isn't it? Well, it makes sense, I suppose. If you want to spread the word of God, then it would be easier to just use the existing festivals. Less of an upheaval for everyone."

Greg was turning out to be a lot shrewder than the usual halfwits that Tone encountered. *Not that it makes any difference*, he thought.

"Can I ask," Greg went on, "if any of you have been born again?"

"Nah," Joker shook his head, "I suggested it once, but my ma told me to fuck off." He looked around at all the blank expressions, then tutted to himself. *Way over their heads*, he decided.

"You all know, of course," Greg continued, "that Jesus Christ died for our sins?"

"No he didn't," said Tone, and, for once, Greg's smile wavered.

"I'm … I'm sorry?" he stammered. "It clearly states in –"

"You Christians don't believe that, do you?" Tone argued. "Doesn't it say in your book, *Jesus ascended into heaven to be seated on the right hand of God*?"

"Yeah," interrupted Joker, trying to ease the growing tension, "you'd think that Jesus could have knocked up a couple of chairs." Everyone ignored him, so he turned to Jamesy. "I'm wasted on these bloody plebs," he said, but Jamesy didn't appear to have heard him.

"Well, obviously," Greg persisted, "the Resurrection forms the basis of our faith. It shows us that we are all –"

"So, if you want to be more accurate, then," said Tone, "you would have to say that Jesus was temporarily inconvenienced for our sins, isn't that right?"

"It clearly states," Greg stated firmly, "in John 3:16, *God so loved the world that He gave His only begotten son*."

"Shouldn't that be *lent* his only son? Doesn't have the same impact, does it? Not so much of a sacrifice when you think about it. The all-powerful, all-knowing, all-seeing creator of the universe has a three-day kip and then buggers off to spend the rest of eternity in paradise. Don't see what the big deal is, myself."

"Yes, but –"

"And what do you mean by God's *only* son? Your man, John, hadn't read his scriptures, had he?"

"What do you mean?"

"Genesis 6:2," said Tone. "*That the sons of God saw the daughters of men that were fair; and they took them wives of all which they chose.* Seems that your God had loads of sons, and they were horny buggers, too. Don't go quoting your book of fairy stories at me, mate. I've read it, so I know what a pile of crap it is."

"Well, I just –"

"And another thing," Tone was approaching full rant, "what exactly was God thinking when he turned himself into a human foetus? As a Christian, you believe in God's omniscience, right?"

"Yes, of course, it's one of the core –"

"So, as a Christian," Tone continued, "you must accept that God was aware of every single event that would play out in human history as a consequence of him being born as a divine, human baby thing – from the slaughter of the innocents onwards. You have to accept that God has been looking down from heaven at all the divisions, the purges, the genocides, the crusades ... the inconceivable misery that religion has given humanity, and you have to accept that your omniscient God must be thinking, *Yep, that's exactly what I was aiming for!*"

"Oh, well that's just –"

"The only thing that Jesus ever gave to the world, is more fucking religion!"

An atmosphere had descended on the scene. The carollers had stopped singing and were listening anxiously to the exchange. The young woman beside Greg looked down at the ground. They were all used to suffering casual abuse and insults shouted by jeering passers-by – it came with the territory – but there was something sinister in Tone's measured words that unnerved the group.

Greg was still smiling, though it now seemed a little forced.

"You have some interesting points to make," he said condescendingly, "but isn't it beyond our mortal comprehension to fully grasp the majesty of God's eternal plan? I know it can be difficult at times, and there are times when we all have our faith tested, but as long as we keep our trust in the Lord, then, in time, all shall become clear and we shall have all the answers we require."

"It's the old get-out clause, isn't it?" Tone sneered. "Whenever the questions get too difficult, or when the contradictions become hard to ignore, then all you religious types fall back on the same old chestnut: *man cannot know the mind of God*, or *God works in mysterious ways*. Well, that's the same as closing your eyes and putting your hands over your ears."

"But it's the truth!" Greg protested. "How can you just dismiss the truth? How can anyone claim to know the mind of God?"

Joker was becoming restless, though he sensed that Tone was just warming up. The young woman kept staring at her feet, which she shuffled uneasily.

"But that is exactly what you do claim," Tone insisted. "When you stand here preaching, aren't you claiming to know exactly what God wants?"

Greg's smile became smug. "We are only here to spread God's message," he said. "God has provided us with all the guidance we need. All we have to do is follow the scriptures that He has given us, and the path shall become clear. These scriptures take into account the limited capacity of our human understanding and have been designed accordingly."

Tone, to the Christians at least, seemed to assume a demonic air. The scarf around his neck, a lurid red against a black overcoat, billowed in the chill breeze. His long, black hair swept back and forth across his dark eyes, which glittered and pierced the dull winter light.

"So," Tone began sweetly, "the Bible is a clear set of guidelines? Is that what you're saying?"

Greg was not to be trapped so easily. "It's true," he admitted, "there are many ways to interpret the scriptures, perhaps that is the clearest proof of their divine origin, but I would say they are all variations on a common belief. The underlying message of our salvation through the love and sacrifice of Jesus Christ is the fundamental basis of all denominations."

"All *Christian* denominations," Tone corrected him.

"Well, yes, obviously."

Tone could feel himself growing angry, which annoyed him. He knew that anger would not get him anywhere, it would only serve to cheapen his arguments.

"Are you really telling me," he said, trying to remain calm, "that all Christian denominations are equally valid? Are you saying that the beliefs of Quakers, of Mormons, of the Plymouth Brethren, Seventh Day Adventists, Jehovah's Witnesses, even Catholics are all acceptable to God? Of course you're not, are you? You wouldn't be standing here if you thought that. Why bother pushing your particular Christian beliefs when *all* Christian beliefs are the same? You don't think that all denominations are the same at all, do you? Even though it's only all about one thing. Regardless of what variety of Christianity you want to label yourself with, you all share the one conviction, don't you? You all believe that some Jew on a stick has given you a Golden Ticket, a Get-Out-of-Jail-Free card. That's what it all boils down to isn't it? Never mind all the fancy interpret–"

"Come on, Tone, for fuck's sake!" Joker had heard enough and was pulling Tone by the arm. "Come on, now! Leave the nice Christians alone!" Tone allowed himself to be led away as his anger came to the boil. Jamesy slowly followed.

"Your man said *shall* a lot, did you notice that?" Joker said as they walked down the narrow lane towards Kelly's Cellars.

"Closed-minded, bloody myopic, bloody fuckwits," Tone was still fuming, and angrily threw the end of his scarf over his shoulder.

"I mean, what sort of bloke says *shall* all the time. Bit weird, if you ask me. Bit creepy."

"Keep up there, Jamesy," said Tone, looking behind him, "there's a good lad."

"Oh yeah, Tone!" Joker said suddenly. "Jew on a stick? Fuck me, even I was offended by that!"

Tone stopped and faced Joker. He jabbed a finger at Joker's chest. "You know why that is, don't you?" he said. "Brainwashing! You've been force-fed this nonsense from birth. That's why you felt offended."

They continued walking to the bar and Tone could feel his anger begin to ebb. He was looking forward to the craic in Kelly's now, and another drink would serve to quell his simmering emotions.

"Yes, indeed," he went on, in a happier frame of mind, "it certainly isn't easy to shake off that level of mental conditioning. Isn't that right, Jamesy?"

But Jamesy, still hanging a way behind, wasn't listening. Because Jamesy, to his astonishment, had just fallen in love.

NINE

To Snatter, everything had taken on an oppressive and menacing feel. The little streets of terraced houses that backed onto narrow alleys – known in Belfast as *entries* – became quieter and more eerie the further they walked from the main road.

Fewer people could be seen and more of the houses looked derelict and abandoned. Despite his breath frosting in front of him, Snatter could feel a few beads of sweat roll down his forehead as Macker led him as far away from his comfort zone as he could imagine.

Finally, Macker stopped at a house that stood in the middle of a row of similar houses, all desolate and overgrown and silent. Macker gave the front door a tentative push, then a firmer shove. Nothing happened.

"Oh, right," he muttered. He crouched down and swept some litter away from the bottom of the door to reveal a large bolt lock. Pulling back the bolt, he tried the door again. This time it opened with a creak that almost shattered Snatter's fragile nerves.

Just inside the door was another door, which was padlocked. Macker looked up to see a baton of wood jammed haphazardly above the door frame. It blended in with the rest of the rubble-strewn hallway, but Macker reached up to reveal a narrow ledge. He felt around for a bit, then he smiled and pulled down a small skeleton key.

"Right," he said to Ding-a-Ling and Snatter as he turned the key in the lock, "as far as I know, all the gear is stashed upstairs. Then, opening the door, he carefully pushed the first door closed.

They entered the house and made their way upstairs. At the top, there was a narrow landing with three doors leading off it. The first door opened onto an empty, dilapidated bathroom. The second door revealed a larger room, in almost total darkness.

Ding-a-Ling went in to look around, followed by Snatter. The darkness was split by a thin line of vertical light, shining dully in the wall opposite the door. Ding-a-Ling approached the light and discovered that daylight was seeping past a sheet of heavy plywood, covering a glassless window frame. He touched the bare brickwork of the wall around the boarded window to find the bricks had been saturated by running water that had dripped from the broken roof above. On closer inspection, he realised the entire wall was bowed outwards. He tutted and looked at Snatter.

"Look at the state of this," he said, giving the wall a kick. "It wouldn't take much for this whole –" There was a huge crash as the wall suddenly disappeared.

"Holy fuck!" Snatter screamed, as every one of his nerves snapped at once. "What the fuck did you do, you stupid bastard?"

Macker came running into the room, a terrified look in his eyes.

"I hardly touched it!" Ding-a-Ling protested. "Anyway, it was only a matter of time before it collapsed. Did you see the state of –?"

"Yeah, it was only a matter of time," said Snatter, the panic obvious in his voice. "All it took was for some dickhead to come along, and kick the fucking –"

"Look, lads," Macker interrupted, "That other door was jammed, but I've been working at it and I think I've nearly got it open. Just leave this shit," he said, gesturing to the destruction as he headed out of the room. Snatter glared at Ding-a-Ling, who simply shrugged as he surveyed the damage. The room was at the back of the house and, where the window had been, there was now a gaping hole that afforded a view of a small backyard, choked with a riot of weeds and a fresh tumble of bricks and shattered wood.

Ding-a-Ling stepped over and glanced down into the yard. "Reminds me of Old Ardoyne," he said. "Remember? When we were kids?"

Snatter could feel his heart pounding in his chest. "Can we just get a move on?" he begged.

"Yeah, okay," said Ding-a-Ling, "I'm only saying."

They went through the third door to find Macker standing in the middle of the room. He was rubbing his hands. "What did I tell you, lads?" he grinned. "What did I tell you?"

"Jesus!" Ding-a-Ling exclaimed.

It was just as Macker had described. All around the room were goods piled as high as the ceiling. Cartons of cigarettes were stacked on top of cases of vodka and whiskey and rum. There were heaps of leather goods and boxes of electrical equipment: portable televisions, video recorders and cassette players.

Macker reached over and cracked open a case of whiskey.

"I think I'll do all my Christmas shopping here," he said laughing.

"Fuck," said Ding-a-Ling, "we should have picked up some bags from somewhere."

"We'll just take what we can, and then split," Snatter told him. "This place is freaking me out."

"You worry too much," said Ding-a-Ling as he ripped open a carton of Benson and Hedges, "you always did."

"Do you see any Regal?" Snatter asked. Ding-a-Ling gave him a look and Snatter shrugged. "Be stupid to leave empty handed," he said.

A sudden noise from downstairs made them all freeze. They heard a man's voice cry out in alarm.

"Hey, this fucking door's open!"

A second voice, "Aye, look! There's the lock on the floor there!"

A third voice, "Do you think there's somebody up there?"

"Listen, you run and get Big Dennis! And tell him to bring a rod!"

They heard footsteps disappear quickly down the street. Snatter stared at Ding-a-Ling, his eyes wide with panic and accusation.

"Right," Ding-a-Ling hissed at Snatter and Macker, "I think there's only two of them. We can rush them!"

Snatter felt a sudden urge to strangle his friend.

"Have you gone fucking mad?" he yelled quietly. He looked at Macker, who was shaking with fear. "*Rush them?*"

"Look, they won't be expecting it. We'll surprise them if we just push past them and split. Come on, I'll go first!"

Ding-a-Ling went to the end of the landing. The top of the stairs lay just beyond the end of the wall to his left. Suddenly, with a yell, he launched himself around the corner and down the stairs. A split second later he came sprinting back.

"Nah," he shouted, "there's fucking loads of them! Leg it!"

Loud footsteps could be heard crashing up the stairs, as Snatter and Macker chased after Ding-a-Ling into the back bedroom. With only the slightest hesitation, all three leapt through the hole in the wall and landed heavily, in a tangle of limbs, amongst the rubble and the weeds. Now they had only the wooden door, in the wall enclosing the yard, to negotiate. Ding-a-Ling hurled himself, shoulder-first, at the flimsy structure, only to discover the door's deceptive solidity. He rebounded past Snatter and Macker to fall backwards into the weeds, from which he had scrambled just seconds before.

Snatter grabbed Ding-a-Ling's hand and pulled him to his feet, then, yanking the door open, he pushed him into the little entry beyond and stumbled after, with Macker following. They could hear the shouts close behind.

"*Quick, round the back!*", "*Cover the entry!*", "*Don't let them get away*!".

Sheer panic propelled them to the end of the entry where Macker turned right and shot off towards the Shankill Road.

"Scatter, lads!" he shouted over his shoulder.

Ding-a-Ling and Snatter sprinted in the opposite direction, which took them past some more derelict houses, until they came to a large expanse of broken, uneven tarmac. They crouched behind a low wall as they paused for breath. Ding-a-Ling pointed across to a clump of overgrown bushes on the far side of the waste ground.

"If we can get to those bushes," he suggested, "we can lie low till things quieten down."

Snatter didn't like the look of it. "We'll be bloody exposed out there," he said, pointing to the waste ground.

"I know, that's why we need to move now. Quick, before they get here. Come on!"

They jumped to their feet and sprinted towards the bushes.

The waste ground that they ran across had been used for many years as the location for the local Twelfth of July bonfire.

This annual event was the most important date in the calendar for the Loyalists of Northern Ireland, and commemorated a battle, fought

300 years previously, when a Dutch king of England defeated an English king of England beside a river in Ireland. It had since been deemed, by Northern Ireland's Protestants, as a victory for Protestantism over Catholicism and a victory that secured the national religion of Britain and Ireland forever.

The people of Northern Ireland have, over the years, found many ways to mark an occasion. Celebrations can take a variety of forms, street parties, parades etc., but their favourite way to celebrate the most important events is to set fire to stuff. And so, every year, on the night before the anniversary of the Battle of the Boyne, loyalist areas all over Northern Ireland become ablaze with carefully constructed bonfires that reach high into the night sky and give light to the celebrations that last until the dawn of the Twelfth.

This was why a patch of waste ground, just off the Shankill Road, was strewn with old and charred bits of scrap wood. One of these scrap pieces had once been part of a wooden pallet, but now all that remained was a small, burnt corner of a former plank that was still clinging to its last remaining nail. This nail, though warped by heat and rusted by rain, now thrust towards the heavens, pointing defiantly at the heavy, grey Christmas sky.

Snatter hit it at full pelt, driving the nail through the sole of his favourite trainer and into the sole of one of his favourite feet. There was a tiny moment of shocked silence before he went down in a flurry of expletives.

Ding-a-Ling stopped and turned around.

"Stop acting the maggot, Snatter," he cried, "for fuck's sake! Come on, we're … Oh, shit!" The little piece of wood that was now nailed to Snatter gave Ding-a-Ling a hint as to what was causing the hold up. He rushed over and pulled the wood away from Snatter's foot, which caused an increase in the volume and intensity of Snatter's swearing. Ding-a-Ling then lifted his friend onto his one good foot and, together with arms around each other's shoulders, they hobbled and tripped and stumbled to the bushes, where they collapsed, sweating and swearing, onto the ground.

TEN

Kelly’s Cellars was built in the early 1700s, right in the centre of Belfast. This would become something of an inconvenience, many years later, when Belfast’s civic leaders decided to celebrate the increasing industrial power of the city by building a series of solid and imposing sandstone edifices that would tower into the sky and shout to the world the might of Belfast's industry.

Kelly's, however, did not fit into this vision of thrusting masculinity. It was little more than a humble, stone shack and it was in the way of progress. It would have to go.

But Kelly’s refused to budge and so, in a spirit of compromise, the town planners built their vibrant, new city around the scruffy little upstart and Kelly’s, sandwiched between the mighty buildings of the modern age, was hidden down its own little alley, nestled quietly in the shadows as the city around it marched boldly into the future.

As Tone, Joker and Jamesy approached the stubborn little bar, they could hear the muffled buzz of conversation and laughter. Tone, his anger now gone, was cheered by the promise of a boisterous and friendly ambience. Joker was rubbing his hands in anticipation of his next drink, while Jamesy felt physically sick.

It didn’t make any sense to Jamesy. He did not believe in love at first sight. In fact, Jamesy was not sure if he believed in love at all. His favourite quotation was an epitaph that WB Yeats had written for his own headstone:

Cast a cold eye,
On Life, on Death,
Horseman pass by.

The phrase, *Cast a cold eye*, had become something of a mantra for Jamesy, not just in his studies, but for life in general.

To look at things from a clear, analytical, almost cynical perspective was important to him in determining the truth of a matter. Even the most nebulous of subjects could be explained if one ‘cast a cold eye’ to see through the superfluous and get straight to the heart.

Emotions, to Jamesy, were no different. He had never given much credence to the traditional notion of romantic love. The image of the tragically lovesick, pining and swooning, that fuelled much of popular culture had always seemed, to him, vaguely embarrassing.

Physical attraction, Jamesy would say, can be explained in terms of chemical reactions in the brain that are born out of basic biological urges. When viewed from a scientific perspective, he would argue, love is no more mysterious than a bowel movement.

Jamesy wasn't popular at parties.

So, what was going on? Why was his stomach churning, and his thoughts jumbled and incoherent? This was a new experience for Jamesy, and one that he was struggling to rationalise.

Yes, he told himself, the girl was pretty, but so what? Lots of girls were pretty. Jamesy had seen pretty girls before, he had seen extremely beautiful girls before, and he could equate his appreciation of their beauty with his appreciation of a pleasant sunset. It was a simple matter of aesthetics.

But no sunset had ever made him want to throw up. No sunset had ever torn him with such irrational despair. The more he tried to cast a cold eye on his feelings the more he was faced with a conclusion that he was finding difficult to acknowledge. He was in love. And he wasn't at all sure that he liked it.

The indistinct conversational buzz became a low roar as Tone shoved open the door into the bar. They pushed their way into the crowd and Tone, as Jamesy went off to get the round, scanned the room. Over to the left, in the far corner, a fiddler and an accordion player were preparing to add to the noise. The smell of a turf fire mingled with the familiar smells of beer and tobacco smoke. Tone spotted something and turned to Joker.

"This way," he said, "Jamesy, we'll be down the back!" he shouted over to the bar, but Jamesy seemed to be in a world of his own.

Tone and Joker made their way through the crowd to a table where a young man and woman were hunched in conversation.

"All right there, Ed?" Tone said to the man. "Thought it was you."

Ed, surprised, looked up. "Tone?" he stammered. "Um, yeah, how's it going?"

"Oh, not too bad. Here, do you think we could squeeze in there? You know Joker, don't you?"

"All right, Joker?" Ed said, then turned to his companion. "Could you move around a wee bit, love?"

The young woman looked a little put out, but she pushed her chair closer to the wall to make space for a few more chairs to be placed around the table. Ed shifted along the bench that ran along the wall and Tone squeezed in beside him. Joker found an unused chair and pulled it next to the girl.

"Bout ye, love?" Joker leered, as he slipped into the vernacular.

Tone tutted loudly and kicked Joker under the table. "You'll have to excuse him," he told the bemused couple. "He's from Sandy Row."

Jamesy appeared carrying three pints and, as he placed the drinks on the table, Tone thought he could detect from him a sense of agitation. Before Tone could say anything, though, Jamesy turned and disappeared into the crowd.

"Of course!" Ed exclaimed. "How could I forget? It's the pub-crawl, isn't it?"

"The very same," said Tone, lifting his pint.

At that moment, Sean appeared with a bag of shopping in his hand. "All right there?" he said. "Ed! How's it going? Long time, no see."

Jamesy came back with two chairs. "All I could find," he mumbled, as he sat down.

Sean took the other chair and sat, placing his bag on the floor beside him. "Bobby's at the bar," he said to no one in particular.

"Here we are, then," Tone stretched as he spoke, "more weary participants in the crushing tedium of existence."

"You ever thought of becoming one of those motivational speakers, Tone?" Sean asked. "I reckon you could clean up."

As Tone had just raised his drink to his lips, he had to reply to Sean visually, using one of his fingers.

"Seriously," Sean continued, "I'm sure people would pay a lot of money to be told their lives are pointless and they should all just fuck off and die!"

Joker sensed Ed's girlfriend squirm beside him. *If she's prudish about the language*, he thought with a smile, *then this should be fun.*

"Imagine the applause," Sean said.

"I think you may be right," Tone replied. "People are getting bored with apathy, so nihilism may be the way to go."

Bobby arrived with a beer in each hand. "No fucking seat?" he moaned good humouredly.

Joker was disappointed by the apparent lack of reaction to Bobby's words from the girl at his side, then he realised she was trying not to stare at Jamesy. He shook his head sadly. *Junkie's eyes*, he thought.

Tone pushed up a bit, squashing Ed against the wall. "Cheers, Tone!" Bobby said, as he took a seat. Joker passed around some cigarettes.

"Is this the full complement for the pub-crawl these days, then?" Ed asked.

"We've got two missing at the minute," Bobby answered. "You know about the pub-crawl?"

"I was on the first two," Ed said proudly, "but then, well you know …" he said, glancing at his girlfriend, "things come up. So, who's missing?"

"Snatter and Ding-a-Ling," Tone told him.

"Oh yeah!" said Sean, suddenly remembering. "I spoke to Karen. Seems there was a bit of an incident at Ardoyne this morning. Her husband – you know, Harry? – was giving Snatter and Ding-a-Ling a lift, but he ended up getting arrested."

"Shit!" said Joker. "What happened?"

"Not too sure. Karen was a bit hysterical, but it sounds like our happy wanderers had to get the bus."

"So, they *are* on their way, then?" Tone asked.

"As far as I know."

"Ding-a-Ling," Ed muttered, scratching his chin, "Ding-a-Ling … What was it I heard about Ding-a-Ling?"

"That he's a total wab?" Joker offered.

Ed shook his head. "No," he said, "it was something I hadn't heard before. Now, what was it? Oh yeah, I know what it was! I heard a while back that Ding-a-Ling got castrated."

Everyone turned to stare at Ed.

"What?" Tone asked. "Where the hell did you hear that?"

"Not sure where it was," Ed said, "but that's definitely what I heard. Just a rumour, then, was it?"

"Yeah, I think it's something that Ding-a-Ling would've mentioned," Sean said, "it's just the sort of thing that might pop up in conversation, you know? Where the hell did that rumour come from?"

Tone seemed to consider this, then he smiled. He leaned forward and placed his drink on the table.

"Perhaps," he declared grandly, "I might be able to shed some light on this grubby little subject."

They all looked at him expectantly.

"You will recall, I am sure," began Tone, assuming the role of narrator, "earlier this year, when Ding-a-Ling embarked upon a brief sojourn to Spain?"

"That's right," said Bobby, "Majorca, wasn't it?"

"Yeah," Joker replied, "I was supposed to go, but my great aunt died." He took a draw from his cigarette and leaned back, deep in thought.

"Well, that's unfortunate," said Tone, "but the –"

"Bitch!" Joker muttered.

"Who did he go with in the end, then?" Bobby asked.

"An old mate of ours from school," Sean told him, "Marty, his name is. From Andytown. In fact, I think it was Marty who organised the –"

"Yes," Tone interjected, trying to regain control of the conversation, "it was, indeed, Marty who got in touch with Ding-a-Ling with the idea of sampling one of those 18-30 deals that were being advertised with subtle, bilingual wordplay at the time."

Joker laughed. "I remember that," he said. "*Beaver España*, wasn't it?"

"Exactly," said Tone. "Now, I seem to remember when Ding-a-Ling got back, he was going on about some sort of knife attack."

"Oh yeah," said Bobby, thinking back.

"Rings a bell," Joker agreed.

"Of course," Tone went on, "given Ding-a-Ling's indistinct relationship with reality, no one paid him much attention and he didn't really mention it again." Tone paused to take a drink and to light up a cigarette before continuing. "Well," he said, "I bumped into Marty, up in Renshaw's, not too long ago, and he told me the whole story. It seems that Marty and Ding-a-Ling, whilst partaking of a few refreshing beverages, became embroiled with some like-minded souls from Glasgow, who were there to commiserate with one of their number on the inevitability of his approaching nuptials.

"Well, as it transpired that the interests of all the concerned parties appeared to be in tandem, it was proposed that they should pursue those interests together in a spirit of Celtic brotherhood." Tone paused to take another sip of beer and to let his inner thespian develop fully.

"They all went out on the piss, you mean?" asked Joker.

"To put it into monosyllabic grunts, yes," said Tone. "And, later that very evening, everyone having arrived at a satisfactory degree of inebriation, they weaved their way home along the town's paseo. At this time, one of the merry Glaswegians was so enamoured by his new-found friends that he decided to treat them to a demonstration of the pocketknife he had recently acquired at the town market.

"But, owing to the generous number of libations consumed during the previous few hours, the unfortunate character was finding the extraction of the implement, from his pocket, to be something of a challenge."

"Jesus, Tone," said Joker, "where the fuck is this going?"

"Ding-a-Ling," Tone persisted, "as we all know, is not a man to turn down a challenge and, as such, offered his capable assistance. During the frantic fumbling that ensued, the knife blade was exposed, and managed to slice Ding-a-Ling's finger, which caused him, with intoxicated exaggeration, to leap backwards, slip on some recent vomit and fall, cracking his head on a public bench."

Tone finished his drink and stubbed out his cigarette.

"Yeah," said Bobby, "so what does that have to do with –?"

Tone held up his hand. "Well, as I said," he continued, "Ding-a-Ling didn't push the whole knife business on anyone who knows him well, did he?"

"No," said Joker, "that's true, he hardly talked about it at all."

"But isn't it true that Ding-a-Ling has a lot of passing acquaintances all over Belfast? And isn't it true that Ding-a-Ling also has a tendency to over-dramatize, to exaggerate, to embellish? In other words, to talk a load of old balls?"

Everyone around the table nodded, recognising Ding-a-Ling from the description.

"So, it's more than likely, is it not, that there are quite a few people around Belfast who are under the impression that Ding-a-Ling, probably while he was saving a busload of disabled orphans, was attacked by a knife wielding maniac? With me so far?" Tone took the blank stares to mean *yes* and carried on.

"You all know about Chinese whispers, don't you? Well, the chances are that the story was passed on and became more distorted with each telling."

"Feel free to arrive at a point any time soon," said Sean, but Tone waved him down.

"Perchance there were those," he went on, "who are more given to drollery, you understand, who simply said that Ding-a-Ling had been stabbed in the Balearics."

"Oh, for fuck's sake!" Sean groaned. Bobby and Joker both laughed, while Ed and his girlfriend smiled uncertainly. Jamesy stared at his pint.

"It's my round, isn't it?" Tone said as he stood up. "Ed, you two okay there?"

"Yeah, Tone, you go ahead."

"Don't get me one either, Tone," Jamesy added.

Tone gave Jamesy a quizzical look, then turned and made his way to the bar. As he waited to be served, he noticed a grey-haired lady, who looked to be in her seventies, take a microphone from the musicians at the far end of the room and launch into a rendition of *Santa Claus is Coming to Town*. When she came to the chorus, virtually everyone in the bar joined in, and even Tone had to smile.

Joker had been watching Jamesy. "What's up with you, Jamesy? You've a face on you like a slapped arse."

"What?" Jamesy exclaimed. "Oh, nothing, just thinking, that's all."

"Ah, you don't want to be getting involved with any of that thinking business," Joker said with an air of authority. "Nothing good ever came from thinking."

Jamesy smiled a weak smile. He wasn't accustomed to the feelings he was currently experiencing and was considering asking for some advice.

It made sense, he decided, to consult with someone who had more experience in the, now very real, matters of the heart. He had already dismissed Joker as a possible confidant for, although Joker possessed many admirable qualities, the ability to dispense tactful and sage advice was not, Jamesy feared, one of them. Tone had once referred to Joker as an abstract collection of noises and smells and the fact that Joker had taken this to be a compliment summed up, for Jamesy, Joker's frivolous approach to life.

Jamesy had also discounted Sean and Bobby as – solid guys though they were – he felt that they were too preoccupied with their own lives to give much more than a passing nod to his problems. Snatter could always be relied upon to devote his full attention to an issue before supplying his thoughtfully considered opinion on the matter. But Snatter wasn't there, so that just left …

Tone returned to the table with a tray of drinks. "I'd better knock this one back," he said. "I just remembered I was supposed to get some tobacco for my da when I was in Queen's Arcade. I'd better nip back."

"Is it okay if I tag along?" asked Jamesy. "I think I could do with some air."

"No problem, Jamesy. Drink up." Tone nudged Sean. "So, where will we meet up?"

"I don't think we'll have time for the Morning Star this year," said Sean, "so what about White's?"

"Yeah, okay, though we might nip into the Globe for a quick one, just to see what the craic is."

Tone knocked back his pint in a few gulps and stood up. Jamesy tried to finish his drink, but still had to leave a little in the bottom of the glass. He pulled on his coat as he stood and followed Tone to the door.

"Well," Ed said when they had gone, "Tone seems in better form from the last time I saw him."

"What do you mean?" asked Sean.

"I bumped into him, a while ago, at the top of the New Lodge," Ed explained. "We were just chatting away and I said I was on my way to Mass. All of a sudden, he calls me a credulous moron and storms off. I thought, what the hell was that all about?"

Sean put his drink on the table and leaned back in his chair.

"That," he said with a sigh, "is a long story."

ELEVEN

Bournemouth lay on the south coast of England, about thirty miles west of Southampton. Tone was faintly surprised that his battered old Ford Fiesta had made it so far, but as he drove past the Royal Bath Hotel towards the seafront, he felt he could relax enough to take in the sights.

Bournemouth, it seemed, was showing off. It was hot, even though it was approaching the end of September, and the sky was unfeasibly blue. It was not yet noon, but the tall pines that framed and fractured the sea and the sky seemed to bake gently in the sun, which put Tone in mind of a Cézanne landscape from the south of France. Only better, he thought, for he wasn't a big fan of Cézanne.

He tried not to stare at the local girls – still dressed in colourful little skirts and shorts despite the lateness of the season – as he drove past the Gardens, heading for the West Cliff. He was driving to a hotel where his friend, Douglas, had arranged a meeting with a young playwright named Matthew Patterson.

Tone had recently received, from Douglas, a copy of Matthew's manuscript, which told the story of the early struggles of a Christian group that had been founded in Bournemouth in the nineteenth century. It was not a subject that would normally have interested Tone, but it had been written so well, and with such gentle humour, that Tone could see a lot of possibilities with it. He thought he could use it for his second-year project.

Ever since Tone had watched, as a schoolboy, a performance by the Royal Shakespeare Company, his main ambitions had all involved the theatre. He wanted to write for the theatre, he wanted to direct in the theatre, he wanted to thrill and entertain and educate and provoke in the theatre and so, for his university drama project for that year, he was planning to direct his first play.

Tone had met Douglas the previous year at Southampton University; a shared passion for drama bringing them together. It had been Douglas' final year and he had already been offered a lucrative position as assistant casting director with a company in London.

"Not going to take it, though," he had told Tone. "Can't see me working for a bunch of poncey twats up in London. Besides I'd always planned to move back to Bournemouth when I finished here."

He had taken a job with the local arts council and was helping to discover and develop new talent. Tone had kept in touch and had let him know that he was going to need an interesting project for the coming year. It looked like Douglas may have found the very thing.

Tone drove past the new conference centre and spotted the sign for the hotel, almost lost in a forest of hotel signs that blanketed the West Cliff. It was hot in the car and he was looking forward to a cold pint of lager in the hotel bar.

Douglas had actually invited Tone to afternoon tea, but Tone had assumed that 'afternoon tea' was some sort of Dorset euphemism, for Douglas was mightily and famously fond of alcohol and, sure enough, as Tone walked up the steps to the hotel reception, he caught a glimpse, through the window, of Douglas standing at the bar.

Afternoon tea! Tone chuckled. *Yeah, right!*

"Yes, two sugars would be lovely, thank you very much," said Tone, and Matthew picked up two little pieces of cane sugar, using tiny silver tongs, and dropped them into a bone china teacup, filled with steaming English Breakfast tea.

Tone glanced at Douglas, who glanced back and gave a slight shake of his head. *Don't ask*, was the message Tone received.

"The hotel was my idea," Matthew explained as he passed around the teas, "I just think they do such wonderful teas here. You really should try the scones. The best in Dorset, I would say."

Tone had taken a liking to Matthew right away. He was a good-looking and well-dressed young man, who was open and friendly, and who made Tone feel immediately at ease.

Douglas, thought Tone, looked out of place in this dainty little side room. His chaotic, red hair and his unruly beard betrayed his Scottish ancestry and gave the impression that his head was in the process of exploding. *He'd look more at home,* Tone thought, *on an ancient Scottish battlefield, swinging a huge claymore and smiting the Sassenach bastards.*

As Douglas reached for his cup of tea, he gripped the delicate handle between his thumb and forefinger and, with his little finger pointing into the air, raised the cup to his lips. Tone suppressed a smile.

"So, where did the idea for the play come from," he asked Matthew.

"Well," said Matthew as he dabbed at the corner of his mouth with a napkin, "it's really just my way of spreading the Lord's message. I don't know if you had ever heard of our little congregation before you read the play?" Tone shook his head.

"No, I'm not surprised," Matthew laughed. "You have heard of Jesus Christ, though?"

"The name rings a bell."

"Tony is a bit of a Godless heathen," said Douglas.

"I'm a Catholic," Tone said.

"Yeah, I know. That's what I mean."

Matthew laughed again. "It was my father who gave me the idea," he said. "He has been concerned, lately, about the dwindling numbers coming to our church meetings. I'm studying English at college at the minute, and I thought that maybe I could use that to help in some way. That's when I came up with the idea for a play."

"So, it's like some sort of recruitment drive, then?" Tone asked.

"I like to think it simply provides information about us in, hopefully, an entertaining way. And perhaps it might lead some people to want to know more."

"Well, with your words and my masterful direction, I'm sure we can manage that," Tone said, and they all laughed. They carried on talking, working out various details, for another hour or so, and then Matthew said he had to go.

Tone and Douglas walked him to the front door and, once they had waved him off, they turned and bolted to the bar.

"Fuck!" Douglas exclaimed, as he handed Tone a cigarette. "I never realised how hard it could be to be on your best behaviour for that long."

"Yeah, I know what you mean," said Tone. He ordered two pints and, sitting on a stool beside Douglas at the bar, he took a puff from his cigarette. "Why, though?" he went on. "Why were we so bothered about offending him?"

Douglas shrugged, as a beer was placed in front of him. "Don't know," he said, "it just wouldn't have felt right, know what I mean?"

"Yeah," Tone agreed, "he was such a likeable wee fucker, it would have been like kicking a puppy."

"Exactly! And he is a nice guy, isn't he?"

Tone took a sip of beer and nodded. "Queer as a bottle of chips, of course," he said, "but that –"

"Oh no, no, no," Douglas interrupted, "he can't be, you see. His god doesn't allow it."

"He should get himself a different god, then."

"Doesn't work that way with these religious types," Douglas explained. "They tend to be stuck with whatever god their parents give them."

"Spoken like a true cynic!"

"That's me!" Douglas said cheerfully. He took a large gulp from his drink and wiped his beard with the back of his hand. "So, anyway, what sort of timescale do you have in mind for this?"

"Not sure," Tone replied. "Off the top of my head, I'd say a short run in the spring."

"Sounds okay, I'll start scouting out some venues."

"Casting?"

"I've got a few people in mind," Douglas said, "although, I think Sarah might be a bit of a bitch to fill."

Tone nodded. "Yeah, I'd thought that myself. He's written her like a cross between Florence Nightingale and Attila the Hun."

Douglas laughed. "We'll sort something out," he said, finishing his beer. "You still planning to stay at my place tonight?"

"If that's okay?"

"Of course," Douglas assured him as he ordered another round. "So how have you been, Tony? It's been a while."

"Yeah, not too bad," Tone answered, "You know, the usual, settling back into a routine and all."

"Seen Adrian lately?"

"Yeah, I called round the other day. He seems well enough."

"That's good," said Douglas. He took a long drink and looked at Tone. "What do you have in mind for the rest of the day?"

"Well," Tone replied, "after you've bought me dinner, I thought you could give me a tour of all the decadent fleshpots of Bournemouth."

And that's what they did.

Tone spent the next few weekends travelling back and forth between Southampton and Bournemouth, meeting with Douglas and Matthew, and slowly bringing together the components that would make his directorial debut a success. Everything was going smoothly, apart from the one issue that both Tone and Douglas had anticipated.

The casting for the role of Sarah, the play's female lead, was proving problematic.

There was no shortage of talented actresses who had auditioned for the role but, for one reason or another, Tone had dismissed them all. Douglas was becoming exasperated with what he called Tone's impossible pickiness and would throw his hands in the air after yet another rejection and shout, "So, what the fuck was wrong with that one, then?"

But Tone was unable to give a satisfactory reply. He wasn't sure what the answer was himself. Technically, all of the girls who auditioned were perfectly acceptable, but perfectly acceptable, as far as Tone was concerned, was not the same as perfect.

"Jesus, Tony!" Douglas would moan. "We're not making *Gone with the Wind* here."

"I know, I know," Tone would reply, "and you're right, but I just want to get this spot on. Don't worry, we've still got time to sort it out."

One evening, during the week, Tone received a phone call from Matthew. He was ringing to invite Tone to lunch with his family on Saturday. It was to be at their home in Poole, on the far side of Bournemouth. Douglas, Matthew informed him, had already accepted his invitation.

Tone was not keen on the idea, but he agreed to come and told Matthew he was looking forward to it. *At least Douglas will be there too*, he told himself.

"Douglas can't make it, I'm afraid," Matthew said as Tone arrived at the house. "He phoned earlier; says he's got a bit of a dodgy tummy."

Bastard, thought Tone. *Wish I'd thought of that.*

Matthew led the way into the house, which was an impressively large, detached building.

"Nice place," Tone commented.

"Thank you," Matthew smiled. "It's been in my mother's family for a long time."

There was a stairway straight ahead as they entered the hall, with two doorways on the left and one on the right. Matthew opened the door on the right and motioned for Tone to enter.

The introductions, Tone thought, were a little formal. A middle-aged man sat, rather stiffly, in a leather wing-backed armchair in one corner, while on the other side of the room a woman with greying hair sat on a leather couch. Her legs were pressed tightly together and she sat rigidly upright with her hands set together on her lap. Beside the woman on the couch was a younger woman, who Tone guessed at being in her late teens, and whose beaming smile provided the only hint of a welcome in the entire room.

"Anthony," Matthew said, "I'd like you to meet my father, Samuel." He gestured to the man in the chair, who gave a polite nod. "My mother, Jessica." Another nod. "And this is my sister, Emily." A smiling nod.

"Nice to meet you all," said Tone. He felt uncomfortable, and he continued to feel uncomfortable through the stilted conversation that led up to the meal.

Sitting at the table, Tone had to wait until prayers were said before he could eat. He was familiar with the practice of saying Grace before a meal – he'd seen it in the movies – but this was interminable. Samuel even went so far as to read some passages from a Bible that lay open on the table. Eventually, though, they were able make a start on the soup course.

"Matthew tells me that you are a Roman Catholic," Samuel said to Tone as they ate their soup.

"Not a very good one, I'm afraid," Tone replied with an apologetic smile. Samuel shook his head sadly and carried on eating his soup. Tone frowned, bewildered. *He seems to be the sombre type,* he thought. *Can't imagine old Samuel here, kicking back with a joint and having a fit of the giggles.*

"You do know," Samuel suddenly resumed, "that idolatry is one of the most wicked of sins."

Tone was taken by surprise. "Aye, well," he stammered, "I've been trying to cut down on that just lately."

Samuel continued to stare at Tone for a few more seconds, before returning to his soup.

Jesus! thought Tone. *It's the fucking Adams Family!*

"Anthony's been having some wonderful ideas about *The Congregation*," Matthew told his father. "It's all beginning to look very professional. You really must come and take a look some time."

Samuel shifted in his seat. "I'm still not sure about all this," he said gruffly. "Parading around on stage seems disrespectful."

"Well, that's where Anthony has been so clever," said Matthew, "I think he's given it just the right touch of dignity. It's very reverential."

Samuel did not reply. He finished his soup and stared into the middle-distance. His wife, Jessica, got up and took the empty soup bowls into the kitchen.

"What do you know of our faith?" Samuel barked, turning his gaze, once more, on Tone.

Tone, again taken by surprise, spread his hands in a gesture of uncertainty. "Only what I've gathered from reading the play," he said. "It's an interesting story."

"I doubt that the full account of our founding can be conveyed in a single play," Samuel said with an intensity that Tone found ridiculous. "Although," Samuel continued, "I have every faith in Matthew."

There was a pause and Tone, assuming that Samuel had finished, turned to make a comment to Matthew. Samuel, however, spoke again.

"The Catholic Church," he said gravely, "has been guilty of the most atrocious of sins. I would imagine that you feel a constant burden of guilt."

Tone met Samuel's accusing stare and felt an increasing sense of irritation. He was tempted to tell Samuel that he could take his opinions and shove them straight up his –

"That's the familiar old cliché, isn't it?" said Matthew laughing. It eased the growing tension, which had been Matthew's objective. "That all Catholics share a burden of guilt?"

"Well, like I was saying," said Tone, grateful for Matthew's intervention, "I've never been a very good Catholic. Although, to be fair, the Catholic Church has been trying to improve things over the years. I mean, we're only allowed to sacrifice a baby when there's a full moon, these days."

"You joke about it?" Samuel raged and Tone thought that his reaction could not have been any more excessive if Tone had climbed onto the table, dropped his trousers and made a faecal deposit in the fruit bowl.

Samuel stared at Tone for a heartbeat and then pointedly turned away. Tone shrugged and allowed his gaze to wander around the table. He caught Emily watching him, but she quickly looked away when their eyes met. Tone's attention then turned to Jessica as she came back from the kitchen.

She was a strong-featured woman, Tone thought, though maybe a little serious. Her face held a strange combination of sorrow and strength, which, though curious, was not unattractive. In this, Emily was similar.

Tone looked once more at Emily and studied her with a little more care. She had a childish, elfin quality, which her smile tended to exaggerate. Her features reminded Tone of illustrations from a book of fairy tales, in a charming but also unsettling way. She did, indeed, share her mother's odd sense of determined melancholy, but in Emily it was less serious and more ethereal, almost haunting.

Under Tone's scrutiny, Emily stared fixedly at the table in front of her.

"Matthew," said Tone, still thoughtfully regarding Emily, "what do you think of Emily for the role of Sarah?" At this, Emily stared harder at the table and blushed furiously.

Matthew folded his arms and leaned back in his chair as he looked at his sister, as if for the first time. He tried to imagine the words he had written coming from Emily's lips and the more he thought about it, the more he realised that Anthony could be on to something.

"Yes," he exclaimed, "I see what you mean!"

"Emily has her studies," said Samuel firmly.

"Oh, but Father," Matthew insisted, "it won't take up a lot of time and I do think she would suit the role."

Samuel seemed to consider this, then his face softened. "Very well," he relented, "if Emily wants to, then I –"

"Yes!" Emily cried out, her face erupting in smiles.

After dinner, Tone and Matthew took Emily along to the Community Hall, where they had been rehearsing, to properly determine her potential. She proved to be a natural, and Tone was delighted that his nagging dilemma had been resolved.

He had found Sarah.

Over the next few weeks, Tone watched as Emily's confidence grew. It seemed strange for such a small and delicate figure to dominate the stage, but Emily had real presence and a flare for acting. During one rehearsal, Emily gave a performance that was so assured, so passionate and so moving, that the rest of the cast simply stood and stared. Tone was stunned.

"How was it?" Emily asked nervously.

Tone felt that his response should be measured and restrained; not wishing to place too much pressure on those fragile shoulders.

"Oh," he said blithely, "it was probably the single greatest thing I have ever seen in my entire life." And everyone laughed.

One Sunday, Matthew invited both Tone and Douglas to attend a meeting of the Dorset Congregation and, having failed to come up with an adequate excuse not to go, they went.

It had turned out to be much more tedious than they were expecting. Dragging on for almost two hours, the relief that Tone and Douglas had felt, when it ended, was palpable. What they hadn't realised, though, was that Samuel had watched them intently throughout the service and every stifled yawn, every roll of the eyes and every mocking smirk was noted and, in Samuel's mind, magnified tenfold.

"What did you think?" Matthew and Emily asked excitedly when they got together afterwards.

"Wonderful," Tone lied. "Very moving."

"Yes," Douglas agreed, "I found it very humbling."

To return the favour or, as Douglas put it, to retaliate, Tone and Douglas persuaded Matthew and Emily to accompany them on a night out in Bournemouth.

And so, one Friday evening, Matthew and Emily picked up Tone and Douglas in Matthew's car and they drove into town. The nightlife in the town centre proved to be suitably lively as they trawled the popular bars and clubs. From the Third Side and Midnight Express to the Vaults and the bars of the Square and the Triangle, they met Teds, reliving the fifties, Mods, reliving the sixties, and punks, reliving two weeks in the summer of 1976. They saw peroxide hairdos, and Mohicans, and Dreadies. They met New Romantics and Futurists and New Wave poseurs. They met Technobillies, Psychobillies and Oriental Rockabillies. They even met the 'Clash girl', a local celebrity who had run away from school to follow The Clash around the country.

At the end of the night, a wide-eyed Emily and Matthew dropped Tone and Douglas at Douglas' flat.

"Well," Tone asked, as he got out of the car, "did you have a good time?"

"Oh, yes, yes," they assured him, "it was … yes it was … it was nice."

As they drove home in silence, Matthew determined to consult the Old Testament when he got back to his room.

Bournemouth, he felt, was bound to be in there somewhere.

The little denomination of the Dorset Congregation had been founded by William Makehurst and his wife, Sarah, in the latter half of the nineteenth century. William and Sarah were part of a growing number of Christians who had become dissatisfied with the direction that the Church of England seemed to be taking.

It was felt that the doctrines of the national church had become diluted and ambiguous, and that a more defined set of instructions would be required for proper Christian guidance. Of course, everyone had their own opinions on what these new rules should be, and lots of opposing little faiths began to spring up around the country.

For William and Sarah, the keystone of their faith was God's direct and immediate influence on Earth. They saw His will everywhere and in everything and so, when Sarah broke her spine, falling from her horse, it was not seen as an accident, but as a part of God's plan. Everything that happened on Earth, they believed, was directed by God.

The fact that Sarah could no longer walk was accepted with a simple faith in God's will, and William and Sarah's evangelical mission continued with just as much fervour as before. They became a popular and recognisable couple as they preached around the south coast.

It was when Sarah's parents got involved, however, that the core teaching of the new church would become cemented in place.

Sarah's mother had heard of a physician in Salisbury who was earning a reputation for his miraculous powers of healing. His new, ground-breaking techniques were showing unprecedented results and Sarah's mother grasped at a renewed hope that her daughter could be cured.

"You must at least go and see him," she begged William and Sarah.

"Yes," Sarah's father agreed, "I feel we should pursue every course that is available to us in aiding your recovery, Sarah. You will let us take you to see him, won't you?"

William had his misgivings, though. "Aren't we attempting to undo what God has done?" he pleaded. "Wouldn't we be trying to subvert His will?"

But eventually he was persuaded to let Sarah travel with her parents to Salisbury, where the miracle physician declared that all Sarah needed, for her to walk once more, was a simple operation.

William never saw his wife alive again and, through his grief, he understood the message that heaven had given him. God's will, William now knew, was absolute, and the foundational doctrine of the First Church of the Dorset Congregation was laid.

God's design must never be opposed. Never challenged. Never questioned.

Samuel had spent much of the day in his study, which faced onto the drive at the front of the house. He knew the history of his Church and he largely agreed with William's interpretation of the events. He accepted the absurdity of mortal man trying to change divine decree but, at the same time, Samuel believed there was a way for God to be swayed, and that way was through the Saviour, Jesus Christ, using the power of prayer.

There were other elders in the Church, he knew, who disputed this line of reasoning; accusing him of using the Son of God in the same way the idolatrous Catholics used their saints, but Samuel was confident that his analysis was correct. Why else, he argued, would God send His Son down to Earth, if not to mediate on our behalf?

There had been many discussions like this one among the elders on various points of the Church's teachings, but they had always been good-natured, and Samuel did not fear the prospect of any serious schisms in the Church in the near future.

He got up from his desk and stretched. He had been poring over the scriptures for several hours, seeking comfort and also looking for some guidance.

Ever since Anthony had appeared in the midst of his family, Samuel had been troubled. There was no one single reason that he could point to for making him feel so uneasy but there was something about Anthony's overall presence that hinted at a lurking menace.

And the Lord said, Simon, Simon, behold, Satan hath desired to have you, that he may sift you as wheat.

It didn't help that Anthony's dark eyes were shrouded and unreadable, or that his general attitude lacked humility. It didn't help that Samuel's children seemed beguiled by Anthony. Mesmerised. Tempted.

But I prayed for thee, that thy faith fail not.

Samuel watched, through the window, as Anthony's car pulled up, and Anthony, Matthew and Emily got out. He watched as Matthew shook Anthony by the hand and then walked, smiling, towards the house. He watched as Emily, laughing and blushing, jumped up to give Anthony a quick hug, before turning to chase after her brother. Samuel picked up his leather-bound Bible and clutched it to his chest. Was God testing him, he wondered. Or was he being tempted by Satan? As he listened to his children's laughter in the hall outside his study, Samuel dropped to his knees and prayed for the strength to face whatever challenges lay ahead.

"Belfast?" Emily asked. "For how long?"

Tone thought she seemed a little crestfallen, but he dismissed it and gave her a smile.

"Not long," he told her. "Just till after Christmas. I'll be staying with my folks. And there just happens to be a pub-crawl with my name on it."

The pub-crawl that year was memorable for several reasons. Tone met Joker for the first time and, later in the evening, Bobby, a friend that Sean had met at university, became absorbed into the group. Everyone, that year, was in high spirits. Tone especially, it was noted, was in good form. He laughed and joked throughout the long day, and the tentative memories that came creeping through the fog of Christmas morning turned out to be pleasant ones.

Tone was finally having to confront the reason for his sense of well-being. It was becoming obvious, anyway. He could not get Emily out of his head. He thought about her constantly, which played havoc with the natural scowl that normally held sway over his features. Unbidden smiles and twinkles would now occasionally flicker across his face. Twinkles, for fuck's sake!

The Christmas and New Year celebrations came and went, and Tone thought of little else but Emily. He pictured her elf-like smile, her infectious laughter and her touching, wide-eyed innocence.

You're wasting your time, he told himself. *An innocent, God-fearing, wee girl like that? And what are you? Some jumped-up scruff from the slums of Belfast, that's what! Dream on, son. Dream on!*

And he did.

By the time he settled into his seat in the coach at Stranraer for the overnight trip down through Scotland and England, Tone had filled his head with silly fantasies. He imagined glittering opening nights, where everyone would be entranced by the beautiful pixie at his side. Or a far-flung beach at dusk, where they would stroll, and Tone would point something out and make a clever remark, and Emily would laugh and tease and run a little ahead – a dark-haired sparkle in nature's red gloom – as above and around them both an ebbing sun would splash the sky with scarlet.

Jesus! thought Tone as he turned over, trying to get comfortable. *What the hell is happening to me?*

Emily had not been feeling well for a while now. It was a terrifying illness that brought waves of nausea and squeezed her lungs, leaving her fighting for breath. It dragged her lower than she'd ever been before, and it swamped her young life with pain and despair and darkness.

And it hurled her into the heavens in rapturous flight to go soaring through sun-kissed days, and nights washed bright by a delirious moon. It would send her from euphoria to hopelessness in an eye-blink and it was making her feel dizzy and sick.

Was this love?

If this was love, thought Emily, then love was horrible. And it was wonderful. Anthony was filling her thoughts and making her heart race and leaving her gasping and breathless in her happy misery. Anthony was an obsession that was becoming all-consuming, and as Emily found herself thinking less and less of the Lord, she was both horrified and thrilled.

Her father had dismissed Anthony as having no faith, and this had worried Emily. She had fretted, at first, over Anthony's immortal soul, but she had come to the conclusion that, as a good person, Anthony would, in time, come to embrace the Lord.

And Anthony *was* a good person, despite what her father said. She was sure of it. And one day in mid-January she found out the type of person that Anthony really was.

Tone phoned Matthew to tell him he wouldn't be able to come down to Bournemouth at the weekend due to problems with his car.

"Then I'll come over to you," Matthew said. "I've done those re-writes we discussed, and I'd like your opinion on them."

"No problem," said Tone. He took a glance around the house that he shared with three other students. "I'll give you the address of a café we can meet at."

When Saturday morning arrived, Matthew threw the bag containing his manuscript into the back of his car, and then he noticed Emily, standing in the doorway, wearing her warm overcoat.

"I thought I could come along," she suggested. "I don't have anything else to do today."

Matthew, glad of the company, motioned for her to jump in the car. They drove off and Emily let Matthew chatter away unheard, as she allowed herself to wallow in the honey-warm glow of anticipation. Just to see him was enough.

Emily had never entertained the notion of revealing her feelings for Anthony. The possibility of a rejection, whether scathing or gentle, was so appalling to her that she didn't consider it worth the risk. The idea of an actual romance with Anthony was so unlikely that she felt content to let it dwell beyond the reach of her imagination. Just to see him was enough. To be near him, to be in his company, was an agony so delicious that Emily craved it without condition.

The café was situated on the Avenue, not far from Southampton Common, and Tone was already seated when they arrived.

"We can get lunch here," he told them, surprised and delighted to see Emily. "It's a decent menu."

It did, indeed, prove to be a decent menu and they had an enjoyable lunch, discussing various aspects of the play. After lunch, Matthew declared that he wanted to visit the city centre.

"There's a shop that stocks rare books that I'd like to investigate," he said, and then he laughed as he saw the look on Emily's face. "Don't worry," he told her, "you don't have to come. I can meet you back here, if Anthony doesn't mind, that is."

"Not at all," Tone shrugged casually. He resisted the urge to punch the air.

"I should only be about an hour," Matthew told them as he got up. "I'll see you both later."

Once Matthew had gone, Tone and Emily smiled shyly at each other and, at first, their conversation was a little stilted. It was their first time alone together, and they both felt awkward and unsure of themselves. Soon, though, they began to open up, and it wasn't long before they were laughing and chatting, comfortable in each other's company. Emily felt a simple contentment just gazing across the table at Anthony as he told her of his studies and his plans for the future.

Behind her, Emily vaguely heard the door to the café open, as someone entered. Watching Anthony, she saw him glance over her shoulder. And then, with a snarl, he suddenly exclaimed. "Look at that bloody spastic!"

Emily slowly turned and instantly felt sick with shock and embarrassment.

A woman had just come into the café. She was pushing a wheelchair, in which was a young boy, his body twisted and contorted, and his hands held, claw-like, against his chest.

The woman had heard Anthony's remark and was staring at him. Emily felt paralysed, her world crashing around her in tortuous slow-motion. She felt a rising sense of panic as Anthony got up from the table and approached the newcomers. She gaped helplessly as she watched him stop in front of the wheelchair and glower down at the boy.

"So, where have *you* been, you wee bugger?" Tone asked the boy as he knelt down. He was patient as the boy stammered out a reply.

"Too busy for the likes of you!"

"Oh, is that right?" said Tone. He glanced up at the woman. "Hiya, Margaret, how have you been?"

"Hi, Tony," Margaret said, "I heard you'd moved to Bournemouth."

"No, it's just something I'm working on. I have to spend a bit of time down there." Tone turned back to the boy. "Right, matey boy," he said, "I think you're well overdue an ass-kicking. I hope you've been practising."

"He's never off that little Spectrum thing you got him, Tony." Margaret said. "Isn't that right, Adrian?"

"You must be getting pretty good, then," said Tone.

"No time for chess," Adrian informed him. "Programming now."

"What?" Tone cried. "You're programming? I don't believe you!"

"It's true," laughed Margaret, "he's becoming a real whizz-kid."

"I'm impressed," Tone told Adrian. He then looked up at Margaret. "Are you sitting down?"

"No, Tony," Margaret replied, "we're going to the Common. We just called in to get some sandwiches and drinks."

"Well, pick what you want, and I'll get it," Tone said as he stood up and reached for his wallet.

"Don't be silly, Tony!"

"Look, I don't want to have to get violent with you, but I can –" Tone began, and Margaret laughed.

"Oh, go on, then, you daft sod!"

When Margaret and Adrian had left, Tone sat back at the table and faced Emily.

"That was Adrian," he said. "A wee mate of mine. His ma's a cleaner at the univers…What are you grinning at?"

"Nothing," Emily replied, her heart singing. "Nothing at all."

TWELVE

Snatter had taken off his shoe and sock and was staring at the little circular hole in the sole of his foot.

"That's going to go septic, isn't it?" he said. "I mean, who knows what the fuck was on that nail."

Ding-a-Ling was lying on his stomach, peering out through a small gap in the bushes.

"I can't see anybody," he said, "but I can hear loads of shouting. I think we might have upset them."

"Some people can be so touchy," Snatter muttered, poking his hole. "Any idea what happened to Macker?"

"No, but fuck, did you see him go?" Ding-a-Ling crawled backwards to crouch beside Snatter. "He took off like two men and a wee lad."

"He probably has to run away from loads of things. He looks the type."

"That's true," Ding-a-Ling agreed. He then looked thoughtful. "I didn't like the sound of that Big Dennis bloke, though," he said. "Sounds like a right laugh, doesn't he?"

"Shit, it's going purple!"

"What? Oh, stop whinging about your fucking foot!"

"Well, pardon me!" Snatter exclaimed. "But it happens to be really fucking sore!"

"I'm sorry if I don't seem too sympathetic," Ding-a-Ling retorted, "but nobody seemed to give a fuck when I got knifed that time in Spain. Anyway, I'm sure you'll live. We need to figure out what we're going to do here. And never mind your bloody foot."

"Maybe we should wait till Big Dennis gets here," Snatter replied sulkily. "We can ask *him* what we should do."

Ding-a-Ling gave Snatter a withering look. "Well, maybe," he suggested, "the *big* is used ironically."

"Of course!" Snatter cried. "It's obvious, isn't it? Big Dennis is a midget! And I'm sure he's the forgiving type who just wants everybody to get along and love each other. Of course," he went on, "that's what the UVF is known for, isn't it? Paramilitary violence, racketeering and a playful sense of irony. That's right, isn't it? I mean –"

"Look, we don't even know if it is the UVF," Ding-a-Ling pointed out.

"True, true," Snatter conceded, "it could be the UDA, couldn't it? Well, if that's the case, then we're fucking laughing, aren't we? Or maybe it's the Salvation Army with a controversial new fundraising initiative. Or the Boy Scouts. Or the Little Sisters of fucking Mercy!"

"You know something, Snatter?" Ding-a-Ling snapped. "You've had a real shit attitude all day, so you have. From the minute we picked you up, you've been in a mood. Just what the fuck is the problem?"

Snatter was taken aback. It was unlike Ding-a-Ling to be so tetchy, and Snatter was momentarily speechless.

"Nothing," he mumbled. He pulled his bloodied sock back on. "There's nothing wrong. It's just that … well, it's Christmas Eve, for fuck's sake! I should be sitting in a warm bar with a cold beer, but instead I'm bruised and bleeding and stuck under a fucking bush on the Shankill Road, with the UVF, or whoever it is, on one side and this … this … actually, what *is* this?"

Ding-a-Ling pulled aside some undergrowth to reveal a corroded section of corrugated iron. "It looks like …" he frowned, and then it came to him. "Shit, Snatter, it's the peace line! We're right at the fucking peace line!"

"So?"

"So, it's got to be the Falls on the other side, hasn't it? We just have to get to the other side and we're home free. We can just jump in a Black Taxi and we'll be in town in no time."

"I could do with calling into the Royal," Snatter said. "Get this foot looked at."

"What about the pub-crawl?"

"What about fucking blood poisoning?"

"Oh, for fuck's sake," said Ding-a-Ling, "I'll buy you some TCP!"

"TCP? Isn't that throat medicine?"

"Oh, it's good for anything. Throats, feet, elbows, anything."

"Doesn't matter, anyway," Snatter said. "I mean, this iron is rusted to fuck and all, but it still looks solid enough to me."

Ding-a-Ling did not reply. He was staring at the peace line and, as his gaze moved upwards, Snatter suddenly realised what he was doing. He was looking for hand and footholds.

"You must be joking, Ding-a-Ling. We're not climbing a fucking peace line!"

"Why not?" Ding-a-Ling asked. "We've climbed harder stuff than this in our time."

"Yeah, when we were younger and fitter. There's been a lot of cigarettes and beer since then."

"Oh, it's mostly about technique. And look, this hedge thing nearly reaches up to the top, so we'll be hidden most of the way. Nobody'll see us."

"Still," Snatter argued, "climbing a peace line? It's just not done, is it?"

"Have you got any better ideas?"

Snatter had to admit that he hadn't. It was clear they had compromised a major criminal operation and, because of that, there would be a concerted effort to find them.

If they tried to negotiate the maze of narrow streets to reach the relative safety of the Shankill Road then, Snatter knew, they would almost certainly be spotted and caught. And if they were caught, then,

Snatter also knew, the type of people who would be involved in such an operation would not hesitate to put a bullet in the back of their heads. *Fuck*, he thought, *they'd do it for fun*.

"All right," he conceded with a sigh. "Lead the way."

THIRTEEN

It was a warm and sunny day at the beginning of May as Tone sat on a hillside overlooking Poole harbour and watched the little boats bob lazily in the shallow bay.

Over to his left, he could make out the yellow ferries chugging back and forth between Brownsea Island and Sandbanks, as the cries of gulls were carried to him on the spring breeze.

There was no good reason for Tone to be in Poole that morning, but he had driven down early and had then wandered along the seafront for a while, before coming to a weary halt on Evening Hill. He took a swig from the half-bottle of whiskey he had brought with him, and then he tried to think about where he had left his car. Somewhere in Bournemouth, he decided. Somewhere.

He wondered if he should get in touch with Douglas to arrange a place to stay that night, but he shook his head and took another drink. It didn't really matter. He didn't care.

It was the day of Emily's funeral.

They had been window-shopping in Bournemouth, when Emily began to complain of a headache. She was smiling when she mentioned it, saying it wasn't really a problem. She just didn't feel that she could do much more walking and maybe she should go home to rest. As Tone walked her back to the car, he asked if he could get her some painkillers, but she declined.

"I do get these headaches from time to time," she told him, "but they usually go away on their own."

Tone drove her home and escorted her to the front lounge where she lay down on the couch. Her mother came into the room and went straight to Emily's side. She barely gave Tone a second glance, which didn't surprise him. He had noticed a certain coolness, over the past few months, from both of Emily's parents, but he wasn't bothered by it. He just assumed they were a couple of uptight pricks and left it at that.

After speaking briefly to Emily, Jessica left the room and came back a few moments later with a blanket that she draped over her daughter. As she fussed over Emily, she looked up at Tone and gave a curt nod. Realising he was being dismissed, Tone tried not to laugh. *Your presence is no longer required*, he told himself. He stopped on his way to the door and called to Emily.

"I'll call later to see how you're doing. Hope you feel better soon."

Emily smiled and waved her goodbyes, and Tone left.

He phoned Emily that evening from Douglas' flat. She seemed better.

"Are you still up for a drive over to the Purbecks tomorrow?" he asked.

"I think so," Emily replied. "What time are you calling round at? Eleven, was it?"

"That's right," said Tone. "I'm going out with Douglas tonight, but I'll see you at eleven in the morning."

That night, Tone and Douglas found a quiet bar, where they settled in for a few beers and a chat.

"All ready for the opening night, then?" Douglas asked.

"As ready as we'll ever be," said Tone. "It's looking bloody good, if I do say so myself."

"I think you're right," Douglas laughed. "That little bit of the dress rehearsal I caught last week was impressive. Emily's a star in the making, don't you think?"

"Absolutely!" Tone replied emphatically.

"You two seem to be getting very cosy. Is there any gossip I should know about?"

Tone looked blankly at Douglas. "No, not at all," he said, shaking his head, "we're just friends. And, anyway, do you not think she's a wee bit out of my league?"

Douglas threw back his head and laughed. "Are you serious?" he asked. "I used to think you had some sense, Tony, but you're actually fucking blind, aren't you?"

Tone was mystified. "What the hell are you talking about?"

"Oh, nothing!" Douglas roared. "Nothing at all."

The next day Tone and Emily strolled along the clifftops of England's Jurassic Coast. There was a strong wind coming off the sea and Emily clung tightly to Tone's arm. With Emily pressed so close to him, Tone was finding it hard to concentrate on their little sightseeing tour of Lulworth Cove and Durdle Door.

"I think I felt a couple of spots of rain," he said. "We should probably start to head back."

Emily looked out to sea. The waves were beginning to crash more vigorously against the shore, throwing a hazy sea-mist around the limestone archway of Durdle Door and the beach below.

"I think there's a storm coming," she said, and instinctively pulled Tone closer to her. Tone looked up to the sky and was shocked by how quickly the clouds had darkened.

"I think you're right," he said. "Come on, we'd better go."

It wasn't too far to walk back to the car and Tone thought they might have a chance of making it before the weather deteriorated any further. The rain, however, became more incessant and, all of a sudden, the storm rushed off the sea and began to scream around them.

Tone searched for some shelter, but the land all around was bleak and empty. *Not even a bloody tree!* he thought. They struggled on, blown by the wind and drenched by the rain, until Tone spotted, up ahead, a large rock, soaring from the ground at an angle, and pointing away from the sea. He pulled Emily towards it.

They reached the rock, breathless and soaked, and huddled beneath it, savouring what little protection it offered from the deluge. Tone looked at Emily's face and was surprised to see her eyes wide with excitement. She was grinning as she threw her arms around Tone's neck and pulled him to her. Her lips were pressed to his ear, but still, with the wind howling around them, he almost didn't hear it.

"I love you."

"What?" Tone cried, as he pulled back to stare at Emily. Suddenly, she looked frightened and confused. She tried to look away, blushing and stammering.

"I … I … nothing, I just …"

"No, don't!" Tone shouted to be heard above the storm. "Don't do that, Emily! I feel the same! Do you hear me? I feel the same! I love you!"

She stared at him, and Tone could see the confusion on her face begin to waver, and the fear in her eyes flicker and die. And there, standing beneath a rock in a storm, with the rain disguising two sets of tears, they kissed.

Back at university, during the week, Tone was finding it difficult to concentrate. He had tried, a few times, to call Emily on the phone, but Matthew had answered and had told him that Emily wasn't feeling well. Her headaches had been getting worse, he said.

"Has she seen a doctor?" Tone asked.

"No, Anthony," Matthew told him, "but with God's will, I'm sure that she'll be fine. Don't worry, we are all praying for her."

Tone wasn't reassured by this, and he began counting the seconds until Friday afternoon when he could finally get back down to Poole. He arrived in the evening and drove straight to Emily's house.

Samuel met him at the door with undisguised hostility. He looked, at first, as if he would deny Tone entry, but he stood aside and allowed Tone to step past him. Matthew appeared in the hall and greeted Tone with a handshake.

"Emily is in her room," he said. "In bed. I'm afraid there hasn't been much change since we last spoke."

"Can I see her?" Tone asked.

"Absolutely not!" Samuel said as he closed the front door and walked past Tone to go into the lounge. Matthew smiled awkwardly. Tone went over to the lounge and stood in the doorway.

"Just for a minute," he pleaded. "I need … I just want to see how she is."

Samuel said nothing. He didn't even acknowledge that Tone had spoken. Matthew stepped past Tone and went into the lounge.

"But what harm can it do, Father?" he asked gently. "Anthony has been a good friend to Emily. I'm sure it would cheer her up to see him."

Samuel seemed to consider this, then relented with a barely perceptible nod.

"Just for one minute," he said. "Remember, Emily tires easily."

Tone followed Matthew up the stairs to Emily's bedroom. When they got there, Tone was surprised at the austerity of the room, the only decoration was a wooden cross, attached to the wall above the bed. Jessica was kneeling at the bedside when they walked in. She gave them a brief glance, before lowering her head and resuming her prayers.

"There is always at least one person praying at Emily's side," Matthew whispered to Tone, to reassure him that everything necessary was being done. Tone, however, didn't hear him. He was transfixed by the figure on the bed.

Emily was almost unrecognisable. Her eyes were open only very slightly, as if she were drifting off to sleep, and her skin, now a ghostly white, had a sheen of perspiration that made her appear translucent. It was like she was disappearing before Tone's eyes.

Tone turned and fled from the room. He plummeted down the stairway, clattering noisily into the hall and skidding across the polished floor to the little telephone table that was set against the wall. He snatched up the receiver and began to dial. Nine … nine … the receiver was ripped from his hands and was placed, with a bang, back in its cradle.

"Just what do you think you're doing?" Samuel was furious. Tone stared at him with incredulity.

"I'm phoning for an ambulance!" he cried. "What do you think I'm doing? Emily has to go to hospital! Can't you see that? Why haven't you called a doctor, or done *something*, at least?"

"Emily is where she needs to be!" Samuel said, struggling to control his anger.

"But a doctor –"

"This has got nothing to do with doctors," Samuel shouted. "It is in the hands of God!"

"Listen," said Tone, "I know you're upset, but this is serious. We have to get Emily to a hospital. We have to –"

"It is not up to us," Samuel said coldly. "Our only duty is to pray to the Lord, our Saviour, so that He may –"

"Look, look," Tone held up his hands in desperation, "I know that you're a man of faith and all, but I don't see how –"

"Faith?" Samuel hissed into Tone's face. "What would you know of faith, Irishman? I know whose orders you follow, don't think that I don't!"

Tone was thrown by this. "What?" he muttered in confusion. "What's that supposed to –"

"You have been thwarted. Don't you see that? God's glory shines in Emily!"

Tone was beginning to panic. He couldn't understand why Samuel seemed to be taunting him. And what the hell was he talking about? Tone forced himself to remain calm.

"Look, beliefs are all well and good," he said, "but this is real life. You have to let her see a doctor."

"Would you defy God?" Samuel demanded. "Doctors are men, and you expect men to stand in defiance of God? God has seen fit to test my faith, and I tell you now that my faith will not be found wanting. You have failed, Irishman!"

Tone was astonished to see a smirk of satisfaction appear briefly on Samuel's face. Samuel then looked straight into Tone's eyes and said in a cold voice.

"You must leave this house. You are no longer welcome here. Do you understand?"

"But –"

"Anthony," Matthew had appeared at the bottom of the stairs. "I think you should go. There's nothing you can do here."

He led Tone to the front door. "It's all right," he said. "I'll let you know if there's any news."

Tone left the house in a daze but, as he drove round to Douglas' flat, he didn't feel too concerned. Even a nut like Samuel, he felt, would eventually see sense. He, surely, could not watch his daughter suffer for much longer.

Tone was back in his house in Southampton when Matthew rang. He told Tone there was nothing that anyone could have done. God had decided to take Emily to live in perpetual peace. There was no need to be sad, Matthew said. Emily would not have wanted that.

Tone put down the phone, walked into the kitchen and vomited into the sink.

As he sat and watched a few small clouds float above the harbour, Tone could feel the demons that fuelled his grief and his anger begin to tug at him. They were tugging him away from here, dragging him out of the sunlight and into the dark places where his nightmares could feed.

They dragged him into the drug-cosy warmth of the bedsits of London, the cold, Stygian alleys of Manchester, of Liverpool, of Glasgow. Eventually, his grief and rage subsiding, they dragged him home.

To Belfast.

FOURTEEN

"Jesus, Mary and Joseph! Can you believe them two fucking eejits? I swear to fuck, when I get a hold of our Gary, I'll … I'm sorry, Rosie love. If I'd known what them two fuckers were up to, I'd have … I mean, going off alcoholicking all over the fucking town and you waiting there like some dickhead! I'm fucking scundered for you, Rosie love."

Karen had been round at her mother's house all day, supposedly to help out with the preparations for Christmas Day. In reality, though, she had spent the day complaining about her husband's incarceration, and how the van that he needed for work was now a write-off. She had also been working her way through her parents' Christmas drinks cabinet, which was why Harry was now driving her car.

Harry was not in a good mood. When he had been released from the police barracks in town, he had taken a Black Taxi back to Ardoyne. His plan for what was left of the day, was to go home, get something to eat and then head round to the League for a few drinks with his mates. He reckoned he deserved a drink, after the day he'd had.

On arriving home, he realised that Karen must have gone to her parents' house, and he thought he should go and let her know that he was back and what his immediate plans were. He walked the short distance to his in-laws and, as he pushed open the gate to the front garden, he could hear Karen's voice from inside the house, thirty feet away. This made him hesitate.

He could be sure that Karen wasn't upset about his earlier brush with the law, for she normally took that in her stride, but she was ranting about something, and experience had taught him that it was best not to get involved. Harry, though, was not a man to shirk his responsibilities, and so, with a heavy sigh, he walked up the path to the house and pushed open the front door. Karen was standing by the fireplace, a drink in her hand, while her friend, Rosie, Harry was surprised to see, was sitting on the sofa beside Karen's mother.

"Harry!" Karen's mother exclaimed. "Thank God!"

"What's happening?" Harry asked warily.

"You can take your bloody wife round to her own house, that's what's happening! She's been doing my head in all bloody day. Not you, Rosie love. It's lovely to see you again, so it is. Right, Karen, you can put that drink down, and you can piss off!"

Karen ignored her mother, and turned to her husband.

"Aye, Harry, wait till you hear this for a fucking geg," she began. "You know our –"

"Tell you what," said Karen's mother as she bundled Karen towards the door, "why don't you tell Harry all about it, round at your house."

She took the drink from Karen, who managed to grab her coat as she was pushed to the door. "There you go now. I'll see you all later." She managed to herd Karen, Rosie and Harry out the door, and she then went off to finish preparing her soup vegetables for the next day's lunch.

Harry could feel the remainder of his Christmas Eve slip away as he accompanied the two girls back to his own house. Once they were inside, he started to prepare some food while he listened to their story.

Rosie, apparently, had waited, at her sister's house, for Seamus Green to show up. When it became obvious that this was not going to happen, she had gone in search of him. This had led to her seek out Karen, who she had managed to track down at her parents' house. Karen, on seeing how upset Rosie was, had told her not to worry.

"He's with our fucking Gary," she had informed her, "away drinking around the town. I'll get Harry to drive us down the town when he gets back. He won't be long, he's only with the Peelers." She had then embarked on the vitriolic rant that Harry had interrupted.

So now, instead of enjoying a drink round the club with his mates, Harry found himself stone-cold sober, chauffeuring a hysterical, half-drunk wife and her friend around the town for reasons that he still hadn't fully grasped. He wasn't in a good mood at all.

"So, what's the plan here?" he asked Karen.

"Well, I think they only go to certain bars," Karen said, "so if we split up, you go to some of the bars, Harry, and me and Rosie will go to some, we should find the two wankers in no time. We'll meet back at the car, is that all right, Rosie love?"

Harry saw Rosie nod in the rear-view mirror and thought, not for the first time, that she could be an attractive woman if it weren't for the anger that clouded her features and gave her a mean look.

As Harry glanced in the mirror once more, he caught a glimpse of Rosie's eyes and spotted something in them that hadn't been there before. He was familiar with the look of fear in people's eyes – he saw it quite often – and he was looking at it now.

FIFTEEN

"So, it's love, is it?" Tone asked the back of Jamesy's head as they walked to their table.

The Globe was situated down one of the entries in the city centre that ran perpendicular to High Street. It was a family-friendly bar, and was crowded with weary parents taking a break from the frantic, last-minute shopping. Children, excited by Christmas and fuelled by sugar, ran between the tables, shrieking and laughing.

Tone and Jamesy weaved their way through it all until they reached some empty chairs around a table. They set down their drinks and settled into the chairs.

"I think so," Jamesy replied. "I mean, I do seem to be exhibiting all the traditional symptoms."

"So, what's the plan?"

"Well, that's the point," said Jamesy. "I'm not sure what I should do."

"Yeah, it's a tricky one," Tone agreed, "what with her mental issues and all."

Jamesy sat back in his chair and sighed. "I don't have a problem with her religion, Tone," he said, "I'm talking about what my next move should be, you know? I don't exactly have a lot of experience with this type of thing."

At that moment, Tone spotted Joker coming in through the door. He raised his arm and Joker nodded in acknowledgement before heading to the bar. Tone turned back to Jamesy.

"Well, it may be out of your hands, you know."

"What do you mean?" Jamesy asked.

"It depends how far gone she is," Tone explained. "If she's become completely obsessed with this Jesus bloke, then she won't be having eyes for anybody else, will she? Especially not somebody who hasn't been washed in the blood of the lamb."

Jamesy shook his head. "I don't think she'd be like that," he said. "I mean, that wasn't the impression I got. She seemed normal enough."

"Aye, they all do, Jamesy," Tone said wisely.

Joker arrived with a pint in his hand. "They're still fucking nattering away there, back in Kelly's," he said, taking a seat. "So, what's happening, then?"

"Jamesy's in love," Tone said as he handed Joker a cigarette.

Joker nodded. "That wee Christian girl?"

Jamesy was astonished. "How did –?"

Joker held up his hand to interrupt. He took a light from Tone before he explained. "My perspicacity is frequently overlooked."

Jamesy and Tone stared at him.

"I mean … well, you know …" Joker was suddenly flustered. "Well, fuck, I'd ride her!"

Tone sighed. "Joker, I know you're trying to stay in touch with your roots, but don't you think you can go too far? I mean, you're back in the fucking Stone Age at the minute."

"It's people like you, Tone," said Joker, pointing with his cigarette, "who are trying to scramble their way into the middle classes, that don't understand –"

"I thought we were talking about me for a change," Jamesy put in.

"Oh, aye, sorry Jamesy," Joker said. "So, what are you going to do, then?"

"I'm getting a pram for Christmas." They all looked down to see a little girl of about seven or eight, holding a doll. She was staring at Jamesy.

"That's brilliant," said Jamesy, "I bet you can't wait!"

"Are you going to put your wee doll in it?" Joker asked her. She turned and looked at him as if he were a simpleton.

"She's too old for a pram," she explained, "she's nearly seven."

"Yeah, Joker, you spo!" Tone laughed. "He's a tube, isn't he, love?"

The little girl giggled and ran off.

"Well, she's going to make some poor bastard's life a misery one day." Joker grumbled.

"Anyway," said Tone, "what about this woman of Jamesy's? I'm not even sure what she looked like. I didn't pay her that much attention."

Jamesy was incredulous. "Didn't you see her smile?" he asked. "I mean, Jesus, you could melt icebergs with a smile like that!"

Joker gave Jamesy a look of concern. "Um, Jamesy," he said, "I think you may be going a wee bit gay there."

"Yes," Tone added, "as much as I'm appalled by the notion, I'm afraid I have to agree with *Homo Erectus* here. You're the dry academic type, remember? Such outbursts of lyricism don't suit you."

Jamesy shook his head in despair. This conversation wasn't going the way he had hoped. He picked up his drink to muddy his thoughts.

"And, anyway," Tone went on, "what about arse-face, needs-his-teeth-kicked-in, Greg?"

"Don't you think Greg looked like Fred from *Scooby-Doo*?" asked Joker.

"Yes!" Tone exclaimed. "Thank you! That's exactly who he looked like. It was bugging me, that."

"He should get himself one of them Great Danes," said Joker. "Maybe start up a wee act. Go on tour."

"Actually," said Tone as a thought struck him, "I know a girl from the Whiterock who's the spitting image of Velma."

"What, like in a sexy way?" asked Joker.

"Why? Did you think Velma was sexy?"

"I preferred her to that other one, to be honest."

"Daphne?"

"Yeah, I always thought that Daphne was a –"

"Jesus Christ!" said Jamesy, rubbing his forehead.

"Oh right, Jamesy," said Tone. "What were we saying?"

"You were talking about Greg," Jamesy said, "What did you mean by that? What about Greg?"

"I think what Tone was trying to say," Joker explained, "is that those two might be blowing trumpets."

"What?"

"Allow me to translate," said Tone. "The troglodyte here is suggesting that Greg and –"

"Yes, yes," said Jamesy, "I know what he's saying, but what gives you that idea?"

Tone shrugged. "Makes sense, doesn't it?"

"I don't know," Jamesy let out a sigh. "It probably doesn't matter anyway, does it? They weren't still outside Primark when we went past, so they've probably gone home."

"They're outside White's," Joker remarked casually. "I saw them on my way here."

"White's?" Jamesy said, considering his options. "Maybe I should just go for it."

"You do that, son!" Joker exclaimed, patting Jamesy's knee. "You just fucking do that!"

"Go for what, exactly?" asked Tone.

Jamesy looked suddenly deflated. "Well, that's the whole point, isn't it? I'm open to suggestions."

Joker, who considered himself a bit of a ladies' man, took the initiative. "I'm your man, Jamesy," he said. "I'll sort you out. What you do, right? What you do is you just walk up to her, and maybe act all shy, right? Maybe even a wee smile, like you're not too sure of yourself and just say, 'All right there, love? Is there any chance of a wee feel?'"

Jamesy turned to Tone. "Any ideas, Tone?"

"I don't know, Jamesy," said Tone, "you just dismissed Joker's advice completely out of hand, so I'm not sure that –"

"Seriously," Jamesy pleaded.

"All right," said Tone, relenting, "here's what you do. First thing, get some mints or something to take the smell of beer off your breath. Then just go up to her and make out that you want to say sorry. Say you want to apologise for your friend's behaviour earlier. Tell her that you didn't think it was very nice of your friend to value logic and reason over made-up, supernatural bullshit. That it was wrong of him to reject the infantile mythology of a –"

"Okay, okay," Jamesy broke in, "I get the gist. Then what?"

"Well," Tone continued, "isn't Delaney's round that way? Tell her you want to buy her a cup of tea, or a coffee, or, I don't know, a French Fancy, or something."

"Oooh," said Joker, "French Fancies!"

"Be persuasive," said Tone. "Insistent. Don't give her much of an option to say no. Then, once you're sitting down together, well then, you'll just have to rely on your own winning charm."

Jamesy thought about it for a second. "That's not bad," he said. "That's not bad at all."

"Yeah," said Joker, scratching his chin, "that could work too, I suppose."

Jamesy stood up. "Right!" he said. "I'm going to do it! Wish me luck!"

"Best of luck, Jamesy!" Tone said, raising his glass in salute.

"A legend like you, Jamesy, doesn't need luck," Joker added.

"Right then," Jamesy said, "I'll see you in White's later. Hopefully I'll be celebrating." He steeled himself and headed for the door, pausing only to have his head blown off by a six-year-old with a ray-gun.

Joker and Tone watched him go. "Hasn't got a hope, has he?" Joker said.

"Nope," said Tone. "Not a fucking hope in Hell!"

SIXTEEN

A popular aphorism states that beauty is in the eye of the beholder, but this is incorrect. That would suggest that beauty is subjective, which, of course, it isn't. A more accurate phrase would be *attractiveness* is in the eye of the beholder, but that does not roll off the tongue quite so well.

Rosie McCann was beautiful. That was just a fact. It was not open to debate. No one would even consider denying it. And yet … and yet, something was not quite right.

Her smile was pretty, it was true, but there was something indefinable in the tiny upturn of her lips, a subtle, almost imperceptible twist at the corner of her mouth that gave the suggestion of a sneer.

Hazel eyes that were generously flecked with gold would, on most people, be considered quite a feature, but Rosie's eyes, that should have sparkled and danced with life and light, shone only with a smouldering fire of passionate, burning rage and hatred towards all of mankind.

And some people found this off-putting.

The happy little world of Rosie McCann came to an end just before her seventh birthday, in the middle of a long summer of childhood glee.

She had always been a cheerful child, and she had much to be cheerful for. She had an older sister, Ellie, who she worshipped, and a younger brother, Jack, who she teased. Her parents loved their children and each other, and the family home was often filled with laughter and joy.

Rosie's mother, Shauna, worked part-time at the local primary school, which gave her plenty of time to spend with her children. With a simple outlook on life and a good heart, Shauna would impart her infectious happiness to Ellie, Rosie and baby Jack; frequently dragging them up to dance with her around the living room as she sang along to the radio.

'Never lie and never steal' was the philosophy that Shauna taught her children. She would repeat it to them often. 'Never lie and never steal'. It became, for them, a kind of mantra, that became mingled with the peals of laughter, and the chatter, and the love.

The blue skies of Rosie's early childhood contained few clouds, and her gold-flecked, hazel eyes were free to sparkle and dance and to smile.

And then the soldiers came.

Summer was at its height and the dawn was promising a beautiful day, the sky bleeding from grey to pink, to baby blue. Rosie awoke to see two soldiers drag her father past the open door of her bedroom.

She wasn't sure what had shocked her the most; the fact that he was just in his underwear, or the look of terror on his face. She never remembered hearing her mother's screams.

Martin McCann was a quiet, hard-working man who lived for his family. He made a good living at the Ardoyne bus-depot, keeping the bus engines in working order, and nothing gave him more pleasure than seeing the look in his children's eyes when he was able to bring them home some small treat. He considered himself a lucky man. He had a job he enjoyed, few money worries and a family he adored.

He had watched with genuine dismay as Northern Ireland, at the end of the 1960s, began to crumble into civil disarray, and he had determined to shield his family, as much as he could, from the unrest.

Northern Ireland's troubles were nothing to do with him and he wanted no part of them, but there wasn't a lot he could do when Northern Ireland's troubles came and kicked down his front door and dragged him out of bed.

Internment was the British Army's attempt to, once and for all, destroy the growing threat of the provisional IRA. The idea was simple. At the same time, all across Northern Ireland, the army would swoop down on the homes of suspected republican activists, and take them off to camps, where they could be held indefinitely.

For this idea to be effective, it was necessary to maintain absolute secrecy in the period leading up to its implementation, and so, the only people who were aware of the plan were the British Prime Minister and selected members of his Cabinet, a few senior figures in Whitehall, and those who would carry out the actual raids. And, also, the leadership of the provisional IRA.

The lack of secrecy, though, was not the only problem with the plan. There was also the fact that the intelligence upon which the army was acting, was hopelessly out of date. One example of this was the case of Michael 'Big Mick' McCain.

Big Mick had fought against the Free State forces during the civil war that had followed the partition of Ireland and had remained a staunch and vocal Republican for the rest of his life. His views would, inevitably, come to the attention of those who had the responsibility of keeping the fragile new state of Northern Ireland intact and, as such, his name and address would make their way onto a list of potential security risks.

Big Mick died at his Ardoyne home at the age of eighty-four. He had no family, and his death was unexceptionable. No one, certainly, thought to note the fact on his security file and so, even in death, Michael McCain remained a potential security risk.

The young McCann family moved into Big Mick's house with great excitement. It was their first proper home and Martin could not conceal his pride. A family home, where he and Shauna could watch their children grow was the fulfilment of his modest dreams. He was not to know that it would be this very house that would bring those dreams to an end.

Had there been a trial, then the error would, more than likely, have come to light, but the beauty of internment was that the whole, unpredictable business of trials was simply removed from the process.

The address had been checked and the name, Martin McCann, was close enough, so Martin was brought to a custom-built concentration camp on the outskirts of Belfast where the British Army was keen to try out some of its innovative, new torture techniques.

One small, poignant moment had occurred when Martin was being taken from his home. A photograph on the wall at the top of the stairs caught the eye of the young officer who was supervising the operation. It was a black-and-white picture, showing a group of young men smiling for the camera. The men had their arms round each other's shoulders and were wearing British Army uniforms. It was dated May 1944.

Martin McCann had always been proud of that photograph.

"Oh, aye," he would boast to visitors, "that was taken just before my da and his wee mates went off and got tore into Hitler over in France."

The young officer had turned away and caught a glimpse of a pink nightdress, a mess of black hair and a haunted pair of hazel eyes, flecked with gold and brimming with terrified tears.

The McCann family struggled to recover from the shock. Shauna tried everything she could to find out what was going on but, as families from all over Northern Ireland were going through the same thing, there didn't seem to be anyone who could help.

As the days and weeks wore on with no word, Shauna realised she was going to have to find new work just to put some food on the table. A series of part-time jobs brought in just enough to keep the family ticking over, while the neighbours would look after the kids and help with any washing or cooking that Shauna couldn't manage. Still, Shauna felt, it was becoming more of a struggle just to make it from one day to the next.

It took three years before the system had finished with Martin and he was allowed to return home.

Shauna and the children were overjoyed, but it soon became apparent that the years away had taken their toll on the mind of Martin McCann.

Before he had been taken away, Martin had been quiet, tolerant and easy-going. When he returned, however, he was prone to sudden, angry outbursts. He was now incapable of holding down a job and would fly into a rage for the slightest of reasons. The children learned to avoid the father they had once idolised, then one day, after school, Rosie came home to hear a strange noise coming from the kitchen. Peeking through a gap in the door, she could see her father lying on the kitchen floor. He was curled up on his side, and was wailing in torment through floods of tears.

That's not my daddy in there, she told herself as she slipped quietly from the house.

And she went to find a shoulder to cry on.

Martin McCann was committed to Belfast's main hospital for the treatment of mental illness, and the McCann family's troubles continued.

The children now found themselves being teased and bullied by the other children of the area. To have a father held captive by the British was a badge of honour, but to have a father who had gone insane was seen as a weakness, a taint on the whole family.

Shauna was rarely at home as she struggled with several jobs, trying to ease the financial pressures of raising three children on her own. Her visits to see Martin became less frequent, mainly due to time constraints, but also because she found the visits heart-breaking. He barely acknowledged her presence.

Although Shauna tried to keep the routine at home as normal as possible, it was becoming harder to disguise the growing sense of despair that threatened to overwhelm her.

The children became more withdrawn. It was easier to retreat into themselves than to face a once-friendly world that was now frightening and cruel. Rosie, especially, would seek solace in the world of television, blankly absorbing an endless maelstrom of children's TV.

Eventually, Shauna had to admit to herself that the current situation couldn't last. Whatever money she earned went to pay off debts, and still it wasn't enough. There were times, she knew, when her children would go to bed hungry and the fact that they never complained just made her weep more. In desperation, she turned to her brother, Mark, for help.

They had never been very close. He had moved to Derry, years before, with his new wife, and any subsequent contact had been sporadic. Shauna knew that Mark's wife had left him when it became apparent their marriage would remain childless and, as far as she knew, Mark still lived alone.

He seemed pleased to hear from her when she phoned, and he listened carefully as she laid out her woes. After several phone calls, back and forth, it was decided that Shauna and the children should come to live with him in Derry.

Shauna hated to leave the home she had come to love, but she accepted there was little choice. She had also fretted about how Ellie, Rosie and Jack would react to such a dislocation, but they seemed to adjust naturally with the fluid adaptability of children.

This came as a relief to Shauna, but what she didn't know was that Rosie would cry herself to sleep every night before they left.

At first, everything was fine. Mark, lonely since his wife had left, was glad to have the company. He was making a decent living, working at a nearby bakery, so Shauna was not under the same pressure to provide for the children and herself.

She took a job at a large textile factory in the town and, to some extent, was able to choose her own hours.

Ellie and Rosie started at the local girls' secondary school and Jack settled into the boys' school, a little further away. Shauna, working the early shift at the factory, was able to pick up Jack from school, and Mark, working nights, could drop the children off in the mornings. Life settled down into a comfortable, if unexciting, routine.

At school, Ellie excelled, while Rosie, although considered to be bright, never seemed to be out of trouble. Shauna would continually be called to the school to discuss Rosie's attitude.

"We know she has the ability," Shauna would be told, "but she just can't seem to settle."

Such worries, however, were insignificant compared to the problems Shauna had faced back in Belfast and life, in general, carried on without much drama. Ellie completed school with good grades in her A-levels and went to Coleraine to study nursing. Jack was planning to leave school at age sixteen, to become an apprentice mechanic at a garage in the centre of town, while Rosie, to everyone's surprise, did well in her O-levels and decided to stay on in school to take her A-levels.

Rosie had been a source of concern for Shauna, ever since their move to Derry. She knew that Rosie had been reserved since her father had been taken away, but her moods had become more brittle and fractious on leaving Belfast. She would fly into a rage for reasons that were unclear to Shauna and the ferocity of her anger was disproportionate, Shauna felt, to the loss she had endured. Rosie had seemed less capable than the rest of the family in coming to terms with their new situation and Shauna had struggled to understand why.

But, Shauna thought, maybe now Rosie was finally beginning to settle down. She certainly hoped so, for Shauna, of late, had been feeling weary. She was feeling more tired these days and she didn't think she would be able to face any further disruptions in her life.

All she wanted now was to watch her children grow and for them to find new joy in their lives. She yearned to see, once more, excitement and hope in their eyes as they raced towards the future, unburdened by the past. She looked forward to the day when she could settle back in her chair and put her feet up, knowing that – her work all done – she could simply close her eyes and rest.

And then the IRA intervened.

Where the rumour had come from, no one knew, but soon it became common knowledge. The bakery, where Mark worked, was supplying bread to British Army bases in Derry and this, as far as the IRA was concerned, was collaborating with the enemy. The bakery was promptly firebombed, and Mark found himself out of work. With the entire country in recession, Mark struggled to find another job, and the household bills began to mount.

Shauna was forced to take on extra shifts at the textile factory just so they could meet their financial commitments, but the strain on her body was beginning to show. The weariness and the hopelessness of an endless treadmill of bills, and work, and despair wore her down and, early one morning, as Shauna trudged home from a night shift, her heart simply gave in.

She slumped lifeless to the pavement. Her work, at last, all done.

There were many tears shed at Shauna's funeral. Ellie came back from Coleraine to stand, sobbing and broken-hearted, at the graveside, and Jack, as his mother's coffin was lowered into the earth, couldn't stop the big tears from rolling down his cheeks. Even Mark wept openly for the sister he had come to admire.

It was only Rosie who stood silent and still in the windswept graveyard as she watched the sad displays of gentle grief. Her grief was not gentle. Hers was a furious, screaming grief, that roared and tore at her. The anger and the hurt and the sorrow all raged within her as one, but there was one feeling that clawed, more than any other, at her shattered heart.

More than anything else, Rosie felt betrayed.

Rosie's sullen bitterness erupted at school, and she stormed out before she could be expelled. She had given up pretending to care.

Mark watched helplessly as Rosie packed her few possessions and moved in with a man she had just recently met. All of their time was taken up with drinking and arguing until, eventually, they both managed to be sober enough to split up.

Rosie then moved into a house with some friends where, with a combination of casual jobs and signing on the dole, they always had just enough money to keep sobriety at bay. Ellie, Mark, and Jack had all tried, at various times, to persuade Rosie to straighten out her life, but she never seemed to hear them.

When Ellie announced, however, that she was moving to Belfast to accept a nursing role, Rosie agreed to go with her. Ellie managed to acquire a mortgage on a place in north Belfast, not far from the Mater Hospital where she worked, and the two sisters moved into the modest little, two-bedroom, terraced house. In Ardoyne.

Ellie spent a lot of her spare time trying to discover what had happened to their father. She found out that, after a fire at the hospital, a lot of the long-term patients had been transferred to other facilities, some of which were in England.

During the upheaval, a lot of the hospital records were either lost or destroyed, and Ellie was finding it difficult to find anyone who could give her a definitive answer regarding the whereabouts of Martin McCann.

"He can't have just disappeared!" she complained to Rosie. "I mean, he must be somewhere."

Rosie pretended to sympathise, but as far as she was concerned, her father had left her when she was six years old, and that was the end of it.

One of the first things that Rosie did when she returned to Ardoyne was track down her best friend from primary school, Karen Lingfield.

"It's Hegarty, these days," said Karen, overjoyed to see her old friend. "Jesus, would you look at you! You're fucking gorgeous! Come in, come in, and tell me fucking everything!"

Rosie told Karen all that had happened since she had left for Derry. Karen cried when she heard about Shauna, and shook her head when she heard how Rosie had gone spinning off the rails.

"I'm not fucking surprised, Rosie love!" she exclaimed. "With all that you've had to fucking put up with."

Rosie told her that Jack was doing well for himself, back in Derry. "Got himself a girl now," she said.

"And Ellie's a nurse?" said Karen. "You know, I can remember even when she was a wee girl, she'd go on about being a nurse."

"Yeah," Rosie agreed, "she's always wanted to be a nurse."

"And she did it! Well, fucking good for her!"

"So, what about you? Married and all?"

"Aye, for fuck's sake!" Karen said. "He's a fucking nuisance, but he's my fucking nuisance, if you know what I mean."

Rosie laughed. "What's all the gossip been in Ardoyne, then?"

"Just the usual," said Karen, and she went on to tell Rosie about the people she would remember from childhood. "And our Gary," she said, "he's living up the Ormeau Road these days."

"Really?"

"Aye, he's living over there with his mate, this mad fucking skinhead from Sandy Row. Joseph, he's called. Mad as fuck, like, but he's a geg."

"What does Gary do?" Rosie asked.

"Him and Joseph used to work in the big electrical place in Royal Avenue, but they … well … we don't really talk about it, to be honest. So anyway, they're on the dole at the minute. Life of fucking Riley, if you ask me. He still sees Sean and Seamus now and again. Remember them two fucking headers?"

Rosie nodded. "So, Gary's on the dole?" she asked.

"Aye," said Karen, shaking her head, "don't know what that stupid cunt's going to do with his life. Sean's doing great for himself, though. He's up at Queen's, doing engineering or something like that. I don't really see much of him these days. He lives up that end of town." Rosie listened with a sad smile as children from a distant past walked back into her life as fully formed strangers, living actual lives.

"Seamus, though," Karen continued, "he's moved into his ma and da's old house. Bought it outright too, I heard."

"Oh, really?" Rosie's curiosity was piqued.

"Aye, he's fucking loaded," said Karen. "He's got a wee shop in the town, and our Gary says he's on his way to being a millionaire."

"Is that right?"

"Aye, he's lovely, like, Seamus is. Very polite, he always says hello whenever I see him."

But Rosie was no longer listening. Because Rosie's sights had just been set.

"Seamus? It *is* Seamus, isn't it? I don't know if you remember me, but –"

"Rosie? Rosie McCann? Of course I remember you. I heard you were back in the district. How are you doing?"

"Oh, not too bad, you know? I'm staying with Ellie, do you remember Ellie, my big sister?"

"Course I do, and wee Jack as well. How are they doing?"

"They're doing great. Jack's still in Derry, doing very well for himself. But what about you, how have you been?"

"Oh, okay, you know?"

"You must come out for a wee drink sometime. We can catch up on all the gossip."

"Yeah, that sounds good."

"I'm going to hold you to it, now."

"I'll look forward to it.

And now Rosie would wake in the night, sobbing in disbelief at the bitch she had become. But it wouldn't last. She would shake it off, wipe away her tears and harden her heart.

Never lie and never steal? Isn't that what you used to say? she would ask her dead mother. *Well, you made me believe in you and that was a lie, wasn't it? Remember, I watched you work yourself to death, so what did your stupid slogan ever get you? A miserable life and an early grave? Well, I've got my own slogan, now*, she would tell Shauna. *No child of mine will ever go hungry.*

And the tiniest voice in the depths of her soul would whisper, *What about love?*

And the shattered fragments of her frozen heart would answer, *Fuck love!*

SEVENTEEN

Tone leaned forward to light Joker's cigarette, then put a light to his own. They puffed away in quiet contentment.

"So, what'll we do, then, Tone?" Joker said at last. "Finish these and head on?"

"Might as well," Tone replied. "Jamesy's probably in White's already. Drowning his sorrows."

"Oh, you never know, you miserable old bastard. Young love and all that crap."

Tone shrugged. "I hear you got a job," he said.

"Yeah, we start in the New Year," Joker told him. "Me and Ding-a-Ling. Some printing place my uncle works for. Should be a good laugh."

"Ding-a-Ling was saying you were having a bit of trouble with some hoods," Tone said. "What was that all about?"

"Aye, for fuck's sake! It was a couple of weeks ago. Ding-a-Ling's da was over at the flat and he'd left his car outside." Joker reached over to stub out his cigarette. "Anyway, Ding-a-Ling had to nip out to the shop, and he caught a couple of wee bastards trying to break into his da's car. He chased them off and gave one of them a boot up the arse.

"We just thought that would be the end of it, but a couple of days later, me and Ding-a-Ling got jumped at the back of the BBC. They were just kids, you know? Teenagers. Well, we just slapped them about a bit and told them to fuck off, but there was one wee slabber who tripped when I gave him a shove." Joker paused to take a drink. "Broke his fucking arm, apparently, but he still gets up and starts giving it all this," Joker opened and closed his hand to mimic a mouth. "Shouting something about his brother-in-law, and how me and Ding-a-Ling would be got."

"His brother-in-law?"

"Yeah, well, it turns out that his sister is married to some sort of top hood. It sounds like all the hoods around the Lower Ormeau answer to him. Even the paramilitaries can't touch him, so they say. Michael McClelland? You heard of him?"

Tone shook his head.

"They call him Sticky Mickey. You heard of him now?"

"The name rings a bell," Tone replied. "Sticky Mickey? Is he covered in jam or something?"

"Something to do with sticky fingers, I suppose," Joker said. "Anyway, he's supposed to be after me and Ding-a-Ling for breaking his brother-in-law's arm."

"I'm sure nothing will come of it."

"Hope so. Oh, look who it is."

Sean and Bobby appeared at the table. "Where's Jamesy?" Bobby asked.

"He had to nip out," Tone said. "He'll catch up with us in White's."

"Still no sign of Snatter and Ding-a-Ling, then?" said Sean as he took a seat. "So what are we doing? Moving on or what?"

"I'm easy," said Tone. "I'm happy to stay here for another."

"Yeah, fuck it," said Bobby, "we'll have one here." He set off for the bar and Joker followed to give a hand.

"So," Sean said to Tone, "guess who's been looking at engagement rings?"

"What?" cried Tone.

"Bobby," said Sean, deciding to ignore the sudden flash of alarm in Tone's eyes, "he seems to have it all planned out."

"Yeah, well, that's Bobby for you," Tone lit a cigarette as he regained his composure. "He's probably allocated an appropriate amount of time for his engagement, followed by a regimented timetable for the wedding. Have you ever met his girl?"

"Once, yeah," said Sean. "So has Jamesy."

"What's she like?"

Sean shrugged. "Yeah, she's okay," he said. "Do you want to hear Jamesy's verdict?"

"Yeah, okay."

"He said she seems nice, and she suits Bobby."

"Aye, that's Jamesy all over," said Tone. "Mister fucking controversial. He doesn't give a shit, does he, that lad? Doesn't care whose feelings he tramples all over, does he? Just blurts out what's on his mind and bugger the consequences."

Sean laughed. "It'll happen to us all at some point," he said. "Settling down, I mean. Bobby thinks it'll be the end of the pub-crawl. Sooner rather than later. What do you reckon?"

"He's got a point," said Tone. "What sort of woman is going to let her bloke go out on the rip with his mates on Christmas Eve?"

At that point, Bobby and Joker came back from the bar with the drinks. They were in the middle of an argument.

"Marine Boy was not fucking gay," Bobby protested. "He had a girlfriend!"

"What? You mean that fish thing?

"She was a mermaid!"

"Oh, right," Joker scoffed, "isn't that the perfect girlfriend for a gay bloke? A woman with no genitals?"

"Fuck off!" Bobby retorted cleverly. "Anyway, what are you? Some sort of homophobe?"

"No, I'm just saying that Captain Scarlet would kick Marine Boy's bahleeks in."

Bobby stared at Joker for a heartbeat, then shook his head. "You know, Joker," he said as he took a seat, "sometimes you can be really childish."

"So, Bobby," Tone began, "I hear you're thinking of settling down?"

Bobby nodded as he accepted a cigarette from Joker. "Yeah," he said, "it's just the next step, isn't it?"

"The next step?" Tone asked. "Are you ticking off some sort of fucking list? What date have you planned your funeral for? I'll stick it in my diary."

"What the fuck's wrong with having plans?" Bobby demanded. "I like to know where I stand, that's all."

"Oh, I'm only messing you about," Tone said. "Actually, I agree with you. It's going to happen sooner or later. You may as well be ready for it."

"You won't catch me getting married," Joker asserted.

"Yes, well," said Tone, "you're the last of your species, aren't you? You don't have much choice."

"You're not talking about getting married next year, are you?" Sean asked Bobby.

"Fuck, no! Of course not, why?"

"Well, with all the talk about Snatter, I was wondering if this year will turn out to be the last ever pub-crawl."

"You wash your fucking mouth out, Sean!" cried Joker, appalled. "And would you all stop talking about fucking marriage. Nobody's getting married. Marriage is for homos, and that's the fucking end of it!"

"That was very moving, Joker," said Tone, "and you make a very good point. All this talk about marriage is getting depressing."

"We could discuss the current political climate," Joker suggested. "That's always good for a laugh."

Sean and Bobby groaned.

"Actually," Tone said thoughtfully, "that's not as stupid as Joker made it sound. Do you remember those two Dutch guys from last year? They wanted to know the history of the Troubles?"

Everyone nodded. "Well," Tone continued, "they came to the conclusion that Northern Ireland was created because you Prods didn't want to be under the thumb of the Catholic Church, isn't that right?" Tone directed this to Joker and Bobby.

"Yeah, so?" Bobby said. "What's your point?"

"No, there's no point, it just got me thinking, that's all. I understand the whole Catholic Church business, and I'm with you on that one, but the hold of the Church down south isn't what it was. Now, there's obviously a long way to go before there's a total separation of church and state, but what if the Republic became totally secular? Would a united Ireland be acceptable to the Protestants under those circumstances?"

"Haven't you always said that the divisions in Ireland were more political than religious?" Bobby asked Tone.

"Yeah, but you can't ignore the religious side of it."

"Well, you can't just boil it all down to one issue either, can you?" Bobby said. "It's religious, it's political, it's about identity. There's a lot of stuff swirling around in the mix, Tone!"

"I'm only trying to find out if there are any circumstances, at all, where the unionist community would accept reunification, that's all."

"Okay," said Bobby, "then I would say yes, there are."

"Really?"

"Yeah, if the entire island was absorbed back into the United Kingdom, then I, for one, would be happy to see a united Ireland."

"Yeah, very funny," said Tone.

"Make your mind up, Tone. Do you want a united Ireland, or not?"

Joker laughed. "So, it does all boil down to one thing, then," he said. "It's not religion, it's not politics or identity, it's all about what colour you want the wee bit of cloth that's fluttering above your head to be."

"Yeah, Joker," said Sean, "that's identity."

"No it isn't, it's tribalism."

"Yes," Sean insisted, "tribalism is fucking identity!"

"I identify as working-class," said Joker. "I identify as a human being. I identify as a citizen of the world. That matters more than any fucking flag."

"A human being?" asked Tone. "Are you sure?"

"I certainly have more in common," Joker went on, ignoring Tone, "with all of you pricks, than with the wankers I went to school with."

"That's very touching," Tone said, "but there can't be many people who would have anything in common with the wankers you went to school with. Anyway, what was I saying?"

"Don't know, Tone," Joker replied, "I couldn't concentrate, because I was distracted by the bizarre properties of this glass. It's got such an unusual –"

"All right, all right, I'll get the fucking round in!" Tone stood up. "Could you give us a hand, Sean?"

"Yeah, no problem."

While Sean and Tone were at the bar, the old Slade song, *Merry Christmas, Everybody*, came over the speakers, and someone behind the bar decided to increase the volume. The entire room erupted.

The children running between the tables, now began jumping up and down. The grown-ups all joined in, dancing and singing along to the music. It was Christmas and people were celebrating. Tone could see Bobby, standing on his chair, waving his arms around. Joker was jiving with the little girl who had been so condescending to him earlier.

The crowd at the bar had forgotten their orders and were swaying and singing *en masse*, even Sean was joining in. Tone, unable to wipe the smile off his face, turned to the bar and ordered another round.

A little while later, when the glasses on the table had almost been drained, Tone pondered the tactics they had been employing. The pub-crawl, this year, had been much less flowing than usual, as they hung around waiting for Snatter and Ding-a-Ling to show up. He knew the idea was flawed, though, for Snatter and Ding-a-Ling were just as likely to be waiting for them in the next bar.

He suggested they make a move.

"We're normally in White's at about this time," he said, "so maybe they're already there."

"Yeah, okay," said Sean. "We've got to meet Jamesy there, haven't we? Where has he been, anyway?"

"He's away chasing some wee Christian girl," Joker told him. "That one that was hassling *you*, Bobby."

"What?" Bobby cried.

"And you let him go, Tone?" Sean asked, amused. "Did you not give him a lecture on the evils of Christianity, then?"

"Why should I?" said Tone, defensively. "It's Jamesy's life, isn't it? It's got nothing to do with me."

"Jesus, Tone," said Sean, "if I didn't know any better, I'd say you were getting mellow in your old age."

And Sean had a point. Because, lately, Tone had been feeling less irritable. Life did not seem so bleak now, and the suffocating bonds of black despair did not feel quite so tight.

He could still be quickly roused to anger, but his rage seemed to subside more readily these days and, just every now and then, he thought he could sense a tiny flickering of hope.

Her name was Claire.

EIGHTEEN

"Yes, I know it's a pain in the arse, but there's nothing I can do about it." Tone was in the lobby of his Dublin hotel, speaking on the phone to Ding-a-Ling.

"Are you sure?" Ding-a-Ling sounded disappointed. "It should be a good party."

"I know, but this asshole can only see me in the morning before he goes back to Kerry. Isn't Joker going?"

"Yeah, but I think Carol's going too," said Ding-a-Ling. "Sean and Bobby are away on a course and Jamesy says he's too busy. Can you believe that? Too busy for a party? I don't know what the world's coming to."

"What about Snatter?"

"Oh, he's all fucking loved-up at the minute. I don't really see much of him these days."

Tone was surprised at the venom in Ding-a-Ling's voice, but he chose to ignore it as he continued. "Look," he said, "I'm sure you'll have a better night than me. I'll be stuck on my tod in the hotel bar with a book. Not exactly my idea of a fun Saturday night."

"You ever get the feeling we're getting old?" Ding-a-Ling asked.

"Speak for yourself," Tone laughed. "Look, I'll have to go here. Have a good time at the party. And keep Joker out of trouble."

"Yeah okay, I'll see you later."

"See you," said Tone as he hung up. His plan for the evening was to go out and grab something to eat, something quick, like a burger or a pizza and then head back to his room for a shower. He then planned to spend a few hours reading a book over some drinks in the hotel bar before bed.

Despite what he had told Ding-a-Ling, he was actually looking forward to it. *Maybe Ding-a-Ling was right,* he thought. *Maybe we are all getting old.*

"Any good?"

Tone was engrossed in his book, sipping his beer and minding his own business, so the interruption startled him.

"I'm sorry," he said. "What?"

"Your book. Is it any good?" the girl repeated, smiling broadly. Tone's usual reaction would have been to tell the girl to piss off and stop bothering him, but there was something about her that made him pause.

"Yes, it is," he told her. "It's very good."

"Bit of a pose, isn't it?"

"What?" said Tone, taken aback.

"Sitting in a Dublin bar, on your own, reading Beckett," she said. Her smile was still wide and friendly which, normally, Tone would have found irritating. "I mean, I'm not saying you're a stereotype, or anything," she went on, "but you certainly –"

"Well, this is my hotel," said Tone. "Where the hell am I supposed to sit?" Despite himself, Tone was becoming intrigued. He couldn't quite figure it out. The girl's frankness was arresting, but she also bubbled with a vivacity that seemed to shine with curious wonder. Finding delight, it seemed, in everything.

These were personal traits that Tone would usually view with suspicion and disgust, but in this girl, he was finding them strangely compelling. He even felt the urge to smile back at her, but he suppressed the foreign impulse as if it were somehow dirty and shameful.

"Claire!" Tone looked behind the girl to see another girl, standing at the bar and arranging some drinks to carry. "Come and give me a hand here!"

Claire turned and called to her friend. "Just give me a minute!" she turned back to Tone. "So, is this you for the night, then?"

"That's the plan," said Tone.

"We're all heading into town for a session," said Claire, gesturing to a table where several girls, dressed for a night out, were waiting. "Why don't you come along?"

The suggestion was so spontaneous, and Claire's fervour so thrillingly subversive, that Tone was flustered.

"Well, I … um … well, you see … oh, what the hell!" he exclaimed. "Why not?"

The next morning as Tone watched himself shave in the bathroom mirror, little shards of memory phased in and out of view.

There had been a lot of bars and a lot of alcohol involved in Tone's first ever girls' night out. He could remember, with a fair degree of clarity, the first two or three bars, but after that the subsequent events became harder to nail down.

Some memories stood out in the hazy gloom; tequila slammers, dancing on tables, vodka shots, an impromptu folk session with stolen instruments.

Quite a night, he thought as he glimpsed through the bathroom door to watch Claire's breasts rise and fall with the rhythm of her gentle snores. *Quite a night indeed.*

The business meeting went smoothly, despite Tone's growing hangover, and a deal was struck which meant that Tone did not have to travel all the way to Kerry that week. The Kerry hotel owner, however, insisted that Tone absolutely had to come down and stay sometime, and Tone, trying to dispel the image of Claire's breasts from his mind, insisted that he absolutely would.

With the meeting concluded, Tone was keen to return to his hotel room, hoping that Claire would still be there. He had left her a note, telling her he wouldn't be long and suggesting lunch together. He had already booked his room for another night, which was an act of spontaneity that surprised him, and he imagined a long, lazy Sunday afternoon unravelling Claire's perplexing personality.

As he opened the door to his room, he could tell she was gone, and the strength of his disappointment unsettled him. He sat heavily on the bed as he examined his feelings on the matter.

I mean, she was nice enough, he thought, '*but I don't see …*' It was then that he saw the note.

Sorry, but I really had to go. Lunch sounds good. See you in the bar at one?

And Tone frowned at the stupid grin on his face.

Claire's smile could be seen from the far side of the room and, as she approached the table where Tone was seated, he tried again to analyse his clashing emotions.

She wasn't his type, he was sure of that. Everything about her was animated and filled with an irrepressible zest for life. And that grated with Tone.

Happiness, Tone believed, should never be the default condition for anyone. Happiness was something that one might occasionally stumble across, or catch a brief glimpse of, as it hurtles off to somewhere else. The natural demeanour for normal human adults, he felt, was a certain grim neutrality that could waver up or down, depending on the circumstances.

Tone knew that he should feel repulsed by this crazy, perky bitch, but he wasn't, and that was leading him to question his feelings. He never questioned his feelings because he knew what the answers were. At least, he thought he did.

Rather than feeling repulsed by Claire, Tone, in fact, was beginning to suspect he felt the exact opposite. Which, according to all the laws of the universe, was just wrong.

"Not too late, am I?" Claire said as she leant to kiss Tone on the cheek. A bit too forward, Tone thought, which, given that he had recently been on intimate terms with her vagina, may have been a little sanctimonious. But still, he felt, wasn't there a certain etiquette to follow? A protocol that should be observed following a night of drunken sex with a relative stranger? What was wrong with sheepish embarrassment, or a bumbling sense of awkwardness, for fuck's sake?

He was forced to acknowledge, though, that Claire's breezy familiarity was giving him an illicit thrill.

"Not at all," he replied. "What do you fancy doing? Eat here, or go out for something?"

"Here's fine by me," she told him.

"Do you have anything planned for this afternoon?"

"Not a thing."

"Well," said Tone, "after lunch I thought we could take in a few sights of Dublin."

Claire looked at him, then cocked her head to one side.

"Oh," she said, "I thought that, after lunch, we could grab a bottle of wine and head up to your room."

This woman is a brazen hussy! thought Tone.

"Now why the hell didn't I think of that?" he said.

"So, you're a student?" Tone was sitting up in bed, watching Claire pull two cigarettes from a pack on the table on the other side of the room. She tossed a cigarette to him and lit her own. Then, walking to the bed, she handed him the lighter.

"Sort of," she said, climbing in beside Tone. "I'm not a full-time student. My boss sent me on a course for work. It's only for six months. I stay in Dublin when it suits my lectures. What about you? What's your story?"

"Oh, it's all a bit boring," Tone said. "I'm a sales rep for a firm up north. They import genuine Irish linen from China and sell it on to the tourist trade around the UK and Ireland."

"You sound like a desperate old cynic, so you do," Claire declared happily.

"Call me a cynic if you want, but it's true." Tone placed his cigarette in the ashtray on the nightstand, and idly brushed a fingertip across Claire's nipple. She reached across him to place her cigarette beside his, then picked up the book that he had been reading.

"I thought he only wrote plays," she said.

"Beckett? He wrote a lot of things."

Claire opened the book and read out the first line.

"*The sun shone, having no alternative, on the nothing new.*" She laughed and turned to look at Tone. "Yeah," she said, "that sounds like the sort of thing you'd be into."

Tone smiled. "That book is actually very funny, I'll have you know."

"Do you read a lot?"

"I stay in hotels a lot, so there's usually not much else to do."

"I have a real passion for literature," Claire said as she snuggled up to him. "Sometimes, though, it can all seem a bit overwhelming. Does that make sense?"

"No, it's total gibberish."

She laughed and gave him a playful nip. "It's just that there never seems to be enough time to read everything that I think I *should* read, you know what I mean? When am I ever going to get a chance to read *Middlemarch*, or *Moby Dick*? And forget about *War and Peace*, for God's sake! But you do know what I mean, don't you?"

"You don't have to read everything, you know. There is no set list."

"I know, but there are so many books that I want to read, and it's not a pretentious thing or anything like that, before you make some snide wee comment." Tone held his hands up in protest, and Claire laughed before continuing. "It's just that these books are so famous that there must be something to them, you know?"

"Well, don't spend your life regretting," said Tone. He reached for the wine bottle and poured what was left into their two glasses. "Not that you're doing that anyway," he said. "You seem to be living life to the full."

Claire sipped her wine. "That's what life's for, isn't it?" she said with a smile. "No, it's like, well, I read once that *Middlemarch* was reckoned to be the best novel ever written in English. So, I mean, that's got to mean something, hasn't it? It must be worth a read, but it's just a bit daunting, that's all."

"Oh, I'm sure you'll get around to it someday and I'm sure you'll be impressed. You might find it all a bit dry, though."

"Have you read it, then?"

"Once, yeah."

"And you didn't like it?"

"I liked it a lot, it's a stunning achievement, but there's not much in the way of sex and violence. I think she missed a trick there."

"She?" asked Claire, puzzled. "I thought George Eliot was a man."

"Yeah," said Tone, "a lot of people think that. Like I said, though, *Middlemarch* is quite an achievement. It's hard to believe she managed to write other stuff as well."

"I felt like that when I read *One Hundred Years of Solitude*," Claire said. "It blew me away, that book."

"I have a friend who reads Marquez in the original Spanish."

"That's pretty cool."

"And Camus and Zola in French."

"Okay, well, maybe that's a bit geeky," Claire said laughing.

"Not to mention Ovid and Virgil in Latin."

"Jesus, are you serious? Is he some sort of freak?"

"He's a working-class hero."

Claire gave Tone a quizzical look, then snuggled closer, being careful not to spill her wine. "Anyway," she said, "so tell me. What are your guilty book secrets? What books have you not read that you think you should have?"

"Probably loads," said Tone. "There's a lot of Hemmingway I haven't read. *The Gulag Archipelago*, I should probably read, and *The Man in The Gray Flannel Suit*, *The Catcher in the Rye*, *Lord of the-*"

"You've never read *Catcher in the Rye*?"

Tone shrugged. "Never got around to it."

"Right, that's it. I'm going to get you a copy. You have to read it."

"I think I'm perfectly capable of getting my own cop–"

"Shut up! It's a present, okay? You'll just have to lie there and take it."

"What, *again*?"

Claire slapped his arm and giggled. "Have you ever read any Joyce?"

"Some. Not *Finnegan's Wake*, obviously."

"*Dubliners*?"

"Yeah."

She lay back and looked at the ceiling. "I read it before I came down here," she said. "That last paragraph is so beautiful."

"Yeah, very haunting," Tone agreed. "Are we out of wine?"

"Looks like it."

"It's starting to get dark. Do you have anywhere to be tomorrow morning?"

"I've got a lecture, but it's not till half-eleven."

"Fancy some dinner?"

"Sounds good."

"And some wine?"

"Sounds good."

"And then …"

"Yeah," Claire said with a filthy grin, "that sounds good too!"

They laughed as they got dressed and went down to dinner. The sights of Dublin, for now, would just have to remain unseen.

NINETEEN

Jamesy was dithering. He was chewing his fifth extra-strong mint while staring at the window display of a men's clothes shop.

Behind him, across the road, the Christians were singing and chatting to passers-by. Jamesy watched them in the reflection of the shop window. He could see Greg, laughing and shaking hands with several people who stopped to talk. He could see other members of the group try to hand leaflets to shoppers rushing past. And he could see the girl.

She was using the smile that had moved Jamesy to poetry, the smile that could melt icebergs. Despite the cold, Jamesy felt suddenly warm and clammy. He swallowed the mint and attempted, once more, to summon up the courage he needed to cross the road.

Right! he said to himself. *This time! This time, just do it!*

To his shock, he found himself striding across the road and, before he knew it, he was standing in front of the girl. He gave a nervous smile.

"Um, hi," he said. "I don't know if you remem–"

"Didn't we see you earlier?" Greg interrupted. "Your friend got very excited, didn't he?"

"Um, yeah," said Jamesy, "well, that's sort of why I'm here. I wanted to apologise and –"

"He seemed to have a lot of anger," Greg went on. "I wouldn't mind meeting him again, to discuss some of his issues."

"That's … well, that's possible, I suppose." Jamesy tried to focus on the matter in hand. He turned to the girl.

"Look," he said, "I want to say sorry for my friend's behaviour earlier. I thought, maybe, I could buy you a coffee or something. Delaney's is just there, and I thought that –"

"That's a good idea," Greg broke in, "We could all do with a break. That would be okay, wouldn't it?"

"Oh, yes," said Jamesy, "that would be fine. Absolutely fine." *Bugger!* he thought.

The interior design of Delaney's café was eccentric. Rows of little wooden booths were surrounded by lush jungle foliage, from which peeped an eclectic mix of stuffed wildlife. An unwary diner could suddenly be confronted by a snarling leopard. Or startled by a grinning gorilla, a flamingo, or a crocodile, lurking in the dark, by the sausage rolls.

Jamesy, as he waited in the queue for coffee, stared dumbly at a bewildered penguin and tried to be pragmatic. The scenario he had constructed in his mind featured just him and the girl, sitting facing each other in one of the wooden booths, heads bowed in intimate proximity over cups of coffee, as they excitedly planned their lives together. He conceded that he may have allowed his imagination to stray a little too far, but these feelings were new to him and he wasn't entirely sure what to do with them.

Still, he told himself, the main thing was that the girl was here, and that he now had a chance to talk to her. The fact that a small crowd of born-again Christians was also tagging along was an inconvenience he would just have to work around.

He sat down at a booth, with Greg and the girl sitting opposite. The rest of the group had found seats in nearby booths and everyone was chattering happily about the day's events.

"I'm sorry," said Jamesy, addressing the girl, "but I don't even know your name."

"It's Hannah," said Hannah.

"Hannah?" Jamesy said, relishing the information. "That's a beautiful name. I'm James, by the way."

She beamed a smile in his direction and he almost dropped his coffee.

"Like I was saying," Greg began, "I found some of your friend's arguments quite interesting, but, ultimately, I think they can be dismissed as rather facile."

"What?" said Jamesy, shaken from his reverie, "Um, yeah, well, he can come across as being a bit aggressive, I suppose, but his heart's in the right place."

"I don't know about that," Greg replied. "If his heart has been hardened against Our Lord, then it can hardly be said to be in the right place, now can it?" He gave a little snort of laughter at his cleverness and Jamesy found himself thinking that Tone may have been right. It did indeed appear that Greg needed to have his teeth kicked in.

"Of course," Hannah interjected, "it is still possible that he can be saved. The Lord turns no one away."

"Yes, but he must *want* to be saved," Greg insisted. "He seems to be in a very dark place at the moment."

"He's had his troubles, I suppose," said Jamesy, "but, like you say, no one is beyond redemption."

"What about you, James?" Hannah asked. "Have you been saved?"

"Well, I'm a Christian," Jamesy replied. He had been brought up as a Catholic but had never given it much thought. "Probably not as good a Christian as I should be," he said with a smile, "but maybe I've been too engrossed in my studies to give it my full attention."

"You're a student?" she asked.

"Yes," said Jamesy, "at Queen's."

"Doing what?"

"Well," Jamesy replied, "my chosen field covers a variety of disciplines, from archaeology to the structures of early societies. Generally speaking, though, the term *ancient history* is a fair enough description."

"I would have thought," said Greg, "that all the history anyone needs to know can be found in the Bible."

"Yes, well, with all due respect to the Bible," said Jamesy, "it tends to focus on a limited geographical area. It doesn't mention the Incas, or the Mayans, for example."

"There could be a very good reason for that," Greg informed him. "It could be that God considers the contributions of those people to be irrelevant. They did worship false gods, remember."

Jamesy considered what Greg had just said to be the most objectionable thing he had ever heard. He tried, however, to keep his objections concealed.

"But, don't you think," he ventured, "that the more we uncover, not just in history but in all fields of knowledge, the better we'll be able to appreciate the full extent of God's creation?" Jamesy shuddered as he thought about how Tone would have reacted to that little sentence.

"The answer to that," said Greg, smiling smugly, "can be found in Ecclesiastes: *He who increases knowledge, increases suffering.*"

Jamesy wasn't sure how he was supposed to respond to such an outrageous comment. He half suspected that Greg was trying to make some sort of joke. The best course of action, he decided, would be to remain silent and focus his attention on the object of his infatuation. He caught her eye, and she looked shyly down at the table.

"Right from the very beginning," Greg continued, "God has been warning us about our curiosity. He explains it all quite beautifully when He shows us how Eve brought about the Fall. We really must pay attention to what God is telling us; that the only worthwhile knowledge is to be found through Him."

"Hmm," said Jamesy, "that's an interesting way of looking at it." He was trying to be as accommodating as possible, but Greg wasn't making it easy. He thought he should try to steer the conversation away from the minefield of faith and onto safer ground. It wasn't that Jamesy didn't believe in God, because he assumed that he did, but the fact that there were so many differing convictions, with regard to belief, made it almost impossible to give an honest opinion without causing some offence to someone, somewhere. It was best to avoid the subject altogether.

"So, what about you?" he asked Hannah. "What do you do? Do you have a job, or do you –"

"I'm at Queen's as well," she said. "I'm doing computing, a bit boring really."

"I wouldn't say that," Jamesy exclaimed, "a lot of people say computing's a good thing to get into. I don't really know much about it, but I'm always keen to learn new things." Jamesy felt that he was slowly groping towards his final objective. "So, what do you like to do? In your spare time, I mean."

"All of my spare time is taken up with doing the Lord's work," she told him, though Jamesy thought she looked a little hesitant.

"Is that what you enjoy?" he asked her. She seemed surprised by the question.

"It's the Lord's work," she answered. "What could be more important?"

"Oh, yes, yes … well, of course, you're right." Jamesy's level of toadying was beginning to sicken even himself. He decided to cut through all the superfluous chit-chat and simply invite Hannah out to dinner sometime. He was framing the proposal in his mind, when Greg spoke up.

"I would imagine," he said, "that there can't really be that much history to look at."

Jamesy stared at Greg in consternation. He couldn't quite process what Greg was hinting at but decided it was best to simply ignore him. He was on the brink of launching his proposition to Hannah, when Greg continued.

"I mean, if the Earth was created in 4004BC, and then had to be started again after the Flood, then, surely, there is only a limited number of events you need to learn."

Jamesy felt that, had he been in one of those old Warner Brothers' cartoons, then his lower jaw would have gone crashing through the table to slam onto the floor below.

He was speechless. Unless he was making a joke, Jamesy thought, then Greg had just made the single most stupid claim that he had ever heard.

"I … I'm … What?" he stammered.

"Well," Greg went on, "you study history, so you obviously know about the work of Bishop Ussher."

"Who?" Jamesy asked, baffled. He thought the name rang a bell somewhere in the back of his mind, but he certainly didn't feel it warranted any great significance.

"You know," Hannah prompted, "Bishop James Ussher?" She looked at Jamesy's blank expression in disbelief.

"He was the Archbishop of Armagh, back in the 1600s," she said, "but you should know this if you study history. He was a great scholar and his research into biblical genealogy led him to pinpoint the exact date of Creation."

"That's right," Greg added, "his ground-breaking work also confirmed the previous conclusions of John Lightfoot."

"Lightfoot?" Jamesy mumbled in confusion. He was beginning to suspect that he had, somehow, been transported to a parallel dimension where a reality existed that was very different from his own.

"Yes," said Greg, "Doctor John Lightfoot. Bishop Ussher's work was able to remove any doubts about the findings of Dr Lightfoot. It was an incredible achievement; to reveal the exact moment of Creation. You've really never heard of James Ussher?"

"Um … no, well, maybe," Jamesy was feeling rattled. "So, let me see if I've got this right," he said as he tried to gather his thoughts. "You're saying that the Earth was created, when was it? 4000BC?"

"4004, to be exact," Greg corrected him, "on the 23rd of October."

Jamesy scrutinised the two people sitting opposite him. They appeared to be perfectly normal human adults. They possessed an obvious intelligence, and were both coherent and articulate. They were able to move around and to operate simple implements, like a cup and a spoon, and they were exhibiting no obvious signs of cognitive deficiency or deterioration.

Why, then, were they saying these things? Why were they saying things that anyone, with even a basic grasp of reality, would dismiss as absolute nonsense?

Jamesy had heard of creationists before, but he had always assumed they were confined to a few obscure sects in some of the more backward states of America. Greg and Hannah, however, lived in a modern European society and were, presumably, exposed to modern European education and understanding. He stared at them, puzzled.

Their obvious sincerity and easy confidence convinced Jamesy that they genuinely believed the things they had told him, and that he would have to venture into this strange new world with some caution.

"So, you're saying," he said, "that someone has used the Bible to work out when the Earth began?"

"Not just the Earth," Greg told him. "The entire universe."

Jamesy realised that the situation called for a delicate touch. He had no desire to offend their beliefs, regardless of how offensive their beliefs were to him.

"You know," he proceeded gingerly, "that a timescale like that doesn't sit very well with current scientific understanding?"

"Scientists!" Greg scoffed. "Scientists are just men, remember. How can any man know more than God? If men choose to ignore the facts of the Bible, then they're simply blundering around in the dark. They're just guessing, that's all."

"Well, to be fair," said Jamesy, "they do have certain evidence they can point to. They can work out the age of rocks, for example, by –"

"Yes, so they say," Greg said, "but they can't prove it, can they? All they are doing is making wild claims that don't make any real sense. It's simple, really. If any of the claims made by scientists, or anyone else for that matter, conflict with what the Bible teaches us, then those claims are wrong. They must be wrong, or else we'd be disagreeing with God." Greg laughed at the absurdity of the notion. "I mean, come on, you can't seriously be suggesting *that* now, can you?"

Jamesy decided to try a different approach. He was having trouble, though, forming rational thoughts, still reeling, as he was, from the scale of the irrationality confronting him.

"Okay," he began, "I can see how you could be satisfied by the information contained in the Bible; there's so much of it, after all. But what about discovering something new? Don't you think that it would be interesting to look for answers to questions that aren't mentioned in the Bible?"

Greg looked dubious. "I'm not sure what it is you're getting at," he said. "What sort of questions, exactly?"

"Oh, I don't know," said Jamesy, frantically trying pull to something from his befuddled, beer-soaked brain. "What about *Why can't dolphins breathe underwater?* or *What causes the auroras?* or –"

Greg held up his hand. "Look," he said, "things like that are irrelevant. Why would you even want to know something like that? You said yourself that we can be satisfied with what's in the Bible. In fact, I would say, if it isn't in the Bible, then God doesn't want us to know about it. The fate of Lot's wife is a good example of where curiosity can lead."

Jamesy glanced at Hannah. She was watching him with a strange look in her eyes. What was it, he wondered. *Scorn? Contempt? Pity?* He felt a sudden surge of anger, which unnerved him. He rarely got angry, and he tried to shake it off.

"All I'm saying," he said, trying to be reasonable, "is that a lot of advancements have been made by science. If you're going to dismiss the scientific process, then you have to dismiss the work of people like Pasteur, or Fleming, or –"

"No," said Greg, "you weren't listening. I said if the claims made by science contradict the Bible, then they can simply be dismissed."

Jamesy looked thoughtfully at Greg. "I probably shouldn't mention Charles Darwin, then, should I?"

Greg laughed. "Old Charlie Darwin, eh? He really fooled a lot of people, didn't he? I just don't know how anyone could have fallen for that nonsense."

"You do know, don't you," Hannah said to Jamesy, "that evolution is just a theory?"

Jamesy nodded and waited for Hannah to finish her point. Then it struck him. "Oh, I see," he said, "you're getting confused with the word *theory*. Well, you see, when it's used in a scientific context, then it means that –"

"Are you seriously trying to defend an idea as ridiculous as evolution?" Greg asked.

"But a lot of Christians have accepted evolution," Jamesy protested. "There's just too much evidence to even try to –"

"No real Christian can possibly accept evolution," said Greg dismissively. "How can they? Evolution says that the Bible is wrong, so how can any Christian accept that? I've been told, anyway, that most scientists have rejected evolution."

"Seriously," said Jamesy, struggling to control his temper, "you've been misinformed."

"I'm sorry," Greg retorted, "but you don't seem to have understood this at all. It's perfectly simple, the Bible has been given to us by God, and if we try to find fault with the word of God then –"

"Look," said Jamesy, exasperated, "God didn't actually write the Bible now, did He?"

"Of course He did," said Greg. "He wrote it with the Holy Spirit."

"Why?" Jamesy snapped. "Couldn't He find a pen?"

Greg stared at Jamesy as an awkward silence descended. Some of the other Christians in the group were casting curious glances in their direction. Jamesy was instantly apologetic.

"Look, I'm sorry," he began, but Greg turned to Hannah. "It's starting to get dark," he told her, "we should probably make a move."

Greg stepped out of the booth, and Hannah slid along the seat behind him. Greg looked down at Jamesy as the rest of the group got ready to leave.

"Well, it's been interesting meeting you," he said insincerely, "but we must be getting along. Have a pleasant Christmas."

Jamesy sat and watched them march out of the café. He felt drained as his mind reeled with emotional turmoil. He sat in stunned silence as he attempted to make sense of what had just happened. A waitress, clearing tables, glanced in his direction and self-consciously tidied away a strand of hair that had come loose from behind her ear. Jamesy didn't notice. He was lost in a whirlwind of thoughts that made no sense to him. Did that all actually happen?

Eventually, he stirred from his trance. *Well*, he thought as he pulled himself out of the booth, *that could have gone better.*

TWENTY

"Snouts!"

The five boys were between seven and ten years old, and they were the only ones around to witness the invasion. They had lived all of their lives in the shadow of the peace line. The high rusting fence that marked the boundary of their world rose grimly over the rubble-strewn tarmac expanse where they played football and skinned their knees and elbows in play-fights and childhood adventures.

They had never met, or even seen, the people who lived on the other side of that imposing barrier. *Snouts*, they were called. Or *Orangies*, or *Prods*, or *Huns*, and now the boys watched in horror as they poured over in their droves, to attack the peace-loving residents of the Falls Road. On Christmas Eve.

The sneaky bastards.

The boys had all grown up with the songs and stories of Irish nationalist heroes. Men who, when the call came, were not to be found wanting. Robert Emmet and Wolf Tone, James Connolly, Padraig Pearse, Kevin Barry and Bobby Sands. Men prepared to stand up to tyranny and to lay down their lives in the name of liberty.

The call now came to them. Five small boys faced their destiny. Perhaps this was happening all over Belfast? All over Northern Ireland? And what, then, would history say of the battle for the Lower Falls? Would it be remembered by Republicans with shame? No! The boys were determined. They would not be found wanting.

"Come on, lads!" The oldest boy rallied his troops. "Get stuck into them!"

They hunted the waste ground for ammo. Stones and broken bricks littered the area and the boys hastily gathered as many as they could. They stood and faced the enemy just as Ding-a-Ling dropped the last few feet to the ground. One of the younger boys wildly threw a couple of stones and then panicked.

"There's too many of them!" he shouted. "I'm going to get my da!" And he fled.

The other boys waited nervously. Fidgeting, they suddenly broke as Snatter jumped to the ground, rolling forward as he landed. The oldest boy was the last to flee. He was armed with a weapon much favoured by the discerning rioter – a half-brick, or *halfer* – and he was reluctant to waste it. With all his strength, he hurled the halfer in the direction of the invading horde, then turned and joined his comrades in retreat.

"Watch out there, Snatter," said Ding-a-Ling, stepping to one side.

"What?" Snatter asked, getting to his feet. The spinning halfer hit the ground in front of him and bounced up to strike his shin with a crack that made Ding-a-Ling wince.

Snatter went down.

Ding-a-Ling lit a cigarette as he listened to the stream of profanities.

"It's starting to get dark, you know." he said needlessly.

"… bastard … fuck … fuck …"

"You know," Ding-a-Ling mused, "I just realised those wee fuckers must have thought we were Prods."

"… cunt and fuck … wanking … shin …"

"So, what do you reckon? Should we go and get a taxi?"

"… bloody … bugger … fuck …"

"Snatter, watch out, there's jeggy nettles there!"

Ding-a-Ling's warning came too late as Snatter, rolling around clutching his leg, rolled face-first into a tenacious little clump of nettles that were growing through a gap in the tarmac.

Ding-a-Ling grimaced and pulled Snatter free from the stinging plant. There were tears in Snatter's eyes now, but he had stopped swearing and Ding-a-Ling took this to be a good sign. He snatched up some nearby dock leaves and started to rub them on the angry red welts that were appearing all over Snatter's face.

"Just take a wee rest there, Snatter," he said soothingly, "and then we'll head on, okay?"

Snatter sat up, dazed, and gingerly rolled up his trouser leg to reveal a nasty looking wound. It wasn't bleeding much, but the pain was excruciating and Snatter was concerned by the amount of swelling and bruising. He looked up at Ding-a-Ling with pleading in his eyes.

"Seriously," he said, "I really need to get to Casualty."

"Yeah," Ding-a-Ling conceded, "I think you're right. Can you stand okay?"

He pulled Snatter to his feet and, supporting his weight, helped him shuffle towards the Falls Road and the Royal Victoria Hospital which, they reckoned, had to be close by.

"Lucky it was on the same leg as your sore foot," Ding-a-Ling noted cheerfully. "Or else you wouldn't be able to walk at all."

Yeah, thought Snatter grimly, *I must be the luckiest bastard in the whole world.*

TWENTY ONE

Tone fished around for a cassette. The radio was getting on his nerves, and he wanted some decent music to listen to. He was driving back from Cork and was planning to spend the night in Dublin at his usual hotel. He had arranged to meet Claire, but he was irritated by his giddy sense of anticipation which, he felt, was out of all proportion.

He popped a tape in the deck and *Barbed Wire Love*, by Stiff Little Fingers, blared from the speakers. He tapped his fingers on the steering wheel in time to the music as he, again, tried to analyse his feelings towards Claire.

He had been doing a lot of this self-examination bollocks, just lately, and it annoyed him. All that spiritual, touchy-feely, inner-self crap left him cold, but, for some reason, he felt a need to pin down the slippery, ephemeral set of emotions that plagued him whenever he thought of Claire.

Tonight was an example. If he was being honest with himself, then he could easily have made it back to Belfast for the weekend, but then he wouldn't get to see Claire. And seeing Claire had, somehow, become important to him.

Tone knew that what had started as a simple fling had become an infatuation, and this was what he couldn't understand. Was it just a sexual thing? He didn't think so. He was no stranger to casual sex and he'd never been hung up on it before. Claire was not unattractive, he thought, but her mouth was a little too wide, and her nose a little too prominent for her to be considered beautiful. He had been with smarter girls before. And funnier girls.

Fuck it! he thought. *Why over-think it? Did it really matter so much?* He made a decision to just sit back and enjoy the ride. He was happy in her company and that, he concluded, was all that mattered.

He glanced at the book on the passenger seat. It was a copy of *Catcher in the Rye*, and had been a present from Claire. Tone smiled as he remembered how he had received it.

He had been staying in Dublin for a few days the week before and, returning to his hotel from an appointment, he walked up to reception to fetch his key. He was pleased to see that the pretty girl, with whom he occasionally flirted, was on duty. He gave her a smile as he approached the reception desk and noted, with satisfaction, the flush of colour that rose in her cheeks.

Still got it, Tony boy, he told himself. *You've still got it.*

The receptionist handed over his key and then, as Tone turned away, she stopped him.

Oh, here we go, Tone thought smugly. *Well, I suppose I'd better let the poor wee girl down gently.*

"Actually, Mr Maguire," the receptionist began, blushing even more, "there seems to be a package left for you here."

Tone was puzzled. He couldn't think of anyone in the city who would leave a package for him. Well, except maybe ... Oh, crap!

Tone stared, appalled, as the receptionist retrieved a small parcel from under the desk. She seemed to be embarrassed just touching it. She placed it on the counter and pushed it towards Tone. He forced himself to look at it. It was a small oblong parcel that, fairly obviously, contained a book. It was how it was wrapped, however, that caught the eye. Or more to the point, repelled the eye. The wrapping paper was the most garish shade of electric pink that Tone had ever seen and was complemented by an elaborate concoction of pink and lilac ribbons and bows. There was worse to come, though, for as Tone guardedly nudged closer to the object, he realised that on top of this gleefully two-fingered salute to good taste was a card.

And on this card was a very visible message.

Tone realised the receptionist was now looking in any direction that didn't have him in it, and he got the impression that the doorman, too, was trying to avoid catching his eye.

Even though he knew he would regret it, he tentatively lowered his gaze to read the message that, apparently, had been read by the entire hotel staff.

As it turned out, the message was worse than he had feared. Much worse.

To Mr Anthony, Fluffybum, Maguire,
For all those stolen kisses and so much more besides,
For frequently letting me into your inner circle,
With all my squidgy-pidgy love,
Forever yours,
Derek XXXX

Tone looked at the receptionist, who was furiously polishing a blank sheet of paper. He picked up his package and gruffly cleared his throat. "Thank you," he said, and strode off towards the lift.

He saw Claire later that night, in a bar near the city centre and, still feeling angry from his humiliation, was prepared to tell her off. As he tried to reprimand her, though, and as he described what had happened, he began to see the funny side. Especially as Claire was doubled over, in obvious discomfort, with tears of laughter pouring down her face.

"Oh, stop it!" she cried. "Please, I can't take anymore!"

Her laughter was so infectious, Tone couldn't help joining in. He started to make a joke of the whole thing.

"Of course," he told her, "I can never go back to that hotel, you know. I'm not actually sure if homosexuality is even legal down here."

"Oh God! Oh God!" Claire was taking huge gulps of air to ease the pain in her sides.

"I've blown my chances with that wee receptionist, as well. Thanks to you."

Claire collapsed into uncontrollable giggles, unable to speak anymore. Tone watched her and grinned. It was impossible to be upset in the face of such unfettered joy. Claire's simple love for life overflowed from her to wash in waves around the room.

Later, as they walked back to the hotel, she gave Tone a sly look.

"Well," she said, "are going to let me into your inner circle tonight?"

"Are you insane, woman?" Tone cried. "What would Derek say?"

They were still laughing when they reached Tone's hotel room where, thankfully, there was no sign of Derek.

Tone reached the outskirts of Dublin, just after three in the afternoon, and arrived at his hotel not long after that. After checking in, he went to his room to get ready for the night ahead.

He had arranged to meet Claire in Temple Bar, just south of the river but, if he was being totally honest with himself, he was having some misgivings. Not about meeting Claire, but about being in Temple Bar on a Friday night.

It would be busy, he thought. Very busy. Crowded and noisy, he reflected. It would be lively and vibrant and exciting and … Jesus! What was wrong with him? He was in his mid-twenties, the perfect age to party in Temple Bar on a Friday night. So why was he so reluctant?

Tone realised he would much prefer to spend the entire evening in his room. With Claire.

I'm turning into Jamesy, he mused. *Only there's sex involved.*

It turned out to be a thoroughly enjoyable evening. Tone felt himself relax quickly after the first few drinks, and he joked and chatted happily with Claire and the friends that she had brought along from Trinity College. They danced between drinks, merging and laughing with the crowds of revellers.

The evening began to cascade, and they lurched through the night from bar to bar, dancing on the cobbled streets as the music blared from all directions and the sights and the sounds blurred with the people and the bars. The bars, the booze, the lights, the music, the dancing, the booze, the bars and the booze.

Tone opened his eyes, then quickly closed them. He craved darkness, but the sun was being a wanker about the whole thing, so he draped his arm over his face to muffle the glare.

He figured he was in his hotel room and assumed that Claire was there too. He groped blindly around the bed but could find no sign of her. The movement hurt his head and he groaned. Which hurt his head.

"So, Wicklow Mountains, then?"

Tone was familiar with all four of those words, but he couldn't quite figure out what they were doing in his room. He rejected the idea of opening his eyes. He wasn't going to fall for that again.

"What time do you want to head?"

More words! It was just pandemonium in here, he thought. He realised, unhappily, that a situation was occurring in his room that would have to be addressed. He was going to have to investigate. He raised his arm slightly, opened one eye, and could make out a shape that was vaguely Claire-shaped. It was rubbing itself with a towel. Tone felt he should probably be paying more attention to a naked woman standing in front of him, but he didn't think he could manage it.

"Wicklow Mountains?"

Why did she keep saying those words? Was she still drunk? That was it, he decided. The poor bitch couldn't hold her liquor. What a state to get into.

"What time do you think we should leave?" Claire said as she walked back to the bathroom.

"Maybe you should sober up before we do anything," Tone murmured from the bed.

"What?"

"What?" Tone repeated, and then it struck him that *What?* may have been a little inadequate. "What do you mean by *leave*?" he expanded.

"Don't you remember?" Claire came and knelt beside him on the bed. "Last night? You said you'd take me to see the Wicklow Mountains today."

"Of course I remember," he lied. "Just give me a minute."

It probably would have been quicker to take the main coastal road past Bray, Tone thought, but they were in no hurry, so he took the slower, minor roads to Glendalough.

Where this idea had come from, Tone could genuinely not remember, but the closer they drove to the mountains, the more he was looking forward to it. It was a beautiful autumn day, just the day that Ireland had been made for, with a few immature clouds childishly teasing the mountain peaks in the distance.

"Nice day for it, at least," he said.

Claire was rummaging around in the glove compartment, searching through Tone's music cassettes.

"Jesus, Tony," she said, "don't you have any music that's a bit more up to date? I don't think I was even born when some of these things were made."

"You weren't born? So what are you? Five?"

"Okay, so I'm exaggerating, but really, Tony, people still make music today, you know!"

"Philistine," said Tone. "Everybody knows that music died the day The Clash split up."

Claire sighed and slipped a compilation tape into the deck. Squeeze came on singing *Up the Junction.*

"You see now?" Tone said. "Proper music."

"You're a sad old fart. You know that, don't you?"

"Yeah, so? What's your point?"

Claire laughed. "What are we going to do for lunch?" she asked.

"Fancy a picnic?"

"Sounds like a good idea, but we haven't brought anything with us, have we?"

"No," Tone conceded, "but there's a blanket in the boot, and we can stop somewhere and load up with supplies. What do you reckon?"

"A picnic lunch in the Wicklow Mountains?" Claire said. "Sounds very romantic."

"You stick with me, Kiddo," Tone told her. "I'll romance your ass off."

They parked the car in the little town of Glendalough and – loaded up with food, drinks and a blanket – they headed off into the hills towards Glendalough's Upper Lake. The scenery they passed through was pretty, if unremarkable, and Claire said that it reminded her of the Glens of Antrim. She did most of the talking during the walk, and Tone was content to do most of the listening. They arrived at the shores of the Upper Lake and Tone began to lay out the blanket. He realised that Claire had gone quiet and turned to see her staring at the lake.

"Jesus Christ!" she said softly. "It's absolutely stunning." Tone followed her gaze and nodded.

The mountains, as if entranced by their own beauty, had gathered to stare at their reflections in the still, clear water of the lake, in a scene that was framed, top and bottom, by a startling crystal blue.

"Yeah," Tone agreed, "but it'll look a lot better with some food in your gob and some liquor down your neck."

Claire laughed. "Is that you romancing my ass off?"

"Well, admit it," said Tone, "you're turned on, aren't you?"

They sat on the blanket and Tone served up the food and poured the drinks: wine for Claire and a weak shandy for him. After they had eaten, they sat side-by-side, smoking cigarettes and admiring the view. When Tone had finished his cigarette, he lay back with his hands behind his head and stared up at the blue sky.

"Well," he asked Claire, "are you having a nice day?"

He watched her back as she shrugged her shoulders. "I've had worse, I suppose," she said casually, and Tone laughed.

She then dropped her cigarette butt into Tone's empty shandy can and turned to lie on top of him.

"Yeah, it's been okay so far," she said as she bit his bottom lip. "Can you think of something we could do to make it better?"

Tone managed to think of something.

"It's getting late," Tone said eventually. "We should think about making a move."

"Hmm," Claire murmured, her head on Tone's chest. "We really should." She snuggled closer to him.

Tone reached down and rubbed her back and shoulders. "What do you fancy doing this evening, then?" he asked her. "Do you fancy an Indian for dinner?"

"Yeah," she said, "that sounds good. Then what'll we do after?"

"Whatever you want really. We could go to the theatre, or maybe see a film. We've got the whole of Dublin to play with. What do you think?"

"I think that, after dinner, we should spend the night in your room, smoking, drinking and having sex."

"Well," said Tone haughtily, "at least I made the pretence of being cultured."

"I know," said Claire laughing, "but how often do we see each other? We need to make the most of it, don't you think?"

Tone sighed. "I suppose you're right," he said. "Life is short and bitter after all. We have to cling to whatever respites we find along the way."

Claire sat up and looked down at him. "That was a gloomy thing to say."

"I know," said Tone regretfully. "I don't know if you've noticed, but I can be a miserable old git sometimes. Being with you helps, though."

"Are you getting all soppy on me there?" Claire teased as she settled back to rest her head on his chest. "What do you know about life anyway? You're only twenty-five, for God's sake."

"What's that got to do with anything?"

"You know what I mean," she said, "it takes a while to build up some life experience."

"Depends what you mean by life experience," Tone said. "I mean, a mate of mine was only eight years old when he saw his ma's head get blown off."

"What? Really?" Claire looked into his face.

"Yeah," Tone shrugged. "It's by no means the most tragic story to come out of Northern Ireland, but try telling my mate that."

"So, what happened?"

"Well, as far as I know, he was off sick from school, mumps or something, and he was lying on the sofa in the front room. His ma had brought her ironing board in so she could watch TV as she did her ironing.

"Anyway, a couple of IRA men were moving some weapons down my mate's street when they were surprised by an army foot patrol. They opened up on each other but nobody was hit, except for my mate's ma, that is. A stray bullet came through the window and took the top of her head off."

"Jesus," Claire whispered. She shuddered and pulled closer to Tone.

"My mate told me once," Tone continued, "that all he could remember thinking, was how angry his ma was going to be when she saw the state of the wallpaper."

Claire remained silent as Tone carried on.

"His da took it badly," he said, "and hit the bottle pretty hard. For a while my mate had to look after his da and himself, though he did have aunts and uncles around. Well, eventually, his da cleaned himself up and things seemed to be going okay. Then he was run over and killed by a police Land Rover that was chasing a joyrider. My mate was fifteen."

Claire said nothing for a few seconds and then she spoke.

"You're right," she said.

"I'm right? What about?"

"We should cling to whatever respites we find along the way."

Tone was thoughtful for a moment, then he stirred himself and shook Claire "Come on, wee girl," he said. "We need to go."

They stood up and Claire stretched as Tone folded the blanket. They then gathered up all of their rubbish into a plastic bag and, making sure they had left nothing behind, they started to walk back to town.

"Your mate's okay now, though, isn't he?" Claire asked as they walked.

"Oh yeah," Tone assured her, "he got a big claim from the government, and he runs his own shop these days. Doing well, by all accounts."

"He's not the one that reads Marquez in Spanish, is he?"

"No," said Tone laughing, "he's a different story altogether. He actually went to Inst.."

"You know somebody that went to Inst.? Really?"

"Hard to believe, isn't it? But, yeah, he did. Hated it, though."

"Is he, like, a real brainbox?"

"Not especially, no," said Tone. "I mean, he's bright enough, don't get me wrong, but …" Tone thought for a moment. "But I think there's something wrong with his brain."

TWENTY TWO

There was something wrong with Joker's brain. Not necessarily in a negative way, but there was something about Joker's brain that made it function a little bit differently from other, more conventional, brains.

It first became noticeable in primary school, where Joker's teacher, Mrs Donohue, became aware that young Joseph Anderson was finding solutions to simple problems consistently faster than any of his classmates.

Mrs Donohue then provided Joker with more challenging problems which, to her delight, he proved able to solve.

Joker was hailed as a prodigy, a child with a God-given gift. A genius.

This turned out not to be true. It soon transpired that Joker was just as stupid as everyone else. It was just that, when it came to problem-solving, Joker's brain – often to Joker's surprise – would simply find a route to the solution that was a little different from the route taken by any of his peers. This cerebral independence would occasionally put Joker at odds with his own brain, but for the most part they enjoyed a congenial, symbiotic relationship that generally suited them both.

Joker wasn't a genius. He was just a bit strange.

Joker was born into a typical working-class, protestant family in Sandy Row.

Despite the pretty name, Sandy Row was neither sandy, nor, strictly speaking, a row. It was a meandering, busy road that ran through the delta of little communities that would come to share its name, and would be, for many, the beating heart of loyalist south Belfast.

Joker's father, Davy Anderson, was, at first glance, a stereotype. Hard-drinking and pugnacious, he seemed to fulfil the usual view of the Belfast working man, but he was also a highly principled socialist and a devout atheist.

He was scornful of all religion, which he regarded as just another burden on the working class, and he would scathingly denounce it every chance he got. This was something that Joker's mother, who preferred to hedge her bets when it came to God, would come to regret on at least one occasion.

Katherine was a spritely and cheerful woman who was not as close-minded as her husband when it came to spiritual matters. She had been raised as a Presbyterian but did not feel any strong ties to that denomination. She had always felt that, with so many varieties of Christianity to choose from, the path to salvation could be a deeply personal decision.

Her son and husband would always be the two most important things in Katherine's life, but she also believed there should be a place in her life and, by extension, her family's life, for faith. It was for this reason that she persuaded Davy to accompany her to the local Community Hall to hear The Fury.

Nigel Linsey Smith was The Fury. He was a preacher from Ballymena who preached in the old style, berating his congregation, condemning them as sinners and vividly describing their futures in the fires of Hell. The path to salvation, he would declare, was not an easy one to take. It required determination and sacrifice. The feeble minds of men, in the aftermath of the Fall, were easy prey for the demons of temptation and the whores of seduction.

The hall was packed with sinners, standing shoulder to shoulder, on the evening that The Fury came to preach to Sandy Row, and Katherine and her reluctant husband took their places in the crowd.

Katherine was keen to see for herself the fiery brand of Christianity that had captivated thousands across Northern Ireland and beyond. Perhaps this would be the light she was seeking to illuminate her path to the Lord.

Davy had grumbled the whole way there, but he couldn't deny that he too was a little curious to see what this 'Fury' had to say. And so, they had arranged a babysitter for Joseph and had come along as good Ulster Protestants to be told what wicked sinners they were.

There was a hush as The Fury entered and slowly made his way to the lectern on the raised stage at one end of the long hall. He took his place and stood facing the crowd. There was absolute silence as he clenched the sides of the lectern and looked down at the upturned, expectant faces.

He smiled inwardly as he relished the ease with which he would transport these simple people to the very gates of damnation. The horrendous images he would place before their eyes, the unspeakable agonies they were sure to face, the burning, roasting, everlasting torture of Hell, and how he would bring them, inch by tantalising inch, back from the brink. Back with him as their guide, leading the way to salvation, to God and to Paradise.

He cleared his throat and began to speak.

"*But the cowards and the unbelievers*," he shouted, and watched with satisfaction as the entire congregation visibly jumped, "*the abominable, and murderers, and whoremongers, and sorcerers, and idolaters, and all liars, shall have their part in the lake which burneth with fire and brimstone, which is the second death*." He paused for effect and to let the words sink in, and then, unbelievably, just as he was about to continue, The Fury was faced with his first ever heckler.

"Look," a voice called from the crowd, "just tell us how much fucking money you want us to give you, and we can all go home early!"

The shock around the hall was obvious in the audible gasps and the cries of disbelief. Katherine took a step back and to the side. Then another and another as she jostled her way through the crowd until she felt at a safe enough distance from her husband to be able to tut and shake her head along with the rest of the congregation.

"That's just shocking, so it is!" she said to the old woman she found herself next to.

"Yes, Katherine," the old woman replied drily, "I've always thought so."

The Fury was speechless. He had thought he had the measure of these people, these lower classes of Sandy Row. They were meant to be God-fearing and pliant, no match for his soaring intellect. What, in the name of the suffering Christ, were they doing with an opinion?

The Fury tried to work himself up to a show of righteous indignation. The crowd, after all, seemed to be as outraged as he was, but he was flustered and could only stammer something about doing the Lord's work.

"Can't the Lord do his own work?" the voice called out. "The lazy bastard!"

Many of the people in the congregation knew Davy Anderson, and they knew him for what he was. He was a man you could trust. A man who would lend a hand without hesitation and spurn any gratitude. There were many in that hall who had been helped out by a timely gift of cash, or had been grateful for Davy's help when moving house, or doing some building work, and in return, Davy would shake his head and say, 'Ach, you can buy a me pint next time you see me.'

Davy Anderson was a man of his word and a man of his people. The Fury, though, was a man of God.

The boos and the cries of 'shame' became louder until Davy admitted defeat. He shook his head in disgust and stormed out through the doors at the back of the hall. Katherine decided to stay and listen to the rest of the sermon and, when it finally ended, she could see no irony in the collection plates that were passed around the congregation.

As the plate came to her, she realised that no one had been prepared to suffer the social stigma of insulting God with a few paltry coins and so she was forced to give away the last pound note in her purse. *It was to help with God's work*, was how she justified it to herself, *and you couldn't put a price on that now, could you*?

Joker grew up with the influence of both his parents. His mother would supplement the religious teaching he received at school with her own gentle and indistinct interpretations of the message of Jesus Christ, while his father would provide him with an alternative set of ideas, content to let his son come to his own view of the world, in his own way and in his own time.

Joker, for his part, was more interested in the stories his father would tell about the heroes of his own family. Davy would tell his son about his own father and grandfather who had worked in the shipyard, building ships that would sail all over the world. He would tell him of the working men from Katherine's side of the family, men who had grafted in the factories and foundries of Belfast to provide for their families.

"Working men," Davy would tell his son, "have to fight for everything their whole lives, because no bastard is ever going to just hand them anything on a plate."

"That's right." Katherine, for whom sarcasm was the only form of wit, would sweetly say. "It's the women who get everything handed to them. The women in your family have always sat quietly at home, waiting for their big, strong men to bring them everything."

Davy would chew on his lower lip. He knew that Katherine's mother had worked twelve-hour days, six days a week in the flax mills of north Belfast, while his own mother had once led a riot through the streets of Tiger's Bay to gain improvements in the working conditions for the men in the shipyard.

Occasionally, therefore, Davy would concede that the roles played by the women of the family were just as important as those played by the men. Only occasionally, though, for, despite his socialist principles, he was still a bit of a chauvinist at heart.

One time, Thomas Anderson, Joker's grandfather, sat Joker down in front of the fire in the living room and told him of his time in the army during the Second World War.

"Oh, aye," he said, "there was a wee gang of us. All from Northern Ireland we were. A real bunch of madmen."

"Is this you and your mates winning the war on your own again, Da?" Davy called from the kitchen.

"I'm telling the story!" Thomas yelled back.

"Well, be sure and tell Joseph there were other people involved."

"Yes, I will, don't worry!"

"The Yanks were there, for one thing," Davy called out. "And the Poles, and the Canadians, and the –"

"Yes, okay, okay!"

"Don't forget the Scots and the Welsh. Even the English showed up to try and –"

"Yes, I know, okay?" Thomas threw up his hands in exasperation. "Of course, your da's right," he told Joker, "there were loads of other people there too. But to be honest," he said, lowering his voice, "between you and me, they just got in the way." And Joker laughed.

"Yes, there was a wee gang of us," his grandfather went on. "There was Scotty from Limavady. Nobody could understand a word that he said, but he was a good lad. There was Geordie Rice and Gerry McCann from north Belfast, and Billy Cavendish from Londonderry." Joker's grandfather paused to wipe something away from his eyes. "I'm sure there was a photograph, taken one time, of us all together," he said. "Long gone now, of course."

And Thomas went on to tell his grandson about the time he and his mates went off, one morning in June, to steal a French beach. And win a world war.

Joker loved to hear these stories. Stories that were filled with humour and spirit. Stories that set the honest working man against a myriad of enemies, from the Nazis to the faceless demons of the ruling classes.

In the streets around Sandy Row, Joker played with the children of other working families. He grew up in the confusion of the Troubles and he learned of other faceless demons. Demons who wanted to kill him and his family and who wanted to destroy Northern Ireland itself. The Taigs.

"Who are these Taigs, Da?" Joker asked his father, and Davy had done his best to explain.

"The Taigs are Catholics, Son," he said, "and they've been conned the same way that we've been conned. The only difference is that their con men want to be in control of everybody. They don't want to be ruled by our con men and that's why they're causing all this trouble.

"Now, I work with Catholics and they're good men. They're working men, like we are, but if it comes down to it, then I'd have to choose our con men over theirs. At least we know where we are with our lot."

Davy worked in Mackie's foundry in west Belfast, where he mixed with Catholics from across the city. There were many that he would consider friends but, despite his ideals of a united working class, Davy would fight against the Catholics' ideal of a united Ireland. A united Irish Republic would be ruled by the Catholic Church, and that would be unacceptable, so Joker learned not to hate the Catholics, like most of his friends did, but to mistrust their leaders' ideologies.

It was the Royal Belfast Academical Institution, or Inst., that opened Joker's eyes to the entitlement and inequality that his father had hinted at his whole life.

It was Joker's upstart brain that had secured him a place at the prestigious school in the centre of Belfast and had made him something of a celebrity in the tight-knit little community of Sandy Row.

Katherine's tears of pride nourished the nervous excitement of her son as she watched him walk alongside his father on the short stroll into town for the first day of school. Davy's pride was diluted by the apprehension he felt as he walked his son directly into the bosom of the enemy. The grasping greed of capitalism, Davy knew, could have a seductive pull, and he feared for the integrity he had tried to instil in Joseph from an early age.

But still, he thought, *Inst.? Bloody Hell!*

Growing up, Joker had often passed the gates of RBAI. It was one of the more obvious landmarks in the city centre, and Joker had, on more than one occasion, gazed through the railings at the grand building beyond. It had never occurred to him that it would ever be possible to be a part of this world.

To mingle with those boys, with their immaculate uniforms and their self-assured swagger, was such an absurd notion that it had never once intruded upon his imagination.

And yet, here he was. Joseph Anderson from Sandy Row, about to join the ranks of the privileged, the powerful and the elite. The cream of society, the best that Northern Ireland had to offer.

Shower of wankers, was Joker's initial impression, and it was an impression that he would cling to throughout his time at the school. He quickly came to the conclusion that he didn't belong.

What did he have in common with these confident boys and their bland acceptance of their right to rule? Their fathers and grandfathers did not build ships. They employed people who built ships, and these employees, in Joker's mind, were treated as little more than commodities. These employees, these people, these human beings, were seen as indistinguishable from the machines that slaved in the foundries, and the factories, and the mills.

Joker came to understand that the boys of Inst. despised him. The guttersnipe who had crawled from the gutter, too stupid to accept his place in the world. He felt the condescension and the disgust engulf him.

And, in this, he was entirely wrong.

The boys of Inst. were no more condescending or aloof than the boys from any other school. There were assholes, certainly, but there were assholes in every school.

As Joker imagined the pernicious social snobbery swirling around him, he failed to recognise the inverted form in himself.

He needed the persecution. He needed to feel ostracised and to feel like an outsider. The faceless demons may not have been faceless anymore, but Joker needed them still to be demons because it gave him an excuse to be angry. And anger, for Joker, was more bearable than fear.

The world that Joker could now glimpse frightened him because he didn't understand it. He did not feel sure of himself, he did not feel confident, he did not feel safely relaxed in the cosy reassurance that his road ahead had already been paved and he couldn't understand anyone who did. More to the point, he didn't want to understand.

So Joker kept his head down, burrowed deep into the world of learning and, with the help of his brain, he excelled. Latin, a stumbling block for generations of schoolchildren was, for Joker, a vibrant, living language as his brain revelled in the rigid beauty of its laws. This helped him to master the structures of modern languages, and, throughout his school career, he never once dropped from the top five percent of his class.

His teachers, therefore, were horrified when Joker announced his intention to leave school at the age of sixteen in order to enter the shipyard as an apprentice.

"What about your studies?" they howled. "Your A-levels? What about university? Please, Joseph, please think of your future!"

But his future was exactly what Joker was thinking of. He had always known what he was and what he wanted to be. He had no desire to prowl the corridors of power or the boardrooms of the shallow, hoarding classes. His history, his working-class history, was his present and his future. His arms and his back were strong, and he yearned to stretch them. He wanted the days ahead to exhilarate and to exhaust him, to smear him with sweat and grime and fulfilment. He was done with school and so, at the first opportunity, he left.

The glory days of the Harland and Wolff shipyard were all in the past, but there was enough work around for Joker to be taken on as an apprentice in the metal shop.

He was there for just over a year, however, when he fell victim to one of the rounds of redundancies that were increasingly sweeping the yard. He was devastated.

For a while, he moped around on the dole, feeling restless and useless until, after saving some of his unemployment benefit and scrounging some money from Davy, he bought a coach ticket to London and set off to find his fortune.

He had been given a contact number by a friend back in Belfast, and with this he was able to get a labouring job helping to build London's new orbital motorway.

Life, for Joker, soon became a happy routine. He moved into a house with some of his workmates and the shared rent allowed him to save a decent percentage of his wages. He spent several years in London, living the life of a young bachelor; working, drinking and fooling around with girls.

He was friendly with all of his housemates but there were two in particular with whom he would spend most of his time.

One of these was Danny, a young guy whose parents had moved to England from Jamaica, not long before he was born. Danny introduced Joker to marijuana and reggae music, and these would become two of Joker's greatest passions.

For his part, Joker introduced Danny to the Ulster fry, with soda and potato farls which Joker had sourced from a shop in Kilburn. He also taught Danny to sing *The Sash My Father Wore*, the unofficial anthem of loyalist Ulster, and they would sing it together in drunken attempts to rile their fellow housemates.

Many of the others in the house were from the Irish Republic, from the western counties of Galway and Donegal. They were the sons and grandsons of the navvies who had torn up swathes of the English landscape to provide the arteries of empire and they were not the sort of men you should want to rile. The spirit of the house, however, remained good-natured, and the boisterous camaraderie never got out of hand.

It was Danny who persuaded Joker to shave off all of his hair. For a while, it had become increasingly obvious that Joker's hair was receding at an alarming rate and he monitored the situation with growing distress.

"For fuck's sake, Danny," he would moan, "I'm only twenty. And look!"

"If you want my advice," said Danny, "just shave it all off, and be done with it."

"How the fuck is that going to help?"

"Okay, so it sounds a bit drastic, but trust me." Danny gave a reassuring grin. "You won't have to worry about your hair anymore, know what I mean? Besides, man, it might suit you. You're okay-looking for a white guy, and who do you think the ladies are going to dig anyway? Some poor fuck who's all sad about his hair falling out, or the cool guy who's got the balls to do a full Yul Brynner?"

Joker was persuaded to take the plunge and he, Danny and their other friend, Francie, decided to take his new head down the pub for a test drive. It was here that a tipsy girl came and sat on Joker's knee and gave the fuzzy stubble on his scalp a sensuous rub. 'It turns me on,' she told him. And at that moment Joker became a skinhead.

The other member of Joker's trio, Francie, was from Glengormley, in Northern Ireland, and he introduced Joker and Danny to a variety of exciting ways they could give all their money to Bookmakers.

He taught them doubles, and trebles, and yankees and all sorts of accumulators, but, as they watched their money disappear at a frightening rate, Joker and Danny decided that gambling wasn't their thing.

"It's just an insidious tax on the working man," Joker declared sanctimoniously, but he was happy enough to help Francie spend his winnings when all four horses came up on a 'Lucky 15'.

As much as he enjoyed his time in London, Joker never felt that it was somewhere he could ever settle. He had finished London's new motorway by now and, as the country struggled with recession, it was becoming harder to find any lasting work.

Danny was now married and was looking forward to the arrival of his first child, while Francie was working in Newcastle, in the north of England. It was time, Joker decided, to go home.

"What the fuck did you do to your head?" were Davy's first words to his son, but he embraced him once Katherine had finally stopped fussing over him.

Back in Belfast, Joker was in no rush to find a job. He had saved enough money from his time in London to take things easy for a while and he felt that he could do with a breather after the hectic pace of the capital. He signed on for unemployment benefit – to keep up his pension contributions more than anything else – and assured the harassed clerk at the benefits office that his time on the dole would be entirely devoted to looking for work.

He spent his time *chilling*, as Danny called it, frequenting the bars of Belfast and taking trips to Windsor Park to watch Linfield FC, his local football team, play. He started getting serious enough with a girl to consider moving in with her and, although he knew he would find a job at some point, he was happy to coast for the time being.

One annoying condition of being on the dole was the occasional job interview that the benefits office would arrange. It was only a minor inconvenience, though, and anyway, Joker reckoned, it could be useful preparation for when he started looking for work in earnest. And so, one afternoon, he cheerfully strolled along to a meaningless interview in the centre of town.

Joker noted, with satisfaction, the looks of dismay on the faces of the two interviewers as he entered the little newsagent's shop. It was just after lunch and the shop was quiet.

"Good afternoon, Mr Anderson," said Snatter, once Joker's identity had been established. He then paused as he referred to the clipboard he was holding. "I'm Mr Green, and this my associate, Mr Lingfield."

"Linfield?" asked Joker, surprised. "I'm a big fan, actually I was –"

"Not Linfield," said Ding-a-Ling. "LINGfield!"

"Oh, sorry. My mistake."

"So, you're a Linfield fan?" Ding-a-Ling asked as he wrote something in his clipboard. "Does it bother you that me and Snat ... um ... me and Mr Green are both Cliftonville supporters?"

"No, it doesn't bother me at all," said Joker, "I've had all my tetanus jabs." He was surprised to see Mr Lingfield suppress a smile, and Joker thought that, while he was here, he might as well have a little fun.

"No, it doesn't bother me," he repeated, "in fact, when I was a kid, I used to have this football game, and I painted one of the teams to look like Cliftonville. There was a terrible accident, though, when the bus taking them to Windsor inexplicably caught fire. No survivors. Shocking, it was."

Snatter and Ding-a-Ling looked at Joker, unsure of how to respond.

"Striker, the game was," Joker told them.

"Striker?" Ding-a-Ling suddenly exclaimed. "You had Striker?"

"Yeah."

"I used to love Striker," Ding-a-Ling enthused. "I had the World Cup edition, all the accessories and everything. It was better than Subbuteo anyway. Striker! My God! That was the game with 'real kicking action', wasn't it?"

"Yeah, I know what you mean about Subbuteo," said Joker, "it was just fancy marlies, wasn't it? Striker was a game of skill."

"I've always said that," Ding-a-Ling agreed, "you really had to judge how hard to kick the ball."

"Excuse me," said Snatter, clearly exasperated, "but can we stop being childish and try to be serious here for a minute? I can't believe you think Striker was a better game than Subbuteo. Anyone with half a –"

"Oh, yeah," said Ding-a-Ling, "I forgot you were into your Subbuteo. Well, tell me this, smartass; what about the time Man United beat Liverpool 48-0 in the FA Cup Final?"

"What the hell has that got to do with anything?" Snatter cried in disbelief. "That was the time you played your wee sister. You told me about it the next day. You had her in tears."

"Are you Man United fans?" asked Joker.

"Yeah," said Ding-a-Ling. "Why?"

"Me too," Joker told them. "We haven't had much to cheer about lately, have we?"

"You're right about that," Snatter said, "I can't see us ever winning the league, not in *my* lifetime."

"Oh, you can't think like that," said Joker, "you have to take the rough with the smooth."

Yeah, but where's the smooth?" Snatter looked a little glum, so Joker thought he would try to cheer him up.

"I have an aunt who thinks she's Bobby Charlton," he said.

"What?" Both Snatter and Ding-a-Ling stared, wide-eyed. "Really?"

"Well, no, I just made that up," Joker admitted. "I thought it would be funny, that's all."

Ding-a-Ling and Snatter looked at Joker, then at each other, then all three burst out laughing.

"It would be cool, though, wouldn't it?" said Joker.

"Do you remember the 1979 Cup Final?" Ding-a-Ling asked Joker.

"Are you kidding? I'm still recovering!"

"Well, me and Snatt … um, I mean, Mr … oh, fuck it! Me and Snatter here, and this other mate of ours, watched it round my house. And when Alan Sunderland –"

"Frizzy-haired bastard," Joker scoffed.

"Exactly," agreed Ding-a-Ling. "Well, when he scored in the last minute, I got so worked up, that I grabbed my ma's clock off the mantelpiece and fucked it at the TV."

"Jesus!" Joker exclaimed. "What happened?"

"Nothing good, funnily enough," Snatter told him.

"The TV exploded," said Ding-a-Ling. "The three of us just stood there and stared, and then we turned and ran like fuck."

Joker threw back his head and laughed, and Snatter and Ding-a-Ling joined in.

"The worst thing about it was," Ding-a-Ling eventually continued, "the clock was an anniversary present from my da. Waterford Crystal. Worth a bloody fortune!"

The three of them laughed even harder and the banter between them flowed until Ding-a-Ling asked Snatter a question.

"What do you think of Mr Anderson here for the job?"

"Well," said Snatter, looking at Joker, "you do seem to be the most suitable applicant so far."

"No other cunt showed up," Ding-a-Ling explained.

"So, Mr Anderson, what do you say? Are you interested?"

Joker leaned across to shake hands. "Call me Joker," he said.

It was a few years later that Joker met Carol. Joker knew that he wasn't bad looking. Despite the years of alcohol abuse, he was still reasonably lean and muscular, and his defined, chiselled facial structure suggested, he told himself, the moody looks of a young Montgomery Clift. Joker reckoned he had plenty going for him.

But Carol was something else. Carol was from another planet.

He first saw her in the Speakeasy Bar of Queen's student union. It was a Friday afternoon and Joker was standing at the bar waiting for his order when Carol walked in with a group of friends.

From the corner of his eye, Joker caught a glimpse of a pale-yellow summer dress, flowing over flawless skin, as she passed slowly behind his right shoulder. His eyes, excited and aroused, then dragged the rest of his head around to his left, in anticipation of the vision's reappearance, which, in turn, caught the attention of certain other parts of his anatomy.

Carol and her friends had stopped and now stood near the end of the long bar, several feet to Joker's left. She could have been standing in the company of Kermit the Frog, Mick Jagger and the Duke of Edinburgh, wearing bikinis, and Joker's eyes would still have been fixed on Carol.

Just standing there, making the slightest of movements, Carol had a poise that would make a stalking leopard look ungainly. Panache, style and class oozed from every perfect pore, and an entrancing, lively face beamed with animated intelligence. Joker was mesmerised. His blank, slack-jawed scrutiny would have been embarrassingly obvious, were it not for the fact that every other man in the room was doing the same thing.

This girl, thought Joker, was the smile on the Mona Lisa. She was the top, she was the Colosseum, a Shakespeare sonnet, the Louvre Museum.

She was the top, she was Napoleon brandy, she –

"Are you fucking deaf, or something?"

"What?" said Joker with a jolt.

"I said, that'll be £1.90," said the grizzled barman. "*Please!*"

"Jesus!" Joker grumbled as he handed over a five-pound note. "95p for a pint? I thought you guys were meant to be subsidised?"

The barman didn't reply, he took Joker's money and went to the till.

When Joker returned to his table, he was giddy with excitement.

"Did you see your woman there?" he asked Ding-a-Ling.

"No, Joker, I didn't," Ding-a-Ling replied, "because I happen to be stone-cold, fucking blind. And the reason why I'm covered in drool, is because I thought I could smell a bacon sandwich." Satisfied that this stream of sarcasm had been delivered with suitable aplomb, Ding-a-Ling lifted his pint.

"Fair point," said Joker. "So, do you reckon I've got a chance?"

"Of not spilling your pint? Stranger things have happened, I suppose."

"Fuck off, you know what I mean."

The Pogues came over the sound system with *A Rainy Night in Soho*. It was one of Joker's favourite songs.

"There you are," he said, "that's got to be a sign, hasn't it?"

"Jesus!" said Ding-a-Ling, shaking his head.

Joker stared at the girl across the room, willing her to glance in his direction. When she did, he gave her a friendly wink. She gave a smile in return, though Ding-a-Ling felt it was just the sort of bemused smile you might give if you were to catch sight of a squirrel wearing a hat.

Joker, nonetheless, stood up and, to the haunting strains of *A Rainy Night in Soho*, he walked towards the measure of his dreams.

It was never going to work, of course. After several months of rapturous, sensual intensity, Joker began to chafe against his illusory chains of oppression.

Had Joker been more of an introspective type, then, perhaps, he might have reflected on the fact that his sense of persecution had been instilled in him from an early age.

When told, continuously, that you face an eternal struggle in an unjust world, then any hint of contentment must seem like mockery.

Perhaps, also, he may have deduced that the conditioning he had received, telling him to wallow with pride in his victimisation, may have clouded his judgement on several significant occasions and, just maybe, he would have concluded that his crime was not being working-class; it was allowing himself to be convinced he would never be anything else.

But indulgence in such middle-class, Freudian wank was not in Joker's nature, and so his natural instinct was to rage against his superiors and to strain against his perceived fetters until they snapped. And they snapped.

To his brain's dismay, every single flaw in his relationship with Carol had been put there by Joker. Like a child with a hammer on a tiled floor, he seemed beguiled by the patterns he created.

His powers of reasoning, as well as his natural intelligence resided in clashing discord with the sense of inferiority that formed Joker's core, and the collateral damage was strewn around for all to see.

To sabotage your own chance of being with someone like Carol could be considered irrational and could prompt some accusatory glances in the direction of a wayward brain, but Joker's brain had played no part in the debacle and had been just as exasperated as everyone else.

Joker had no one to blame but himself.

TWENTY THREE

"Right! Up against that fucking wall!" The angry voice that barked the command came from behind them, and Snatter slumped against Ding-a-Ling and groaned.

Now what? he thought.

They were about to turn around, when they were roughly pushed up against the gable wall of an abandoned house. They heard the voice of a young boy call out.

"Aye," it said, "that's some of them."

"What?" Ding-a-Ling asked, confused.

"Shut it!" Snatter and Ding-a-Ling felt their feet being kicked apart as a hand was run up the inside of their legs, searching for concealed weapons.

"Where the fuck's the rest of you?" the original angry voice shouted.

"Seriously," said Ding-a-Ling, "what the –?"

"Did you two fuckers just come over the peace line there?"

"What? Well, yeah, but –"

"There was fucking loads of them," the young boy insisted. "I saw them!"

"Right," said the angry voice, "there's something going on here, and I'm going to make fucking sure that … Is that you, Gary?"

Ding-a-Ling turned his head. "Frankie?"

"Aye," said Frankie, "what the fuck are you … it's all right, Paddy, you can let them go."

Snatter and Ding-a-Ling felt the hands that were pressing them to the wall relax and they were able to turn around. Ding-a-Ling recognised the young boy who had thrown the halfer.

He was standing between two anachronisms.

Frankie and Paddy could easily be identified as two men who had sacrificed a large part of their youth to the paramilitaries.

There were men like Frankie and Paddy all over Northern Ireland and, regardless of side or faction, they were instantly recognisable, for they all wore the same uniform. The uniform of the seventies.

When the sectarian tensions in Northern Ireland had finally erupted into full-scale violence at the end of the 1960s, young men, on both sides of the divide, flocked to join the ranks of the paramilitaries. They were desperate to defend their own communities and, at the same time, to either preserve the union with Britain or to free Ireland, once and for all, from the tyranny of British rule.

The paramilitary organisations, however, struggled to cope with the scale of the influx and, with regard to discipline and security, the various groups became increasingly unwieldy.

It became routine, therefore, for the security forces to round up many of these young and inexperienced volunteers, and the prison population grew accordingly.

Now, in the 1980s, these men, having served their sentences, were being released to wardrobes that were no longer fashionable.

Frankie and Paddy were both wearing bell-bottom jeans with high waistbands, garishly coloured shirts with flared collars, and brown anoraks. They also had shoulder length hair, sideburns and handlebar moustaches.

"What the fuck do you mean, there were loads of them?" Ding-a-Ling addressed the young boy, who suddenly realised he may have made a mistake. He spun around and sprinted into the distance.

"Did you really come over the peace line?" Frankie asked Ding-a-Ling.

"Yeah," said Ding-a-Ling, "they didn't seem too friendly over there."

"You mad fuckers!" Frankie declared, laughing loudly. "You know, to hear that wee cunt, you'd have thought the whole fucking Shankill Road was attacking."

"You know what kids are like," said Ding-a-Ling. Snatter bent down and rolled up his trouser leg to re-assess his wound.

"You alright there, mate?" Frankie asked. "Looks bad, that." Snatter stood up, grimacing.

"Is the Royal near here?" he asked.

"Aye, it's not far at all. You going to Casualty?"

"That's the plan," Ding-a-Ling said cheerfully.

"Well, we're heading back that way," said Frankie. "We were in the Laurel Leaf, so we can dander back with you as far as the Falls."

So, Snatter and Ding-a-Ling set off, once more, for the Royal Victoria Hospital, only this time they were being escorted by the IRA. From the 1970s.

TWENTY FOUR

"It's a bit bloody obvious, though, isn't it? Marcia Brady? I mean, everybody fancied Marcia Brady, for fuck's sake!"

"Okay then, smartass," said Bobby, feeling a little aggrieved, "who was *your* crush, then, when you were a kid?"

Joker thought about it for a second. "Remember *The Double Deckers*?" he asked, and everyone nodded. "Well, I used to fancy the wee one with the stuffed tiger."

"She was only about six, for fuck's sake!" said Sean in disgust.

"Well, I wasn't much fucking older, was I?" Joker protested. "Anyway, it wasn't like a sexual thing, or anything like that. I just thought she was, well, you know, pretty."

"Aw, that's so sweet," said Tone. "Did you want to hold her hand? Did you want to share your sweeties with her?"

"Piss off!"

"What about you, Tone?" asked Bobby. "Who did you fancy when you were a kid?"

"Not really sure," Tone replied, "apart from Marcia Brady, obviously. Although, wasn't there a good-looking girl in *Black Beauty*? Remember? The TV series?"

"Oh, yeah," said Sean, "yeah, I fancied her."

"What about Marcia Brady?" Joker asked.

"Well, of course, Marcia Brady," Sean replied. "Marcia Brady goes without saying. And your woman from *It's a Wonderful Life*? What was her name? Mary, was it?"

"Yeah," Tone told him. "Played by Donna Reed, who also played a prostitute in *From Here to Eternity*."

"Thanks, Tone," said Sean. "You just ruined that memory for me."

"*It's a Wonderful Life*," mused Bobby. "That's a good film, isn't it? I think it's on BBC2 tonight, actually."

"I'm sure my ma will be watching it," Joker told him, "although she can never remember the name of it. She just calls it the film with the bells."

"*Every time a bell rings, an angel gets its wings*," Tone quoted.

"That's right," Bobby said smiling.

"And Ingrid Bergman," Joker suddenly remembered. "I used to fancy her in *Casablanca*."

Everyone agreed, then Sean added, "*Little House on the Prairie*. The older one."

"Didn't she go blind?" Bobby asked.

"What the fuck has that got to do with anything?"

"Nothing. I'm just saying, that's all."

They were now in White's, one of Belfast's oldest bars, and, just like every other bar they had been in, there was a noisy, festive atmosphere.

When they first arrived, there had been no room to sit down, so they had stood at the bar as they waited for a table to become available. As the tightly packed crowd at the bar swayed around them, they had to hold their pints close to their chests, making it difficult to drink. Joker had a brainwave. He reached over and plucked a plastic straw from a box on the bar, which meant he could now sip his beer in comfort.

Classy, thought Tone with a smile.

Eventually, Sean managed to secure a table and they all sat down. Joker brought his straw with him.

"Become attached to that, have you?" Bobby asked him.

"You can't go wrong when you've got a straw, Bobby," Joker intoned gravely. And he popped it into his pocket.

The first round of drinks was coming to an end, just as the *Little House on the Prairie* discussion was starting to get heated, and Sean and Joker went off to get the next.

When they returned, and took their seats, Bobby handed cigarettes to Tone and Joker, and they lit up. Tone leaned back as he exhaled.

"Did Jamesy ever tell you about the plan he's got for his future?" he asked.

"Yeah," said Joker, "he wants to sit in the middle of a field, freezing his balls off, rubbing a bit of crap off another bit of crap with a tooth-brush."

"Thank you, Joker," said Tone, "for that fascinating insight into the world of archaeology, but I'm talking about after that."

"What, later that night?"

"No," Tone said, rolling his eyes, "I mean when he's done with all that sitting in a field business. He was talking about lecturing at some university. Queen's, or Trinity, maybe. Or even somewhere across the water."

"Lecturing in what?" Sean asked. "Archaeology?"

"Yeah, or ancient history, or something. I don't really know, I stopped listening after a while. You know what he's like when he gets started."

"Who's your man he's always banging on about?" asked Sean. "Themos ...Themis ..."

"Themistocles," said Joker.

"Aye, that's right," Tone said. "I think that maybe Alexander the Great is a wee bit too racy for Jamesy. Anyway, in this fantasy of his, he'd come home every night to his wee wife, and they'd sit in front of the fire and chat about their day."

"Crazy wee bastard!" said Joker in wonder.

"Yeah," said Bobby, "that's Jamesy for you, always shooting for the stars."

"Well, obviously, that's what I thought," Tone said, leaning forward, "but, when you actually think about … Oh, talk of the devil."

Jamesy, looking dejected, was making his way through the crowd.

"I think he's had his eyes opened," said Tone.

On reaching the table, Jamesy slumped into a seat and looked around him, a haunted, gaunt expression on his face.

"Not go well, then?" Tone asked him.

"She's a creationist," Jamesy said. Tone simply nodded, then told Joker to go to the bar and get Jamesy a drink.

"I'm just back from the fucking bar," Joker grumbled as he got up and went to the bar.

"What's a creationist?" Sean asked.

"Creationism," said Tone, "is the belief that every word in the Bible is literally true. So, you know, Adam and Eve, Noah's Ark, all that stuff? Well, creationists believe that it all really happened just the way the Bible says it did. And just like every other branch of religion, creationism has a broad spectrum of opinions. What about your woman, Jamesy? What's she, then? *Old-Earth* creationist? *Young-Earth* creationist? *Flat-Earth* creationist?"

"Well, she thinks the universe is six thousand years old."

"Fuck!" said Sean. Tone nodded again and turned back to Jamesy.

"A Young-Earth creationist, then. Did she mention James Ussher?" he asked.

Jamesy looked at Tone. "How did you ...?" he began, but then he looked down and shook his head. "Doesn't matter, but, yeah, James Ussher."

"Who?" asked everyone.

"He's a big deal with these types," said Tone. "Back in the 1600s, he worked out from the Bible – *scientifically* worked out, that is – that God created everything in 4000BC. So, ironically, at about the same time that Galileo was dragging the western world out of the Dark Ages, this prick was trying to push it back in."

"4004BC, to be precise," said Jamesy miserably. "On the 23rd of October."

"Are you sure?" Bobby was shocked. "She actually said that?"

"Yeah," Jamesy told him, "although Greg was doing most of the talking."

Joker came back from the bar and put a pint in front of Jamesy. "There you go Jamesy," he said, "get that down your neck."

"What the fuck was Greg doing there?" Tone demanded.

"Who's Greg?" asked Sean.

"Greg invited the whole lot of them," said Jamesy. "Wasn't much I could do about it."

"Who's Greg?" Sean repeated.

"He was in *Scooby Doo*," Joker told him.

"Maybe it wasn't meant to be," Bobby told Jamesy, but he was moved by the pain he saw when those strange blue eyes turned to face him.

"Yeah, cheer up, Jamesy," said Joker. "Do you want to see my straw?"

"What?"

"So, Jamesy," said Sean, "do you want to talk about it? What happened exactly?"

"We were all in Delaney's," Jamesy began, "and it was going okay, you know? I was trying to just get to the point when, all of a sudden, they start spouting all this nonsense at me. It came as a bit of a shock, actually."

"I suppose they had a go at Darwin," said Tone, "He's one of their big yapping points, isn't he?"

"Yeah, they didn't seem to be fans," Jamesy said as he took a drink. "It's funny, though," he went on, "but Greg mentioned the Holy Spirit and it just occurred to me that I'm not sure what the Holy Spirit actually is."

"It's whatever you want it to be," Tone told him, "just like everything else in religion, it can be anything at all. It can be an essence, or a type of mist, or God's butler, or a twenty-foot-tall rhinoceros with banjos for ears. It can be anything you want because it isn't fucking real."

Sean bristled at Tone's remarks. His faith was important to him, and he often took offence at Tone's angry dismissal of what he believed to be meaningful. He remained silent, however, and reached for his beer.

"When I was a kid," Joker said, "I used to think that the Holy Spirit was God's nickname for his dick."

Everyone gaped at Joker as if he had suddenly sprouted antlers.

"Have you been drinking out of the toilet again?" Tone asked.

"No, seriously," Joker protested, "doesn't it say somewhere that God impregnated Mary using the Holy Spirit? Well, when you're a kid, then you –"

"Christ!" Sean exclaimed, looking up to the ceiling.

"Why would God even need a dick?" Bobby asked.

"Well, for just such an occasion," Joker informed him.

"Oh, for fuck's sake!" cried Sean. "I think it's safe to assume that the Holy Spirit is not some euphemism for God's wab!"

"Why do you say that, Sean?" asked Tone. "The Bible is open to an infinite number of interpretations, so Joker's theory is just as valid as any other."

"Balls!"

"Well, yes, presumably."

"It's an interesting point, actually," said Bobby, "I mean, if we're made in God's image, then it does suggest that God would have a penis."

"And a belly-button," Joker pointed out.

"Yeah," Tone joined in, "you can just picture God, up in Heaven, wondering just what the fuck his nipples are for. Anyway, in light of evolution, *made in God's image* doesn't make any sense."

"Why not?" Sean asked.

"Because we're still evolving, that's why not. I mean, we didn't look like this a million years ago, and we won't look like this a million years from now. So, at what point are we made *in God's own image*?"

"Maybe the phrase refers to the soul," Sean suggested. "Maybe the essence of God is in harmony with the human soul."

"Why, Sean!" Tone pressed his fingertips to his chest with exaggerated theatricality. "That sounds like excrement from a male cow!"

"Yeah okay, Tone!" Sean snapped. "We all know why *you* hate God, don't we?"

"Who hates God?" Tone asked. "I certainly don't hate God, in the same way that I don't hate Thor, or Isis, or the bloody pixies that play with the elves in fairyland. The existence or non-existence of supernatural beings is of absolutely no concern to me."

"Then what's your fucking problem?"

"My problem, Sean," said Tone, "is the snivelling, grasping, lying bastards who claim to know exactly what their God wants. Before St Patrick came along, we were all a bunch of happy, drunken bastards in this country. Jamesy, what did you call that Greek bugger?"

"You need to be a bit more specific there, Tone."

"He wrote about the Celts."

"Strabo? Is that who you mean?"

"Aye, that's him. Well, he said that the Celts were *madly fond of war*, in a good way, like. Then along comes St Patrick and tells us we should all be on our knees, and we've been crawling ever since."

"Well, that's a simplistic way to –"

"Yes, yes, okay, Jamesy," Tone interrupted, "the point is, that for every religion on Earth, there are a million shades of opinion on how the holy words should be understood. That's because we're all individuals, with our own ideas. Take you, Sean, for example. You consider yourself to be a good Catholic, right?"

"Yeah, so?"

"But you still use condoms, don't you?"

"Well, yeah, but –"

"I'm not having a go; I'm just saying that you take the teachings of the Church and you pick and choose the ones that suit you. Everybody does, to some extent, and that's okay because everybody's different. But it's the priests, the vicars, the rabbis, the imams, the druids and the other shit-talkers who piss me off because they have to have *their* individual views forced on everybody else."

Sean sighed. "Yeah," he said, "it's easy to have a go at the Church, isn't it? But you have to have some sort of authority, and the Church has done a lot of good in this world."

"Oh, has it, Sean?" said Tone, getting riled. "Oh, fucking has it? So what happened when the Republic broke free from the UK, then? Was the whole country suddenly all happy and free, do you think? Or did the Catholic Church stamp on the country's fucking neck? One of the first things the Church did, when they got into power, was ban books. Isn't that right, Sean? The land of saints and scholars actually banned more books than the Soviet fucking Union, and that's because the biggest enemy to any religion is freedom of thought. *Don't question your faith*, that's what they keep telling you, isn't it? That's because ignorance and superstition are the only things that keep religions going. Reason is the biggest enemy that any religion can have."

There was a tense silence as Sean considered his reply. Joker had taken out his straw and was twirling it around his fingers. He turned to Jamesy, who was just putting his pint to his lips.

"Have you ever bubbled a frog?" he asked. Jamesy managed to spit most of his beer back into his glass, but the rest came down his nose.

"It's easy to focus on the negative, Tone," said Sean, "but what about all the achievements of the Church? What about all the advancements, in art, in architecture, and even in science?"

"They'd fuck all choice after Galileo!"

"I've never done it myself," Joker continued as Jamesy tried to clear the rest of the beer from his nostrils, "but I'm familiar with the procedure. Apparently, you take a straw and …"

"And what about morality, Sean?" Tone said. "Isn't that what you religious types harp on about? We all get our morality from religion, isn't that what you all say? Well, would you agree, Sean, that one of the strongest bonds in nature is between a parent and a child?"

"Yes," said Sean wearily. "What's your point?"

"Well, the fact that this bond can be seen all over the animal kingdom would suggest that it's a natural instinct, right? Some sort of evolutionary device."

Sean shrugged. He could tell where this was going.

"But it's only with religion," Tone went on, "that we break this natural instinct to safeguard our offspring. It's only with religion – isn't it, Sean? – that parents can stand by and celebrate while they watch some disgusting old bastard mutilate their baby son's penis with his fucking *teeth*. And it's only with religion that parents can watch their daughter's clitoris get ripped off because some ignorant, fucking wankstain has decided it's a sin for women to enjoy sex."

"Yeah, but aren't you –?"

"And it's only with religion," Tone continued, "that parents can sit and watch their child die in agony and do nothing except mumble nonsense at an empty sky."

"I would imagine, though," Joker concluded to Jamesy, "it's not something you'd want to do if you've got your good clothes on."

"What would you do, then, Tone?" Sean sneered. "What's your answer, then? Ban all religion?"

"Of course not," Tone replied, "I think it's a basic human right that people can believe whatever they want."

"Then what the fuck are –?"

"What I *would* do, though," said Tone, "is ban religion for anybody under the age of eighteen."

"What?"

"Well, think about it. Children should be free to have a childhood. They should be allowed to get used to *this* life without having to worry about the potential of another one. It should be no more acceptable to impose religion on kids than it is to force-feed them whiskey. I mean, let's face it, religion has killed more people than cigarettes and booze combined, but it's considered okay to expose new-born babies to it.

"I say that when everybody turns eighteen, they should be taught all the religions of the world and then told they're free to choose whichever one makes the most sense to them. Or, if they want, they can make up their own. Of course, they'll also have the option to choose no religion at all.

"Now, you can't deny that that is a perfectly reasonable idea, but can you imagine the uproar? Religious leaders all over the world would squeal like pigs because they'd know the game would be up. Without the impressionable minds of kids to fuck around with, all religions would wither and die in no time at all."

Joker suddenly roared with laughter. "That's brilliant, Tone," he exclaimed, "I think you've got something there. You can just picture all these eighteen-year-old blokes going; 'Hand me those scissors, I've decided to become a Jew.' You and me, Tone, we should start a campaign."

"I would imagine," said Tone, "that there would be some blokes attracted to the misogyny of Islam, but how many girls do you think there would be? How many eighteen-year-old girls are going to say; 'Yes I'd like to be covered in a sack for the rest of my life, and the thought of having my head cut off for having a shag just adds a wee element of danger?'"

Tone stood up. "Anyway, it's my round," he said. "Who's going to give me a hand?"

"I'll come with you," said Bobby, "there's something I want to talk to you about."

"Well," Sean said, once Tone and Bobby had gone, "Tone didn't say much about eighteen-year-olds accepting Christianity. Do you think that's a flaw in his plan?"

"Course not," said Joker, "were you not listening? He said you get shown every religion in the world and, to be honest, they're all just as unfeasible as each other. Why would Christianity stand out?"

"You can't just dismiss the beliefs of a billion people, Joker," Sean said.

"Course you can," Joker told him. "Most people used to believe the world was flat, so are you saying we should have respected *their* beliefs?"

Sean gave a sigh and leaned back in his seat. "What about you, Jamesy?" he said. "Are you turning into one of these mad atheists?"

"I don't think so," said Jamesy with a sad smile, "though I wish I'd had Tone with me in Delaney's."

"Yeah, he can be a clever bugger, I'll give him that," said Sean, "and we know he's got his reasons for all the anger, but I don't think there can be any excuse for rejecting the whole Bible."

"Have you read it?" Joker asked innocently.

"Fuck off, Joker," Sean replied.

"I'll take that as a no, then."

"Take what as a no?" asked Tone as he placed three pints on the table.

"Sean, here, is sticking up for a book he hasn't read."

"Well, that doesn't narrow it down," Bobby laughed, taking a seat.

"I'm just saying," Sean said, exasperated, "that you can't reject a book that's given us the Ten Commandments."

"You think the Ten Commandments are important?" Tone asked as he accepted a light from Joker.

"Come on, Tone," said Sean, "even you can't have a fucking go at the Ten Commandments, can you? They're a profound set of moral guidelines. They form the basis of all of our laws. They mean that –"

"Name them."

"What?"

"These profound moral guidelines," Tone said, "if they give us instructions on how we're supposed to conduct ourselves then you should be able to tell me what they are."

"I can't name all of them," Sean said petulantly, "Not off the top of my head anyway."

"I'll start you off with some clues," said Tone. "The first commandment should be a fucking cracker, right? Really grab your attention, you know? Something like, 'Thou shalt not mentally, physically or sexually abuse a child, under any circumstances. Ever!' Does that ring a bell, Sean? Does that sound like the first commandment?"

Sean didn't answer, he lifted his pint and took a sip. Bobby took a perplexed look around the table.

"That's really weird," he said, "I learned the Ten Commandments in Sunday School, but I can't remember what the first one is."

"Fondling your neighbour's ass," said Joker. "Isn't that one of them?"

"Don't you mean covet?" asked Jamesy.

"You're just splitting hairs, Jamesy."

"Okay, Tone," said Bobby, "it's bugging me now, just tell me the first one."

"Right," Tone said, "Here we go! Everybody ready? Then I'll tell you that number one in the list of the most important rules that we should all live our lives by is ..." he paused for dramatic effect and to take a drink, "*Thou shalt have no other Gods before me.*"

"Well, that was an anti-climax," said Joker.

"Bit pointless, too," Tone added, "if there's only supposed to be one God anyway."

"Oh yeah, I remember now," said Bobby, "in fact, I think the first four are all about God, aren't they?"

"Yes, Bobby," said Tone, "not that God's self-absorbed, or needy, or anything."

"There must be something in the Bible you approve of," said Sean.

"Now that you mention it, Sean," Tone replied, "yes, there is. In the entire Bible, there is only one line that I would keep. *Do unto others, as you would have them do unto you*, but that phrase isn't unique to the Bible. Just about every human society in history came up with their own version of it, independent of Jesus. In fact, Jesus even contra…" Tone's words trailed away as something caught his attention. A fierce-looking beauty seemed to be approaching their table. She was accompanied by another girl that Tone recognised. It was Karen. Ding-a-Ling's sister.

"Right!" said Karen. "Where the fuck are they?"

"What?" said Tone pointlessly.

"Gary and Seamus! What the fuck have you done with them?"

"They're not here, Karen," said Sean. "All right there, Rosie?"

"What the fuck are you talking about? They were supposed to be meeting up with all you hoor begs."

"Yeah, but they never showed up. We haven't seen them all day."

Karen frowned and turned to face Rosie. Rosie was looking pale, she thought. She turned back to Sean.

"Where the fuck can they be, then?" she asked.

Sean shrugged. "Don't know," he said. "We know as much as you do, to be honest. We haven't heard anything since I talked to you earlier on."

Karen looked thoughtful. She wasn't sure if she should be worried or not, but she thought she should reassure Rosie.

"Don't you worry, Rosie love," she said. "They're bound to turn up somewhere, sooner or later. And when they do ..." she turned back to the table. "If you see our Gary, you can tell him he'll be getting my fucking toe up his hole! All right there, James love?" Karen had a soft spot for Jamesy. She turned and took Rosie by the arm, and they marched off towards the door.

"Lovely turn of phrase, Karen has," said Joker. "Don't you think?"

"So that's the future Mrs Green?" asked Tone.

"Yeah, that's Rosie," said Sean.

"Not exactly Snatter's type, I would have thought."

"Yeah," Bobby agreed, "she looks like she'd eat Snatter for breakfast."

"You've been very quiet about this whole business, Sean," said Tone. "Is there something you're not telling us?"

Sean put up his hands. "Nothing to do with me," he said. "Anyway, I'm away for a piss."

Joker leaned over and tapped Tone on the shoulder. "Black," he said.

"What?"

"The colour of her hair. It's black."

TWENTY FIVE

"Rosie's pregnant." Snatter was surprised at how easy it was to say out loud, and how natural it sounded. "I'm supposed to keep it all a big secret till after Christmas, but fuck it, what difference can it make?"

The casualty department of the Royal Victoria Hospital would certainly have heard much more shocking statements, but Snatter had expected more of a reaction from Ding-a-Ling.

They had been in Casualty for nearly two hours and were almost ready to go. Snatter's various wounds had all been tended to and they were just waiting for the results of his leg X-ray. Snatter glanced at Ding-a-Ling, who was staring straight ahead.

"Did you hear what I said?" he asked. Ding-a-Ling seemed startled.

"What?" he blurted out. "I mean, um, are you sure it's yours?"

"What the fuck is that supp–"

"All right, all right, I didn't mean anything by it. It's just, well, it was a bit of a shock, that's all."

"Yeah, well."

"So that's what all the marriage talk is about, then?"

"Aye, for fuck's sake," Snatter said wearily. "Rosie's idea. It's all getting a bit out of hand. I could have really done with a day out with the lads today.

"Mmm," said Ding-a-Ling unhelpfully.

"They must be wondering where we are. Do you think we should ring somebody? Are you even fucking listening?"

"What? Um, yeah, yeah. Ring? Ring who?"

"I don't know. Your Karen maybe. Find out what happened with Harry at least. Or your ma. Somebody might have rung her, looking for us, so she might be worried."

"Yeah, you're right. I'll go and make a couple of calls."

Ding-a-Ling got up and walked over to some payphones that were attached to the far wall. A nurse came and called Snatter to the treatment room. When he got back, he found Ding-a-Ling sitting with his elbows resting on his knees, staring at the floor.

"Well," said Snatter, "it's not fractured."

"What? Oh, right, okay. We going, then?"

"Yeah. What I think we should do, is get a Black Taxi into town, and then just get a private taxi straight up to the Bot. There's no point trying to intercept them before that, and we know they'll end up in the Bot at some point."

"Okay," said Ding-a-Ling. "Makes sense, I suppose."

When they got outside, they were surprised to see it was snowing.

"Well, it has been cold enough today," Snatter said. "White Christmas, then?" Ding-a-Ling didn't respond. When they reached the Falls Road, they crossed at the pedestrian crossing and stood waiting by the roadside for a Black Taxi to appear.

The Falls Road Black Taxis operated like a bus service, following a set route to ferry the nationalist community of west Belfast to and from the city centre. Snatter, shivering against the cold, turned to Ding-a-Ling.

"So, did you get through to anybody?" he asked.

"What?"

"On the phone."

"Oh, yeah, I spoke to my ma. Turns out Karen, Harry and Rosie are on the warpath. They headed into town, looking for us."

"Fuck!" Snatter was suddenly worried.

"You don't seem all that excited about becoming a father," Ding-a-Ling ventured.

Snatter hesitated. He looked up and watched the falling snowflakes.

"To be totally honest," he said, "it's my worst nightmare. I don't want to have a kid, and I don't want to get fucking married." He shook his head in wonder. "It's all taken on a life of its own, and I don't seem to have any say in it. It's like I'm watching my whole life disappear, and there's fuck all I can do about it."

Ding-a-Ling was watching him carefully.

"Sounds like you needed to get that off your chest," he said. "I thought you and Rosie were happy together."

Snatter gave a long sigh. "Not really," he said. "*I'm* not, anyway. And to be honest, I don't think Rosie is either. I don't really know how it all happened, you know? I mean, one minute I bump into her in the street, and the next minute I'm about to have a fucking wife and kid."

Ding-a-Ling seemed to be about to say something, but he spotted a Black Taxi approaching and held out his hand. As the taxi pulled into the kerb, he turned to Snatter.

"Yeah," he said, "bit of a bugger that, isn't it?"

TWENTY SIX

It was almost seven when they got back to the hotel. Claire, in the car's passenger seat, yawned and stretched.

"Can we just skip dinner?" she asked. "And go straight to bed?"

Tone looked at her and shook his head.

"No, I'm starving," he said. "You just need to get your second wind. A good meal, a drink of wine and an invigorating cigarette should do the trick."

"Will you carry me into the hotel?"

"The answer to that question would have loads of swear words in it, not to mention a lot of violent, slapping actions, so I'll pretend I didn't hear you."

Claire laughed. "My hero."

"Come on, like I said, I'm bloody starving!"

They decided against going out for an Indian and had dinner in the hotel instead. Afterwards, they settled down in the bar with a lager for Tone and a glass of wine for Claire.

"So, did you get around to reading *Catcher in the Rye,* then?" Claire asked.

"Yeah," Tone replied, "I enjoyed it."

"I thought you'd like it. You remind me of him."

"Who? You mean Holden?"

"Yeah," Claire smiled, "you both take everything so seriously. No, wait, that's not exactly what I meant. I think it's more that you don't suffer fools gladly. You know what I mean? People annoy you, don't they?"

"Well, I wouldn't say that. That sounds a bit harsh."

"But they do! Oh, I know you try to hide it, but it's obvious."

"Well, *you're* annoying me, if that's any help."

"I'd say, at best, you tolerate people, but I think there's a real resentment there. Is resentment the right word? Disgust, maybe?"

"Are you just making this stuff up? I thought it was journalism you were doing, not psy–" Tone stopped suddenly as Claire leaned forward.

"I'm going to find out what makes you tick, Mr Maguire," she said intently. "I'm going to explore the murky depths of your soul."

"Sounds like a fun evening."

"It will be," she assured him. "There's more to you than meets the eye, and I think you're worth getting to know."

"I'm worth getting to know?"

"I think so. I'd like to make the effort at least."

"You're not getting all soppy on me there, are you?" Tone gently mocked, making Claire laugh. She then lowered her head, letting her eyes flirt with him through her eyelashes.

"Maybe I am," she murmured, and Tone felt his heart beat faster.

"What do you want to know?"

"Everything!" she exclaimed. "Now go and get some wine, and we'll head upstairs. And be quick, we've got work to do!"

"It was a normal enough childhood," said Tone. He sat in the one chair in his room while Claire sat facing him, propped up on pillows, on the bed. "Or as normal as you can expect, growing up in Divis. My parents were pretty old when they had me. I think I may have been a bit of a surprise. They already had a son, you see. My brother's about ten years older than me, he lives in Australia now, and I don't really hear from him much."

"Does that bother you?"

"Not even slightly. Nice try, though," Tone smiled and took a packet of cigarettes from his shirt pocket. "No, I think there was too much of an age gap for us ever to be close," he carried on as he handed a cigarette to Claire. "I was only about twelve when he left, so I never really got to know him. Maybe that's something for the future, some big reunion when we finally get to know each other," he shrugged. "At the moment, though, I don't even think about it."

Claire looked thoughtful for a second and then she reached for the wine. She topped off her glass and passed the bottle to Tone.

"So, there's no big juicy childhood trauma we can dredge up and pick over?"

"Sorry," said Tone.

"But there is something that rattles your cage," Claire insisted, "and I'm going to find it. Let me see," she said, "I know you've got a bee in your bonnet about religion. I can tell from all the bitter wee comments you make. I'm not sure if that's the problem, though, but we –"

"What makes you think there's a prob–?"

"Shut up!" said Claire. "I'm analysing here. Right then, religion. What's that all about? What have you got against religion?"

Tone took a sip of wine as he studied Claire's face. He took a draw from his cigarette and sat back, resigned, in his chair.

"You're going to make a big deal out of this," he said.

"Really?" Claire was suddenly intrigued. "Well, go on then. Let's hear it."

"To be honest," said Tone, "I don't know what it is you're looking for, but I don't think this is it."

Claire shifted on the bed, making herself more comfortable. She drank some wine and stared at Tone in anticipation.

"I met a girl," he began, "when I was at university in England. Her family belonged to some obscure Christian cult that's got all these weird rules about not interfering with God's plan. Anyway, to cut a long story short, she got an aneurysm, a blood vessel, that burst in her brain. Well, it could have been sorted out in hospital but, of course, that would have been interfering with God's plan, so her family just sat and watched her die."

"Jesus!" Claire said quietly. "Did you love her?"

Tone looked away, a sudden, uncomfortable lump in his throat. "Does it matter?" he asked.

Claire did not reply, she just sat still and watched him closely.

"I probably did, I suppose," he said finally. "But who knows? Who knows where it would have gone? No point thinking about it really, is there? I mean, I think about it less and less."

"And you blame religion? All religion?"

"Of course I blame religion. Wouldn't you?" Tone waited for Claire to reply, but she remained silent. He sighed. "I'd never really thought about religion," he went on. "It was something that was there, you know? Something that everybody has, to one degree or another. But when Emily died, then –"

"Emily? Was that her name?"

"What? Yes. Look, do you want to hear this, or not?"

"Sorry," Claire smiled. "Go on."

"Well, when she died, I sort of lost the plot for a bit. Did the usual old clichés, you know, drink and drugs? But, eventually, I got back to Belfast, and I started to take more of an interest in religion. I did a lot of research and stuff and I have to admit, it was a bit of an eye-opener. It all just seemed to be such an obvious con."

"What do you mean by that?"

"Well, it seemed to me that every religion in the world was started for a reason. Either to make money, or to manipulate people."

"What about God?"

"What's God got to do with anything?"

Claire tilted her head to one side and gave a sardonic smirk.

"So, religion is a con, then?" she said. "Christianity? How is that a con?"

Tone stubbed out his cigarette and leaned forward to rest his elbows on his knees. He felt he was growing tired of the whole argument. All he wanted was to climb into bed beside Claire and help her out of her clothes.

"It's only my opinion," he said.

"Well, I'm nosy," said Claire, "so tell me your opinion."

"Okay then," Tone leaned back in his chair as he spoke. "Christianity was founded by a guy, who'd never even met Jesus, called Saul of Tarsus."

"Saul of Tarsus? You mean St Paul?"

"Yeah," said Tone. "He changed his name after his *miraculous* conversion. Probably hoping that people wouldn't associate him with his previous reputation for persecuting heretical Jews."

"Heretical Jews?"

"You'd call them Christians. Don't get me wrong," Tone went on, "I'm sure Saul did have a revelation on the road to Damascus, but I think it was more of a financial opening of the eyes than a spiritual one. He was a big fan of opening up Christianity to non-Jews by telling them they didn't have to stick to the old Jewish laws, like circumcision and not eating pork. This, obviously, would have increased the number of sheep he could fleece."

"But didn't St Paul get killed for his beliefs?"

"Yeah, but what are you getting at? Are you trying to say his execution makes him somehow more genuine?"

"Maybe. Oh, I don't know, I'm just trying to play devil's advocate."

"Yeah, well, it's impossible to know what really went on back then, but I think my take on it is the most logical. Saul's version doesn't make any rational sense at all."

"Yeah," said Claire, "but isn't that the whole point of religion? Faith and faith alone is all that's needed?"

"Then why do these people make such a big deal about so-called miracles. Why do they need to see moving statues? Or the face of Mary in a bloody hedge?"

"Okay, Tony, but don't you think you're oversimplifying it? I mean, isn't your attitude a bit out of proportion? When I look at the clergy, I see –"

"Con men," said Tone.

"What?"

Tone smiled. "A friend of mine, the one I told you about, went to Inst.. Well, his da is a bit of an atheist, and the way he describes the clergy of any religion is *con men*."

"Sounds like you two would get on very well together."

"We do, actually," said Tone laughing.

"That reminds me," said Claire. "I meant to ask you earlier. Didn't you say there was something wrong with your mate's brain? What did you mean by that?"

"Oh, nothing really. It's just that, well, I don't know if it's some weird form of autism, or whatever, but there do seem to be some things that he's unusually good at. He's got a flair for languages, for example."

"A cunning linguist, eh? I'm a fan already."

"You, my dear, are incorrigible. In fact, I've never met anyone so incapable of being corriged."

Claire laughed and held out her glass for Tone to fill with wine.

"So, what does he do with himself, this mate of yours?" she asked.

Tone paused before answering. "He's on the dole at the moment," he said.

Claire was suddenly alert. She leaned forward.

"Well that hit a nerve!" she said.

"What? What are you talking about?"

"You flinched, just before you answered. It wasn't very obvious, but it was there. Now why would you do that?"

"Are you already drunk?"

"Now you're being defensive," Claire said. "Tell me about him. Tell me about your mate."

"Christ," Tone muttered. He stood up and paced about the room. "There's nothing to tell." He took a deep breath and ran his hand through his hair. "I don't really know what you're after here. Like I said, he's gifted at certain things. Of course, at other things, he's just an asshole." He smiled, but Claire thought it was a nervous smile.

"So, he's got a talent that he doesn't use," she said. "Is that right?"

"I'm not even sure he wants to use it." Tone gave a shrug. "He's just drifting, you know?"

"Is he happy?"

"Is anybody?" That nervous smile again. Tone leant against the desk that was on the opposite side of the room to the bed. He looked down into his glass and swirled the wine around it.

"He shouldn't be," he said finally. "He's just prepared to settle, and what he's settling for is nothing. Is he happy? He probably is, but that doesn't make it any less of a waste."

Claire was silent as she debated with herself whether or not she should ask the obvious question. *Oh, what the hell*, she thought. *In for a penny ...*

"Are you talking about *him* or *you*?" she said. Tone's head jerked up and he glared at her.

"Oh, spare me the amateur bloody psychology!" he snapped. Claire jumped off the bed, her eyes wide and her anger flaring.

"Well, you bloody tell me, Tony," she barked, "just what the problem is, because I don't get it. What is it that's holding you back? It's obvious you hate your bloody job. You moan about it often enough! So what is it, then? Do you have a wife and kids up north?"

"Of course not!"

"Then what is it, Tony? You must have a bit of money in the bank, so what's stopping you? There must be something you want to do, besides selling bloody tablecloths! So why not just do it? Why not just ..." Claire slumped back onto the bed, her anger fading, "... just grasp the fucking nettle."

Tone looked down at her. He knew she was right. He had been thinking the same thing for a while now. What *was* holding him back? Was it fear? He was aware that his memory of Emily was beginning to blur and to fade away, but what else had he lost in Bournemouth? His ambition? His self-belief?

He watched Claire as she sat on the edge of the bed, staring at the carpet, sulking.

"Did you find what you were looking for?" he asked sheepishly.

"Maybe I'm too nosy for my own good," she said, not looking up.

"You know that cheesy old phrase; *You look beautiful when you're angry*?" Tone asked her. She turned to face him, her look was sullen and guarded. She remained silent.

"Well, *you* don't," said Tone. "In fact, you look like shit."

Claire leapt from the bed with a pillow in her hand. She managed to catch Tone a blow to the side of his head before he grabbed her by the waist and they struggled and wrestled each other across the room. They wrestled against the wall and they wrestled each other's clothes off and they wrestled each other down onto the floor. Where they stayed for a while. Wrestling.

TWENTY SEVEN

Jamesy drained his glass and placed it on the table.

"We're not staying here for another one, are we?" he asked.

"No," said Tone, "we should probably make a move. You knocked that back quick. What's the rush?"

"I just fancy a walk, that's all. Get a bit of air."

"Want some company?" Tone asked him.

"If you don't mind."

"Course not." Tone knocked back the rest of his drink and stood up. As he pulled on his coat, he spoke to the three still sitting. "See you in the Crown, then?"

"Yeah, we shouldn't be long," Sean told him.

"Right, Jamesy, lead the way."

The cold hit them as soon as they stepped outside, so they walked quickly, trying to generate some warmth. They made their way through the dwindling crowds, heading towards Donegall Place.

Most of the shops were now closed and those people still in the city centre were either making their way home or were heading to a bar.

Parties would be erupting all over town as the end of the working day signalled the start of the countdown to Christmas. The centre of town still had a buzz to it with crowds milling around the bus stops and taxi ranks. Alcohol-fuelled singsongs could be heard bubbling up here and there amidst the shouting and the laughter.

The Christmas lights completed the festive scene, with the giant Christmas Tree in front of the City Hall at its heart. Tone and Jamesy strode past oblivious.

Tone had been expecting Jamesy to unburden himself about what had happened in Delaney's from the moment they left White's, but Jamesy waited until they were close to the Crown before he spoke.

"What if she was the one, Tone?" he asked.

"The one?"

"You know what I mean. I've never felt like that before, what if I never feel like it again?"

"Are you talking about one true love?" asked Tone, surprised. "You don't believe in all that nonsense."

"I know," said Jamesy, "at least, I thought I didn't. What else am I supposed to think, though? It's shaken me up a bit, to be honest."

"You think your woman's a lost cause, then?"

"I don't know what to think," said Jamesy miserably. "I'll probably never see her again anyway."

"Never say never, Jamesy boy," Tone exclaimed. "Make it your New Year's resolution. Set her in your sights and just go for it."

"Yeah, like it's that easy. Anyway, what about all that stuff she believes. That's a bit of a hurdle, isn't it?"

"Well, hurdles are there to be cleared. Fuck, it's cold! Take her on a journey, Jamesy. Show her the real world. Bring her into the light. Make it a wee project for yourself."

"Not sure if I'm up to that," said Jamesy. "You wouldn't believe some of the things they were coming out with."

"Oh, I've heard it all," said Tone. "Trust me. Anyway, you're being a wee bit of a hypocrite there, aren't you, Jamesy?"

Jamesy stopped dead. "What's that supposed to mean?" he asked.

"You're having a go at poor old Greg and his cronies for having views that fly in the face of reason, aren't you?" They started walking again, eager to get out of the cold.

"Yeah, but why does that make –"

"Going to Mass tomorrow, Jamesy?"

"Yes, you know I always …" Jamesy's voice trailed away as the penny dropped.

"So, *their* irrational beliefs are bad, but *your* irrational beliefs are perfectly okay, is that it? You're a bright lad, Jamesy," said Tone as he pulled open the door to the Crown, "but only up to a point."

"Oh shit!" said Joker, as they got up to go. "I forgot to get my ma a bottle of vodka."

"Bit late now, Joker," Bobby said. "The shops will all be closed at this time."

"There's an offy beside the Crown," Sean suggested, "that might be open."

"No, I know a better place," Joker told them. "Let's get going."

They walked silently through the evening air, feeling it was too cold to waste energy on idle chit-chat. As they turned left into Donegall Place, Bobby stopped and gave a wolf-whistle. Some girls, waiting at a bus stop, laughed and waved to him. One of the girls peeled away and walked over, giving Bobby a warm embrace.

"Hello, beautiful," Bobby said, "are you coming round tomorrow?"

"Of course," she said, "probably late afternoon."

Behind him, Bobby heard Joker loudly clear his throat. He laughed and turned around.

"You've met Sean, haven't you?" he asked the girl. "Well, this is Joker. Joker, this is Claire."

TWENTY EIGHT

It was late afternoon and the unfashionable little bar in the centre of Dublin was filling up with traders from the market in nearby Moore Street.

Tone could guess how cold it was outside by the actions of the newcomers. They would rub their hands and stamp their feet as they made their way to the bar to order hot whiskies and pints of Guinness.

"Do you want another one," he asked Claire, pointing to her empty glass.

"Oh, yes please," she replied. "I could get very settled here."

Tone smiled, then he picked up the two empty glasses from the table and went up to the bar. They had spent much of the day wandering around Dublin, finally getting around to seeing the sights, but a sudden drop in temperature had forced them to take refuge in the Barrow Inn.

Claire watched Tone make his way back from the bar with fresh drinks. He placed the drinks on the table and sat down facing her.

"Pretty rubbish Christmas decorations, aren't they?" she said, nodding to the bar. Tone turned to take a quick glance. Behind the bar, a single length of straggly tinsel was pinned up. It swayed half-heartedly each time the door was opened.

"Yeah, I noticed that," said Tone. "To be honest, though, I think it suits this place. You know, understated?"

"Understated?" Claire laughed. "Do you think that's their mission statement?"

"You never know with bloody theme pubs these days," Tone said. He took two cigarettes from a pack on the table and passed one to Claire. She accepted a light, and settled back in her chair, relaxed and content.

"This year's flown in," she said. "I can't believe it's only two weeks till Christmas."

"Got any plans?"

"What? For Christmas?"

"Yeah, for Christmas."

"Oh, just the usual stuff. A traditional family affair. I'll be staying with my parents, same as every year. Nothing out of the ordinary, but I like it, you know? The whole corny Christmas thing. What about you?"

"Same for me, really," said Tone. "I stay at my flat, but I usually spend all of Christmas Day round at my folks' place in Divis. Just the usual family stuff." He gave Claire a hesitant glance. "Any chance we could meet up over the holidays? If we're both going to be back in Belfast, then we can –"

Claire shook her head. "I'd love to," she said, "but I don't think I'm going to have any time for myself when I get back home. You know what families are like. Plus, I'll probably have to call into the *Telegraph* at some point. It's getting hard to keep up with all the news at the minute. I still can't believe the Berlin Wall has gone."

"Yeah," Tone agreed, "that was bit of a shock." They had both watched the news coverage, in Tone's hotel room, a few weeks back. "I noticed you were getting a bit emotional over it."

"Yeah, I was," Claire laughed, "and so were you."

"I don't know what you're talking about," Tone said dismissively.

"Oh yeah, right!" Claire teased. "What was all that; *I'm just going to the bathroom to do some man's stuff*? I heard the wee quiver in your voice."

"Nonsense, woman," said Tone. "Like I said, it was man's stuff. Women don't understand these things. And, trust me, it isn't really something you'd want to know about. All that scraping, and poking, and scooping." Tone feigned a shudder. "Very unpleasant."

Claire cocked her head to one side. "So, you're telling me," she began, "that you didn't have to wipe a wee tear away when you saw all those people dancing on the wall?"

"Course I didn't wipe a tear away. I'm a bloke, remember?"

"Yeah, okay, I believe you," Claire mocked. "But doesn't it give you some hope for Northern Ireland? I mean, if it can all work out in Germany, then maybe there's hope for *us* too."

"Not really," said Tone as he drained his pint. "The more you know about Northern Ireland, the more you realise there is no bloody hope at all."

"Oh, it's Mr Cheery Optimist," Claire laughed.

"Mr Miserable Realist, you mean. Anyway, drink up, and we'll go and see if we can find somewhere for dinner."

Later that night, as they lay in bed together, their meandering conversation happened to stumble onto the subject of past relationships. Tone had told Claire about a variety of different girls that had passed through his life, none of whom, apart from Emily, had created much impact.

"So, what about you?" he asked. "I've told you all about the tragic farce that passes for my love life. It's your turn to dish the dirt. Anybody waiting for you back in Belfast?" He tried to make it sound like a casual inquiry, but he was aware of just how much significance he was placing on her answer. Claire hesitated, and Tone's heart sank.

"To be perfectly honest," she said finally, "I'm not really sure." She gave a nervous little laugh. "That doesn't make sense, does it?"

"Oh, I don't know," said Tone. "There have been times when I wasn't sure if I was in a relationship or not."

"It's something like that, I suppose." Claire sat up to light a cigarette. "We grew up together, you see. We met in primary school and just became friends from the beginning. It sort of grew from there, you know? We'd call round each other's houses and hang out together. We had this wee gang, and we'd just do everything together, and things grew from there, I suppose. We did all the usual teenage experimenting together, and all that stuff, but I never thought there was anything serious to it, you know? As we grew up, I had other boyfriends, and he had other girlfriends, but we always seemed to end up back with each other. Some sort of unspoken thing, I don't know."

Tone lay beside her, listening quietly and intently, as Claire continued.

"And then he went off to Queen's, and I went off to Jordanstown, and I think, at the time, I just assumed we'd drift apart. That's what usually happens, isn't it? But it's weird, it's like we never got around to drifting apart, you know? So that's it. I'm not really sure how things stand at the moment."

"Do you love him?" Tone blurted out, then inwardly cursed himself. Again, Claire took a little time to compose her answer. Eventually, she nodded.

"I love him for who he is," she said carefully, "for his goodness. That's not too corny, is it? He's always been there for me, so I love him for that, you know? For his friendship. He's a genuinely lovely person so, in that way, I suppose I do love him. In other ways, though?" She gave a little shrug. "Does that answer your question?"

"Yeah," said Tone, pulling her down to lie beside him.

Yeah, he thought, *because he sounds like a bit of a wab.*

TWENTY NINE

"Nice meeting you, love." Joker nodded to Claire, and turned to Sean and Bobby. "I'm going to shoot off here," he said. "I want to get that bottle of Smirnoff for my ma, so I'll just see you in the Crown, okay?"

"Okay, Joker," said Bobby. "We'll see you in a bit."

Joker took off. He knew of a little off-licence behind the City Hall that sold cheap spirits and he was keen to complete the one chore that he had for today. He assessed his level of inebriation as he crossed the road in front of the City Hall. *Not too bad*, he thought, *Feeling pretty good actually*. He walked past the City Hall's Christmas Tree and was cheered by the sight. *You can't beat Christmas*, he told himself.

The part of town at the back of the City Hall was a lot quieter than the busy retail area that blazed brightly down Royal Avenue and Donegall Place. Most of the buildings here were comprised of office blocks, closed now for Christmas. Joker found the off-licence in a small side street.

"Just in time," the elderly man behind the counter told him. "I'm closing up now."

"Aye," said Joker, "you'd want to be home by this time on Christmas Eve, if you'd any sense."

"Is that where you're off to, then?"

"No," Joker laughed, "but then, nobody ever accused me of having any sense."

He wished the old man a Merry Christmas and set off for the Crown, a plastic carrier bag containing the vodka clutched in his hand. He shivered and quickened his pace, keen to be back in the warmth, surrounded by friends and beer.

Joker was familiar with this part of the town and he remembered there was a shortcut to the Crown that would take him down a twisting alleyway.

The entrance to the alley was formed on one side by a tall office block and on the other by the remains of an old warehouse that had recently been demolished. At this time of the evening, and with the rubble from the warehouse casting grotesque shadows, the alley would be silent, dark and uninviting. Not that Joker was bothered by this, of course. It was Christmas Eve after all.

Sticky Mickey watched from the back of his car. Jippo, his right-hand man, sat in the car's front passenger seat.

"I wanted the two of them together," Sticky Mickey said grimly. "It's getting too fucking late now."

"I'm sure they were meant to meet up earlier," said Jippo defensively. He had been following Joker for most of the day, waiting for Lingfield to show up so that he could contact his boss and get everything moving. Lingfield, however, had failed to appear.

"I don't know what's happened," he said. "It's jolly odd."

"Yes, it is *jolly odd*," said Sticky Mickey, mimicking Jippo's accent. "So, what do you want to do?"

Sticky Mickey thought about it. He had wanted to have this all sorted out by now, but he had been busy lately. Today should have been the ideal opportunity to get the whole business done and out of the way, but just getting one of these assholes seemed messy and unfinished. He was tempted to leave it for another day, but he had made promises and so felt obliged to do something tonight.

The situation, at the moment, was perfect for his plans. The streets around the back of the City Hall were deserted, and his target was approaching the entrance to a quiet alleyway.

He was still mulling it over, when Jippo stirred in the seat in front of him.

"Just a sec!" Jippo suddenly exclaimed. "Who's that?"

Sticky Mickey looked and saw someone stop and talk to Joker. They obviously knew each other.

"Fuck it!" he said. "I don't care who it is. We're getting this over with. Give the word."

Jippo quietly got out of the car and gave a signal to a group of men waiting in the shadow of a doorway on the far side of Joker and his companion.

"Hey, Joker! The main man!" The voice came from behind Joker and stopped him in his tracks. He turned around.

"Johnny Gee?" he said. *Fuck!* he thought.

"Yeah, how's it going?" said Johnny Gee. "Last-minute shopping?"

"Um, yeah, sort of," Joker replied. He had only met Johnny Gee once and, as far as Joker was concerned, that had been one time too many. He was already trying to think of a way he could break off from this encounter as quickly and as politely as possible.

He certainly took no heed of the three men he could see approaching from behind Johnny Gee, and Johnny Gee, in turn, paid no attention to the three men who were walking up behind Joker.

"Listen," Joker began, but he was startled when an arm was thrown around Johnny Gee's neck, and a hand was clasped over his mouth. Before Joker could react, his right arm was grabbed from behind, and pushed up his back. A hand covered his own mouth, and both he and Johnny Gee were roughly manhandled into the dark and empty alleyway. They were pushed, faces first, against a brick wall. Someone spoke.

"Is this the other one?"

"Let's see. Fuck, no. I don't know who this is."

"Shit!"

"What do you want to do?"

"Just hit him a slap and tell him to fuck off."

Joker heard a cry and managed to turn his head enough to see Johnny Gee reeling to the end of the alley. It was beginning to dawn on him just what was going on.

"Mr Anderson, I presume?"

"Let me guess," said Joker. "You're Sticky Mickey?"

Joker's head was banged against the wall, and his arm was pushed further up his back. He felt the bag containing his mother's vodka being wrenched from his hand.

"Nobody fucking calls me that!" said Sticky Mickey angrily. "Especially not a pointless piece of shit like you!"

"I'm sorry," said Joker. "What do you prefer? Just Sticky? Or Mr Mickey?"

A fist was driven into Joker's back, making him wince. He made a mental note to keep his big mouth shut.

"Where's your gobshite mate?" asked Sticky Mickey.

"Could you be more specific? I've got loads of gobsh–" Again Joker's head was banged hard against the wall. This time he felt a little blood trickle down the length of his nose.

You really need to shut the fuck up, he scolded himself. He turned his head and finally caught a glimpse of his tormentor. He was shocked. Sticky Mickey was tiny. He had small, delicate features with a smooth, unblemished complexion that gave him a distinctly feminine appearance.

Joker looked beyond him, trying to fully appreciate the situation he was in. He could see one hood at the end of the alley, about twenty feet away, and two more were standing by Sticky Mickey. If he added the two who were pressing him to the wall, then Joker reckoned the odds were six to one. Not good. Sticky Mickey then made the situation a whole lot worse when he produced a black automatic pistol.

"Aye, I had one of them too, when I was a kid," said Joker. "Does it fire wee bits of potato?"

Joker received a violent slap that made his head ring. Despite his bravado, he was beginning to wonder where his kneecaps would be spending Christmas.

"My wife wants me to cut your balls off and bring them back to her," Sticky Mickey said.

"She sounds lovely," said Joker.

"She took it as a personal insult when you broke her brother's arm. So you can understand her being upset. And when she's upset, I have to fucking sort it out, you know? She made me promise to bring your balls and your dickhead mate's balls to her on a plate."

The thought of losing his kneecaps now struck Joker as being wildly optimistic.

"Personally," Sticky Mickey went on, "I thought that was going a bit too far. A good fucking kicking should be enough."

The hood at the end of the alley had been rummaging around in some building debris and had found a three-foot long piece of broken banister which he was now weighing up in his hands. Joker didn't want to think about what the hood had in mind for his makeshift weapon, but he wanted to think about his balls on a plate even less.

"But your dickhead mate's not here, is he?" said Sticky Mickey. "And that fucks things up a bit."

"Well, if it's easier for you to wait and do us both together, then –" A sudden bark of laughter from the hood at the end of the alley made everyone turn and look.

"Look at this cunt!"

The new figure that had entered the alley had his face in shadow, making it difficult to make out his features, but Joker grinned.

"You couldn't give us a hand here, could you, Harry?"

THIRTY

The Crown Liquor Saloon was well aware of Thomas Edison's new-fangled electric lightbulbs but wanted no truck with them. There was nothing wrong with gas lighting, it was felt. Gas lighting was honest and easy to understand. What could be more natural, it was argued, than pumping combustible material into your premises and setting fire to it?

Electrical lighting was clearly witchcraft, and so, Mr Edison, a minion of Satan if ever there was one, could go fuck himself.

The gas lighting also gave the bar a distinctive yellow glow which provided Bobby and Sean with an instant sense of warmth as they walked through the door.

The Crown had a central floor space that was surrounded, on three sides, by a series of enclosed wooden booths, or 'snugs', and on the fourth side by the bar itself. The central area was crowded with people standing, smoking, drinking and chatting, but Sean spotted Tone waving to him through the open door of one of the snugs. Sean and Bobby pushed their way through the crowd and stepped into the snug.

"How did you manage this?" Bobby asked. When the Crown was busy it could often be difficult to acquire one of the snugs which, apart from some stools at the bar, contained the Crown's only seating.

"We arrived just as some people were leaving," said Tone. "Bit of luck really. Where's Joker?"

"He had to go and pick up a bottle of vodka, he shouldn't be long," Sean said. He gestured to the two almost-empty glasses on the table. "Ready for another one?"

"Yeah, cheers," said Tone, and Sean set off for the bar.

"I thought Joker would have been here by now," Bobby said as he sat down. "He left us a while ago, we were talking to –"

"There's an off-licence just outside," Jamesy pointed out. "Why didn't he just go there?"

"This is Joker we're talking about. He probably knew somewhere cheaper."

"So, Bobby," said Tone, stretching his arms out to the side, "you and Sean will be normal, civilised human beings this time next year, and not the work-shy, scrounging bastards you are at the minute."

"That's one way of putting it," Bobby said. "You know we've both got placements in the same firm, don't you?"

"I thought Sean was planning to go abroad?"

"The Far East, yeah. It's still with the same firm, though. They've got places all over the world."

"You and Sean building skyscrapers, eh? Imagine that."

Sean came back with a tray of drinks, which he placed on the table. "Did I just hear my name being mentioned?"

"Tone was just pointing out that we won't be lazy bastard students anymore, next year." Bobby told him.

Sean rolled his eyes. "I don't know why you keep having a go at students," he said. "Although, I can't remember you ever giving Jamesy any jip."

"Oh, you know I'm only messing you about," Tone said. He accepted a cigarette from Bobby and put a light to it. "Actually," he went on, "I'm considering a return to the academic world myself."

"You?" said Sean, surprised. "Back at university? To do what?"

"Not sure yet," Tone replied. "English? Drama? I don't know. Like I said, I'm still considering it."

"It's about time," said Jamesy.

"What's brought this on?" asked Bobby. "Bit out of the blue, isn't it?"

"Just something that somebody said, that's all," said Tone. "So, yeah, I'm looking into becoming a mature student."

"At Queen's?" Jamesy asked.

"Probably," said Tone, as he stifled a yawn. A few flakes of ash fell from his cigarette.

"Feeling the pace there, Tone?" asked Sean, amused.

Tone nodded. "Getting old, you see."

"Yeah," Sean agreed. "Tell me about it."

After a while, Tone noticed that everyone's drinks were getting low. He pushed open the door of the snug and peered into the main bar.

"Where the hell is Joker?" he wondered aloud. "It's his round, isn't it?"

"Fuck knows whose round it is," said Sean, "but, yeah, that's a point, he should be here by now."

"It does seem a bit weird," Bobby agreed. "It's not like Joker to be late for a drink."

"The same with Snatter and Ding-a-Ling," Jamesy said. "There's still no sign of *them*, is there?"

"Maybe somebody's bumping us off one by one," Sean suggested. "And who's going to be next, eh? Maybe we should make sure we stay together."

"Is this some elaborate ploy, Sean, to get someone to go into the bogs with you and hold your willy?" Tone asked.

"Do you think we should ring somebody again?" Jamesy said "See if we can find out what's going on?"

"I think I'm too drunk to care," said Bobby. "Does that make me a bad person?"

"Yes, Bobby, it does," Tone told him. "But to get back to more important matters, what are we going to do about the whole drink situation? It's nearly time for another round, so do we hold on for Joker, or just say *fuck him*?"

"*Fuck him* sounds good to me," said Sean. "It's what he would have wanted."

"Okay then," Tone decided. "I'll get a round in." He picked up the tray, stood up, and stepped out of the snug.

"I'll come with you," said Sean.

They stood side-by-side at the bar and waited for one of the bar staff to become available. Tone got the impression that Sean had accompanied him to the bar for a reason, but sensed he was being hesitant.

"Something on your mind, Sean?" he asked.

"Oh, I don't know," said Sean. "It may be nothing."

"Is it about Snatter?"

"How did you know?"

"You've been acting cagey all day," Tone told him, "whenever Snatter's engagement came up."

"Well, I don't like to gossip, but some things need to be said."

"Okay then, spill it."

"Well," Sean began, "it was back in the summer, at the Ardoyne Fleadh. This was before Rosie appeared on the scene. I'd arranged to meet up with Snatter in the GAA one night when there was a band on that I wanted to see. Well, Snatter had been on the sauce all day, so he was rightly by the time I got there. He kept calling me Tommy Gun, for Christ's sake! Anyway, we're sitting there in the GAA, with Snatter rambling away, when all of a sudden, he blurts out that he thinks he might be gay."

"Really? Jesus!"

"And you know what sort of men think they might be gay, don't you?" asked Sean.

"What sort of men?"

"Gay men."

"You an expert, are you?"

"Oh, come on, Tone! Have you ever thought you might be gay?"

"Yeah," Tone replied. "I once thought about becoming gay, but then I thought *Why bother my arse*?"

"Oh, that's very funny, Tone," said Sean. "Quality material, mate. Really hilarious, but don't you think this is serious? This a mate we're talking about."

"Yeah, you're right. Has Snatter mentioned it since then?"

"No," Sean said. "I don't think he even remembers saying it. I ended up carrying him home that night. He barely even remembers being in the GAA. And I've never mentioned it because, well, it's his business, isn't it? If he wanted to bring it up, then okay, but I wasn't going to force it. But then, bloody Rosie shows up out of nowhere."

Tone managed, at last, to catch the attention of a barman, and he placed his order. When the barman had gone off to pour the drinks, Tone turned back to Sean.

"So what the hell is Snatter doing getting engaged?" he asked. "Unless …" Tone raised an eyebrow at Sean, but Sean remained tight-lipped.

"Are you trying to say," Tone said, piecing things together, "that Snatter has got some girl pregnant, and has decided he has to marry her? Even though he's gay? That's a bit of a fuck-up, isn't it?"

The barman returned with four drinks, and Tone paid for them. He was about to pick up two of the glasses, when Sean stopped him.

"There might be something else," he said.

"Jesus!" said Tone. "Now what?"

"It may be nothing, but do you remember Weasel, from school?"

"Of course, how could I forget?"

"Well, I bumped into him in town, a few weeks back, and we got talking. He was telling me about this party he was at, down the Markets."

"Charlie's party?"

"Yeah, you weren't at it, were you?"

"No, I was meant to go, but I was in Dublin that night."

"Yeah, well, Weasel was at this party …" Sean related Weasel's story as he and Tone carried the drinks back to the snug. When they reached it, they could hear Jamesy inside, trying to assure Bobby that he wasn't a bad person. Tone and Sean paused before opening the door to the snug.

"But you can't be sure?" said Tone.

"Well, no, but I put two and two together."

"It's not like you to be jumping to conclusions, Sean."

"No, it's not, but it's like I said. I know Rosie from way back."

THIRTY ONE

Harry did not consider himself to be a violent man. It was true that he was prone to what some people might describe as violent outbursts due his short temper, but Harry saw himself, essentially, as a peaceful soul.

It didn't take a lot to keep him happy, really. All he asked for was a couple of evenings a week, when he could enjoy a few drinks with his mates, round the Ardoyne Working Men's Club, known as the League.

That's where he should be now, he had been thinking. Not traipsing around town on some wild-goose chase.

What the hell did Seamus Green's whereabouts have to do with *him*? Bugger all, that's what. Harry's mood had been growing darker as he had been walking around, thinking about the injustice of it all. Now, at least, it looked like he had found the pub-crawl. Or a bit of it, anyway.

Joseph Anderson, in Harry's opinion, was a decent enough bloke. They didn't know each other very well, just on nodding terms really, but Harry thought that Joseph was okay.

More importantly, Joseph was a friend of Karen's brother which, in Harry's view of things, made him part of the family, and Harry was unimpressed by anyone who tried to interfere with his family.

Now, just who was this asshole?

Clint Eastwood. That was the picture of himself that Sticky Mickey had in mind as he posed in the middle of the alley.

With the pistol held loosely in a hand that rested, ever so coolly, on his right hip, Sticky Mickey was Clint Eastwood facing down a Tiger tank at the end of *Kelly's Heroes*. He was feeling arrogant. He had two men behind him, who were pinning Anderson to the wall, Jippo was to his left, and he had another man on his right, while back down the alley, behind the gorilla, was a fifth man.

Besides, he reminded himself, he was armed. He took a casual step forward.

"I don't know who the fuck you are, mate, but this is none of your business. So, do yourself a big fucking favour and –"

Harry, who was a man of few words, reached out and clamped his right hand over the front of Sticky Mickey's head, and, as he picked him up by his face, he threw a straight left in the direction of the hood to Sticky Mickey's right. The hood walked into Harry's fist, and as he made his way to the ground, he realised his cheekbone had been fractured, and determined, therefore, that, on reaching the ground, he would close his eyes and take no further part in proceedings.

Sticky Mickey had dropped his gun as both his hands flew instinctively to his face. His delicate fingers clawed uselessly at the huge hand that held his entire face in its grip, and his legs flailed wildly below him, occasionally connecting with Harry's thighs.

Harry, though, appeared not to notice. Using Sticky Mickey as a club, Harry thrust him at the oncoming Jippo. Jippo's nose connected with the back of Sticky Mickey's head with a sickening crunch, and Jippo went down, his vision exploding in white, searing pain.

Harry, fully aware of the threat from behind, spun around, still holding a gyrating Sticky Mickey at arm's length, and realised he had timed it perfectly. The piece of broken banister came down hard on the back of Sticky Mickey's head and Harry felt him go limp. He dropped him and snatched the banister from the hood, who stared in horror at what he had just done.

In the meantime, the two hoods holding Joker had been agonising over whether they should risk releasing their captive to join in the fight or wait to see how things turned out. It was soon obvious, though, that things were not turning out well at all. They both let go of Joker and went after Harry. As the hood to Joker's left ran behind him, Joker turned, managed to grab a handful of hair and, with a tug, he jerked the hood's head backwards.

With the hood's throat now exposed, Joker chopped his left hand down onto his bulging Adam's apple, and, at the same time, let go of his hair. The hood pitched forward, choking and retching, to land on all-fours in front of Joker. Joker happily accepted the invitation, and sent the toe of his DM boot sailing into the hood's unsuspecting genitalia. The hood seemed to freeze for a second, then, with a sad little whimper, he collapsed onto his side.

While this was going on, Harry stabbed one end of the broken banister into the face of its former owner and, in the same moment, spun the makeshift weapon around to catch Joker's other captor on the side of his face. The first hood rocked backwards with a mouth full of blood and broken teeth, while the second went spinning into the wall as blood poured from a split in his cheek.

It had all taken less than ten seconds.

"All right there, Joseph?" said Harry, who was not easily flustered. "Have you seen our Gary and Seamus Green?"

"What?" cried Joker, a little flustered. "I mean, fuck, what? Fuck me, Harry!"

"What?"

Joker gestured to the carnage in the alley. Harry looked around him and shrugged.

"Who were they?" he asked.

"Have you heard of Sticky Mickey?" said Joker as he picked up his carrier bag. He was surprised and delighted to discover his vodka was still intact. He looked around for the gun, but couldn't see it.

Fuck it! he thought. "Come on Harry, let's get the fuck out of here."

"Sticky Mickey?" Harry asked as they walked to the end of the alley.

"Yeah, he's some top hood," Joker explained. "They reckon even the paramilitaries can't touch him."

Harry's silence reflected his lack of interest in the matter, so Joker went back to Harry's earlier question.

"Um, Seamus and Gary?" he began, "To be honest, there's been no sign of them all day. We heard you had a wee bit of trouble with the cops earlier."

"Yeah, but as far as I know, Gary and Seamus got the bus into town hours ago."

"Then I don't know, Harry," said Joker. "If they were in town then I'm sure they would have found us. I mean, your wife managed it."

"You saw Karen?"

"Yeah, her and Snatt … Seamus' girl nabbed us round in White's, so they know that Gary and Seamus aren't with us. Look, Harry, I'm heading to the Crown, have you time for a quick one?"

Harry looked tempted, but he declined.

"Nah, I'd better find the women and get them home," he said. "No point hanging around town, is there?"

"Okay. Here, look, thanks for helping me out there, Harry." Joker grabbed Harry's hand and shook it. "Seriously, I thought I was fucked there for a minute."

"No problem, I'll see you later," said Harry as he strode off into the night.

"Yeah, Harry, see you." Joker mopped the blood from his nose and forehead, and set off for the Crown.

THIRTY TWO

Ding-a-Ling and Snatter had arrived in the city centre and were now making their way to a taxi firm they knew to be reliable. Snatter's limp was less pronounced than before and the wind had dropped, making the temperature feel less bitter. Snowflakes still drifted in the air, and Snatter, hopeful that his day was finally back on track, felt cheered by the sight.

Ding-a-Ling had been quiet during the taxi ride into town and remained silent for the short walk to the taxi firm's base.

From the outside, the taxi firm was uninviting. At some point in the building's existence, it had been a prosperous shop, but sheets of plywood now covered the windows and a hand-painted sign was placed above the narrow door proclaiming the taxi company's name and phone number.

The taxi firm was widely known to be one which catered mostly to the nationalist community and, as such, was vulnerable to sectarian attacks from the paramilitaries on the loyalist side of Northern Ireland's divide. For this reason, precautions had been taken.

Inside was stark and imposing, with only a few plastic chairs to break up the, otherwise empty, expanse of bare concrete floor. The walls, lovingly painted in the distant past, now provided an abstract display of faded, peeling colours and broken plaster, adding to the overall sense of dereliction.

High up on the wall that directly faced the entrance was a small rectangle of scratched and misted Perspex, behind which – and unseen from the room below – sat the taxi controller.

"Where to?" asked a disembodied female voice as Snatter and Ding-a-Ling entered.

"Could we have two taxis please, love?" Ding-a-Ling called up to the window. Snatter shot him a confused glance.

"What the –?"

"One going to the Botanic Inn and one going to Ardoyne."

"They'll be about twenty minutes."

"Aye, that's dead on."

"What the fuck's going on?" Snatter demanded.

"Sit down over here," said Ding-a-Ling, gesturing to the plastic chairs that lined the walls. "There's something you need to hear."

They sat down beside each other, and Ding-a-Ling leaned forward, rocking slightly, as he tried to think of a way to proceed.

"I don't know how you're going to take this," he began, "but there was a party in the Markets a while back, and I was –"

"Charlie's party?"

"Yeah."

"Yeah, I remember that. I was meant to go but I had a dose of the Gary Glitters that night, and I thought that –"

"Jesus, okay, Snatter, thanks for filling in the details, but I'm trying to fucking tell you something here."

"Okay, okay. Charlie's party. What about it?"

THIRTY THREE

It was actually a double house-party. Charlie lived next door to his cousin, in the small nationalist housing estate, known as the Markets, that lay in a loop of the river Lagan, south-east of Belfast city centre. They had opened up both houses for the party, including the two large back gardens, which were linked by a gate in the middle of a wooden fence.

Most of the neighbours in the cul-de-sac were also invited so, as they moved between the party and their own homes, the boundaries of the party became indistinct, giving the overall feel of a street party.

Joker, standing in Charlie's kitchen, had decided that at some point he was going to have to punch the dickhead who had been talking to him, non-stop, for the last fifteen minutes. Ding-a-Ling, he reckoned, also deserved a slap for introducing him to the little prick.

"Joker, my old mate!" Ding-a-Ling had called eagerly when Joker had strolled into the kitchen. "Come over here and meet somebody."

Joker, beer in hand, and content in the embrace of a great party, ambled, unsuspecting, over to where Ding-a-Ling stood alongside an unassuming, but cheerful young man.

"Joker, this is Weas ... er, Johnny," said Ding-a-ling. "We were at school together."

"Johnny Gee, actually," Johnny Gee corrected.

"All right there, mate?" said Joker, shaking hands. He failed to notice Ding-a-Ling quietly slip away to the other side of the room, where he engaged in conversation with a couple that he knew.

"Here, Joker, you'll love this," said Johnny Gee. "Why did the pervert cross the road?"

"What?" said Joker dumbly. He glanced across the room to see Ding-a-Ling's innocently smiling face.

"He couldn't get his dick out of the chicken!" Johnny Gee threw back his head and laughed the laugh that had been making Joker's skin crawl for nearly a quarter of an hour.

"What do you call a rabbit with a bendy dick?" Johnny Gee continued his relentless onslaught as Joker stared into the bleak chasm of despair that was now his life.

"Fucks Funny!" Johnny Gee roared.

Right! thought Joker decisively. *Fuck this!*

"Hey!" he shouted as he pointed through the open door that led into the garden. "That's the woman that stole my hat!"

Joker then set off in pursuit of his imaginary hat, pausing only to grab a can of beer from the fridge as he passed. Ding-a-Ling watched Joker's audacious escape with admiration, but then he dropped to the floor in a panic as he realised that Johnny Gee's head was swivelling round in his direction.

As the couple he had been chatting to looked all around in consternation, Ding-a-Ling crawled through the crowd towards the door to the hall.

Shit! he thought as he realised he was moving away from the fridge and, again, he had to admire the thoroughness of Joker's plan. Once he reached the hall, he got to his feet and made for the front door. He planned to go to the house next door where, he assumed, Joker would be and, besides, he needed to find another fridge.

As Joker passed through the gate into next door's garden, he heard a slap, and turned to see a girl, holding a hand to her face, rush past him in tears. She was running from a small group of men who were standing and drinking beside a plastic patio table. One of the men was shaking his hand up and down and laughing, though his friends seemed shocked.

Joker had no illusions about the use of violence. Everyone, he believed, had the capacity for violence to some degree, but he had always felt that the application of violence should have some inherent challenge to it. In other words: punch up, not down.

This, of course, made no sense. It would be a lot more logical, he was aware, to direct your violence towards someone who was unable to reciprocate, rather than to launch yourself into a situation where the chances of having your reproductive organs kicked clean through the top of your head were high, but Joker's opinions on the matter were firm.

He had no time for words like honour or chivalry, but he sensed, on some visceral level, that directing violence towards a weaker opponent was somehow wrong, and so he gave instructions to his contrary brain to come up with a plan of recompense.

The kitchen was crowded, so Ding-a-Ling had to squeeze his way through to the fridge. He took a four-pack of beer and headed out to the garden for some air. Once he had had enough air, he lit a cigarette. There was no sign of Joker.

It was unusually mild, for an autumn evening, and the garden had a few groups of revellers milling around. Ding-a-Ling stood in a tiled patio area that was shielded from the rest of the garden by a tall trellis. He placed his three spare cans of beer on the ground and leant against the back wall of the house, smoking and sipping his beer. Along the wall from him, at head height, was a yellow glow from a small, frosted window. Ding-a-Ling's eye was drawn to it when it went suddenly dark.

A few seconds later, the window opened, and Ding-a-Ling was amused to see Joker's head appear. Joker wriggled and squeezed through the tiny gap until, finally, he fell through onto his hands, and landed with a forward roll onto the patio.

"Yeah, I get sick of those fucking doors too," said Ding-a-Ling. Joker stared at him, then turned ostentatiously away.

"I'm busy," he told Ding-a-Ling as he walked off. "I don't have time for your nonsense."

"Did you get your hat?"

"Fuck off!"

Ding-a-Ling picked his beer up from the ground and hurried after Joker.

"So, what is it you're doing, then?" he asked.

Joker stopped and turned around. He jabbed a finger into Ding-a-Ling's chest.

"Not that it's any of your business," he said, "but I happen to be serving a bit of justice to a complete cunt."

Ding-a-Ling wasn't sure what he had been expecting, but he didn't think it was that. Joker turned and strode off, leaving Ding-a-Ling to catch up.

"Well, can I watch?" Ding-a-Ling asked.

"It's a free country."

"That's a matter of opinion," said Ding-a-Ling politically.

Joker walked around the trellis, then hurried over to the group by the patio table. He tapped the shoulder of the man that Joker's brain had decided to christen *Slappy Boy*, and gasped excitedly.

"Here, mate," he said, "you couldn't give us a hand here, could you?"

"What?" said Slappy Boy.

"You're just about the right size," Joker told him.

"What?"

"Perfect fit, I'd say!"

"What?" Slappy Boy was turning out to be a fairly limited conversationalist, but he was clearly intimidated by Joker's size and physique, so he was trying to be accommodating.

"I think some poor bastard's got locked in the bogs," Joker explained. "There's no answer, and the door's locked. Somebody's probably passed out, or had a heart attack or something."

"What?"

"Good man!" Joker enthused as he led Slappy Boy to the back of the house. "You're a fucking legend, so you are!"

Joker pointed to the little window as Ding-a-Ling looked on, intrigued.

"You could squeeze through there, couldn't you?" Joker asked.

"Well, I –"

"Fucking legend, you are! Come on, I'll give you a hand." Joker leant his back against the wall, bent his knees and let his hands form a cradle in front of him. Slappy Boy seemed perplexed, but Joker's manic grin persuaded him that the best course of action would be to stay on the good side of the large skinhead, so he put his foot in Joker's hands, and heaved himself up. He was halfway through the window, when he paused.

"Hold on," he said, "I can't really see anything."

"What was that?" asked Joker. "You need a shove?" He thrust his hands up and, with a muffled yelp, Slappy Boy disappeared into the darkness beyond. There was a tremendous crash as he collided with the collection of shampoo bottles and other toiletries that Joker had carefully positioned earlier. Joker dusted his hands and turned to Ding-a-Ling.

"My work here is done," he said.

"And fine work it was too," Ding-a-Ling assured him as he handed him a beer. They strolled into the garden.

"Where's your wee mate?" Joker asked.

"Yeah, sorry about that," said Ding-a-Ling laughing. "We used to call him Weasel at school, although he seems to prefer, what was it? Johnny Gee? Fuck knows why, though. His name's Kevin."

Joker laughed. "Yeah, that sounds about right."

"Carol not here yet?"

"Haven't seen her," said Joker. They were standing close to the end of the garden, in front of a large hedge. A sudden noise made them both turn in time to see a young couple emerge from the other side of the hedge. They spotted Joker and Ding-a-Ling and burst into raucous, drunken laughter. They staggered on past, into the garden, heading towards the house.

Curious, Ding-a-Ling and Joker peered through the hedge.

"Fucking hell!" cried Joker. "You wouldn't know that was there, would you?"

Behind the hedge, almost hidden from the house, was a large garden shed. On closer inspection, it looked more like an outside room than a shed, with an old sofa along the far wall, a little table, and some rugs and cushions scattered around.

"Very cosy," said Ding-a-Ling.

"Maybe me and Carol could sneak in here later on," said Joker.

"Oh, please let me be there when you ask her," Ding-a-Ling laughed. "Fancy a shag in a shed, love?"

"I like to think I'm a wee bit more subtle than that."

"Oh, you are, Joker, you are." They were both laughing as they drifted back towards the house. It was nearly time for another visit to the fridge.

The kitchen was almost empty when they entered. A couple of girls were standing at the worktop, filling some glasses with vodka, while a young man was asleep under the kitchen table. Joker and Ding-a-Ling went to the fridge, and Joker pulled open the door. One of the girls turned round on hearing the door open and gave a sudden gasp. Ding-a-Ling glanced at her and froze.

"Rosie?" he exclaimed. "What are you doing here?"

Rosie quickly regained her composure and regarded Ding-a-Ling with almost haughty disdain. Joker grabbed two cans of beer and straightened up. He took out a packet of cigarettes and handed one to Ding-a-Ling. As he gave Ding-a-Ling a light, he looked at him quizzically.

"Oh, Joker, this is Rosie," Ding-a-Ling explained. "Snatter's girlfriend."

"All right there, love?" said Joker. "Is Snatter with you, then?"

Rosie rolled her eyes and tutted.

"Still using those stupid nicknames, Gary? You're not bloody kids anymore, you know!" She turned to Joker. "His name's Seamus," she told him. "And, no, he isn't here. He wasn't feeling too well."

"Who are you here with, then?" Ding-a-Ling asked.

The girl beside Rosie turned around. "This is Sheila," said Rosie. "We knew each other back in Derry."

"Aye," said Sheila, "living in the Short Strand these days, though." She looked at Joker. "Fuck, you're a big one, aren't you?"

"You don't know the half of it, love," said Joker, giving her his best leer. Sheila laughed.

"Fucking typical, isn't it, Rosie, love?" she said. "Here we are at a party with two good-looking fellas, and we're both fucking spoken for."

Rosie was about to reply, when a group of men came into the kitchen and made for the fridge. An elegant woman came in behind them, and suddenly the kitchen began to fill up.

"All right there, Gary?" One of the men recognised Ding-a-Ling.

"Oh, hiya, Joe. How's it going? Ding-a-Ling replied. "Still at the *Irish News*?"

"Yeah, still working away. What about you, though? I heard you got your balls cut off."

"What?" Ding-a-Ling was stunned. "Where the fuck did you hear that? No, I'm sure I would have noticed something like that."

"Oh, right, okay," said Joe. "You still at that place in Royal Avenue?"

"Nah, that didn't work out," Ding-a-Ling told him. "Just bumming about on the dole at the minute."

"Well, I'm sure something will turn up. Anyway, I'll see you about, okay?" Joe and his mates, having stocked up on drinks, drifted off to the garden. Ding-a-Ling couldn't help noticing that Rosie and Sheila had also gone. Joker was talking to the elegant woman.

"Hiya, Carol," Ding-a-Ling said. "Feeling any better?"

"Yeah, not too bad, thanks, Gary," said Carol. "I'm just explaining something to Joseph."

"Yeah, wait till you hear this," said Joker in disbelief. "She says she doesn't want to spend the evening standing in a stranger's kitchen, watching me drink beer."

"Oh, I'm sure she's only messing with you," said Ding-a-Ling. "I mean, who wouldn't want to do that?"

Carol laughed. "I'm going to have a couple of drinks here," she said, "but then I'm going to have to drag him away, if that's okay."

"Aye, go on, Carol, love," Ding-a-Ling told her. "He's only holding me back, cramping my style, you know?"

"Style?" Joker cried. "Is that what you call it?"

"What do you want to drink, Carol?" Ding-a-Ling asked as he stepped over to the worktop which was piled with all kinds of bottles. "I'll be barman."

"Bacardi and white, please, Gary."

Ding-a-Ling poured Carol's drink, and the three of them strolled out to the back garden where a makeshift dancefloor had been marked out. They chatted happily as they stood watching some partygoers flailing around to *Wings of a Dove*, by Madness.

Rosie watched from the house. She was alone by the window in the dining room, Sheila having gone upstairs with her boyfriend.

"Are you sure, Rosie love? You'll be okay on your own? I can tell Jim to fuck off, if you want. It'll probably do him good to wait for a bit, anyway. The horny bastard."

Rosie laughed. "No, go on, really. I'm all right, you go ahead."

As she stood, sipping her drink, Rosie was feeling on an upward curve of alcohol's little rollercoaster. She felt relaxed and at ease as she watched Gary and his friends laughing together. She guessed that the tall skinhead was Gary's flatmate, Joseph, and the woman appeared to be Joseph's girlfriend.

Even from this distance, she could tell that the woman was absurdly glamorous, making Rosie feel dowdy by comparison. When the woman turned to Gary to say something into his ear, she touched his arm and Rosie was shocked by her own reaction. She took a gulp from her drink, and wished she had a cigarette. She had been trying to quit, on and off, for a while now, though she secretly believed it was impossible.

Oh, to hell with it! she thought. *I need a smoke*. And she went off to scrounge a cigarette.

"Don't you stay out too late," Joker was telling Ding-a-Ling. "And don't drink too much. And stay away from strange women. You know, like funny-shaped ones."

"Carol, for Christ's sake, will you take this eejit away with you?"

"I'm trying to, Gary," Carol said, as she pulled on Joker's arm. "Come on, you bloody lump."

"And don't do anything that I'd be willing to have a bash at. You'd only hurt yourself."

Eventually, Joker was bundled into the back of a taxi, and he and Carol left. Ding-a-Ling shook his beer can and decided that a trip to the fridge was in order.

The kitchen, he was surprised to see, was empty. Even the sleeper, under the table, was gone. The party, he figured, had now spread all over the cul-de-sac, so he had the fridge to himself. He took out a beer and opened it as Rosie walked in. She gave him no more than a glance as she went to refill her glass.

"You settling back okay, Rosie?" Ding-a-Ling asked. "In Ardoyne, I mean."

Rosie turned to face him. She stood by the worktop on the opposite side of the kitchen.

"Karen tells me you're scrounging off the dole," she said, a strange bitterness in her voice.

"Yeah," he replied. "Hopefully not for long, though."

"Seamus is doing very well for himself," she told him.

"Yeah, I'd heard."

"He might even look for more shops to run."

"Good for him."

The kitchen fell silent, making Ding-a-Ling feel slightly uncomfortable. Rosie stared at the floor. She seemed to be almost simmering.

"How was Derry?" Ding-a-Ling asked, to break the silence more than anything. "I heard you didn't have an easy time of it."

"It was all right," Rosie said with a shrug. "At least in Derry we didn't have everybody laughing at us because our da was in fucking Purdysburn!"

Ding-a-Ling felt hurt by her sudden anger. He looked down at his can of beer.

"Not everybody was laughing, Rosie," he said quietly.

Rosie felt chastened and shook her head.

"No, not everybody," she admitted. "*You* never did. You and Seamus and Sean, you three never laughed." She gave him a quick look. "You always stuck up for me and Ellie, and Jack."

Feeling embarrassed, Ding-a-Ling took a drink of beer. When he looked back to Rosie, she gave him a broad smile. It came from nowhere and it knocked him sideways.

"You were my *Three Musketeers*," she said, and then blushed.

"Um, what?" he stammered.

"Nothing, nothing," she insisted, suddenly flustered. "Just kid's stuff, that's all."

"No, really, go on."

"Well, do you remember the old cartoon?"

"Cartoon?" Ding-a-Ling thought for a moment. "Oh, was that the one in *The Banana Splits*?"

Rosie laughed as she nodded.

"God, I remember it now," Ding-a-Ling went on. "Wasn't there a really annoying kid in it, with a stupid wooden sword? I can remember hoping, every week, that the wee bastard would get killed. Never was, though. Funnily enough."

"That's right," said Rosie. "It was my favourite show when I was a kid. I used to fancy D'Artagnan."

"Well, who wouldn't?" cried Ding-a-Ling. "He was bloody gorgeous!"

Their laughter rang around the kitchen, mingling with the memories of childhood that fizzed and popped in the air between them before drifting into a companionable silence.

A silence that Ding-a-Ling shattered.

"I was gutted when you left, you know."

Rosie's head snapped back as if she'd been slapped. *Fuck him!* she thought furiously. *Fuck him! Why did he have to –*' And suddenly she was kissing him.

What the hell are you doing, you stupid bitch? her mind was screaming, but the screams were muffled by alcohol and, besides, her heart wasn't listening.

All that Rosie's battered heart knew was that she was in the arms of the one she had never forgotten. The shoulder she had cried on and the reason she had cried herself to sleep. Her defender and protector. Her childhood crush. Her musketeer.

Her D'Artagnan.

One good-looking couple, thought Johnny Gee from the hall as he watched Ding-a-Ling and Rosie slip through the back door into the garden. He raised a cigarette packet to his mouth and, using his teeth, pulled out a cigarette. Then, using one hand, he took a match from its box, placed it in the crook of his forefinger and flicked his thumbnail across the matchhead which flared into life. It also flew off the match and landed on the carpet, where it started a happy little fire.

"Shit!" Johnny Gee cried as he stomped it out.

He took out another match and tried again. He made sure the match was sitting lower in his finger to prevent the head from becoming detached, but this also meant that he managed to burn a neat little hole in his flesh.

"Shit!" he cried again as he ran to the sink. After he had run some cold water over the burn, he dried his hands and took out a third match. This time he struck it against the side of the box and lit his cigarette.

He languidly stroked the match through the air to extinguish the flame and, sauntering to the back door, he flicked the dead match to spiral a trail of smoke out into the darkness.

Cool as fuck, Johnny Gee, he assured himself. *Cool as fuck!*

THIRTY FOUR

"In a fucking shed?"

"That's hardly the point, is it?" said Gary softly.

Snatter wasn't sure how to react. A part of him had been shocked by his friend's betrayal. The rest of him, though, was jumping up and down and cheering.

"She was fucking furious afterwards," Gary continued. "I mean, she went mental. Told me to never mention it, or she'd never forgive me. Said she was ashamed of herself, can you believe that?"

Snatter let Ding-a-Ling's words sink in. "You're saying the kid's yours, then?" he asked.

"Come on, Snatter," said Gary. "I know what you're like. You put on a condom just to shake hands with a woman, for fuck's sake!"

And that's what had been bothering Snatter. His relationship with Rosie had not been overly physical, but on the few occasions when alcohol and loneliness had pushed them both over the edge, he had been careful to use protection. Caution was almost an obsession with Snatter.

He knew that no form of contraception was completely effective, but just how unlucky could he have been? Voicing these concerns, however, had proved impossible, caught up, as he was, in the storm of Rosie's raging moods. Had Ding-a-Ling really just solved his problem?

"Wait a minute," he said, "Rosie's not stupid. She must know the kid's yours, so why would she –"

"I've been thinking about that," said Gary. "Like you said, Rosie's not stupid, but I think she just panicked. Were you supposed to make the engagement official round at Ellie's today?"

"Yeah, I think so," Snatter replied. "To be honest, I never really paid that much attention. Rosie was running around, making all these mad plans, and I was just sucked along by it all."

"She must have known me and you were still in touch, though."

"I don't think she did," said Snatter. "I mean, I never really talked about you, what with you being an asshole and all."

Gary laughed. "Can you picture the look on her face when she found out you were going drinking with me all day?"

"So, what are you going to do?" Snatter asked, remembering the two taxis.

Gary stood up and stretched. He looked down at his oldest friend and smiled.

"I think me and Rosie McCann have got some things to discuss," he said.

"What about the pub-crawl?"

"Well, maybe some things are more important than the pub-crawl."

Snatter almost jumped to his feet to slap this imposter. This was a Ding-a-Ling he didn't recognise.

"What about Rosie's lies?" he asked. "She was being so fucking – what's the word – mercenary! Are you okay with that?"

Gary sighed. "She hasn't had it easy," he said as he sat back down beside Snatter. "Okay, okay, I know that doesn't make her unique, but you know how I felt about her. You know what state I was in when she left."

"Yeah, but that ..." said Snatter as he looked at Ding-a-Ling, "... that was a long time ago, wasn't it?"

"I know, but as soon as I saw her at Charlie's party, it didn't matter. It was like we were kids again. Jesus! Would you listen to me!" He leapt to his feet again, unable to sit still.

Snatter couldn't help but smile as his friend crackled with excited energy. This was a new Ding-a-Ling, he realised. A revitalised Ding-a-Ling. This was Ding-a-Ling running through Bedford Falls at the end of *It's a Wonderful Life*.

"Taxi for Ardoyne!"

"Right!" Gary cried happily. "That's me!" He grabbed Snatter's hand and shook it. "Merry Christmas, my old mucker! And wish all the lads a Merry Christmas from me as well."

He rushed out the door, but a few seconds later he popped his head back in, a look of concern on his face.

"Um," he said to Snatter. "We're okay, aren't we?"

Belfast was not, by any stretch of the imagination, Bedford Falls.

"Fuck off, asshole!" said Snatter.

Gary was still grinning as he got into the taxi.

A pretty woman was both laughing and crying, in a corny old black-and-white movie, on the television. Rosie switched it off. She hadn't been watching.

Karen had pleaded with her to come along with her and Harry, for the evening, to their house where they were having some friends round for drinks. But Rosie couldn't face any company.

She had got back to Ellie's, just as her sister was heading out to her night shift at the hospital and now she sat alone in the house as the lights blinked silently on the Christmas Tree in the bay window.

There were no sounds to help distract her fears as she sat numb and bewildered by the chaotic web of lies she had spun. The belligerent rage that had propelled her forwards through life was now peeling away, along with the years, to leave her sitting, lonely and lost and afraid.

A dishevelled little girl, in a pink nightdress, dragged from happy slumber into a new world of confusion and fear.

Wanting, needing, begging for someone just to come along and hold her.

The doorbell rang.

THIRTY FIVE

"What the hell happened to you?" Tone asked as Joker appeared.

"I had a run in with Sticky Mickey," Joker explained, "but I'm going to need a beer before I can say any more than that. Did you know it's snowing out there?"

"Snowing?" asked Sean. "Is it heavy?"

"Not really. Very festive, though. Really gets the old bells jingling."

"I'll get a round in," said Bobby, and got up to go to the bar.

Joker sat down and dabbed at his forehead. "Does it look bad?" he asked.

"Well, it doesn't look life-threatening, if that's what you mean," Tone said. "We'd just about given up on you. We were going to head on."

"Well, fuck you!" said Joker.

Tone looked at his watch when Bobby got back with a tray of drinks.

"It's knocking on a bit," he said. "We could do with drinking these up."

"What's the rush?" Joker protested. "I've just had a very traumatic experience, thank you very much, and I could with a bit of time to relax and savour this pint."

"Yes, and I'm sure you'll be boring us with all the details of your traumatic experience at some point but, seriously, we don't want to leave it too late to get to the Bot."

"Why not?" asked Joker. "Anyway, it's not that late, is it?"

"No, it's not that late," said Tone patiently, "but we need to go soon because, for one thing, we need to get something to eat."

"Oh, for fuck's sake! If you're hungry, then get a pint of Guinness," said Joker. "That's food, isn't it? Guinness is food."

"But I also happen to know," Tone continued, "that Janty isn't working a full shift tonight. He's going to be finishing shortly."

"Janty?" said Joker, puzzled. "The bouncer? What has that got to … oh." Joker happened to catch a glimpse of his reflection in one of the little painted mirrors that adorned the inside of the snug. With his shaven head, black eye, and cut forehead, he looked exactly like the sort of person who would not be welcome in a respectable nightclub.

"That's a bloody good point, Tone," he said. "Right, everybody, drink up!"

Despite Joker's protests, they called into a nearby fast-food restaurant and filled up on burgers and chips, setting themselves up for the night ahead.

"Maybe we should get a couple of taxis," Jamesy suggested when they stepped outside. It was only a fifteen-minute walk to the Botanic

Inn, but it was snowing, and they were all quite drunk, so he thought that taxis would be a sensible option.

"Yes, Jamesy," said Joker, "that's a great idea, but this is supposed to be a pub-*crawl*, remember. Not some bloody pub … sitting in a bloody taxi … bloody thing."

"That was beautifully put, Joker," said Sean, "but we're hardly going to be *crawling* up to the Bot, now are we?"

"You know, Sean? It's just that type of pedantic attitude that –"

"Will you all just shut the fuck up and start walking!" Tone was getting impatient. He wanted to get settled down in the final bar of the day, and to ease himself into the last few hours of Christmas Eve. He set off along the road with the lads grumbling in his wake.

Janty, luckily, was still on the door when they got to the Bot. He rolled his eyes at Joker, but nodded for him to go in.

"For fuck's sake, Joker! Just find a dark corner and stay there, okay?"

Once inside, they climbed the stairs to the disco, where they found a booth which would serve as their base for the rest of the night. Jamesy and Joker went off to the bar, while Tone, Sean and Bobby made themselves comfortable. Tone had a look around.

There was a decent amount of people in tonight, but they were all well-spaced around the room and the place did not feel overcrowded or claustrophobic. Even the volume of the music was at a bearable level and Tone felt it was just the right atmosphere in which to end the night.

He watched a group of girls, no more than teenagers, gyrate on the dancefloor. Their slim figures balanced elegantly on high, slender heels. Joker and Jamesy returned from the bar and everyone prepared themselves for the evening ahead. Cigarettes were passed around and glasses raised.

As Tone drank his beer, he was aware of different voices and conversations merging and tumbling around the booth. Bobby seemed to be addressing him directly, while Joker was rambling away to Jamesy. Sean was singing.

"*You'd better watch out, you'd better not cry …*"

"… lamped him so hard in the ging-gangs, that his eyeballs popped out. Swear to fuck! You can ask …"

"… *Santa Claus is coming to …*"

"… meet up with her some time. She …"

"… *sees you when you're sleeping. He knows …*"

"… there was no time to waste, because Harry was in trouble. Help me, Joker! Help me! he shouted, so …"

"… whenever you're both in Dublin together, you can …"

"… *be good, for goodness' sake!*"

"She works at the *Belfast Telegraph*," Bobby went on as Tone's attention began to focus entirely on just what Bobby was saying. "But she's on a course down there at the minute."

Tone turned and looked Bobby in the eye. "What?" he asked flatly.

"My girlfriend," Bobby said. "I was just saying you could meet up with her some time in Dublin."

Tone felt as if he were rising from the table, to go careering across the room and go crashing through the tottering, dead-eyed slappers on the dance floor.

"Claire, her name is. Claire Masterson."

Hitting the stairs and spiralling into the night, spinning amongst the drunks, and the dregs, and the fucked-in-the-head.

"I think I've got her number here somewhere. Her Dublin one, I mean."

Anonymous and alone, puking and raging at an empty sky. Spewing anger and bitterness into a city that overflowed with anger and bitterness.

"I reckon you'd get on really well."

Pouring bile over the streets and the silent fields. Over all the hatred and the mistrust, over the fear and the violence, and all the laughter and the love. Over all the living and all the fucking dead.

He stubbed his cigarette out in the ashtray.

"Oh, yeah," said Bobby, "I hear you're seeing some Dublin girl. How's that going?"

"Have you ever read any Joyce, Bobby?" asked Tone.

"What? What the fuck has that got to do with anything? No, of course I haven't. Why?"

"Oh, nothing. I've just always thought he was overrated, that's all. What were you saying?"

"Your girl in Dublin? How's it going?"

Tone gave a shrug. "Just wasn't meant to be, I suppose."

"Really? I'm sorry to hear it."

"Just one of those things," said Tone. "Still, that's not *your* problem, is it?"

"I know, but I thought … Hey! *Dickhead!* It's *your* fucking round!"

Snatter had arrived.

Jamesy stood up. "Sit yourself down, Snatter," he said. "You look like you need a seat. I'll get these." He set off for the bar as Snatter sat down.

"Where's Ding-a-Ling?" asked Joker.

"It's a long story," Snatter told him.

"Ah, fuck it, then."

"Your girlfriend was looking for you earlier," Tone said.

"Not my problem anymore," Snatter told him happily.

"False alarm?"

Snatter looked at Tone in surprise, then smiled. "Not for Ding-a-Ling," he said.

Jamesy appeared, put some drinks on the table, and went back for the rest.

"This calls for a toast," Sean suddenly exclaimed.

"What calls for a toast?" Bobby asked, and Sean looked confused.

"Okay, then," he said, "*I* call for a fucking toast!"

Jamesy returned from the bar and sat down. "A toast?" he asked. "What are we toasting?"

Sean raised his glass. "What about, *Ireland united, Gaelic and free*?"

"Well, I don't know about that," said Bobby. "Wouldn't the Unionists in the company find that offensive?"

"Fuck them!"

"How about," Tone said, looking at Snatter. "How about, *Freedom*?"

"Well, freedom from what, though?" Bobby persisted. "I mean, that's just –"

"Oh, give it a rest, Bobby!" said Joker laughing.

Freedom? thought Seamus as he lifted his first drink of the day.

"Yes," he said. "Yes, I'll drink to that!"

EPILOGUE

It was the type of morning that Jamesy would normally have relished.

A grey, cold, wet and miserable Sunday morning in mid-January, when he could stand at his window and regard the empty streets with satisfaction.

He could anticipate a long day of cosy solitude, as the wind shrieked and lashed the quivering little houses with freezing rain. He would put the kettle on to make tea, and feel comfortable enough to be magnanimous to every tiny raindrop.

Each one, a perfect little sigh of melancholy, come to make a monochrome world all blissful and sad.

But now, the little bastards were just making him wet.

As he stood and waited for the lights to change on the pedestrian crossing, a van sped past, splashing through a puddle and soaking his feet. Not for the first time that morning, he cursed Bobby and Tone.

Jamesy's mood was not helped by an encroaching hangover which, he felt sure, was down to all the whiskey that Seamus had forced upon him the night before. Jamesy was partial to a glass of whiskey every so often, but it had seemed to be an endless supply that Seamus was providing throughout the entire evening.

So, here he was, cold, wet and hungover, shuffling and sniffling through a rain-swept Sunday morning in Belfast, and feeling that he should have stayed in bed. He was beginning to think he was getting a cold as well, and that was something else he could blame Tone and Bobby for.

Still, he thought, it had been a good night.

It had been Gary's engagement party.

"So, you're an actual, real-life homo, then?" Joker was standing at the bar with Jamesy and Seamus. They were in the upstairs function room of a city centre bar that Rosie and Gary had booked and Seamus had insisted on paying for.

"It certainly looks that way," said Seamus. "Why, does it bother you?"

"Of course not!" said Joker, a little offended. "I'm just curious, that's all. I mean, do you know what you're supposed to do, for instance?"

Seamus raised an eyebrow. "What? You mean –?"

"Oh, fuck, no! I don't mean the actual … I mean … Like what's your next move, you know? Do you know any clubs or bars to go to?"

"I've got a couple of contacts," Seamus told him, "but I just have to work up the courage, that's all. Something to work on for the New Year, I suppose."

"Well, if you need any moral support," said Joker, "then just say the word."

"You, Joker?" asked Jamesy, amused. "In a gay bar?"

"Aye, no bother," Joker insisted. "Listen, Seamus, if I come with you, then you don't have to worry, okay? I'll make sure the gays don't give you any jip."

Jamesy and Seamus both smiled at Joker.

"Oh, you know what I mean!" he said.

Seamus could see Rosie approaching from behind Jamesy and, as she reached them, Joker tactfully nodded to Jamesy to back away a little, to give them some privacy.

"All right, Seamus?" Rosie said. "I haven't seen much of you lately."

"No," Seamus agreed. "It's been a hectic couple of weeks, hasn't it?"

She hesitated, and then gave him an awkward smile. "We're okay, aren't we?" she asked, concern in her voice.

Seamus pulled her to him in a hug. "Of course, we're okay!" he told her. "Look!" He gestured across the room to where Gary was entertaining a small group with a story that involved a lot of elaborate arm movements. He was in his element.

"I don't think I've ever seen him so happy," Seamus said. "So, how could we not be okay? And if there's anything you need, you just have to ask. You know that, don't you?"

Rosie nodded. Each one of Gary's friends had told her the same thing.

"So, how's Gary's job going?" Seamus asked her. "I haven't had a chance to talk to him about it."

"He loves it," she replied. "Him and Joseph are just like big kids with new toys to play with." Seamus laughed along with her.

"Hey, Jamesy, come over here a minute!" Tone and Bobby were seated at a table near the bar. Jamesy went over and joined them.

"What is it?" he asked.

"I was round at Bobby's flat during the week," said Tone, "and his wee cousin was there. I don't know if you know him."

"Nah," Bobby said, "you wouldn't know him, but he's doing an A-level in ancient history."

"Oh, okay," said Jamesy. "Smart lad, then?"

"Yeah, well," Tone explained, "he's doing some work on this Greek fella. What's he called, Bobby?"

"Um, Themistocles, I think."

"Aye, that's him. And some battle he was at."

"Salamis," Bobby added.

"Yeah, that's right," said Tone. "Well, anyway, Bobby's cousin reckons that this Themistocles character may have been a bit of a double agent at the time."

"What?" Jamesy was appalled. "That's bloody nonsense. I mean, it's true that in later life –"

"Yes, Jamesy, okay," Tone interrupted, "but this is me you're talking to, and I don't give a shit, remember? The thing is, though, this guy has actually heard of you, from some lectures, or something, that you gave somewhere, and me and Bobby said we could introduce you."

"Well, of course," said Jamesy. "Somebody needs to put him straight."

"Good man!" Tone exclaimed. "We're all meeting up in Maggie's, the coffee shop. You know it, don't you?"

"In Shaftesbury Square? Yeah, I know it."

"That's it. So, ten o'clock, tomorrow morning?"

"Tomorrow? Come on, Tone! Tomorrow's Sunday. It's a day of rest."

"I know, but I'm driving to Donegal on Monday morning," Tone told him. "Come on, Jamesy, I'll treat you to lunch afterwards. One of the hotels up round Queen's, we'll make a day of it."

"All right, I suppose," Jamesy grumbled.

"You okay there, Rosie?" Gary had finally got the chance to speak to his fiancée. She had been sitting at a table with Karen, but Karen had now gone to look for Harry, and Rosie was left on her own.

"Yeah," she said smiling. "I'm happy just sitting here."

"No worries, then?"

"Worries?" She looked around the room. Sean and Seamus were at the bar, laughing at Joker who was blowing bubbles into his beer with a straw. Tony and Bobby were shaking some enthusiasm into a glum looking Jamesy. "Why would I have any worries?" Rosie continued. "I have seven musketeers."

Gary moved closer to her, and they kissed.

Later on, Rosie found a quiet little corner of the room, where she could sit by herself and be alone with her thoughts. She smiled indulgently at Gary, laughing at the bar, surrounded by his friends as she placed a hand on the growing bulge of her stomach and gave it a gentle rub.

You okay in there? she asked her unborn child. *We all can't wait to meet you, you know. You're going to love your daddy, so you are, with all the silly things he does. And his friends are all going to spoil you rotten. So when you're ready to arrive, we'll all be here for you. And there's something you'll need to know*. Rosie said the next words aloud.

"Never lie and never steal, sweetheart."

I'll be telling you that when I see you. I'll be telling you that a lot.

Bloody Tone, and bloody Bobby! Jamesy was soaked as he approached the coffee shop. Just before he entered, he shook himself like a wet dog. He sniffed, and shivered, and pushed open the door.

He knew right away that he'd been set up.

There was no sign of Tone, nor of Bobby. Nor of Bobby's bloody cous... *Wait, Bobby's cousin?* Jamesy struggled to force the blurring jumble of thoughts in his head to coalesce into something he could understand, but nothing was clicking into place, as he stood, dripping onto the black and white tiles, feeling nauseous, and sniffing, and shivering, and swaying.

And caught in the full and blinding glare of a smile that could melt icebergs.

"So, tell me," said Hannah. "Why can't dolphins breathe underwater?"

RISE

PROLOGUE

The city slumbered in the pre-dawn, unaware of the cautious approach of spring. There was no fond anticipation for this renewal of old acquaintance. No sense of warm familiarity in spring's playful heart as the dark brute loomed through the mist. Just weary acceptance of the inevitable.

The feeling was mutual.

The brooding metropolis, mistrustful of giddy frivolity, much preferred to huddle beneath the murky mantle of winter than to frolic in the gauzy threads of spring.

The stabbing cold was a cleansing penance, and the city cherished the frost and the gloom and the rain. The drenching, piercing rain.

Proper rain.

Not the anaemic drizzle of an April shower, nor the oxymoronic monstrosity of a sun-shower, speckling the warm, dusty pavements with cheery black spots of paradox.

Proper rain.

Rain birthed by the gods of thunder and rage as they thrashed and flexed in the full-throated roar of a winter storm to punish and to pound, with fearsome deluge, the grim, granite-faced stoicism of the city below.

Belfast just didn't suit Springtime.

Also approaching the city in the misty dawn – and making much more of a fuss about it – was the overnight ferry from Liverpool.

With lights smearing the fog and propellers churning the water, it made a boisterous entry into Belfast Lough just as the eastern sky brightened enough to pull the veil from the timorous creep of spring.

In the ferry's tiny cafeteria, a woman in her late middle-age picked up a cup of tea from the counter and turned to look around her. She had friendly eyes, a long, pointed nose and greying hair that was pulled back into a bun. As she gazed around the small room for a place to sit, she regarded her fellow passengers with some dismay.

Most of the people gathered around the few tables in the cramped space were long-distance lorry drivers, who were eating noisily and communicating with each other using a complicated system of grunts, burps, farts and whistles. The woman was considering taking her tea out to the cold deck when she spotted a man sitting at a table on his own, idly stirring his tea and gazing through a porthole at the silent dawn.

He seems nice enough, she thought as she made for his table.

"Do you mind if I sit here?" she asked. The man looked up, startled.

"What?" he stammered. "Oh, I'm sorry, of course I don't mind.

Please sit down."

The woman took a seat and gave the man a warm smile. He smiled back, then looked down at his tea.

"Did you sleep all right?" she asked after taking a sip from her cup.

"I'm sorry?" he asked, startled again.

"On the crossing," she said. "I sometimes have trouble sleeping if the sea's a wee bit rough. Although, I have to say, it felt very smooth last night. I slept right through."

"Oh, right," the man said. "Um, yeah, it was okay, I think. To be honest, though, I don't sleep great at the best of times."

"Really? That's something I've never had a problem with. Except in the middle of a rough sea, of course." She gave another smile.

"Do you make this crossing a lot?" The man forced himself to make conversation, hoping to make the time pass more quickly. The ferry seemed to be taking forever to reach the dock and he was beginning to feel the blank, soulless fog close around him, clouding his mind and his shivering nerves.

"A couple of times a year, I suppose," the woman replied. "I go to see my daughter and her family. They live in Birmingham, you see. I've tried Larne-Stranraer before, but I just hate that long coach journey. I'd rather sleep on the ferry than the coach." The woman's chatter was incessant and the man was grateful for it, calmed by it. "Of course," she went on, "I keep telling Sally – Sally, that's my daughter – to come and visit me, but her husband says no. He's English, you see, so he thinks everybody in Belfast is a mad bomber. He thinks he's going to get shot or blown up or something if he comes over."

The man shuddered and turned away. He looked through the porthole at the patches of mist and felt suddenly terrified that his demons were crawling towards him through the fog. Instinctively he closed his eyes and placed the fingertips of his right hand on the inside of his left wrist. The feel of the steady pulse was reassuring and he let his breathing slow to the gentle rhythm until his consciousness was able to embrace the peace he had learned, the peace he had been shown, the peace of the universe pulsing in time to the beat of his own heart. He opened his eyes.

The woman was watching him thoughtfully, compassion and understanding in her eyes. She slipped a hand across the table to lightly touch his arm.

"Are you okay?" she asked.

"Um, yeah," he said shakily, "yeah, I'm fine."

"Sure?"

"Yeah, really, I'm okay," he said, smiling now. "I'm fine, thanks."

"Do you live in Belfast?" she asked, her voice soft and sympathetic. "Are you heading home?"

"I don't know," he replied, then laughed at her puzzled expression. "I'm sorry, it's just that I've been away a long time … I mean, I used to have a home here but whether I still do or not . . ." he shrugged. "I suppose that's where I'm going," he said. "I'm going to find out."

The woman nodded pensively as the ferry's engines changed pitch and the ship slowed and turned in the water. The lorry drivers all stood and stretched before they grunted, burped and farted their way to the vehicle deck. The woman grimaced and grinned and then made a quick decision. She reached into her handbag and pulled out a pen and a piece of paper.

"Look," she said, "I'm going to give you my phone number. If you need a hand with anything, or even if you just fancy a moan, then give me a shout."

She scribbled down her number and handed him the slip of paper. The man took it, genuinely touched by the gesture.

"Thank you," he said. "Thank you very much."

She stood and held out her hand. "I'm Stephanie," she said.

The man got up from the table to shake her hand.

"Martin," he said. "Martin McCann."

ONE

Several weeks earlier.

Joseph Anderson, known to his friends as Joker, was fantasising about punching the old woman in the back of the head.

He had been standing behind her in the queue for what felt like a million years, and now watched with exasperation as she slowly picked up her change and dropped it, one coin at a time, into her purse.

Of course, Joker knew, she was perfectly entitled to take all the time she needed – her slow, deliberate movements hinted at painful arthritis – and he was well aware that she did not deserve to be harried by an impatient wanker like himself. But still.

The old woman finally snapped her purse shut and placed it into her bag. She turned and gave Joker an apologetic smile.

"Sorry for holding you up there, son," she said.

"No trouble at all," Joker told her. "You just take your time."

She made her way to the door and Joker, with a sigh of relief, stepped forward and placed the card he had chosen on the counter. The young shop-assistant seemed nervous as the tall skinhead approached and glowered down at him.

"All right there, mate?" said Joker. "Just this card. Oh, and twenty Regal as well."

The nervous young man, no older than sixteen, picked up the card and entered the price into the till. He then turned and scanned the rows of cigarette packs behind him, making it obvious that he wasn't at all sure just what he was looking for. Joker rolled his eyes.

"There, mate," he said, pointing. "Just there."

The shop-assistant followed the invisible line from Joker's outstretched finger but, for some reason, seemed incapable of spotting the little blue and white pack, upon which the word *Regal* was emblazoned in gold. He put a tentative hand on a red pack and gave Joker a hopeful glance.

"No," Joker said, exasperated. "To your left. No, down a bit. Now go right, bit more, bit more."

The shop-assistant seemed to touch every single pack before finally alighting on Joker's preferred brand.

"Aye, there you go," Joker exclaimed. "You're really getting the hang of this, aren't you, mate?"

Joker paid for the card and the cigarettes and left the shop. As he walked across the car park he could see his father impatiently drumming his fingers on top of the car's steering wheel. Pulling open the rear door, Joker clambered onto the back seat.

"Took your bloody time, didn't you, Joseph?" Joker's father

grunted as he started the car.

"Oh, leave him alone, Davy," said Joker's mother, Katherine, who sat in the front passenger seat. "Don't be such a grump." Joker felt grateful for her maternal support.

"I mean," Katherine went on, "you know how buying a sympathy card can really take it out of you, don't you? Is that what it was, Joseph? Did you get worn out? Did you have to have a wee lie-down? A wee nap?"

Joker, too much of a dutiful son to rebuke his mother with profanity, remained silent as he pulled the cellophane wrapping from the card he had bought. Katherine held out her hand.

"Let's see it, Joseph," she said.

Joker passed it to her and Katherine ran her fingers over the embossed lilies and the silver, foil-blocked lettering.

"Aye, that's lovely," she said, holding it up for Davy to see. She then handed it back to Joker.

"Would you see if there's a pen there?" Joker asked his mother. "In the glove box."

Rummaging through the little compartment, Katherine found a pen and handed it to Joker. She then sat back in her seat and looked through the window at the unfamiliar surroundings passing by outside. They were only a few miles from their own home, but Katherine felt they might as well be on the other side of the world. The kerbstones here were painted a hostile green, white and orange instead of the reassuring red, white and blue of her own patch of Belfast. She saw the Irish tricolours and the yellow and white papal flags hanging limply from lampposts and from the upper windows of some of the terraced houses and she gave a shiver of trepidation.

The colours here were too garish, she thought, too bright and gaudy compared to the comforting warmth of the purples and blues and the reds and blacks of protestant Ulster. Stripped of all the colours, though, the little streets became recognisable, reminding Katherine of the streets in which she had grown up, the streets of her city and her home, and she felt a touch of sad regret.

"It's not that different from Sandy Row, is it?" she said.

"Aye, but you still have to be careful," Joker told her. "Remember, if you see any priests, then you have to keep really still. Their vision is based on movement."

"Joseph!" said Davy, suppressing a grin. "Stop trying to scare your mother."

Katherine sighed and turned round to face Joker.

"Have you written that card yet?" she asked.

"Yeah, here you go." Joker placed the card inside its envelope and gave it to his mother. He then sat back in his seat, content to spend the rest of the short journey up the Falls Road lost in his own thoughts.

He was aware of how much more pensive he had been just lately and felt that it was something that he needed to have a think about. He didn't see himself as someone who thought too much; someone who dithered and examined and analysed, someone trapped in the pointless exploration of his own mind, considering options, probing and poking at feelings and emotions that were best left undisturbed.

As far as Joker was concerned, he was a man of action. The image he held of himself was a dashing, gung-ho figure. Carefree, rakish and handsome. Decisive and unbound by the cloying grasp of overthinking. A free spirit. A swashbuckling cavalier, dynamic and debonair.

This was not the image, however, that formed in the minds of most people on first encountering Joker. Immediate impressions of the six-foot-four skinhead cast rather a different picture in the eyes of those who lacked a familiarity with Joker's nuanced personality.

The word 'oaf' has largely fallen from common usage, but if it were still to enjoy the popularity of its heyday, then it would likely feature prominently in the uninformed opinions of new acquaintances. There were many who, on first meeting Joker, would instantly judge his shaven head and intimidating muscularity as belonging to a knuckle-dragging moron who would only feel at home in the company of like-minded morons in an environment of unfocused anger and potential violence.

But this image would be wide of the mark.

"What does that say, Joseph?" asked Katherine. She was pointing at some graffiti daubed in white paint on a wall beside the main road.

Náisiún arís
Tiochfiadh ár lá

"I think it's meant to say," said Joker, "*A nation once again. Our day will come*, but, for one thing, it's spelt wrong."

"It's so different from English, isn't it?"

"Yeah," said Joker, "it is." At this point, Joker could have explained to his mother that Irish Gaelic, although sharing a language root with English, had arrived in the British Isles having travelled along the southern coasts of Europe with the Celtic tribes of the east, while English had taken a different route via the Germanic tribes of the north.

However, he had surmised – correctly – that his mother would not appreciate a lecture on linguistics at this point in her life, and so he said no more.

Joker's peculiar knowledge and natural intelligence were, for those who knew him well, a source of wonder, but also a cause for some dismay at his blank refusal to use his talents to achieve anything tangible in the world. Language, for Joker, was a hobby and nothing more.

None of this, however, was what was bothering him. Joker cared not at all for the preconceptions of strangers, nor for the despair of his friends at the apparent waste of his abilities, but there was something lurking in the depths of his mind that he was finding increasingly difficult to ignore.

Joker had seen a lot of changes over the past few months that had impacted on his normally unruffled ramble through life. His good friend and flatmate, Ding-a-Ling, had suddenly acquired a pregnant fiancée and was now calling himself 'Gary' for some reason. Another friend, Snatter, was now using the name 'Seamus' and had decided to become a homosexual, while yet another friend, the once reliable Jamesy, had discovered girls and could now be seen walking around with one as if it were the most natural thing in the world.

Perplexing though all of these events were, they were not what was keeping Joker awake at night. Something else was doing that.

It was there and it was not there. A slippery little irritant that shimmered just below his consciousness, whispering, giggling and teasing. Playing with his memories and stroking his emotions and ultimately forcing Joker to take action. He would have to consult his brain on the matter.

Joker's brain had a mind of its own. There were those who said that Joker's brain didn't work properly and, in a sense, this was true. His brain, on tackling any particular issue, preferred to adopt an approach that would never have been considered by more conventional brains, but would, invariably, turn out to be the more efficient choice. It was this kink in his thought process that allowed him to catch many unawares by his insight and also gave him such a clear perception of the structure of language.

Joker felt, however, that getting his brain involved would probably be unnecessary because, deep down, he knew what was troubling him. Or he had guessed. Or suspected. He just wasn't sure what he was going to do about it.

"Do you think you should write something on the envelope?" Katherine turned round to address her son.

"Oh yeah," said Joker, and leaned forward. Katherine passed the card back to him and he placed it in his lap and wrote neatly on the blank envelope.

To the Maguire Family.

TWO

Rosie McCann's self-imposed withdrawal from nicotine, combined with her increasingly obvious pregnancy, was making her a little irritable.

"For the last time, Gary," she told her fiancé, "I'm not walking down the aisle in a bloody tent."

Gary, in Rosie's opinion, had lately been the source of most of her irritation. His constantly cheerful attentiveness was beginning to grate on her nerves as she grew more bloated and miserable. Rosie liked being miserable. It suited her moods at this moment in time. It made her happy.

But Gary had no time for any glum introspection or self-pity. The world he preferred to inhabit was filled with upbeat optimism, with no room for wavering doubts or negativity. Gary wore the same smile today as the one he had worn as a child when the world seemed to bask in the sun and blue skies of an endless summer. The same smile that had dazzled a little girl as her own world crumbled around her, the smile that had cheered her breaking heart and warmed her childhood dreams. The smile that had made her fall in love.

But now it was just getting on her tits. Gary's irrepressible chirpiness rubbed hard against her own moody grumblings but, she told herself, she possessed enough grace and serenity to rise above the persistent aggravation. She prided herself on her restraint in the face of Gary's provocation, and on her ability to remain steady and calm, composed and tranquil and sedate.

Rosie had lately become something of an unpredictable psycho-bitch, thought Gary, but he had to concede she did have a point.

"Yeah, all right," he said. "I can see how that would look in the photographs, but I just thought that it may be better to get it all over with."

"Get it over with?" Rosie shrieked. "That's bloody lovely, that is! Did you hear that, Ellie? Gary's really laying on the charm over here, I'm not sure I can resist." Rosie glanced over to where her sister sat, but Ellie was poring over some letters that lay on the coffee table in front of her and seemed oblivious to all around her.

They were in the front room of Ellie's house in the Ardoyne area of north Belfast, with Gary standing by the window and Rosie sitting by herself on the sofa. Ellie was more than happy to share the house with her little sister, but there were times when she would have liked some time to herself. Ellie had always been the quiet one and was usually to be found engrossed in her work, either in her occupation as a nurse or in the more personal project on which her attention was now focused.

"Oh, you know what I mean," said Gary. "But I suppose you're right. There's no harm in waiting till after the baby's born."

"Well, thank you, Gary," said Rosie. "I don't understand what the rush is anyway. If you had it your way, my waters would be breaking when we're standing at the altar. That's really classy, Gary." Rosie grinned and turned to her sister, expecting Ellie to be similarly amused by the notion. Ellie, however, did not even look up.

"So, yeah, Gary," Rosie went on, "what's the big bloody rush all about?"

"No rush," said Gary hurriedly. "There's no rush at all, it's just that me and the lads were talking about maybe having a bit of a stag do and we thought that –"

"A stag do?" Rosie exclaimed. "A fucking stag do?"

"Well yeah," Gary explained, "I mean, you have to think about these things, don't you?"

"Yeah, because we don't have anything else to think about, do we?"

"You know what I mean."

"Okay, Gary," said Rosie, her suspicions aroused. "What exactly did you have in mind, then?"

"Don't know really." Gary shrugged. "Oh," he said, as if a thought had just struck him, "I think somebody might have said something about Italy. Not really sure, though. Sometime in June, I think it was, maybe, or something like that, I don't know but I thought that –"

"Italy?" Rosie asked, her suspicions now fully erect. "Why Italy?"

"What?" said Gary defensively. "Why Italy? Well, why not Italy? It's as good a place as any, isn't it? I mean when you think about –"

"Isn't the World Cup in Italy this year?" Ellie asked as she looked up from the papers on the table. Gary felt that Ellie had really picked her moment to take an interest in the conversation.

"Is it?" he asked in all innocence. "Is it really?" He knew he wasn't fooling anyone but he decided his best plan would be to forge ahead.

"The World Cup?" Rosie said as she looked from Ellie to Gary. "The bloody World Cup? I wonder when that would be, then? No, no wait … let me guess! It wouldn't be June by any chance, now, would it?"

Gary dumbly shook his head as if the looming occasion of the world's biggest football tournament had somehow slipped his mind. Rosie gave him a look that would have withered a smarter man.

"Oh, Gary," she suddenly sighed, "I'd be only too happy for you to go to the World Cup, but you know what money's like at the minute. We'd struggle to get to Ballycastle, never mind Italy."

Gary nodded. He had actually been having similar concerns. It had taken a few informal enquiries to let him know that attending even just one game at the tournament would be much more than he could afford. In fact, out of all of his friends, he was sure that only Seamus Green, his oldest friend, would be able to raise the necessary finances for such a trip. Everybody else, he reckoned, was just fantasising. He was about to make a comment when the squeal of the garden gate being pushed open caused him to glance out the window.

"Here comes Sna … um, Seamus," he said. "Are you sure you don't want to come?"

"No, you two go ahead," said Rosie as she pushed herself up from the sofa. "I just wouldn't feel right."

The main front door to the house was already open, exposing a little square of hall at the foot of the stairs, so there was just a quick knock on the lounge door before Seamus pushed it open and stepped inside.

"All right there?" he said as he closed the door behind him. "Hiya, Ellie. Rosie, how's it going?"

"Yeah, okay, Seamus," said Rosie, arching her back, "but I'm crawling the bloody walls gasping for a smoke."

"Oh, I'm sure you are," said Seamus, "but you know it's for the best, don't you? You okay there, Ellie?"

Ellie looked up as if taken by surprise. "What?" she exclaimed. "Oh sorry, Seamus, I'm just trying to sort through all these letters from places in England to see if there's anything useful about daddy."

Rosie, Seamus noted, looked at Gary and rolled her eyes while shaking her head.

"Well, is there?" Seamus asked. "Anything useful, I mean?"

Ellie sat back with a sigh. "Not really," she said. "You'd think there would be something, you know? Some trace, or some sort of lead or something."

Ellie and Rosie's father had been torn from his family almost two decades before and had been missing for over fifteen years. He had been caught up, through no fault of his own, in the turmoil of internment at the beginning of the 1970s.

The British had introduced internment – imprisonment without trial – in a desperate attempt to quell the eruption of militant Irish republicanism that had been largely dormant since the partition of Ireland in the 1920s.

Martin McCann, like many others, was an innocent victim of circumstance and his experiences in custody had contributed directly to a complete emotional breakdown, which led to him passing through a variety of mental health institutions until the trail went cold during the turbulence of the seventies.

Ellie, Rosie and their younger brother, Jack – now living in Derry – had been brought up by their mother, Shauna, who had eventually succumbed to the effort and had died when Rosie was a teenager. Jack had no memories of his father and any memories that Rosie may have had were either discarded or suppressed, which meant the legacy of Martin McCann lived on only in the heart of his eldest child. And Ellie preserved that legacy with a firm resolve.

"Well, I'm sure something will turn up," said Seamus.

"I know," Ellie said, "but hopefully it'll be soon. I just wish that –"

"Oh, for God's sake, Ellie," Rosie snapped, "just let it go, will you?"

"What do you mean let it go?" Ellie was shocked by Rosie's outburst. "How can you say that about your own father?"

Rosie, standing by the window, turned on her sister. "My own father?" she shouted. "My own bloody father? Then where was he, Ellie? Where was he when we had to leave home? Where was he when ma died? Where was he when …?" Rosie stopped as she tried to control her anger. Seamus and Gary began to shuffle towards the door.

"You can hardly blame him for any of that," Ellie insisted. "How can you –?"

"I don't care!" Rosie cried. "I don't care whose fault it was! He left us!"

"But –"

"He left *me*!" Rosie banged a fist against her chest. "I was only fucking six!"

Seamus had a hand on the door handle but, despite Gary's silent urgings for him to turn it, he felt frozen; helplessly caught up in the moment. Tears had begun to well in Rosie's eyes, but she forced them back. She wouldn't cry over this, she thought. Never over this.

"Just move on with your life, Ellie," Rosie said grimly. "I have. And as far as I'm concerned, he's already dead. In fact, I hope he is."

"Rosie!" Ellie cried. "God forgive you!"

Rosie shrugged and sat down in the chair by the window, her face hard and dark.

"Right then," said Gary, clapping his hands together. "We should make a move here. You ready there, Seamus?"

"What? Oh, right, yeah." Seamus was still getting used to Ding-a-Ling, or rather Gary, calling him by his name. There was a lot to get used to this year, he thought, so an unstable pregnant woman was just par for the course. He opened the door and turned to address the chilly silence in the room.

"Well, all the best," he said. "See you later."

"Yeah, see you," Gary added as he and Seamus hurried outside and pulled the door closed behind them.

"Jesus!" Seamus exclaimed as they walked down the path towards his car. "What the hell was that all about?"

"Don't know," Gary replied. "And I'm not sure I *want* to know." They got into the car and pulled on their seatbelts. "Did you get the Mass Cards?"

"Yeah," said Seamus. "They're on the back seat there. Have you heard from Tone lately?"

"Yeah, he seems okay."

Seamus simply nodded as he drove out of Ardoyne and crossed to the Woodvale, heading for the west of the city and the Falls Road.

THREE

Tone was standing, in the midst of a small crowd, in the front garden of his parents' house in a housing estate just off the Falls Road when Joker's father's car pulled into the street. Tone waved in acknowledgement as Davy parked in the nearest available space, and then he, Katherine and Joker got out and walked towards the house.

Davy and Joker took turns to shake Tone's hand while Katherine gave him a quick hug.

"So sorry to hear about your daddy, Tony," she said.

"Thanks," said Tone.

"We got a wee sympathy card," Katherine told him, holding up her handbag. She then stepped closer and lowered her voice, "but I'm not really sure what to do with it, you know? Is there somewhere I'm supposed to leave it?"

The system of political and religious segregation in many parts of Northern Ireland meant that Katherine, a Protestant, would be unfamiliar with the customs and procedures that Catholics would normally adopt in situations like this. Removed from her own environment, her own little patch of the same city, she was self-conscious and fearful of standing out from the crowd.

"No problem," Tone assured her. "My da's laid out in the front room, so you can just put it in the coffin with the rest of the cards. You don't want to go in just yet, though, there's a priest in there saying a decade of the rosary."

"A decade of the rosary?" Katherine whispered conspiratorially. "What's that?" Katherine was fascinated by all forms of spirituality, searching, as she was, for her own personal enlightenment.

"Oh," said Tone, "it's nothing, really – just mumbling the same words over and over again."

Davy passed some cigarettes to Tone and Joker and proceeded to light them up, while Katherine wanted to learn more about the whole rosary business.

"So, what's it for?" she asked. "Is it supposed to do anything? Or serve some purpose, or something?"

"Yeah," said Tone mischievously, "I think if you do it right, then it's supposed to bring the corpse back to life."

"Tony!" cried Katherine. "That's terrible! You're as bad as Davy, so you are!"

"Yeah, you're right," Tone smiled. "Sorry, Katherine."

"So, what does it do, then?" she persisted.

"I have no idea," Tone told her. He shrugged. "Unless it's to give the priest something to do." Tone looked over Katherine's head to see a small, portly figure emerge from the house. "Here's somebody who can answer your question, Katherine," he said. "All right there, Hugh?"

Father Hugh was the type of priest who gave the priesthood a good name. He served his parish with self-effacing humility and good humour. He was widely loved by his parishioners and even Tone held a grudging respect for him.

"What's that, Anthony?" Father Hugh asked as he approached. "A question, you say? Something furrowed your brow, has it? Well, I'm always one to enlighten the bewildered." He gave Katherine a friendly wink. "Anthony here is a Godless heathen," he told her, the lilting brogue of his native Galway had been bludgeoned over the years by the staccato snarl of west Belfast. "A shocking man, he is. Just shocking."

Katherine grinned; she had warmed instantly to this jocular priest.

"So, tell me, Anthony," he went on, "what is it that's troubling you? Has something cast some doubt in your sceptical mind? Something punctured your certainties and scattered a few clouds across your sunny sky?"

"As you can see, Katherine," Tone said, "Father Hugh, here, suffers from an affliction that ails many a priest. He's addicted to the sound of his own voice."

"And sadly," Father Hugh observed, "I'm one of the few people who will actually listen. So, what was your question, Anthony? I'm all ears."

While Tone, Katherine and Father Hugh discussed the finer points of catholic protocol, Joker ambled through the front gate and let his attention wander. It strolled across the street and became transfixed by an empty crisp packet that was tumbling along the pavement. It then got distracted by a scruffy cat wandering past and was finally aroused by the sudden appearance of a sleek, black Mercedes that pulled up just behind Joker's father's car.

Damn! thought Joker as a young man emerged from the driver's side and walked towards him. Joker had met Johnny Gee on only a few occasions but had still managed to form a less than favourable opinion of him. Though harmless enough, he thought, it was Joker's firmly held belief that Johnny Gee was a cloying and eager-to-please little prick whose ingratiating manner was intensely irritating.

"Johnny Gee," said Joker. "How's it going?"

"Joker?" Johnny Gee replied, a little surprised. "Yeah, I'm not too bad, really. What about yourself?" Johnny Gee, Joker felt, seemed more subdued than normal, not quite as annoying, which, given the circumstances, was understandable.

"Yeah, I'm doing okay," Joker told him. "Not as well as you, obviously," he said, nodding to the shiny black car with the three-pointed star on the bonnet.

"What?" Johnny Gee followed Joker's gaze. "Oh right, well it's not mine of course."

"Doing a bit of joyriding, are you?"

"It's my da's car," said Johnny Gee. "My folks are away in Spain at the minute, so I thought I could –"

"Spain?" Joker interrupted. "Bit early in the year for a holiday, isn't it?"

"Well, it's not that," Johnny Gee explained. "They're looking for some places to buy over there. They've already got a beach-house there, you see, and they're looking to –"

"Your folks have a beach-house?"

"Yeah, it's sort of a –"

"In Spain?"

"Yeah, it's –"

"A beach-house?"

"Yeah."

"On a beach?"

"Yeah."

"In Spain?"

"Yeah."

"So let me see if I've got this right. Your parents have a –"

"Look, Joker," Johnny Gee said hastily, "I just noticed Tone there, so I should really go and pay my respects."

"Oh yeah, no probs," said Joker. "You go ahead there." As Joker watched Johnny Gee enter the garden he began to think.

Yeah, I know, he told his excited brain. *He's a great lad, that Johnny Gee. I've always said so.* Joker's firmly held beliefs were, of course, infinitely flexible.

At that moment Seamus drove past and parked a little way down the street. Joker watched as he and Gary got out of the car and walked towards the growing crowd outside the Maguire home. They each punched Joker on the arm and then went into the garden to shake hands with Tone and to say a few words of condolence. They then, along with Katherine and Davy, stepped into the house to place their cards and to take a final look at the shell that had been abruptly emptied of a lifetime's worth of ideas and tears and memories and dreams.

"Not going in, then?" asked Tone as he stepped to one side of Joker.

"Don't fancy it, myself," Joker told him. "If that's okay?"

"Can't say I blame you," Tone replied. "There's something a bit morbid about death, really." He offered Joker a cigarette.

"No, I'm all right, Tone. I've just put one out."

"Yeah, so have I," Tone said as he lit his cigarette. "Just seem to be chain-smoking at the minute."

"It's to be expected, I suppose," said Joker. "The funeral's the day after tomorrow, isn't it?"

"Yeah, ten in the morning."

"Have you heard from your brother?" Tone's elder brother had moved to Australia when Tone was only twelve years old, and they hadn't seen each other since then. "Is he planning to get back for the funeral?"

"Yeah," said Tone, "he's already on his way. He's due to get to Heathrow early tomorrow, so he should be here tomorrow afternoon. I'll pick him up from the airport."

"That's going to be weird, isn't it? After all these years?"

Tone shrugged. "Don't know," he said. "Just have to wait and see."

Katherine and Davy reappeared to let Tone know they were going to head on.

"You staying, then, Joseph?" Davy asked Joker.

"Aye, I'll get a lift with Seamus," said Joker. "I'll see you later." He watched his parents walk off towards their car then turned to see Johnny Gee emerge from the crowd.

"I'm going to shoot on here, Tone," Johnny Gee said as he shook Tone's hand again. "If there's anything I can do for you, then just let me know, okay?"

"Yeah okay, thanks Kevin," said Tone.

"Oh, it's not Kev ..." Johnny Gee began, but then stopped and simply nodded. As he stepped onto the road to walk to his car, Joker chased after him.

"Hang on there, Johnny Gee!"

"They seem very pally," said Gary when he and Seamus appeared beside Tone. The three of them watched, bemused, as Joker and Johnny Gee stood in the middle of the street, deep in conversation. After a few moments, Joker gave Johnny Gee a pat on the arm and turned back towards Tone's house. Johnny Gee got into his car and drove off.

"What the fuck was that all about?" asked Gary when Joker stopped in front of him.

"You'll just have to wait and see," said Joker before changing the subject. "Bobby said he was going to call over at some point," he said to Tone. "Have you seen him?"

"Yeah, you just missed him. He drove over with Sean and Jamesy."

"Jamesy?" said Seamus. "I haven't seen him in ages."

"Aye," Joker agreed, "he's been lying low, hasn't he? Horny wee bugger."

"Oh, I don't think there's anything like that going on," Tone said. "Can't really imagine it with those two, can you? Jamesy and Hannah?"

They all fell silent as they began to imagine it.

"Okay, okay," said Tone, "maybe we *can* imagine it, but I think that says more about us than about them. I mean, I don't think Hannah's the type that would even think about sex before marriage, and Jamesy's hardly a wild stallion, is he?"

"Oh, you never know, Tone," said Gary. "Still waters run deep and all that."

"Yeah right," Tone grunted. "How's Rosie doing these days, anyway?"

"Dead on," replied Gary. "Does my head in a wee bit like, but you know how it is, hormones and all."

They quietly nodded. They had all heard of that word. Dusk began to creep over the rooftops, so Seamus, Gary and Joker took their leave and drove off towards Gary and Joker's flat near the city centre, leaving Tone to chain-smoke in the encroaching gloom.

The number of people who came to the house to pay their respects eventually dwindled until it was just Tone and his mother sitting together in the front room, with the open coffin by the window. They sat quietly with their own memories of the man that once was until Tone persuaded his mother to go on to bed.

"Are you sure, Anthony?" his mother asked, breaking Tone's heart with the sadness in her voice. "You'll be okay on your own?"

"Yeah, you go on," Tone told her. Convention dictated that he would stay up to keep vigil throughout the night and he thought he would prefer to do so alone. "You could do with trying to get some sleep," he said. He watched his mother head off to bed then he got up and went into the kitchen. He took a beer from the fridge, set it on the kitchen table and sat down. He lit a cigarette and opened the beer and then, to his astonishment, he silently and uncontrollably wept.

FOUR

Nigeria, 1963

Dr Maher locked up the surgery for the day and made his way across the road, weaving through the noisy, static traffic of rush hour. He had still not got used to the heat, despite being in the city for more than a month, and he could feel the sweat begin to prickle the skin on his back.

He thought back to a cold, wet morning in February, when, on a visit to the library near his home in south London, he had searched for Kano in an atlas and had been shocked by the city's proximity to the southern edge of the Sahara Desert. Even on the flat, lifeless map, the desert seemed to be on a relentless march to engulf the city, nudging ever closer to the bustling outpost in the far north of Nigeria's Northern Region. Dr Maher realised then that, even for Africa, Kano would be hot, but still he was unprepared for the furnace that greeted him as he disembarked from his flight from the capital, Lagos, down on the south coast.

He was not entirely sure what had made him volunteer for this Pan-African initiative. He had been perfectly comfortable working as a general practitioner in London, but there was something about the new initiative, when he first heard of it, that fired his imagination. The idea was to spread modern medical practices throughout Africa, paying particular attention to the former colonies that were beginning to emerge as new independent states, and it had come along at just the right time.

He had been thinking about becoming involved in some teaching role and was considering looking into the possibility of taking up a position at a university or a teaching hospital when Dr Henry Rafferty, his old friend from college, had shown him the article in a medical journal.

The idea of spending several years in Africa helping to educate and train a new generation of medical students had a sudden appeal for him. Africa especially, for it was his continent after all.

Benjamin Maher, despite training and working in England for much of the last ten years, had been born in Cairo and had witnessed, as a child, the ebb and flow of a world war that would come to devastate his life and leave him orphaned and alone.

He took a quick glance at his watch as he jostled through the crowds on the busy pavement. The heat of an early evening in April discouraged rapid movement but he walked briskly, keen to reach the café in time.

"Benjamin!" Dr Maher's friend, Odi, was already seated at a table outside the café and called to him as he approached. "Don't worry," said Odi as he stood to embrace his little Egyptian friend. "You have plenty of time."

"What?" Benjamin exclaimed, taking a seat at the table. "What do you mean by that? Plenty of time for what?"

Odi roared with laughter. "You are so obvious, my friend," he said. "A blind man would be able to see it."

"I don't know what you mean," Benjamin said primly. He pushed his glasses up the bridge of his nose and sat back in his chair dismissively.

"Of course you don't," mocked Odi, laughing all the more. "Anyway, what would you like to drink, my friend? I will go and order."

"Just a glass of palm wine, thank you," said Benjamin. Odi got up and, still laughing, went inside. *Have I really been so transparent?* Benjamin wondered. *Surely not. Surely Odi is simply having some fun.* He looked along the pavement and saw Adanna, Odi's girlfriend, approaching with a few of her colleagues from work.

"Good evening, Dr Maher," she said formally. "Have you seen Odi?"

"Hello, Adanna. Yes, he's just gone inside."

Adanna embraced two of her workmates and they went off on their way. A third colleague, Zara, stayed behind.

"I will share a drink with you, Adanna," said Zara, glancing at Benjamin. "I'll have a tea, if you're going inside."

Adanna smiled and went to find Odi. Zara took a seat at the table beside Benjamin.

"How are you today, Benjamin?" Zara smiled sweetly.

"I'm well, thank you, Zara," said Benjamin. He liked Zara. Her pretty face was constantly enlivened by a broad smile. "And you?"

"Yes, I am very well," At that moment Odi and Adanna appeared with drinks and they joined Benjamin and Zara at the table.

"So, Dr Maher," said Adanna, "has your Hausa girl passed by yet?"

Benjamin was aghast. "What?" he stammered. "What do you mean?"

Odi shook with laughter. "He thinks that we haven't noticed," he said, slapping his knee. "Oh, Benjamin, do not look so surprised."

Benjamin felt himself flush with embarrassment. Zara smiled sympathetically at his discomfort.

"Do not worry, Benjamin," she told him. "I think she is very beautiful."

"How can she be beautiful?" Adanna snapped. "She is Hausa."

"You must not say that, Danna," Odi gently scolded. "We are all Nigerians."

"So I have been told," Adanna said coldly. Zara laughed at the serious look on her friend's face.

"Yes, Adanna," she said, "do not be like that. It is the weekend. We must make some plans for our days off."

"Very well," said Adanna with a brief smile. "Perhaps we should help Dr Maher pursue his *beautiful* Hausa girl. He is clearly incapable of doing so himself."

Zara clapped with delight. "Yes!" she cried. "That is an excellent idea."

Benjamin would normally have squirmed at being spoken of in this way, but he had spotted the approach of a familiar figure. It was the girl again, and he could no longer hear the teasing of his friends. It was the girl. His girl. His beautiful Hausa girl.

FIVE

Jamesy had never been one for romantic love in the traditional sense. Love, for Jamesy, was a straightforward, biological process that was responsible for the release of identifiable chemicals in the brain. The whole concept of love was nothing more than a mechanism which slavishly followed natural laws in order to perpetuate the species.

When such clinical scrutiny is brought to bear on a subject, then the mystery vanishes, but that, Jamesy believed, was no bad thing. No subject had ever been diminished by the truth. In fact, he thought, once the mechanisms for driving the human race forwards were revealed, then those mechanisms could only appear to be more wondrous and more inspiring than if they were still veiled in ambiguous mysticism.

Jamesy knew all this. He knew these things and he understood them. And he also understood that the embellishments to this biological urge, symbolised by a hopelessly inaccurate representation of the organ for pumping blood around the body, had given rise to an entire industry. An industry that drove the myth of love's throbbing heart through most of popular culture.

This, of course, was nothing new. Words of love had been around for as long as words had been around, and love had always been seen as an ephemeral, spiritual experience rather than a mundane, physical one. The subtle deceit was, Jamesy understood, probably necessary from an evolutionary standpoint. Those groups of early humans that cherished the notion of love as a heightened state of personal bonding, rather than as a simple, and often aggressive, physical act, would likely have been more successful than those that didn't, and this benign philosophy would then be passed down, becoming more ingrained with each generation. Ideas that benefited society would naturally thrive.

Necessary and harmless the deceit may have been, but it was deceit nonetheless and that, for Jamesy, was unacceptable. Jamesy needed to peek behind the curtain. He needed to see the structure and the clock-work. His inquisitive nature demanded nothing less. He needed to know. He needed to understand.

But now, it seemed, he could not only accept the lies, he could willingly embrace them.

Meeting Hannah had shaken Jamesy's cool restraint, and his detached, analytical approach was struggling to cope. He could still, of course, cast a cold eye on the reasons for his physical attraction to this particular girl. The components of her face, he understood, were arranged in such a way as to appeal to that part of his brain that dealt with aesthetics. And that part of his brain, Jamesy could imagine, would experience a surge of neurological activity when those same components of Hannah's face were temporarily rearranged when she smiled.

Such a sterile evaluation, however, no longer seemed appropriate. It was no longer an adequate description. And when Hannah smiled, Jamesy felt, it was not even close. What Jamesy was experiencing was unfamiliar and intriguing and had left him unsure about things that had once been firmly established.

His frustration at being unable to neatly interpret his feelings for Hannah was leading to some unwelcome ambiguity and uncertainty, but there was one thing that Jamesy was sure of. He was certain that at some point in the very near future – at a time convenient to them both – he would very much like to have sex with her.

Hannah walked quickly along Botanic Avenue, propelled by a cold wind and by her eagerness to see James. She had been thinking for a while now about what exactly her feelings were towards him and she had come to the conclusion that a large part of what she felt was gratitude.

Hannah was not so naïve as to believe that James would turn out to be the one great love of her life, but he had undeniably alerted her to the fact that such a thing might be possible.

She had grown up in the small town of Saintfield, just south of Belfast, and had lived her life closely tied to a local branch of Presbyterianism that held firm views on biblical scripture. The path that led to her future had been, up to now, clearly defined. She had, over the years, grown close to a boy named Greg who was in the same youth group of her Church and, though never mentioned outright, it was assumed that they would one day join their lives together in a union bonded by their shared love of Jesus Christ. There was no great passion there, but that had never bothered Hannah as she happily accepted the wisdom of an arrangement that would be safe and sensible and would provide a framework for them both to come to a greater understanding of Christ's love.

Then, last Christmas Eve, she had met James and everything had changed. She understood her immediate attraction to him, for James was extremely good-looking, but it soon became apparent that her passive acceptance of a future of bland domesticity had, in that very instant, evaporated.

James had aroused feelings in her that she hadn't been aware of before, but she now believed that the fuel for these new feelings had always been within her, just waiting for a spark to drift by and set it alight. And James had come along with a flamethrower.

She was still coming to terms with the strength of her new passions and the unexpected stirrings of – dare she even think it? – *lust*. The thoughts that James had sent spinning through her mind were thrilling and frightening, but it was the actual existence of these thoughts, rather than the cause, that excited her the most. She accepted that James could turn out to be little more than a catalyst, a first step on a new journey of possibilities, but she was also painfully aware that he was the first person she had ever met who had managed to push some wicked thoughts into the forefront of her mind. She was beginning to seriously contemplate committing a sin.

Jamesy occupied the ground floor of a student house in a quiet street that ran directly off Botanic Avenue. He sat at the kitchen table, glancing continually at the clock on the wall. The minutes ticked past nine o'clock until, finally, the doorbell rang and he jumped to his feet in happy anticipation of a certain smile.

"Not too late, am I?" asked Hannah as Jamesy led her into the small front room.

"No, not at all," said Jamesy. "In fact, we've got time for a cup of tea if you fancy it."

"I'd love a cup of tea," she told him, and Jamesy ushered her into the kitchen.

"We can have it at the table," he said. "There's a bit more room in the kitchen."

Jamesy's front room, Hannah had noted before, was filled with books of all sizes and subjects, piled in stacks of various heights, at seemingly haphazard locations all around the room. Outside of a library, Hannah thought, she had never seen so many books. Her family home in Saintfield had only one bookcase, in the hallway, and even that was not completely filled. It contained a Bible, of course, and a few other books concerning theology and scriptural analysis, as well as the writings of John Calvin and the philosophy of Presbyterianism. For anyone to possess so many books not related to Christianity was, for Hannah, something of a revelation.

She sat at the kitchen table and watched as Jamesy filled the kettle.

"Don't tell me you've read all those books," she said smiling.

"Well, not cover to cover," Jamesy told her. He switched on the kettle and reached for two cups that were hanging on hooks below one of the cupboards. "but I've certainly dipped into most of them. You know, for reference?"

"But they're not all about history, are they?" As far as Hannah understood things, James was at university to study history, though the truth was a lot more varied than just *history*.

"No," Jamesy admitted, "they're about all sorts of things."

"Then why have you –?" The kettle came to the boil and Jamesy turned his back to pour the water into a teapot. He then placed the teapot along with the cups on the table and sat down to wait for the tea to brew.

"Why have I got books that aren't about history? Is that what you were going to ask?"

"Well, yes."

"It's just something I do," Jamesy explained. "Like, I'll be reading about something and I'll come across a reference to something completely unrelated that might arouse my curiosity. Especially if it's something that I've vaguely heard of but I don't really know anything about. So then, of course, I have to investigate. I need to find out all I can about it." He poured the tea and got up to get some milk from the fridge.

"You need to?" asked Hannah, bemused.

"Well, maybe not *need* to," Jamesy said as he placed a carton of milk by Hannah's cup, "but it's certainly something that I like to do. You're looking a bit perplexed."

Hannah laughed. "I am a bit perplexed, actually. I can't imagine just going off on a tangent like that. Especially not when I'm studying. I try to stay focused on the subject in hand."

"Yeah, but knowledge is knowledge, isn't it?"

"Mmm," said Hannah. "I'll write that in my next exam. It'll go down well in a programming assignment."

"Okay, fair point," Jamesy conceded, grinning. "Maybe it's just me, but I seem to be curious about just about everything."

"Maybe it is just you," said Hannah, though, to Jamesy, she seemed a little thoughtful. She splashed some milk into her tea and took a sip. "I've got more than enough to keep me occupied," she said, "with my course, and with Scripture too. There can be times when I really struggle with God's message, you know? I can spend a whole day going over the same passage again and again, just trying to work out what the true meaning is." Hannah smiled, assuming that James would be knowingly sympathetic.

Jamesy had a sudden picture of himself grabbing the lapels of Hannah's overcoat, shaking her and screaming, *But there's so much more!* Instead, he drank his tea and nodded.

"So, what sort of things are you talking about?" asked Hannah.

"Oh, anything and everything," Jamesy said. "For example, the other day I was reading about eels, and that got –"

"Eels?"

"Long story," said Jamesy laughing, "but it got me thinking about the Sargasso Sea, you know?"

"The Sargasso Sea? That name rings a bell. Is that where all the eels come from?"

"A lot of them, yeah, but I suddenly thought that I had no idea where the Sargasso Sea actually is."

"So, where is it, then?"

"Well," Jamesy said, "I'd always assumed that Sargasso was a place, you know? An actual geographical location."

"But it isn't?"

"No, not really. The Sargasso Sea is an area in the Atlantic Ocean."

"A sea in the ocean?"

"Yeah, apparently it's full of a weird sort of seaweed called sargassum. And that's where the name comes from."

Hannah looked at Jamesy and laughed. "Well," she exclaimed, "that actually was pretty interesting. And I was expecting to be bored to tears."

"Well, don't be getting too used to that sort of wild entertainment all the time," Jamesy told her. "I mean, I am fairly boring most of the time."

They laughed and chatted as they drank their tea and, after a while, Jamesy stood up. He carried their empty cups over to the sink and glanced at the clock.

"We should make a move," he said. "We'll just walk down and get a taxi in Botanic. You're looking lovely by the way."

"Thank you," said Hannah as she stood up. "And you look very handsome too, James," she added with an accompanying smile. "Black really suits you."

SIX

Wee Paulie was a coming man. He could sense it. He could feel it in his water. He had worked his way up with quiet determination, always making sure he was there when needed, always happy to do whatever was asked of him, becoming more and more indispensable, nudging his way ever closer to the top. And it was all starting to pay off.

He liked to think that he was already the right-hand man to the right-hand man; the person who was called on for tasks of the highest importance. This particular job was a perfect example. It was true, he supposed, that one of the reasons he had been selected for the mission was that he was originally from Ardoyne, and so would be able to mingle in some of the drinking clubs without arousing too much suspicion. But that detail, he was sure, was just a minor consideration. He was sure that it was his discretion and cool professionalism that had really swayed his selection and he felt confident that a successful outcome would confirm his position in the upper echelons of the organisation.

He watched his girlfriend, Gemma, rush between the bedroom and the bathroom as she got ready for work. He sat up in bed and stretched, leaving his hands behind his head and leaning back against the headboard.

"You know," he said as Gemma hurriedly assembled the persona she used for work, "I reckon this could be the big one."

"The kettle's on," Gemma told him during a brief appearance in the bedroom. "Can you finish making the tea. Where the fuck are my shoes?"

"What? Oh yeah, okay." Wee Paulie got out of bed, pulled on a dressing gown and walked to the kitchen. Their one-bedroom flat was on one level, so he didn't have far to go. As he dropped some teabags into two large mugs he continued with his observations.

"Yeah," he went on, "I think I'll really be on my way after this one."

"Can you stick some toast on?" Gemma called from the bathroom. "Have you seen my other earring?"

As the kettle came to the boil, Wee Paulie placed some bread in the toaster before filling the two mugs.

"Very important, by all accounts," he said. "In fact, it's even –"

"Got fucking mascara in my eye," moaned Gemma as she burst into the kitchen, holding a tissue to her eye. The toast popped up and she grabbed a slice, spreading some butter as Wee Paulie finished making the tea. "What were you saying?"

"I was just saying that –"

"Shit! Is that the time?" Gemma took a few gulps of tea to wash down a mouthful of toast, then rushed back to the bathroom. A moment later she reappeared, grabbed her bag and keys from the worktop, then paused briefly on her way to the front door to give Wee Paulie a quick kiss. "I'll see you later," she said and, pulling her coat from a hook on the door, she was gone.

Wee Paulie took his tea and went back to the bedroom. He got into bed and sat up sipping the hot drink and thinking about how his mission had been going so far. It was a straightforward job of surveillance and information-gathering and was centred on a monstrous figure by the name of Hegarty in the nationalist enclave of Ardoyne in north Belfast.

Having managed to escape from Ardoyne in his late-teens, Wee Paulie had been loath to return there, but he could see the sense in having a known face in an area where the unfamiliar was viewed with suspicion.

As far as the residents of Ardoyne were concerned, their exuberant sense of freedom and independence was viewed as seditious by the British, and that, coupled with the close proximity of hostile unionist communities, had given them something of a siege mentality. Strangers to the district tended to stand out and were treated with mistrust until they could be vouched for by someone *known*. And this was why Wee Paulie could go and drink in the local clubs without having to face any awkward questions, for, despite no longer living there, his face was still *known*.

Wee Paulie had been working on the group of friends and work-mates with whom Hegarty tended to socialise. Hegarty had assembled a gang of tradesmen that worked together in building sites around Northern Ireland and Wee Paulie had been getting to know them as individuals and as a group, slowly building up their trust. Wee Paulie knew how to play the long game. He was assembling a wealth of information to bring to his superiors that, he hoped, would provide them with what they required.

Hegarty himself, Wee Paulie had learned, was a skilled carpenter who, despite his enormous size, was capable of the most intricate and delicate feats of woodworking. Wee Paulie had managed to have the odd casual word or two with this uncommunicative brute, but it was the other members of the gang that were proving to be more open.

There was Plumber Pete, loud, raucous and friendly. Darren, the self-proclaimed God's gift to women, who also did some plastering, the two brickies, Andy and Tom, both surly when sober, and Terry the Spark, whip-thin and cool as Elvis. Wee Paulie was on friendly terms with them all by now and was confident that he was working towards a satisfying result to his mission.

What, exactly, that result would be, remained to be seen. Wee Paulie wasn't entirely sure what Mr Jippsen-Phillips was looking for, but he seemed to be happy enough with all of the reports he had received so far. There was a chance, Wee Paulie felt, that this job was in some way related to Mr McClelland's stay in hospital over Christmas and if that was the case then Wee Paulie was linked to the very head of the firm, and the thought made him giddy.

He finished his tea and lay back in bed, allowing the dreams and the little fantasies of a glorious future play around in his head. Wee Paulie was a coming man.

SEVEN

Tone watched the motorway traffic hurtle in and out of the city, far enough away to be eerily silent. Probably wouldn't be able to hear it anyway, he thought, over the priest's endless droning. A chill wind brushed a shiver through the crowd and Tone found himself thinking it was always cold at funerals. Maybe it was because Milltown Cemetery was situated on an exposed hillside, but Tone was sure he had always shivered at funerals here, even on the hottest of days. His mother would probably say it had something to do with the spirits of the dead or some other such nonsense that Tone would dismiss. He had no time for paranormal explanations but still, he had to admit, it was always cold at funerals. The priest droned on.

Tone glanced at the mourners gathered around the graveside. They were mostly friends of his parents that he had known from childhood, but he could just make out, lurking at the back, a small group of his own friends. He could see the shaven head of Joker and, further back, standing even taller than Joker, he recognised the huge figure of Harry, Gary's brother-in-law. Tone smiled inwardly. Harry, he assumed, had been dragged along by Karen, Gary's sister, who had, no doubt, been dragged along by Rosie, Gary's fiancée, who, in her present condition, would have needed more support than even a mad rip like Gary could provide. The priest droned on.

Tone's drifting thoughts eventually settled on his father and how, without warning, he was shockingly no longer there. A heart attack, a little defect in a physical muscle, had bridged the gap between existence and oblivion and had turned a normal morning into a maelstrom of grief and loss and uncertainty. Tone looked at his mother standing at the graveside and saw her, for the first time, as an old woman.

He found it impossible to equate this sad, tiny figure, almost fading away before his eyes, with the woman who had shaped his childhood. The woman who could both ease his fears and cause his fears. The woman who could scold and terrify, and praise and hug and reassure. A tyrant, a teacher, a bully and a friend.

There are memories from childhood, Tone thought, that blaze forever through life. Moments that stay with you. He would never forget, for instance, one summer in Donegal when he and his brother had walked with their father across a meadow in search of a river to fish from and had stumbled upon a sun-dappled paradise. A slow, shallow stream trickling over rocks and hidden from the world by broad, leafy trees.

They had all stood and quietly gaped. Guilty, almost, for catching nature with her hair down in tranquil, private repose. Tone could still picture the clear water in the shallow pools between the little rapids of the river with the occasional buzz of an insect that only intensified the silent beauty of the scene.

But there are other memories, Tone mused, that sit quietly between the big moments of walking in the world; memories that come gently to the surface at a sudden sight, or a taste, or a scent. New pyjamas at Christmas or the welcome oasis of a hot water bottle in a freezing bedroom or the tending of wounds earned in summer escapades, and Tone knew, glancing at the diminishing figure beside him, that all of those unassuming moments were filled with her.

The droning of the priest finally came to an end and the mourners relaxed. A few took their leave of Tone's mother and began to drift away to their cars, but most stayed behind to chat and to catch up with old acquaintances. Tone lit up a cigarette while his mother and his brother went over to talk to Father Hugh.

"You flashing the ash there, Tone?" asked Bobby, pushing through the crowd.

Tone handed over his cigarettes and lighter. "Well, did you enjoy that?" he asked.

"He did go on a bit, didn't he?" said Bobby, taking and lighting a cigarette before handing back the pack. "But apart from that it was okay."

Jamesy appeared and shook Tone's hand. "All right there, Tone?" he said. "How are you bearing up?"

"Yeah, not too bad, Jamesy. Thanks."

"Is that your brother over there with the priest?" asked Jamesy.

"Yeah, that's Donal."

"So, how have you been getting on, then?"

Tone shrugged. "Don't seem to have much in common, to be honest."

"He seems a bit serious, doesn't he?" said Bobby, glancing over at Donal.

"Well, this is a funeral," Jamesy pointed out.

"I know, but even so …"

"You've got a point, Bobby," said Tone. "I don't think I've seen him smile since he got here."

"Be fair, Tone," Jamesy said. "The guy's just flown halfway around the world to bury his father. He's hardly going to be in a mood for the giggles, is he?"

Bobby looked at Jamesy. "What have you done with Hannah?" he asked. Hannah was Bobby's cousin and he felt that maybe he should show some concern for her wellbeing.

"I left her talking to Rosie," Jamesy told him.

"I was surprised to see Hannah here today," said Tone. "Fair play to her, though. It showed some guts coming here and mixing with a load of priests and rebels."

"Yeah, it was her idea," Jamesy said. "I certainly didn't suggest it."

"Probably curiosity," Bobby suggested. "See what you Taigs get up to."

"We're all heading to the Foresters after," Tone told Jamesy, "if you fancy it."

"Probably not, Tone," said Jamesy. "I was just going to say we're going to be heading on soon."

"Aye, no problem, Jamesy. Tell Hannah I really appreciate her coming today, will you?"

"Yeah, of course. All the best, mate, and I'll see you later."

Back at the flat, Jamesy surveyed the contents of his kitchen cupboard.

"I've got a tin of Spaghetti Hoops," he told Hannah, "some tuna, a half a jar of marmalade and … some dog food, apparently. I could probably rustle up some sort of casserole from all that."

"I'm not very hungry," said Hannah.

"Or we could go out somewhere."

"Oh yeah, I'm starving."

Jamesy laughed. "It's still a bit early, though," he said. "Fancy a cup of tea?"

"Love one."

Jamesy picked up the kettle, went to the sink and, as he turned on the tap, he let his mind wander over to a subject that had lately been attracting a lot of his attention. He wanted to make Hannah aware that he was not averse to the notion of taking their relationship to a more physical level, but he was struggling to think of a way of doing so without coming across as a ravenous sex beast. He just wasn't very good at this sort of thing.

Jamesy had played a fairly passive role in all of his previous sexual encounters, even, on a few occasions, going along with the whole thing only out of politeness. It may have been that he didn't have a particularly strong libido, or maybe it was because he had never had to try too hard, but he had never felt the same overwhelming urge for sexual release that he had observed in all of his peers once puberty had hit.

Now, though, he was beginning to appreciate the sexual frustration that had plagued his friends, as he tried desperately to come up with an appropriate way of broaching the subject with Hannah. It didn't help, of course, that Hannah's religious views would, presumably, make her less amenable to the idea and would make raising the topic so much more delicate than it would normally have been. He certainly would not be able to use the approach of someone like Joker who would simply come straight out and ask to have a little rummage around in her underwear. Jamesy smiled to himself at the thought.

"I was talking to your friend, Joseph, at the funeral," said Hannah from her seat at the table.

"Oh, sweet Jesus!" Jamesy muttered.

"What?"

"Oh nothing, nothing." Jamesy placed the kettle on its base and switched it on. He then sat down facing Hannah. "So, um, so, what was he saying?"

"Well, I think he said he was going to be taking somebody to a gay bar," said Hannah. She frowned. "He's not gay, is he?"

"Joker? No, no, he's not gay." Jamesy assured her. He didn't quite know how to proceed. He had a sense that fundamentalist Christian types were not well disposed towards the homosexual community, but as he had so far avoided any deep religious discussions with Hannah, he wasn't sure what her own feelings would be on the matter.

"Then why is he –?"

"You've met Seamus, haven't you?" he asked.

"Seamus? Yes," said Hannah. "I like Seamus. He's nice."

"Well," Jamesy explained, "Seamus has recently come out as being gay and, for reasons best known to himself, Joker has decided help him out."

"Help him out?"

"Yeah, it doesn't bear thinking about, does it?" Jamesy got up to finish making the tea, relieved that Hannah didn't pursue the matter. She leaned back in her chair and stretched lazily.

"You never answered my question, you know," she said as Jamesy sat back down at the table with two cups of tea.

"What question?"

"Why can't dolphins breathe underwater?"

"What?"

"Don't you remember?" Hannah said. "It was something you said when you were having that argument with Greg."

"I wouldn't call it an argument," said Jamesy defensively. "More of a discussion really."

"Well anyway," Hannah went on, leaning forward to gaze into those mesmerising, milky-blue eyes that were Jamesy's most striking feature, "you came up with that question as some sort of example, I think, as the type of thing we should want to find out about. Remember?"

"Sort of," Jamesy replied. "What's your point?"

"Well, it sort of stuck with me," she told him. "The more I thought about it, the less sense it made."

"What do you mean?" Jamesy was uneasy about the direction this conversation seemed to be taking.

"Well, fish can breathe underwater, right? And that makes sense because they live in water their whole lives. But then, so do dolphins." Hannah looked at Jamesy and frowned. "But if dolphins don't keep jumping out of the water every so often then they'll drown. Whales too, for that matter. It doesn't seem fair."

"Doesn't seem to bother the dolphins," said Jamesy.

"I know, but it's the same as us having to stick our heads in a bucket of water every now and then just to stay alive. It's mad! I just don't understand why God would make dolphins that way."

"Yeah, well," Jamesy said as he finished his tea, "we should probably make a move. I reckon we should try that new Italian place in Botanic."

Hannah gave him a curious look. "You're still avoiding the question, aren't you?" she said.

"What makes you think I know the answer?"

"You said it yourself. You need to know everything."

"I thought you said you were starving?"

"Wow!" said Hannah laughing. "You really don't want to answer the question, do you?"

"Come on." Jamesy stood up. "We can talk about it over lunch."

"Are you going to tell me the answer, then?" Hannah got up and they both headed for the front door.

"If you want," Jamesy told her. "Although," he said as he pulled open the door, "it's more of a theory."

EIGHT

"Father Hugh was telling me you've lost your faith," Donal said as he sat down at the table across from Tone.

"I didn't lose it," said Tone. "I threw it away."

"Why?"

"I just never felt comfortable kneeling in front of a man in a dress."

Donal sighed. "What happened, Tony?" he said. "I can remember when you wanted to be a choirboy at St Peter's."

"Yeah, well, they do say youth is wasted on the young."

"You're still young," Donal told him, "but you've got really cynical. So, what happened to you? What made you reject your faith?"

"I read the Bible," said Tone. Donal was beginning to irritate him. They were supposed to be celebrating the life of their father with drinks and songs and memories, not going over all this old nonsense again.

Tone had been surprised to learn that Donal had become more religious since moving to Australia. He had assumed the opposite would be true, believing Australia to be a lot more secular and forward-thinking than Northern Ireland.

"Never mind *me*, Donal," he said. "What the hell happened to *you*? I don't remember you going to Mass much when I was a kid."

Donal took a sip of his beer and leaned forward, resting his elbows on the table. "I think the Church really helped me," he said, "when my marriage broke up."

"What? When did this happen?"

"A couple of months ago," Donal explained. "One day Donna just took the kids and left. They're staying with Donna's parents in Melbourne."

"Why, though? What happened?"

"A lot of things really," said Donal with a shrug. "Maybe I should have put in a bit more effort. I don't know. It looks like it's over, though."

"Does ma know?"

"Not yet. There hasn't really been the right time, you know? I'll tell her before I head back, though."

"Jesus, Donal," said Tone. "You really know how to bring down a funeral."

Seamus and Sean were talking with Tone's mother on the other side of the room, so Bobby joined Tone and Donal's table.

"All right there, Donal?" he said, sitting down. They had been introduced earlier. "Have you noticed many changes since you've been back?"

"I haven't really been here long enough," said Donal. "Although from what Tony's been telling me, the town seems to have got a lot livelier.

When I left, the whole city centre would shut down at five o'clock every day. Didn't open at all on Sundays."

"Yeah, I know what you mean," Bobby agreed. "It has all opened up a lot in the last couple of years. I can remember a lot of the Bible-Bashers on our side being up in arms about places opening on Sundays."

"Donal!" someone called from the bar. "Come and see your Aunt Jessie."

Donal got up from his chair and melted into the crowd. Tone threw a cigarette across the table to Bobby and lit one for himself.

"Cheers, Tone," Bobby said. "So, how's it going with you and Donal, then?"

Tone shrugged. "He's got his problems," he said. "Like everybody else."

"Mmm," Bobby muttered. He took a sip of his beer and looked intently across the table at Tone. "Did I ever tell you," he began, "that I was planning to get engaged this year?"

Tone gave him a look. "Uh, yeah," he said with as much nonchalance as he could muster. "I'd heard."

"Well, it didn't work out," said Bobby.

"Really?"

"Yeah, it turns out," Bobby casually replied, "that she met somebody down in Dublin last year."

Tone said nothing. He simply looked at Bobby and took a draw from his cigarette.

"Yeah," Bobby continued, "a bit of an arsehole by all accounts."

Tone remained silent, waiting for Bobby to go on.

"He's actually from Belfast, apparently." Bobby paused to take a long drink before continuing. "Some cunt by the name of Tony Maguire. Sounds like a right wanker."

"Look, Bobby," Tone quickly interjected, "I had no idea that –"

"I know, I know," Bobby waved away Tone's protestations, "I'm only messing with you." He seemed amused by Tone's reaction. "So, when did you realise?"

Tone looked uncomfortable as he answered. "You were rambling away about her at the pub-crawl," he said miserably, "and it just clicked."

"Really?" said Bobby. "I don't remember that."

"I haven't seen her since," Tone admitted.

"No, you haven't, you dickhead!"

"What?"

Bobby leaned forward. "That's what I want to talk to you about," he said. "Claire's really confused about why you haven't been in touch. She thinks she's done something wrong."

"I know, but I just thought that …" Tone stopped and thought for a second. "Did you tell her that you knew me?" he asked.

"No," Bobby told him, "I thought I should see you first. Got to say it was a hell of a shock, though, when it all came out."

"I'm sure."

"So, what are you going to do about it, Tone?" Bobby went on. "You can't just leave it like that."

"Well, what about you two? Did you actually propose?"

"Never got a bloody chance, did I?" Bobby leaned back in his chair with a smile. "You managed to fuck up that plan, didn't you? Lucky I never bought a ring."

"Sorry about that."

"Yeah, well," Bobby shrugged, "you know me, Tone. It was just the next step, really."

"Even so …"

"Anyway, shit happens, but you still need to talk to Claire."

"Yeah, you're right," Tone said, an unfamiliar glimmer of hope flickering within him. "I'll do that."

Seamus and Sean arrived at the table with a tray of drinks. They had to shout to be heard above the shouts and laughter of the crowd as old friends met up and hugged and reminisced and drank to a man that used to be.

"It's a pity Joker and Gary had to work this afternoon," Sean said as he and Seamus sat down. "They'd have been in their element here."

"Yeah," Tone agreed. "Gary was saying he doesn't think he can manage the World Cup this year."

"No, I'm not surprised," Sean said, "There's no way I can afford it either."

"I'm out too," Bobby added. "Bloody skint."

"Yeah, it was a nice idea," said Tone, "but it was always going to be a long shot." He looked at Seamus. "I hear you've got a big night coming up," he said with a grin. "You and Joker, then?"

Seamus nodded. "Saturday night," he said.

Bobby laughed. "I'd love to be a fly on the wall that night," he said. "Are you looking forward to it?"

"Of course," Seamus replied. "Well, you know, sort of." He wasn't sure how he was feeling about Saturday night. It was going to be, for him, a leap into the unknown and he was both excited and apprehensive about what he would encounter. He was also unsure about Joker's offer of accompaniment.

On the one hand, he would be glad of the support, but on the other hand, it was Joker.

Anything could happen.

NINE

The Front Page bar was so-called because of its proximity to two of Belfast's main newspapers; the *Irish News* was across the road and the *Belfast Telegraph* was just around the corner. It was an upstairs bar, elegantly furnished with seating areas off to the right of the entrance and another, raised area, across the way from the bar. There was also a small stage in the left-hand corner that looked to be set up for some live music later in the evening, with microphones and instruments already in place.

Joker sat at the bar by himself. It was still early, so the place was quiet with just a few people dotted here and there. An elderly couple sat in silence at the far end on the right, while a gang of women, with bags of shopping at their feet, gossiped around a table a little closer to the bar.

Joker glanced in the large, ornate mirror behind the bar and saw a couple of cool, young dudes sitting at a table in the middle of the raised section. They were huddled in deep conversation.

As Joker watched, one of the cool dudes got up and walked furtively to the left of the bar. He then leapt onto the stage and, grabbing a microphone in its stand, made a request of the smattering of disinterested punters around the room.

"Ladies and gentlemen," he said with enthusiasm, "could you please put your hands together for 'Blues Boy' Morrison!"

Then, to no applause, the other cool dude – presumably 'Blues Boy' Morrison – bounded onstage, picked up a guitar, and launched into a hurried version of *Drink That Bottle Down,* before a red-faced bouncer came through the door and began remonstrating with 'Blues Boy' and his mate. After a heated exchange, the dudes were bundled out the door and down the stairs to the street below.

Under normal circumstances, Joker would have been highly amused by such shenanigans but his current, reflective state of mind had curbed his fondness for mischief and so he simply gestured to the barman to refill his glass.

As a fresh pint was placed in front of him, Joker lit a cigarette and pondered this strange new contemplative condition. It was clear that his attempts to suppress his feelings – to bury them in the darkest of depths – had not been entirely successful by the fact that his brain revelled in nagging him about it. There were times when Joker wished his brain would just fuck off and leave him alone. Especially when it was being, he believed, largely unreasonable.

It was all very well, Joker felt, to constantly highlight the issue, but if his brain had nothing constructive to offer, then what was the point? Just what did his brain expect him to do about it?

"Right there, Joker? Been here long?"

"Hiya, Seamus," Joker replied as Seamus arrived beside him. "Nah, not long. Just a couple of pints."

"You okay there?" Seamus asked, nodding to Joker's pint.

"Yeah, you go ahead."

Seamus ordered a drink and sat up on the barstool next to Joker.

"Still up for it, then?" he asked Joker as his pint arrived.

"Aye, no problem." Joker grinned. "What's the worst that can happen?"

Seamus winced. "For fuck's sake, Joker," he said. "Don't say things like that."

"So, what time do you want to head round at?"

"Well," said Seamus, taking a drink from his pint and holding it up, "not till I've had several more of these."

"Good plan."

The evening wore on, and Seamus could not help noticing that Joker was a lot more enthusiastic about his drinking than normal. He had never been much of a slouch in that regard, but tonight he seemed to be attacking each beer with an almost solemn intent.

"Take it easy, Joker. We've got all night," he said as Joker downed another pint.

"Just thirsty, Seamus, that's all," Joker told him. "Besides, you can't expect me to walk into a gay bar sober, now can you?"

"God forbid."

The Parliament was Belfast's first openly gay venue and so, being a new thing, people were naturally against it. The problem for the people who disliked new things, though, was that, over the last few years, Belfast had been trying to catch up with the rest of the United Kingdom and so new things were happening at an increasing rate. It was hard for the protesters to keep up.

It also meant that the protesters were having to spread themselves ever more thinly to ensure that they covered every new thing that appeared. But the protests, the protesters believed, were necessary because if groups of people who were not the same as them were to be given the same rights as them, then other groups of people who were not the same as them would want to be given those rights too. All sorts of groups. Even women. And then where would we be?

So as Seamus and Joker headed towards the Parliament, they were confronted by a sign-waving mob of three people who tried to explain to them that they were both abominations in the eyes of God and if they did not repent, then, after they had died, things would start to get very unpleasant indeed.

Seamus had to restrain Joker from voicing his opinion, so Joker contented himself with putting his fingertips to the tip of his thumb and showing the protesters the universal sign of the wanker.

Once inside, they found a booth close to the bar and Seamus sat down while Joker went off to get the drinks. When he returned, he sat down and looked around him.

"I'm a wee bit disappointed," he told Seamus.

"Why?"

"Well, I don't know what I was expecting," said Joker, "but these people are all just sitting around being dead boring."

"What else would they be doing?" Seamus asked with some amusement, though, in truth, he hadn't known what to expect either.

"I don't know," said Joker thoughtfully. "Maybe I was expecting a wee bit more flamboyance, you know? A bit more pizzazz, a bit more *joie de vivre.*"

"You thought they'd all be in drag, didn't you?"

"No, no, it's not that," Joker insisted, passing a cigarette to Seamus. "Well … you know, maybe a bit."

Seamus rolled his eyes as he lit his cigarette. He looked around. Everything did indeed appear to be perfectly ordinary, and he wondered if he too felt disappointed. When he looked a little closer, though, he could spot a few obvious differences. On the dancefloor men were dancing with other men, and then it suddenly hit him. These men were gay. They were gay men. And *he* was a gay man. He felt almost sick with nerves. He was a gay man in a room with other gay men and he had no idea what he was supposed to do.

"See anybody you fancy?" asked Joker.

"What?"

"You're sussing out the talent, aren't you? What about your man over there? He looks like a bit of a ride."

"Jesus Christ, Joker," said Seamus, gulping down his pint. "Stop fucking pointing."

"Fuck, I think I might be in there," Joker exclaimed. "That would be funny, wouldn't it?"

Seamus was squirming as the reality of the situation began to sink in. He stared at the table, thankful that, apart from the odd curious glance, no one seemed to be paying him much attention.

"These bloody pints don't last as long as they used to," Joker moaned, holding up an empty glass. "Do you want another one, Seamus?"

"No, Joker, I'm okay. You go ahead." Seamus was beginning to regret the whole thing. He felt out of his depth. He felt like an imposter, an intruder. He had no right to be here, in this place where everyone was smiling and confident and self-assured.

"The barman likes my shirt," said Joker on his return from the bar. "*Very sexy*, he said. And some other fella called me *Darling*. I must say, they seem like a friendly bunch."

Seamus felt a sudden surge of gratitude that Joker had come along with him tonight. It could be just a normal night out, he thought. No pressure. He could simply spend the rest of the evening drinking and chatting with his friend, and feel under no obligation to do anything else. He began to relax. It could turn out to be a good night, he reckoned. Just a couple of old mates, out on the beer on a Saturday night. You could always rely on your mates. He turned to Joker who was resting the back of his head on the plush upholstery of the seating. He was snoring loudly.

Seamus stared in disbelief. This had never happened before. He could not recall a single occasion when Joker had passed out in a bar while the bar had still been open.

"Is your boyfriend okay there?"

"What?" Seamus turned to see a concerned young man with wispy red hair gesturing at Joker. "Um, yeah, he's just … oh, he's not my boyfriend," Seamus said hurriedly, "He's my …" *My what?* he thought. *My chaperone?* "He's just a friend," he said finally.

The red-haired guy smiled. "Bit of moral support?"

"What?"

"Well, I haven't seen you here before and you were looking a wee bit nervous."

"Um, yeah," Seamus stammered, "I suppose so, yeah."

"I'm Alan, by the way," Alan leaned over to shake hands.

"Um, Seamus," said Seamus.

Alan smiled. "Do you mind if I join you?"

Joker was leaning heavily on Seamus as they both stumbled along the Dunbar Link on their way to Joker's flat. Gary had arranged to stay with Rosie for the night, so Seamus was going to stay in Gary's room to save having to get a taxi back to Ardoyne.

"We showed them, didn't we Seamus?" Joker slurred. Alan had gone by the time Joker had woken up and Seamus had decided not to mention him. On waking, Joker had picked up his pint and had simply carried on as if nothing had happened. "We showed them gays, didn't we? They won't mess with us again in a hurry."

"Isn't that missing the point?" asked Seamus, trying to keep Joker walking in a straight line.

"You're right, you're just fucking right, me old mucker," said Joker, patting Seamus on the chest. "I've missed more points than you've had hot dinners."

"I don't doubt it."

Joker then lifted his face to the sky and, to the dismay of Seamus, began to sing.

"*Ooh…ooh… Carol, I am but a foo…ooo…oool.*" It was sung with passion and heart, but with no discernible ability. Joker then seemed to forget the song as he stared at the night sky.

"Fuck me!" he exclaimed in wonder. "Look at the size of the moon!"

Seamus followed Joker's gaze. "That's the Albert Clock," he said.

"What? Oh fuck, so it is," said Joker, and then he giggled. "I'm fucking hammered."

"I hadn't noticed," said Seamus untruthfully.

"*Daaarling, I love youuu, though you treat meee cruuueeeel…*" Joker sang with obvious feeling, but soon the cacophony petered out and he fell silent, becoming almost morose. "Do you remember Carol, Snatter?" he asked. "Do you remember? She was class, wasn't she?"

"Of course I remember Carol," said Seamus. "How could anybody forget Carol?" When Seamus had first met Carol, his cautiously emerging sexuality had almost been sent scuttling back to the closet, slamming the door closed behind it. "How is she these days? Have you heard at all?"

"Oh, she's gone," Joker told him. "Gone far, far away." He drunkenly waved his arm in the direction of far, far away.

Seamus remained silent, lost in his own thoughts. Joker was enigmatic enough at the best of times, but when he was this inebriated it was wise not to get too involved. They stumbled on through the night.

When Seamus finally managed to pour Joker into bed, he went into Gary's room and lay down. He reached into his pocket and pulled out the little scrap of paper that had Alan's phone number written on it.

Staring at it, as he played it around between his fingers, he could feel his heart beating with anticipation. And exhilaration. And fear.

TEN

His companions were getting up to go, but Michael McClelland remained seated. He watched his associates shuffle out with the rest of the Kitchen Bar's lunchtime crowd and then sat back and rubbed his eyes. He had a few moments to himself before his next appointment and he took the time to dwell on his growing sense of unease.

It seemed to him that there would always be one more score to settle. There would always be someone who needed to be put in their place, taught a lesson, forced to show respect. It would never end, he realised, and he sighed as he sipped his wine.

The macho posturing and endless retributions were beginning to wear him down and, as he thought more about the future, he was learning to despise the life he led. He had started to hate the secretive dealings and the single-minded thugs with whom he was forced to mix. He hated the snobbish condescension of his neighbours, the constant police harassment, the hypocrisy of the paramilitaries. He hated the need to keep to the shadows, knowing he would never be accepted by the 'legitimate' business community. He hated telling his wife to be more discreet with their wealth and – perhaps more than anything – he hated his bloody nickname.

Throughout Belfast, especially among certain elements of society, he was known simply as Sticky Mickey, and he cringed every time he heard it. Still, he soberly reflected, in his line of work it was best to keep a low profile. Better to remain anonymous behind an embarrassing nickname than to have your own name bandied around the streets.

Thinking of it led his thoughts to what his line of work actually was and how he had ended up in such a profession.

He preferred to think of himself as a businessman, but how did others see him? As a thief? He was more than that. A dealer in stolen goods? He was more than that too. A gang boss? A criminal? A hood? He supposed he was all of these things, but wasn't there something more to him – more to his life – than all of that?

And how was it, he wondered, that he had ended up like this? As a child his small stature had prompted some people to suggest he could be a jockey, but he was not a great lover of horses. In fact, one time, during a school visit to riding stables in north Down, he had been bitten on the arm by a horse and had since developed a passionate hatred for the vicious, four-legged bastards that would likely be frowned upon at the Jockey Club.

Not that Michael would dream of trying to link one traumatic event in childhood to his drifting into a life of crime as a teenager, though he could imagine some psychologist, or psychiatrist somewhere drawing all sorts of excited conclusions, while trying to shoehorn in abandonment issues or issues with his father or his mother or some other such nonsense.

There were no dark, complex reasons for his involvement in crime, he decided. He was simply good at it.

At first it was easy money, selling goods that had mysteriously filtered through from the docks, but Michael had been shrewd enough to spot opportunities where others had seen only a quick profit. He had been shrewd enough to see that the real money could lie a little further down the line if you were prepared to make investments. He had been smart enough to stay below the radar and smart enough to keep one step ahead of the authorities.

Bit by bit he had built his empire but, he was now asking himself, to what end? The wealth and the power had always been enough for him. He had never craved social acceptance. Even his dopey wife had understood the wisdom of discretion and had curbed her natural instinct for showing off. Money had a tendency to compensate for a life on the shadowy fringe of society.

Now, though, Michael realised, everything had changed, and it had come from an unexpected quarter. It was his son, Peter.

When Peter had been born, a little under ten years ago, Michael had given him little thought. He was not planning on having much to do with a child who, he assumed, would grow up to be a typical brat, spoilt by a rich, soft-headed mother who would lavish upon him everything he demanded. Michael had seen it all before, and he knew that he couldn't, and wouldn't, be bothered to make any effort to prevent it. It was inevitable anyway, he believed.

Maddy, his wife, would now have something to focus on. The long dull days married to Michael would now have meaning, and Maddy would now be able to watch her own life spread out beyond the restrictive household. She could develop and grow as the child grew, and the child, Michael knew, would feel the burden of the extra life and would grow to resent it. He was wrong, though.

Peter was a joy. Michael would find himself rushing home as often as he could just to spend time in his son's company. Despite the heavy-handed soppiness of his mother and the initial disinterest of his father, Peter flourished.

To Michael's great surprise, the boy was selfless, clever, funny and polite. He charmed all who met him, and Michael's cynical old heart warmed with every smile and softened with every unselfish gesture from a child who seemed to give nothing but happiness.

And that was why Michael was feeling compelled to question his life. The thought of Peter, as he moved into secondary education, being teased, bullied or ostracised simply because of his father's 'business' dealings caused Michael genuine pain. Would he be the cause of his son's journey into adolescence being a nightmare of mockery and rejection? The idea that the light that Peter brought to everything in life could be dimmed because of him was agony for Michael and he had lately begun to explore his options.

Michael had a passion for cinema and he saw his life echoed in the struggles of Michael Corleone in the *Godfather* movies. His namesake wanted to distance himself from the criminality at the heart of his empire and to make the Corleone family business entirely legal and legitimate, and Michael McClelland harboured similar ambitions. Breaking free from the myriad of complicated, interwoven little ties, however, would not be easy.

Jippo, Michael's right hand man, entered the bar and sat down facing Michael. He didn't order a drink – Jippo rarely drank, and never during the day – but got straight down to business. They discussed a variety of pressing topics and upcoming dealings until Jippo finally brought up the current status of the ongoing Hegarty situation.

"Not a great deal to report from the Ardoyne side of things," Jippo told Michael. "I've still got a close eye on things, though. But I do have something you should be aware of."

"Oh?" said Michael, trying to generate some interest. He would rather not have to deal with this matter, but Jippo had been pushing it and he reluctantly could see the sense of it. Michael, Jippo and several of his men had been completely humiliated by Hegarty, and a guy called Anderson, at Christmas, leaving Michael with a fractured skull and Jippo with a broken nose, and in this business, Michael knew, reputation was everything. There would need to be some payback.

"Yes," Jippo replied, "Anderson was seen going into the Parliament, on the Dunbar Link, on Saturday night."

"The Parliament?" Michael asked, surprised. "That new gay place?"

"Exactly."

"Is Anderson gay, then?"

"Looks like it."

"I have to say I never thought he was the type."

"Well, you can never tell, can you?"

"Suppose not. Who was he with?"

"Seamus Green," said Jippo, "You know? He owns a shop in Bridge Street."

"Yeah, I know who you mean," Michael replied. He thought for a moment. "So, is there any way we can use this?"

"Not sure," Jippo said as he leaned back. "If anything, though, it may be something that we want to keep quiet about."

"Oh yeah," said Michael, "I see what you mean." His reputation, he felt, would be tarnished even more if it came out that he had been hospitalised by a gay bloke.

"I'll have a think about it," Jippo told him.

"What about that other gobshite?" Michael asked. "Lingfield, isn't it?"

"Gary Lingfield, yes," said Jippo. Gary Lingfield, along with Anderson, had been the original target when everything had gone wrong at Christmas. "It sounds like he's planning to move back to Ardoyne to be with his girlfriend. She's pregnant, by the way."

"Yeah, I know that," said Michael. He looked at Jippo. "Why? You're not suggesting we use that, are you?"

Jippo said nothing, but gave a tiny shrug.

"Jesus Christ, Jippo!" Michael shook his head. He had complete faith in his right-hand man but he knew that Jippo could be a ruthless bastard. Jippo had even suggested that they should make a move on their targets when they had recently all gathered together for a funeral, but Michael had instantly rejected the idea on the grounds that too many people would be around.

That was the excuse he had given Jippo, but on top of that it was a funeral, for God's sake, and Michael liked to think he still had some shred of decency.

"Anyway," he said, "there's no rush. I'd rather wait for exactly the right moment and do it properly."

"Of course," said Jippo. "You're the boss."

ELEVEN

Gary had been on the early shift and had arranged to call up, after work, to Ardoyne to see Rosie. She was looking at some brochures when he stepped through the door. Ellie was at work and Rosie was listening to some music on the radio.

"Jesus, Rosie!" Gary shouted. "Turn it down a bit, love. You can hear it at the end of the path."

Rosie turned down the volume on the radio and looked at Gary. "It's supposed to be good for the baby," she told him.

"What is?" Gary asked. "Being born deaf?"

"Music in the womb, Gary," Rosie explained. "It's the latest thing. It's meant to be very soothing. Relaxes the baby."

"I've never heard Motorhead described as soothing before."

"That just happened to be on when you came in," she said. Gary sat down beside her on the sofa.

"What's that you're looking at?" he asked.

"Hannah got me them," she said. "They're all about different computer courses you can do."

"Computers?"

"Yeah, Gary," Rosie sighed as she leaned back on the sofa. "I've been thinking that I'm going to have to do something, you know? We're going to need the money when the baby's born, especially if we're going to be getting some place of our own."

"Why computers, though?"

"It was one of the few things in school I was actually interested in," Rosie said. "I got talking to Hannah about it at the funeral and she said she'd look into some courses that would suit me."

"See anything you fancy?"

"Yeah, there's a couple of things that look really good. I mean, I won't be able to do anything about it till next year, but it's worth getting an idea, isn't it?"

"Yeah, absolutely," said Gary. He stood up and headed for the kitchen. "Fancy a cup of tea?" he asked.

"I'd love a cup of tea," she said. "There's some biscuits in the cupboard there as well."

"KitKats and Penguins!" Gary called from the kitchen. "Now I know how the other half lives. Me and Joker are happy with the odd Jammie Dodger."

"Oh yeah," Rosie shouted back. "how did it go with Joseph and Seamus the other night at that gay bar?"

Gary popped his head through the door. "I haven't seen Seamus," he said, "but Joker reckons it went well."

"Did Seamus meet anybody?"

"Don't think so," Gary answered, "but I would imagine that Joker would have scared anybody off. You know what he's like."

Gary went back to finish the tea. He returned with a plate of chocolate biscuits and then brought in two mugs of tea. He sat down again beside Rosie.

"What are you thinking of doing on Saturday?" he asked, taking a sip of tea and unwrapping a Penguin.

"Well," Rosie began, gesturing at her pregnancy bump, "I'm not going to be going out drinking all day, am I?"

Gary patted her hand in what he assumed was a gesture of sympathy. It was unfortunate, he thought, but it was hardly *his* problem.

"So, I thought," Rosie continued mischievously, "that me and you could go to early Mass together and then go over some of the wedding plans the rest of the day."

She watched with sadistic amusement the look of horrified panic on Gary's face. Her heart went out to him as she saw the confusion and the anguish in his eyes.

"But … but …" he spluttered.

"I don't think Ellie's working that night," Rosie went on, seemingly oblivious to Gary's turmoil, "so the three of us could just have a wee quiet evening in."

"Evening in?" Gary dumbly repeated, the words falling automatically from his mouth as his mind raced in frenzied alarm. "But … but …"

Rosie could hold it in no longer and shrieked with laughter. "The look on your face!" she screamed. "I'm only messing with you, Gary."

Gary gave a weak, uncertain smile as the relief flooded through him.

"I wouldn't do that to you, Gary," Rosie said, wiping the tears from her cheeks, "I just couldn't resist it."

Gary's heart had started beating again after the shock and he turned to stare at his fiancée. He did love this mad bitch, he thought, but there were times …

"No," she assured him, "I'm just going to spend the day with Ellie. Though we might call down the Short Strand to see Sheila. She was saying she's got nothing planned, so the three of us could just sit around slegging off men."

"Um, yeah," Gary put down his tea, as he felt his hands were still shaking, "that's a good idea."

"Because, obviously," Rosie teased, "women have got nothing better to do than to just sit around slegging off men."

"Um, no … no … of course not."

"Are you okay?"

"Yeah, yeah," Gary said, putting a hand to his chest to check his heart was still going, "just give me a minute, that's all."

TWELVE

Hannah was worried that she might be a sex maniac. At first it was just a tiny flicker of an image, a spectre in her mind that was gone before she realised it was there, but now it seemed to be growing in intensity and becoming ever more frequent. It had even happened at the funeral.

At a funeral!

She had been respectfully standing by the graveside, aware of James at her side and thinking of nothing in particular when, from nowhere, a thought flashed vividly in her mind. It was a stark picture of the tips of James' fingers. And they were stroking the top of her inner thigh.

It had come so suddenly and so shockingly that she was terrified she may have gasped aloud. A quick glance around, however, assured her that no one was staring at her. Her mind was still reeling as the service ended, and she was grateful for Rosie coming over to talk to her, giving her a chance to regain her composure.

It had happened again just now. She was in the library of the university's IT Department, supposedly studying, when she felt – physically felt – James' lips on the back of her neck as he unhooked her bra.

She closed her books in exasperation. It was impossible to study when you were a sex maniac.

She decided she had done the right thing when she'd told James that, for a while at least, they should stop seeing each other.

It had not been an easy decision for her to make because James was becoming an obsession. But then, that, Hannah told herself, was exactly the point. It would be impossible for her to go any further into a relationship with someone who could not see the truth.

Hannah may still have been struggling with many points of Scripture, but she knew that all of the things she'd been told to believe were true. It followed, therefore, that those things that others had been told to believe, if different, were clearly untrue. But there was so much ignorance in the world, so many differing beliefs, that Hannah began to wonder why God would allow it. And that had led her to think that maybe it wasn't God. Maybe it was Satan who was flooding the world with blindness. Which brought her round in a circle. Why would God allow Satan to have such sway over His Creation?

She prayed to God every night to let her understand. To give her just a glimmer of insight. But the continuing silence suggested that God wished her to make the journey using her own abilities, and she accepted the wisdom of such a strategy. It was cheating, after all, to be given the answers.

The casual discussion she had had with James over lunch had shaken Hannah and had made her see him in a new light.

She had always suspected, she supposed, that James had held beliefs that were antithetical to the true Word of God, but she had suppressed those suspicions because of … because of what? Because of lust? Her selfish desires? Temptation? Sin?

Hannah knew – knew in her heart – that the evil seed that would become the lie of evolution had been planted by Satan in the mind of the unfortunate man, Charles Darwin, but what she couldn't understand was why the idea had so strongly taken root. It seemed that God's Word was receding from the Earth, while Satan's lies were spreading unchecked and unstoppable throughout all the peoples of the world.

Her little church group was doing its best to stem the tide of wilful ignorance, but it seemed an impossible task. Hannah was able to see for herself the insidious rise of secularism, of humanism, of atheism, of sheer disbelief in everything that was true, and she despaired that God was allowing it to happen.

She understood, of course, that she should never question His plan, but the fact she found it difficult to see even the simplest points of Scripture was leaving her deflated. She didn't even feel she could approach anyone in the Church about her concerns because she was embarrassed by her own ignorance. The elders of the Church, she felt sure, would be appalled by her lack of insight, by her inability to grasp what small children could happily absorb from the outset.

One of the things from Scripture that Hannah struggled to comprehend was God's omniscience. God was perfect. She knew that. That was easy. God was without flaw. And, Hannah also knew, He was all-powerful and everywhere at once. Nothing was beyond God.

So, why then did a plan that was conceived and executed by a perfect, all-knowing deity go so catastrophically wrong, right at the very beginning?

It was the fault of the serpent.

But God would have been fully aware of the serpent and the serpent's intent. God was omniscient.

It was because Adam and Eve had been given free will.

But God would have known exactly what they would do with their free will. God was omniscient.

God got angry by the actions of Adam and Eve. God got *angry*? But God was omniscient. He would have foreseen these events, so why would He be surprised enough to get angry?

Hannah knew that all of those parts of Scripture that she perceived as contradictions were deliberately shrouded to test her comprehension. Enlightenment required effort, dedication and focus, and that was why she despaired. Because she was failing.

She could feel James' lips in the small of her back and she leaned forwards onto the desk, put her head in her hands, and shuddered.

She had laughed when James had told her how some people explain why dolphins can't breathe underwater. He had said that some people believed that the ancestors of dolphins weren't dolphins at all, but had walked on the land and breathed air. As she was laughing, however, Hannah couldn't help noticing that James wasn't.

"Surely *you* don't believe that, do you?" Hannah asked.

Jamesy shrugged. "Well, it's the theory that's currently accepted by the scientific community."

"Theory!" Hannah declared triumphantly. "It's just one guess after another, isn't it?"

"Well, to be honest," Jamesy explained, "that's sort of how science works. If you observe something that doesn't have an obvious answer then you make a guess, then you test that guess to see if it's viable. If it is, then it might lead to the next step in a process that leads eventually to an answer that's the most likely to be right."

"So," Hannah said dismissively, "just lots of guesses, then?"

Jamesy's analytical mind bridled at Hannah's rejection of the scientific method, but he suppressed his distaste and tried to carry on as diplomatically as he could.

"That's one way of putting it," he ventured, "but, you have to admit, the process seems to work. We never would have walked on the moon otherwise."

"Yes, okay," Hannah said smiling. "Don't you think, though, that if more people searched for answers in Scripture, then the world would be a much better place?"

"But surely Scripture can only provide answers up to a point," Jamesy replied. "Can it give you the square root of two, for example?"

It was Hannah's turn to bridle at Jamesy's attitude. "I was talking about meaningful answers," she said. "Answers to important questions about life and about the real things that matter."

"Of course," Jamesy muttered, "I should have realised."

"Are you being patronising?"

"No, no," he frantically tried to explain, "it's just that there's nothing wrong with broadening your horizons, is there? *Seek and ye shall find.* Isn't that in the Bible?"

"Yes," Hannah replied, a little uncertainly, "it's a verse in Matthew." The verse haunted her because she *had* been seeking. She'd been seeking for a long time. It was the finding part she was having trouble with.

"And that phrase doesn't restrict you to Scripture," Jamesy continued. "Does it?"

"No, I don't suppose it does," said Hannah. She looked troubled. "Okay then," she exclaimed. "Educate me! Explain your theory."

"What theory?"

"Evolution."

"It's not my theory."

"You know what I mean."

"Really, Hannah?" Jamesy sighed. "You want me to explain the

Theory of Evolution over lunch?"

"Why not? We're not in any rush, are we?"

"Okay," he said wearily, "but first you have to open your mind a bit."

"What do you mean?"

"Well, you have to accept the possibility that not every word in the Bible is literally true."

Hannah sat up straight. "It's the Word of God," she said. "How can it not be true?"

Jamesy pointed to her lunch. "You're eating a seafood salad," he said.

"Yes, but what does …? Hannah's words trailed away.

"Look, I've read a fair bit of the Bible," said Jamesy, "and doesn't it say in Leviticus that you can't eat prawns?"

Hannah gave a sigh. It was just one of the many passages in Scripture that she had problems with. Greg had once pointed to passages in both Matthew and Mark where Jesus dismisses the notion of any food being unclean, but then why would God set down instructions that He knew – God was omniscient – He would later rescind?

Greg also explained to her that certain passages of the Bible belonged primarily to a specific period in history and should not be transferred to modern times with any great significance. But then how was she meant to distinguish which passage to follow and which to reject? What criteria should she use? Leviticus describes both homosexuality and shellfish as abominations, but Greg had insisted that one description could be accepted and the other dismissed. On what had he based his conclusions, though?

Hannah had never felt comfortable with the discrimination of people based on their sexuality. She accepted that homosexuals who acted on their desires were sinners, but then the sexual act outside of marriage was a sin for everyone. If gay people were allowed to marry, she wondered, would homosexuality cease to be a sin?

It was just this type of quandary that was causing Hannah's anxiety over her failure to reconcile the words of Scripture with what she experienced in life. She hesitated to believe it might be Satan who was deliberately clouding her understanding, but then what else could it be?

"All right," she relented. "My mind is open."

"You sure?" Jamesy looked uncertainly at Hannah.

"Yes! Go ahead!"

"Okay then," Jamesy began, "I would imagine you've already heard what the basic idea of evolution is."

"Yes," Hannah told him, "we're all descended from monkeys, isn't that right?"

"Well, not exactly."

"But that doesn't make sense, does it," she went on, "because there are still monkeys around, aren't there?"

"You're talking about the modern species of monkeys, aren't you?

Well one modern species can't evolve into another modern species. That doesn't make any sense."

"That's what I'm saying."

"But it's not what evolution is saying."

"Okay then," Hannah said, exasperated. "What is evolution saying?"

"Evolution," said Jamesy, trying to collect his thoughts, "simply gives an explanation for how all living things on Earth have developed over billions of years. The progression can be traced in the fossil record and in the different layers in the ground. In the very simplest of terms, the most basic forms of life are found in the bottom layers, which obviously are the furthest back in time, and as we go up through the layers then the different forms of life become ever more diverse and complex." Jamesy glanced at Hannah. "Like I said, though, that's a very sketchy outline. You'd really need to ask a biologist if you want to get more details."

"So, what were Adam and Eve, then?" said Hannah testily. "Hamsters?"

Jamesy rubbed his forehead. "You're still thinking in terms of modern species," he said. "You've seen dinosaur fossils, haven't you?"

"Yes, of course."

"Well, dinosaurs don't exist anymore, and there are thousands of other fossils of creatures that also don't exist anymore and that's because over time they evolved into something else. We know this because we can see the progression of one form, in a lower layer of earth, to a slightly different form in a slightly higher layer of earth. Then the higher up the layers we go, the more different the form becomes. Evolution can be a very, very gradual process."

"But that's just the thing," said Hannah. "Where did all these billions of years come from? The Earth hasn't been around that long, has it?"

"Yes," Jamesy stressed, "it has."

"What are you talking about?"

"We know how old the Earth is," said Jamesy. He had known this discussion would happen at some point and he had not been looking forward to it. How was he supposed to convince someone that their ideas about the universe were not just wrong, but wrong by an unimaginable margin. "And it's a wee bit older than you thought it was."

"What do you mean by a 'wee bit'?" asked Hannah.

"About four thousand million years."

"Oh, come on, James," Hannah scoffed. "Seriously?"

"Look, okay," Jamesy conceded. He felt he'd gone as far as he dared. "I'm just letting you know what the mainstream understanding is, all right?" He knew he was ducking out of the argument, but he felt it would be wise to take it slow. One small step at a time.

"So, why would the *mainstream* come to an understanding as mad as that?"

"Well, that's another story," Jamesy said, "for another day. Do you want me to order you a coffee?"

"You're being evasive again," Hannah told him.

"I know," he said, "it's one of my more endearing quirks."

Hannah laughed and Jamesy breathed a sigh of relief. He wondered, though, just what the next step in Hannah's journey would be.

Hannah gathered her books together and stood up. She had decided to give up on studying for today, her thoughts were too jumbled. As she left the library, she convinced herself that she had been right to call James to tell him that she didn't think they should see each other anymore, for it had become inescapable. The whisper-soft breath she could sense on her skin could only be one thing.

It could only be the breath of Satan.

THIRTEEN

Nigeria, 1963

Benjamin arrived at his surgery in the afternoon and sat down with a sigh. He had spent yet another fruitless morning at the university trying to discern the reasons for the latest hold-up.

Everyone had been very polite, very courteous, but had told him exactly nothing, and he had returned to his surgery still no further along than when he had first arrived in Kano.

The task he'd been set had seemed simple enough when he and a team made up of various medical professionals and administrators had been briefed by members of the World Health Organisation back in Lagos.

They were required to open up a new medical department at the university in Kano that would eventually serve as a template for similar faculties to be set up all over the North. The people of the North, however, seemed to have other ideas.

What Benjamin had gathered from his discussions with Odi was that this was to be expected. The people of the North, Odi had told him, had a distinct character from the people who inhabited the other regions of Nigeria. The majority of the North was formed by the Hausa-Fulani people who had been drifting southwards for centuries from their origins far to the north of Nigeria's current border, bringing with them their religion of Islam.

Nigeria, Benjamin was coming to understand, was a country in name only. Like many countries in Africa, Nigeria's borders had been drawn by Europeans with no regard for existing tribal boundaries, and had thrown together a host of different peoples, tribes and traditions. The country had three distinct regions: the North, which had the largest geographical area; the West, which was actually in the south-west, and which was where the capital, Lagos, was situated and was home mostly to the Yoruba people; and the East, actually in the south-east, where the majority of people were Igbo. The south coast of Nigeria formed the southern border of both the West and the East and held the country's sea ports; Lagos in the West and Port Harcourt in the East.

"So you see," Odi cheerfully explained, "we have the Hausa in the North, the Yoruba in the West and the Igbo in the East. Simple, you see?"

Adanna snorted loudly from her seat at the kitchen table. They were in her and Odi's small apartment in Sabon Gari. She sat reading at the table while Odi and Benjamin were in the lounge area on the other side of the room.

"Did you say something, my sweet?" Odi called to her. He smiled and winked at Benjamin.

"You are the only thing here that is simple," Adanna said. "Have you forgotten the Ebu, the Ouguri, the Bashiri, the Tiv, the –"

"Yes, yes, yes," Odi waved his hand impatiently and looked at Benjamin. "My beautiful girlfriend is pointing out that, yes, there are many tribes besides the Hausa, the Yoruba and the Igbo, but my point is this, you see," he leaned closer, "my point is that we are all Nigerians, and the –"

"Ha!" exclaimed Adanna.

"I fear my delicate flower may be developing an ailment of some sort," Odi told Benjamin. "Did you cough, my cherub?"

Adanna stood up and walked towards the lounge area. She had an intensity that Benjamin found unnerving.

"We are all Nigerians, do you say?" she asked, not expecting an answer. "Then why must we live in Sabon Gari, eh? If we are Nigerians and the Hausa are Nigerians, then why do we live in the strangers' quarter? Why can we not live where the Hausa live? Why are Igbo children not allowed to go to Hausa schools? Are we unclean?"

"Of course not, my beloved," Odi grinned, "but you know that the Hausa have their traditions just as we have ours. They are a proud people and they like to do things their own way." Odi turned again to Benjamin. "It's just what I was telling you," he said. "I think you will find it very difficult to make your changes at the university. The Hausa do not like change, you see. They are very set in their ways. Not like the East now. The East is very different. We Igbo demand to be educated, you see. We must always be learning. You will find more schools in the East than in all of the rest of Nigeria."

"Is that true?" Benjamin asked.

"It is probably true," said Odi with his habitual grin. "There is a distinct possibility that it is true."

Adanna sat on the arm of Odi's chair. "Perhaps," she said to Benjamin, "you should have gone to the East to set up your medical school. You would have found it much easier there."

"Maybe," said Benjamin, "but I've been sent to Kano, so I have no choice but to do what I can here, in Kano."

"But didn't you say," Odi interjected, "that other members of your team have already left Nigeria? They have given up, isn't that right?"

"Maybe they aren't as stubborn as I am," said Benjamin smiling. "But, yes, some of my colleagues have been reassigned to other projects, but I believe it is only until the issues at the university have been resolved."

"*If* those issues are resolved," Adanna said.

"Oh, I'm sure they will be," Benjamin replied, "and in the meantime I have the surgery to keep me busy."

"How are things going at the surgery?" Odi asked him.

"Fine," said Benjamin, "It gets busier every day."

"Do you have many Hausa patients?" asked Adanna.

Benjamin thought about it. "Actually, no," he said. "Now that I think about it, most of my patients are from Sabon Gari."

"You see!" Adanna declared firmly. "It is like I told you. The Hausa do not trust strangers."

Benjamin was feeling nervous as his final patient of the day left the surgery. The receptionist at her desk offered to lock up for him, but he told her she should just go on home as he had a few things in his office he needed to see to.

When she had gone, he went back to his office and sat at his desk. He felt like a schoolboy waiting to go on a date that his friends had arranged for him.

Odi, a telecommunications engineer, had talked with some of his Hausa workmates and had discovered that the girl Benjamin liked was called Jamilah and that she was the daughter of a Kano haulage contractor.

Zara worked as a secretary and was able to make use of a network of other secretaries in the town to make contact with Jamilah and to see if she would be interested in meeting with a handsome Egyptian admirer. It turned out that Jamilah had already noticed the exotic young doctor who would cast furtive glances in her direction as she walked back from the market every day, and arrangements were made for them to meet at a nearby park.

Benjamin felt embarrassed by all the infantile zeal involved on his behalf but still he could not deny his own childish excitement at the prospect of finally speaking to Jamilah. He changed into the crisp, short-sleeved, white shirt that was hanging in his office and, when the specified time approached, he locked up the surgery and walked along Abuja Road to the little park, where he sat down on a bench and waited.

He was not waiting for very long when he saw Jamilah appear from the other end of the park. She was walking with two friends, which Benjamin had expected. It would not have been seemly for a Muslim woman to approach a strange man unaccompanied.

As they got closer, however, Jamilah's friends held back, giggling, to allow Jamilah to make the final few steps to the bench on her own. Benjamin stood and gave a polite bow, to which Jamilah gave a coy smile and a nod of her head.

"I'm very pleased to meet you," said Benjamin. "My name is Benjamin."

"Nice to meet you. I am Jamilah."

"Would you like to walk with me for a while, Jamilah?"

Jamilah smiled again and nodded her assent, so they walked side-by-side along the dusty path that meandered around the park.

"Tell me about yourself," Benjamin suggested. He was beginning to feel a nervous exhilaration to be actually walking alongside the beauty that had been distracting him almost since he had arrived in Kano. She was even more beautiful up close, he thought.

"What would you like to know?" she asked shyly, before glancing back to her friends who were following a few steps behind.

"Anything at all," Benjamin happily replied. "What are your interests, for example? Do you have work that you do? Is there anything that you wish to do in the future?"

"My!" Jamilah laughed. "That is a lot of questions."

"Sorry," Benjamin said smiling.

"I have a stall at the market," Jamilah said after a while. "I don't make a lot of money from it, of course, but it is something that I like to do."

"That sounds very interesting," Benjamin told her seriously. "What sort of things do you have on your stall?"

"I sell jewellery. It is just silly stuff that my friends and I make when we have some spare time."

"You make jewellery? Then you are an artist," said Benjamin.

Jamilah laughed. "Not really. It is just a hobby, but we enjoy it all the same. We like to listen to music as well," she said, "especially the new music that is coming from England. Do you like music?"

"Yes, I like music," he answered, "but I'm afraid my tastes are rather more classical than popular."

"Have you heard of The Beatles? They are a wonderful new group from England."

"Yes," he said, "when I was living in England, everyone was talking about The Beatles." In Benjamin's opinion The Beatles did little more than make a lot of painful noise. "They seemed to be very popular."

"You lived in England?"

"In London, yes."

"I would love to live in England," Jamilah said. "I could go to see all these wonderful bands play whenever I wanted to."

"Well, there are many other things that one could see and do in England."

"Yes, of course," she enthused, "my father has visited London and he has told me of streets that are filled with shops devoted only to clothes, or to jewellery, or even just to hats." Jamilah laughed. "Is this actually true?"

"Um? Oh yes, quite true," said Benjamin, feeling a little distracted. Jamilah carried on discussing her love for popular music, for fashion and jewellery and shoes. She spoke quickly and without pause, allowing Benjamin little room for reply, and after a while his eyes glazed over. Closely followed by his ears. And then his brain.

After their first date, they went through the motions of several more polite and increasingly awkward meetings until Benjamin began to feel like someone who had been entranced by dancing patterns of sunlight, only to realise that, as a cloud passes overhead, he has been staring all the while at a blank wall.

He soon came to view Jamilah as a decorative wine glass that held no wine. Or a shapely violin that was lacking its strings.

Such comparisons, Benjamin knew, were unfair. He was sure that, in the right company, Jamilah would be a positive delight, but he knew that he was not, nor ever would be, the right company.

It came as a great relief, therefore, when Jamilah eventually fluttered away, distracted by the next shiny object that caught her eye.

Odi found this all highly amusing and illustrated the fact by throwing his head back in riotous laughter. Adanna looked at Benjamin with wry amusement and gave Odi a playful slap.

"Do not be so insensitive," she said. "Can't you see the poor doctor is broken-hearted."

"Yes, I can tell," laughed Odi, "by the huge smile on his face."

Zara was the only one who seemed distraught.

"Are you sure, Benjamin," she asked with a look of concern in her eyes, "that you are not upset?"

"Oh no, not at all," Benjamin was quick to reassure her. "I think it was good to discover so quickly that Jamilah and I are incompatible. I believe that it has saved me a lot of trouble."

Zara smiled. "In that case," she said, "I am very happy for you. Perhaps we should celebrate."

"This woman," Odi stated, suddenly very serious, "is a woman of great wisdom." He turned to face Adanna. "My beloved," he said, "would you do me the great service of going up to the bar and purchasing many beers so that we can celebrate the liberation of our great friend here?"

"My beloved," Adanna replied softly, lowering her gaze, "it is my humble and respectful opinion that the mighty lion that has captured my unworthy heart should get off his fat, lazy behind and go and do it himself."

Odi looked at Benjamin. "This is also a wise woman," he said. "Perhaps we should listen to the women."

Benjamin laughed. "I will give you a hand at the bar," he told his friend. They had found a little place in the middle of Sabon Gari, well away from Jamilah's normal route home, and as Benjamin followed Odi to the bar, he realised that he did feel liberated. He felt that he could now devote his full attention to his problems with an intransigent university, and his task in Kano could begin in earnest.

At the bar, Benjamin listened to all the voices of the crowd. There were some that spoke English, of course, but there were many conversations in Igbo, in Yoruba, in Fula, in Edo, all spoken in a host of different variations and dialects that was the sound of Sabon Gari, the stranger's quarter in the middle of Kano.

Sabon Gari was home to many of the tribes that were now fellow countrymen in the country of Nigeria that had only recently become independent from Britain.

They were now in control of their own destiny. All together. All Nigerians.

And, here in Sabon Gari, all strangers in their own land.

FOURTEEN

Sean knelt with his hands clasped together and touching his lips. He then pushed himself up and back to sit once more on the hard, polished wood. After a while he stood and rested his knuckles on the back of the wooden bench in front. His body was automatically going through the familiar routine of the Mass as his mind wandered onto other things. Looking across the aisle, he caught a glimpse of Gary standing beside Rosie and looking uncomfortable in his stiff-collared shirt and tie. Gary turned to see Sean watching him and gave an exaggerated grimace. Sean smiled, then turned to the front as the familiar old hymn began and everyone sang along.

After the Mass, the crowd of worshippers, smiling, laughing and looking their best, milled around in the grounds of Holy Cross, the pompous old chapel that gazed down, as if in disapproval, at the little streets of Ardoyne. Sean stood chatting with his parents and his sister, Siobhan, but took his leave as he spotted Gary and Rosie coming down the chapel steps.

"Hiya, Rosie," Sean said as he walked over to greet them. "Right there, Gary?"

"Hiya, Sean," said Rosie. Gary tugged dramatically at his shirt collar, then loosened his tie and undid his top button.

"Jesus!" he said. "How do people wear these things?"

"How's it going with you, then?" Sean asked Rosie. "You're looking well."

"Aye, I'm sure I am, Sean," Rosie said, pressing her hand to the small of her back, "but thanks for letting on. Those seats are murder on the back," she went on. "I feel stiff as hell."

"Pews," said Gary.

"What?"

"Pews," Gary repeated. "The seats. They're called pews."

"Jesus!" Rosie turned to Sean. "See what I have to put up with, Sean?"

"I'm only saying," Gary protested. "The bloody things are called pews!"

"You really put the 'dick' in dictionary, don't you, Gary?" said Rosie. "You trying to show me up in front of Sean?"

"No! Look, I'm just saying that –"

"All right, all right," Sean interrupted, laughing. "So, what plans have you got for the rest of the day, then, Rosie?"

"Quiet day," Rosie told him. "Ellie finishes work at lunchtime so we're just going to spend the day together. I'd rather be going out with you two, though."

"I'm sure you and Ellie will have a nice enough day together," Sean assured her.

"If you two can stop gabbing away there," said Gary, "We need to head on here."

"Yeah okay, Gary," Rosie grumbled, "I know you can't wait to get away from me."

Gary put a comforting hand on her shoulder. "It's good that you can see things from my point of view," he said. "It's why we make such a great wee team."

"Piss off!" Rosie said with a grin.

Sean and Gary walked Rosie round to Ellie's house, then headed off towards the Ardoyne Black Taxi rank.

"Where's Seamus, then?" Sean asked as they walked.

"Haven't seen him since the funeral," said Gary, "but he phoned the other night and said he'd see us in Lavery's."

"Is he working this morning?"

"Must be."

They joined the taxi queue and Gary pulled off his tie and stuffed it in his pocket. Sean gave him a glance.

"Everything okay with you and Rosie?" he asked.

"Yeah, dead on," Gary said, puzzled by the question. "Why?"

"Oh, no reason," Sean replied. "Just asking, that's all." He looked thoughtful. "You know," he said, "I've never called the chapel seats pews in my life."

"No, neither have I," said Gary. "It's still their fucking name, though, isn't it?"

So, what had he been expecting? Fireworks? A sweeping orchestral score? A choir of angels? Seamus walked through the centre of town, thinking about the night he had spent with Alan.

It was always going to be a memorable occasion, he thought, being such a new experience, but was it what he was looking for? And what, exactly, *was* he looking for? Was it love's great adventure he sought? Or was it something of a baser nature?

It had been an enjoyable evening, and Alan had been just what Seamus had needed him to be – relaxed and funny and understanding – but Seamus had always felt it would be nothing more than a brief physical interaction with a like-minded individual. And was that it? Was that enough?

Seamus stopped to light a cigarette and then smiled to himself. If some further research was needed, he decided, then that wouldn't be a problem, for if there was one thing that the night had confirmed to him, it was that he was definitely gay.

Any few remaining doubts regarding his sexuality had been dispelled and because of this he felt a new sense of liberation that was exhilarating in its unfamiliarity. He was now free to experience life on his own terms and to experiment with his own desires.

He felt a spring in his step as he strode along Great Victoria Street heading for Lavery's. There was a new confidence to his manner, and he enjoyed the sense of happy anticipation for the day ahead.

"What?" Claire was incredulous. "You know Tony?"

"Known him for years," said Bobby.

"Why didn't you say when I told you about him?"

"I'm not sure," Bobby told her. "Well, I wanted to make sure, for one thing. There's more than one Tony Maguire in Belfast, you know."

"More than one Tony Maguire who occasionally works in Dublin and supplies linen to the catering trade?"

"Yeah, okay, fair enough. Maybe I just wanted to see how Tone felt about the whole thing. You said he'd stopped getting in touch."

"Well, now we know why, don't we?"

"Yeah, we do." Bobby had explained to Claire that Tone had backed off once he realised that Claire and Bobby were involved.

"Very noble of him," Claire said bitterly.

"Well, it sort of is, isn't it? And anyway, at least you know it had nothing to do with you."

"What did he say, then?"

"He said he'd be in touch."

"Oh great," said Claire, "I can hardly bloody wait." She was trying to feign anger, but her sudden burst of happiness was thwarting her efforts and she knew she could never fool Bobby.

"Are you sure you don't want to come along today?" Bobby asked her. They were in Bobby's flat in Belfast's university area and Bobby was just about to head out for the day.

"No, I can't," Claire said, picking up her bag, "I said I'd call up home today."

Bobby walked her out to her car, gave her a hug, and watched her drive off. He then turned and set off in the opposite direction. Towards Lavery's.

You'd better behave yourself today, Joker warned his brain. He was looking in the bathroom mirror as he got ready for the day ahead, but he was bothered by his muted sense of excitement. He would normally be hopping eagerly from foot to foot on a morning such as this, but his mood today was sanguine, almost sombre.

Still, he reckoned, he knew of a perfect remedy for such despondency and, besides, there was always the secret idea that he was planning to unveil. That should generate some interest, he decided.

The thought of it seemed to cheer him and, as he checked his pockets for keys, wallet and cigarettes before leaving the flat, he felt his mood begin to brighten and the prospects of the coming day began to assume the significance that he would normally have expected.

If only his brain would stop nagging him, he thought. If only for just one day.

Tone had called round to see his mother, but was surprised to see her getting ready to leave the house.

"Are you going out again?" he asked as she pulled on her coat.

"Yes, I am," she said, annoyed by his attitude. "Why shouldn't I go out? You're going out today, too, aren't you?"

"Well, yeah, but ..." Tone wanted to say that he could go out because he hadn't recently buried a spouse, but he stopped himself. Although, if he were being honest, what he really wanted to say was that he could go out because he was young and vibrant and he had his whole life ahead of him, whereas she was ... She was what? Just hanging around waiting to die? Was that what he believed? The thought was unworthy of him and it was unfair because his mother was not old. She had not yet turned sixty, so why shouldn't she go out? Why shouldn't she enjoy her life? Her husband's life had stopped, but hers was still going on, so why was Tone being so negative?

"Look, Anthony," his mother said, "life is too short. Your daddy dying showed me that. Donal too, for that matter."

"What did Donal say?"

"He told me about Donna. He says he doesn't think they're going to get back together, but you never know, do you? But I told him that even if it is the end of his marriage, then it doesn't have to mean it's the end of the world. Life goes on, doesn't it?"

Tone felt that his brother had given up on this life and was pinning all his hopes on there being another one, but he kept the thought to himself.

"So, where are you off to?" he asked.

"I'm meeting Jessie and Maureen round the club. There's a wee band on today, so, come on, Anthony, I don't want to be late."

Tone left the house with his mother and accompanied her as far as the Falls Road. He gave her a hug and watched her as she set off for the club. She seemed all of a sudden to be filled with strength and life and purpose, and Tone wondered at his feelings on the matter.

He needed a drink, he thought as he held out a hand to hail a Black Taxi, so it was lucky, then, that the prospect of such a thing was looming large.

The towering spire of the gloomy old Gothic chapel looked incongruous in the little street of shops and showrooms and offices, and the colourful clothes of the worshippers spilling into Donegall Street contrasted with the soot-blackened sandstone of a building that seemed to be sinking under its own weight.

Jamesy had gone back to his childhood parish of the New Lodge to attend Mass with his family and was now standing on the pavement outside listening to the chattering of his sisters and the gossiping of his mother. He and his father exchanged rueful glances, both keen to get away and to start the day's drinking.

Eventually, after much hugging and well-wishing, he was able to peel himself away and make his way through the town, heading towards the south of the city. Hannah dominated his thoughts.

He supposed that he shouldn't have been too surprised when she had called to essentially break up with him. Break up? Was that the right phrase to use? That would suggest they had been in a relationship and Jamesy wasn't sure if that had been the case. Apart from friendly hugs and the occasional chaste kiss on the cheek, there had been no intimate physicality to their … companionship?

Of course, he accepted, they had not been together for very long but, even so, Jamesy felt that it would have required a considerable amount of effort to penetrate Hannah's sense of religious propriety.

And that was why he shouldn't have been surprised that it had all ended so quickly. Hannah's beliefs.

Jamesy had initially been carried away by the strength of his attraction to Hannah, and had believed, naively perhaps, that love would conquer all. Nothing, he had felt, was insurmountable. There was nothing that couldn't be overcome by the sweeping grandeur of his newly discovered passion, but it had not taken long before he had come to understand the scale of the task confronting him.

He soon came to realise that Hannah's beliefs were so entrenched, so intractable and so deeply woven into the fabric of who she was, that his tentative attempts at chipping away at them were ineffectual. But then, he asked himself, what right did he have to chip away at Hannah's beliefs at all?

Who was he to judge which beliefs were valid and which weren't? Were his own beliefs, as Tone had once pointed out, just as irrational as Hannah's? Hannah's faith was certainly a lot more robust than his own, but then wouldn't that make her faith more valid than his?

Jamesy had never given his faith much thought. His Catholicism, for him at least, was more of a cultural experience than a firmly held set of opinions. So, did that make his faith less offensive? Less harmful? Less real?

He knew that the dry theological discussions tumbling around in his head were only there to distract him from the fact that he was in pain.

Nonsensical, irrational pain. He hated feeling this way. There was no physical reason for the clenching agony in his guts, or the overwhelming sense of despair and torpor that draped over him like a blanket. He had always despised the term 'lovesick' and now found himself desperately trying to rationalise the heaviness he felt when Hannah's face, electrified by her smile, came suddenly to mind.

Was that it, then? Was that the one great love of his life? And was it now doomed to come to a clattering halt because of irreconcilable differences over beliefs? It seemed unfair to Jamesy. Stupid and pointless and unfair, but he could see no way around it.

He tried to put the matter out of his mind as he reached Shaftsbury Square. Instead of taking the road to the left which would lead to his flat, he went to the right which would take him to Lavery's bar.

He forced himself to focus on the day that now beckoned. There was a time, he thought, when a Saturday spent in a bar with his friends would not have been considered unusual. A bar would be nominated, a time agreed, and everyone would arrive with the unspoken understanding of being in this together to the bitter end. Which would be, generally speaking, closing time. But no longer.

It seemed to Jamesy that life had managed to slither its insidious way into the little circle of friends, corrupting the group dynamic and pulling everyone in different directions. It was no longer usual to lose an entire day to drinking, carousing, cajoling and laughing. It just didn't happen anymore. Jamesy pulled open the door to Lavery's and was greeted with chaos.

Today was different, though, he thought. Today was Saint Patrick's Day.

FIFTEEN

He had never had any great desire to go to Dartmouth, but, he thought bitterly, it was a family tradition. His father had served as a midshipman on escort missions during the Battle of the Atlantic, while his grandfather had fought at Jutland.

If he delved back far enough, he supposed, then he would likely find some ancestor who had taken a three-decker through the French and Spanish lines at Trafalgar or had sailed with Drake into the Bay of Cadiz. The history of the Royal Navy was irrevocably entwined with the history of his own family so it was only natural that he should continue the tradition.

It had come as a bit of a shock, therefore, when the Britannia Royal Naval College at Dartmouth had quietly but firmly insisted that, halfway into his second year, he should pack his bags and leave. A shock to his parents that is, for as far as Simon Jippsen-Phillips was concerned, it hadn't been a shock at all.

Too many complaints to his superiors, he reflected. Too many little incidents, too many personal items that went missing, too many suspicions and accusing whispers, too many pointless misdemeanours that accumulated to the inescapable conclusion: he was not Royal Navy material.

From the window of his south Belfast apartment, he watched the river make its unhurried way to the docks and to the sea beyond, and he remembered how he had looked down, from his parents' back lawn, to another river in another life as he broke the disappointing news. He remembered how he had enjoyed his father's spluttering anger and his mother's speechless disbelief. He had relished their shock. Revelled in it.

He knew that the senseless acts of disobedience that coloured his time in Dartmouth could be put down to youthful rebellion, but he had hated the Royal Navy. He hated the idea of it, the stuffiness of it all, the stultifying aura of propriety and protocol. And he hated his parents for their blithe assumption that he would toe the line, that he would simply do what he was told with no questions asked.

He sighed as he sipped his tea and went to sit down. There were many things in his life that he hated, or had hated, or would probably hate at some point in the future, but there was one thing he hated most of all; he hated his bloody nickname.

It was only Michael who called him Jippo – no one else would dare – but it still grated. He knew that he had a lot to be thankful to Michael for, but he didn't feel that that should excuse such disrespect.

Simon had landed in Belfast over five years ago, after a spate of menial jobs on a variety of cargo ships, and had met Michael in a bar by the docks. They had discovered an instant rapport and Michael had taken him under his wing and had introduced him to the city's underworld, where Simon had thrived. He had often wondered if criminality, or malevolence, or whatever you wanted to call it, was something that a person is born with. He certainly could not point to a deprived upbringing, or any of the other standard excuses, for his own tendency to lean towards the less legal side of life, so was it just in his nature? Was it who he was?

There were those who would accuse him of dodging his responsibilities, of taking the easy way out to coast through life. If that were true, though, then he was working awfully hard to avoid working hard. Simon liked the fine things in life. His beautiful apartment was furnished with impeccable taste, he had his eye on a new Porsche, even the tea he was drinking was a special blend that was sent over from Fortnum and Mason in London, but, he understood, he could have acquired all of these things and more if he had simply followed the road his family had laid out for him. So why all the crime? He shrugged. Maybe it was just something he enjoyed.

He was now second only to Michael in the organisation, helped, he believed by the respect afforded by his English Home Counties accent and by his natural officer-class bearing – a family tradition and all that – but he could never feel satisfied; there were always things that needed to be done. He gingerly put a finger to the bridge of his nose. It still felt tender and misshapen, even though the attack which had shattered it had taken place months ago, at Christmastime.

That was something that would have to be addressed at some point, but he believed that he had that matter well in hand and was simply waiting for a suitable opportunity to present itself.

A few other tasks shuffled for priority in his mind, though there was one idea in particular that kept coming to the fore. He had given only brief consideration to this idea in the past but, just lately, he had been looking upon it with a cooler eye.

Plans began to form in his mind. Possibilities and consequences were played out and addressed, and a coherent strategy took shape.

He would need to involve someone from the organisation, he thought. No one significant, of course. No one important. In fact, it would be preferable if it were someone who was almost invisible. A nonentity. Someone completely pliable and easily coerced.

A halfwit, in other words.

He already had someone in mind.

SIXTEEN

Wee Paulie knew that wearing anything green today would mark him out as a Catholic, so he felt that the dark green socks he wore would be a concession to his heritage while still being subtle enough to go unnoticed in loyalist Tate's Avenue.

Mr Jippsen-Phillips had told him he could have the night off, so he told Gemma to get herself dolled up because she was about to get wined and dined.

"You *have* to go out on Saint Patrick's Day," he told her. "I think it's actually the law."

"Where did you have in mind?" Gemma asked.

"We could go to that new French place on the Lisburn Road."

"Oh, very fancy," said Gemma. "It'll probably be expensive, though."

"Doesn't matter," Wee Paulie declared grandly. "Like I said, I'm becoming a bit of a big deal these days. Mr Jippsen-Phillips talks to me all the time, you know, and not just about work stuff either. He asks me about all sorts of things."

"As long as you're not getting involved in anything too dangerous," said Gemma. She had long ago accepted the fact that her boyfriend was a hood, but she felt that as long as Wee Paulie confined himself to those areas where the distinction between what was and wasn't legal remained a little hazy, then there shouldn't be a problem. And, besides, everyone had to make a living in some way, didn't they?

"Nah, me and Mr Jippsen-Phillips are above all that sort of stuff," he explained. "We leave all the dirty work to the goons."

"Well, in that case, I'd better start getting ready. I'm not sure I've got anything classy enough to wear to that French place, though."

"You'd look classy in anything," Wee Paulie said sincerely. He really knew how to turn on the charm, he told himself. Gemma laughed dismissively, though she was pleased, and she went off to get ready.

"I can't believe all the different places that are opening up these days," Gemma said as they walked, arms linked, along the Lisburn Road. "I can remember when I was a kid there'd just be a chippy, and that would be about it."

"Aye," Wee Paulie agreed, "I know what you mean. Belfast has really taken off the last couple of years, hasn't it? It's starting to look like a proper city all of a sudden, instead of the ghost town it used to be."

"Why do you think that is, though?"

"Money!" said Wee Paulie with some authority. "It's all about money. The paramilitaries have had their day, you see. They're just a spent force these days and people are fed up with them, so now it's the hoods' turn to come forward. The future is ours for the taking.

"I reckon Mr McClelland and Mr Jippsen-Phillips have got big plans for the future, you know. They'll know exactly where the big opportunities are going to be, you can take my word for it. I would say they're really going to take off in the years to come, and guess who's going to be right there along with them."

"Ooh, let me think," said Gemma laughing. She knew she shouldn't get too carried away by Wee Paulie's wild flights of fancy, but maybe on this Saint Patrick's Day, as they strolled along to a fancy restaurant, looking their best, she could indulge him just a little.

She held him a little closer and allowed herself to dream that, just perhaps, the future really was theirs for the taking.

SEVENTEEN

"And the bar was still open?" Tone was asking.

"Yeah, that's what I'm saying," said Seamus. "The bar was still open, and there he was, out like a fucking light."

"Jesus!"

"I know!" Seamus exclaimed. They were trying to hold on to their place at the bar as the crowd jostled and swayed around them. "Do you not think he's been acting a bit weird lately?"

"More than usual, you mean?"

"Yeah, do you not think he's been a wee bit subdued, a bit quieter than normal?"

Tone glanced behind him to see Joker standing on a table. He was stomping his feet and clapping his hands while singing *The Star of The County Down.* Tone turned back to Seamus.

"Now that you mention it," he said, "I suppose he has been a bit subdued. What do think it is, then? Anything in particular?"

"Well, he was going on about Carol for a bit."

"Carol?" Tone finally caught the attention of one of the harassed-looking bar staff and was able to place his order. "You think he's still hung up on Carol?"

"Could be," said Seamus. "I mean, wouldn't you be?"

"Yeah, but …" Tone thought for second. "He hasn't said anything to me about it."

"I know, but this is Joker we're talking about. He probably doesn't even realise it himself, does he? He only mentioned her when he was totally out of it, probably doesn't even remember."

"So, what was he saying about her, then?".

"That's the funny thing," Seamus said, "he said she was far, far away."

"What?" Tone frowned. "Far, far away? What the fuck is that supposed to mean?"

"Who knows?"

The last two pints of the order were placed on the bar and Tone handed over his money. Once he had received his change, he and Seamus ferried the drinks back to their table.

"Get that eejit off the table," Tone demanded. "He's going to fucking spill something."

Joker, realising that beer had arrived, was only too happy to sit back down. He passed around some cigarettes and lit one for himself. The table served as a little island of relative calm in a stormy ocean of drunken, dancing revelry as a nation celebrated its conversion from one set of beliefs to another.

"Cheer up, Jamesy," said Joker. "You miserable wee bastard!"

"Yeah, so, what the hell happened?" asked Sean. "I thought everything was going okay with you two."

Jamesy took a sip of his beer and shrugged. "I don't know," he said, "maybe I was moving things a bit too fast."

Joker nodded with understanding. "Did you slip the hand?"

Jamesy gave Joker a look. "No, I don't mean that," he said. "I was just trying to open her eyes a wee bit, you know?"

"What do you mean?" Seamus asked. "Open her eyes? What, like in a sexual way?"

"What? No! What's wrong with you? There was nothing like that going on."

"Yeah," Bobby exclaimed, "this is my cousin we're talking about here, so just watch what you're saying." He turned to Jamesy. "So, when you say there was nothing going on, do you mean absolutely nothing?"

"Yes," Jamesy sighed, "there was nothing going on."

"Told you!" Tone declared smugly.

"What?"

"Oh nothing, Jamesy," said Tone hurriedly. "What was it you were saying?"

"So, what you're trying to say, Jamesy," Joker began, "is that, apart from you having a wee grope, there was absolutely no sex involved with you and Hannah? Is that right?"

Everyone at the table leaned forward. Jamesy rolled his eyes and took a drink.

"Well?" Gary prompted.

"Well, what?" said Jamesy. "There's nothing to say about it. We never had sex, okay? Is that what you wanted to hear?"

"You mean apart from you –?"

"No, Joker, there was nothing, okay? In fact, we never even …" Jamesy paused.

"Never even what?" asked Bobby.

"Well, we never even really had a kiss, to be honest."

Everyone stared at Jamesy. "So, when you say you've split up," said Tone, "you mean you were never really together in the first place."

"Not really," Jamesy replied glumly. "Not in the way that you mean anyway."

"So, what did you mean by 'opening her eyes', then?" asked Seamus.

"Well, I think it was at lunch the other day," Jamesy told him. "I was trying to explain the Theory of Evolution to her and I was probably –"

"Well, there's your problem," Joker exclaimed. "You've over-stimulated the poor wee girl. Jesus, it's no wonder she split up with you, is it? She probably couldn't handle any more excitement."

"She didn't take it well, then?" Tone suggested.

"Obviously not," Jamesy reflected.

"Pity, that," said Tone. "I actually thought she had a bit of potential. She didn't come across as being completely brainwashed, you know? So how much reality did you explain to her? Did you point out all of the mass extinctions in history that the Bible fails to mention."

"No, Tone," Jamesy said miserably. "I didn't want to overwhelm her with talk of asteroids or Ice Ages, you know? I just thought it would be best to take it slow. Although, for all the good it's done me …"

"Well, you know, Jamesy," Tone said decisively. "If you want to knock over a house of cards, then it's best to just open a bloody window."

"Well, Jamesy," Joker suddenly exclaimed, "you know what you could with, don't you? You know what we all could do with, don't you?"

"Bobby," Tone said, "could you not have a word with Hannah?"

"Don't see what it has to do with me," Bobby told him. "I don't really have much to do with that side of the family."

"Yeah, I know, but –"

"Did nobody fucking hear me?" Joker said loudly.

"What the fuck is he waffling about?" asked Tone from the other end of the table.

Everyone around the table looked at Joker.

"Thank you," he said, straightening up. "Well," he went on, "I suggest that we could all do with a holiday." He paused to observe the expectant faces around the table.

"You've obviously got something in mind," said Gary.

"I certainly do," Joker proudly announced. "We all knew that the World Cup idea was never going to take off, didn't we? Well, it just so happens that I took it upon myself to make alternative arrangements." He calmly took a drink to build up a little bit of tension. "I've been talking to Johnny Gee," he continued, "and it turns out that –"

"Who?" asked Sean.

"Johnny Gee," Joker repeated. "You know Johnny Gee, he's the –"

"He means Weasel," Gary said to Sean.

"Yeah, well anyway –" said Joker.

"Who's Weasel?" Bobby asked Gary.

"Weasel was a guy we knew at school," Sean told Bobby. "He was sound enough, like. Can't remember where his nickname came from, though."

"Aye," Bobby said thoughtfully, "nicknames are like that. I knew a guy once, from round our way, and he was –"

"Look, would you all just shut the fuck up and listen!" Everyone turned back to Joker. "Right," he said, "Where was I?"

"You were talking about Johnny Gee," Gary reminded him.

"Why are you calling Weasel Johnny Gee?" asked Tone. "His name's Kevin."

"Well, that's the thing," said Gary. "Me and Joker met him at –"

"Oh, for fuck's sake!" cried Joker. "Look, it doesn't fucking matter, okay? It doesn't matter what he's called. Johnny Gee, Weasel or whatever. He could be called Percy Fucking Titwhistle for all I care, but the point is –"

"Titwhistle?" asked Bobby. "Where the hell did that come from?"

"I think it was one of those old Ealing comedies," Sean said to Bobby. "*The Titwhistle Express* or something, it was called."

"No, Sean," Tone corrected. "You're thinking of *The Titfield Thunderbolt*, which starred Stanley Holloway. He was one of the –"

"Shut up!" Joker shouted. "Would you all just shut the fuck up, okay? Look, the point is this, right? The point I'm making is that Johnny … is that this wee mate of mine has got access to a beach-house in Spain."

That got everyone's attention. "A beach-house?" Gary asked. "What sort of beach-house?"

"Well, it's …" Joker hadn't been expecting the question, "it's, well it's, you know, it's just your normal sort of beach-house. It's got all the …What kind of stupid, fucking question is that? What sort of beach-house? It's in a tree, halfway up a bloody mountain, it's *that* sort of fucking beach-house!"

"When you say he has access," Tone began, "then what do –?"

"His parents actually own it."

"Well, this is starting to get interesting," said Tone, getting interested.

"Do you have anything specific in mind, then?" Seamus asked Joker.

"As a matter of fact, I do." Joker leaned forward and rested his elbows on the table. Everyone else leant closer. "What I suggest is this," said Joker. "We're all going to be off on the Monday and Tuesday after Easter, right? So, I say we take off the rest of that week and head off for a holiday in the sun. The accommodation's already sorted, so we just need flights and beer money."

Everyone was silent as they mulled it over. The idea, they all decided, had actual potential.

"And we can still use the stag do excuse, can't we?" Gary suggested.

"I don't see why not," said Joker.

"What does Kevin say about this?" asked Tone.

"Who?" said Bobby with a grin.

"Don't start that again," Joker groaned. "Anyway, you can ask him yourselves."

"What do you mean?"

"I told him to meet us here today, so he said he'd be along later."

"Well, I'm up for a week in Spain," Tone declared.

"Yeah," said Sean, "I'm free that week."

"And me," Bobby added.

"Count me in," said Seamus.

"Well," Gary joined in, "I'm hardly going to miss my own stag do, am I?"

Everyone looked at Jamesy. He looked at each of them in turn and shrugged. "I obviously have nothing on that week," he said.

"Right," Joker announced as he stood up. "This calls for a drink."

Johnny Gee arrived a few hours later and joined the company at the table.

"Right," said Tone, once a new round of drinks had been acquired, "first things first. There'll be no more of this Johnny Gee business, okay? It's either Kevin or Weasel. Your choice."

"Kevin," said Kevin.

"Kevin it is, then," agreed Tone. He passed his cigarettes around the table and the smokers all lit up. "Right, so," Tone looked at Kevin, "presumably you're aware that Joker only asked you to come along today because of his shamelessly mercenary attitude with regards to a beach-house in Spain, is that right?"

"Well, yeah, I'd figured that," said Kevin with a hesitant smile.

"Okay then," said Tone. "Now Joker has suggested the possibility of us all spending the week after Easter in this beach-house, and I want to hear what your opinion is on the matter."

"What do you mean by 'shamelessly mercenary attitude', Tone?" asked Joker, disgruntled. "Johnny Gee's a mate of mine."

"Kevin!" said everyone.

"Oh right, Kevin. Why does everybody keep changing their fucking names around here?"

"Never mind that," said Tone, turning back to Kevin. "Well, Kevin, what do you reckon?"

Kevin seemed a little nervous under Tone's interrogation. He shifted in his chair before answering. "Yeah," he said, "Joker's already talked to me about that week and it shouldn't be a problem. In fact," he went on, "it could actually work out well because my folks have just bought a townhouse in the area and I was supposed to go out there anyway to make a start on clearing it out. You could all give me a hand with it."

Tone nodded. He liked the sound of that. He had been feeling slightly uncomfortable with the thought that they would be taking advantage of someone with whom they would not normally socialise, just because of his parents' money, but now they would be doing him a favour and that, thought Tone, was something he could go along with.

"Sounds good to me," he said, and everyone agreed. "So, whereabouts is it, then?"

Kevin explained that the beach-house was on the east coast of Spain, just south of Valencia, in a place called Tavernes de la Valldigna. The beach and the town, where Kevin's parents had bought their new townhouse, shared the same name, though the town lay several kilometres further inland.

Kevin went on to paint a picture of uninterrupted blue skies, of hot sands and lazy, lapping waves, and smiling señoritas and sangria and ice-cold San Miguel, and, while outside the gentle tears of Saint Patrick lovingly washed the Emerald Isle, the thoughts and dreams around the table turned south to the golden glow of Saint James.

To where the scents of jasmine and orange blossom mingled in the warm air and danced to the chirping of cicadas.

To Spain.

EIGHTEEN

Nigeria, 1963

As the weeks wore on, Benjamin became increasingly frustrated. The authorities at the university had finally consented to the allocation of some buildings he could use to set up his new facility, but when he had gone along to inspect them he realised they were totally unsuited to his needs. They were little more than dilapidated cattle sheds, but when Benjamin had raised his objections, it was made to look like he was the one who was being unreasonable.

He had tried to explain the situation to his superiors in Lagos, but it was impossible to convey, over the telephone, the apparent lack of interest and the sometimes open hostility he faced from the university administration.

It also didn't help, he thought, that the whole initiative was so unwieldy. Co-funded and partly backed by the World Health Organisation, the project was hugely ambitious as it tried to encompass the entire continent in a spirit of cooperation between the established and emerging African states. Which in itself, Benjamin believed, was based on deliriously unfounded optimism.

There seemed to be no coherent guidelines to follow, no proper set of protocols to abide by in what was little more than a chaotic structure, seemingly riddled with in-fighting and corruption.

In fact, it was a surprise to Benjamin that he was still able to draw a salary, and that was probably why he had held on for so long in Kano. But his patience was beginning to run out. He was contemplating taking a flight to Lagos to try to find someone in charge who could tell him exactly what was going on, and if he could get no satisfactory answers there, then it might even be time to return to England.

This, he felt, would be a last resort, however, for he had given up his job there and had sold his flat, so returning to London would be like starting from scratch.

He had learnt that his old friend, Henry, had also left London to go and care for his ailing parents back in his hometown, so there was not much remaining in London to tempt Benjamin back there. And besides, he thought, he had come to love being in Africa.

These were the thoughts going round in his head when the door to his apartment shook with a furious hammering.

"Benjamin! Oh, Dr Maher! Please! Please!"

Benjamin pulled open the door and was surprised to see Zara standing, tearful and shaking on the threshold.

"Zara," he said as he led her inside and closed the door. "What is it? What's happening?"

"It is Odi," she managed to say between sobs, "I think that they will kill him."

"What do you mean?" Benjamin guided her to an armchair, while he knelt in front of her and held onto her hand. "Where is Odi?"

"We do not know," she cried. "He went out to try to help but he has not come back. Adanna is terrified. Odi has not come back and Adanna is afraid of what has happened."

"All right, Zara," Benjamin said soothingly. "Take it slowly. Try to calm down and explain what is going on."

Zara nodded, gave a weak smile through her tears, and tried to explain.

Whether the rumours were true or not was irrelevant. It was believed that a young Hausa woman had been attacked and raped in broad daylight by a gang of young men. According to the rumours, Zara told Benjamin, the young men were all Igbo from Sabon Gari and the Hausa were now looking for vengeance.

Zara explained that several groups of Hausa men had entered Sabon Gari and were attacking any Igbo that they found. As the Igbo tried to defend themselves, the violence had escalated and was threatening to engulf all of Sabon Gari, so Odi had gone to see if he could help to calm the situation.

"But he has not returned," cried Zara.

"Where is Adanna?" Benjamin asked calmly.

"She is in their apartment. She wanted to look for Odi but I said it was too dangerous. I said I would come and find you. I said that you would know what we should do."

"Yes, yes, Zara, you did the right thing." Benjamin tried to be reassuring but he wasn't sure what he was expected to do. "What about the police?" he asked.

Zara shook her head. "The police are mostly Hausa," she said, "and the crowds are too big for them to control. Oh, Benjamin, what should we do?"

Benjamin crossed the room and opened a window. Odi and Adanna's apartment was on the other side of Sabon Gari, but as he listened, he could make out distant shouts and muffled crashes and bangs. A sudden terrified scream chilled him.

He closed the window and turned to Zara. "Come," he said. "We must go to Adanna. We'll make sure she is safe. What are the roads like? Should I take the car?"

Zara, still shaking, took a tissue and wiped her face. "Many of the roads between here and Adanna's apartment are blocked with burning vehicles," she said. "I think it will be much quicker to walk."

Benjamin nodded and then led her by the hand as they tentatively walked outside and into the madness of the night.

Adanna was frantically pacing the floor of her apartment, alert to every sound that rose from the streets, when there was a loud knock at the door.

"Adanna!" Zara called. "Let us in! Please!"

She opened the door, and Zara and Benjamin hurried inside. Zara, weeping, threw her arms around Adanna.

"What is happening?" Adanna pleaded. "Have you seen Odi?" She then noticed that Benjamin was holding a blood-stained handkerchief to his left ear. "You are hurt?" she cried. The desperation and panic were clear in her voice.

"It's nothing," Benjamin told her. "Some people were just throwing stones, that's all."

"Oh, Adanna," Zara cried, "we saw many places that had been set on fire. There are Hausa everywhere."

"Did you see any police?" Adanna asked.

"Some," said Benjamin, "but they seemed to be keeping well back. I don't think we can expect much help from them."

"And Odi?" she begged.

Benjamin shook his head. "It is impossible at the moment," he said. "There are too many crowds, too much chaos."

"Then what do we do?" she demanded, suddenly angry. "We have to do something. We can't just sit here."

"We have no choice," Benjamin insisted. "It is far too dangerous to go outside. The best thing we can do for Odi is to be here when he gets back. We would not be helping if we went outside and got … and got caught up in the violence."

Adanna slumped into a chair. Zara sat on the floor and put her head in Adanna's lap.

"Trust me," said Benjamin. "The only thing that we can do is to sit tight and hope that this insanity will run its course."

As they waited through the long night, the sounds of the unrest came clear and harsh from the streets and ensured that their eyes remained open and their nerves remained taut. On top of the screams and the crackling flames and the gunshots and the shattering glass, came the constant chanting of the Hausa.

"Allahu Akbar! Allahu Akbar!"

Benjamin sat with his head in his hands and prayed for the dawn.

After a sleepless night, they ventured out to a to scene of destruction, with smouldering fires and broken glass everywhere. Benjamin suggested they all go to the police station to see if they could garner any information regarding Odi's whereabouts. They first made their way to Benjamin's apartment to pick up his car and then Benjamin drove them to the station on Sabon Gari's southern fringe.

Zara preferred to wait in the car while Benjamin and Adanna went inside. They were greeted with crowds of angry people from Sabon

Gari remonstrating with harassed police officers, demanding to know why the night's events had been allowed to rage unchecked.

Benjamin and Adanna made their way through the crowd and eventually encountered a senior official at a desk in the back. He appeared nonchalant and relaxed, and responded to Benjamin's enquiries about Odi with a wave of his hand.

"We are holding no one of that description," he told them.

"But, surely you must know something," Benjamin insisted. "It is most unusual for him not to return home all night."

"Then I suggest that you try the hospital," the official replied impatiently. "Many of the injured have been taken there."

"The hospital?" The thought had already crossed Benjamin's mind, but he hadn't wanted to voice his fears to Adanna. She stood quietly by his side as he turned to face her. "Perhaps we should try the –"

"Or you could try the market," the official continued.

"The market?" asked Benjamin, puzzled.

"Yes," the official said, "some of the sheds there have been allocated to hold the bodies."

Benjamin sensed Adanna physically weaken at his side. *Bodies?*

"Now, as you can see, we are extremely busy so if you could just …" Benjamin and Adanna were ushered outside and they slowly made their way to the car.

"Well?" Zara asked as they climbed into the front seats. Her cheeks were still streaked with tears. "Did you find out anything?"

"Odi is dead," Adanna said flatly.

"We don't know that," said Benjamin. "We will try the hospital."

They went straight to the hospital, but after more than an hour of desperate searching they could find no trace of Odi. As they walked back to the car, Benjamin insisted they should eat something before they continued their search. He found a stall and bought them all some roasted corn which they took back to eat in the car.

"You look tired, Zara," Adanna said, looking in the mirror. "You should go home to try to get some sleep."

"How can I sleep?" Zara pleaded.

Adanna did not reply. She took small nibbles of food and stared blankly through the windscreen, already resigned to what she would find at the market.

She spotted Odi almost immediately. He lay close to the end of a row of broken and disfigured corpses. Despite the mutilation inflicted on his body, Adanna could recognise the shirt she had bought him at this very market, the wine stain still visible on the pocket. She made her way calmly through the hysterical wives and daughters and mothers who were crowding the shed, and identified Odi to one of the officials trying to impose some order.

Benjamin caught up to Adanna and stared in disbelief at the body of his friend. None of it seemed real.

"Very well, then," the official was telling Adanna, "but you must take him. You cannot leave him here."

"Adanna," Benjamin put his hands on Adanna's shoulders and looked into her eyes. She gazed at him without seeing. The light in her eyes was gone. "Adanna," he repeated, "I'm going to take you and Zara home, you understand? You must go home and try to rest. I will come back here and see to all the … all the requirements. Do you hear me?"

Benjamin led her to the car and then drove her and Zara to Adanna's apartment where he left them both to their grief and shock. He got back in the car and, resting his forehead on the top of the steering wheel, he began to physically shake.

Once he had calmed down, he started the ignition and, with a deep sigh, headed back to the market.

After the attack on the Igbo, all of Kano felt heavy with menace. It was as if the true feelings of the North towards the people from the East were no longer held in check and were now exposed like an open wound. Adanna and Zara, on returning to work, had both felt an unspoken hostility in occasional glances or deliberate stares from the Northerners of Kano.

Benjamin made all the arrangements for Odi's burial, consulting occasionally with Adanna, who had been behaving in a resigned, almost serene, manner since the day at the market.

As the arrangements were being made, Zara asked Adanna if it would not be preferable to take Odi back to the East for burial in the Igbo homeland, but Adanna had said no.

Odi, she said, did not have any family back in the East and, besides, he had always regarded himself as Nigerian.

"This," she told Zara, as she gestured all around her, "this is Odi's homeland."

There were few mourners at the graveside. Some of Odi's workmates had come along, though none of them, Adanna noted, were Hausa. A few of Adanna's friends and colleagues were there, standing with Benjamin and Zara, as the pastor said the usual words of condolence and consolation, and then, before anyone truly had time to process the fact, Odi was gone.

It was in the days that followed that Benjamin made a decision to leave Kano. It wasn't just the intransigence of the university that had swayed him; he had also been witnessing a rise in patients at the surgery who had been victims of random attacks in and around Sabon Gari. They had all been Igbo and had suffered unprovoked beatings from groups of young Hausa men who had begun to roam the area. Benjamin felt that someone should make a direct report of the incidents to the authorities in Lagos.

Adanna also came to the conclusion that she could no longer stay in Kano. Without Odi's salary she would have to find a cheaper apartment and, even though Zara had suggested she could move in with her, Adanna decided it was time for her to return to her family in the East. It had always been her intention to return there with Odi once they had made enough money in the North, but now she could see no reason for her to remain in a city that was now pulsing with an atmosphere of dread and persecution.

When the day came for Adanna to leave, Benjamin and Zara placed her luggage in Benjamin's car and they drove to the train station together.

"I cannot believe you are going," Zara said as she hugged Adanna on the station concourse. "And Benjamin will be leaving too. What am I going to do without you both?"

"You will be fine," Adanna told her. "And you have my mother's address so we can keep in touch." She turned to Benjamin. "Thank you for everything you have done, Dr Maher," she said, shaking his hand. "I don't suppose I shall see you again."

"No," said Benjamin, "I hadn't thought of it, but I don't suppose you shall. I'm not sure where I will end up after I've been to Lagos."

Zara wept as she watched her friend board the train while, beside her, Benjamin waved as he felt a sudden surge of admiration for the tall, stately figure who had unsettled him with her intensity.

Adanna found a seat, made herself comfortable, and then broke down in tears as the train took her south and east to the land of the Igbo, to her family and her people, and to where the Hausa could not reach.

NINETEEN

"Well? What do you reckon?" asked Joker. He was holding up a pair of swimming briefs.

Tone gave them his consideration. The thought of those tiny, fluorescent yellow speedos stretched over Joker's pasty skin was making him feel queasy.

"Yeah," he said, "I can see you in those."

"Really?"

"Yeah, you'd look class."

"Not sure about the colour, though."

"What, jaundice? You don't like jaundice?"

"Don't know if it would really bring out my eyes."

"Good point," said Tone. "You're looking for more of a bloodshot with a hint of nicotine shade, aren't you?"

"You're just taking the piss."

"I thought we both were."

Joker sighed and placed the briefs back on the rack. "It's important to make an impression on the beach, you know."

"I don't think you've got anything to worry about there," said Tone as they strolled down the swimwear aisle. "Not with your general demeanour."

"You think I've got a demeanour?"

"Well, it's more of a misdemeanour."

"What do you think of these?" Joker had stopped to look at a pair of shorts. Tone stared hard at the fluffy clouds and cartoon palm trees that were splashed all over the garishly coloured shorts, then turned to look at Joker.

"Seriously?" he asked. "Did you forget to bring your eyes out with you today?"

"You're not helping, you know," said Joker.

"Well, what is it that you're looking for?"

"Oh, I don't know," Joker said wearily. "I was just thinking I should maybe shake things up a bit for going away, you know? Go for a new image. A new *me* type of thing."

"And you think that looking like a wanker is the way to go?"

"Is that your idea of constructive criticism?"

"It is, actually, yes."

"Well, what have *you* got, then?" Joker pointed to the two items of clothing that Tone was carrying. "A blue T-shirt and a white T-shirt? Do you not think you've gone a wee bit too crazy there, you flash bastard?"

"What's wrong with these?" said Tone defensively. "These are classics! You can't go wrong with classics!"

"There's nothing classic about playing it safe. It just means you can't be bothered to make an effort, that's all."

"Look, just pick a pair of bloody shorts, will you? It can't be that difficult."

Joker picked up a standard pair of blue shorts. "These'll have to do," he said grumpily.

"Right then, are we done?"

"Oh, hang on," Joker said suddenly. "Now we're talking!" He walked over to a rail that held a row of short-sleeved shirts. "Now this is what I'm talking about."

"That's actually not a bad shirt," said Tone.

"Not a bad shirt? You're kidding me, aren't you? It's bloody spectacular."

"Right, okay then, just grab it and we'll go."

"You know what?" Joker was admiring the shirt as they walked to the tills. "They'd love this round at the Parliament. I'm actually going to feel sorry for all of you, having to walk beside me wearing this shirt. You're all going to look like a bunch of sad losers, aren't you?"

"Well, we all have our crosses to bear, don't we?"

"Is there anywhere else you wanted to go after Primark?"

"What, shopping wise, you mean?" asked Tone. "Nah, I think I'm all shopped out for the day."

"Yeah," Joker agreed as they waited in the queue, "I know what you mean, makes you thirsty, doesn't it?"

"It certainly does."

They walked with their shopping through the centre of town until Joker, realising that Tone had come to an abrupt halt, stopped and looked behind him. He could see Tone staring through the window of a café, and, curious, he walked back towards him.

"Fancy a cup of tea?" Tone asked him. It wasn't what Joker fancied at all.

"A cup of tea? What do you …?" He looked in the window. "Oh," he said.

Hannah thought about pretending she hadn't seen them, but it would have been pointless, as they walked straight over to the table.

"Hannah!" Tone cried happily. "And Greg too, my old mate. How are you doing?"

"All right there, Hannah love?" said Joker. "Right there, Greg? Solved any mysteries lately?"

"What?"

"Oh, nothing, nothing," Joker said as he pulled a chair over to the table. "Don't mind if we barge in, do you?"

"Actually, we were –"

"It's funny, so it is," Tone began as he sat down at the table, "but we were just talking about you, weren't we, Joker?"

"Were we?"

"We were just saying that …" A waitress came over and placed a teapot and two cups down on the table.

"Your food's on its way," she told Greg and Hannah, and then looked expectantly at Tone and Joker.

"I'll just have a cup of tea too, please," Tone told her.

"Aye, me too," said Joker. The waitress went off, and Tone carried on.

"We were just saying that it's a real shame that you and Jamesy split up," he said to Hannah. "You seemed to get on well together."

"I know," said Hannah, "but it was never going to work."

"Why's that, then?" Joker asked her.

"Well," she said, "I just think that we were too different. I don't think that James is able to accept the truth of the Bible."

"Yeah, he's a bugger for that, isn't he?" said Tone, slapping his knee. "I've always said that, haven't I, Joker?"

"No."

"I've always said that Jamesy's a real bugger for not accepting the truth of things."

Greg gave Hannah a quick glance. He seemed uncomfortable, which surprised Tone. Tone had assumed that Greg would relish any opportunity to confront the ungodly, but he looked as if he wished he were elsewhere.

The waitress appeared with a tray. She placed two plates of food in front of Hannah and Greg, along with tea for Tone and Joker. Tone paid for the tea and turned back to Hannah as the waitress left.

"You know what you should do, you know?" he began, but then Greg interrupted.

"It sounds to me that James, whether he's aware of it or not, is being influenced by Satan."

"Why would Satan want to do that?" asked Tone.

Greg gave Tone a pitying look. "Satan is a constant force in the world," he explained. "We have to be vigilant for any signs of temptation. It was lucky that Hannah recognised her tempter before it was too late. It's possible that Satan was trying to work through James."

"You've really got it in for this Satan character, haven't you?" said Tone.

"Satan was never meant to be a proper noun, by the way," Joker interjected, sipping his tea. "It's just an old Hebrew word that means adversary, so you may want to slip a wee definite or indefinite article in there somewhere."

"Oh, I'm sure Greg knows that," Tone said, looking at Greg. "The Bible even refers to an angel of the Lord as being a satan at one point, isn't that right? Although, it does depend on what version of the Bible you're reading."

Greg gave a dismissive gesture with his cutlery as he chewed his sausage roll. "It has become a proper noun, though, hasn't it?" he said.

"Yeah," said Joker. "Funny the way language evolves, isn't it?"

"The name isn't relevant anyway," Greg continued.

"No," Tone agreed, "but whatever you want to call him, I still think you're being a bit hard on him, you know. I mean, it's not as if he flooded the whole planet and drowned everybody on it, now, is it?" Tone realised he was getting side-tracked. "Look," he said, "I'm not trying to stick up for Satan – we all need our bogeymen, don't we? – I just wanted to make a suggestion to you, that's all."

Hannah looked up from the salad she'd been picking at. "What suggestion?"

"Well," Tone explained, "I reckon you should take Jamesy on at his own game."

"What do you mean?"

"Does it not bother you," said Tone, addressing both Greg and Hannah, "that the world seems to be moving further and further away from God? I mean, society is a lot more secular these days than it was a couple of hundred years ago, isn't it? And despite both of your valiant efforts, secularism always seems to be on the rise."

Greg eyed Tone suspiciously. "What's your point?"

"My point is that you should try to find out why that should be. You should make a point of learning about the stuff that's turning people away from God. You know, find out what it is they've been stuffing their heads with so you can combat it more easily. Know thine enemy, that sort of thing." Tone gestured to Greg with his cup as he lifted it to his lips. "Know thine enemy, Greg."

Greg, realising what Tone was getting at, gave a condescending smirk. "The Bible is very clear on that subject," he said. "In Ecclesiastes it states that *he who increases knowledge increases suffering*."

"Well," said Tone, turning to Joker, "that's certainly pretty clear, isn't it?"

"Can't get much clearer than that," agreed Joker.

"How do we get around that, then?" Tone pondered.

"We could do what everybody else does," Joker suggested.

"And what would that be?"

"We just ignore those bits of the Bible that don't suit us."

"You may be on to something there," said Tone, "and then we could find a bit in the Bible that does suit us, couldn't we?"

"If we were that way inclined, then yes, we certainly could."

"Like the bit in Proverbs that says, *get wisdom, get understanding*, perhaps?"

"Perhaps indeed."

"Wisdom and knowledge are two different things," said Greg.

"What about understanding?" Tone said, and then held up his hand as Greg was about to reply. "Look, I'm just trying to help you out here," he insisted. "Put it this way; if you want to argue with a cosmologist about the age of the universe, then wouldn't it make sense to be familiar with where his arguments are coming from?" He turned to Hannah. "I'm only referring to the cosmologist as a *he* for the sake of convenience."

"And because you're a bit of a sexist as well," Joker pointed out.

"Well yes," Tone conceded, "there's that, too."

Hannah smiled, while Greg gave a snort of bemusement.

"Are you suggesting I take a degree in cosmology, then?" he asked derisively. "Hardly very practical, is it?"

"No, Greg," Tone explained patiently, "but it wouldn't take much research to find out why cosmologists have settled on such a definite age for the universe, now would it? They haven't just plucked a figure out of thin air, have they? There's a reason for the conclusion they've come to and all you have to do is find out what that reason is, you see? Know thine enemy, Greg."

Greg shook his head disdainfully. Tone, however, was not bothered about Greg. As far as Tone was concerned, Greg was a lost cause, and so, despite directing most of his arguments to Greg, it was to Hannah that Tone was speaking.

"I don't see what difference it would make," Greg said. "It doesn't matter what the reasons are. If the conclusions conflict with Scripture, then the conclusions are wrong, and that's all there is to it."

"But doesn't it bother you that poor wee kids in school are being taught all these things that contradict what the Bible says?" asked Tone.

"Of course," Hannah replied, "it's terrible."

"Well then, don't you think it would be easier to discuss the things they're being taught if you understood what those things were? What harm can it do?"

To Hannah, what Tone was saying made sense. She had often wondered what it was that had made society in general decide to turn its back on Scripture. It couldn't simply be because some scientists, influenced by Satan, had led everyone astray with a few outrageous lies.

There had to be something seductive in those lies, something subtle and sinister that had driven a wedge between God's Word and His people, and Hannah felt a need to understand what it was.

"But you're a non-believer, aren't you?" Greg said to Tone. "So why would you care what we should or shouldn't understand?"

Tone shrugged. "I'm familiar with both sides of the argument," he said, "so I just don't think you can make a convincing case for your own position if you don't fully understand the position of the other side."

"It's a fairly transparent ploy, isn't it?" Greg suggested, pointing out Tone's fairly transparent ploy. "You're expecting us to just abandon the teachings of the Lord once we've been exposed to the *truth* of the scientists, isn't that it?"

"Not at all, Greg," Tone said, half-truthfully, "I believe that your faith is too strong for that, I really do."

Greg eyed Tone thoughtfully. "It isn't just a matter of faith, anyway," he said. "A lot of the claims made by scientists are just too spurious to be given any proper consideration in the first place."

"Well, how do you know that?"

"Because I *have* done the research," Greg explained. "At least I've done enough to know as much as I need to. For example, I know that scientists don't have a clue about how the universe began, do they?"

"I wouldn't say they don't have a clue," said Tone. "The most widely accepted theory at the minute is the inflationary model of the –"

"You mean the Big Bang Theory?" sneered Greg.

"That's the popular name for it, yeah."

"Well, don't you have to admit that it's nothing more than a guess? It's just the best guess that scientists have, isn't it?"

"That's one way of putting it, I suppose."

"Well then," Greg declared, "that's where their argument collapses, isn't it? You see, I don't have to *guess* how the universe began, because I already *know* how it began."

"You do?"

"Of course," Greg smugly went on. "Everything was created by God in six days in –"

"Why did it take him so long?" asked Joker.

"What?"

"Well, if this God of yours is so –"

"That's not the point, Joker," Tone said excitedly. "The point is that Greg here is about to make us all very rich."

Greg narrowed his eyes as he regarded Tone.

"Right, Greg, if you know how the universe began," Tone exclaimed, leaning forward, "this is what you should do. You first need to gather all of the evidence that you've accumulated to support your hypothesis, along with the results of any experiments you may have carried out, and then you need to assemble it all together into a manuscript that you can then submit to the relevant journals for a rigorous peer review.

"Then, once your findings have been verified and accepted, you'll become the most famous person in all of history. I would imagine the Nobel Committee will be tripping over themselves to bestow every award that's going."

"Yes, well," Greg said, wiping some ketchup from his mouth with a napkin, "it's easy to be sarcastic, isn't it?"

"I thought I was being facetious," said Tone.

"Anyway," Greg pushed his chair back from the table and looked at Hannah, "I think we need to get going here."

They both got up, gave some polite nods to Joker and Tone, and made their way to the door.

Joker watched them leave and then turned back to Tone. He stretched, raising his arms, and idly rubbed the stubble on the top of his head.

"If it's any consolation, Tone," he said, "I thought you were being facetious, too."

TWENTY

It was just like when they were kids, thought Seamus. They would often, as children, find themselves shuffling reluctantly along to stand before an authority figure, steeling themselves to face the consequences after Gary's recklessness had, once again, dragged them both into trouble.

"I still don't see why I have to come," he moaned.

"Well, it's safety in numbers, isn't it?" said Gary. "I wanted Sean to come too, but he told me to fuck off."

"At least you know who your friends are," Seamus told him as he wondered why it hadn't occurred to him to use Sean's tactic. *That's the trouble with us gays*, he grumbled to himself. *Too bloody nice!*

"It'll catch her off-guard, you see," Gary went on. "We can come at her from different directions, so she won't know where to turn."

Gary had earlier called to Seamus' house, and they were now walking the short distance to Rosie and Ellie's place.

"It won't be that bad, will it?" Seamus asked nervously. "You make it sound like we're trying to corner some sort of angry bear."

"You're not scared of her, are you?"

"What sort of question's that? You know I'm fucking scared of her."

"Oh, you worry too much," said Gary. "Anyway, she's carrying a lot of weight at the minute, so she can't move all that fast."

They stopped at the garden gate and Gary turned to Seamus. "Right," he said, "let me do the talking. I'll just work my way up to it, gently like, and then you can weigh in and back me up. Okay?"

"Okay," Seamus mumbled, unconvinced. The squeal of the gate, as Gary pushed it open, made him jump. "Fuck!" he hissed.

"Yeah," Gary agreed thoughtfully, "I should probably oil that at some point."

They walked up the path and Gary opened the door to the front lounge. It came as a surprise to see his sister there.

"Oh, here's that useless fucker now!"

"Karen?" Gary stepped inside, followed by Seamus. "What are you doing here?"

"I don't need a fucking reason, do I?" said Karen. "I'm here to see Rosie."

Gary's mind began to race. This was an unexpected complication. There were two of them now. It would have been much simpler to tackle Rosie on her own, he thought, especially as Karen, who was known to be quite opinionated, could tip the delicate balance of Rosie's fickle moods. This, he realised, would require a lot more tact and subtlety than he had planned to employ.

"Well, how's it going?" he said cheerfully as he took a seat on the sofa beside Rosie. Seamus sat down on the chair by the window.

"Oh, the usual," Rosie replied. "Hiya, Seamus."

"All right there, Seamus?" said Karen.

Seamus panicked. "Gary wants to go to Spain!" he shouted. Gary stared at him in disbelief.

"What?" Rosie said.

Gary jumped to his feet. "I'm going to put the kettle on," he declared. "I don't know what the fuck he's talking about."

"What was that, Seamus?" asked Karen.

"Who wants tea?" said Gary, heading for the kitchen.

"You just hold your fucking horses!" Karen said to Gary. "What was that about Spain?"

"It's all *his* idea!" Gary exclaimed, pointing to Seamus.

"What?" cried Seamus.

"What the fuck is all this about Spain?" Rosie said loudly.

"He wants me to go Spain with him," Gary explained, looking accusingly at Seamus. "But I said I couldn't go. I've got too much to do here, I told him."

Rosie and Karen both turned to Seamus who was squirming in his seat and staring hatefully at Gary.

"Are you going to Spain, Seamus?" Rosie asked.

"What?" he exclaimed, startled. "Um, yeah," he said, "all the lads are going." He then pointed frantically at Gary. "He said we could use his stag do as an excuse!"

Rosie and Karen then turned to Gary. Gary glowered murderously at Seamus as he tried to think fast. He suddenly clasped his hands together and turned to face Karen and Rosie.

"So," he said happily, "what do you reckon?"

"What the fuck are you on about?" said Karen.

"Well, it was supposed to be a surprise," he said, "but bloody Seamus here …" Gary rolled his eyes and tutted unconvincingly.

"Gary," Rosie began menacingly, "what's going on?"

"Look," said Gary, thinking fast, "I was thinking that after the baby's born, you could probably do with a bit of a break, right? A wee holiday in the sun, you know? Well, a mate of ours has got a beach-house in Spain, and –"

"Who?" Karen demanded. "Who's got a fucking beach-house?"

"Oh, you wouldn't know him. He was from school, but, anyway, he –"

"What do mean, *after the baby's born*?" said Rosie. "Do you not think we'll be a wee bit busy, Gary?"

"Well, I don't mean right away, do I?" Gary explained. "I'm not saying you should just drop the pup and then head off to the airport, am I?"

"I don't know, Gary. What exactly *are* you saying?"

"I'm just saying we can wait for a bit until my ma's happy to look after the kid for a couple of days and then we can –"

"Does my ma know this?" asked Karen.

"What? Um … yeah, yeah, I'm sure she'll be … You know what, Karen? You and Harry could probably do with a holiday as well."

Seamus considered sneaking off towards the door while the girls were distracted by Gary digging an ever-deeper hole for himself, but he was too afraid to move.

"Oh," cried Karen, "don't you fucking think you can just … what sort of beach-house?"

"Well, that's the thing," said Gary, getting into his stride. "Me and Seamus here, and the rest of the lads, were thinking that we could go over and suss it out, you know? Make sure it's up to scratch and all that."

"That's good of you," Rosie told him.

"I know," Gary continued, ignoring the sarcasm, "but that's just the type of guys we are. Selfless, we are, bloody selfless. It's just the sort of –"

"What was that about a stag do?" asked Rosie.

Seamus could not help but admire Gary's uncanny ability to adapt instantly to the fluidity of any situation. He didn't even blink.

"Well, that's what you call killing two birds with one stone," he told Rosie. "So when you think about it, we'd actually be saving money. In fact, not going would be an act of financial stupidity. We might as well be just throwing money away."

Both Karen and Rosie found themselves in a quandary. On one hand it felt unnatural not to be ripping into Gary for being an underhand, self-absorbed dickhead, but on the other hand they were both intrigued by the promise of a private beach-house in Spain.

"So, when were you planning to go and *suss it out*?" Rosie asked cautiously.

"The week after Easter," said Gary. "We're really only going to help out a mate, you see. He needs a hand moving some stuff from some other place he's got out there, so it's not like it's going to be a holiday at all really. The plan is to head over, suss out the beach-house, have a couple of beers for a quick stag-do, and then work the rest of the time. Not a holiday at all."

Seamus thought that Gary was probably stretching the concept of his selfless altruism a little too far, but the girls now seemed to be too enraptured by the idea of cheap holidays in the sun to pay Gary's ramblings any close attention.

As they left the house, having decided to call into the Star for a drink, Gary and Seamus had formed different opinions on how the encounter had gone.

Seamus thought that Gary had made a lot of promises he had no right to make. They had left the two girls excitedly making plans for long, leisurely breaks in the summer and beyond, but there could be no guarantee that Gary would be able to deliver any of the increasingly outlandish situations he had promised. Gary, as usual, was only thinking of the present. The thought that any of his words or actions would have any repercussions at a later date was little more than a vague and abstract notion that Gary had no time for.

"Well," Gary enthused as he rubbed his hands together, "That went really well, didn't it?

TWENTY ONE

Jamesy climbed the stairs to the Speakeasy Bar in the Student Union. It was Friday afternoon and his lectures were all finished for the day.

As he walked through the door to the bar, he nodded briefly to acknowledge a smile from a girl as she passed going the other way, and then made his way through the Friday crowd until he found Sean and Bobby at a table close to the bar. Putting his bag under the table, he sat down.

"All right there, Jamesy?" said Sean. "Perfect timing, Bobby was just about to go to the bar."

"Well, now that you mention it …" Bobby stood up. "The usual, Jamesy?"

Jamesy nodded and Bobby set off.

"How's it going?" asked Sean. "All set for Spain?" They had all gone into town the weekend before to buy their plane tickets. It had been decided that their best option would be to fly from Dublin to Barcelona, and then take a train to Valencia where they could then take another train on to Tavernes. It would be a long day, but they were all young enough to view the travel as part of the adventure.

"Yeah," Jamesy said. "Looking forward to it."

"I think it's already starting to get hot over there, so it should be roasting by the time we get there."

"Well, I've packed my shorts."

Bobby came back from the bar and set three pints down on the table.

"You've packed, did you say?" he asked Jamesy as he took his seat. "That's a bit organised, isn't it?"

"No, I mean I've only just started packing," Jamesy told him. "But I think I've bought everything that I need to take, so I'm near enough ready to go."

"Well," said Sean, taking a sip of beer, "there's not long to go now, is there? Though we still don't know how we're getting to the airport."

"I thought Gary had it all in hand," said Jamesy.

"Yeah, but that's just according to Gary, isn't it?"

"That's right," Bobby agreed. "You can just picture us all standing there early on Easter Monday with all our luggage, and Gary shows up on a fucking skateboard."

"You don't have a lot of faith in him, then?"

"No!"

Jamesy shrugged and picked up his drink. He was sure they'd work something out, one way or another. A band started to set up on the stage over by the row of windows, and Jamesy watched them with little interest. It was the same band that played every Friday afternoon and Jamesy had heard the same set many times over the years. There was still something comforting, though, in the familiarity. Jamesy turned to Bobby.

"Have you seen Hannah lately?" he asked nonchalantly.

"No, not at all. Why?"

"Just asking."

"That's definitely all over, is it?" asked Sean.

"Looks like it."

"Well then," said Bobby, "a holiday is just what you need to take your mind off things."

"Hope so."

"You feeling a bit low, then, Jamesy?"

Jamesy looked thoughtful as he picked up his drink. "You could say that," he said, taking a sip. "But the worrying thing is I seem to be having trouble concentrating as well."

"In what way?" asked Bobby.

"Well, I'm supposed to be revising, but I just can't seem to focus on anything for more than a couple of minutes at a time. I'll just be, like, staring at a page and then realise I haven't actually been taking anything in. My head's all over the place at the minute, just don't know what I'm going to do, really."

"Well, that's not good," said Sean. "That's your one superpower, isn't it? Studying?"

"Yeah, let's face it, Jamesy," added Bobby, "you've got fuck all else going for you."

Jamesy didn't react, he just stared at his drink, so Bobby carried on. "It's weird, isn't it?" he said. "You and Hannah both go really well together. You belong together because you're both … well, you know … a wee bit dull. But a long time ago, a bunch of people, herding goats in a desert, wrote some stuff down, and now that means you and Hannah can't be together. Funny, when you think about it."

"Funny's not the word I would have used," Jamesy said glumly.

"Aye, well, like I said," Bobby told him, "a holiday in the sun should cheer you up."

"Maybe it'll work for Joker too," Sean suggested.

"Yeah," said Bobby with sudden awareness, "he has been a bit miserable, lately, hasn't he?"

"Aye, I don't know what the fuck's wrong with everybody at the minute."

"Tone seems to be in good form these days," Jamesy ventured.

"He does, doesn't he?" said Bobby. "And I've got a fair idea why."

TWENTY TWO

She had it all planned out. She was going to march straight in, call him an asshole, and march straight out again.

But when it came to the crunch, it was her face that let her down.

"You're an asshole," she told him through a beaming smile.

"Well, it took you long enough to work that out," said Tone as he rose to greet her. "What do you want to drink?"

Claire sat down at the table. "I'm not staying long," she said. "So I'll just have a small red wine. I was sorry to hear about your daddy, by the way."

"Thanks," said Tone. He shrugged. "Just one of those things, really." He went off to the bar and Claire watched him as she put a light to her cigarette. She was surprised at how pleased she was to see him again. When he had suddenly broken off all contact just after Christmas, she had been, at first, confused, and then she had felt angry. She had no right, she knew, to feel that way, for their relationship had only ever been casual, but Tony's inexplicable silence still felt like a hurtful rejection and she wanted him to feel as bad as she had felt.

But now she was beginning to understand just how much she had missed him.

"There you go." Tone placed a glass of wine on the table and sat down. "So, how have you been keeping?"

"Is that all you have to say?" she demanded, annoyed by his easy manner.

"Well, I didn't think I'd need to explain anything," said Tone. "I mean, hasn't Bobby told you all about it."

Claire was trying to maintain her irritation, but her stupid face broke out in another broad smile. "That was a shock, wasn't it?" she beamed.

"Jesus! You can say that again."

"When did you find out?"

"Christmas Eve. We have this –"

"Oh, Bobby's pub-crawl!" Claire exclaimed. "Of course. So, you're one of his wee drinking buddies?"

"That's one way of putting it."

"It must have come as a real shock to Bobby too."

"He seems to be taking it well enough, though."

"Well, I did tell you, didn't I?" Claire said as she stubbed out her cigarette. "He's a lovely guy."

"Have you seen him lately?"

"Not since St Patrick's day, no. Why?"

"Did you know we're going to Spain on Monday?"

"No. Who's *we*?"

"Me, Bobby and all our wee drinking buddies."

"What for?"

"Just a holiday. We got the chance of a cheap week in the sun, so we all just thought we could do with a break."

"It's all right for some."

"Well, like I said, it's just for a week."

There was a brief, stilted silence as they each sipped their drinks and wondered what they were doing there. Were they expecting to pick up from where they had left off before Christmas, when they had torn each other's clothes off in a Dublin hotel room? Or was this an ending? Was this an opportunity to draw a conclusive line under something that had been little more than a passionate, but passing, fling, and could now be left forever back in a Dublin hotel?

"You've finished your drink," Tone pointed out needlessly when Claire placed her empty glass on the table. She didn't reply. She stared accusingly at her glass and wondered why she had asked for a small one. She never asked for a small glass of wine; she could never see the point.

But then she realised that this was her chance. This was her opportunity to stand up, to say something clever and final, and to simply leave. 'Well, it's been nice knowing you,' she would say, and then maybe shake hands, as Tony looked into her eyes with longing and a desperate pleading. 'We'll always have Dublin,' she would tell him as their fingers slipped slowly apart and she turned and walked steadily away into the swirling black and white mist.

Tone was becoming uncomfortable as he looked at Claire. He had never been aroused by just a person's face before, but Claire's hilarious attempts to stifle her natural exuberance were turning him on. He had always felt vaguely unsettled by her irrepressible cheeriness, believing it to be somehow unnatural, but watching her now try to impose some sort of discipline to her face, he realised that her smile shone all the more brightly, and it now seemed right. It seemed right and natural and perfect. And undeniably sexy.

The tension between them began to grow. Claire raised her eyes from her glass to stare into Tone's face. She could see confusion and doubt in his eyes, and guessed that he could see the same in her eyes too. The silent tension stretched.

"Well," she said finally. "Are you just going to sit there?"

Tone grinned. "A large one this time, I take it?" he said. She lit another cigarette in reply and watched as he went back to the bar.

Later that night, Claire was still trying to convey a sense of aggrieved indignation, but as she peeled off her pants before climbing on top of Tony, she had to concede that she wasn't being entirely convincing.

TWENTY THREE

Hannah was having trouble with smallpox. She was in the reference section of Belfast Central Library and she was learning about one of the most devastating infectious diseases in human history.

Smallpox, it seemed, had a fatality rate of thirty percent, and those that survived were left heavily scarred and often blind. But that was not why Hannah was having trouble.

Hannah's problem was that smallpox was now in the past. It was a disease that had been officially eradicated, and that was giving Hannah some cause for concern.

She knew that all of the ailments of mankind could be traced back to God's displeasure at Adam and Eve's disobedience in Eden.

As well as being cast out from Paradise, humanity would have to face punishments in the form of illnesses for the remainder of its history.

She remembered the long and confusing discussions that she and her church group had had regarding the varying degrees of God's wrath. Bone cancer in children had raised a lot of harrowing debate. And malaria. And dysentery. And heart disease. But what about tooth decay? Was that one of God's punishments? Or dandruff, even?

God had sprinkled His punishments seemingly at random throughout His creation, as if it were mankind as a whole, and not the individual, that mattered.

But His creation, it seemed, was fighting back.

What did God make, she wondered, of such disdain for His will? And what about medicine in general? Were doctors and nurses not constantly subverting His will? Hannah was worried that mankind was unwittingly fuelling God's anger. The story of the Tower of Babel was an example of how God viewed the hubris of humanity but then, for Hannah, it all came back to God's omniscience. God knew how every event in human history would play out. He must know; He's omniscient. So why, in Scripture, is He so often moved to anger?

The reference books she was browsing covered a wide range of topics, but none that she could see made any reference to Scripture. She had largely dismissed those books that dealt with evolution, for they were obviously just disgraceful propaganda, but there were other books that covered broad topics such as geography, geology, history, science and astronomy that seemed not only to ignore the Bible, but to go way beyond its scope, almost as if the Bible was not a comprehensive enough resource. For one thing, every reference book seemed to make casual reference to the Earth being older than six thousand years. Much older.

She flicked through some books dealing with the natural world of flora and fauna, and was astonished and appalled to learn that nature was little more than an unending struggle for survival, and was filled with slaughter, suffering and unimaginable cruelty. There were insects that laid their eggs in the eyes of mammals, and parasites that slowly devoured their hosts from the inside out; not to mention the teeth and slashing claws, ripping and tearing at terrified prey in every corner of the world. Nature was not in balance; it was at war.

She knew, of course, that all of this was a direct result of the Fall, but it seemed, to her, to be wildly disproportionate. All of this because some people ate a piece of fruit six thousand years ago?

It seemed that no matter where she turned, she was faced with questions she couldn't answer.

A glimpse at a scientific magazine informed her that a new volcanic island had just appeared in the Pacific Ocean; a fact that left her dumbfounded. She had always believed that God had created the Earth fully formed, so why were new bits of it suddenly popping up from nowhere? Feeling perplexed, she was drawn to a glossy and colourful book on astronomy, attracted by pictures that showed the jaw-dropping majesty of the full extent of God's creation. She was starting to read about the Solar System when she felt Jamesy's teeth nibble gently at her earlobe and she had to close the book in frustration. She looked up and let her mind wander aimlessly while she allowed her body to have its moment as tiny prickles rippled across her skin in all sorts of confusing ways. The moment passed and she went back to her book.

The sun, she already knew, was a star. It was the only star in our Solar System but was just one of at least a hundred billion other stars in the galaxy that was called the Milky Way. Hannah stopped. She had to read that again. At least a hundred *billion* other stars? She was barely beginning to comprehend such a number when she read about the distances involved in outer space.

The closest star to our own, she learned, was Proxima Centauri, but it would take over six thousand years to get there using current technology. Even travelling at the speed of light, which, she read with growing disbelief, was more than six hundred *million* miles per hour, it would still take over four years to reach our closest stellar neighbour. And what about the hundred billion other stars? It was all on a scale that Hannah found impossible to grasp, but she found herself becoming intrigued.

She was just putting the fragments of her blown mind back together when her imagination exploded once more. She had had only a vague notion beforehand of there being other galaxies in the universe besides the Milky Way, but when she learned that there were at least a hundred billion other galaxies in the universe, each containing a hundred billion stars, she calmly closed the book and stared into the middle-distance.

God, it seemed, had been much busier than the Bible suggested. The Solar System was far more massive than she could comprehend, but it was a mere speck in the Milky Way galaxy, and that, in turn, was entirely insignificant in the wider universe.

She discovered that it was unlikely that humans would ever be able to travel very far within the Solar System, let alone being able to travel to another star. And the idea of humans travelling to another galaxy was far-fetched even for science fiction. The scale of everything was just so far beyond anything she could even begin to imagine that it begged a simple question in Hannah's mind.

Why?

TWENTY FOUR

Nigeria, 1963

The first time that Benjamin set foot on the campus, he felt at home. He could sense a greater desire for new medical teaching and training, among both students and faculty at the university in Enugu, than he had ever felt in Kano.

When he had returned to Nigeria's capital, Lagos, he had been met with blank indifference and a simple lack of understanding for the difficulties he had been facing in Kano, and he had begun to suspect that an ignominious return to London was now inevitable. It was during his second week in Lagos, however, that a chance encounter with a university administrator from Enugu in the East had alerted him to a shortage of training staff in the Faculty of Medicine at Enugu University, and he had then broached the subject with the committee that was overseeing his placement in Nigeria.

Even though Benjamin suspected the committee had seized upon the suggestion of his reassignment to Enugu as an ideal way of getting rid of him, he didn't mind because it meant he could finally step into the role that had tempted him to Nigeria in the first place.

His first tour of the facilities had confirmed to him that this was truly what he wanted to do with his time in Africa. The students he encountered at the Enugu University Faculty of Medicine possessed an almost manic eagerness to learn, and as Benjamin was helping to address the faculty's chronic under-staffing issues, he felt that he could make a real difference.

The position also provided him with accommodation on campus which, to Benjamin's surprise and delight, turned out to be a pretty little bungalow with sizeable gardens to the front and back. He bought a new car, having sold his old one back in Kano, and he set about furnishing the bungalow to his own, fairly traditional, tastes, with plenty of bookshelves and comfortable chairs for reading. He even decided that he could try his hand at gardening, now that he had been given some decent-sized plots to work with, and his mind raced ahead into the future with all sorts of plans for his gardens and his house. *His* house. His home. He smiled at the thought. He was home.

It was the enthusiasm of his students during his first weeks in the job that made Benjamin sadly reflect on the words of his friend, Odi. Odi, Benjamin realised, had been accurate when he had described the hunger for learning among the people of the East, and the memories of that beaming grin and infectious laugh made Benjamin smile and want to weep. He hated his grief. He hated missing Odi and he hated that Odi was gone, and it was thoughts of Odi that led him, one evening after several beers, to think of Adanna and where she had gone, and it was thoughts of Odi that had led him to pull an atlas from a bookshelf and to tearfully flick through the maps looking for the name of a village. A village that Odi had once told him about and which was, as far as Benjamin could remember, close to Enugu. After a while, he found it.

This coming Saturday, Benjamin decided, he would take a drive down there to look around, to perhaps get a sense of where Odi had come from and maybe even see if he could re-establish contact with Adanna, to see how she was doing.

He parked close to the village square and then strolled past the bars and cafés that bordered the square's western side. To the north of the little square was a church that huddled in the shade of a corkwood tree and, as Benjamin stood and looked around the Saturday afternoon crowds, walking, shopping, eating, drinking, he began to wonder why he had come.

He could feel no special connection to Odi here, and the chances of somehow bumping into Adanna in this busy little town now seemed slim. He sighed and sat down at a table outside the nearest café and ordered a tea. As he waited, he became aware of someone approaching him from the side and then a voice spoke to him in Igbo.

"*Ndeewo*."

Benjamin turned and was surprised to see a white face smiling at him. The face belonged to a catholic priest.

"*Ndewo*," Benjamin replied, "but I have to say," he went on, "that's about as far as my Igbo goes, I'm afraid."

The priest laughed. "Yes," he said in a strong Irish accent, "I didn't take you for a local. Are you waiting for someone?"

"No, I'm … I'm not sure why I'm here, actually."

"I'm Father Jerome," the priest said, holding out his hand for Benjamin to shake. "You don't mind if I join you, do you?"

"Oh no, of course not. Please do. I'm Benjamin, by the way."

Father Jerome sat down at the table. "Well, Benjamin," he explained, "it's just that I can tell you're not Nigerian, you see, but I can't quite place your accent and I'm a shockingly nosy man, so I am."

"I'm Egyptian," said Benjamin smiling, "but I've spent several years in England."

"England, you say?" Father Jerome shuddered. "You have my condolences, but then I suppose we've all had our troubles."

Benjamin laughed. "I have a good friend who is Irish," he said. "We were students in London together. We still try to keep in touch."

"I'm very glad to hear it," Father Jerome told him. "So, tell me, Benjamin, what brings an interesting and exotic man like yourself to this little backwater, then? Like I said, I'm a very nosy man."

Father Jerome ordered a beer from the waitress who brought Benjamin's tea, and then listened intently as Benjamin explained what he was doing in Nigeria, how he was living and teaching at the university in Enugu, and how he had come, on a whim, to the village where his friends had grown up.

"Odi Mbanefo?" Father Jerome reflected sadly. "Yes, I knew him," he said, "though not terribly well. And Adanna too, of course. They were with the Anglican congregation in the village," he gestured to the church on the other side of the square. "The news of Odi's death came as a real shock to everyone. As you can imagine in a small place like this, everyone knows pretty much everyone else."

"I believe that Adanna has moved back here," said Benjamin.

"Yes, I believe so," agreed Father Jerome. "I can get you her mother's address, if you like."

Benjamin nodded as he finished his tea. He was beginning to have some doubts about tracking down Adanna now that it had become a possibility. They had never been friendly in the same way that he and Odi had been. His relationship with Adanna had always been stiff and formal, he felt, and he wasn't sure he wanted to reacquaint himself with the simmering ferocity that he sensed in her.

"That beer looks good," he said, gesturing to Father Jerome's almost empty bottle.

"Then why don't you join me in one?" Father Jerome suggested. "And we'll raise a toast to the memory of a fine man."

"Well, when you put it like that," said Benjamin with a smile.

They drank and chatted until well after dark when it occurred to Benjamin that it would be foolish for him to drive back to Enugu.

"Oh, you can stay with me tonight," Father Jerome assured him. "I've got a wee place, not far from here, over by St Patrick's."

"St Patrick's?" asked an amused Benjamin.

The café began to close so Father Jerome directed Benjamin to a nearby bar where they could continue their conversation.

"Yes, St Patrick's," Father Jerome said, "it's the chapel and the charitable mission for the Holy Ghost Fathers in the village. St Patrick, of course, is the patron saint of Nigeria."

"What, really?" asked Benjamin. He managed to prop himself up against the bar as Father Jerome ordered the next round.

"Yes, really," Father Jerome replied. "The British, you see, go around the world, planting their flag in places, while we Irish go around planting our saints."

Benjamin gave the priest a long look. "Well, tell me, Father," he said, "what's an interesting and exotic man like yourself doing in a backwater like this, then?"

"Oh, there have always been missionaries in Africa," Father Jerome told him, "whether the Africans want them or not. I like to think that we do more good than harm, though, but then I would say that, wouldn't I?"

Benjamin found it easier to raise his drink as a response rather than try to formulate words into a coherent sentence. He had been enjoying the company of this easy-going priest, but he was beginning to feel the evening slip away from him, as it slurred and stumbled into night.

It took a while for Benjamin to understand where he was when Father Jerome shook him awake the next morning.

"Good morning, Benjamin," the priest said as Benjamin opened his eyes. "I'm going to have to go soon, but you can stay as long as you like. There's some bread in the kitchen if you want breakfast."

The events of the previous day slowly assembled themselves in Benjamin's consciousness as he sat up in the small cot-bed. He was still fully dressed, his head hurt, his mouth was dry and he blinked uncontrollably in the harsh morning light.

"How are you feeling?" asked Father Jerome. Benjamin thought that the priest was looking obscenely bright and cheerful, considering the amount of alcohol he had consumed.

"Did you say you were going out?" he managed to ask.

"Yes," said Father Jerome, "I must go and say Mass later on. I got that address that you were looking for, by the way. I left it on the kitchen table for you."

"Um, thanks," Benjamin said as he stood up. Father Jerome showed him where the bathroom and the kitchen were and then left him on his own in the house. After a trip to the bathroom, Benjamin sat down at the kitchen table, picked up the slip of paper that had been left for him and stared at the address. He did not think he was up to seeing anyone today, but it would be useful to have the address for the future.

He made himself a quick breakfast and a cup of coffee and spent some time in the bathroom trying to make himself look and feel more human. Eventually, though still queasy, he felt he could make his way to his car and then suffer the drive back to Enugu, where he planned to climb into bed and stay there for the rest of the day.

Before he left, he scribbled a thank-you note to Father Jerome and, adding his address and phone number to the bottom, he placed it on the table. He then stepped outside and, blinking in the sun, made his way to the village square.

He walked through the square, feeling glad that he didn't have to see anyone today for, despite his best efforts, he still looked dreadful. He was unshaven and his clothes were all wrinkled and beer-stained. He tried to focus his thoughts on his bath and his bed back in Enugu as he stumbled groggily towards his car.

"Dr Maher?" The woman's voice made Benjamin freeze. The congregation from the Anglican Church was pouring into the square, jostling Benjamin as he slowly turned to face the source of the inquiry. It was Adanna, though she now seemed to be a lot more blurry than Benjamin remembered.

"Adanna!" he exclaimed, struggling to convey surprised enthusiasm. She stepped towards him and gave him a tentative embrace.

"But … but what are you doing here?" she asked, and then took a step back. "And why are you …?" She gave him a quizzical look.

"Well, it's … um," Benjamin was only too aware of how he must look in a crowd of people who were dressed in their Sunday best. He probably smelt quite differently as well. "I'm living in Enugu now," he finally told her. "At the university."

"Enugu?" Adanna said, surprised. "Are you teaching, then?"

"Adanna!" The voice came from behind her. "Who is this man you are talking to?" An older woman, heavier than Adanna, and not quite as tall, appeared at her side.

"This is Dr Maher, Momma," said Adanna, "I told you about him. He was in Kano with us."

"A doctor?" Adanna's mother cried in disbelief. "You are a doctor?"

Benjamin's discomfort was approaching a crescendo. He wished he could just slip away and crawl under the covers of his bed at home, but instead he was sweating uncomfortably under a mocking sun whilst trying to make small talk with two intimidating women in a crowd of chirruping churchgoers.

"It's nice to meet you, Mrs …" Benjamin realised, with horror, that he couldn't remember Adanna's surname. "Mrs …?"

"Obiaka," said Adanna with an amused grin.

"Oh yes, of course," he stammered, "Mrs Obiaka." He extended a hand which, after a hesitant pause, Adanna's mother briefly shook. "I know I'm not looking my best," he continued, "but I drove down here yesterday, you see, because I've been living in Enugu and, well, I had heard Odi speak of this place and I just thought that … well …" Benjamin was running out of words, though he wasn't sure what he was trying to say. "Well, I got talking to a Father Jerome, you see, and –"

"Father Jerome?" Mrs Obiaka gave a sudden burst of laughter, which made Benjamin wince with pain. "You do not have to say any more, Dr Maher," she said as she walked past him, still laughing, to go and speak to someone in the crowd.

"So, you have had an interesting night with Father Jerome, then?" Adanna asked smiling.

"Well, yes, you could say that," said Benjamin, mopping at his brow with a handkerchief. "It's good to see you again, Adanna."

"It is good to see you too, Dr Maher," she replied. "How are you finding Enugu? Did you say you were teaching?"

"Yes, yes," he said, suddenly enthused, "I'm teaching, and the faculty at Enugu is wonderful. Just what I had been hoping to establish in Kano, actually."

"I'm glad that you are happy in Enugu."

"And what about you?" asked Benjamin. "How have you settled back home?"

"Yes, I am well," Adanna said with a shrug. "Life goes on, does it not?"

Benjamin could sense the same lifelessness in Adanna that had settled within her after Odi had died, but now was not the time to probe deeper. They stood for a little while longer exchanging standard pleasantries until Benjamin saw a chance to take his leave.

"Well, Adanna," he said, "I must get back to Enugu, but I would be happy to visit you again if that is something you would like."

Adanna nodded without much enthusiasm. "Of course, Dr Maher. I would like that very much."

Benjamin gave her his telephone number, while she gave him the number of the bar where she worked, and he then set off to find his car.

As he drove back to Enugu, Benjamin reflected on the chance meeting and he realised with some surprise that he had actually told Adanna the truth. It *had* been good to see her again.

It was a few weeks later that Benjamin went back to the village. He had been invited by Father Jerome to inspect the little cross-congregational clinic that had recently opened in the square, so he drove down early one Saturday morning. He had not heard any word from Adanna since his first trip to the village, but he was keen to renew his friendship with Father Jerome.

"Benjamin!" the priest called to him as he crossed the square. "Good to see you again."

"You too, Father," said Benjamin, shaking the priest's hand. "You've been busy, I see."

"Oh, we've all been involved in this," Father Jerome told him. "All the congregations from miles around have chipped in something. Come, have a look around."

The clinic, though small, was neat and professional, and Benjamin voiced his approval and made a few helpful suggestions to the staff. After the tour, Benjamin was invited to lunch with Father Jerome and a few of the protestant ministers.

"That sounds like an excellent idea," he said, "but do you think it would be possible for me to invite a friend?"

"Of course," said Father Jerome. "Are you talking about Adanna?"

"Yes, if that's all right? I fear I may have made a rather poor impression on her when last we met."

Benjamin made his way to the address he had been given and knocked on the door. Adanna's mother answered, and when she recognised who it was, she stepped outside with a condescending smile.

"Dr Maher," she said. "How nice of you to call."

"Hello, Mrs Obiaka. I just called to see if –"

"Adanna!" Mrs Obiaka shouted back inside. "It's your drunken doctor friend!"

"Well, I … I …"

"Who?" Adanna appeared in the doorway. "Oh, Dr Maher. What

are you –?"

"I think he has come to take you drinking with him," Mrs Obiaka suggested mockingly.

"Oh no, I just thought that …" Benjamin wavered. Mrs Obiaka folded her arms and glared at him.

"Momma," said Adanna, "why don't you go back inside?"

Adanna's mother hesitated, then, still staring at Benjamin, she walked slowly inside and closed the door.

"Yes, Dr Maher?" Adanna asked, raising an eyebrow.

"Adanna, I … I was wondering if you would like to come out for lunch. I mean, not just with me … with some of the local church leaders, I mean …"

"Church leaders? Have you found religion, Dr Maher?"

"Yes. I mean no … I mean …" Benjamin mopped at his forehead. "Adanna," he said, "won't you please call me Benjamin?"

She looked at him thoughtfully and then smiled. "Very well, Benjamin," she said. "Now, if you will give me a minute to get ready, then yes, I will have lunch with you."

Initially, it seemed odd to Benjamin to be joining a table of clergymen for lunch, but he knew Father Jerome, and Adanna was familiar with most of the others to varying degrees so they were able to blend in quite naturally.

The conversation, at first, was dominated by the new clinic, but during the meal it began to fracture into individual chats around the table. Benjamin and Adanna talked amongst themselves.

"I have received several letters from Zara," she told him. "She says that the situation in Kano has settled down now. She wants to know if I would return there."

Benjamin nodded. "I went to the police headquarters when I was in Lagos," he said. "I thought that they would want to have as much information as possible about what had happened, but they dismissed it all as a local disturbance. They showed no interest at all."

"Welcome to Nigeria," Adanna said with a sardonic smile.

"Yes," Benjamin returned her smile, "I have to say I have noticed a lot of differences between the regions. Especially between the North and the East. There does seem to be a much greater desire for change down here than in Kano."

"Of course, Dr …" she smiled. "Benjamin. Do you believe in national traits? Or racial traits? Or tribal traits?"

"Do certain groups of people behave inherently differently from other groups, is that what you mean?" he asked. Adanna nodded, and Benjamin seemed to consider it. "I don't think so," he said. "I mean, there are superficial differences, of course, but I believe that people are all essentially the same."

"What about cultural differences that have been ingrained for generations?"

"Well," Benjamin began. He was wondering how a light chat over lunch could have suddenly become so intense. "I think cultural differences are still superficial," he said. "The species *Homo Sapiens* is, after all, just one species."

"Then it depends on how deep you believe the superficiality descends."

The other conversations around the table had begun to tail off as theological ears pricked up at the hint of a philosophical discussion.

"Would you listen to you two!" said Father Jerome. "And here's me discussing the chances of Glasgow Celtic winning the league this year."

"Perhaps," suggested Benjamin, "it is not a suitable discussion to have over lunch."

"Oh, I don't know," ventured an elderly pastor at one end of the table. "If it saves us all from another one of Father Jerome's rants about some obscure football team, then I say we should give it a try."

"Obscure?" cried Father Jerome. "I'll have you know that –"

"So, Adanna," the elderly pastor continued, "I'm curious to hear your thoughts on the matter. It sounds like you have some firm opinions on the differences between people, is that right?"

"I'm sorry, Pastor Osawe," said Adanna, "I'm afraid I may have spoken out of turn."

"Not at all," the elderly pastor assured her. "We all know how much you have suffered, and how it is natural for you to bear ill will towards our neighbours in the North but, of course, you know what Our Lord has to say on the matter of turning the other cheek."

Adanna smiled. "If only it were that easy."

"No one ever said that forgiveness is easy," said a burly Methodist who sat facing Benjamin. "To do so means striving against our natural human impulses."

"Ah," Father Jerome interjected, "but from what I gathered earlier, it sounds like Adanna is saying that not all humans have the same impulses."

"I am only going by the evidence of my own eyes," Adanna said defiantly.

Benjamin sighed. He just wanted to have a nice lunch with pleasant company, but he could already tell that things were about to get heated.

"I would like to hear the argument from a scientific point of view," said Pastor Osawe, looking directly at Benjamin. "What does a doctor of medicine have to say on the matter?"

"What?" Benjamin said, taken by surprise. "What matter?"

"It's just the old question of nurture versus nature, isn't it?" said Father Jerome. "So, Benjamin, what's your take on it?"

"I've already said that there is only one human species," Benjamin explained. "That's simply from a biological point of view. Recent discoveries in molecular biology have only confirmed that viewpoint. Of course, some groups of humans will exhibit certain characteristics that differ from other groups but the same can be said of individual humans as well. It doesn't change the fact that on a very basic, fundamental level, we are all exactly the same."

"So, nurture, then?" Father Jerome said with a smile.

"Of course," said Benjamin. "No child is born a Christian, or a Muslim or even a fan of Glasgow Celtic."

Everyone laughed, but Benjamin could sense that Adanna, beside him, remained tense. The conversation moved on and, when lunch was finished, Benjamin offered to walk Adanna back home.

"So, have you replied to Zara's question?" he asked her as they walked.

"Which question?"

"About returning to the North."

"Ah, no, I have not answered her yet, but I do not think I will return to the North."

"Why not? Wouldn't you make more money there?"

"Money is not everything," Adanna said softly, her head bowed.

"No, no, of course not," said Benjamin. It was obvious to him that Adanna was still suffering, still consumed by a grief that seemed to be dragging her down. He felt compelled to help.

"So, you're working at a bar in Ngwo?" he said. She turned to look at him, suspecting his disapproval, but his face was neutral.

"I am the manager there, yes," she said defensively. "Why? What of it?"

"Oh, nothing," said Benjamin hastily, "but I was just wondering if you had ever considered teaching, that's all."

"Teaching? Teaching what?"

"I don't know," he said, "it needn't be anything specific. You could teach children to read and write, for example. Or you could teach English, or geography, or anything you –"

Adanna stopped and stared at him. "What are you suggesting?" she demanded.

"Well," he explained, "there is a shortage of qualified teachers throughout Nigeria, so the university at Enugu is running several courses for anyone who wants to get into teaching. And I just happen to think that you would make an excellent teacher."

"Why?"

"Well, because you … um … well, you know … you have such strong opinions."

Adanna laughed as they walked on. "And that makes a good teacher, does it?"

"You know what I mean," he said. "You're smart, you could be a real help to children. You would certainly make them think, that's for sure." Benjamin smiled, but Adanna walked along with her head down, quiet and thoughtful. When they arrived at her home, she stopped, still silent, and then looked into his eyes.

"What do I have to do?" she asked.

TWENTY FIVE

Michael was not a fan of sports, and rarely engaged in any form of physical activity, so Simon was surprised to see him in a pair of shorts, running around his back garden. He raised an eyebrow at Michael's wife, who had shown him through the patio doors.

"I know," said Maddy laughing, "he thinks he's Maradona."

"What on earth is he doing?"

"It's Peter," Maddy explained. "He loves his football, so his daddy said he'd have a wee kick-about with him. Michael's a bit crap, though. He's getting hammered."

"Yes," Simon agreed, "he looks like he could do with some practice."

"What are you two gabbing about?" Michael called from the lawn.

"We're just admiring your fancy footwork," Simon shouted across the garden. "Poetry in motion, we were saying."

"Aye, very funny," said Michael, walking towards them. He picked up a towel from a chair on the patio and began to mop his sweating face. "Jesus!" he gasped. "That's bloody killing me."

"Do you have a few minutes?" asked Simon.

"Yeah, no problem," Michael turned back to his son. "Just going to take a wee break here, Peter," he said. Peter waved in acknowledgement and carried on practising his dribbling.

Michael and Simon went into the house and made their way to Michael's home office. Maddy offered to make them tea but they both declined.

"Well?" asked Michael as he closed the office door and went to sit at his desk.

"I've received some interesting information," Simon began, "regarding Hegarty and those other two … nuisances."

Michael sighed and ran a hand through his hair. "Go on," he said.

"An opportunity may have presented itself," Simon told him, "just after Easter."

"Easter? Why? What's happening?"

"Well, apparently, Anderson and Lingfield have arranged to go off to Spain for a week."

"Just those two?"

"No," Simon admitted, "there'll be a group of them going." Michael frowned at this, so Simon hurried on. "It isn't ideal, I know that, but hear me out."

Michael leaned back in his chair, waiting to be convinced.

"They're going to be flying from Dublin Airport," Simon continued, "and who do you think will be taking them there and back again?"

"Hegarty?"

"Yes," said Simon. "Hegarty has agreed to drive them all down in his van, and then pick them up again the Sunday after Easter."

Michael remained silent as he mulled over this new information. He had been half-hoping that the whole Hegarty business would just quietly go away as the months dragged on with no viable opportunity becoming obvious, but now it looked like he would have to give the matter some thought. He disliked the thought of others being involved, but the idea of the targets being grouped together on quiet Sunday roads in the Irish Republic was too tempting to be dismissed.

The fact that the matter could be dealt with, safely out of the way, on the other side of the border, held a strong appeal for Michael.

"What have you got in mind?" he asked.

"Well, I was thinking that the Sunday when they're coming back would give us more time to prepare," Simon told him. "The roads should be quieter too, so I was thinking we could slip over the border, early on Sunday morning, and pick our spot to wait for them coming by. Obviously, I'll have the area scouted out beforehand to make sure we choose the perfect place."

"Who do you have in mind for this?" Michael asked.

"Just you and I, and two others."

"Weapons?"

"Pistols only, I would have thought."

Michael pondered this, and then gave another nod. Pistols made sense, he thought, for they would be making their way through some of Northern Ireland's most sensitive regions to get to the border. It would be best to be discreet.

"Two others?" he asked. "Who are you thinking of?"

Simon seemed to hesitate. "Um … I'd thought of maybe Wee Paulie and Big Dennis," he muttered.

Michael exhaled slowly. "Not exactly the cream of the crop, is it?" he suggested.

"No," Simon admitted, "but they're both fairly dependable, and Big Dennis has just got that new car, so it would be completely clean. There's no way it could be traced back to us."

"Big Dennis will be driving, then?"

"Yes, it's still early days, of course, but that's the plan so far."

Michael thought some more, then came to a decision.

"Okay," he said, "you sort out the rest of the details, and let me know how you get on."

"Fine," said Simon, getting up and walking to the door. He turned at the door and smiled. "I'll let you get back to your football."

TWENTY SIX

The tiny ticking accusations of an unseen clock. Brooding, featureless walls of threatening blue. The cry of a child, shrieking like a thousand demons.

Martin had his eyes squeezed tightly shut, but it was no use. The voices were still there. He could still *see* the voices. But how was that even possible? How could he see –?

It's all for you!

He didn't want to scream. Screaming hurt. But screaming was so seductive. The shaking started again. He looked at his hands and they were motionless. Pale and still, like …

For you, Martin. All for you.

He didn't understand. But he did understand. He knew he deserved it all. The voices nodded. Everything was because of him. Because of his sins. Because of … the voices were nodding faster now. And laughing. And accusing. And they were … the bed shook violently as he jolted awake.

He lay still for a moment and listened to the ticking of his wrist-watch on the bedside cabinet. The hotel room was small but comfortable with walls of soothing blue, washed pale by the streetlights from the road outside.

Martin sat up and looked at the digital display on the clock beside the bed. 4:33am. He was sleeping much better these days, he thought, and the nightmares were now confined to when he was asleep. He had made a lot of progress in the last six months. He got up and went to the bathroom.

He had spent his first few days in Belfast reacquainting himself with the city centre and was surprised to find that not an awful lot had changed. The security gates that ringed the main retail area were, he supposed, inevitable, and the Grand Central Hotel that had once graced Royal Avenue was now a garish new shopping centre, but most other things were familiar to him.

The famous department stores of Robinson and Cleaver, and Anderson and McAuley had ceased trading, but the decorative old Victorian buildings were still there, now hosting new retail outlets for fashion and entertainment.

The City Hall still stood, unchanged, at the very heart of the city, and Martin was cheered by the sight of buses darting constantly around the pale grey building. He had once worked as a mechanic at the bus depot in Ardoyne and, even though these buses were updated versions of the ones he had worked on, they brought back some distant memories, and he looked on them fondly.

Ardoyne was now at the forefront of his mind as he stood looking out of his hotel window at the empty city. The streetlights still illuminated the roads outside, despite no one being around to appreciate their glow. Martin preferred this time of day. He preferred it to when the city had shaken itself awake to shatter the peaceful calm with the scurrying, shouting, insidious infestation of humanity. At this time of day, it was just him and the redundant streetlights, and just as the lights would quietly fade as the city stirred, he would retreat a little into himself as the noise and the bustle of the day increased.

He sighed as he sat back on the bed. He was trying not to think of the day ahead, but he could avoid it no longer. Today was the day when he would go back to Ardoyne.

So, what would he find there? That was the question that was causing little ripples of anxiety to wash back and forth through his thoughts as he played out a host of scenarios in his mind. Would he be welcomed with open arms back into the happy warmth of his family? This, he felt, was the least likely of all the scenarios, but it was the one that he played with the most. What could he expect from their reactions, he wondered. Would it be disappointment? Anger? Disgust? Blame? Or would they be happy to see him? Would there be celebrations? Would there be joy?

Or would there be indifference? Would that be the worst reaction, he wondered. An apathetic shrug? He shuddered as he tortured himself with events that most likely would never happen. Not today at least.

Martin knew that it was unlikely he would find his family in the same little house that he had been dragged away from all those years ago, but he believed it could provide a start to his search. He had sent a speculative letter to the address several weeks ago but had received no reply, and he could find no listing in the phone book, so he decided he would simply call to the house, knock on the door, and see where it led him.

His fears, though, were crippling him. The clock told him it would soon be time for the brash day to sweep away the night that the steadfast little streetlights still pointlessly held at bay, so he forced himself to prepare for whatever he was about to face. He would have a wash and a shave. He would dress and he would have breakfast, and he would stride with confidence and with purpose into the coming day.

And he would go to Ardoyne.

There were two Ardoynes. There was the original village, built in the 1800s to house the workforce from the mills that wove flax plants into linen, with houses that were simple brick two-storey boxes packed tightly together in rows of tiny streets.

This village gradually expanded further from the mills, but the structure of the houses remained the same – four roomed, two storied dwellings, with a lavatory out in the backyard and a front door that opened straight onto the street.

This was 'old' Ardoyne, and by the time the McCann family had moved in, the mills had been abandoned and the homes adjacent to them, sitting on cobbled streets, were largely derelict. The McCann's house, however, was still in a vibrant part of the area, and from his front window, Martin was able to look straight up Elmfield Street and see the Saunders' Club on the left hand side. If he stepped outside his house and turned directly to his right, he would see the little gap in a row of larger houses that led to the most recent part of Ardoyne that was known as the Glenard Estate.

Martin and his wife, Shauna, had once held ambitions to one day move the short distance to Glenard, where each house, though still terraced, had a spacious front garden and, more excitingly, an indoor bathroom. It was in Glenard where the bus depot was situated where Martin had once been employed, and he had admired the gardens as he walked through the area every day on his way to and from work.

And so, he decided, it might be pleasant to approach his old home by strolling through Glenard on his way to the little gap that led to the older terraces of Herbert Street and beyond.

It was a bright spring day when the bus dropped him at the Oldpark Road end of Alliance Avenue. The houses here were large, detached properties, surrounded by tall, established trees, and a world away from the terraces of Ardoyne that lay less than half a mile away along the avenue.

Alliance Avenue ran through the leafy suburbs until it eventually became the eastern boundary of Glenard, running parallel to Brompton Park, a quarter mile distant, that formed the western boundary. It was Brompton Park that was split in half by the gap through to Old Ardoyne. If Alliance Avenue and Brompton Park could be said to form the two uprights of the capital letter 'H' then the bar in the middle was formed by the arrow-straight Berwick Road, from which ran, left and right, the streets of Glenard.

As Glenard was built on the side of one of Belfast's many hills, then anyone walking along the Berwick Road from the Alliance Avenue end towards Brompton Park would see the streets on their left run steeply downhill and the streets to the right rise uphill. This was Martin's plan, to walk along the Berwick Road towards the Brompton Park gap.

As he made his way down Alliance Avenue towards the Berwick, he was saddened to see the tall, corrugated iron barriers of the 'Peace Lines' filling in any possible gaps along the right hand side of the avenue and preventing any contact with the people of the Glenbryn Estate on the other side who were, judging by the Union flags showing just above the Peace Line, loyal to Britain and therefore hostile to the Irish Nationalists of Ardoyne.

Martin could remember how these streets had once been all open, and how people could move freely wherever they liked. He felt, as well, that everything seemed cleaner back then, or more cared-for at least.

Back in the sixties, before that decade's end had ushered in the Troubles.

He reached the Berwick Road and paused. To his right, the gap in Alliance Avenue that echoed the gap at the other end of the Berwick was blocked off by a Peace Line. Ahead, the avenue carried on to eventually meet one of the main roads that circled Ardoyne, which meant that Martin turned left and set off towards the gap that he could just make out at the far end of the Berwick Road.

Many of the gable walls, Martin noted, of the end houses on the streets that ran at right angles to the Berwick Road contained colourful murals. These murals featured images either of nationalist politics, supporting the revolutionary efforts of Irish republicanism, or of Mary, the goddess of conservative Catholicism, which gave the impression that the Queen of Heaven was a passionate advocate of armed resistance.

This mixture of politics and religion was also evident in the Easter decorations that Martin could see in the streets to the right and to the left as he strolled along. The colours of the buntings that ran from the upper windows of many of the houses, down to the wall or fence at the front of their gardens, fell into one of two categories.

One of these was the green, white and orange of the Irish national flag which served to commemorate the Easter Rising in Dublin in 1916, when Irish Republicans had launched an armed insurrection against British rule. Though quashed by an overwhelming British military response, it would lead eventually to the formation of an independent Irish Republic, and also to the partition of the island which left six counties still under British rule.

The other type of bunting was yellow and white. The colours of the Pope. This was to commemorate the most important date in the Christian calendar, when God sacrificed Himself, in human form, to atone for the sins of Man.

It all gave the district a colourful, festive air, thought Martin, which was only enhanced by the warm sunshine and the sense that spring had finally begun.

Walking along in the sunshine, Martin began to entertain all kinds of silly notions. He thought of taking Shauna for a drink at the Wheatfield, the bar they had frequented during their courting days. In his mind, Shauna was stunned but ecstatic to see him. She would catch a glimpse of him at the end of the street but would look away and then slowly turn back as recognition widened her eyes and caused her to gasp aloud. She would walk towards him, and then run, and then she would throw herself into his arms and … he shook his head, bemused by his own foolishness. He knew that it was nothing more than a corny romantic fantasy, but still, he thought, he could dream at least, couldn't he?

As Martin got closer to the gap, he started to feel uneasy. This wasn't because of the apprehension he should have been feeling as he approached his old home, it was something else. Something was wrong.

He walked through the gap with growing disbelief. Where was Herbert Street? He could still see it in his mind. The pavement on the right hand side of the narrow street was higher than the pavement on the left and had a kerb of large granite blocks that formed a double step. He could see Elaine and Rosemary sitting together on the step, sharing a bag of sweets. He could see the housewives, gossiping at their front doors as their children kicked a ball and chased each other around the street. He could see the corner shop at the bottom of Elmfield Street where he bought his cigarettes before going for a drink in the Saunders' and … where was Elmfield Street? Where was the Saunders'?

A street sign informed him he was in something called Butler Place, which made no sense to him. He could remember a Butler *Street*, but not a Butler Place. He then found a Butler *Walk* which made sense, he supposed, for the paving tiles beneath his feet seemed to be for pedestrians only. He walked on with increasing despair. The houses here were all clean and modern and, he imagined, perfectly pleasant, but why were they all placed in such a haphazard fashion? The straightforward system of one street after another had been abandoned for a more random placement of homes that seemed to follow no obvious pattern. He eventually found something called Elmfield Street, but it bore no resemblance to the one he remembered.

Martin became more and more disorientated as he made his way through the unfamiliar and surreal environment. Disillusioned, and in something of a daze, he eventually found the Oldpark Road where he turned to his right and trudged back towards the city centre.

Back at his hotel that evening, Martin lay on his bed and wondered what he should do. It all seemed hopeless to him at the moment, but maybe he just needed some advice. Someone he could talk to. He fished out the little piece of paper that the woman, Stephanie, had given him on the ferry, and stared at the phone number.

After a few moments of internal debate, he made a decision.

Why not?

TWENTY SEVEN

There was no reason why Hannah should not meet up with Rosie but, as she approached the café in Great Victoria Street, she still felt a sense of unease about Rosie's connections to James.

It shouldn't matter, she told herself. She liked Rosie. She liked the thought of having Rosie as a friend, so she could see no reason at all for them not to meet.

Rosie had phoned to ask for more details on possible programming courses that she could take and it was decided that they should meet in town in order to speak face to face. Hannah had brought along some prospectuses and brochures that she thought might be of interest to Rosie and she found herself warming to the idea of helping someone embark on a new career.

When Hannah had first met Rosie she had initially been wary of her terse manner, but she soon came to appreciate Rosie's sharp humour and shrewd intelligence, and was now only too happy to encourage her desire for improvement.

She pushed open the door to the café and was surprised to see Rosie seated at a table beside another girl.

"Hiya, Hannah," said Rosie. "You remember Karen, don't you? From the funeral? She gave me a lift into town today."

"Karen, yes, of course," Hannah said, taking a seat. She gave Karen a warm smile. "Harry's wife, right? I could hardly forget your Harry."

"Aye, I know, Hannah love," Karen replied, "he is hard to forget, isn't he? God knows I've tried."

They all laughed as the waitress came to take their order. Once the order of tea and pastries had been brought to the table, Hannah and Rosie discussed the pros and cons of various courses while Karen watched and listened with great interest.

"I might try one of these courses myself," Karen told them as she flicked through the brochures. "I mean, I don't mean computers, like, I don't have the brains, but some of these other courses sound class."

"Well, why not?" said Hannah. "It can't do any harm, can it?"

The conversation and the easy laughter flowed freely around the table until, inevitably, the subject of Jamesy came up.

"It's a real shame about you and James," Karen told Hannah. "You looked really well together."

"I know," Hannah sighed, "but I think there were just too many differences. I still think about him, though." And then, to her surprise, Hannah began to reveal how she had been having inappropriate thoughts about James at inconvenient times of the day, and how they were making it difficult for her to concentrate.

"Awk, you're just horny, love," Karen told her. "Just have a wee wank. That'll sort you out."

Hannah could only gape, open-mouthed at Karen, as Rosie searched for somewhere to look. Rosie was no stranger to bawdy banter, but she believed there should be a time and a place for such remarks. Karen had no such filter.

"What?" asked Karen, puzzled by their reactions. "It's totally natural."

"I know," Rosie began, "but …"

"I … I … well …" Hannah was still wide-eyed and tongue-tied.

"I mean, I know it's not the same as having a –"

"Anyway, Karen," Rosie hastily interrupted, "I'm sure Hannah doesn't want to hear about all that."

"I'm only trying to help."

"But … but …" Hannah managed to stammer, "isn't it sinful?"

"Is it?" Karen asked with genuine curiosity. "Is it really?"

"Well, I … I …" Hannah thought about it. "I'm sure it must be," she concluded.

"So, are you saying, then," Karen went on, "that somewhere in the Bible, it says *Thou shalt not finger yourself?*"

"Oh, holy fuck!" Rosie muttered under her breath as she raised her eyes to the ceiling.

Hannah had got over her initial shock and was now, despite herself, becoming fascinated by the discussion. "Well, not those exact words," she said, "but then a lot of Scripture is implied."

"Implied?" asked Karen "What does that mean?"

"It means that you have to work out for yourself what the meaning is. Scripture doesn't spell everything out for you."

"I still don't know what you mean."

"Well, for example," Hannah explained, "you're talking about female masturbation, aren't you?"

"No, I'm talking about having a wank."

Hannah laughed. "Okay then, that. But the Bible implies that male masturbation is a sin, so from that we can –"

"Does it really?" Karen was intrigued.

"Well, yes, it's called the sin of Onan."

"Why is it a sin?"

"Because it's wasteful to spill your seed on the ground."

"Hannah!" Rosie exclaimed with shock and amusement and some new-found admiration. "You dirty bitch!"

"Aye, Hannah, that's just shocking talk, so it is," Karen told her solemnly, and they laughed. "Anyway, women don't spill their seed, do they?"

"Well, no but …"

"It sounds like you're reading a wee bit too much into the Bible there," said Karen.

"Maybe it's all about having wicked thoughts, though," Hannah suggested.

"Don't think about it, then. Just do it."

"I don't think it's that easy."

"Then you're doing it wrong."

"Jesus!" said Rosie. "I can't believe I have to listen to this. Can you two hear yourselves?" She steered the conversation back to less contentious topics and later, once they had finished up, Karen offered Hannah a lift back to her flat at the university.

"No, it's all right, thanks, Karen," Hannah told her, "it's not too far to walk."

They said their goodbyes and Hannah made her way thoughtfully back to her flat.

That night, in bed, Hannah lay awake thinking about the talk she had had with Karen. She couldn't fathom how Karen could be so unconcerned about the fate of her soul, and so uncaring about where she would be spending eternity. The words of Paul's letter to the Ephesians kept playing in her head:

But fornication, and all uncleanness, or covetousness, let it not be named among you.

Karen's liberal use of profanity was, according to Scripture, sinful in the eyes of God, and it bothered Hannah that anyone could be so dismissive of God's laws. Hannah, for most of her life had been terrified of incurring God's wrath.

There was a time in her childhood, she remembered, when she had been friendly with a little girl called Rebecca, who lived in the same street as her. At that time, they each owned a Sindy doll, a popular girls' toy, which they would play with constantly in each other's homes and gardens.

Rebecca, though, Hannah noted, possessed a lot more of Sindy's accessories than Hannah. In particular, Rebecca owned Sindy's pony. A beautiful Palomino horse that Hannah craved. She never seemed able to persuade her parents to buy one for her, though, so she would secretly burn with desire to possess Rebecca's pony. It was only later, when she had learnt the meaning of the word 'covet', that Hannah realised with horror that she had been continuously breaking the Tenth Commandment; *Thou shalt not covet thy neighbours' goods.*

She could still remember the sheer terror she had experienced as it became clear she would be going to Hell. She knew that committing a sin was enough to arouse God's fury, but to repeatedly break an entire Commandment could have only one consequence. She was going to Hell. She was going to burn forever in everlasting agony. Her childhood was suddenly a nightmare of fear, her imagination feeding with increasing intensity the torments she was certain to face.

The paralysing anxiety that she had felt had led to a spate of bedwetting, which only made things worse, for she knew that God must look with disapproval on such behaviour. It didn't matter that she could find no direct reference to bed-wetting in her Children's Bible, her paranoia was self-fulfilling. She was beyond redemption.

It had taken years for her to accept that there was a way for her to earn God's forgiveness, through the understanding and love of Jesus Christ, but the memories still haunted her. She still suffered from debilitating panic attacks, always fearful of causing some inadvertent offence.

As she lay on her back, her right hand resting on her lower abdomen, her fingertips lightly touching the skin through a gap in her pyjamas, she tried not to think of James. She tried not to think of Karen's frivolous words. She tried not to think at all. She knew that God was watching her. She knew that He could see and hear everything, but more than that, she knew despairingly, He could read her thoughts.

And how was she supposed to manage her thoughts, she wondered helplessly. Surely everyone experienced unwanted and unbidden thoughts that they could not control. She couldn't be the only one, could she?

She had been told, her whole life, that God's love was infinite and unconditional, but what were the Commandments, if not conditions? She felt God's disapproval more often than she felt His love. She felt His perpetual judgement, and, more than anything, she feared His wrath and His eternal damnation.

She turned over onto her side and tried to sleep, wondering if James felt as miserable as she did.

TWENTY EIGHT

"The back of the bus is in the huff,
Barney Boo!
The back of the bus is in the huff,
Barney Boo!
The back of the bus is –"

"That's enough, Gary," Harry's voice was soft, and held no obvious hint of menace, but Gary stopped singing, nonetheless.

"Aye, no problem, Harry," he said. He turned round to address the back of the van. "Just trying to get the holiday mood in full swing, isn't that right, lads?"

"Bit too early in the morning," said Seamus.

"Yeah, fuck off, Gary," Tone agreed. "Some of us are still asleep."

Gary grinned and turned back to look through the windscreen, tapping his fingers on his knee as he finished the song in his head.

Harry, in the driver's seat beside him, also stared ahead. The early morning roads were devoid of traffic, and they were making good time as they headed for Dublin Airport. Despite himself, Harry was quite enjoying the drive. He was pleased with his new van, which replaced the one he had lost at Christmas. It was larger than his previous van and, in the back, he had fitted wooden benches down the sides to accommodate his work crew as they went from job to job. Gary's friends now occupied the seating, with their luggage taking up the space in between.

The sun was shining and the road ahead was clear, so Harry was in good spirits. He was looking forward to the drive back, when it would just be him on his own, listening to the radio and lost in his own thoughts. Such tranquil moments were rare in Harry's life and so, when they did occur, he made a point of embracing them.

When they arrived at the airport, Harry stepped down from the driver's seat to help unload the luggage.

"Cheers for that, Harry." Everyone took turns to shake Harry's hand or pat him on the arm. Tone handed him a wad of notes. "Here you go, Harry," he said. "We had a wee whip-round for the petrol."

"Nah, don't worry about it," Harry told him. "That's too much, anyway."

"Now look, Harry," Tone insisted, "we don't want to have to fucking slap you about a bit, but if you keep up that auld nonsense, then –"

"All right, all right," said Harry with an exasperated smile. He took the money, got back in his van and drove off. Bobby, standing by Tone, watched the white van weave through the airport traffic until it was out of sight. He waited a little longer. Then a bit more. Then, when he felt sure that Harry was no longer in the same county, he turned to Tone.

"I reckon we could have taken him," he said.

"Aye, I know," said Tone. "Did you see the look on his face? Looked like he was going to shite himself, to be honest."

Everyone picked up their bags and walked into the airport. Once they had checked in their luggage, they all turned and automatically headed for the bar.

"Best thing about going on holiday," said Gary, lifting his pint, "is early morning drinking at the airport."

They all nodded in agreement.

"Got a long day ahead of us, though," Kevin pointed out.

"Well, that's why it's important to get off to a good start," Gary told him. "So, what's the deal, then, Kevin, with this place in Spain?"

"My folks bought it a couple of years ago," Kevin explained. "They'd been going on holiday to Spain every year and they just thought it would make sense to buy their own place out there."

"Was it expensive?"

"Well, it wasn't cheap, but it was reasonable compared to other parts of Spain. That bit of the coast doesn't get the same number of tourists that you get in the Costa Blanca or the Costa Brava, you see."

"Why not?"

Kevin shrugged. "Don't know," he said. "It's got some spectacular beaches. Maybe it just hasn't been developed as a tourist spot yet. It's where the Spaniards go on holiday, though. They come from all over Spain to the region, especially Gandia. That's the big holiday town there."

"So, the Spanish people go on holiday to a place where they don't have to put up with drunken arseholes from the rest of Europe, then, is that what you're saying?"

"They're going to love *us,* then," said Seamus.

Kevin smiled. "It's not like that," he said. "Everybody's dead friendly there. It's all really relaxed, a lot more relaxed than all the mad tourist places, anyway."

"Sounds like just what we need," Tone said, looking around him. "Somewhere we can all just chill out for a few days."

Joker stood up. "Well, I'm going to get a round in," he informed everyone. "Who wants to give me a hand?"

"I'll go with you," said Jamesy, standing up. "I want to have a look in the bookshop as well."

"You want to pick up some nudie books?" asked Joker as they set off.

"What? No, no, I just …"

"It's all right, Jamesy, I'm not judging …"

Gary turned back to Kevin. "So, do you speak Spanish, then?" he asked.

"I wouldn't say I'm fluent, but I can get by okay."

"I suppose it's still the Easter holidays there."

"Yeah, I think so."

"So, how do you say Easter in Spanish, then?"

"Mmm...*Pascua*, I think."

"*Pascua*? Really?"

"Why, Gary?" said Tone. "Did you think it would be something like 'Eastero'?"

"Well yeah," Gary replied. "Or something a bit closer to Easter anyway. *Pascua* is completely different, isn't it? Where did *Pascua* come from?"

Kevin shrugged. "Never thought about it."

"Ask Joker," Sean suggested. "He'll know."

"Not that I'm all that curious," said Gary, "but it just seems a bit weird, that's all." He drained the last of his pint and put the empty glass on the table. "Now that's what I call timing," he said as Joker and Jamesy returned from the bar. Drinks were distributed and everyone settled down for the fresh round.

"Did you go to the bookshop, Jamesy?" asked Bobby.

"Yeah, I just had a quick look, I might go back later on."

"Are you looking for anything in particular?"

"I don't know," Jamesy sighed, "I just thought I might try a bit of light fiction."

"Fiction? Really?" Bobby was surprised. "That's not like you, Jamesy. I thought you'd be after something like a thousand-page account of what the Babylonians got up to."

"Well, I'm having a bit of trouble concentrating these days," Jamesy explained, "so I thought I could use this week to try and take it easy, you know? Just chill out for a bit."

"Yeah," said Bobby, "I think that's the plan for us all."

"Right well, if you two have finished boring the shite out of everybody," said Gary, "I have an intellectual question I'd like to pose to Joker here."

Joker gave Gary a quizzical glance.

"Why is the Spanish word for Easter," Gary began, "so different from everybody else's word for Easter?"

"Everybody else's?" asked Joker, amused. "Do you know what the French word for Easter is?"

"No."

"It's *Les Pậques*," said Joker. "And what about Italian?"

Gary shook his head.

"*Pasqua,*" Joker told him.

"What?" asked Gary. "The same as Spanish?"

"Near enough."

"So, Easter is the odd one out, then? Is that what you're saying?"

"Not quite," Joker explained. "French, Spanish and Italian are all classed as Romance languages, and the Romance languages take their names for the resurrection story from the Latin and Greek variations on the old Hebrew word for *Passover*."

"*Passover*? Isn't that a Jewish thing?"

"Yeah, *Passover* was already an established festival for that time of year, so the Christians just adapted it."

"Yeah," said Tone, "they did the same thing with Christmas."

"So, where the hell does the word Easter come from, then?"

"Well," said Joker, "English is classed as one of the Germanic languages, you see, and it seems that, back in the day, the pre-Christian tribes of northern Europe had a load of different gods and goddesses, and one of these goddesses was called *Oestre*. That's spelt O, E, S, T, R, E. She was the goddess of spring, or the dawn or something. So anyway, when they all became Christians, they just said, *Fuck it! We'll just use that*. You know, because it had that whole rebirth, Springtime sort of vibe going on."

"You could make a claim," Jamesy suggested, "that *Oestre* evolved from an earlier Mesopotamian goddess, *Inanna*, whose name later became *Ishtar*."

"Yeah well, we're not going to go down that rabbit hole, are we, Jamesy?"

"Just saying."

Kevin stared at Joker with a mixture of puzzlement and awe. "How do you know all that?" he asked.

"Oh, it's just a wee hobby of mine," Joker told him. "Languages, linguistics, that sort of thing."

"Sounds like you'll come in handy over in Spain, then."

"Well, Castilian's not a problem," said Joker, "but I'm looking forward to finding out a bit more about Valencian."

"Valencian?" asked Seamus. "What the fuck is Valencian?"

"You've heard of Catalonia, haven't you?" Joker asked. "And the Basque Region?"

"Yeah but –"

"And you know they speak their own languages, don't you?" Joker carried on as Seamus nodded. "Well, as far as I know, in the region around Valencia, they speak their own language too. It's not as famous as Basque or Catalan, but it –"

"For fuck's sake!" Gary exclaimed. "Does *anybody* speak bloody Spanish in Spain?"

"Yes, Gary," Joker patiently explained. "Everybody speaks the official language of Castilian Spanish, but Castile is just the middle bit of Spain. The other regions have their own sense of identity, and some of them have their own language too."

"It all sounds a bit fucked up, if you ask me."

"It's like if you go to Wales," said Joker. "Everybody there speaks English, but a lot of the time they just talk to each other in Welsh."

"Or if you go to north Belfast," Tone suggested. "Everybody there talks bullshit."

"Fuck off!" the natives of north Belfast told Tone, who was grinning into his beer.

"I would imagine," Joker went on, "that Valencian isn't that much different from Catalan, which, as I'm sure you all know, is another Romance language from the Proto Indo-European root."

"Well, obviously!" tutted Bobby, rolling his eyes.

"Unlike the Basque language," said Joker. "Nobody knows where the fuck that comes from."

"You see, Kevin," said Tone. "And you thought this was just going to be a week of mindless boozing."

"It *is* just going to be a week of mindless boozing," insisted Gary. "All this educational bahleeks needs to be nipped in the bud."

"Look," Tone explained hastily, "nobody is suggesting for a minute that there won't be any boozing going on, but you have to –"

"I don't know how you can say that," said Sean, holding up an empty glass. "I've run out of booze already."

"Oh, for fuck's sake!" cried Tone. "Right, okay, I'll get this round."

"They'll be calling the flight soon," Bobby pointed out, "so you should get a move on."

The flight to Barcelona was almost full, with the holiday mood in full swing, and the time passed quickly in a haze of vodka and beer and banter and sing-songs.

At Barcelona Airport, Kevin led them to the trains, where they boarded an Express to Valencia. This proved to be the perfect opportunity for everyone to catch up on some much-needed sleep as they were whisked, in air-conditioned comfort, down the east coast of Spain to the next stage in their journey.

At the train station in Valencia, they caught another train for the short trip to the station at Tavernes de la Valldigna. Where some confusion arose.

"What the fuck do you mean, 'we're not there yet'?"

"Well, I told you," Kevin tried to explain, "that Tavernes beach is obviously on the coast, but the actual town is a few miles further inland."

"So what's your point?" asked Gary as they walked outside the tiny train station to be greeted with … nothing. "Shit!"

"The train station," said Kevin, "is between the two."

"In the middle of nowhere, you mean?"

"Well," Kevin looked around him. The plain stretched wide and empty, and was bathed in a sumptuous, early-evening light that was a parting gift from the sun as it dipped behind the mountains in the distance off to the left. "You could say that."

Gary considered launching into a thoughtful tirade, laced with some choice expletives, but the sheer tranquillity of the scene demanded reverential silence, and so they simply stood and watched as the light faded gently away into an evening that rippled with cicada song.

It almost felt like an intrusion when the shuttle bus came rattling along the road, but they all clambered aboard and by the time they arrived at the beach, it was dark.

They were dropped off at one end of a palm tree-lined paseo that ran behind a row of buildings facing directly onto the beach. Many of the buildings were apartment blocks, but there were several among them that were just single, private properties, and it was to one of these that Kevin headed.

"Jesus Christ!" said everyone at once when Kevin had unlocked the door and led them inside. The large interior was all open-plan, with marble floors and luxurious furnishings. A kitchen area, off to one side, was spacious enough to contain a grand, French-polished dining table, while the lounge area held lavish seating, all tastefully upholstered in cream-coloured leather. At the far end of the room was an impressive set of double doors that could be opened to provide direct access to a veranda and the beach beyond.

"All built on the backs of the workers, no doubt," sniffed Joker.

"Oh, that's right," said Tone. "I forgot that the multi-national corporation that you work for gives all their profits away to charity. Isn't that right, Joker?"

"Piss off, Tone."

"Well, stop being such a fucking hypocrite, then."

Kevin led them on a tour of the house. Upstairs they were shown the bedrooms, the lavatory and a separate wet-room, where they could shower.

"Where do these stairs go?" asked Gary, pointing to a staircase at the end of a corridor.

"I'll show you." Kevin led them up the stairs and onto a wide terraced roof with a floor of terracotta tiles. There was a wall along one side of the roof that held the door to the stairway, and which had a wooden bench set against it. A table and chairs sat in the middle of the tiled floor, and around the other three sides of the roof ran a low, ornamental balustrade.

Beyond the balustrade directly opposite the wall with the stairwell lay the quietly shimmering Mediterranean Sea.

"All the shops," said Kevin, "are just on the other side of the paseo, behind us. There's a wee supermarket that'll still be open, so if anybody fancies some beer, then –"

Joker shocked Kevin with a spontaneous hug. He then clapped his hands together. "Right," he said, "I'm away to the shops. Who's coming?"

"We'll all go," said Tone.

"Well," Bobby sighed as he looked around him. "this'll just have to do, I suppose."

TWENTY NINE

Nigeria, 1964-1967

Adanna decided to enrol at Enugu University to begin a course in teacher training. Initially she had planned to take the bus every day to and from the university but, after a while, Benjamin persuaded her that it would make more practical and financial sense for her to move into the spare room in his bungalow on campus.

And it was there that the fates, inevitably, threw them together as lovers.

After several months of needy, clinging, almost dream-like love-making, Benjamin blurted out a clumsy proposal of marriage, and Adanna accepted.

Later, though, she wondered why.

Even though she was now working towards a career in teaching, Adanna still felt listless and unsure of her place in the world, and had accepted Benjamin's proposal with the same unthinking compliance that had led her into accepting her previous job offer in bar management.

Her introspection reached heavenward.

Adanna had always had an informal relationship with God – rather than pray she would prefer to have a casual chat – and it was to Him she turned for answers.

Lying awake at night, Adanna discussed how the easy assumptions of her future had all been shattered in Kano, and how she had drifted onto an uncertain path with little sense of direction.

Is this where my life is meant to go? she asked God. *Is this the purpose that You have for me now?* Feeling untethered, disconnected, from her life, Adanna no longer trusted her own decisions. What was it that she wanted, she wondered. She tried to examine her desires, but they were vague and fleeting; drifting, like herself, on an aimless breeze.

She was not expecting any answers from God, but she asked for them, nonetheless.

Her feelings for Benjamin were just as hazy as everything else in her life. Was she simply fond of him? Was it nothing more than admiration? Was she confusing her gratitude for his help in Kano for something else? Or did she love him? Was she actually in love with him? She couldn't say.

There was one night, however, when all of her feelings towards Benjamin became focused and resolute, as they all formed together into a blistering furnace of hatred.

That night she had screamed obscenities at him, loathed the very thought of him. She had sworn and cursed his name, his birth and his very existence. She didn't love him at that moment, that was for sure.

But it was not much later – that very same night, in fact – when her daughter had slipped into the world, and mother and child had gazed upon each other in silent wonder, that Adanna had thought that maybe she did love Benjamin after all.

She certainly felt that, at that moment, she had more than enough love to go around.

"She will have an Igbo name," Adanna insisted.

"Of course," said Benjamin, as he cradled his daughter in his arms. "Did you have something in mind?"

"Chiaza," she said firmly. "It is short for Chiazacam."

"Chiaza," Benjamin said, testing the feel of the name on his lips. "I like it." He stared at the tiny, sleeping face and whispered.

"Chiaza."

Benjamin and Adanna were already a popular couple on campus, and that popularity was only cemented by Chiazacam's arrival.

As she grew, the entire university fell before her. It was an unfair contest, after all, for not only was she blessed with a wistful blend of her father's Nilotic golden bronze and the dark fire of the sub-Sahara, she was also armed with a giggle that could squeeze hearts. No one stood a chance.

Benjamin arrived home one day from work, to find Chiaza in the kitchen, helping Adanna's mother to bake bread.

"Hello, Ijemma," he said to Mrs Obiaka as he lifted Chiaza into the air, "and how has my little girl been today?"

"She has been fine, Benjamin," Ijemma replied. "We've had a very busy day, haven't we, my sweet?"

"I thought that Adanna would be home by now," said Benjamin as he lowered his daughter back to the floor.

"No, she told me she would be late getting back today. She said she had something to do after class."

"Did she say what?"

"No, not to me."

Benjamin shrugged and poured himself a glass of water. He leant against the kitchen worktop and chatted to Ijemma while Chiaza tugged at his trouser leg for attention. After a while, they heard the front door, and then Adanna appeared.

"Good afternoon, everyone," she said smiling. Chiaza ran to her and Adanna picked her up and carried her into the living room. Benjamin and Ijemma followed.

"Where have you been?" Ijemma asked Adanna as they sat down.

"Oh, Momma, that is my business."

"So, you have secrets from your mother?" Ijemma cried passionately. "From your husband, I can understand, but from your own mother?"

Benjamin was about to say something, but Ijemma motioned for him to shush.

"You will know soon enough," said Adanna, "but, Benjamin, you said this morning that you wanted to talk to me about something."

"What? Oh, yes," Benjamin said, "I was just thinking that we could go on holiday when the term is over. I thought it would be nice to visit Europe, perhaps see Paris, or London maybe. What do you think?"

"Does this include me?" asked Ijemma.

"Yes, of course," Benjamin told her.

"Then I think it is a very fine idea!"

They turned to Adanna who was playing on the sofa with Chiaza. She acted as if she hadn't heard.

"Well?" Ijemma prompted.

"Well," Adanna finally spoke. "That all sounds well and good, but what will we do with Chiazacam's baby brother?"

"Chiazacam's …?" Benjamin stared at her. "What?"

Adanna simply smiled, and Benjamin jumped up to cross the room and embrace her.

"But, how can you be sure it will be a boy?" he asked.

"It will be a boy," Adanna stated firmly.

It was a boy.

They named him Ikeobi, and his big sister was delighted with her new toy, taking charge to fuss over him and to teach him all the things that he would need to know.

This was a happy time in Benjamin's life. Adanna was now teaching at a school in the centre of Enugu, and had found satisfaction and a contented peace in the role. Chiaza and Ikeobi thrived, and Benjamin arranged for a young girl from a nearby village to look after them during the day while he and Adanna were at work.

In the evenings, after the children had gone to sleep, Benjamin and Adanna liked to take some drinks out to the back garden and sit at the little table on the lawn, quiet and comfortable in each other's company. They would often have friends call to the house as well. Adanna's mother, Ijemma, would drop by several times a week, and both Father Jerome and Pastor Osawe were regular visitors. Adanna would often leave Benjamin and Father Jerome chatting outside long into the night as they discussed everything from football to science and religion to the bewildering machinations of Nigerian politics.

It was not long after Ikeobi had taken his first steps in the world that the initial reports of the massacres came in.

Adanna and Benjamin listened with growing disbelief to the confusing news bulletins, but it was the visit of Father Jerome that brought home to them the full horror of the events.

"It's bad all right," Father Jerome admitted as they sat at the table in the back garden, Chiaza and Ikeobi playing nearby. "The stories are coming in from all over the North. It seems to be mostly Igbo who are being attacked, but there are reports of other non-Hausa people also being killed."

"But why?" Benjamin asked.

"Do the Hausa need a reason?" Adanna said bitterly.

Father Jerome sighed as he shook his head. "They say it's to pay the Igbo back for the political killings at the start of the year, during the attempted coup."

"But that doesn't make sense," Benjamin insisted. "It was because of Igbo officers in the army that the coup failed."

"I know," said Father Jerome, "it's a flimsy excuse, and, in any case, it doesn't have the feel of simple acts of vengeance. It all seems to have been carefully planned. Many of the Igbo people in the army have been killed by their former comrades, and it's the Hausa soldiers who have been responsible for many of the civilian deaths."

"Benjamin," Adanna suddenly cried, "Zara is still in Kano!"

Father Jerome looked at her. "If you have any Igbo friends in the North," he said, "then I would recommend that you urge them to leave as soon as possible. If you can reach them, that is."

"She should be at work at this time," Adanna said. "I should try to phone her." She got up and went inside.

"What does Gowon have to say about the killings?" Benjamin asked Father Jerome.

"Nothing that's any use," Father Jerome admitted. "You have to remember that Gowon is from the North, so there's not much chance of him cracking down on the troubles in the North, is there? Besides," he went on, "Gowon is an idiot. He may be nominally in charge at the moment, but I would say he's just a puppet for the Emirs in the North."

"But isn't Gowon a Christian?"

"He is, Benjamin, he is," said Father Jerome. "But like I said, the man is an idiot. There does seem to be an intelligence behind all of this, and intelligence is not something you can accuse Gowon of having."

"What about Ojukwu?" Benjamin asked. "Can Gowon recall him from the East?"

"I don't know," Father Jerome told him. "I'm not sure what the legal position is at the moment, but for now Ojukwu is still the governor in the East, and I don't think that will change anytime soon."

"I can't get an answer at Zara's work," Adanna stated as she came back outside. "I don't know what we can do." She looked pleadingly at Father Jerome.

"Well, you can't go to Kano, that's for sure," said Father Jerome. "It's far too dangerous."

"They say on the radio that it is not just in the North," Benjamin said to Father Jerome. "Is that true?"

"I believe so," Father Jerome sighed. "I've heard of sporadic attacks against Igbo people even in Lagos. Ojukwu has demanded that Gowon do something, but I'm not convinced Gowon would be able to do anything even if he wanted to."

Adanna sat down and looked at Father Jerome. "What do you think Ojukwu will do?" she asked.

"It's hard to say, Adanna. It's hard to know what he *can* do. I've met Ojukwu, you know, and I believe he's a good man. Maybe too good, to be honest."

"What do you mean?"

"I mean that I think he's too honest to be a politician. He's a soldier, really, and that's fine up to a point, I suppose, but when he assumed command of the East, I don't imagine that even *he* thought it would be anything other than temporary."

"What do you know about the reports of the refugees?" asked Benjamin.

Father Jerome paused as he scratched at his chin. He was a tall, well-built man, but Benjamin could swear he had shrunk since they last met. "Well," he said, "according to my colleagues, the reports, if anything, haven't gone far enough. People are coming in from all over the country, fleeing for their lives. The train stations of Onitsha, Nsukka and Port Harcourt are all swamped with walking wounded, all telling their stories and spreading the fear. I don't mind telling you both that I think it's just the beginning. I do believe it's going to get a lot worse."

The trickle of refugees became a flood. The Igbo fled from persecution from all corners of Nigeria. Even those who had never even been to the East, saw their traditional homeland as the only place where they could be safe.

The East buckled under the influx of over a million people, but managed to hold firm. The people who sought relief and sanctuary were seen, by the Igbo, as their own people, their family, and for the Igbo, family was everything. The refugees were welcomed and accommodated. But they brought with them tales that were fuel for nightmares.

"There is still no word from Zara," Adanna informed Benjamin.

"Have you spoken to her family in Port Harcourt?"

Adanna nodded. "Her father has driven to Kano to search for her."

"I don't know if that's wise," said Benjamin. "You've heard the stories, haven't you?"

"I know, but what else can her father do?"

Everyone in the East had now heard the stories. Of children being hacked to death. Of pregnant women being cut open, the contents of their wombs stomped into the ground. Of people being locked up without food or water and taunted as they died.

The systematic slaughter was seen as an attempted genocide against the entire Igbo race, and as 1967 began, the fear and the terror of the people in the East had turned to outrage. The demands began to grow for what many felt was the only option left open to them. Independence.

Benjamin was alone in the house when Father Jerome pulled up. They greeted each other warmly and then Benjamin took two bottles of beer from the fridge and led his friend out to the table in the back garden.

"Adanna not home, then?" asked Father Jerome.

"She has taken the children to visit her mother," Benjamin told him.

"And how is Ijemma these days?"

"She is busy," said Benjamin. "You know how she has taken in some refugees, don't you?"

"Ah, yes," Father Jerome said with a smile. "The distant cousins."

"That's right."

"And how are you, then, Benjamin? I haven't seen you in a while."

"Same as always, really. Still teaching at the university."

"Mmm," Father Jerome said thoughtfully, "and what would you say is the mood there? Among your students, I mean."

"They all say the same thing," said Benjamin, "that we must have a country of our own. That the Igbo will never be safe in a Hausa-controlled Nigeria. That the East has no alternative but to secede and to forge a new destiny. But I am sure you have heard all the arguments yourself."

Father Jerome nodded. "Yes," he agreed, "no matter where you go, you hear the same things. The calls for independence grow louder every day."

"What do you think will happen?"

"Well, I know that Ojukwu will do everything in his power to keep Nigeria together." Father Jerome held up a hand as Benjamin was about to speak. "Oh, it's not that Ojukwu has any great idealistic notions about One Nigeria, of course, but he's smart enough to know what the alternative would be. Gowon can't afford to let the East just walk away."

"Because of the oil, you mean?"

"The oil plays a big part of it, Benjamin, yes, but think of the bigger picture. Nigeria is not the only country in Africa to be cobbled together from the old colonies. There are borders all over the continent that cut through tribal lands that have existed for millennia. Ancient tribes have been thrown together here, there and everywhere and they've been told they're now part of this country or that country, and they're now called this or that. Did you know the name *Nigeria* was made up by an old British woman?"

"Yes," Benjamin smiled. "Thanks to my wife, I now know my history."

"So just imagine, Benjamin, if the Igbo were allowed to declare their independence and simply go off on their own. What message do you think that would send to the tribes all over Africa who feel persecuted, or unheard, or who just want to decide their own fate?"

"But it isn't just the Igbo, is it? Ojukwu has made a point of including all the tribes of the East. The East is a region, not a tribe."

"Yes, I know that, but that is not how it will be perceived by the outside world, now, is it? No, Benjamin, it will be looked upon as nothing more than a rebellion by the ungrateful, upstart Igbo, and it could spark uprisings right across the continent."

"You don't agree with independence, then?"

Father Jerome sighed and scratched his head. "Look," he said, "I'd be something of a hypocrite if I claimed that armed insurrection is morally unjustifiable – sure didn't my own father rise against the Brits in 1916? – but this would be suicide. Like I said, Gowon would have no choice but to go to war if the East declared independence, and the British would side with him. In fact, any European power with a vested interest in African stability would side with him too. Gowon would have access to whatever military hardware he needed to crush any uprising. And what do they have here in the East, Benjamin? Little more than shotguns and bloody muskets, that's what."

"It may be inevitable, though," Benjamin said sadly.

"If that cretin, Gowon, reneges on the Aburi Accord," said Father Jerome, "then I would have to agree with you."

A diplomatic solution to the crisis had been sought at the neutral venue of Aburi in Ghana, where Colonel Ojukwu presented a set of proposals designed to pull Nigeria back from the brink of civil war.

These proposals were accepted by the delegation, led by Colonel Yakubu Gowon, representing the Federal Government of Nigeria. And war was averted.

Until Gowon returned to Lagos, where he reneged on the entire accord.

And the calls could no longer be ignored. A new nation would rise. A nation that would take her name from the bay that washed the southern shore. A nation that would stride onto the world stage, with her people filled with pride and hope and belief. A nation, alive with the glow of liberty, that would shine like a beacon for Africa and for the world.

An independent sovereign state with a burning urge for self-determination.

Biafra.

THIRTY

Joker was the first one up. Standing at the bottom of the stairs he paused to take in, once again, the opulence of the room. He shook his head in wonder that this was considered just a little holiday get-away. He had been informed that Kevin's father had grown up impoverished in the working-class housing estate of Ballymurphy, and Joker had been forced to admit that his achievements since then had been worthy of appreciation and, indeed, praise.

Kevin had explained that his father made a point of using his chain of hair and beauty salons around Ireland to employ only the most vulnerable and the most disadvantaged from those sections of society that were generally overlooked, and had initiated a generous profit-sharing scheme that benefited the entire workforce. That information had certainly poured cold water on Joker's attempted rant about the callous exploitation of ordinary working people and had led him to go into a bit of a sulk. He just wasn't prepared for altruistic capitalism.

He walked across the room and, turning the lock, pulled open the patio-style, double bi-fold doors to take a look at the beach. It was early and the sun had just cleared the horizon, smearing the sky with a chaotic mess of oranges and pinks and reds. He walked across the veranda and strode out onto the sand, enjoying the cool sensation on his bare feet.

The sea, whilst mimicking the sky in its silent surface, was making nonchalant little ripples against the shore, as if kicking its heels waiting for the world to wake up and come along to play. Joker sat down at the water's edge. As he gazed at the empty horizon, he wasn't sure that he liked all this peace and serenity. It seemed unnatural. The silence was almost unnerving.

"I could get used to this."

Joker turned to see Gary standing beside him, looking out across the water.

"Not missing Belfast, then?"

"You're kidding, aren't you? It's going to be hard to go home," said Gary as he sat down. "In fact, I might squeal like a pig."

"Yeah," said Joker. "It's some place, isn't it?"

"Unbelievable," Gary agreed. "I was thinking of bringing Rosie here over the summer for a wee bit of a break."

"Bit presumptuous of you, isn't it? Anyway, aren't you and Rosie going to be busy this summer?"

"Fuck's sake, Joker, don't you start as well. It's just a baby we're having, it's not like it's the end of the world or anything."

Joker stared at Gary for a second, then turned away. "Yeah, maybe you're right," he said. He knew there was no point in trying to unveil the true nature of reality to Gary; it would be like trying to teach quantum theory to a bag of squirrels. "What about Kevin, though? Or his folks, even? Do you think they'll be happy with you just moving in?"

"Oh, I'm sure it won't be a big deal," Gary assured him. "Kevin seems sound these days, doesn't he? Totally different from the wee prick he used to be."

"Yeah, well, he's not Johnny Gee anymore," Joker mused idly.

"Yeah, what was that all about? Did you ever find out?"

"Not that interested to be honest."

A few muffled noises of people stirring back at the house made them both turn around. Joker stood up and wiped the sand from his shorts.

"Well," he said, "I think we should go back and find out what the plan is for today."

After breakfast it was decided that, after the exertions of the previous day, they should take the opportunity to spend the day relaxing at the beach, and so by mid-morning they stepped onto the sand with their towels, and sunglasses, and swimming gear, and sun-tan lotion, and paperbacks, and bottles of water and sunhats and various inflatables.

They spent some time finding the optimum position before laying out their beach-towels in a long row and placing all the items required for a day at the beach in strategic places around the area.

It looked like the day would get hot, even though it was only late April, so they slapped on some sun-tan lotion and then, finally, they all lay down on their towels to gently sizzle in the golden Iberian sun. After ten seconds, Joker sat up.

"Fuck this," he said. "I'm going for a beer."

"I'll come with you."

"Yeah, me too."

"Yeah, this is boring."

"Yeah, I've had enough now."

They all stood up and spent some time packing away all of the beach paraphernalia – the paperbacks, the sunhats, the bottles of water, the sun-tan lotion, towels, etc., and marched off to find a bar.

THIRTY ONE

India was once an island, apparently. But then, using something called *plate tectonics,* it crashed into Asia, causing the land to ruck up into the air and create a mountain range. And that's how the Himalayas were made.

Hannah shook her head in disbelief. How could such nonsense come to be written, she wondered. All of the land on Earth, she knew, had been created and fixed by God in a single day, but this book was trying to tell her that the land was moving about all over the place. And *had* been for hundreds of *millions* of years.

According to the book she was reading, the surface of the Earth was made up of different plates that moved around like lily pads on a pond. Sometimes these plates would rub against each other, causing earthquakes. And that made Hannah stop and think.

She knew that earthquakes were a powerful demonstration of God's wrath, and were sent as punishment for sinfulness, but she had never understood why earthquakes were prevalent in some parts of the world and not in others. The notion that earthquakes would occur mostly in those places where two of these plates met would explain that phenomenon, but that just raised all sorts of questions. Why, for example, would God create a world that was inherently unstable?

Hannah then noted with some disdain that the whole business of plate tectonics was just another scientific *theory*, and she closed the book with a sigh. Just more guesswork, she thought wearily, though she could see how the scientists would think it was a good explanation. She sat back in her chair and let her mind wander.

She had long known, of course, that much of society had dismissed Scripture as a reliable source of knowledge, but her time spent going through all these books at the library brought home to her just how pervasive the rejection of the Bible truly was. In fact, a lot of the information contained in these books flagrantly contradicted the facts given in the Bible. But then the Bible, Hannah thought guiltily, had a tendency to contradict itself.

It was the old conflict, she reflected miserably. The problems that she had with Scripture that pulled her in different directions. Biblical inconsistencies, Greg had told her, were probably just down to the scribes, who copied the original manuscripts, making silly mistakes, but why, she wondered, would God allow that to happen?

And besides, she thought, that might explain things like Saul's daughter, Michal, in the second book of Samuel, who remains childless all her life while, at the same time, having five sons, but it could not explain away the one obvious contradiction with which Hannah continued to struggle: the Sixth Commandment; *Thou shalt not kill.*

It is the clearest, the most straightforward, the least ambiguous guideline in all of Scripture, she thought, so why does God consistently ignore it? According to God, any woman who is not a virgin on her wedding night, must be stoned to death. *Must!* Anyone caught working on the Sabbath, *must* be stoned to death. Cursing your parents: death. Blasphemy: death. Adultery: death. Fortune-telling: death. Worship of other gods: death. The demand for slaughter in Scripture is relentless.

Hannah stood up to clear her thoughts. Knowing she was under constant divine scrutiny always made her feel anxious when such nagging doubts crept into her head. She wandered over to what was becoming her favourite section in the library; astronomy.

The absurd scale of the cosmos seemed to speak to her on a level that she didn't fully understand, she just knew that it held her enthralled. She picked out a few books and went back to her desk.

They say that nothing in the universe can go faster than the speed of light, but there were no speed limits in Hannah's mind. Moving at a trillion miles per hour, she soared clear of the Milky Way and out into intergalactic space, heading for Andromeda. The tip of James' tongue circled slowly around her naval before moving down towards her … she brushed it away dismissively. This was getting interesting.

The Andromeda Galaxy was the closest galaxy to the Milky Way and Hannah was looking forward to becoming more acquainted. Had she been plodding along at the sluggish old speed of light, then it would have taken her over two million years to get there, so it was just as well she was really motoring.

She had learned that the galaxies themselves were not exactly standing still, they were positively racing through space. In fact, the Andromeda Galaxy, she discovered, was following a graceful arc that would send it crashing into the Milky Way in about … wait, what?

Hannah stared at the words on the page. The Milky Way Galaxy, it seemed – the galaxy in which she was currently living, and where she kept all of her stuff – was on a collision course with the Andromeda Galaxy. It wasn't due to happen anytime soon – she still had a few billion years in which to brace herself – but still, the idea of galaxies going around bumping into each other was a little unsettling. It suggested some fairly sloppy planning, for one thing.

Leafing further through the books, she came across the subject of asteroids, where she found even more food for thought. The asteroid belt was situated between Mars and Jupiter and was estimated to contain around a billion lumps of rock of all shapes and sizes. These were believed to have once been trying to form a planet but had been pulled apart by the immense gravity of Jupiter, and again Hannah wondered at the purpose of such planning. She knew she had no place to go questioning God's divine plan, but a lot of His work was beginning to strike her as a little haphazard. Of course, it was possible that God just wanted to have a handy source of ammunition floating around in space for when He was in the mood to do a bit of smiting, but Hannah was learning that even the direction of God's fury could be a little perplexing.

In 1908, Hannah read, one of these asteroids entered the Earth's atmosphere and exploded with a force of up to 30 megatons of TNT. That figure didn't mean much to Hannah, but it sounded like quite a lot.

So, what was the target of such violent retribution? Who or what had provoked God's fury to such a cataclysmic extent?

It was trees.

This catastrophic explosion had occurred in a remote and unpopulated region of Siberia and had done little more than wipe out a lot of trees. An awful lot of trees. Around eighty million, in fact.

Now Hannah knew that a lot of God's actions in Scripture could appear baffling to the mortal mind, but sending a thirty megaton fireball to destroy a forest in the middle of nowhere seemed quirky even for God.

She shuddered as she realised her flippant thoughts could once again be construed as disrespectful, and she hurriedly closed her books and sat back, gripped with anxiety. She began to breathe faster and more heavily and, as she tried to bring her breathing under control, the image of James' smiling eyes came into her head and it seemed to calm her. To comfort her. She felt herself relax.

As she walked around the shelves, returning all the books she had taken, she thought again of James and it made her smile. She smiled at his gentle earnestness, his infectious passion for learning, his pompous assertion that he needed to know everything. She smiled at his gorgeous eyes, at his smile, at the way he would … she put her head down and walked quickly from the library, her mind clouded by discordant, confusing notions and the disapproving glare of God.

Making her way through town, she remembered Rosie telling her that James was in Spain this week and she imagined him drenched in warm sunshine. What was he thinking right now, she wondered. Was he thinking of her? What was he doing today, and how was he getting on? She strode along Royal Avenue, anxious, and miserable, and smiling.

THIRTY TWO

"Squeal, little piggy! Squeal!" Joker was taunting the pork sausages, as they hissed in the hot oil, with his criminally underrated impression of an American hillbilly.

Although it was still early, Joker had already been to the supermarket on the other side of the paseo, and had now taken it upon himself to cook breakfast for everyone. Tone and Sean had yet to appear, but everyone else was up, sitting around the dining table, bleary-eyed and yawning, stretching and idly scratching bits of themselves.

"Who was on at the shop?" asked Kevin.

"Some wee redhead," Joker told him. "Funny looking bake, but in a sexy sort of way."

"Sounds like Gabriela," Kevin mused. "I know her."

Joker stopped tormenting the sausages for a second and looked at Kevin. "Know her?" he asked. "What? Like in a biblical way?"

"What?" Kevin flushed. "No … no … I was just …"

Gary leaned forward, intrigued by Kevin's reaction. "That hit a nerve, didn't it? Are you sure you're not slipping her a length?"

"Jesus! No! I only –"

"What's for breakfast?" Tone appeared at the bottom of the stairs wearing just a pair of shorts and some flip-flops.

"Sausages," said Joker. "Hey, did you know that Kevin and the wee redhead from the shop are blowing trumpets?"

"Good for them," remarked Tone, taking a seat at the table. "Sausages and what?"

"Sausages and ketchup," Joker replied.

"Genius!" said Tone appreciatively. "Absolute genius! So, who's this wee redhead, then?"

"Gabriela," said Gary. He turned to Kevin. "That's her name, isn't it? Are you going to introduce us all later?"

"Seriously," Kevin stammered, "there's nothing going on. I've met her a couple of times and, like, we've said hello and all, but there's nothing going on."

"Well, far be it from me to question your veracity," said Tone as he lazily stretched his arms above his head, "but your redner would suggest otherwise."

"Yeah, what's the deal?" pressed Gary. "Do you fancy her, is that it?"

"If that's the case," said Joker, "then you've come to the –"

"For fuck's sake, leave the guy alone!" cried Bobby. He was concerned that Joker was becoming distracted from his breakfast-making duties.

"I'm just saying," Joker persisted, "that if Kevin needs a bit of relationship advice, then we're the very lads to come to. Isn't that right?"

"Yeah," said Bobby, "because we're all such fucking experts when it comes to relationships, aren't we?"

"Exactly, Bobby."

"What's keeping those fucking sausages?" demanded Seamus. He felt he should try to deflect some of the attention away from Kevin, who was becoming more and more flustered.

"All right, Seamus," said Joker, "we all know how you love a good sausage, but don't panic. They won't be long."

"I've heard that Seamus likes them long," quipped Tone, and all attention shifted away from Kevin, as everyone dusted off their favourite old double-entendres, and held them up as breakfast-time entertainment.

Jamesy, sensing there was something unspoken in Kevin's suddenly subdued bearing, determined that he would try to have a casual chat with him at some point later. When it was quieter.

After breakfast, everyone was lounging around, smoking, drinking tea and making plans for the rest of the day. Sean had appeared earlier and had been surprised to learn that a vote had been taken to decide the person who would be doing all the washing-up for that day.

"What can I say, Sean," said Tone, handing Sean a cloth, "it was completely unanimous."

"Wankers," Sean grumbled as he trudged off to the kitchen sink.

"So, what's the plan, then?" asked Bobby.

"I reckon we should go and check out the town," Tone suggested. "We need to go there sometime this week, anyway, to sort that house out, so we might as well get it over with."

"Yeah," Kevin agreed, "I wouldn't mind doing that, to be honest."

"Sounds good to me," said Bobby, and everyone else nodded their approval.

"We could either go after lunch," Kevin said, "or go now, and get lunch in the town."

Tone turned to address Joker. "Did you get anything for lunch," he asked, "when you were at the shop earlier?"

"I did, actually," Joker replied. "I got some stuff to make ham and cheese baguettes."

"Right then, we'll have lunch here, and then head off to the town after."

"And I even got some salad," Joker went on, "for Seamus here."

"What?" said Seamus, hearing his name. "What was that?"

"I got you some salad."

"And what the fuck is that supposed to mean?"

"Look, don't take this the wrong way," Joker began.

"Oh, fuck," muttered Gary. "Here we go …"

"But I was thinking that it's about time you started taking this whole gay thing a bit more seriously. You're just not making the effort, are you?"

"What? What are you talking about?"

"Well, do you not think you should start by embracing your feminine side a bit more?"

"Fuck off, Joker!" cried Seamus. "I may be gay, but that doesn't make me a poof!"

"You see!" said Joker. "That's exactly what I'm talking about! How are you supposed to get your hole with that sort of attitude?"

"Get my hole?" gasped Seamus. "Jesus Christ! Not everything's about sex, you know."

"Now you're getting the hang of it."

Seamus looked over at Tone with exasperation. "Can you have a fucking word with him?"

"Well, I don't know," said Tone, sipping his tea. "I think he might have a point."

"What?"

"It's all about being comfortable with your sexuality, isn't it?"

"Oh, for fuck's sake!"

"What's the salad got to do with anything, though?" asked Kevin.

"Well, it's a woman's thing, isn't it?" said Joker.

"Is it?"

"Actually," Jamesy interjected, "if we're having ham and cheese baguettes, then I'd be happy with a wee bit of salad in mine."

"Well said, Jamesy," Joker enthused. "We can all have a bit of salad just to show there's no shame in it."

"What the fuck are you on about?" asked Seamus.

"Look, I'm only trying to help you out here, you know," Joker insisted. "I mean, think about it. You haven't told me that my shirt looks nice, have you? You've never called me darling. You don't –"

"I'm sorry, which one of us is gay, again?"

"You've never called *me* darling either," said Bobby grinning. "My feelings are a wee bit hurt."

"Look," Joker said placatingly, "remember your man at the *panadería* yesterday?"

"Who?"

"You know who I mean. He called Jamesy his *hermosito*. Good-looking fella, he was."

"Oh yeah," said Seamus. "What about him?"

"Well, that's what I'm talking about," Joker explained. "Now you could tell that he was gay, couldn't you? He was completely at ease with his sexuality. And all that confidence really came across, didn't it? That's what I'm getting at, that's all. Actually, I thought that you and him would look good together."

"Don't know about that," Seamus said thoughtfully. "He was a bit too gay for my liking."

"*Too* gay?" cried Joker. "*Too* gay? You don't like being too gay? What the fuck are planning to do, then? Just stick it in a wee bit?"

"You don't know what the fuck you're talking about!" Seamus snapped. "You just think gay sex is all about the arse, don't you?"

"Well, isn't it?"

"No, it fucking isn't!"

"How the fuck would you know?"

"Because I've ..."

During the pause, everyone turned to stare at Seamus. Sean strolled over from the kitchen area. Tone's teacup was frozen halfway to his lips. Joker's right eyebrow rose slightly. A cheeky breeze flicked a few grains of sand through the open doors, and the sounds of the sea slapping the beach came along in slow regular beats.

Seamus looked around at the expectant faces and sighed. "Because I've already done the deed," he said.

Everyone erupted. "Good man yourself!" they cried as they patted Seamus on the back and shook his hand. "Good fucking lad!" Seamus, grinning, disappeared beneath all of the clamorous congratulations and the whoops of victory and joy.

The first thing that everyone noticed as they stepped off the bus, was the mountain. It dominated the town that sat at its base and could be seen from miles around. Everyone stood at the side of the main road that ran through the town and gazed up at the distant peak.

"Can you see the cross?" asked Kevin.

"What? Oh fuck, yeah, right enough." Right at the very top of the mountain, outlined against the blue sky, was a little black silhouette of a Christian cross.

"That's cool," said Sean, squinting up at the familiar shape.

"Right then, Kevin," said Tone. "Do you know where we're going?"

"Yeah, I've got a fair idea where it is," Kevin told him. He gestured across the road. "I think it's up that way."

The pavement on the street that Kevin led them to was only wide enough to accommodate two abreast, so they walked along in pairs as Kevin checked the house numbers. It was siesta time so the street was quiet, though a few residents could be seen sitting on the pavement by their front doors hoping to catch a cool breeze. Kevin halted.

"This is it, I think. Number Forty-Two."

"Bit creepy, isn't it?" said Bobby, looking up at the high façade.

"Atmospheric, you mean," Jamesy corrected. "Look at the size of those doors. Now, why would they –?"

"Well, are we going to go in, or what?" Tone asked impatiently.

"Right, right," said Kevin as he fumbled in his pocket for the key. Set in the huge double doors that made up a large proportion of the house-front was a small, single door. Kevin tried the key in the smaller door's lock and was mildly surprised when it turned and the door creaked open.

"Now we know how Howard Carter felt," said Bobby lightly.

"Who?" asked Kevin.

"Howard Carter," Bobby repeated. "Him and his mates opened the tomb of Tutankhamen."

"Yeah, and we all know what happened to them, don't we?" said Joker.

"What do you mean?"

"Well, it was the curse, wasn't it? Killed them all."

"Oh, come on, Joker," said Jamesy. "That's a myth."

"They all died, didn't they?"

"Well, yes, eventually, but that –"

"Oh, for fuck's sake!" cried Tone. "Are we going to go in or not? I'm sure there's not going to be any mummies waiting to give us all a plague of fucking boils."

"You can't be sure, though, can you?" said Joker.

"Jesus," muttered Tone, stepping through the door. The others filed in after him and then they all stood silently in the gloomy interior.

They were standing in a high-ceilinged reception area, with a door on their left, leading to the front room of the house, and an open dining area, complete with table and chairs further along, also on the left.

Straight ahead was another set of huge double doors, more ornate than the first pair, with decorative panels of painted glass. There was a sense of dark, oppressive age all around them, with the sun-bright street now reduced to an incongruous rectangle in the gloom behind them.

"Nice and cool in here," Joker whispered.

"Why are you whispering?" Tone whispered back.

"I don't know."

Tone caught a sudden movement in the corner of his eye on the wall to his right and he jumped.

"Shit!" he cried out, and everyone turned and bolted for the bright little rectangle in the door. They all crashed into the doorway at the same time, causing a jam until, one by one, they popped out onto the street, panting and cursing and shaking from the sudden release of tension.

A few doors down, a plump middle-aged woman sat on a chair on the pavement and watched impassively as they spilled out onto the road.

Sean looked accusingly at Tone. "That was just a lizard, wasn't it Tone?"

"A lizard?" asked Bobby. "A fucking lizard?"

"You fucking big Scaredy Baa!" said Joker.

"Okay, okay," said Tone. "Everybody calm down. It's no big deal. Right, I reckon we should have a quick look around the house and then go and explore the town for a bit. It looks like a lively wee place, so we could sit and have a beer somewhere and work out what our options are."

Everyone agreed and they all stepped back inside. As their vision adjusted to the gloom, they began to take more of an interest in their surroundings. Joker gave Kevin a hand to open the big interior doors and they discovered a small but functional kitchen that led to a third set of tall doors at the far end. Jamesy examined the grooves in the stone floor that ran from the front of the house to the back.

"Well that explains that," he muttered.

"Explains what?" asked Kevin.

"This would have led all the way through to some sort of courtyard at the back," Jamesy explained, gesturing from the doors at the front of the house to the third set at the back. "That's why these doors are all so tall. Whoever lived here would have brought their horse and cart, or wagon or whatever, all the way through the house to …" Jamesy unlocked the third set of doors and opened them onto a large courtyard with a two-storey outbuilding at the far end. "… to these stables."

"Why couldn't they just park it out the front?" asked Bobby.

"Joyriders," Joker told him.

"Well, something like that," said Jamesy. "It obviously would have made more sense to have your horse and cart safely tucked away for the night. It's fascinating when you think about –"

"Do you think we should check it out up there?" interrupted Tone, pointing to the upper floor of the stable block. "I'm only saying because I think Jamesy was about to bore the tits off everybody."

"The stairs look a bit rickety," said Kevin.

"Yeah," said Tone, "but the alternative is standing here listening to one of Jamesy's lectures on the social history of rural Spain, so come on."

They all crossed the courtyard towards the little wooden staircase at the side of the stables.

"Don't you listen to him, Jamesy," said Joker. "I thought it was very interesting."

Jamesy laughed as they made their way gingerly up the steps.

"Just a load of old crap, really," said Sean, and everyone agreed. The room above the stables was littered with ancient agricultural implements, as well as old equestrian equipment. Nothing looked useful, or even usable.

"So, what do you want to do, Kevin?" asked Tone.

"Well, I need to organise a van or something to come and take away a lot of this stuff. What we could do," said Kevin, "is have a bit of a look around today to see what can go and what can stay, and then come back tomorrow and pile all the stuff that's going in the hallway by the front doors. Then I'll make a couple of phone calls and that should be that."

"Sounds good to me," said Tone. "And we can get dinner around here this evening, can't we? Before we head back to the beach."

"Yeah, there are some really good bars around here."

"Perfect!" Tone declared, rubbing his hands. "Well, the sooner we get started …"

Later that night, the stable block was silent in the moonlight. The only movement came from the twitching ear of a ginger tomcat as it shuffled ever closer to a small lizard, dozing in the cool of the night. A sudden crash caused the cat to flinch and to turn, hissing, at the intrusion. Further loud noises persuaded the cat to abandon his hunt, and he sloped off over the wall of the courtyard to find somewhere less busy to indulge his passion for stealth and murder.

"What dickhead left that there?" Seamus winced as he rolled on the floor clutching his shin.

"It was you, wasn't it?" said Gary. "You were dead smug about it too, actually."

"Fuck's sake!"

"Yeah, you thought you were being dead clever," Gary reminded him, "putting all the stuff out today, to save having to do it tomorrow."

"Don't lie there too long," said Tone as everyone filed past Seamus. "You'll probably get covered in ants."

They all assembled around the old dining table, upon which they placed some carrier bags containing various bottles of alcohol.

"What made you buy gin?" Sean asked Joker. "You don't normally drink gin, do you?"

"650 pesetas for a litre of gin?" said Joker, "I could hardly leave it there at that price, now, could I?"

"Yeah, but at that price," Sean pointed out, "it must be undrinkable."

"Well, that's what the lemon Fanta's for," Joker explained. "Really, Sean, you just don't think ahead, do you?"

Seamus limped over to the table. "Has anybody checked that the fridge is working?" he asked.

"Seems okay to me," said Bobby, coming through the open doors from the kitchen. "Well, it made a noise when I plugged it in, so …"

"Well, you're the engineer," said Tone, "so that's good enough for me."

They had bought beer and vodka and whiskey, as well as some mixers, so they placed the beer in the fridge and then settled around the dining table and opened the bottles of spirits.

"Are we really going to stay here tonight?" asked Kevin. "We could always order some taxis."

"That would cost a fortune," said Tone. "And anyway, we fucked up, and when you find yourself in a situation like that, you just have to accept it and make the best of it."

"How much did we miss the last bus by, again?" asked Seamus.

"Two and a half hours."

"So, skin of our teeth, really?"

"Yeah," said Bobby. "And Joker proved that we're in no fit state to hitchhike anywhere."

"Yeah, Joker! What the fuck?" Sean exclaimed.

"I'd just found a litre of gin for 650 pesetas, Sean," said Joker. "What was I supposed to do? *Not* dance in the middle of the road? Yeah, Sean, that's realistic, isn't it?"

"It doesn't matter now, anyway," Tone said as he passed around some cigarettes. "We're stuck here and, to be honest, it's probably for the best. It means that tomorrow we can do what we need to do early on, and then we've got the rest of the day to ourselves. Jamesy, what's the bed situation?"

Jamesy came down the staircase that ran up the wall to one side of the dining area.

"Same as it was earlier," he said. "I can't find any sheets or anything, but there's no shortage of beds, and it's warm enough to not need sheets. Besides, I think we'll all be too comatose to care."

"That's settled, then," Tone declared. "We'll hole up here for the night, and then we'll already be here first thing. Couldn't have worked out any better."

"I'll drink to that," said Joker, drinking to that. Gary got up and went over to a large wooden chest of drawers that had been pushed into an alcove under the stairs.

"Did we check out these drawers earlier?" he asked. "I can't actually remember."

No one else could remember so Gary began to pull open the drawers one by one. "Just more old crap," he said, picking up and examining various items. A hairbrush. Old newspapers and magazines. A framed monochrome photograph. "That's a weird picture to frame, isn't it?" He passed it to Tone who gave it a cursory glance. It depicted a simple, low-roofed building in a bleak, rocky environment, and with a tall black cross set against the sky in the background.

"Mmm," said Tone, "it is a bit weird." He set it down on the table and took a puff from his cigarette. "I was thinking if we get a chance tomorrow," he went on, "we could explore the town a bit more."

"We could do with getting back to the beach at some point, though," Kevin pointed out.

"Yeah, no problem, Kevin. Don't worry about it."

"Some good wee bars around here," said Joker. "It seems like the proper, authentic sort of Spain around here, doesn't it? That *Tres Hermanas* bar was class earlier."

"Yeah," Gary agreed, "I reckon we should check out the rest of the town."

"But we do need to get –"

"Yes, yes, Kevin, all right," said Tone. "I said don't worry about it. What's that gin like, Joker?"

"It's going down well."

"So I see."

"It goes really well with lemon Fanta."

"Not the traditional mixer for gin, though, is it?"

"No," Joker conceded, "but we'd all still be stuck in caves if nobody bothered to try anything new."

"So, is that what you're doing, then? Pushing back the boundaries of humanity?"

"I like to think so."

The night wore on into the early hours. The conversation around the table had slowed to intermittent mumblings. Tone sat quietly, staring at the photograph that Gary had found earlier. Sean nudged Bobby. "Do you think he's asleep there?" he asked, nodding to Joker who had one side of his face resting on the tabletop.

"Either that," said Bobby, "or he's wearing a really heavy, invisible hat."

Sean giggled drunkenly. Seamus took a closer look at Joker.

"He's definitely asleep," he said. "He's been doing that a lot lately."

"Well, he's knocked back most of that gin," said Gary. "Hardly surprising he's passed out."

"I know, but that's the point," said Seamus. "It's the fact that –"

"You know where I think this is?" Tone suddenly exclaimed. "I reckon this is up that mountain."

"What is?" asked Sean.

"This building." Tone passed the photograph around. He looked at Kevin. "What do you think, Kevin? Do you know anything about it?"

"No," Kevin told him. "First I've heard of it."

"There you go, then!" Tone declared triumphantly. "That's settled it!"

"What are you talking about?" asked Jamesy.

"No, no. I think he's got a point," said Sean excitedly. "You see, from down here you can just make out the cross, right? But it looks exactly like the cross in this picture, doesn't it?"

"But all crosses look the –"

"So it's obvious that this building is up the mountain, isn't it?" Sean insisted. "On the other side of the cross."

Tone slapped the top of the table to confirm that Sean's logic was irrefutable.

"So?" asked Jamesy. "What's your point?"

"The point is, Jamesy Boy," said Sean firmly. "The point is …" He looked at Tone.

"The point is," said Tone as he took a gulp of beer. "The point is that it's got to be a monastery up there, hasn't it?"

"Has it?"

"Of course! What else can it be?"

"Well, it could be –"

"And you know what they've got in monasteries, don't you?"

"Monks?"

"Well yes, monks obviously. But you know what monks do, don't you?"

"What?"

"They make strong wine."

"Do they?"

"Of course," Tone insisted. "Everybody knows that. They're always at it. Let's face it, they've got fuck all else to do, have they? Especially stuck on top of a bloody mountain."

"Yeah, that makes sense," said Sean.

"Does it, Sean?" Jamesy demanded. "Does it really?"

"Right," said Tone, standing up and raising his glass, "so we're all decided, then?"

No one around the table knew what Tone was talking about, but they held up their drinks and nodded in drunken agreement.

"Drink up, lads!" Tone exhorted. "For tomorrow, come the dawn, we rise!"

THIRTY THREE

Martin thought that Stephanie had sounded pleased on the phone and, as he waited in the city centre café for her to arrive for their arranged meeting, he realised he was looking forward to the encounter. He felt that he had run out of ideas in his search for his family, and he was hoping that sharing the burden with another person might unveil a fresh perspective.

Stephanie, he assumed, would also have a better understanding of what sort of official channels they could try that would be of use in pointing him in the right direction, but even just having someone to talk to, Martin felt, could prove to be beneficial.

Stephanie arrived on time and smiled when she saw Martin sitting at a table by the far wall.

"Hello, Martin," she said cheerfully. "Been waiting long?"

"Not at all," he replied as he stood to shake her hand. "Just got here, really."

They both sat and a waitress came and took their order. They made general small talk about the weather while they waited for the waitress to return and then, once Martin had poured out two cups of tea from the little teapot, Stephanie settled back in her seat and gave Martin a sympathetic look.

"So, how have you been getting on, then?" she asked.

"Not very well," he admitted. He explained how he had gone looking for his old home, only to discover it no longer existed, and how he had wandered around, bewildered, in a world he didn't recognise. "It's all been changed since I was last there," he told her.

"When were you last there?"

"Well, that's a bit of a long story," he said with a sigh, and he went on to explain how he had arrived at his current situation. How, nearly twenty years before, he had been inadvertently caught up in the chaos of internment. How a subsequent mental collapse had thrown him into the confusing machinery of mental health treatment in the seventies, and how he had eventually found himself abandoned and lost on the streets.

Of Glasgow.

"Glasgow?" cried Stephanie. "How did you end up in Glasgow?"

Martin gave a wan smile. "I'm probably not the best person to ask," he said. "Like I said, I wasn't exactly aware of what was going on at the time."

Stephanie nodded. "Yeah," she told him, "I recognised the look in your eyes when we were on the ferry. It didn't last very long, just a flash, really, but it was there all the same."

"You recognised it?"

"Mmm," she said, sipping her tea. "My husband had a severe breakdown about ten years ago. Came as a real shock, I can tell you. It just came out of nowhere and was really bad for a while."

"How is he now?"

"Oh, he's okay these days," she assured him. "But even after all this time you still have to take it one day at a time, you know? You can't get complacent."

Martin smiled. "I know what you mean."

"What shocked me when it happened, though," Stephanie went on, "was how nobody really seemed to know what they were doing. You know, the doctors and psychiatrists and all these people who you just expect to be experts, and who'll know exactly what to do; they didn't have a bloody clue. It was like 'try these drugs' and 'if these don't work, we'll try these ones'. It was like it was all trial and error."

"Yeah," Martin agreed, "I think I must have been under heavy medication for most of the time. There's just so much I don't remember."

"It's strange, isn't it? You just assume that the health experts all know everything, don't you? But when it comes to the brain, nobody has any idea. Or, at least, not much of an idea."

"That's true, actually," said Martin. "It's only in the last year or so that I've really been making any progress, and that's only because I was lucky enough to get hooked up with this psychotherapist who's helped me out a lot. He's been doing a lot of new, experimental stuff, but he once told me that trying to cure mental health issues was like trying to rewire and solder an electrical circuit using only a lump hammer."

Stephanie laughed. "I know," she said. "It still amazes me how nobody seems to know how the mind works. So, where is this psychotherapist, then? Is he in Glasgow?"

"No, no, I left Glasgow years ago," Martin told her. "I fell in with a couple of homeless alcoholics – which means I was a homeless alcoholic myself – and they came up with a plan for us all to make our way to London where we would all be, somehow, set for life. Of course, I didn't really know what was going on, I just went along with it, but eventually we must have made it to London because I have some vague memories of sleeping rough near King's Cross."

"So, you don't remember much about it, then?" asked Stephanie. "Is that because of the alcohol, or were you still suffering from mental health issues?"

"Probably a bit of both, really," said Martin. "I mean, I was still having all sorts of hallucinations – they call them *psychotic episodes,* apparently – but how much of that was down to the booze and the drugs, it's hard to say."

"You were taking drugs as well?"

"Yeah well, anything to make it through the day," he said. "Jesus! I don't know how I survived, to be honest. I think my two mates from Glasgow were looking out for me. They had their own problems, obviously, but they did see me through some bad times."

"Where are they now?"

"I've no idea."

"Why? What happened?"

"I had a bad overdose," Martin explained, "and ended up in hospital. It was touch and go for a while, but I managed to pull through and then I was placed in a homeless shelter that was being run by a mental health charity. That's probably what saved my life, because that's where I met Dr Sedgewick."

"Is this the psychotherapist?"

"Yeah, he happened to be working in London at that time, but he told me of a place in Sussex where he did most of his work. It was an old stately home that had been converted into a modern clinic devoted to mental health, co-funded, apparently, by charities and the private sector.

"Well, anyway, to cut a long story short, Dr Sedgewick pulled some strings and the next thing I knew I was living in a stately home on the south coast of England. I mean, I was just a glorified guinea pig for some wacky, experimental therapies, but what did I have to lose?"

"Sounds like you were a very comfortable guinea pig."

"Oh yes, absolutely," laughed Martin. "It was lovely."

"You've only mentioned therapy," said Stephanie, "does that mean you weren't on any medication?"

"Oh no, I've had to go onto anti-depressants, but Alex doesn't like to –"

"Alex?"

"Oh yeah, sorry, Alex is Dr Sedgewick. We've spent so much time around each other that it's just easier to use first names."

"What were you going to say?"

"Oh, just that Alex doesn't like to focus on the medication side of things. His therapies are more geared towards practical exercises, you know? Almost as a way to retrain your brain, sort of."

"And you think it's helped?"

"I think so." Martin looked thoughtful. "Or it could just be the medication. Or coming off illegal drugs. Or just chilling out in a peaceful environment."

"Or a combination of them all," ventured Stephanie.

"Who knows?" said Martin, spreading his hands wide. "All I know is, I'm thinking clearly now for the first time in years, and there's a family out there somewhere that could probably do with some answers."

"You've looked in the phone book, I take it."

"Yeah," Martin replied. "But I couldn't find anything obvious in there."

"Well then," said Stephanie decisively, "once we've finished this tea, maybe we should go about finding this family of yours."

THIRTY FOUR

As they made their way through the town, it became obvious that the neighbourhoods were becoming less affluent the higher up they climbed, as if the poor were being pushed into the foothills to huddle out of sight of the prosperous town centre that languished on the valley floor.

Had Joker been more aware of his surroundings, then he may have held forth on the inherent inequalities of the capitalist system, and how the fat cats with most of the wealth could wallow in all the amenities the town centre could offer while the most vulnerable and the most in need were shoved to the fringes of society and forgotten.

But Joker was scarcely aware that he was even awake, and so the poor, huddled masses could only watch as their potential champion shuffled past in silence.

At the very top of the town, where the mountain could finally shake off the clinging attentions of man and rise unhindered to meet the sky, the weary group arrived at a walled cemetery. It was silent here. The busy town centre was far below, and the town itself had petered out into a few dusty and deserted alleyways that had almost made it to the walls of the cemetery, only to give up and lie spent and exhausted in the baking heat.

On the other side of the cemetery was a small grove of ancient olive trees, and it was here that Tone decided to make base camp, to rest and to make preparations for the final assault on the summit. He walked with Sean to the top of the grove to scout for possible pathways up the mountain. Everyone else collapsed onto the ground, grateful for the shade afforded by the trees. Plastic bottles of water were passed around to appreciative throats that were, despite the early hour, already parched.

"Why are we doing this, again?" asked Gary.

"Doing what?" Joker mumbled. He was lying on his back with his forearm covering his eyes.

"Climbing a mountain," Gary said casually.

Joker wasn't sure that he had heard that correctly. Climbing a *what*?

"Right lads," said Tone as he and Sean came back to stand in the middle of the group. "It looks like there's a path that winds up around the back of the mountain. It should take us up to the top."

There was that word again, thought Joker. *Mountain*. Just what the buggering fuck were they doing climbing a mountain? In this heat? He considered framing a question that might shed some light on the subject – something along the lines of, *what the buggering fuck are we doing climbing a mountain? In this heat?* – but he needed his brain for that, and his brain, at the moment, seemed to be ignoring him.

"You know," said Jamesy, "I'm starting to wonder if this was such a good idea after all."

"Yeah," Seamus added, "it seemed reasonable enough last night, but that's because we were all –"

"What the fuck are you talking about?" Tone demanded. "This isn't a debate. We all agreed to do this, didn't we?"

"Well, yeah, but –"

"And anyway," Tone went on, "think about the poor wee monk. He's probably sitting up there waiting for us with all that booze he's made. We can't just leave him hanging, can we? Think how happy he'll be when we all show up. And don't forget about all the buxom serving wenches there'll be. Come on! Don't be such fucking faders!"

Joker relaxed as he understood what was happening. He realised now that he wasn't actually lying on the lower slopes of some Spanish mountain in the blazing sun. He was still curled up somewhere, fast asleep, snoring and dreaming. *Boozed-up monkeys? Swervy witches?* It was a little more surreal and more vivid than his usual dreams, but he was still happy to go along with it. In fact, it occurred to him that now he knew it was a dream, he could do whatever he wanted. He could even fly up to the summit. He stood up, feeling altogether in a better frame of mind. Tone was still talking. "I think we might have even sworn an oath on it," he concluded.

"Well, I do remember a lot of swearing," said Bobby.

"Yes," Jamesy argued, "but look at how hot it is already. It's only going to get worse, isn't it? Do we even have enough water with us?"

"Typical Jamesy," laughed Joker, "always fucking moaning about something or other. Come on, Jamesy. We may as well get this over with."

"Right, are we all ready?" called Tone. He could tell there was a growing sense of mutiny in the ranks and, although Joker's attitude confused him, he decided to run with it. It was best to use the momentum to get everyone up and moving and focused on the task in hand.

Which was what, exactly? Why had he become so intent on climbing this stupid mountain? He wasn't entirely convinced by the idea of an isolated monastery, but even if he was, would that justify what he was doing? All he knew was that he was determined to reach the summit and if sheer bloody-mindedness was his only reason for doing so, then so be it.

Everyone got up and, stretching their tired limbs, trudged out from the shaded grove and into the harsh and unforgiving sunshine.

It didn't take long for the truth to dawn on Joker and, struggling through his own little rainstorm as the last of the gin trickled through his pores and dripped onto the front of his shirt, he decided that something needed to be done.

THIRTY FIVE

Ellie was at work, which meant that Rosie was free to wander around the house on her own. Even after all these months of abstinence she still craved a cigarette. It was bad enough, she thought, being so heavy and creaky, but not having the comfort of a little bit of nicotine was just making it all worse.

Of course, no one had forced her to stop smoking, but the risk of harming her child just about outweighed her cravings, and she reckoned that it only added to the sense of anticipation for the first cigarette she would have after the birth. She imagined slipping quietly away somewhere and putting a light to the tobacco and sucking in that first lungful of soothing smoke. Or maybe she wouldn't.

Maybe she would be able to build on this time during her pregnancy to finally quit once and for all. She had tried many times in the past but each time the addiction had proved too strong and her willpower had crumbled. This time might be different.

She roamed aimlessly around the front room, restless and irritable, wishing that Gary was with her so she could have a moan at him. The thought of him, though, made her smile.

She idly picked up a small glass ashtray from the mantelpiece and examined it. *Why had Ellie kept this thing for so long?* she wondered, though she knew the reason why.

It was a memory.

The colourful picture on the bottom of the ashtray was now faded and worn but the logo was still legible and it still told of a time before. A life before. The words *Butlin's at Mosney* tried to drag a resistant Rosie back to that summer, the summer that was the happiest time of her life and the summer that had torn her childhood into nightmarish shreds. *That* summer.

Rosie frowned at the memories that were trying to nudge their way through the armour she always wore. They were persistent, though, and to Rosie's dismay, and despite her best efforts, they came tumbling through.

Her heels bumped pleasantly against her father's chest. She was barefoot. Her white leather sandals were held in her right hand, while her left arm was wrapped tightly around her father's forehead. The buckles of her sandals jingled and glittered in the sunlight as her father strode across the expanse of manicured grass towards the building that filled Rosie with excitement and nervous anticipation.

Although she had been here for little more than a day, Rosie had firmly decided that this was the best place she had ever been. The holiday camp was in the Irish Republic, just north of Dublin, and was a world away from Ardoyne where, at the moment at least, everything seemed to be on fire.

The cute little shops along the pedestrianised streets were all filled with sweets and toys and comics. There were amusement arcades and playgrounds, a boating lake and a beach, a theatre and a free cinema that showed cartoons all day, a glamorous ballroom and cafés and restaurants and parks and happy people and music everywhere. And the building to which they were now headed. The swimming pool.

"You're not scared, are you?" Her father asked her as they got close enough to see the arms and legs of children thrashing around in the water behind the strengthened glass window panels.

"No," she shouted defiantly. She was terrified, but she refused to let her daddy know that. She could do this, she decided.

On arrival at the entrance, Martin lifted Rosie down from his shoulders and, taking her by the hand, led her inside. The sudden rise in the noise level made Rosie's heart beat faster as crowds of children ran here and there, shrieking and laughing and yelling.

They were both wearing their swimming costumes under their clothes so Martin led Rosie past the changing rooms to a row of plastic benches by the side of the pool. Rosie took off her top and her shorts and placed them on a bench. Martin also got undressed and then put all of their clothes into a hold-all that contained their towels.

"Just put your sandals under the bench there, Rosie," said Martin, "and I'll just stick the bag under there as well."

Rosie did as she was told, then turned with trepidation towards the pool.

"Those tiles might be a wee bit rough on your feet," Martin told her. "So, do you want me to carry you to the pool?"

Rosie took a few steps on the hard non-slip surface and grimaced. "It is a wee bit rough," she said.

"No problem." Martin scooped her up and carried her to the shallow end of the pool. He sat her down at the edge and eased himself into the water. He then reached up to lift Rosie and lower her into the pool beside him.

The cold water came as a shock. She had been told the pool was heated and had expected it to be warm, like a bath, but she gasped and struggled to catch her breath, which only added to her rising sense of panic.

"You're okay there, sweetheart," Martin assured her. "We're just going to take it easy now."

With the shock of cold and fear, Rosie could only nod. Her right hand was clasped in her father's as she allowed him to gently lead her further into the pool. The water level rose to her chest.

"Bend down a wee bit and splash your arms about," said Martin. "It'll warm you up a bit."

She realised she had been walking stiffly, her arms and legs held straight, and she had to make a conscious effort to loosen up. She bent her knees until the water came up to her neck and she made slow awkward movements with her left arm. The paralysing cold began to ease, and she could feel herself start to relax. Her confidence was growing, but she still kept a firm grip of her father's hand.

They moved into deeper water until Rosie could barely feel the bottom with the tips of her toes and then, still holding on to her father's hand, she was treading water. With infinite patience and soothing encouragement, Martin would briefly let her go, proud of the fierce determination on his daughter's face, and she would splash about frantically until he held her again. After repeating the process for a while, Rosie was finally able to keep herself afloat with more controlled movements of her arms and legs, and a little later she felt confident enough to lie on her back and enjoy the sensation of floating.

They stayed in the pool long enough for Rosie to take a few strokes in the water and, knowing that her father was right beside her, she eventually could make her way from one side of the pool to the other. She could swim.

It didn't matter that her efforts were clumsy and ungainly. *She could swim.* And as they made their way back to where they had left their clothes and towels, Rosie's eyes shone with exhilaration. She couldn't wait to tell Ellie.

Outside, Martin looked at his watch. They were due to meet up with the rest of the family for lunch, but it was still early. He turned to his daughter.

"We've still got over an hour before we have to meet your mammy," he said, "so do you fancy going for a drink in Dan Lowry's?"

Rosie couldn't believe it. She and her brother and sister had been to Dan Lowry's Bar the night before, but they had just been running around playing, like all the other kids in there, while the adults sat at tables, chatting, smoking and drinking. This was different. She was being invited to go for a drink with her daddy. They would walk into the bar together, and they would sit at a table together, and they would talk and laugh as they sipped their drinks together. She had never felt so grown up.

Martin sat with a glass of Guinness on the table in front of him, and Rosie sat beside him with a glass of Coke which, she decided, looked almost like a glass of Guinness. She took delicate sips of her drink – not gulping it down like a child would do – as she surveyed, with a new-found pious detachment, the antics of the silly little children, rushing chaotically between the tables. She couldn't wait to tell Ellie.

The rest of the fortnight went by far too quickly. Before they left Belfast, Rosie and Ellie had both been given some holiday money to spend on treats for themselves during the two weeks they were at the camp, and as they were packing up to go home, Rosie rather ashamedly realised that Ellie had used some of her money to buy gifts for each of the family.

Jack had received a toy car, and Rosie, a doll. Their mother, Shauna, had been given a souvenir tea towel, and Martin had received a glass ashtray emblazoned with the Butlin's logo set over some colourful pictures of the camp.

Rosie ran her fingertips over the long-faded image on the ashtray, and then gave an exasperated sigh as if to physically dislodge her memories. They didn't belong to her, she decided. They were the memories of a childhood that should have carried on, unbroken and uninterrupted. They were memories that should have been added to over the years as new experiences and happy times collected and accumulated on the carefree walk of a child through a world of comfort and wonder. But those few memories stood glaringly alone, and only served to highlight the scarcity of reckless joy from Rosie's past, like a few grains of sugar sprinkled in coal dust.

Rosie had told Ellie that she hoped their father was dead, but that was not true. Rosie secretly hoped he was alive so that, one day, she could march right up to him and spit in his face. A dark anger had settled on Rosie's heart, an anger for the life she'd never lived and for the memories that never were.

Ellie insisted that their father could not be held responsible for what had happened, but Rosie didn't see it that way. She needed someone to blame. She could never hope to match Ellie's generosity of spirit, but she didn't want to. She embraced the darkness within her. More than that, she nourished it. It gave Rosie an almost perverse pleasure to feed her demons, to keep alive the notion that the day would come when she could stand in front of Martin McCann and cause his heart to break in the same way her own heart had been broken. In this, she was resolute.

A squeal from the garden reminded her to nag Gary, when he got back, to oil the hinges on the gate. She squinted through the window at the strange familiarity of the figure who stepped nervously into the garden. She frowned at the man's hair. There was grey in it now, she thought, but those hazel eyes of his were still … she froze with shock.

And the glass ashtray slipped from her grasp to bounce gently on the thick rug. It rolled crazily, wobbling and teetering, before coming to rest, with a tiny clink, against the cold marble of the hearth.

THIRTY SIX

"Competitive?" scoffed Gary. "Is that what you call it? I call it a couple of stubborn wankers, that's what I call it."

"Well, it's all a question of semantics," said Bobby as he sipped his Coke. "Competitive. Dedication. Single-mindedness. Stubborn wankers. It's all much of a muchness, really."

"Do you think they'll be okay?" Kevin asked, concerned.

"Probably not," said Seamus. "Jesus! This fucking ice cream is unbelievable. What's it called again?"

"*Turrón,*" Kevin told him. "You don't think they'll be okay, then?" They were all sitting around a table on the town's paseo, enjoying drinks and ice cream from the nearby *horchatería*, though Joker had wandered off somewhere.

"No, they're fucked," Seamus answered. "If they don't actually fall off the mountain, then they'll just end up killing each other."

"The thing you have to remember about Tone and Sean," Jamesy began, "is that they –"

"What's that dickhead up to?" asked Bobby, gesturing across the paseo. They turned to see Joker apparently staring at a wall. After a while, he turned and walked back towards the group.

"What were you doing?" Gary asked when Joker joined them.

"I was just reading a poster on the wall there," Joker replied, "about a *Feria de la Pascua de Resurrección*, in a place called Benifairó."

"Benifairó?" said Seamus. He looked at Kevin. "Where's that, then?"

"It's a wee village further down the valley. Not too far from here."

"*Feria de* what? That's an Easter Festival, isn't it?" said Gary.

"It is indeed." Joker told him, "And tomorrow night they've got something called a *Dance with Cows*."

"Well, fuck," said Gary, "we didn't have to come to Spain to do that."

"What?"

"Shamrock disco on a Friday night," explained Gary. "You can dance with all the –"

"Yeah, ha, ha," said Joker, "but I reckon we should go. It sounds like it could be mental."

"It'll be our last night, really, won't it?" Jamesy pointed out.

"Well, yeah, we'll be travelling all the next night."

"It's got to be something to think about," Joker added. "Do you know much about these *ferias,* then, Kevin?"

"Well, the ones in the summer are a good craic," said Kevin. "They're just big parties where everybody stays up all night drinking."

"Sounds like the Fleadh," Gary suggested.

"Same sort of thing, yeah."

"Well, I'm up for a bit of that," said Seamus.

"An all-night party?" asked Bobby. "You can count me in too."

"Well," said Jamesy, "it does sound like an authentic cultural experience."

"That's the spirit, Jamesy," cried Joker. "You mad old bastard!"

"What are we going to do about Hillary and Tensing, though?" asked Gary.

"Yeah," said Kevin, "I'm a bit worried about them, to be honest."

"No, it's not that," Gary told him, "we can't let them get away with not helping us move all this furniture, can we? I mean, I don't mind doing my bit, but if those lazy –"

"Well, we're not going to be doing anything before lunch now, are we?" said Joker. "I'm sure they'll be back by then, so we'll just meet them back at the house."

THIRTY SEVEN

"I'm not going to lie, Sean," said Tone, "I'm a wee bit disappointed."

Sean didn't reply. He walked forward onto the rough, uneven plateau that formed the mountaintop. On the far side of the plateau, overlooking the town, stood a solitary cross.

Sean looked around. Aside from the cross and a few tendrils of mist that had drifted down from a low, passing cloud, there was nothing to be seen. No kindly old monk. No monastery. No building of any kind. Nothing but an eerie silence. He made his way over to the cross, quietly followed by Tone, then stopped and gazed up at the familiar silhouette, stark against the hazy blue of the sky.

"Buxom serving wenches?" he asked without turning round.

"Okay," said Tone, taking out a cigarette, "there's a chance I may have overstated things. But let's be honest, Sean, there were a lot of mitigating circumstances."

"You know what Joker has to say on that matter, don't you?"

Tone put a light to his cigarette. "What?"

"Under no circumstances," Sean expanded, "do you ever, ever blame the alcohol."

"Yeah, well," Tone looked over the edge of the plateau. "Hell of a view, isn't it?" he said, changing the subject.

Sean couldn't argue with that. The entire valley was spread out below them. Off to the right the valley floor was dotted with the occasional town or village as it wound its way through the mountains, while to the left the valley gave way to a wide coastal plain that led to the Mediterranean which could be seen, glittering, in the distance.

"Yes indeed," Tone concluded. "Well worth the effort, I would say."

Sean shook his head and took a closer look at the reason they were there. The cross stood about twenty feet tall and was embedded deep in the rock of the mountain. It was made of wood and had a patchy covering of a grey, weathered material that had a black, tar-like backing. It was clear that the cross had once been covered completely in the material which, after a closer examination, looked more silver than grey.

"Must have been quite a sight, back in the day," Sean muttered.

Tone nodded as he pictured the cross fully attired in shining silver. It would have caught the Spanish sun and shone like a beacon for miles around. "Yeah," he agreed, "not quite Sugarloaf Mountain, but still, it would have been something. Just looks a bit sorry for itself now, though, doesn't it?"

The cross, Sean conceded, did look sorry for itself. Where the covering had peeled away, the bare wood had been exposed to the wind and the rain and the scorching sun, and had twisted and warped as if trying to dispense with its man-made guise and revert to its true origins.

"For the glory of God, eh?" said Tone. "Looks like nobody thinks it's worth the effort anymore."

"Suppose not."

"I could never understand why it's never occurred to Christians that Jesus probably wouldn't want to be reminded of the thing he was tortured to death on. Seems a bit insensitive really, like waving a noose around."

"Your cynicism gets a bit boring after a while, you know that, Tone?"

"Not to me it doesn't." Tone dropped his cigarette butt and stamped it out. "I can't let you Christians have it all your own way, can I? If I did, you'd all just lie there and have the Holy Men force-feed you bullshit all day."

To Tone's surprise, Sean did not react to this deliberate goading, but instead turned back to look down into the valley. Tone usually enjoyed provoking Sean into a passionate defence of the faith that was close to his heart, but there was nothing but a strange silence now between them.

"You all right there, Sean?"

"You don't know what you're talking about," Sean said quietly.

It wasn't like Sean to be so subdued, Tone thought, at least not on a topic like this, so he decided to give him a bit of a poke.

"Well, that's the thing," he said, "I do know what I'm talking about. I know how it works, you see. It's a business, well actually it's more of a scam than a business, with those self-righteous bastards selling something that –"

"Oh, fuck off, Tone!" spat Sean as he spun around. "Fuck off! You don't know anything. You think you do, but you don't. You've got a fucking cheek calling anybody self-righteous. What does that make you, then? You know fuck all!"

Tone was shaken by the outburst. He was used to having heated debates with Sean, but this was different. This was raw, emotional, vitriolic. It was more than just anger. Sean turned away again and slumped down to sit at the base of the cross. He leaned forward to rest his elbows on his knees and gazed down at the town, silent and unreal on the distant valley floor.

Tone lit another cigarette and sat down next to Sean.

"Something on your mind, Sean?" he asked casually.

"Fuck off!"

"Well, there's not much else to do up here, is there?" Tone said lightly. Sean remained silent. "You know I'm not going to let it go, don't you?"

Sean looked at Tone, then looked away again. The anger in Sean's eyes had gone, Tone thought, only to be replaced by something else. Something wistful. Something sad. The quietness of the scene intensified and Tone was about to say something else when Sean spoke up.

"I was only about eight or nine," he began, and Tone felt a sudden urge to hear no more. "It was in Donegal," Sean went on, "at one of those retreats, you know?" Tone nodded. "You know the deal, don't you? You book in for prayer and reflection and all that stuff."

"Yeah," said Tone, "I know the sort of thing you mean."

"It was my ma's idea. She thought we could all do with a weekend away, to get closer to God and all, so we all set off – me and Siobhan and my ma and da – and we got there one Friday evening.

"It was all really sound at the start. For me and Siobhan, it was just like a holiday, really, and the place we were staying was dead cool. There was a seminary there as well, so there were loads of trainee priests knocking about, and me and Siobhan got friendly with one of them – Duncan, his name was – he was a good laugh like, always joking, you know?

"Well, on the Saturday night, I headed off to bed. I felt like a big lad because I had a room to myself, the boy's dormitory was full apparently, but anyway, I must have been knackered because I fell asleep right away." Sean paused as he tried to focus on the memory. Tone sat quietly and waited for him to continue.

"So, then I wake up," said Sean, "because there's somebody beside the bed. It's Duncan, and he's kneeling down, and I think he's saying his prayers, and then I realise he's got my dick in his mouth."

"Fuck!" Tone exclaimed.

"When he saw I was awake, he just got up, dead calm like, and walked to the door. And then, before he left, he turned to me and smiled. That's what really got to me, Tone, the way he just fucking smiled."

"So, what happened?"

"What do you mean, what happened? Nothing happened. We went home the next day and that was it."

"What did your ma and da say?"

"I didn't tell them. I didn't tell anybody. You're the first person I've ever told."

"Jesus Christ, Sean!" said Tone. "Why didn't you tell your folks?"

"Well, because …"

"Because what?"

"Because …" Sean hesitated. "Because I was … because I was ashamed, I don't know, I was only a kid, for fuck's sake!"

"So, that was what? Nearly twenty years ago?"

"Yeah, Tone," Sean said quietly, "I know what you're saying."

"So, how many kids do you think –?"

"Yeah, I know," Sean replied angrily. "I fucking know, okay? Do you think I haven't thought about it?"

"Jesus!" said Tone. He turned to look at the sunlight flickering on the distant sea. He then turned back to Sean. "So, why are you always sticking up for the Church, then? I would have thought something like that would have put you off a wee bit, but you're always at Mass, aren't you?"

"You just don't get it, Tone, do you? That's just who we are."

"What? What the fuck does that mean?"

"It's our identity, isn't it? We're both Catholics, whether you like it or not. It's our heritage. Take away the Church, and what have we got?"

"Unmolested kids?"

"Yeah, very funny, but you went to your da's funeral Mass, didn't you? You can't stop being a Catholic, Tone, it's in your blood. It's who you are. It's the same for Joker and Bobby. They're Protestants, and that's *their* heritage. That's who *they* are."

"That sounds just like the sort of sectarian bullshit that's got Northern Ireland into the fucking mess it's in today."

"You know me better than that."

"Yeah, but that's just Northern Ireland, Sean," Tone insisted. "It's Northern Ireland that's polarised people like that. Not everywhere is as fucked-up as that."

"Yes, Tone," Sean said patiently, "I know it's Northern Ireland but, let's face it, that happens to be where we live." He turned away to let his next words drift into the wind. "For the time being, at least."

"Is that why you're moving abroad, then? To get away from it all?"

Sean stood up and brushed the dust from the back of his shorts. "That's part of it, I suppose," he said. "But it's a big world out there, Tone, and I fancy seeing at least some of it."

"Makes you one of the lucky ones, then," Tone said as he stood up to join Sean. "Getting out, I mean."

"Well, that remains to be seen. Who knows what the future will bring. Anyway, what about you? There's nothing keeping you in Northern Ireland, is there?"

Tone shrugged. "I suppose not," he said. "I mean, my ma's on her own now, but she's got all her mates to play with, so that's not a big deal, but … I don't know, maybe I'm just stuck in a rut."

Sean was about to mention Claire, but decided it was none of his business. Above them, the cross creaked mournfully in the stiffening wind. "Think we should get off this mountain?"

"Yeah," said Tone, "I don't know what possessed us to climb the fucking thing in the first place."

As they made their way to the path that led down the mountain, Sean glanced over at Tone.

"I can't believe I told you about Donegal," he said.

"Maybe you needed to get it off your chest."

"Can't think why, though. I mean I haven't even thought about it in years. Obviously, it was a bit of a shock at the time. It took Gary and Seamus ripping the piss out of me to snap me out of it when I got back to Belfast."

"Good to know they're useful for something," said Tone. "So why do you think you brought it up after all this time?"

"No idea," Sean replied. "Like I said, it's not something I've dwelt on all these years. Maybe it's a subconscious, Freudian sort of thing. Maybe I need to see a therapist."

"You could take Joker with you," Tone suggested, and Sean laughed.

"Yeah," he said, "what the hell was all that about earlier on, when he was running around flapping his arms up and down?"

"Who knows?" said Tone. "This is Joker we're talking about, so who the fuck knows?"

Jamesy and Kevin were clearing out the stable block. Seamus was in the house, rearranging the items he had tripped over the night before, while Joker, Gary and Bobby were seated around the dining table. Jamesy decided to take the opportunity of being alone with Kevin to have a quiet chat.

"Everything okay with you, then, Kevin?"

"Yeah, no problems," said Kevin. He stopped what he was doing and looked at Jamesy. "Why?" he asked.

"Just asking," Jamesy said nonchalantly. "So, what's the deal with your woman at the shop? Gabriela, was it?"

Kevin coloured. "There is no deal," he muttered. "Like I said, there's nothing going on."

"Okay," said Jamesy, "it's just that you seemed to go very quiet when her name was mentioned."

Kevin took a deep breath and looked around him. He knew that if he could trust anyone, it would be Jamesy, but he still seemed unsure. Eventually he sighed and leaned back against a battered old cupboard. "You won't tell anybody, will you?" he asked.

Jamesy shrugged as if to suggest that it went without saying.

"It's just that," Kevin continued hesitantly, "it's just that I've never actually had a girlfriend."

Jamesy stared impassively ahead, but was then suddenly struck by the significance of what Kevin had just told him.

"What?" he said, stupefied. "*Never*?"

"No."

"So, you've never actually …?"

"No," Kevin said miserably. "Never."

"Jesus!"

"Yeah, exactly."

"Mmm," Jamesy was thoughtful for a moment. "I'm probably not the best person to talk to about this," he said. "I don't have much success in that department myself."

Kevin stared at him. "You're kidding me, aren't you?" he said. "Women fall over themselves for you! It's actually embarrassing at times."

"Oh, well yeah," Jamesy stammered, "I mean, I don't have a problem *acquiring* women, it's just that I don't know what to do with them once

I've got them." He tried to make light of it, but Kevin just looked away.

"I'd rather have your problem than mine," he said.

Jamesy wasn't sure how to respond. "You know," he said after a while, "it may be worth mentioning it to the lads."

Kevin shot him a look of disbelief. "Seriously? Wouldn't they just rip the piss out of me?"

"Oh yeah, they would," Jamesy assured him, "but then they'd all look at it as a problem that needed to be solved, and they'd all hunker down and try to find some way to help. I mean, okay, that help would probably be a bit cack-handed and misplaced, and totally inappropriate, but … actually forget I even mentioned it."

"Cack-handed? You mean like that whole salad business?"

"Yeah," said Jamesy. "Really, though, just forget what I said."

"I don't know, though," Kevin said thoughtfully. "I'm desperate enough to try anything at this stage."

"Well, just be sure you've thought it through," Jamesy told him. He turned his head towards the house. "They're being very quiet," he said. "Probably deeply involved in some heavy intellectual debate."

Kevin grinned. "I'm sure," he said.

"*Wacky Races* was fucking shite, Bobby, and you know it!" Joker was standing up and angrily pointing a finger across the table at Bobby.

"How the fuck can you hate *Wacky Races*?" cried Bobby. "It was a classic!"

Gary was chewing on a sandwich as he followed the discussion. "Yeah, I liked *Wacky Races* too," he said, "so I don't know what the hell you're on about."

"What the fuck's your problem, Joker?" added Seamus as he came over to the table. "*Wacky Races* was class."

"Oh, is that right?" Joker demanded. "Then tell me this; what was the coolest car in the whole show?"

They thought about it for a bit and then Gary piped up. "Well, the Double Zero, obviously."

"Yeah," Bobby agreed. "The Double Zero."

"Absolutely," said Seamus.

"Then tell me," Joker continued. "How many times did the Double Zero actually win a fucking race?"

"Well, obviously, it never won a race," said Bobby. "Dick Dastardly was the bad guy. You can't have the bad guy winning, can you? It sends the wrong message to kids."

"Fuck that, Bobby," said Joker passionately. "What about me, then? I was a kid! And every week I'd be sitting there, cheering on the Double Zero, thinking; *Just this once! Just this once!* But every bloody week Dick Dastardly would get to within a couple of inches of the finish line, and then something would happen, and every other cunt would go flying past. *Every* fucking week! Broke my wee heart, it did."

"Yeah, now that you mention it," Seamus mused, "I remember that used to annoy me too."

"Yeah, fair point," said Gary.

"Actually, thinking about *Wacky Races*," Seamus added. "Wasn't Peter Perfect's car just one big phallic symbol? Or is that just me?"

Everyone looked at Seamus. "Yeah, I think that's just you," said Bobby.

"You fading bastards missed it all!"

"Well, if it isn't the wild men of the mountains," said Gary as Sean and Tone came through the door. "Hope you brought us some of that strong wine."

"What? Oh, the monastery was closed."

"Yeah," said Sean, "closed and non-existent."

"Yeah, that too," Tone conceded.

"Is there any food on the go?" asked Sean, heading for the kitchen.

"We got you some *bocadillos*," Joker told him. "They're in the fridge."

"Good lads."

Jamesy and Kevin came in from the courtyard and sat down at the table.

"How was it?" Jamesy asked Tone.

"Brilliant, Jamesy, you would have loved it."

Sean came back from the kitchen with a baguette for him and one for Tone.

"We thought we'd wait till you two got back before we did any work," said Bobby.

"That's good of you."

"We're thinking of going dancing with cows tomorrow night," Joker declared.

Tone looked at Joker, then looked around the table, hoping that someone would translate.

"There's a festival on in a wee town along the valley," Bobby explained. "There was a poster in the paseo that said something about dancing with cows, whatever that means. We thought it would be something we could do for our last night."

"Dancing with cows?" asked Sean.

"I think there's a bullring in Benifairó," said Kevin, "so that might have something to do with it."

"Well, I'm not going to go and watch somebody stab an animal," Sean decided.

"Yeah, fuck that," said Joker.

"No, I don't think there'll be anything like that," Kevin told them. "They'll probably just run some cows around the ring and people can run around getting chased by them. You know, like the running of the bulls in Pamplona."

"But cows, though?" said Tone.

"Yeah, you all know what the big, black Spanish bulls look like, don't you?" Kevin explained. "Well, the cows are the same as that, only smaller, faster and more agile."

"Sounds dangerous."

"It can be, yeah, but I think that's the point."

"Right then, I reckon we should check it out," said Tone. "What was the place called again?"

"Benifairó."

"Benifairó it is, then. Right, that's tomorrow night sorted, what about tonight?"

"I'm happy to just chill out back at the beach-house," said Seamus, and everyone nodded in agreement. Tone looked around at all the furniture and bits and pieces lying around.

"This is going to take a while to sort out," he said. "We could end up missing the last bus again."

"It'll be easy enough to hitchhike," said Kevin. "If we split up into groups and go separately, it won't take long at all."

"Okay," said Tone as he finished his lunch. "We'd better get started, then."

THIRTY EIGHT

They started off at the City Hall, where they discovered they were in the wrong place. They were then redirected to a different building that was just a short walk away and Martin used the opportunity, as they walked, to voice his concerns.

"I've just got no idea what to expect," he explained. "I mean, technically I'm still married, but I'm sure that Shauna's found somebody else by now. The kids will all be grown up as well, and they'll be living their own lives. Probably without ever giving me a second thought."

"It's still best to know, though, isn't it?"

"Oh yeah, absolutely," said Martin, "but I'm just not sure how I'll feel, if me turning up completely out of the blue turns out to be a real hassle for everybody, you know? What if I'm just an inconvenient embarrassment?"

"I think your children will want to know what happened to their father."

"You think so?"

"Of course!" Stephanie stopped and turned to Martin. "Don't you think they would have been curious? Surely they would have been wondering over the years what had happened to you."

"Yeah, I know," Martin said as they walked on, "but I just think that as time has gone on, they would have been more preoccupied with getting on with their own lives, you know? Maybe they'd think about me from time to time, but that would be less and less over the years, wouldn't it?"

"Maybe, but like I said, it's still best to know."

They entered a large office block and were directed by the receptionist to a room where they could access the electoral roll for Belfast. At first it was looking promising as they found several matches for Elaine McCann, Rosemary McCann and Jack McCann, but none of the dates of birth were the right ones. After half an hour of fruitless searching, Martin stood back and stretched in exasperation.

"It's looking a bit hopeless, isn't it?" he suggested.

Stephanie chewed on her lower lip with frustration. "There must be a way," she declared helplessly. She went over to talk to someone sitting at a desk on the other side of the room as Martin paced thoughtfully back and forth. He was feeling increasingly torn by his desire to see his family and by his fear of what he would find.

"We could try the Land Registry," said Stephanie, striding back with her new suggestion.

"How do we go about doing that?"

"Well, it's in another building," she said, "but it's not far from here."

Martin looked at her. "Look, I'm really sorry for dragging you into all of this. I'm sure this is the last thing you could be doing with."

"Nonsense!" Stephanie told him happily. "I'm just as desperate to get to the bottom of this as you are. It's turning into a bit of a quest, isn't it?"

"Well, anyway, I appreciate it."

"I should tell you, though," Stephanie said as they made for the exit, "this is probably a long shot. I don't know what the deal will be for Housing Executive properties." She paused. "Actually, that's not a bad idea. We could try the Housing Executive."

"What's the Housing Executive?"

"Well, it's just council housing, really. The Executive organises all of the affordable rental properties in Northern Ireland. They might have a list of their tenants we can have a look at."

"That sounds well worth a look," said Martin. "We'll give it a try if we don't have any luck with this Land Registry thing. And I'm not sure we will, to be honest. I can't imagine Shauna or any of the kids being able to buy their own place."

"We should still try every option we can think of," Stephanie decided. "Leave no stone unturned, that's what I say!"

Her enthusiasm was contagious, and Martin was feeling quite optimistic by the time they pushed open the smoked glass double-doors of the imposing office block and stepped into the offices of the Land Registry for Northern Ireland.

Where they found Elaine McCann.

Martin stared at the name, next to an Ardoyne address, and tried not get too hopeful.

"There's no date of birth," he pointed out.

"No, but …" Stephanie gave him a glance. She could tell he was trying to suppress his excitement. "there's no harm in trying it out."

"No, I suppose not," he said as he noted the address. "I could call up this afternoon. You're welcome to come too, if you want."

Stephanie smiled. "No, Martin," she told him gently, "if this turns out to be your daughter, then I'll only be in the way. This is something that should be private, with just the two of you."

"Yeah, you're probably right," he admitted. "You've been a huge help, though. I don't know how I can thank you."

"It's been a pleasure." She reached out and patted his arm. "Just be sure and let me know how it goes, okay?"

"Of course," he said. "Absolutely."

As he made his way along the street, counting down the house numbers, he could see that his destination lay just ahead. Just a few more houses along. Nearly there. He started to feel anxious. The tension was building in him and his heart was thumping in his chest.

He stopped at the gate and, pushing it open, he almost cried out at the unexpected squeal of the iron hinge. He stared ahead to the front door at the end of the path as he hesitatingly put one foot into the garden.

He took one step at a time along the path, half-hoping it would be a false alarm. Half-hoping the encounter would end with an apologetic smile, and a shrug and a 'sorry to have bothered –' the front door crashed open causing his heart to jump. He stopped as a crazed figure burst into the garden. Martin's eyes bulged in his head, and he instinctively stepped backwards as the pregnant woman hurtled towards him, with black hair flailing behind her and blazing eyes that were wild and wide and spilling tears that threatened to choke the cry that fell from her lips. *Daddy!*

THIRTY NINE

Nigeria 1968

The war had been raging for a year when Father Jerome disembarked at Lagos airport. After a brief spell in Portugal, he had taken a direct flight from Lisbon and was planning to meet with representatives of Caritas, an amalgamation of Catholic charities, as well as interdenominational groups who were attempting to provide help to the people of Biafra. He had also been granted an audience with the Papal Legate to Western Africa.

The Biafran Army had shocked the world by not immediately capitulating to the superior Nigerian forces, but had instead pushed the Federal Army back almost as far as Lagos itself. Eventually, though, the greater numbers and the far greater firepower of Nigeria began to take their toll and the war had shrunk back to within the borders of Biafra, where the Biafrans were forced to rely on hit-and-run guerrilla tactics against the encroaching enemy.

As the noose tightened around the neck of the independent little nation, it became increasingly obvious that a crisis was looming. Biafra had already struggled to feed the millions of refugees that had poured across her borders since the massacres of 1966, but the war and the almost total blockade of supplies into the country by the Nigerian Armed Forces meant that the deprivation only accelerated and, by now, people were starving.

"What the hell do you mean he doesn't trust the Red Cross?" Father Jerome raged across the table at the Papal Legate. The legate looked impassively at the agitated priest and then waved his hand dismissively.

"Commander Gowon is understandably concerned about military supplies being smuggled to the rebel forces under the cover of humanitarian aid," he said. "It is an unfortunate situation, of course, but until a way can be found to guarantee that only supplies of sustenance are being transported to the East, and then that they are only being supplied to the civilian population and not to the military, then there is little that can be done."

"Supplies of sustenance?" roared Father Jerome. "You mean food? You mean food that can prevent innocent people from dying, is that what you mean?"

"There is no need to become so emotional, Father. Negotiations are still ongoing, but the situation is delicate."

"I know what the situation is! People are starving to death, that's what the situation is! And you're worried about Gowon?"

"Commander Gowon has shown great restraint as he tries to contain an armed insurrection, and there is absolutely nothing that …" The Papal Legate stared open-mouthed as Father Jerome, in a shocking breach of protocol, stormed from the room.

The rest of Father Jerome's appointments proved equally fruitless, and he was in a sombre frame of mind as he drove back to Biafra. He was held up on several occasions at military checkpoints, but his clerical status, as well as his white face, allowed him to cross the border without too much trouble. He was keen to reach Enugu.

Father Jerome knew that the Nigerian Army had captured Enugu a few months earlier, and he had been hearing some disturbing, if unconfirmed, reports of massacres committed against the civilian population. He hadn't heard from Benjamin in months.

He pulled up outside the bungalow and his heart sank. Benjamin's house and all of the houses around had clearly been abandoned. They stood silently derelict, in overgrown gardens, with broken windows and a few sad possessions scattered on the ground. Father Jerome walked thoughtfully around his friend's former home and tried listing the possible events that could have led to the sorry state he had discovered.

The worst case scenario was that the residents of the university campus had all been rounded up and taken off somewhere to be shot, but Father Jerome refused to countenance such a possibility. It was more likely, he decided, that they would have fled in advance of the Nigerians' approach and were now staying at one of the refugee camps that Father Jerome knew had been set up around those parts of the country still under Biafran control.

He got back in his car and decided he would make his way to Umuahia, which he understood to be the current capital of Biafra, and where he hoped he would find some answers.

"You're looking a wee bit lost there, Father, if you don't mind me saying."

Father Jerome stopped and looked behind him. He saw a young white man wearing the uniform of the Biafran Army's 4th Commando Brigade.

"You're Irish?" Father Jerome asked.

"Awk, sure isn't that a grand accent you've got yourself there, Father." The young man walked forward and held out his hand. "Put it there, Father. The name's Malrooney, Louis Malrooney."

They shook hands, then Father Jerome took a step back to look the young man up and down.

"You're a long way from home, Malrooney," he said.

"Sure, didn't I hear there was a fight to be had?"

Father Jerome laughed. "Well, you got that right."

"So, what is it you're after, Father? If you don't mind me asking."

Father Jerome explained how his friends had been living in Enugu before the war, but now seemed to have disappeared since that city's occupation.

"I think you're right, Father," said Malrooney, "they're more than likely at one of the camps." They walked, side by side, along the main corridor of the Government building in Umuahia. "I don't know if there's any sort of official list you could have a look at, but I do know someone you should probably talk to." Malrooney led Father Jerome to a large office that was filled with noise and confusion. They made their way through the chaos until Malrooney stopped at the desk of a young woman.

"Now, Father," he said with a grin, "if this gorgeous creature here can't help you, then I don't think there'll be anyone else in all of Biafra who can."

The woman looked coldly at Malrooney, then gave Father Jerome a quick glance.

"Yes, Father," she said politely. "What can I help you with?"

"Well, I'm looking for some people that may have been evacuated from Enugu," Father Jerome told her. "If I were to give you their names, would that be helpful at all?"

"No, Father," she said. "We don't have the time or the resources to file the names of everyone who is in transit at any given time."

"In transit?"

"But I can get you the locations of several centres where the civilians from that region may have been taken."

"That would be very helpful, thank you."

The girl got up and searched through one of many large filing cabinets that lined the wall. She pulled out three folders and returned to her desk. As she wrote down the names and locations of the relevant refugee centres, she glanced at Malrooney.

"Are you still sober, Malrooney?" she asked. "And it's almost eleven am. Are you ill?"

"Oh, my sweetheart," said Malrooney. "Just to look into those eyes is intoxication enough for me."

She folded the paper she had written on and handed it to Father Jerome. "These are the places where your friends are most likely to be, Father," she said. "I wish you luck. Oh, and Father, you may want to reconsider the company you keep in Umuahia."

"I'll bear that in mind, my dear. And thank you. Thank you very much."

As they walked towards the exit, Father Jerome turned to Malrooney. "She seemed nice," he said. "And she seemed very taken with you."

"Oh, they all are Father. It's my Irish charm."

"What's her name?"

"Now don't be getting me bogged down with details, Father," Malrooney said dismissively. "And did I just hear her say it was nearly eleven o'clock?"

"You did."

"Well now, Father. Do you fancy a drink?"

It was in the second refugee centre that he visited that Father Jerome spotted Adanna. She was sitting on the ground, reading a newspaper, at the doorway to one of several long, low huts.

"Adanna?"

She looked up and gave a shriek of surprise. She got to her feet and rushed over to embrace him.

"Father Jerome," she cried, "it is so good to see you."

"And it's great to see you too, Adanna. Is Benjamin here as well?"

Adanna shook her head. "He is with the army."

"He hasn't been conscripted, has he?"

"He volunteered," she told him as she led him to a makeshift bench where they could sit. "He is a medic with the army now, but I don't know any more than that. I don't even know where he is."

"I could do some snooping around if you'd like. See what I can find out."

"Thank you, Father, but I don't think it will be necessary. I'm sure Benjamin is fine. He knows that we have been relocated to this camp, so he knows where we are at least. Actually, now that you've mentioned it, I haven't had any news from my mother in a while, so if you could ..."

"Ijemma? Yes, of course. Consider it done."

"Thank you."

"So, how have you been keeping, Adanna? Are you all right?"

"Yes, we are doing fine," she said. "Of course, I worry about the children not getting enough to eat, but I think we are doing better than most, so I won't complain."

"Where are the kids?"

"Oh, they'll be off playing somewhere with the other children of the camp."

Father Jerome looked around at the camp's residents. It was just the same as in the first camp he had gone to; people brought to the very brink of starvation. He had been shocked by Adanna's almost skeletal appearance, but he had thought it best not to comment on it.

"What's the food situation like at the moment?" he asked casually.

"We are allowed a handful of boiled rice, twice, sometimes three times a day."

"And that's it?"

"That's it."

He shook his head. "The bloody food is there, Adanna, do you know that? The Red Cross and the other relief agencies have stockpiled all the food you need, but the Nigerians won't let them bring it in."

"Well, what would you expect, Father?" Adanna said wearily. "They are trying to win the war."

"That's a fairly sober view of things."

"I just want it to be over now, that's all. They keep telling us that we are winning, but look around you, Father. Does it look like we are winning?"

"No," he said softly. "No, it doesn't look like that at all."

It wasn't the ripped and shredded limbs that bothered Benjamin. It wasn't the eyeballs torn from sockets or the heads blown from bodies. It wasn't the dribbling ravings of the shell-shocked or the senseless mutilations. It wasn't even the bodies of small children impaled on the spikes of iron railings, designed to taunt and to terrorise the beleaguered Biafran populace. As horrific as these things were, there was something else, something more sinister, more insidious, that stalked the misty edges of Benjamin's consciousness. It was called *kwashiorkor.*

As he travelled around the war-weary nation, Benjamin began to realise the true import of what was going on. He knew that, even though food supplies were desperately low, there was still enough rice to make sure that most people could get something to eat most days. But, for Benjamin, that wasn't the problem.

The problem was the lack of protein. Most of Biafra's protein-rich foods were imported, but that supply had now been cut off by the Nigerian blockade, which meant that the diet for much of the population was almost exclusively starch. Over any extended period of time this was unsustainable. The result was kwashiorkor.

The obvious effects of kwashiorkor, caused by protein deficiency, were wasted limbs and a grotesquely swollen abdomen, leading ultimately to death. Children were especially vulnerable.

Benjamin could see the signs of the affliction everywhere he went, and he knew that if the issue were not addressed soon, then Biafra would face a disaster of unimaginable proportions.

But no one would listen.

He had tried on numerous occasions to raise the matter with his superiors, but the few who were sympathetic had insisted there was nothing they could do. The only realistic answer, it seemed, would be the lifting of the blockade, but that appeared to be increasingly unlikely.

If anything, the noose was tightening.

Father Jerome, now working as part of an inter-faith action group, was touring Uli airport, west of Umuahia, in order to learn how some of the stockpiled aid was managing to get through the blockade. It was only a tiny fraction of what was needed, but just the fact that it was able to break the Federal stranglehold gave Father Jerome some cause to hope.

He spoke to the construction gangs who kept the runway serviceable, despite constant attention from Nigerian bombers, then met with the flight administrator for the airport.

"Yes, Father," the administrator told him with a smile. "The Federals blow holes in the runway during the day, then we hurry to fill in the holes before the night comes."

"So, the flights come in at night, then?"

"They have to, Father. They would be shot down otherwise."

"Even planes that are clearly marked as humanitarian aid?"

"That is correct. The Federals have said as much."

"Is there a flight scheduled for tonight?"

The administrator looked uneasy, and Father Jerome raised his hands. "No, no, of course, you don't have to tell me. I'm being far too nosy."

"Oh no, Father, it isn't that. There is nothing officially scheduled, but we do have pilots that will decide to come if they believe there is no activity from the Nigerian aircraft. Then, at the last minute, they will send us a radio signal and we will turn on the airport lights just long enough for them to land."

"The lights are kept off at night?"

"It is safer that way."

"Mmm, it all sounds very risky."

"Of course, Father, we are at war. And now that Port Harcourt has fallen, it is essential that we remain operational. We are Biafra's only real lifeline now."

The administrator appeared cheerful, but Father Jerome could sense the strain he was under and just how precarious his position was. The loss of Port Harcourt was a major blow to the Biafrans. The territory that was still in Biafran hands had now contracted to the interior of the country and was becoming ever more bloated with refugees.

"Thank you for your time," Father Jerome told him. "You're doing an excellent job under difficult circumstances."

"Thank you, Father."

Later that night, the dark airport bloomed suddenly and shockingly bright in the pitch-black Biafran night and, moments later, a Lockheed Super Constellation swooped in low from the surrounding gloom. Once the plane had landed, the airport went dark once more.

Father Jerome could appreciate the delicate timing. Once lit, the airport would be visible from the sky for miles around, easy prey for one of the Russian MiGs that Nigeria sent regularly into the skies over Biafra.

The Lockheed taxied into a waiting hangar and Father Jerome headed that way, hoping to intercept the pilot. The young man climbed down from his cockpit and walked towards the administration desk. Father Jerome watched him approach and grinned.

"Andrew," he called. "It is Andrew, isn't it? We met in Lisbon."

"Yes, Father," Andrew replied with a smile. His accent had a strong Australian lilt to it. "How are you doing?"

"I'm good. Would it be possible to have a word once you've finished here?"

When Andrew had completed his paperwork, he went with Father Jerome to a small reception area where they sat down at a table.

"It's good to see you again, Father," said Andrew, "but I think you're crazy for coming back here."

"I sometimes think we're all crazy, Andrew. Every last one of us. But I wanted to ask you about all that food we saw being stored back in Lisbon. What are the chances of it getting here anytime soon?"

"Very little, I would say. There just aren't enough aircraft."

"But doesn't your boss have –?"

"Oh, hold on there, Father," Andrew interrupted. "Hank is being paid to fly in equipment for the Biafran Army, and that's what he's doing. He's got three planes at the moment, and their space is mostly taken up with arms shipments."

"Mostly?"

"Well, yeah, the relief agencies keep putting pressure on us to carry aid on our flights and, to be honest, Father, we do what we can, but it isn't what the Biafran Government pays us for. If they paid us to bring food, then we'd bring food."

"I've heard that the charities are trying to purchase their own planes, how is that going?"

"Not as quickly as they'd like," Andrew told him. "I think the Canadians might have offered something, or the Yanks, maybe, but who knows?"

"Yes, I see."

"And there's always the added complication of the Nigerian Air Force, Father. Having enough aircraft won't solve that little problem."

"Dr Maher, is it?"

Benjamin turned to see a Biafran soldier, clearly a mercenary, sitting on a camp bed in the hospital tent. His left hand was heavily bandaged, and in his right was a bottle of wine.

"Yes, I'm Dr Maher," said Benjamin. "Have we … um …?"

"Put it there, Doc," the soldier said, placing the bottle on the floor and holding out his hand. "I believe we have a mutual friend. I had a wee chat with a Father Jerome back in Umuahia," the soldier explained as Benjamin shook his hand. "He was having a hard time finding you, you know."

"Father Jerome?" asked Benjamin excitedly. "He's back in Biafra?"

"He is indeed. The name's Malrooney, by the way. Louis Malrooney, though everyone just calls me Paddy."

"It's good to meet you, um, Paddy. How is your hand?"

"Oh this?" scoffed Malrooney. "It's nothing at all. A wee bit of shrapnel just took a chunk out of it, that's all."

"And how was Father Jerome?" asked Benjamin. "What's he up to now?"

"Father Jerome," Malrooney began, "is a man who likes to keep himself busy. He's here, there and bloody everywhere." Malrooney picked up his wine and offered a swig to Benjamin.

"No, thank you."

"Yes, indeed," Malrooney went on, glugging from the bottle, "trying to save the whole damned world, if you ask me."

"Do you know where he is?"

"Not at this very minute, no. Like I said, Doc, he's a man who gets around."

"Do you think there is any chance you will see him again soon?"

"Anything's possible, Doc," said Malrooney. "I'll be happy to keep a wee eye out for him, if that's what you're after."

"I'd appreciate it, thanks."

"Don't mention it. And you'll be based around here for a while, is that right?"

"Yes. At least I believe so."

Malrooney held up the wine. "Then here's to the impending renewal of your acquaintance," he said as he took a swig. Benjamin thanked him again, then moved on down the long row of beds. His mind raced at this stroke of good fortune. If he could meet up with his old friend to let him know how things stood at the moment, then he felt sure that Father Jerome would do everything he could to help. And Benjamin needed help, for he had arrived at a fateful decision.

He needed to save his young family, he realised. He needed to pluck them from the nightmare, from the apocalypse that he knew was coming, and to do that, he knew they had only one choice.

They would have to flee Biafra.

Adanna no longer had the strength to scream. Nor to cry. Nor even to grieve. She stood, fragile and numb, as Ikeobi, her baby boy, was lowered into the shallow grave, just one of several children to succumb in the night.

She put an arm around the little girl standing quiet by her side and wondered when it would be her daughter's turn to weaken, and to collapse and to slip sadly away. Or would it be herself who deteriorated first? Would the little four-year-old Chiazacam have to sit in the squalid, overcrowded hut and watch her mother slowly die? And did it even matter?

Adanna had watched the population of the camp grow day by day, as people swarmed in from the countryside, desperate for food. The various charity groups, spurred on by a tireless Father Jerome, had lobbied for all available resources to be directed immediately to the refugees, but it was not enough. It would never be enough. They would all die.

She knelt down in front of Chiaza, and her broken heart broke a little more, for she could see that the light in her daughter's eyes – a light that had once blazed with the joy of youth – was now little more than a pale, ghostly flicker.

Benjamin had to wipe away a tear as he greeted Father Jerome. It was more than just the meeting of an old friend; it was a hopeful embrace of happier times. Of times before the war. Of cold beer and warm nights. Of wandering conversations and boisterous debate. Of giggling children and future plans. Of hope and friendship and joy.

"It's so good to see you again, Benjamin," Father Jerome said happily.

"You too, Father," said Benjamin. "A lot has happened, as you can see."

"Yes, yes, a shocking business entirely."

"I hear you've been keeping busy."

"I do what I can, Benjamin, but I fear it is nowhere near enough."

They sat at a table in an open plaza, close to the army base where Benjamin was currently deployed, and talked of the war.

"There is no war," said Father Jerome, "at least not as far as the rest of the world is concerned. I was at a big football match in Lisbon and I got chatting to loads of Scottish and Irish lads. Most had never even heard of Biafra, to be honest."

Benjamin nodded sadly. "It's understandable, I suppose. The world has got its own problems, but it still seems hard to believe that all this madness can go unnoticed."

"Have you seen Adanna lately?" Father Jerome asked.

"No," Benjamin admitted, "I haven't been able to get away for months now, but I heard she's been moved to a different camp."

"Yes, I managed to catch up with her there a few weeks ago. She seemed fine but, Jesus, Benjamin, she looked awful thin."

Benjamin leaned forward and lowered his head. "Well, that is kind of what I wanted to see you about, Father," he said, and then paused as if unsure about how to proceed. "I know that I don't need to explain to an Irishman anything about the word *famine*, but I believe that famine is exactly what Biafra is facing."

"Yes, Benjamin," Father Jerome agreed, "I can see it everywhere I go."

"And I don't think the war will end anytime soon," Benjamin continued, "which means that everything will only get much, much worse."

Father Jerome nodded but said nothing.

"I have to get them out, Father," Benjamin stated flatly. "My wife and my children need to get out of Biafra. If they stay they will die."

Father Jerome showed no reaction as he considered Benjamin's words. "What have you got in mind?" he asked finally.

"Well, it means deserting from the army," Benjamin said quietly. "I thought of taking my car to pick up Adanna and the children, and then trying to make it across the border into Cameroon."

"That would be suicide, Benjamin, and I think you're well aware of that," said Father Jerome. "You would be trying to get through hundreds of miles of enemy held territory."

"I hold a British passport," Benjamin explained. "I had hoped that maybe it would be enough to confuse any checkpoint we came across."

"No piece of paper is going to hold any sway out there in the bush, Benjamin. You know that."

"Well, I don't know what else I can do, Father. I'm open to suggestions."

Father Jerome was thoughtful for a moment, then he grasped Benjamin's arm.

Adanna was lying listless and dozing with Chiaza by her side when she felt herself being shaken.

"Adanna," a voice hissed in her ear.

"Benjamin?"

"Come on, we're leaving."

She sat up and stared at her husband. "What do you mean?"

"There's no time, come on. Where's Ikeobi?"

Adanna lowered her gaze and slowly shook her head. Benjamin's heart froze.

"No!"

"I'm sorry, Benjamin. I'm so sorry. I couldn't save him. I tried, I ..."

"Later, Adanna," Benjamin urged. "We need to go now!" He carefully picked up Chiaza, wrapped in a shawl, and was shocked by how weightless she felt. He then led Adanna out to the waiting car and helped her into the passenger seat before placing Chiaza in her lap. He jumped into the driver's seat and started the engine.

"Where are we going?" Adanna asked as they drove out of the camp.

"If we can make it to the airport by two am," Benjamin told her, "then Father Jerome believes he can get us on a flight to Lisbon."

"Lisbon? But what about passports? We don't –"

"We'll worry about that when we get there. Maybe the British Consulate can help. I don't know, we'll think of something, I'm sure. At least we'll be safe, that's the main thing."

"Benjamin. Ikeobi ... I ..."

"It's all right, Adanna," he assured her. "It's all right." But he knew he was lying. How could it be all right? His son was dead. It would never be all right.

They drove through the night, skirting the ever-changing front line, with the ghost of their little boy stifling their words and clouding their thoughts.

Benjamin spun round a sharp bend, only to see a Land Rover parked across the road just up ahead. He slammed on his brakes to avoid a collision, then watched in dismay as Nigerian troops jumped from the Land Rover and surrounded the car. They wrenched open the car doors and dragged out Benjamin and Adanna. One of the soldiers yanked the bundle from Adanna's arms and threw it onto the roadway where it rolled in the dust. As Adanna rushed forward to save it, a bayonet was thrust into her midriff and she folded over in shock. She slowly slumped to the ground. Someone was screaming.

Benjamin tried to run around the car to reach his wife, but a rifle butt smashed into his glasses causing his vision to explode in searing red agony. The screaming stopped, and Benjamin could hear the soldiers laughing as he scrambled through the blood and dust to get to Adanna. His blurred vision could just make out the look in Adanna's eyes as her wasted body succumbed to the appalling violation and her life force seeped away into the Biafran soil. The screaming started again and continued through the bursts of automatic gunfire that ripped through the night.

"Come on, man, she's gone!" Benjamin felt someone tug at his shoulder. "Come on, you need to be quiet now."

Benjamin stopped screaming. He turned to see a young soldier in a Biafran Army uniform standing over him. Behind him, his colleagues were looting the bodies of the ambushed Nigerians, taking all of their weapons and ammunition. Benjamin made a hurried shuffle over to snatch up the bundle that lay lifeless in the moonlight.

The young soldier made to stop him, but then paused and turned away. The soldiers had all borne witness to the very worst that humanity had to offer over the last year, but there was something especially unbearable in the sight of a broken father clinging with wretched determination to the corpse of a child.

FORTY

London 1969

Winter's weary end threw some half-hearted snowflakes at the window of Benjamin's rented apartment in south London. He watched them flutter moth-like against the warm glass as he replaced the phone receiver in its cradle. He had a decision to make.

He stood at the window and stared down at the sad dusting of snow trying to persuade an unconvinced Streatham Common to cling to winter and to ignore the cheerful inevitability of the coming spring. Reaching up to scratch an imaginary itch beneath his eyepatch, he considered the offer that his old friend, Henry Rafferty, had just made him.

The Biafrans were still fighting, he knew. Still dying. But *his* war was over. He had sacrificed enough for a country that was never his, for a struggle that was never his, and all he wanted now was to find some peace.

He had already made up his mind. He craved a refuge. He needed a place where he could begin again, a place to shelter and a place to heal his wounds, both in body and spirit, and so he would turn away from the all the anger and the hatred, all the bigotry and pain, and he would go and find his peace.

In Belfast.

In the spring of 1969.

FORTY ONE

Tone and Joker made their way up the steps and onto a rooftop made bright by a mournful moon that sat like a bulbous blemish on the star-freckled face of night.

"*O sovereign mistress of true melancholy*," Tone quoted in praise of the plump, silvery orb, gifting her morose beauty to the sombre sea below. "*The poisonous damp of night disponge upon me*."

Joker followed Tone's gaze and silently nodded. "Reminds me of the Albert Clock," he said.

Tone did not reply. He knew from experience not to pry too deeply into the dark, twisting spirals of Joker's mind, so he decided to redirect the conversation onto safer ground.

"Right," he said, "break out the beer."

Joker pulled out two bottles from the bag he was carrying and placed them on the table.

"We won't need any more for a while, will we?" he said.

"Nah, these'll last us for a bit," Tone told him as he took out his cigarettes. Joker brought the other bottles of beer back down the stairs to the kitchen and placed them in the fridge. He came back upstairs and accepted a cigarette from Tone.

"Still really warm, isn't it?" he said as he stood sipping his beer and looking out across the water.

"Yeah," Tone agreed, "makes you wonder why our ancestors left the Med. I mean, what the hell were they thinking?"

"You'd need to ask Jamesy that question. He'd probably give you a long and detailed explanation about all the environmental and migratory pressures faced by Neolithic tribes of hunter-gatherers in their great quest for who the fuck knows what."

"Remind me to never, ever to ask Jamesy that question."

Joker turned from the edge of the little terrace and walked back to sit down on the bench. He seemed restless, Tone thought. Distracted, almost.

"What's your verdict on Valencian, then?" Tone asked.

"It's just Catalan," Joker replied with a shrug. "Don't know why they call it Valencian."

"I've noticed they seem to be fond of the letter 'x'. It pops up everywhere."

"Yeah," agreed Joker, "though it's probably more noticeable because it isn't used much in Castilian. What about tomorrow night, then? Are you up for a bit of cow dancing?"

"Yeah, it sounds like a laugh," said Tone. "It's our last night, so we might as well do something different." He hesitated as he tried to think of the best way to approach the question of Joker's, increasingly obvious, lack of motivation. "You know," he began, "I was talking to –"

"Best fucking lift ever!" The exclamation accompanied loud footsteps at the bottom of the stairs.

"Yeah," said Seamus, "but it was only because we had Jamesy with us."

"Fuck off!" Gary retorted as he, Seamus and Jamesy made their way onto the rooftop. "Your woman was all over me."

"You?" Seamus demanded. "You? Then why did she make Jamesy sit in the front?"

"Well, that's just –"

"Why did she stare at him the whole way here?"

"Because –"

"Why did she talk to him the whole time? And we just sat in the back like a couple of fucking gooseberries."

"You really don't know much about women, do you?" said Gary in a condescending manner. "She was just trying to make me jealous. Anybody could see that. Isn't that right, Jamesy?"

"What? Um … yeah, probably," Jamesy replied, sitting down at the table.

"And who did she give her phone number to?" asked Seamus.

"Jesus! Are you really that fucking dense?" cried Gary. "She was shy! She didn't want to make it too obvious, did she?"

"Well, you've got a point there," said Seamus. "She didn't make it fucking obvious at all."

"Did you dickheads get any beer on the way?" asked Tone. "I mean, as fascinating as this discussion is, don't you think that –?"

"Yeah, we got beer," Gary told him. "It's in the fridge. Why?"

"Didn't occur to you to bring any up here, then?"

Gary and Seamus looked at each other, then shook their heads and trudged back down the steps, grumbling at each other under their breath.

"Get me one too!" Jamesy called after them.

"Good lift, was it?" Tone turned to Jamesy.

"Good-looking German girl in a convertible BMW?" said Jamesy smiling. "So, yeah, you could say that."

Seamus and Gary reappeared and, handing a beer to Jamesy, sat at the table. After a while Sean, Bobby and Kevin arrived with more beer and grabbed some folding chairs from a storage container that sat to one side of the rooftop.

"Jammy bastards!" Bobby exclaimed. "Did you see the fucking car they got into?" he asked Tone.

"Heard about it."

"Jammy bastards!" Bobby repeated. "And your woman driving it? Jesus Christ! Jammy bastards!"

"Marta, she was called," Seamus told him. "German girl. She gave Jamesy her phone number because she fancied Gary, apparently."

"Really?" asked Sean. He looked at Jamesy. "Are you going to call her?"

"Not much point, is there?" Jamesy replied. "Besides, it was Gary she was after."

Gary gave Jamesy a salute with his beer. "Too fucking right!" he said.

"You looking for the meaning of life there, Joker?" Kevin asked. Everyone turned to see Joker, lying on his back on the bench and staring up at the night sky. His bottle of beer on the terracotta tiles beside him.

"What makes you think there's a meaning to life?" he said.

"Isn't there?"

"You can sum life up in four words," said Joker, still staring at the stars, "but you won't find much meaning in them."

"What four words?" asked Seamus.

"Born, eat, shag, die," Joker answered. "Anything else is just killing time."

"Well, that's fucking bleak," said Sean. "So, you're just dismissing everything that anybody's ever done in all of history? Michelangelo shouldn't have bothered painting the Sistine Chapel, then? Just killing time, was he?"

"Do you think that, ten thousand years from now, the Sistine Chapel will still be there?" asked Joker. "Or Rome, even?"

"Well, Rome's the eternal city," Kevin suggested.

"*We are butterflies that flutter for a day,*" Joker quoted, "*and think it is forever.*"

"What?"

"Nothing's eternal," Joker expanded. "Nothing's permanent. Everything dies."

"And that, Ladies and Gentlemen," said Sean, "is the Second Law of Thermodynamics."

"Jesus Christ, Joker!" cried Gary. "What the fuck is wrong with *you*?"

"Yeah," said Bobby, "that doesn't sound like the Joker we know and tolerate."

Joker lay on the bench and gazed at infinity. Lost in his own thoughts, he elected not to answer.

So Tone decided to answer for him.

"He's missing Carol, that's what's wrong with him."

Joker sat bolt upright. "What?" he cried. "What the fuck did you say that for?"

"It's true, isn't it?"

Joker glared at Tone, then sighed and shook his head. He picked up his beer, stood up and walked to the edge of the rooftop to look out at the silent, empty sea.

"You're a bit of a dickhead, Tone," he pointed out. "You know that, don't you?"

"Yeah," replied Tone, "but is it true about Carol?"

"Probably," Joker admitted. He then turned to face Tone. "But there's fuck-all I can do about it."

"Why not?" Bobby asked.

"Because the last I heard," Joker explained, "was that she'd gone to Nigeria, which is just a wee bit out of the way."

"Has she finished her training, then?" asked Tone.

"I don't think so," said Joker. "At least not completely, but I think she once said she could finish her training in Africa."

"Do you think she's gone for good, then?" asked Seamus, and Joker shrugged in reply.

"For a while, anyway," he said. "So, it's a bit pointless me missing her, isn't it?"

Kevin looked around at the others' faces. "I don't know Carol," he began, "so I may be missing something here, but why Africa?"

Joker walked back to the bench and sat down. He took a sip of beer and looked at Kevin. "Carol is her middle name," he informed him. "She was christened Chiazacam, which, as I'm sure you know, is an Igbo name."

"Eeboh?" asked Kevin, confused.

"Yes," Joker continued, "Carol was one of those wee Biafran kids we all used to make jokes about when we were at school. Nearly died too, apparently. Anyway, she'd always talked about going back there at some point. Don't know why exactly, but I'm sure she's got her reasons."

"I've always thought that Chiazacam was a fucking cool name," mused Gary.

"Yeah," Kevin agreed, "does it mean anything?"

"The closest English translation," Joker said, "would be *God has answered me well.*"

"That makes it even cooler," said Gary.

"So, what are you going to do, Joker?" Bobby asked. "You can't just keep on moping about her, can you?"

"Why not?" Joker smiled, but it was unconvincing. He gave another sigh. "I don't know, Bobby," he said. "I'll just have to get over it, I suppose. Just takes time, that's all."

"How do you know she's in Africa?" asked Jamesy.

"I bumped into one of her mates a while back – Susie, remember her? – and she told me that Carol had buggered off to Africa. It was probably then that I started feeling some sort of … oh, I don't know … regret? ... is that the word?"

"Actually, I think I know who you mean," Kevin said. "Was she at Charlie's party?"

"Yeah, she was there for a bit," said Joker. "That was the night we split up. I think I was annoyed that she made me leave early so I made up some excuse to pick a fight with her."

"You're a dickhead," said Tone, and everyone nodded in agreement.

"You think I don't know that?"

"Well," Tone decided, "nothing is insurmountable. We've got enough beer to help us come up with some sort of solution to Joker's wee problem, so let's get to it."

FORTY TWO

Rosie was almost hugging herself with anticipation. She couldn't be sure how long she and her father had spent sobbing in each other's arms as they stood in the garden, but now she was energized with forming a plan.

"You know what to do, now, don't you?" she asked.

"Yes, love," said Martin. He was still trying to process the flood of information he had received from his daughter – *his daughter!* – after they had eventually made it into the house and had sat in the front room, babbling incessantly, trying to fill a twenty year gap in their lives.

Shauna was dead. Martin was stunned by this. In every scenario he had played out in his mind, Shauna was alive. She was alive, and she was angry. She was smiling. She was confused, she was crying, she was laughing, she was yelling, swearing, blaming. She was alive.

But Shauna was dead.

Rosie had held him as they both stood and sobbed once more until their shared grief tip-toed quietly into the background to leave them alone with new possibilities in an unexpected new future.

Ellie would come first, Rosie decided. Miss Goody-Two-Shoes was about to get the shock of her life. Rosie loved her sister dearly, but she struggled to match Ellie's simple goodness, resorting instead to teasing her relentlessly. She couldn't live up to her sister's piety, but then who could? Ellie was the very best of souls. Gentle and caring and kind.

"She'll fucking shit a brick!" Rosie declared happily, and Martin winced as he tried to reconcile his little Rosemary with this brash, feisty fully-grown woman who could swear with the best of them. And she was *pregnant.*

"I think you'll like Gary," Rosie told him. "I mean, he'll drive you mad sometimes, but I think you'll like him. I'm not sure if you would remember the Lingfields."

Martin shook his head.

"No, I didn't think so," said Rosie. "I knew them because Karen was in my class at school."

"And you were saying Gary's in Spain at the minute?"

"Aye," said Rosie. "He's another one who's in for a bit of a shock."

"So, what about Jack?" asked Martin. "Are you sure you don't want to give him a ring yet?"

"No, we'll ring him later," Rosie insisted. "Ellie should be the first to know – well, after me, anyway. She never gave up trying to find you, you know. Not for a minute."

The emotions brought on by the thought of his eldest child's quiet but dogged determination threatened to overwhelm Martin. He cursed the wasted years. The years he had spent lost in a maelstrom of psychosis, clinging to whatever would quell the waves of anxiety and fear that ebbed and flowed and threatened to pull him under the surface, to darkness and madness and oblivion.

"You found us again," Rosie said softly as she understood his anguish, "and we've got our whole lives ahead of us. And, anyway, you've got this wee thing to look forward to." She gestured to the bump that strained against her T-shirt.

Martin looked at her and smiled. "Yeah, you're right, love." He was going to be a grandfather. He was stupefied by the abrupt turn his life had just taken.

"Right!" Rosie suddenly exclaimed. "She won't be long now, so you'd better get ready."

"Right you are," Martin laughed as he made his way into the kitchen. It somehow did not feel unnatural to be bossed around by his youngest daughter. He was fine with it. It felt good. He was happy. And he was about to meet Ellie.

It was only natural she felt tired. She had just completed a twelve-hour shift at the hospital, so it would be surprising if she didn't feel some fatigue, but as she stepped off the bus for the short walk home, Ellie felt almost crushed by weariness.

She was off work for the next few days, as her shifts rotated, but rather than look forward to the time off, she was hoping to spend as much time as possible curled up in bed under the covers and seeing no one. She was beginning to feel some concern for her own wellbeing as her natural optimism seemed to drain more quickly these days.

Rosie's mood swings did not help, but it would be wrong to blame her little sister's volatile hormones on the fact that Ellie was no longer able to find joy. She simply no longer looked.

As she listened to the garden gate shriek in protest at her audacity in wanting to enter her own garden, Ellie hoped that Rosie would be in a mellow mood. She didn't think she could face any angry sarcasm this evening. She could do without the sullen grumblings, the dark disdain and the constant, pointless arguing.

Ellie had long felt there was a lot more to Rosie's moods than just the shock of pregnancy, but on those occasions when whatever was eating at Rosie would shatter into brittle shards of emotion, she had found rational discussion impossible.

She pushed open the door and, as she stepped into the front room, she saw Rosie sitting on one side of the sofa with a grim, hard look on her face. Ellie sighed and walked across the floor to sit in the armchair against the far wall. As she sat down, she failed to notice the little glance that Rosie flicked towards the kitchen door that was set in the wall to Ellie's left.

"What do you fancy doing for dinner tonight?" Ellie asked Rosie.

"Oh, I don't know," Rosie replied distractedly. "We could get something from the chippy."

"Sounds good to me," said Ellie.

"Have you got any plans for later on?"

"No, I could really just do with an early night, to be honest."

"Mmm," muttered Rosie. "You're not planning on doing any more of your stupid searching tonight, are you?"

"What? No!" Ellie sounded exasperated. "In fact, I don't think –"

"I don't see the bloody point of it myself," spat Rosie, her voice harsh and cold.

"Okay, Rosie. Look, I just want to –"

"Just a bloody waste of everybody's time."

"I know, Rosie, it's just that I –"

"I mean," Rosie exclaimed indignantly, "he can't even make a bloody decent cup of tea!"

Ellie sighed and closed her eyes. She leant back in her chair. "Oh, Rosie," she said wearily, "I don't know what you're talk–"

"Not enough milk, apparently," declared Martin as he stepped through the kitchen doorway.

Rosie pushed herself tight against the back of the sofa to fully appreciate the chaos that was erupting on her sister's face.

It was as if Ellie's emotions had all gathered together at once, uncertain as to which one was due to take precedence over her features.

Surprise, of course, made the smug assumption that it would be taking charge from here on in, but anger made an unexpected early bid, only to trip over confusion, which was curled up in a ball, whimpering.

Panic, running around in circles, was tackled from behind by belligerence, and they tumbled off to the side, while scepticism raised a tentative finger before getting tangled up with anxiety and fear. At this point, apathy strolled casually onto the scene, but on realising its presence would not be required, sauntered nonchalantly away.

"Hello, Elaine," said Martin. "How have you been keeping?"

Joy romped home unopposed.

FORTY THREE

For countless aeons, the driving force behind life on Earth has often been envisioned as a benevolent, maternal figure, so it is possible to imagine a wizened crone, gnarled and weary from three and a half billion years of ceaseless toil, shuffling around in her slippers, in a front parlour lit only by a crackling wood-fire.

And it is then but a small step to picture this ancient, twisted old biddy cast a glance in the direction of Carol and then, nodding with satisfaction, stretch her worn and jaded limbs, put a light to her pipe – ornately carved, perhaps, from the horn of a Triceratops – and settle into a comfortable armchair with a final contented sigh.

Job's a good'un.

Possessed of a languid elegance that slipped, almost lazily, in and out of poetry, Carol was an obvious target for the envious, spiteful bullies that seem to infest all schools but, in this respect, Carol's schooldays were trouble-free. The snide put-downs, the subtle shoves, the insidious intimidation, all simply failed to materialise. Perhaps it was just that everyone could see in Carol something they recognised – or hoped they recognised – in themselves.

The dour misunderstood, the cool kids, the rebels; they all could see, in Carol's exotic appearance, the mark of the true outsider, shunned by the mainstream and forced to lurk on the fringe of society, with head held defiantly high in haughty, independent disdain. It was only Carol's enormous popularity, they reasoned, that held her back from her true calling as the lonely outcast.

And the beautiful people recognised Carol as someone who could truly appreciate the pressure that afflicts those cursed with perfect features. They looked to her as the one person who could understand their torment, someone who could listen to their woes with empathy and understanding. A queen of calm surrounded by delicate princesses.

For the jocks, Carol embodied the African stereotype of lithe athleticism, panther-like in her supple muscularity, loping with easy grace from class to class.

The bright kids worshipped her. The high-achievers, the swots, the nerds, the dweebs, the geeks and the dorks were all enchanted by Carol's intellect. And her sexuality, of course. Many an inadvertent emission had been caused by her overt sexuality, though it was considered vulgar to dwell on such things. It was her mind that mattered. It was Carol's sharp intelligence that was deemed the greatest stimulation for the school's top performers.

And so, the potentially stormy seas of adolescence were, for Carol, a millpond upon which she sailed serenely towards the beckoning haven of further education where she coasted, unflustered, into harbour on half-sail and dropped anchor before the metaphor became tortuous and unwieldy.

It was here that she could no longer ignore the glaring, Joker-shaped, void in her existence, and so entered a tall, broodingly handsome stranger. A majestic mountain of a man with piercing gunmetal grey eyes and cheekbones that …

"Okay, okay, we get the bloody point! Jesus Christ, Joker!"

"Who's telling the story?" Joker asked indignantly.

"I know," said Bobby, "but you're going a wee bit over the top, aren't you? So, Mother Nature smokes a pipe, does she?"

"Well, she's hardly going to smoke fucking roll-ups, is she?"

"Okay, but you still need to tone it down a bit."

"I liked the bit about the metaphor, though," said Jamesy smiling.

"Thank you, Jamesy. Now where was I?"

"I'm still wondering about Biafra," Kevin interjected. "I mean, I can remember the name from when I was a kid and all, but that's about it. I don't know anything else about it."

"That's true," said Seamus thoughtfully. He turned to Jamesy. "Well, Jamesy," he said, "what's the story? You must know something about it."

"Modern history isn't really my thing," Jamesy told him. "Anyway, I'm sure Joker knows more about it than me."

"Yes," said Tone as he put a light to a cigarette, "but I think we've all heard enough of Joker's flights of fancy for one evening. Go ahead, Jamesy. Fill us in on all the details."

"Well," Jamesy began, "as far as I know, the people of one part of Nigeria –"

"The Igbo people," said Joker.

"Yeah," said Jamesy, "the Igbo. Well, they started to get persecuted in some of the other parts of the country not long after Nigeria became independent from Britain in the sixties. I think a lot of them were killed, actually. Thousands, even. Anyway, the survivors all headed back to the region where the Igbo originally came from, to get away from the persecution. We're talking about millions of people here, so it caused a bit of a refugee problem.

"Well, then they reckoned that they were never going to be safe in Nigeria so they formed their own country, Biafra, and tried to go it alone. The rest of Nigeria refused to let them go, though, so they ended up going to war. Britain, and a lot of other countries, backed the Nigerians, so the Biafrans never stood a chance. Even so, it took a couple of years and it was only when Nigeria surrounded the Biafrans and cut off their food supplies that Biafra fell."

"Wait a minute," said Sean, "are you saying that the starvation was deliberate?"

"Yeah," Jamesy said, "the Nigerian government even said that starvation was a legitimate tactic of war."

"Fuck!"

"How many died, then, Jamesy?" asked Gary. "Do you know?"

"All together? About two million."

Everyone stared at Jamesy.

"Two fucking *million*?"

"Give or take," said Jamesy. "And most of them were children."

"Kids? Why?"

"Adults can survive longer without protein than children can, so it was the kids who died first."

"Jesus!" Bobby muttered.

"Well, that explains why you don't hear about Biafra anymore," said Sean. "It doesn't exist."

"So, what about these days, Jamesy?" Seamus wanted to know. "There must still be a lot of tension there. I mean, you don't easily forget two million dead, do you? Do you think Carol will be okay there?"

Jamesy took a sip of beer and let out a sigh. "Hard to say," he said. "It just seems to be one coup after another in Nigeria, so you don't really know where you stand. I wouldn't fancy it myself, to be honest."

Joker, who had been sitting quietly listening, jumped to his feet. "That's it," he decided, "I'm going to Africa!"

"Well, finish your beer first," said Tone.

"I'm serious."

"Well, if you're going," Gary exclaimed, standing up to add emphasis, "then so am I."

"What about Rosie?"

"I won't tell her."

"Good man!"

"You two wankers will only get into trouble in Africa," said Seamus, also standing up, "so I'll have to go, too."

Bobby stood up. "*I'm* Spartacus!" he said.

"What the hell," Tone declared. "Count me in, too."

Sean and Jamesy, who both understood that it was all just drunken bluster, stood and raised their bottles in solidarity. Everyone turned to Kevin.

"Well, Kevin?" asked Sean. "It wouldn't be the same without you."

"No," said Gary with a grin, "it would be much better."

Kevin felt moved by the realisation that he was being fully accepted into the group, and the fact that it was happening without him having to pretend to be someone else made it all the more emotional. He stood and raised his beer.

"To Africa!" he said, and everyone answered.

"To Africa!"

But first, they had a date with some cows.

FORTY FOUR

Calling it a bullring, thought Sean as he and Bobby made their way through the crowds, was a bit of a stretch.

The circular arena of bare earth was surrounded by a series of vertical steel poles that were placed just far enough apart to allow one person to squeeze through. Behind this barrier, and circling the round space in the centre, was an area where the public could stand and where several little bars, spaced at regular intervals, were selling cold beer and strong local spirits.

Above this area, and running around the entire ring, several rows of tiered seating had been constructed, and it was to these seats that Sean and Bobby were heading. They were the last to arrive and had been dropped off close to Benifairó by a bad-tempered old Spanish man.

"How come we have such shit luck with lifts?" asked Bobby. "Your man looked like he wanted to kill the two of us."

"Yeah, makes you wonder why he even bothered to pick us up."

"It just seems to be the natural thing to do around here. Sort of expected, like."

"Well, maybe on the way back we can stay close to Jamesy and get a lift with him."

"That's an idea. Jesus! This is all a bit ramshackle, isn't it?" Bobby and Sean would soon be graduating as civil engineers and their sensibilities were somewhat offended by the rough and ready construction of the 'bullring'.

"It's seen better days," Sean agreed, "but it seems functional enough."

They purchased some beer from one of the bars and climbed the steps to the rows of seats. It was busy upstairs, and it took them a while to pinpoint Tone and the others.

"There they are," said Bobby, "right round the other bloody side."

They made their way around to join the group.

"You made it, then?" exclaimed Tone. "Class wee place, isn't it?"

"Seems like it," said Sean as they both sat down. "Really good atmosphere. All the bars were packed when we came through the town, loads of music too. So, what's going on here, then?"

"There's a bit of a lull at the minute," Tone told him, "but every now and then they seem to let some cow into the ring, evil-looking bastard it is, too, and all the young Spanish lads try to slap it on the arse. They've got a wee three-wheeled van as well, and they drive that around the ring with a couple of lads standing in the back. It's all a mad bit of craic."

"A wee van?"

"Aye, Kevin reckons it's normally used to get around the citrus groves or the olive groves or whatever, but tonight they're using it to irritate a cow."

Suddenly the crowds that were milling around the centre of the arena rushed off to the perimeter and ducked behind the barrier of steel poles.

"Oh, here we go," said Tone. "Looks like they're starting up again."

The ring below was momentarily deserted, and then a lean, jet-black beast strutted into the centre and shook its head angrily from side to side. It snorted as it pawed at the ground, and then it stood still and raised its head, displaying a particularly vicious set of horns. A young man rushed into the ring, but the beast turned quickly to meet him and he had to veer away and scramble, just in time, through one of the gaps between the poles. The crowd jeered.

Several more attempts were made to touch the back of the cow, but she seemed fresh and fast, and only a few intrepid souls were successful. After a while Tone nudged Sean.

"Here's that wee van I was telling you about," he said.

Sean looked down to see a tiny Citroën van appear below him. It had an open back that was crowded with just five or six revellers, standing and waving and drinking beer. Suddenly, Gary jumped to his feet.

"What the fuck does that dickhead think he's doing?" he demanded.

Joker was celebrating. He had come to a decision. He was going to Africa. He was going to go and snatch the lovely Carol from the perils of the dark continent, and then … well, he hadn't got that far yet, but his brain seemed happy enough with the plan as it stood, and that was what mattered.

He had just acquired a bottle of beer from the bar and had then got caught up in the joyous atmosphere of the excited crowd. He had felt a sudden, warm affinity with these mad, drunken bastards and had not taken much persuading to join them on their quest to vanquish the beast in its lair.

He stood, exhilarated, in the back of the little van alongside his Spanish comrades as they trundled towards the centre of the ring. The crowd applauded their noble endeavours and Joker raised his bottle in salute. The cow eyed the strange vehicle cautiously as it trotted around the edge of the ring and then, shockingly, it burst into a sudden charge at the intruder.

The van driver swerved in panic and just managed to avoid a collision as the cow roared past. The van carried on, careering wildly, and Joker, clutching his beer, rather than the side rail of the van, was thrown clear. He landed on his side and rolled along the sand before jumping to his feet. He was laughing as he noted with satisfaction that he had spilled none of his drink. He spotted his friends in the seating area upstairs and, smiling, walked towards them.

He could see they were all waving and chanting his name, and he acknowledged their appreciation by raising his beer. As he got closer, however, it began to dawn on him that they were not so much waving, as gesticulating wildly. And they were not so much chanting his name, as yelling, "Run, you dopey wanker!"

FORTY FIVE

Any misgivings that Martin may have had about accompanying Rosie faded away when he saw the baby moving around on the ultrasound monitor.

Despite his doubts, Rosie had insisted he come with her for her six-month scan and, as he was beginning to understand, his daughter could be very persuasive.

"But shouldn't it be Gary who goes with you?" he had argued.

"Yes, it should," she had retorted, "but he's not bloody here, is he? So come on, don't you want to see your grandchild?"

"Yes, Daddy," said Ellie, relishing the word on her lips, "and we can all head into town afterwards and make a day of it." Ellie's reinvigoration, Rosie thought, had been astonishing. She no longer walked with her shoulders slumped, and her eyes, once dulled and defeated, now shone with a happy resolution. Rosie felt cheered by the transformation in her sister, and she had to acknowledge that she herself could sense that a cloud had lifted. Her overall mood was lighter somehow. Less intense. It was a confusing sensation but not, she had to admit, unwelcome.

"Yes, all right," said Martin, "but I just want to use your phone before we go."

"Oooh," the girls teased. "Phoning your girlfriend, are you?"

Martin reddened but smiled. "Don't be silly," he said. "I told you she's married. I just want to let her know that I'm going to see my grandchild. Why aren't you in the phone book, by the way? I had a look, but I couldn't see you."

"I only had the phone put in a couple of months ago," Ellie explained. "So it won't be in until the new book comes out."

Rosie's friend and Gary's sister, Karen, had driven them across town to the new tower block at the City Hospital, and then let them go off to the appointment.

"I'll just meet you back at the wee cafeteria," she told them, before giving Martin a playful slap on the arm. "I still can't believe Rosie and Ellie have got their daddy back," she said.

"Can't believe it myself," said Martin.

In the treatment room, they stared at the grey, fuzzy blob on the screen, and Martin had to fight back a tear when he felt his little girl squeeze his hand.

"Would you like to know if it's a boy or a girl?" asked the nurse.

"No," said Rosie. "I'm happy to wait. And I really don't mind either way."

They all walked back to the cafeteria and as they approached, Rosie could see Karen standing by a corridor on the far side of the open area.

She was talking to a young doctor that Rosie felt she recognised. Karen spotted them appear on the other side of the room and broke off her conversation to come and join them. The young doctor disappeared down the corridor.

"Who was that you were talking to?" Rosie asked when Karen came over.

"What? Oh, that was Dr Maher," said Karen. "She used to go out with that stupid cunt, Joseph."

FORTY SIX

A person traditionally has fewer legs than a cow, but this was not Joker's only disadvantage. His reflexes were rendered sluggish by alcohol, and he was also slowed by having to set off from a standing start, so he should have been much less surprised than he was when the cow's horn punctured his right buttock and hoisted him into the air to balance precariously like some grotesque cow ornament.

He bounced and flailed with shock and pain as the triumphant cow thundered across the arena with her trophy held high until, feeling that her point had been made, she came to an abrupt halt in front of the steel barrier that circled the ring. Joker's momentum carried him onward towards the row of uprights, where he managed to miss every single one of the gaps between the poles.

His forehead struck one of the uprights with a loud, vibrating *bong* and he rebounded back into the arena to land heavily on his back. Joker's nemesis, her blood fired up from her recent victory, sensed an easy kill and spun around with her head lowered to make the final charge. The people in the crowd closest to the action rushed forward to grab Joker's helpless, writhing form and were able to pull him back behind the barrier just as the cow raced past in snorting fury.

Joker, lying on his back surrounded by anxious Spanish faces, saw Tone appear, then Sean and Gary and everyone else. He noted with some surprise that he still held the bottle of beer in his right hand, and he smiled as he looked up at his friends.

"Didn't spill any," he said, as the world turned blissfully black.

Joker spent the night in the emergency room at the Tavernes paramedic station where bovine related injuries were apparently not uncommon. His wounds were cleansed and treated, and he was pumped so full of painkillers that, when Tone and Kevin picked him up in a taxi the next morning, he was smiling.

"So, what's the plan for today?" he slurred happily.

"Remember," said Tone, "we're catching the train tonight, so you need to get some sleep back at the beach-house while we all pack."

"Are we going to Africa now?"

"Not yet, Joker, no. We have to go home first."

"That's good," said Joker. "Home is good."

"How's your arse?"

"Are you flirting with me?"

"Never mind."

Back at the beach-house, they carefully put Joker to bed, where he soon nodded off, and then everyone assembled around the dining table. The atmosphere was subdued.

"Hopefully he'll sleep for a couple of hours before we have to shoot off," said Tone.

"What was the verdict?" asked Gary.

"Well, the medics seemed more concerned about his head injury than what the cow did to his arsehole, but it's not fractured, at least, and I think they were happy enough with it. He'll need to get it looked at when we get home, though."

"Stupid bastard," Sean muttered.

"Yeah, well," said Tone, "we need to get this place tidied up before we leave, and we still need to pack, so we can get all that done while he's out of the way."

A little while later, Joker appeared at the bottom of the stairs, looking confused.

"You're alive, then?" Seamus shouted over to him.

"Is that what it's called?"

"How do you feel?" asked Bobby.

"Sore."

"Are you not sitting down?"

"I don't think I will, actually, thanks all the same."

"Oh, you're up," said Tone, as he walked past holding a broom, heading for the veranda. "Don't forget, you need to pack at some point."

"Yeah, I know."

Jamesy was in the kitchen area. "Do you want a cup of tea, Joker?" he asked.

"Love one, Jamesy. Thanks." Jamesy filled the kettle while Joker stood by the stairs as if lost in thought.

"Actually," said Joker, "I could go and get my packing done while you're making the tea. It won't take me long."

"Yeah, no problem. I'll just have it here for you."

Joker turned and went back upstairs while Jamesy carried on making the tea. Kevin, quietly observing, felt moved by the unspoken concern the group of friends had for Joker's wounds. Despite the laddish banter, he thought, and the barbed comments and insults, it was obvious they were all gently grieving for their stricken comrade.

"Where's Ermintrude's hat?" asked Tone, returning from the veranda.

"He went back upstairs to pack," Jamesy told him. Tone set down the broom and climbed the stairs. A few moments later, the subsequent exchange, though muted, could still be heard downstairs.

"Hey, Joker!"

"What?"

"Mooooo!"

Kevin sighed and went back to tidying up.

FORTY SEVEN

Gemma walked into the living room and placed her bags of shopping on the floor. Wee Paulie was lying on the sofa watching the football results on the television. Gemma gave him a quick kiss.

"How's the birthday boy?" she asked.

"Okay," he told her. "How was work?"

"Oh, the usual," Gemma said as she carried some of the shopping through to the kitchen. "I got you a couple of presents in the town."

"Thanks," Wee Paulie called after her. He sat up on the sofa and tried not to look at the remaining bags of shopping that Gemma had left on the floor. "But remember," he said when Gemma came back to sit beside him, "we can't really celebrate tonight because I need to be up early in the morning. Big day tomorrow."

"No problem. What do you fancy doing tonight, then?"

"Just an early night," he suggested, "but then we can have a proper celebration tomorrow night."

"Sounds good," said Gemma, "I booked Monday off, so we can even go out somewhere if we want."

"Yeah, we could," said Wee Paulie, his gaze wandering over to the mysterious bags on the floor. "You know," he said, looking back at Gemma, "tomorrow could turn out to be a bit of a double celebration."

"Why?"

"It could be a big step up in my career," he declared. "All going well, that is."

"Is that right?"

"Yeah. Mr Jippsen-Phillips thinks I've got a lot of potential. There's a big shake-up coming, and he said I can expect big things to come my way."

"That probably just means you'll have heavier stuff to carry," said Gemma, but then regretted it when she saw the crestfallen look on his face. She squeezed his leg. "I'm only messing you," she told him. "Look, I got some lasagne for dinner, and there's some wine there as well. We can have a glass of wine with our dinner, can't we?"

Wee Paulie brightened up. "I don't see why not," he said.

"Right then, I'll stick the dinner on and then we'll sit down and you can tell me all about it."

"Okay, but I won't be able to tell you too much, you know. It's all a bit top secret."

"Oooh, sounds important," said Gemma as she got up and headed into the kitchen.

"Well, it's just about knowing what your options are," said Wee Paulie. "About being in the right place at the right time."

"This is going to take about forty minutes," Gemma informed him.

"Why don't you open the wine?"

Wee Paulie got up and joined Gemma in the kitchen. He grabbed a bottle opener from the drawer and picked up the bottle of Shiraz. "You know," he began as he twisted the corkscrew into the top of the bottle, "it is my birthday today, so I don't see why I can't open at least one of my presents."

Gemma laughed. "Well, we'll see," she told him, "but it'll have to wait till after dinner. Now pour me a glass of that wine."

After dinner, they sat together on the sofa and Gemma teased him that they should wait until the proper celebration tomorrow night before any presents could be handed out. Wee Paulie began to whine so much that she relented, laughing. She reached down beside the sofa and began to feel around in one of the bags until she found what she was looking for.

"Happy Birthday!" she said as she handed Wee Paulie a small package.

"Thanks, love," he said, pulling away the wrapping to reveal a pair of boxer shorts.

"Boxers!" he exclaimed. "Very sexy."

"I know he's your favourite."

Wee Paulie gave the boxers a closer inspection. "Daffy Duck boxers!" he cried happily. "They're class, love. Cheers!"

"You're welcome."

"Yeah," he said, "Daffy Duck was the best of all the Looney Tunes characters."

Gemma had heard all this before, but she nodded and smiled, then settled back in the sofa to sip her wine.

"Not like that smug bastard, Bugs Bunny," Wee Paulie continued. "Daffy was more for the man in the street, you know. He had to put up with all sorts of shit, too. And remember, all those old Warner Brothers' cartoons were never meant to be for kids. They were made to be shown in cinemas with the main film. For grown-ups, like." He was warming to one of his favourite themes, so Gemma thought she should intervene.

"Why don't you try them on?" she suggested.

"Try them on?" Wee Paulie repeated, holding up his new underwear shorts. They were made of a white, sheer material covered with little pictures of Daffy Duck in a series of action poses. "Aye, why not?" he decided. He stood up and started to unbuckle his jeans. "Do you know what my favourite Daffy quote is?" he asked.

Gemma knew exactly what his favourite quote was, but she shook her head and smiled indulgently.

"*With me, it's not the principle that counts; it's the money*," Wee Paulie grinned. "Fucking genius!"

"Yeah," said Gemma, "very good."

"Well, what do you think?" Wee Paulie stood, modelling his new boxers, in front of Gemma. He had taken off his top to let her have the full effect. "Sexy, or what?"

"Aye, dead sexy," Gemma laughed. She picked up the wine bottle and stared at it. "Jesus!" she exclaimed. "That went down well!"

Wee Paulie stopped striking sexy poses and looked, perplexed, at the empty bottle. The wine had just got him warmed up, but he was only too aware of the importance of having all his wits about him in the morning. He decided to be sensible.

"Right," he said firmly, "there's a ten-glass bottle of vodka in the kitchen, but we can only have one drink each out of it, okay? And then we need to have an early night."

"I got another bottle of vodka in town today," Gemma told him, "so that can do for tomorrow night." She set off to find the vodka while Wee Paulie went to admire himself in the full-length mirror in the hall.

FORTY EIGHT

Fergal surveyed his troops with some dismay. He felt that things had slipped beyond his control but – he was reluctant to admit – he only had himself to blame.

It had only been a suggestion, he was sure, rather than a direct command that had come down from the Army Council a few weeks ago, but Fergal was shrewd enough to know that such distinctions were negligible.

The Irish Republican Army had decided to create a short promotional video to showcase some of their latest acquisitions, and Fergal had been offered the chance to volunteer for the job. He had accepted readily enough, considering it a simple enough task, but now he was having some doubts. Not about his ability to do the job, but because he knew that he had left it all too late.

He had believed the project to be of such low priority that he had put it to the back of his mind while he attended to matters that he felt were more pressing. In truth, he had largely forgotten about the whole thing until yesterday when he had been informed that a video cassette was expected to be delivered by 3.00pm on Monday, without fail, to the offices of RTÉ in Dublin.

Today was Sunday.

The words 'without fail' were at the forefront of Fergal's thoughts as he inspected his men. It wasn't much of an active service unit, he thought. He had received some bad news earlier that morning which meant that half his squad was missing but, even so, he felt particularly uninspired by the two men standing in front of him.

Morris 'The Cat' Donnelly and Gerry Cleary were decent enough men, Fergal knew, but he had always had his doubts about their unwavering commitment to the cause. Fergal himself was entirely focused on the goals of the IRA – Irish reunification following a British withdrawal from the north-eastern corner of the country – and he expected similar dedication from all of the volunteers in the organisation.

Morris, he felt, was a little too soft-headed to be a truly hardened guerrilla fighter, and his penchant for having frequent daytime naps did little to conjure up the image of the tireless and vigilant soldier of the revolution that Fergal liked to nourish.

Gerry, on the other hand, was sharp and clever, but Fergal reckoned that the armed struggle against British oppression did not feature quite high enough amongst his list of priorities.

Gerry Cleary made his living from producing video tapes of people's special occasions – weddings, birthdays, etc. – and his skill and his natural instinct for film-making gave his work a quality that was in high demand. He enjoyed his work so much that he harboured dreams of becoming a true professional and had made tentative enquiries at the BBC offices in Belfast. This had earned him a reprimand from Fergal and a stern lecture on the true spirit of resistance to British intransigence and brutality in Ireland. Gerry had replied that it was important to keep one's options open.

Fergal shook his head and turned away to pace around the courtyard of the farmhouse where they had met up earlier that morning. Gerry and Morris had arrived together in Gerry's car, which was now parked up against the gable wall of the house.

"We'll need to get that car into the barn," said Fergal. "All the equipment is in the Land Cruiser, so we'll be taking that."

"Righty-ho," chirped Gerry. "I'll just get my gear out first." He was happy at the thought of a day's filming and he had brought along some new filters that he was keen to try out. He was already composing the shots in his head; a heavy brooding sky with the stark silhouette of an assault rifle held aloft in defiance, a lone volunteer, wearied by the struggle, a wistful breeze gently stroking a desolate hilltop, a … "Wait a minute," he said suddenly, looking around him. "I thought Tommy and Rab were meant to be here."

"They're not coming," said Fergal testily. "It's just the three of us."

"Not coming? Why the fuck not?"

"Because they …" Fergal rubbed the back of his neck as he turned away from Gerry. "They phoned in sick," he said.

"They fucking *what*?" cried Gerry. "Phoned in sick? In other words, they were out on the tear up in Drogheda all night and they're still fucking blootered, that's what you mean, isn't it?"

"Look, it doesn't matter," Fergal insisted. "Like I said, it's just the three of us, so just hurry the fuck up."

Morris, who up until that point had been reminiscing about the particularly fine sausages he had had for breakfast that morning, spoke up. "Weren't they meant to be keeping dick, though?"

Fergal spun around to face Morris. "I fucking told you before," he snapped, "it is not *keeping dick*, it is providing surveillance and assistance to volunteers operating in the field."

"Yeah, okay, but they were still meant to be keeping –"

"Aye, that's right, Mo," said Gerry. "So, it's just going to be the three of us wandering around like a bunch of dickheads, not knowing what the fuck we –"

"Oh, for fuck's sake!" cried Fergal. "It won't be a problem, okay? Who the fuck is going to be out at this time on a Sunday? We'll just shoot on up to that wee spot by the bridge, get the filming done, and we'll be back here in no time."

"You know, you can't rush these things." Gerry was about to protest about the need for artistic integrity, but a savage glance from Fergal forced him to reconsider. "Right, I'll just get my gear," he said, "and we'll head on."

As Gerry went to retrieve his equipment, Morris opened the back of the Land Cruiser and pulled an assault rifle from under a tarpaulin.

"I'll hold onto this," he said. "Just in case, like."

Fergal nodded impatiently. "Fine, fine, just get a move on."

Gerry approached with his camera bag and placed it carefully on the back seat. Morris climbed in beside the bag while Gerry got into the front passenger seat. Fergal jumped up into the driver's seat.

"Right!" Gerry said happily. "Here we go, then. The media wing of the IRA. The Irish Republican Broadcast–"

"Don't say it!" Fergal growled. He turned to stare at Gerry as he turned the ignition key. "Just don't fucking say it!"

Gerry grinned and gave Fergal a wink as the Land Cruiser lumbered out of the courtyard and into the quiet country lanes.

The Irish Republican Broadcasting Corporation was off to make an outside broadcast.

FORTY NINE

Wee Paulie gripped the edge of the sink in the kitchen. He was half-hoping that the next wave of nausea would result in a burst of vomiting that might herald the beginning of his recovery. The thought that maybe he should force the issue by sticking a finger down his throat briefly occurred to him, but he didn't feel up to it. An empty vodka bottle mocked him from the kitchen worktop as the room revolved around his quivering form. He put his face to the water tap and let the cold water trickle over his lips and into his mouth. It felt good, but the respite was temporary, serving only to increase his sense of disorientation.

The doorbell rang and Wee Paulie squeezed his eyes closed in desperation. The doorbell rang more insistently, and he forced himself to stagger to the intercom, accompanied by the sound of Gemma's snores coming from the bedroom.

"Come on to fuck!" Big Dennis' voice over the intercom helped Wee Paulie to sharpen his focus. Today was the big day. Today was the day when he needed to have his wits about him. He looked stupidly around the floor by his feet, as if searching for his scattered wits, before replying into the intercom.

"Hold on," he said, "I'm on my way down."

"Don't know why we have to use *my* fucking car," Big Dennis grumbled as Wee Paulie strapped himself into the front seat of the silver Ford Sierra. "You know what the bloody roads are like down south, don't you?" he continued. He started up and set off towards the Lisburn Road. "Might as well take a fucking hammer to the suspension. This car's not even a year old, you know. There's not even five thousand miles on the clock, and here's me taking it into the fucking wilderness."

"Mmm," Wee Paulie was trying to control the shivering and the queasiness that gripped his insides while he attempted to keep up the conversation. "Hopefully it won't take too long."

"Nah," Big Dennis agreed, "it won't take long at all. Here, are you okay? You look like shit."

"Yeah, I'm dead on," Wee Paulie assured him. "It's just a bit early in the morning, that's all."

"Aye, for fuck's sake. Still, at least there's no traffic about at this time. We've got the roads to ourselves."

Wee Paulie let Big Dennis ramble on while he concentrated on not throwing up. He felt quite sure that Big Dennis would not appreciate the inside of his new car being covered in foul-smelling sick. Eventually they pulled up at Mr Jippsen-Phillips' apartment. He was already waiting outside.

"Good morning boys," he said cheerfully. He climbed into the back seat and buckled his seatbelt. "How are you both today? Good God, Paulie, you look terrible, are you feeling okay?"

"Oh yeah, no problem, I'm dead on." Wee Paulie forced a smile. "Thanks for asking, though."

"Right then," said Simon uncertainly. "So, you're both still up for this, I take it?"

"Yes, yes," Wee Paulie assured him. "Absolutely!" Big Dennis nodded.

"Very well, then. Let's go pick up the Boss Man!"

Michael stepped out through the front door when he saw the car approach and then walked down the drive to the gate. He looked tired, thought Simon. Deflated almost. He got into the back seat beside Simon and nodded to Big Dennis and Wee Paulie.

"Right, lads," he said.

"You carrying?" Simon asked him.

Michael shook his head. "If it's all the same to you lads, I'm happy to just stay in the car and watch. I'm not feeling up to it today."

Big Dennis caught Simon's eye in his rear view mirror, but Simon looked away, turning back to Michael.

"Of course," he said cheerfully. "It's fine by me. But it's going to take a while to get there and you might have perked up by then. We'll see how it goes."

"Yes, fine," said Michael. "Whatever."

Big Dennis pulled out onto the empty main road and headed south.

FIFTY

It hadn't been a pleasant flight for Joker. The plan had been for everyone to get some sleep on the overnight train up from Valencia, but Joker, with his injuries, had found it impossible to be both pain-free and comfortable for more than a few moments at a time and so had slept little by the time he boarded the plane.

"Did you get any sleep at all," Jamesy asked him as they went through the arrivals hall at Dublin Airport.

"I think I might have dozed off for a couple of minutes here and there," Joker replied, "but nothing to write home about."

"Well, it won't be long now till you can crash out in your own bed."

"Can't wait."

Harry was already waiting when they cleared customs, so they went straight out to the car park.

"Here, Harry," said Gary. "I was talking to Rosie on the phone the other night and she said she had a big surprise waiting for me. I was just wondering if I should be worried or not. Do you know anything about it?"

"I've been told not to say anything," said Harry as he helped to load the luggage into the van.

"Right …" Gary prompted, then waited expectantly. Harry gave him a look and Gary realised the matter was now closed.

Shit! he thought.

"Maybe she's found out the baby isn't hers," Bobby suggested.

"Yeah, very funny, Bobby," said Gary, "but I could be in the soup here."

"Why, what have you been up to?"

"Well, that's the thing," Gary moaned, "it could be anything."

If Harry thought it was odd that Joker was limping and had a bandage around the top of his head, he didn't say, but when Joker struggled to sit down while trying to keep his right leg straight, he decided to make a comment.

"You all right there, Joseph?"

"Yeah, Harry, I'm great, thanks."

"You sure? Do you not want to sit in the front?"

"Nah, the back is better," said Joker, "in case I have to stand up."

"Why? What's wrong?"

"Let's just say," Tone interjected, "that Joker's coming back with more holes than he went away with."

"What?"

"It's a long story, Harry. We'll tell you all about it over a couple of pints. It's worth hearing."

At this point, Harry seemed to lose interest. He climbed into the driver's seat and, once everyone had settled, they headed for home.

FIFTY ONE

The old wooden fence had long been left to rot, and just a few uprights with some warped horizontal bars in between could still be seen. It ran alongside a track that led to an ancient stone bridge. On the far side of the bridge, a forest lay brooding and still in the lush morning light.

The ground behind the fence rose steeply to form a ridge that looked across the track to another, less steep, rise in the terrain, giving the impression of the road threading along the floor of a small valley as it made its way to the bridge and the woodland beyond.

On one of the decrepit old bars that ran between the fenceposts sat a pair of blackbirds. The male blackbird was nuzzling the female – his mate of many years – in an attempt to arouse a little friskiness within her. Mrs Blackbird was by no means averse to some spontaneous canoodling, but she felt it was only right for her partner to make a bit more of an effort.

She was not the type of bird to just give it away – not like those sluts, the sparrows – so she was acting aloof as she worked out a strategy, wondering if maybe she could persuade him to stand on one leg and puff out his chest like she'd seen the male pigeons do.

Not that she would be impressed by such behaviour, she thought, but it would give her a laugh, at least. She was about to make her proposal when a sudden noise drew her attention. She turned to see a silver car appear slowly along the track and pull up in the little clearing across from the fence. She frowned with disapproval at this unwelcome interruption to the peace of the morning. She frowned even more when all four doors opened.

"I still don't see what we're doing here," Michael grumbled as he got out and walked a little way towards the bridge. "We're nowhere near the main road."

"Yes, I know," Simon explained, "but we're still early and we would look a tad conspicuous if we just sat waiting by the roadside. Besides, this gives us a chance to stretch our legs a bit, don't you think?"

Michael stopped and gazed ahead at the distant woods. He would be happy to get this whole business over and done with, he thought. He had other, more important, matters that had been keeping him distracted just lately, and there were some things on his mind that he …

"Oh, and Michael?" Simon went on. "Consider this a hostile takeover."

"What?" Michael turned to see Big Dennis and Wee Paulie both produce handguns and raise them towards his head. At that moment, the Irish Republican Broadcasting Corporation appeared on top of the ridge just behind and to Michael's left.

Wee Paulie had walked around the car to stand beside Big Dennis. His head was spinning as he stood quivering and nauseous when, all of a sudden, he caught sight of the unmistakeable outline of a Kalashnikov assault rifle. Panicking, he squeezed the trigger of his 9mm several times, making himself jump at the sudden noise.

On the ridge, Morris reacted instinctively and, swinging the AK onto his hip, fired a short burst towards the enemy before ducking behind the skyline. His bullets all sailed harmlessly into the scenery, apart from one, which took a brief but eventful detour through Big Dennis.

"Hold your fire!" Simon yelled. "Hold your fucking fire!"

The clipped south of England accent carried across the valley and convinced Fergal that the British forces had finally caught up with him. He crouched alongside Gerry and Morris below the ridge, hidden from the roadway, while his mind raced.

"Fucking SAS bastards!" he cried. "Fucking sneaky bastards!"

"SAS?" asked Gerry.

"Who the fuck else would it be?" Fergal demanded. "Bastards have been after me for years."

Gerry considered this for a second and decided it was highly unlikely that the Brits would send a crack unit into the Irish Republic, just to take out Fergal. *Fergal,* for fuck's sake! He was about to share this opinion with the others when Morris spoke.

"I think I got one of the bastards!"

"Good man!" said Fergal. "Good man yourself! Don't worry, lads," he went on, "I'll get us out of this."

Gerry thought that this was only fair, considering it was Fergal who had got them into it in the first place, but he couldn't say that he had any great confidence in Fergal's abilities in a crisis. Then again, he thought, he had never witnessed Fergal reacting to any real pressure before and there was always the possibility that Fergal would surprise him.

"I'll tell you one thing, lads," Fergal shouted maniacally, "they won't fucking take us alive!"

"*Us?*" Gerry yelled in alarm. "What the fuck do you mean *us*? I'm more than happy to be taken a–"

A fresh volley of shots from the valley floor caused them all to duck instinctively.

"Jesus Christ!" shouted Gerry.

"Fuck this!" cried Fergal, and he reached for the suspiciously long canvas holdall that Morris had been carrying, and which was now lying at their feet. "Death or glory, lads," Fergal yelled. "Death or glory!"

When the first shots had been fired, Michael, believing he had just been executed, had dropped to the ground and had adopted what he felt was the correct position for the recently murdered. It soon became apparent, however, that he was unharmed and so, confused but relieved, he jumped to his feet and took off in the direction of the old bridge, hoping to find refuge in the woods on the far side.

Simon, panicked by the automatic gunfire, had run back behind the car, glancing briefly at the bulk of Big Dennis, crumpled in the roadway, and had clambered over the high ground on that side of the road. As he settled into the cover provided by the shape of the land, he struggled to make sense of what was happening.

It was unlikely, he decided, that some local farmers would be out hunting rabbits with an AK-47, so the chances were that they had inadvertently stumbled upon an IRA unit out on manoeuvres, or whatever the hell an IRA unit did on a Sunday morning. He was just about to curse his own rotten luck when he remembered why he was there. He slowly raised his head above the natural parapet and was horrified to see Michael making his escape.

Simon had been planning this for weeks, and all of his machinations, all of his plots and dealings and schemes, and all the little details of his complex manoeuvrings were entirely dependent on one simple fact: Michael McClelland needed to be dead.

He fumbled in his pocket for the pistol he hadn't planned on using and, taking aim at the fleeing figure, he emptied the clip just as Michael disappeared below the bank of the stream that flowed under the bridge. Simon swore helplessly and then turned to see Wee Paulie twist one way and then another as he vacillated in the road, paralysed by panic and sheer terror. He seemed to be especially confused by the car which barred his way to the relative safety of the hill where Simon lay.

Simon thought he could hear someone shout *Death or glory* as he waved to Wee Paulie and gestured for him to go around the car. "Around the side!" he shouted. "Go around the side!"

"Bastards are trying to outflank us!" Fergal shouted through a wild and crazy grin. He hadn't expected it to be like this, he thought. He hadn't expected the adrenalin surge, the feeling of exhilaration, the undeniable joy of battle.

Through Fergal's veins coursed the blood of an ancient warrior race and, in his head, he could hear the old rebel songs. Songs of resistance and defiance. Songs of freedom. He pulled from the canvas holdall something that Gerry initially mistook for a large rifle, but the bulbous, diamond shape on the end betrayed it to be a shiny, new, Soviet-made rocket propelled grenade – designed, primarily, for punching through armour plate.

"What the fuck?" Gerry was becoming increasingly concerned about the way the morning was panning out. "What the fuck do you think you're going to do with that?" he yelled.

"Cover me, lads!" cried Fergal with a mad gleam in his eye. They would remember this day, he was certain. Poems would be written, and tales would be told of his actions on this day. A great ballad, no doubt, would be composed. *The Battle of the Old Stone Bridge* would be sung, Fergal was sure, for as long as men remembered heroes. He hoisted the

RPG onto his shoulder.

"*Tiocfaidh ár lá!*" shouted Morris as he sent another burst from his AK down onto the road.

"Don't *you* fucking start!" Gerry cried. "I'm going to tell Molly on you!"

Fergal rose above the ridgeline and, making some slight adjustments, sent the armour-piercing warhead straight at the unarmoured and completely defenceless Ford Sierra. The grenade entered the car with ease and then proceeded to spray the interior with molten metal, causing a significant reaction when it reached the petrol tank.

Mrs Blackbird, flapping around the sky in fury at all the commotion, was considering a particularly loud chirp of outrage when the sudden and unexpected appearance of a gearstick from a 1989 Ford Sierra caused to her to veer away and to swoop back down towards the ground.

Wee Paulie's anal sphincter had had enough. It had been having a fairly torrid time of it already today – trying to keep a lid on things, so to speak – but the latest explosion had convinced it to take the unilateral course of jettisoning all extraneous material in preparation for imminent flight.

Wee Paulie, his eyebrows and fringe now smouldering and crispy, was in two minds about this latest turn of events. On the one hand, the noxious swill that had lately been infesting his lower intestines had now gone. But on the other hand, as Daffy Duck could testify, it hadn't gone far. He stood beside the corpse of Big Dennis as the quickly cooling effluent trickled down the backs of his legs and, as the car settled down into a cosy blaze, he reflected upon the fact that, as far as life decisions went, he may have recently made some poor ones.

Michael was feeling exuberant. He pounded across the meadow towards the tree line, now well out of the bullet range of that treacherous bastard, Jippo, and his goons. Surviving the attempt on his life had made him feel more alive than ever, and he made a vow that he would do right by his boy. He would do whatever it took to divest himself of all criminal ties, and he would do all that he could to make Peter feel proud. He felt good. He felt better than good. With his legs pumping away beneath him, he felt free. He felt more free than he had done in years, and it was glorious.

As soon as he reached the woods, he tripped on a tree root and smashed his face into the trunk of a stately old elm.

In Fergal's mind, it was a tactical withdrawal of the highest order. It was a textbook retreat in the face of overwhelming enemy odds. Covering all directions with a variety of weapons, they backed steadily across the field towards the Land Cruiser with a calm and ordered discipline that gave Fergal a feeling of intense pride in his men.

They made it to the car in good time and, with everyone on board, Fergal gunned the engine and set off, exulting in the fact that the imperial might of Britain had been thwarted by the plucky little rebel force of the Irish Republican Broadcasting Corporation.

FIFTY TWO

"That's all well and good," said Gary, "but what if I need to leave the country sooner, rather than later? I think you're being a wee bit selfish there, Joker, with all this *hospital treatment* business. You should try thinking of others for a change."

"Jesus, Gary," Seamus said, exasperated, "you don't know for sure that it's something bad. How did she actually sound on the phone?"

"Hard to say, really," Gary answered thoughtfully. "Bit weird, to be honest."

"In what way?"

"I don't know. It was like … it was like she was *happy*."

"Happy? Rosie sounded happy? Really?"

"Yeah."

"Shit," said Seamus, "maybe you *are* fucked!"

"Hey, Joseph," Harry called out, as he peered at the road ahead. "Isn't that your man there?"

"Who?" Joker asked as he pulled himself up to stand between the two front seats. He stared through the windscreen for a moment and then nodded. "Yeah, it is," he said. "Yeah, it's Sticky Mickey."

Michael had managed to stumble, dazed and bleeding, into the woods for a little way before realising he would have to double back if he wanted to reach the main road. He knew he would have to be cautious as it was likely that Jippo would still be out to get him.

He had watched, bewildered, as the car had exploded, and he had a vague notion of seeing Big Dennis lying on the ground, so he reckoned that Jippo would be on foot with just Wee Paulie for support. The odds were still in Jippo's favour, he knew, but they were better now than they had been earlier.

He still couldn't figure out what had happened. What should have been a treacherous but perfectly straightforward assassination had gone completely haywire. Jippo had obviously planned it all down to the last detail – Michael could only admire how cleverly he had been manipulated – but then at the very last minute it had all gone chaotically wrong. At least it had for Jippo.

For Michael, it had given him a new lease of life. Despite the fact that he had probably just fractured his skull, he was thinking more clearly now than he had done in years. He now knew what he wanted to do, what he wanted to have. He wanted the tedium of normality. He wanted the security, the banal routine, the family life. He wanted legitimacy, transparency and acceptance. He wanted the parents' evenings, the camping trips, the chilly Saturdays standing on touchlines, and whatever it took to achieve this, he decided, he would do.

But first things first. He had to get back to Belfast. He turned left and walked for a bit through the trees and then turned left again. After a while, he came upon an open field surrounded by overgrown hedgerows. By crouching down and skulking gingerly along the hedges, he eventually emerged onto the main road. It was quiet, but then he had known that it would be at this time on a Sunday, so all he had to do was wait for someone to come along.

He knew he wasn't looking his best, but he reckoned that he was in such a state that some kind soul would see him as someone in urgent need of help, so he sat himself down by the roadside and waited.

A while later, he spotted a vehicle cresting a hill in the distance and he groaned with relief. He got to his feet, held out his hand, and tried to look as needy as possible. As the van got closer, however, he could only stare in horror.

The van pulled up beside Michael and the passenger window was wound down. A familiar face appeared from the back.

"All right there, Mickey Boy?" said Joker. "Need a lift?"

Michael shrugged. "Nah, it's okay," he said. "I'll just wait for the next one."

Joker laughed. "Wise up, you stupid fucker, and just get in the back!"

Michael understood he had little choice. The longer he waited around here, the more chance Jippo would have to catch up with him. As he dithered, the back doors of the van were flung open and he made up his mind. He climbed into the back.

"Been in the wars there, mate?" said Tone as he moved to let Michael sit down. "You can sit beside Joker there, and the two of you can compare brain damage."

Michael sheepishly took a seat.

"Nasty cut, that," Joker pointed out. "What happened?"

"Um, nothing really. I just bumped into a tree."

"Bumped into a tree? You must have been going at a fair old clip."

"Yeah, well, I sort of tripped."

"This here?" Joker pointed to his own head wound. "A cow threw me at a pole."

Michael took this to be gay slang. He deduced that Anderson and his homosexual lover – his 'cow' – had got into some sort of altercation with a Polish lad – a love triangle that had gone wrong, perhaps – and Michael decided, as they plunged northwards, that today could hardly get any more surreal.

FIFTY THREE

"Hello, Joseph. You're looking well." The voice came from behind Joker and was apparently addressing his exposed buttocks. He was lying face down on the treatment room bed and wasn't able to turn his head far enough to see the speaker. It didn't matter, though. He recognised the voice.

"Carol?"

"Been through the mill a bit, haven't you, Joseph?" said Carol, before turning to the nurse who was cleaning Joker's wound. "Hi, Jenny," she said. "How's it looking?"

"It looks a lot worse than it is," Jenny replied. "They did a good job over in Spain."

Carol leaned forward to get a better look. "Mm, there's quite a bit of tissue damage, but you're right, there's nothing too serious there."

"Well, it's bloody painful," said Joker, feeling that he ought to contribute something to a conversation that revolved entirely around the condition of his rear end.

"Oh, I'm sure it is," Carol sympathised, "but we'll get you fixed up with some painkillers. What are you taking at the minute?"

"Just paracetamol," said Joker.

"*Just* paracetamol?"

Joker's shoulders seemed to slump in resignation. "Paracetamol and whiskey," he admitted.

"Yes, well," Carol said primly, "I'm sure we can do better than that."

"Is this going to take much longer?" asked Joker. He couldn't help thinking that under different circumstances he would be flattered by two attractive women discussing the various merits of his backside which, in his opinion, was one of his best features. But this was too clinical, the scrutiny too intense, and besides, his backside, he had to admit, wasn't looking its best at the moment. He wanted it over with.

"Not long now," Jenny assured him. "Just finishing up."

Carol moved forward a little, and Joker could take a look at her by turning his head to one side. She was absorbed in his notes, frowning slightly with concentration, and Joker made a mental note to have a stern word with his memory for being so hopelessly inadequate.

He furtively devoured every tiny detail of Carol's face, while reflecting on his own stupidity for having lost her. Just what the hell was he thinking, he wondered. Just what exactly –?

"Bullfighting?" Carol asked suddenly as she looked up from the notes.

"What?"

"You were in a bullring? What were you doing in a bullring? Was alcohol involved?"

"Alcohol had nothing to do with it," Joker said defensively. "Why do you have to blame the alcohol?"

"Well, generally speaking, people don't normally run around bull-rings getting gored by bulls."

"Well, that's where you're wrong," Joker declared, triumphant in his small victory. "It wasn't a bull, it was a cow!"

During the brief silence that followed, Joker felt that maybe he should have kept his mouth shut.

"I'm sorry?" said Carol. "What was that? A cow? Did you just say you were gored by a cow?"

"That's right," said Joker, deciding to brazen it out, "it was a cow. And for your information, the cows in Spain are more dangerous than the bulls. They're faster and more agile, you know."

"What? Um, yeah." Carol looked serious as she nodded her head. "Of course," she said. "I see what you mean." She handed Joker's notes to Jenny who had started to clear away the used swabs and empty wrappings from the bedside cabinet.

"Could you just excuse me for a second?" said Carol as she slipped quickly from the room.

Joker had to admire Jenny's professionalism as she carried out her duties with a quiet and impassive efficiency, apparently oblivious to the howls of laughter coming from the corridor.

Sullen and tight-lipped, Joker lay on the bed and stared at the wall.

Carol came back into the room as Joker was getting dressed behind a curtain. When he was ready, he pulled back the curtain and stood by the bed as the nurse gave him a prescription for his medication along with some details of the outpatients' clinic.

"There you go, Mr Anderson," said Jenny cheerfully. "All done."

"Thank you," he said, then glanced sulkily at Carol. "Right, I suppose I'll see you about, then," he said as he headed for the door.

Carol laughed. "Oh, don't be like that," she said. "Come on, I'll buy you a coffee."

"Why?" he demanded. "So you can have a good laugh at me?"

"Well, yes, obviously."

"Fine, then," he conceded. They set off for the cafeteria with Joker limping slightly at Carol's side. "I thought you'd gone to live in Africa," he told her.

"What? Really? Why did you think that?"

"Just something I heard, that's all."

"No, I just went over for a couple of weeks," said Carol. "I went to see my Nana Ijemma, but I wasn't planning on staying. I think you just got the wrong end of the stick." She looked up at him and laughed. "As usual."

"Yeah, well …" he said gruffly.

"Funny, though," Carol went on, "I met this woman when I was over there, when I went to Lagos. I was staying at a hotel she was working in, and she noticed my surname. Well, it turns out she knew mummy and daddy way back, like before I was born. When I got back to Belfast, I asked daddy if he remembered a woman called Zara, and he just got really teary."

Joker looked at Carol. "Really?" he asked.

"Yeah. And then he went straight out and booked a flight to Lagos."

"Jesus!"

"I know! Mad, right?"

Joker limped on thoughtfully. He felt embarrassed and humiliated. His pride and his dignity had been shredded by the woman he … he tried not to think about it. He felt mentally drained. He was battered, bruised and weary, and his arse was killing him.

But his heart was squeezed by the music of Chiaza's giggles.

And Joker's brain was singing.

EPILOGUE

She thought of a forest. No, she decided, that wasn't enough. She thought of two forests, but still that wasn't enough. She wasn't particularly good at coming up with analogies, she realised, but she was determined to persevere, believing it to be a worthwhile exercise.

She thought of *every* forest. She pictured the vast coniferous forests of Scandinavia, the sweeping rainforests circling the equator, the majestic sequoias of North America and the dark, deciduous woodlands of central Europe and Asia.

She could see every palm grove, every orchard, every copse, every jungle, every dappled glade. She imagined the evergreen timberlands of the Arctic tundra, stretching silently from horizon to horizon, and the tree-lined avenues and manicured parklands of the world's great cities.

Oaks and elms, willows, elders, sycamores and silver birches. The exotic baobabs of Africa and the gingkoes of China. The great green blanket of life that was draped around the Earth.

And all of it, she imagined, for the sole and solitary benefit of one tiny insect, spending its entire existence on the underside of a single leaf, hanging from a lowly twig on an unremarkable shrub that pushed through the broken concrete of some desolate and long-abandoned waste ground. And suddenly God – *her* God, the tyrant of her childhood – the God of Scripture, squabbling with His creation in the dust of an ancient desert, now seemed somehow … *small.*

She exhaled slowly as she stared at the far wall.

And then, pushing her chair back from the desk, Hannah started to rise.

RACE

... told me that we did it for love, but what did I know of love back then? I was just a young girl, and Meklios and I were both slaves. I could only do what I was bidden to do ... yes, Meklios was my friend and I trusted him, but I do not feel that I had any ...

... And, of course, we believed the world was ending, so what did it matter? ... Did Eumenes know what we were planning? Did he help in some way? I cannot say ... everything was easy that night, maybe it was too easy, so perhaps Eumenes did know after all ...

... the palace was quiet that night. The city was quiet ... the night I crept from my bed to help my friend ... the night we stole the King of Kings ...

... for love.

PROLOGUE

1976, North Belfast

The city blinked in confusion at the alien sky. The unfamiliar blue was broken only by a harsh yellow eye that gazed relentlessly at the baking streets, melting the very roads and blistering any unprotected skin.

It gazed fiercely at the people of Ardoyne, the little nationalist enclave in north Belfast, as they gasped in their gardens and unconsciously turned from pasty-white to red to golden brown. It gazed at the soldiers on foot patrol, crouched and nervous and sweltering in their uniforms. It gazed down upon cats and dogs that would collapse, panting into shade, and it gazed at children shrieking in paddling pools and splashing with the energy of youth.

And it gazed upon Snatter and Ding-a-Ling. Who were in trouble.

Being in trouble was not an unusual state of affairs for Snatter and Ding-a-Ling. In fact, they were in trouble so often, their troubles would often overlap, leading to some difficulty in keeping track.

"What's this all about, then?" Snatter shouted over Ding-a-Ling's shoulder.

"I don't know," replied Ding-a-Ling. "Just keep pushing!"

They were both kneeling on a guider, with Snatter just behind Ding-a-Ling who had his hands clamped to the steering bar. They knelt with their right knees on the guider itself and their left legs pushing against the ground in an attempt to flee from the angry boys who were rushing up from a street that sloped down at a right angle from the Berwick Road.

They had been returning along the Berwick from visiting their friend, Tommy Gun, when they heard a shout on their left.

"That's them, lads! After them!" They turned to see a gang of boys abandon their game of football and run up the street towards them. Snatter and Ding-a-Ling reacted instinctively. They pushed off quickly and the guider lurched forward. Though they quickly gathered speed, they were never going to outrun the chasing pack over level ground.

"They're gaining on us!" Snatter shouted as he took a glance over his shoulder.

"It's all right," replied Ding-a-Ling, "don't worry about it."

"What do you mean?"

"It's all in hand."

"What?"

"The entry!"

"What entry?" Snatter stared past Ding-a-Ling's left ear. He could see the entry up ahead. Entries, in Ardoyne, were alleyways that separated the backyards of one street from the backyards of another. High brick walls with doors leading into the yards of the terraced houses ran down either side. "Shit! Are you mad? What the hell do –?"

"I said don't worry about it." Ding-a-Ling took the guider into a wide arc, aiming to hit the top of the entry head on. With Snatter holding on tight to the sides, the guider swerved and juddered as they veered towards the narrow opening – their pursuers rushing ever closer. Snatter closed his eyes and prayed. He could hear the approaching feet slapping the dry, dusty ground, closing in, getting ready to pounce, just as the guider creaked over the lip of the slope.

And then gravity took over.

A guider, in its simplest form, was a plank of wood with a pair of wheels attached at either end. A wider sheet of wood could then be attached to provide a more comfortable area on which to sit or to kneel. It was a concept familiar to generations of children the world over. In Ardoyne it had long been established that the best guiders would have large, rubber-tyred, pram wheels at the front and smaller wheels at the rear, which meant the guider would slope downwards from front to back.

The front wheels' axle was attached to a wooden baton which was then fixed to the guider with a single bolt to provide a simple steering system. This could then be operated by the hands, with the driver kneeling forward, or by the feet, in a sitting position.

The acquisition of a good pair of front wheels was, by far, the most important aspect of constructing a guider. The back wheels were of lesser importance as they could be improvised from a variety of sources. It was not unknown for roller-skates – stolen from sisters – to be crudely nailed to the backs of guiders, so for back wheels, a general rule of thumb was that if they were round then they would probably be fine.

Front wheels were different. Front wheels were the key to a good guider. For one thing they needed to have a decent clearance off the ground. This made it more comfortable for any driver using the kneeling position and also made it less likely for knuckles to receive damage from small stones thrown up from the road. Large, good quality front wheels also contributed greatly to a guider's speed, which was perhaps a more important consideration.

The only wheels, therefore, that any serious guider enthusiast would consider for the front of his vehicle would be those wheels with solid, white rubber tyres that could only be found on old-fashioned, quality prams. And that was the problem.

Because prams were becoming scarce.

The traditional pram, with its bouncy suspension and four properly-sized wheels, was already beginning to be supplanted by the modern buggy whose hateful little plastic wheels – echoing those of a supermarket trolley – were entirely useless for guider construction. This was a fact that an increasing number of parents were selfishly failing to appreciate, and the pram was in danger of becoming extinct. Good pram wheels were hard to come by.

Which was why, early one Sunday morning, at the beginning of what was promising to be a decent summer, Ding-a-Ling could not believe his luck.

He had risen early and had set off to fetch the Sunday papers with the money his da had left on the mantelpiece the night before. He was to purchase a copy of the *Sunday World* as well as the *News of the World,* and he was also allowed to pick up a copy of the *Victor* comic for himself and the *Bunty* for his sister. As he walked up the street, warmed by the morning sun, he could imagine that he was the only person awake in the whole of Ardoyne. Everywhere was quiet and deserted, with blinds and curtains, like drooping eyelids, still shielding the street's watchful windows. Then, walking past the front gardens at the top of the street, Ding-a-Ling stopped and stared.

There, sitting in one of the gardens, was a gleaming pair of the most beautiful pram wheels he had ever seen. The wheels had already been detached from the pram to which they had once belonged and now sat, gleaming, on the dew-bright lawn just waiting to be put to proper use.

Ding-a-Ling's mind raced as he sprinted to the newsagent to get his shopping task out of the way. It was remarkably negligent, he thought, to leave such a pair of wheels just lying around for anyone to come along and take. It showed such a flagrant disregard for the wheels' worth, he told himself, that it would be stupid – criminal, really – *not* to take them.

By the time he arrived back at the garden with its shiny treasure, he had worked himself into a state of righteous indignation. *How dare they?* he thought. *How dare these people be so dismissive of their own personal property? How careless! How irresponsible!*

As he quietly slipped the latch of the gate and crept into the garden, he had convinced himself that he was performing a moral and civic duty. He was showing the – soon to be former – wheel owners that such a cavalier approach to ownership could not come without consequences. He came to the conclusion that he was providing a service. It was a lesson, he decided. A harsh lesson, perhaps, but ultimately it was for their own good.

A few moments later, Ding-a-Ling strolled down the street with the Sunday papers under his arm and a pair of wheels in his hand, and he reflected on how the wheels' previous owners would be waking this morning with a new understanding of their responsibilities.

And, in Ding-a-Ling's reality, they would be grateful.

The slope of the entry was steepest at the very top, causing the speed of the guider to increase rapidly and leaving the pursuers to give up the chase in foul-mouthed frustration. It quickly occurred to Ding-a-Ling, however, that he may have made a mistake. The entry ahead was strewn with bags of rubbish that gave the impression of an impenetrable assault course. The decision, though, had already been made and, thanks to gravity, Ding-a-Ling and Snatter no longer had any say in the matter. All they could do was hold on and hope.

Snatter opened his eyes, saw what lay ahead, and quickly closed them again. He also kept his lips firmly shut and would have covered his nostrils as well if both of his hands weren't already clasped so tightly to the sides of the guider. Instead, he tried to bury his face into Ding-A-Ling's back as the guider bounced wildly over and through the detritus that had been dumped all over the entry. Swollen plastic bags burst under the speeding wheels, spewing various materials and releasing swarms of outraged flies and other insects to create a noxious cloud, through which Snatter and Ding-A-Ling grimly hurtled. Bottles and jam-jars skittered away or else shattered to add tiny shards of gloop-smeared glass to the mix.

Snatter could feel the fragments of glass and flecks of refuse – discarded food, used nappies, etc. – ping off his forehead and become lodged in his hair as the guider thundered chaotically downhill. Ding-A-Ling was making no attempt to steer, he was simply holding on and trying to keep the guider in a straight line, squinting towards the bottom of the entry and wincing at the smell and the globs of mess that were speckling his face and arms.

Snatter had long suspected that Ding-A-Ling would, at some point, end up killing them both, but he had always assumed that it would happen sometime in the distant future. The violent manner in which the guider was now rocking and shaking, however, made him feel that he should be making his peace with God much sooner.

The guider hurtled on, startling the occasional plump rat that would scurry quickly out of the way, and splashing Snatter and Ding-A-Ling, as well as the entry walls, with an unpleasant collection of fluids, condiments and suspiciously brown solids that combined to provide an aroma that had been ripening in the hot sun. Snatter was not enjoying himself. He knew, however, that he would be much better off staying on the guider than to go rolling off into the putrid mess of the entry and so he tightened his grip and prayed for the nightmare to end.

And eventually it did.

The ground began to level out as they neared the bottom of the hill and the guider slowed and then rolled, squeaking, to a halt, leaving Snatter and Ding-A-Ling looking out onto Etna Drive which ran perpendicular to the bottom of the entry. Snatter prised his fingers from the sides of the guider, and he and Ding-A-Ling stood up to look back at the trail of scattered rubbish they had left behind.

"Look at the state of youse two!"

Ding-A-Ling turned to see, on the pavement on the other side of the road, his little sister, Karen, striding purposefully past with a group of her friends, their arms linked together at the elbows. They walked on with a sense of haughty disgust, with Ding-A-Ling staring after them. He stood motionless … watching … waiting … hoping.

And then it came. One of Karen's friends – little Rosie with the long black hair – glanced back. Her eyes met those of Ding-A-Ling. Flustered and blushing at his gaze, Rosie quickly looked away.

Ding-A-Ling grinned and turned to face Snatter who stood quivering with terror and rage.

"That was mad!" he said happily, nodding to the entry. "We should do it again."

ONE

July 1990, Belfast

Considering she was attempting to expel something akin to a watermelon through her vagina, Rosemary McCann was feeling remarkably calm. The sensation was unexpected, though not unwelcome, as if some billowing strands of gossamer had come along to drift around in her memories. Had she been more prone to lyricism then she might have described herself as floating in pastoral serenity to the sounds of birdsong and lilting harp-strings. There were blissful little tingles of euphoria that washed through her like the gentlest of waves lapping a sandy beach in an empty, sun-bright morn. Not that she particularly cared, but Rose began to give some idle speculation as to the source of this wonderful sense of peace and wellbeing. Could it possibly be due, she wondered, to the soothing presence of her fiancé, Gary, who stood quietly and reassuringly at her bedside?

Yes, that could be it, she decided with a languorous decadence. Gary was lovely, she thought dreamily. He draped the room in love and warmth like a blanket made of sparkles and rainbows. Yes, Gary was lovely, reflected Rosie. He was lovely and gentle and caring and … no, wait … that was Ellie! It was her sister, Ellie, she was thinking of. Ellie was the one who was gentle and caring and kind. That's right, Rosie remembered now … Gary was a prick.

Gary, she recalled, could never be described as a calming influence – quite the opposite, in fact – but then what could be causing the almost mystical sense of mellowness that Rosie was experiencing? Not that it mattered, she mused happily. She was just a little curious.

Maybe, she lazily mused, it was down to the amount of drugs in her system.

Rosie had been quite insistent to anyone at the hospital who would listen that she would be having every single type of medication that was available to her. In fact, she had heard of some women who eschewed all forms of artificial suppression, fearing that it would detract from the natural miracle of childbirth, and Rosie had made it quite clear that she would happily accept any of the drugs that were allocated to those morons as well.

It was possible, then, she decided, that all of the delightfully fuzzy levels of consciousness that she was slipping through were a result of her medication.

Did she care?

Rosie almost laughed out loud. What a ridiculous question! She smiled condescendingly at the rather stern-looking panda in the corner. That's just the sort of question you would expect from a panda, she thought.

At times she began to think that she might be hallucinating, but how would she know? How would she be able to tell? She thought about asking Sara, from the pop group Bananarama, about it, but Sara seemed to be taking a rather inappropriate amount of interest in Rosie's fanny. This surprised Rosie as she didn't think Bananarama was that type of girl group. You just can't tell these days, she told herself.

Something that could possibly be described as brain-melting agony ripped through the lower half of Rosie's body and she gave Gary's hand a little squeeze. He smiled lovingly down at her which made Rosie think that she needed to remember something. Was it about her daddy? Was that it? She began to wonder if her daddy had made it back in time, but then she realised he *must* have made it back. Gary was here after all.

Was that a guarantee, though? Gary's presence certainly suggested that her father would also be around, but Rosie couldn't be sure. She wasn't sure that she had that much confidence in her fiancé's ability to carry out simple tasks. Gary had been set the task of bringing Rosie's father back to Belfast, but Rosie would not have been at all surprised if Gary had come back with nothing more than a tin of soup and a golf ball.

No, that was unfair, she thought. Gary wasn't all that bad. Sara, from the pop group Bananarama, was becoming rather excited about something, but Rosie decided that it had nothing to do with her. No, Rosie concluded, Gary wasn't all that bad. She was feeling a genuine sense of warmth towards him, and now that she thought about it, Gary had been accompanied on the trip by Seamus Green, and Rosie knew that Seamus could usually be relied upon to make good on his promises.

That was settled, then.

What was settled? Rosie tried to focus. Tried to remember. And then she smiled as it came to her. She remembered that her daddy had been back for days now. Gary and Seamus had done it. They had managed to get back in time.

For a while, though, it had been touch and go.

TWO

Several weeks earlier

In his own mind, Gary Lingfield was the Fonz. He was Arthur Fonzarelli from the TV show, *Happy Days,* arching his right arm over his head and dragging a comb through his hair while simultaneously smoothing it down with his left hand.

The reflection in the mirror that hung above Ellie and Rosie's mantelpiece suggested that he was mistaken in this perception, but Gary had always preferred his own reality to the one in which most other people lived, and so he gave his reflection a thumbs up and popped the comb back into the inside pocket of his jacket. He then walked across the floor, pulled open the door to the hall and, standing in the doorway, shouted up the stairs.

"You nearly ready there, love? The taxi won't be long."

"Aye, I'm coming!" Rosie called back, impatient tension in her voice. "I'll only be two seconds!"

Gary considered this as he closed the door and walked back into the lounge. Experience told him that in those two seconds he would have ample time to make a cup of tea, bake a Victoria sponge and create a scale model of the City Hall using only his toenail clippings. He sighed and sat down, glancing at his watch.

Eventually, after the continents had drifted a little further around the globe, Gary heard heavy footsteps on the stairs before the door was pushed open and Rosie stepped into the lounge.

"Well, do I look okay?" she asked uncertainly.

Gary stood up to better scrutinise Rosie's appearance. She was now in her eighth month of pregnancy and was clearly uncomfortable with the size she had become. The subtle make-up she had applied, however, served to enhance the natural glow of her skin and her thick black hair, blown back in waves, framed her face beautifully.

"Aye, you look class, love," Gary told her. Rosie gave a sigh and looked down at the floor.

"I'm really not sure about tonight," she admitted nervously.

"Why? What's wrong?"

"Well, it's ..." Rosie was uncertain about how to proceed. "Well, I think it's just that Carol and Claire are so smart and successful, you know? I just don't know what I'm going to say to them. I'm scared I'm going to make a real dick of myself."

"I wouldn't worry about it," said Gary dismissively. "Carol and Claire are dead on, you know. They're both really sound."

"I know, but ..." Rosie began to chew on her lower lip. "Well look at Carol, for God's sake!" she cried. "She could be a bloody supermodel.

And look at me!" Rosie gestured at her pregnancy bump.

"Look, I don't know what your problem is," said Gary. "You're the best-looking girl in Belfast. You always were."

Rosie hesitated, thrown by the unexpected compliment.

"So come on," Gary continued, "why don't you waddle on over here and give us a kiss?"

"You bastard!" Rosie exclaimed, though she waddled over to him and put her arms around his waist. Gary kissed her forehead as she rested her head on his shoulder.

"Everything's going to be okay, isn't it?" Rosie asked quietly, seeking reassurance. For Gary, the question was meaningless.

"Of course it is," he said, pulling back to look into her eyes. "What sort of question is that?"

"I don't know," said Rosie, "I've just started to feel really worried about everything. I don't know if I'm having some sort of panic attacks or whatever, but I seem to start crying at anything these days."

"Oh, it's just your hormones, love," Gary assured her. "They're bound to be all over the place at the minute."

"I know but … well, I wish my daddy was here for one thing. I worry about him."

"Yeah, but it won't be long before he's back, will it? He'll be back before you're due."

"I know, but …"

"And Jack and your uncle Mark said they'll come back down again in time for the baby, so you're going to have your whole family around you. I think you're just worrying for the sake of worrying, but like I said, it's just your hormones." Gary considered himself to be an expert on such things. A car horn sounded from outside. "Right, that's us," said Gary, glancing out the window. "You all set, then?" Rosie nodded and they both made for the door. "It was a good wee night we had up in the Star, wasn't it?" Gary said as they made their way down the garden path. "With your da and Jack and all?"

Rosie smiled at the memory. "Yeah," she agreed, "it was a great wee night."

Martin paced anxiously across the floor as Ellie and Rosie sat and watched from the sofa. The two sisters would occasionally catch each other's eye and try to stifle an amused grin. It still felt strange to have their father back in their lives after so many years, but it was a happy strangeness and a strangeness they were excited to turn into a familiarity.

"I don't know what you're so nervous about," said Ellie. "It's only your son that you haven't seen in about twenty years, after all. Nothing to worry about at all, really."

Martin stared at his eldest daughter before realising she was gently mocking him. He shook his head with a smile and sat down in the chair by the fireplace. He then got up again and continued his anxious pacing.

As he paced, he tried to focus on his memories of Jack. He wanted to grasp the most recent memory of his son, but he wasn't sure just what that memory might be. He was confident he could remember the happy, gurgling infant, beginning to crawl and to get into mischief, but were there other memories? Later memories? Martin couldn't say for sure, but a persistent image would swirl suddenly from the mist before fading and disappearing, only to come again, unannounced and unexpected, an image clear and vague. A young boy walking, strong and sure. A pair of blue shorts. A yellow T-shirt, white socks and grey plimsols. A smile.

A movement from outside made him stop to look through the window. A car had pulled up.

"I think that's them," he told the girls.

Ellie got up to take a look. She nodded, smiling, and went to open the front door "Uncle Mark!" she called out, rushing down the path.

"All right there, Ellie love," said Mark, greeting her with a hug. Ellie and Rosie's brother, Jack, followed close behind, hand-in-hand with a dark-haired girl flashing a friendly smile. Ellie broke off from Mark to embrace them both.

"You've met Tina, haven't you, Ellie?" asked Jack.

"Of course, we met ages ago. How are you doing, Tina love?"

"I'm all right, Ellie. What about yourself? It was some shock about your daddy, I'm sure."

Ellie laughed. "You can say that again! Well, come on in." She led them towards the house.

Martin and Rosie were standing side-by-side in the middle of the floor when they all came through the open door.

"Martin!" Mark exclaimed as he grasped Martin's hand and patted his shoulder. "Jesus, but it's grand to see you again!"

"Thanks, Mark. It's good to see you too." Martin took a glance over Mark's shoulder and saw a young man waiting nervously. Mark tactfully moved to one side and embraced Rosie while Martin stood in front of the man, his son, who was a stranger to him.

For a heartbeat they stood regarding one another, unsure of what to do, until, like a dam bursting, they threw their arms around each other in a tearful flood of emotion. Everybody else looked on, smiling and wiping away tears. Jack then introduced Tina to his father and everyone began talking at once while Ellie went off to the kitchen to make tea.

After the greetings had been made, they all found a seat in the living room and the chattering became constant while Ellie kept up a supply of tea and sandwiches and plates of biscuits.

"So, I hear you're a mechanic," Martin said to Jack. "I couldn't believe it when Rosie told me. A real chip off the old block, then?"

"Aye, that's right," Jack replied. "It's something I've always been into, so I suppose I get that from you. And what about you? Have you been managing to keep your hand in?"

"Well, sort of," said Martin. "I've been working part-time at a garage near where I live in Sussex. They do a lot of work with motorbikes, you know, racing bikes? That sort of thing."

"Sounds like high-end stuff," said Jack. He sensed Rosie bristle on the sofa beside him and turned inquisitively towards her.

"Aye, well," said Rosie firmly, "I'm sure we can find something like that around here."

Martin laughed. "Rosie and Ellie weren't too happy when I told them I was going to have to go back to England at some point."

"You're going back?" asked Mark.

"Well, yeah, I've just started to get back on my feet in the last year or so, you know, what with work and all. And I'm renting my own flat now as well."

"So, what's the plan?"

"I haven't thought that far ahead. To be honest I wasn't sure what I was coming back to over here, so I'd only planned to come for a couple of weeks. I've had to extend that obviously, but I'm still going to have to go back to sort things out eventually."

The conversation pinballed around the room, veering from topic to topic, until it was time for dinner, which Ellie and Mark fetched from the local chip shop.

"Oh, I brought some stuff down from Derry for you," Mark told Martin when he came back from the chippy. "It's in the boot, I'll just go and get it." Mark went out to the car and came back a few moments later with an old cardboard box. Everyone else had begun to tuck into their food, so Mark set the box on the floor and sat on the sofa with his own meal on his lap. "It's just some stuff that Shauna kept," he said, nodding to the box. "Old photos and stuff I thought you might want."

"Thanks," said Martin. "It'll be interesting going through them. Maybe jog a few memories."

After they had eaten, Martin took a quick look in the box.

"I don't remember this," he said, holding up a battered old teddy bear.

"*Pandy!*" shrieked Ellie. "Jesus, I haven't seen him in years!"

Martin handed her the old black and white toy and turned back to the box.

"Oh my God!" he said, holding up a framed photograph. "I never thought I'd see this again." He showed it to Rosie and Ellie. "It's my da and his army mates during the war. I thought this was long gone."

"Yeah, I remember it from when I was a kid," said Ellie. "Set it up on top of the fireplace there."

Martin placed it carefully on the mantelpiece and glanced at the remaining objects in the box.

"I'll go through the rest of these tomorrow," he said. "We don't want to keep Gary waiting, do we?"

"Aye, we should probably make a move," said Rosie. They had arranged to meet Gary and his parents for drinks in the Star.

"You two are going to be staying with Gary's mummy and daddy tonight," Rosie told Jack and Tina. "You'll meet them up in the Star. They're lovely, so they are. You'll get on really well with them."

It didn't take long for everyone to be ready, and they set off in a group for the short walk to the club.

Once inside the maze-like complex of the Crumlin Star Social Club, they made their way to the long, narrow lounge known as the Carriage Room. The larger bar downstairs was for men only.

"I can't believe they can get away with that in this bloody day and age!" Tina fumed. She was dissuaded, however, from making a fuss and they walked into the lounge where they found Gary and his parents already seated in one of the booths. Hands were shaken and hugs given as all the necessary introductions were made, before Gary, Jack and Mark went up to the bar to get the drinks in. The Carriage Room wasn't too busy so the company was able to sprawl out over several tables. This proved to be useful when Gary's sister, Karen, and her husband, Harry, appeared. Harry would normally have been found in a different Ardoyne club and his appearance in the Star caused a few bemused glances.

"What's the matter, Harry?" someone called out as he walked past. "Is the League closed?" Harry simply scowled in response and kept walking to the bar while Karen found a seat beside Rosie.

As the drinks were being distributed, Tina frowned at the murky brown liquid that was placed in front of Rosie.

"Jesus, Rosie, what's that you're drinking?"

Rosie held up her glass and smiled. "It's tomato juice and Worcester sauce," she said. "With a wee bit of tabasco in it."

"It's a Bloody Mary without the vodka," explained Gary, taking a seat with a pint of Bass in his hand. "Or a *Bloody Shame* as they call it in Australia."

"A *Virgin* Mary, it's known as," said Rosie. "I've got really into it since I've been pregnant."

"Looks disgusting," said Karen just as Harry pulled up a seat beside her.

"Aye, it's weird looking, isn't it?" said Tina. "How did you get into that, then?"

"A wee friend of mine got me into it," said Rosie. She looked at Karen. "You know Marina don't you, Karen? From over the Bone?"

"Aye, I know Marina," replied Karen. "She drinks in the Glenpark, doesn't she?"

"Over the Bone?" asked Tina. "What's the Bone?"

"The Bone," Gary interjected, "is where they put all the people who aren't good enough to live in Ardoyne."

"Watch it!" Harry growled. "My granny lives on the Bone."

"I know, Harry," said Gary cheerfully. "I've met your granny and, to be honest with you, the Bone's the best place for her."

"What's that supposed to –?"

"Here, Martin!" Karen called across the tables. "When are you heading back to England?"

Martin looked over and gave a shrug. "Probably in the next couple of weeks."

"You'll be back for the baby being born, though, won't you?"

"Hopefully, yes."

"Bloody better be," muttered Rosie.

"It's not going to be long now, is it, Rosie love?" said Sadie, Karen and Gary's mother.

"When are you due?" asked Jack. He had already been told Rosie's due date, but had clearly not considered the information worthy of retention.

"July," said Rosie.

"Aye," Gary added. "Round about the Twelfth too! That's going to be a laugh, isn't it? Trying to get across town on the bloody Twelfth!"

"Well, I think we're planning to be back down in Belfast by then," Jack told him, "so I'm sure we'll work something out."

"Can you imagine it, though?" continued Gary, warming to the idea. "A kid from Ardoyne being born on the twelfth of July? We could tell him every year that they're having a parade for his birthday."

"Yeah, a parade he's not allowed to go to," grunted Rosie. The parades that took place every summer throughout Northern Ireland were generally not considered to be a welcoming environment for someone with a catholic, nationalist background. They were a way for the loyalist community to commemorate and to celebrate the victory of the protestant King William over his father-in-law, King James, at a battle by the banks of the river Boyne in County Meath. King James had been deposed by the British for leaning a little too far towards Catholicism. The battle, now long forgotten by the rest of the UK, was still deeply rooted in the loyalist culture of Northern Ireland and was seen as symbolic of the conflict between the true faiths of Protestantism and the idolatry of Catholicism.

This religious conflict – also long forgotten by the rest of the UK – had, in Northern Ireland, become further complicated by the absorption of the political differences over the sovereignty of the island of Ireland. This political slant ensured the gaping wound would remain open and weeping and would lead, particularly during the parade season, to a continuing source of friction.

One problem was that the policy of the parades dictated that the marchers must strictly adhere to the same routes they had followed for years, even if it meant marching past areas, like Ardoyne, that now had large nationalist populations. The Nationalists of these areas would then loudly express their disapproval of this policy.

The Loyalists, for their part, would stress that they were simply following the traditional routes they had followed for centuries, and the

Nationalists would counter this by insisting that the Loyalists could go and fuck themselves.

It was a tense and finely balanced argument.

"There's nothing stopping him going," Gary pointed out.

"Aye, he'd look cute, wouldn't he?" said Karen. "With his wee sash, and his wee Union Jack."

"Joker once took me round the Eleventh Night bonfires," said Gary. "Wasn't a problem at all."

"Did you tell anybody there that you were a Fenian from Ardoyne?" asked Karen.

"Course not! Do I look stupid?"

Harry looked like he was about to say something, but Karen slapped his arm.

"You all keep saying *he*," Tina noted. "So do you know if it's going to be a boy?"

"No," said Rosie. "It's just an expression. I mean we can hardly just call the baby *it*, can we?"

"Don't see why not," said Jack.

Gary lit a cigarette and picked up his beer. "Well," he said, "we'll be finding out soon enough if it's a boy or girl."

"How's your pregnancy been, Rosie?" asked Tina. "You haven't had any problems, have you?"

"No, it's all been straightforward, thank God." Rosie smiled and gestured towards Ellie. "It probably helps living with a nurse, though."

"Aye," said Karen, glancing at Gary, "it's good you've got somebody you can rely on."

"Same again?" asked Gary's father as he stood up holding an empty glass. Harry pushed himself up from his seat.

"I'll go up with you," he said. The Carriage Room was beginning to fill up now and the volume increased as friends and neighbours boisterously gathered for the evening, greeting and cajoling, laughing and shouting.

"Hey, Harry!" Someone, seeing Harry at the bar, gave a shout. "What's wrong? Is the League closed?" The comment now had a larger audience, and a ripple of laughter ran around the room. Gary set his pint down on the table, took a puff from his cigarette and leaned back contentedly. He caught Rosie's eye and gave her a wink and a rogue's grin. Rosie tried to reply with a smouldering glare but, as she took a sip from her glass, she found she couldn't help smiling back.

Life, Gary decided, was good.

THREE

Tone had just finished shaving, when the intercom buzzed.

"You're early," he said as he let Claire into the flat. "You're looking good, though." Claire smiled, although she thought it was the very least Tony could have said after she'd put so much thought and effort into her appearance. She was wearing a simple, navy-blue box jacket over a blue, patterned, Chinese-style silk dress that came to just above her knees. She was wearing her hair up and held at the back with a large clip and, unusually for her, she had clearly spent some time on her make-up.

"Thanks," she said, taking a seat. "I wasn't really sure what the protocol was for this evening, but I thought I should at least make an effort."

"It's just dinner," Tone said, checking his reflection in a wall-mirror. He then made his way back to the bathroom for some fine-tuning.

"I know, but …" Claire paused, unsure of what to say.

"But what?" Tone called through the bathroom's open door.

"Well, it's just …" Again, Claire hesitated as she considered her reply. "Well, Rosie's very pretty, isn't she?"

"Is she?"

"You know she is. And she's got such … oh, what's the word?"

"Well, I don't know," said Tone, showing his face in the doorway. "You're the bloody wordsmith." Claire worked as a journalist for Northern Ireland's biggest newspaper. She gave Tone a sardonic, lopsided smile.

"Swagger?" she suggested. "Is that the word?"

"No idea," Tone said as he disappeared back into the bathroom. "Depends what you're trying to say, doesn't it?"

"You know what I mean, though, she's got a real confidence about her, hasn't she? But in a brittle sort of way. She's got a bit of harshness about her."

Tone came back into the lounge, rubbing his hands on a towel. "I don't know about that," he said. "She's had her fair share of knocks, I suppose, and now she has Gary to put up with as well. That's got to colour your outlook, hasn't it?"

"Mmm," said Claire, "I think I just find her a bit intimidating."

"Oh, Rosie's dead on when you get to know her."

"I know, but …" Claire chewed nervously on her lower lip. "And there's Carol as well!" she exclaimed.

"What the hell is wrong with Carol?"

"Oh, come on, Tony! Just look at her! She looks like she's on loan from heaven!"

"On loan from heaven?" Tone asked amused. "I like that. Have you ever thought about writing for a living?"

"Oh, ha, bloody, ha!"

Tone frowned as he looked at Claire. All of a sudden she seemed vulnerable, and vulnerability was not a condition that Tone would ever have associated with Claire.

"Are you okay?" he asked.

"Yeah, it's just … I just feel a bit nervous, that's all."

"Nervous? Why? That's not like you. You're normally the bubbly, life and soul of the party type. It's actually a bit sickening, to be honest."

Claire laughed. "I know, I don't know what's wrong with me," she said. "I just feel really desperate to make a good impression. Jesus, that doesn't sound like me at all, does it?"

"No, it doesn't." said Tone. He sat down beside her on the sofa. "I don't understand what the problem is. We're just calling up to a mate's house for drinks and a meal, it's not a big deal at all."

"I know, but …" Claire turned to look Tone in the eye. She suddenly shook her head and allowed her face to light up with a smile. "You're right, obviously. I'm just being stupid. I'm sure it'll be a laugh. I don't know what's up with me."

"God knows," said Tone. He stood up to check his reflection again, flicking a few strands of hair across his forehead. "Like I said, it's just dinner."

"I hear that Joseph's helping to make it," said Claire smiling. "Is that something we should be worried about?"

"Actually," Tone turned to face her, "he's a surprisingly good cook. It's a bit of a hobby of his."

"He's full of surprises, isn't he?"

"He is," agreed Tone. "Not all of them are pleasant, though."

"He was telling me he's read the whole of *The Canterbury Tales* in the original Middle English."

"He's read a lot of weird shit."

"That's impressive, though, isn't it? I mean I haven't even read the modern translation."

"I suppose it's impressive if you like that sort of thing," said Tone dismissively. "It's not something that *I'd* go around bragging about."

Claire laughed. "You sound jealous!"

"Wise up!"

"Well at least there'll be some stimulating conversation over the dinner table."

"Don't get Joker started on the evolution of language," said Tone. He leaned forward to look Claire in the eye. "Seriously, you'll regret it."

"I don't know what you mean," Claire said primly. "I'm sure it would be very interesting."

"Aye, I'm sure." Tone straightened up and headed towards the kitchen. "Do you fancy a glass of wine before we head out?"

"I think we both know the answer to that question."

Tone grinned and set off down the narrow corridor that led to the kitchen. He came back with a bottle of red wine and two glasses.

"Have you ever heard of *The Decameron*?" he asked, pouring the wine.

"*The Decameron*?" Claire frowned. "I don't think so. Why? What is it?"

"It's an old book," Tone explained. He picked up his glass of wine and sat down in an armchair facing Claire. They both lit a cigarette. "Italian, I think," said Tone as he made himself comfortable. "And when I say *old*, I mean really old. It was an influence, apparently, on Chaucer when he wrote *The Canterbury Tales*."

"Jesus!"

"Yeah, exactly!" said Tone. "Well Joker's read that as well, in whatever bloody language it was written. I mean I'm pretty sure it's Italian, but it would be as close to modern Italian as *The Canterbury Tales* is to modern English. Probably closer to Latin, now that I think of it."

Claire looked thoughtful as she sipped her wine. "Yeah, okay," she said. "But that's what I'm talking about. Don't you think that that sounds really interesting?"

Tone shrugged. "I'm just letting you know what you'd be getting yourself into. You may find yourself a wee bit out of your depth."

Claire made a face at Tone. "I can look after myself," she said indignantly. "I'm always happy to learn new things."

"I'll tell you what," said Tone. "I'll be ready to jump in as soon as I see your eyes start to glaze over."

"Don't you worry about me, Bucko!" retorted Claire, gesturing to Tone with her wine glass. "Like I said, I can look after myself."

"Okay, you're on your own," said Tone laughing. They bantered good-humouredly back and forth as they drank and smoked until Tone decided it was time to order a taxi. It arrived fifteen minutes later and they both made their way downstairs to the street below.

The stirrings of a cool breeze could now be felt which made Claire glad she had brought a jacket. Tone held open the door of the taxi.

"Are you feeling any better, then?" he asked.

"Oh, much better now I've had a drop of wine."

"That's good." Tone climbed into the back seat beside Claire and then leaned towards the driver. "Malone Road, mate" he said.

The driver nodded and they set off.

FOUR

Rosie eased herself slowly from the back seat and stood staring up at the house while Gary paid the taxi driver.

"Jesus, Gary," she said once the taxi had gone, "would you look at that house!" The large, detached house was set back from the street at the end of a short, tree-lined driveway. It looked imposing from the bottom of the drive, making Rosie shiver with trepidation.

"Class, isn't it?" said Gary. "You could probably fit half of Ardoyne just in the front room."

Rosie smiled at the exaggeration in an attempt to hide her nerves. As they made their way towards the house, she tugged at Gary's arm. "You'd better not embarrass me here tonight," she hissed half-jokingly. "I know what you're like."

Gary stopped and was about to protest when a car pulled up at the end of the drive.

"That looks like Tone and Claire," said Gary. "That's good, we can all go in together."

Rosie nodded uncertainly. She stood beside Gary and watched Claire and Tone emerge from the taxi and then walk, smiling, towards them.

"That was a good bit of timing," said Gary. They all greeted each other, then eased into friendly chat.

"I love your dress," Rosie told Claire.

"Thanks," said Claire. "You're looking lovely. Your hair's gorgeous, where did you get it done?"

"What? Oh, I just blow-dried it myself, it only took ten minutes."

"You're kidding! Really?"

"Right, well come on," Tone said hurriedly. "We'd better go and see what they've got in store for us."

"I'm looking forward to this," Gary said to Tone as they walked to the front door. "It's something a wee bit different for a Friday night, isn't it?"

"You can say that again." Tone rang the doorbell.

"Good evening!" Carol exclaimed on opening the front door. "Come on in." She led them into a long hallway. "Joseph's in the kitchen," she told them, "stewing his plums."

"Well, if we've come at a bad time, then …" Gary began and Carol laughed.

"It's what we're having for dessert," she said. "Stewed plums and ice-cream."

"That sounds lovely," said Rosie, shooting Gary a warning glance.

"Oh, you all made it, then?" Joker appeared from a doorway at the other end of the hall. "I was just in the kitchen," he told them, "stewing my –"

"It's all right, Joseph," said Carol, "I've already done that joke."

"What? Awk, but I wanted to –"

"Never mind, you can take everybody's coats while you're here."

"Well, what if I don't want their bloody coats?"

"There's no need to sulk."

"I'm not sulking," said Joker sulkily. He took a closer look at Gary. "Jesus!" he exclaimed. "You've really cleaned yourself up, haven't you? You must be a good influence on him, Rosie love."

"Yeah, it's been a lot of work," said Rosie grinning, "but I'm getting there."

Joker took everyone's jackets and hung them up in a cloakroom under the staircase.

"Your house is absolutely gorgeous," Rosie told Carol.

"Yeah," Claire agreed, "It's unbelievable."

"Thanks," said Carol. "My daddy got it really cheap at the start of the seventies. He's done a lot of work to it since then."

"So, your da's not here at the minute, then?" said Gary.

"No, he's away down south for the weekend. Visiting an old friend." Carol gestured towards a set of tall double doors to the right of the entrance. "Dinner should be ready in about half an hour," she said. "So I thought we could have drinks in here first."

"Lead the way," said Gary.

Tone experienced a strong sense of déjà vu when Carol pushed open the doors. He pictured the shining smile of Emily as she perched, pixie-like, on the leather sofa, and he remembered that first unyielding stare of her father, Samuel, coming from the wingback chair on the right. He gave a tiny shudder.

"Nice room," he said to Carol.

"Thanks. We use it as a sort of library and a music room. You can stick on some records if you want."

Gary walked over to a set of shelves that were set into an alcove in one of the walls. Most of the shelves were taken up with music albums, and Gary browsed their spines while Rosie and Claire sat down on the sofa.

"So, it's just us tonight, is it?" asked Gary as he read the album titles.

"Yeah, just us," Carol confirmed. "I think Joseph had asked a couple of other people, but they couldn't make it tonight."

"Well, Bobby had to go to that meeting, didn't he?" said Claire. "Him and Sean, for their new jobs. They're going to be heading off soon."

"Yeah," said Tone, flopping down in the armchair. "In the next couple of weeks."

"Who's the Beatles' fan?" Gary asked, picking an album from the shelf.

"My daddy," said Carol. "Though he once told me that he hated them the first time he heard them. So, what drinks can I get everyone?"

"I'd better check on the dinner," said Joker as he headed back to the kitchen. Tone watched him go then turned to Carol.

"Did he just ignore the offer of a drink?" he asked bemused.

"He's got a beer on the go in the kitchen," Carol told him.

"Ah, that makes sense," said Tone. "I'll have a red wine, if that's okay."

"Me too," Claire piped up.

"Beer for me," said Gary. He'd found a compilation album of chart hits and was positioning it on the turntable.

"Rosie?" asked Carol. "What can I get you?"

"Just a Coke or a lemonade, please, Carol. Or just a glass of water if you don't have any."

"No problem." Carol set off for the kitchen just as the first few bars of *Robert De Niro's Waiting* drifted from the sound system. Gary, standing by the record player, began to gyrate rhythmically to the music.

"You're a great wee mover there, Gary," said Tone.

"Aye, Gary," agreed Claire with some amusement. "You could be a professional."

"Nah," said Gary. "I just dance for my own enjoyment. And to sexually excite women, obviously."

"Obviously," said Claire grinning.

Rosie looked on impassively. She would normally be amused by Gary's antics, but she was still feeling anxious, unsure of herself in these unfamiliar surroundings. Carol and Joker came back into the room with the drinks.

"Here you go, Rosie love," said Joker, handing her a glass of Coke. "Hey, Dancing Dan! Grab this!" he passed a can of lager over to Gary. "You don't need a glass with that, do you?"

Gary replied with a withering look as he popped open the can and put it to his lips.

"No, I didn't think so," muttered Joker.

"Rioja okay?" asked Carol, handing Tone and Claire each a glass of wine.

"Yeah, that's lovely," said Claire. "Thanks Carol."

"Cheers, Carol," said Tone.

Gary took a seat, content now that he had some alcohol. "Is it okay to smoke in here?" he asked Carol. "Or should I go out to the garden?"

"No, smoke away," Carol insisted. "There's an ashtray by your chair there."

Gary lit up, closely followed by Tone and Claire.

"So, does your course start in September, then?" Carol asked Tone.

"Yeah, I can't wait."

"You do realise," said Gary, "that all the people in your class are going to be calling you granda?"

"I'm not that much older!"

"Yeah, but to an 18-year-old, Tone, you're bloody ancient."

"That's true, Tony," Claire gently mocked. "Maybe I should come with you on your first day, to make sure they all don't pick on you."

"Yeah, very funny," said Tone. "Do you want me to get you a ticket to the Fresher's Ball or not?"

"It's drama you're doing, isn't it?" asked Rosie.

"Yeah, at Stranmillis." Tone gave Rosie a nod. "I hear you're planning to go to college as well, Rosie. Computers, isn't it?"

"Mmm," Rosie nodded with a half-smile. "I was thinking about it, anyway."

"Oh, just go for it, Rosie love!" Tone told her. "Sometimes you just have to …" he gave Claire a quick sideways glance. "… grasp the nettle."

"I suppose I'm going to have to wait and see how it goes," said Rosie, rubbing her stomach. "I've got a couple of other things to think about first."

"Aye, one thing at a time," said Gary.

"Oops!" said Joker suddenly. "I'd better check on dinner!" He hurried back to the kitchen.

"I must say, Carol," said Tone, "you seem to have him well trained. He's got very domesticated, hasn't he?"

"No, he's just missing his beer, that's all."

"Right, everybody!" Joker called through from the kitchen. "This is nearly ready, so you might want to head on into the dining room."

"Okay, whenever you're all ready," said Carol.

Tone stood up. "After you," he said, and Carol, smiling, led them through to dinner.

FIVE

Jamesy was beginning to wonder if he should be panicking. He still had another year left before he completed his master's degree, but it was what would come after it that was causing him some concern.

In order to achieve his ultimate goal of entering the world of field archaeology, in order to gain the respect of his peers in his chosen career and to be fully accepted, Jamesy believed he would have to complete his doctorate. He would need a PhD.

And that was where he was struggling. Jamesy had never been particularly competitive. He had never been driven to be the best, to be first in all things, to reach the very top, but this, he felt, was different. A PhD, he believed, should reflect his passion. It should shine. For Jamesy, a PhD – *his* PhD – should not simply be another worthy but unremarkable rung on the ladder, it should make people sit up and take notice. He had always believed his PhD would boldly announce his arrival on the scene by shaking up the world of archaeology. Even if it turned out to be little more than a gentle shake, it should be, he felt, a statement of intent. A declaration that there was a new kid in town, someone with radical new ideas, someone to drag the ancient past into the present, someone to … He stood up with a weary sigh. Maybe Tone was right, he reflected. Maybe he did want to be Indiana Jones.

Not that it mattered anymore, he thought ruefully, because for the first time in his academic career, Jamesy's mind was blank. He was all out of ideas.

He knew, of course, that there was no rush. There was nothing that said he had to go straight into a PhD thesis once he had completed his master's. He could as take as long as he liked. Years even. But that, for Jamesy, was missing the point. He had never before lacked inspiration. He had always been focused on his goal, knowing with clarity where he was headed and how he would get there, one step at a time. Now, though, it felt like he was staring into a void. He simply had no clue as to what he should base his thesis on.

He picked up the kettle and walked over to the sink. He wasn't even sure that he wanted a cup of tea, but the familiar motions gave him something to do. Another wild Friday night, he told himself. Sitting alone in his kitchen, drinking tea. Crazy times.

And that was another sensation that was unfamiliar to Jamesy. Self-pity. Where had that come from? He could have gone to Joker and Carol's dinner party tonight, but he wasn't in the mood for company. Besides, it had sounded more like a cosy gathering of happy couples than the usual banter-filled drinking session.

Jamesy sat back down at the kitchen table and waited for the kettle to boil. He understood the reasons for his current malaise, of course, but that did not make it any easier to bear. He had had only a few, fleeting encounters with Hannah over the past few weeks, and those had been rather formal and awkward affairs, as Hannah would make some mumbled apology before rushing off.

Having to accept the fact that the only relationship he had ever really cared about was crumbling away to nothing had led him to dwell increasingly on the bleak and pointless monotony of human existence. And not in a fun way.

The kettle bubbled excitedly before clicking off in a cloud of steam. Jamesy, deep in thought, barely noticed. He hated this black, despondent apathy that seemed to burrow every day deeper into his core, but he felt incapable of finding a way to fight it. That was the problem with apathy, he thought darkly; he just didn't care anymore.

He let his mind wander aimlessly, allowing it to stroll into the past to poke lethargically at some old memories while it tried to ignore the blinding smile that screamed from every direction. Hannah's smile. The smile that could melt icebergs. The smile that had ensnared him, but now served only to … Jamesy was suddenly alert. His mind, shuffling around in his childhood, had found something. A memory. An idea.

He leapt to his feet and began to pace around the kitchen. His mind was racing now, throwing around ideas and fizzing with excitement. A plan was starting to take shape, and Jamesy could feel the first stirrings of the old joy, the old passion. That old unquenchable thirst. He raced into the front room, grabbed the phone receiver, and began to dial. He assumed that Seamus would be out at this time on a Friday night but he knew that Seamus had recently purchased a fancy new answering machine, and Jamesy's sudden excitement was urging him to do something, anything, to set his plan in motion right away.

He was surprised when Seamus picked up on the third ring.

"Hello!"

"Oh, Seamus, I wasn't sure if you'd be in."

"Jamesy?"

"Yeah. I thought you'd be going down to the Parliament tonight."

"Nah, I was going to, but then I just couldn't be bothered," said Seamus. "It was starting to get a bit boring, you know? Just the same old faces every week."

"Oh, right."

"So, what's up?"

"Well, I was just wondering something," said Jamesy. "You're still planning to drive Sean and Bobby over to their induction course, aren't you?"

"Yeah, why?"

"When were you planning to go?"

"The ferry's booked for the first week in July. Why? Is something wrong?"

"No, no, I was just wondering if you had room for one more." There was a slight pause before Seamus replied.

"One more?" he said. "You mean you? Do you want to come too?"

"If that's all right."

"Um, yeah, I don't see why not. There's plenty of room."

"Brilliant!"

"Is there any reason why you want to tag along?"

"Yeah, sort of. I'll tell you all about it when I see you. You're going to Sean and Bobby's send-off, aren't you?"

"Of course, yeah."

"Right then, I'll see you then."

"Oh, okay then. I'll see you."

Jamesy put down the phone and headed back to the kitchen. He fancied that cup of tea now. The old energy was returning. The intellectual curiosity that had driven Jamesy for much of his life was not dead, he realised, it had simply become sluggish and dormant, in need of a shake-up. Some sort of spark.

Jamesy poured his tea and smiled to himself. He needed some inspiration, he decided. And he now knew exactly where to find it.

SIX

Joker held up the wine bottle to confirm it was empty. "That went down well," he said. "I take it you want a top-up?"

"If you insist," said Tone. "And compliments to the chef, by the way. That was class."

"Yeah, it was really lovely," Claire added, and Gary and Rosie nodded their agreement while Joker went off to fetch more drinks.

"Yes, it certainly hit the spot," Gary said as he stretched his arms above his head. "Thanks for that."

"You're welcome," said Carol. "I hope you're ready for Joseph's plums."

"Well, there's got to be a first time for everything."

"What are you up to at the weekend, Carol?" asked Claire. "Are you working?"

"Not tomorrow, but I'm going in for a few hours on Sunday."

"I keep hearing all these stories about junior doctors having to work all hours of the day and night."

"Well, yeah, it can be a bit hectic," agreed Carol. "But it's not too bad, really."

Joker came back into the room with some cans of beer and a bottle of wine. "You okay with your Coke there, Rosie?" he asked.

"Yes thanks, Joseph. I've got plenty here."

"Cheers, Joker," said Tone, taking the opened bottle of wine and pouring for Carol, Claire and himself. "I was just wondering," he said as he poured. "Did you ever hear any more from Sticky Mickey?"

"Who, me?" asked Joker. "No, not at all."

"What about you, Gary?"

"Me? No," said Gary. "But apparently he's been giving Harry some jip."

"Harry? Why?"

"Who's Harry?" asked Claire.

"Oh, he's my sister's husband," Gary told her.

"So, why Harry?" Tone persisted. Gary turned and gave Tone a rather pitying look.

"Now, how would I know that?" he asked. "Do I look like I pay attention to things?"

"Oh, that's true, I suppose."

"Right," said Joker, standing up. "Is everybody ready for dessert?"

"Bring it on!" demanded Tone, and Joker set off for the kitchen.

"I hear there's been some big shake-up at your work," Carol said to Gary when Joker had gone. "Some big takeover, is it?"

"Yeah," said Gary, "apparently some American firm has bought out the packaging arm of the business. That would be four sites altogether; us, a place in Scotland and two sites in England."

"What's that going to mean for you and Joker, then?" asked Tone.

"Probably nothing," Gary shrugged. "They've said they'll be putting a lot of investment into all four sites, but our place has already expanded a fair bit just since me and Joker have been there, so who knows? I'm sure they'd be happy to leave things the way they are. I mean, we're making plenty of profit at the minute."

"You talking about work?" asked Joker as he came back with a tray of desserts. He set down the tray and began passing bowls around the dining table.

"What's *your* take on it, Joker?" asked Tone. "This whole takeover business?"

"Don't know," Joker sighed, taking a seat. "We'll just have to wait and see."

"You don't sound too optimistic."

"I think it's too early to say how it's going to go." Joker glanced around the table. "Well, tuck in, everyone!"

After dessert, Carol and Joker cleared away the empty bowls and everyone settled back to enjoy their drinks and to let the meal go down.

"We could finish off these drinks in here," suggested Carol, "and then go back to the music room. It's a bit more relaxed in there."

"Sounds good," said Tone contentedly.

Carol took a quick glance at Rosie. She had noticed how subdued Rosie had been throughout the meal and guessed that she'd been feeling a little intimidated. "You all right there, Rosie?" she said, then nodded to Rosie's stomach. "I bet you can't wait to get it all over with."

Rosie looked at Carol and gave a nervous smile. "No, it's not long now," she said. "I just hope I'll be able to fit into all my clothes again."

"I wouldn't worry about that," said Carol. "I'd say you're the type that'll just snap back to their old weight in no time at all."

"Hope so," said Rosie quietly. "But it's …" she paused and looked around at everyone, "it's just going to be really weird, isn't it? Having a baby to look after?"

"No worse than looking after Gary," said Joker. "And you've had plenty of –"

"Well obviously it's going to be a massive change," said Carol, "but I'm sure you'll be able to cope no problem."

"Yeah," Claire added. "It's not like you'll be on your own, is it? You've got Gary here for one thing. I'm sure he'll be very supportive."

"Supportive?" Rosie stared at Claire, trying to detect some hint of sarcasm but, finding none, she went on. "Me and Gary were in town the other day," she said, "and we stopped at Mothercare to look at the prams in the window. So I asked Gary what sort of pram he thought we should get. And do you know what he said?" Everyone looked at Rosie, waiting for her to continue. "He said, 'Judging by the size of you, love, we'll be needing a bloody wheelbarrow'."

Joker and Tone howled with laughter. Carol and Claire shook their heads and looked sympathetically towards Rosie. "That's shocking," muttered Carol as she and Claire both tutted and sneered in sisterly solidarity with Rosie. The three boys had now jumped to their feet and were high-fiving each other over the table, while Claire and Carol reached over to pat Rosie on the hand and on the shoulder.

Eventually, Tone, Joker and Gary returned to their seats, the raucous laughter now replaced with easy smiles. A companionable silence descended over the room.

"Still," said Claire, glancing at Rosie, "he does have a point."

"I know!" shrieked Rosie. "I'm bloody huge!" The three girls roared with laughter, then collapsed into uncontrollable giggles to the bemusement of Gary, Tone and Joker.

After a while, they all made their way to the music room to round off the evening drinking, smoking, chatting and listening to records.

"It's good to have a night with no bloody football," said Rosie, beginning to feel a bit more at ease.

"You can say that again," agreed Claire. "It's been non-stop, hasn't it?"

"You not enjoying the World Cup, then, Rosie?" asked Tone.

"Oh, it's okay," Rosie told him, "but like Claire said, there's just been too much of it."

"Yeah, well it'll start to ease off a bit after tomorrow when the knockout rounds start. So, who do you fancy in it?"

"Well, I'm glad the Republic got through," said Rosie, "but I think I want Cameroon to win."

"Yes!" cried Carol. "Since Egypt went out, we've been supporting Cameroon."

"They do say an African team will win it someday," said Gary as he changed albums on the record-player. "No reason why it can't be this year."

As the haunting vocals of Enya began to fill the room, the conversation moved onto the wide variety of music genres that were starting to become more accessible. Gary mentioned that there would be some good folk bands playing at the Fleadh in Ardoyne at the beginning of August, and Claire, raised in a unionist community, frowned.

"A flah?" she asked. "What's a flah?"

"A Fleadh," explained Gary, "is a festival of traditional Irish folk music. They've started to hold one in Ardoyne in August every year. It goes on for a week."

"It's not just music, though," enthused Joker. "We went up to it last year and the bars stayed open all night. It was mental!"

"So, it's a festival of music and drinking?" asked Claire.

"No," said Gary, "they try to get everybody involved, so it's sort of like a festival of culture, you know, with arts and sports and stuff. And they've got loads of stuff for kids as well. Street parties and competitions and things like that."

"Sounds like a good laugh."

"It is. There's a really good atmosphere. And one of the best bits of craic is the Guider Race."

"Guider Race?"

"Oh, that's right!" said Carol. "I remember it from last year. I'd never heard of a guider before, until I found out it was just a box-cart."

"Um, yeah," said Gary, "I suppose that's what you'd call it if you lived in a *Charlie Brown* cartoon."

"So, it's just a race for box-carts?" asked Claire.

"No, it's a race for guiders."

"Okay, so what happens at it, then?"

"Well," said Gary, "anybody can enter a guider, so all the clubs in Ardoyne enter one to represent them."

"But it's for kids, right?"

"No, it's for men."

"Drunk men," Joker added.

"So, it's just an excuse for a bunch of drunkards to mess about, then, is it?"

"No!" Gary insisted, slightly offended. "It's a proper sport. They have it on the longest, steepest street in the district, and they hold proper heats and everything!"

"Ooh, sounds very professional."

"I don't think you'll be able to go to much of the Fleadh this year, Gary," Rosie pointed out. "The baby's only going to be a couple of weeks old by then."

Gary, who had yet to fully appreciate the impact that a new baby was going to be having on his life, stared uncomprehendingly at Rosie. "I don't see why that would be a problem," he said.

"Well, we can't just go out and leave a new-born baby with somebody else, can we? For one thing, Ellie works long shifts, and your mummy has her own things to worry about, so I –"

"Yes, yes," said Gary, waving away Rosie's concerns. "Don't worry about it, love. I'm sure we'll be able to work something out."

Rosie stared at Gary and then quietly took a sip of her drink. There was no point in trying to reason with him, she decided. He would, after all, be having his eyes opened soon enough.

SEVEN

On Monday morning, Rosie had just got off the phone to her father when there was a quick knock at the door. Before Rosie could shout a reply, it was pushed open and Karen entered.

"All right there, Rosie love?" she said. "I'm just going up the road here to get some messages in for the match. Do you want me to get you anything?"

Rosie looked thoughtfully at Karen. For anyone in Ardoyne, *going up the road* meant a trip to the row of shops fronting the main road that passed by the northern edge of the district. It was where the people of Ardoyne got their *messages*, or, in other words, did their shopping, and it was also where people could meet acquaintances, to socialize and to chat and to pass on any gossip there might be.

"Is it okay if I come with you?" Rosie asked as she eased herself off her chair.

"Are you sure?" asked Karen. "I thought you'd just want to put your feet up."

"No, I could do with getting out of the house," sighed Rosie, leaning against the mantelpiece. "I won't need a coat, will I?"

"No, it's lovely out," said Karen. "I suppose a wee walk will do you good."

Rosie grabbed her keys, her purse and a small shopping bag, and she and Karen stepped outside with Rosie pulling the front door closed behind them. It wasn't far to the shops, but Rosie struggled to walk at her normal pace, so Karen adjusted her own pace to keep in step. There was no rush, however, and, as Karen had mentioned, it was a lovely day, with just a few light clouds in the sky and a warm sun that felt good on Rosie's face.

"So, you had a good time on Friday, then?" asked Karen as they walked. "Over at Carol's?"

"Yeah, it was a good laugh," Rosie replied with a smile. "I got on really well with Carol and Claire."

"Aye, Carol's lovely, so she is," said Karen. "I don't really know Claire."

"I think you'd like her. She's really down to earth. I think Tony's bringing her to the wedding, so you'll probably meet her there."

"What about your hen night?"

"What hen night?"

"Rosie, you have to have a hen night!" cried Karen. "I've been looking forward to it."

"Do you not think I've got enough on my plate without having to worry about a bloody hen night?"

"Don't worry about it, then. Just let me organise it."

"You? Really?"

"Aye, why not?"

"But what about the baby?" asked Rosie. "It'll only be a couple of weeks old, won't it?"

"Why can't our Gary look after it?" demanded Karen. "The useless fucker!"

"Isn't that sort of answering your own question?"

Karen stared at Rosie and then burst out laughing. "Aye, I suppose it is," she said. "But he's going to have to learn sometime, isn't he? Anyway, your daddy will be around to help out."

"I don't know if he will," said Rosie.

"What do you mean?"

"Well, he was planning to get the ferry over at the end of next week, but he was telling me that the coach drivers are all planning to go on strike around about that time, so he's not sure how he's going to get up to Liverpool."

They turned the corner onto the pedestrianised area in front of the shops and decided to head first to the bakery. Karen spotted one of her neighbours and waved to her.

"All right there, Maeve love?" she called out. "How's it going?"

Maeve gave a weak smile and nodded to Karen and Rosie before disappearing into the butcher's shop.

"Maeve looks awful tired," said Rosie.

"Aye, God love her," agreed Karen. "She's run off her feet with that wee job of hers." As they approached the bakery Karen looked at Rosie. "Can your daddy not get the train?" she asked.

"Probably," Rosie replied, "but it would cost a fortune, and he's not sure he wants to spend that much money just to get to the ferry." They carried on into the bakery and when they came out, Karen said she needed to go to the greengrocers for some vegetables to make a stew.

"I might have an idea for my daddy," said Rosie as they stood in the queue for the grocers, "but I'll have to have a think about it."

"Aye, I'm sure you'll work something out," said Karen. "So, do you want me to organise your hen night, then?"

Rosie laughed. "Aye, why not?" she said. "Go ahead!"

Karen was suddenly brimming with ideas. Once she had paid for her vegetables, and she and Rosie were making their way to the news-agents, she began reeling off names. "It'll have to be a night that Ellie's off," she said, "unless she can take some holiday. I'll have to ask her. And what's your mate's name, Sheila, is it? From the Short Strand? I can give her a ring. And I'm sure my ma will be up for it." Rosie just smiled to herself, content to let Karen ramble on. "I could ask Marina too, couldn't I? And Carol, she's game for anything. What about Claire, then?"

"I don't see why not."

"Hannah?"

Rosie stopped. "Oh," she said. "I hadn't even thought about Hannah."

"To be honest," said Karen, "it may not be her type of thing."

"No, probably not," Rosie conceded, "but there's no harm in asking, is there?"

"No harm at all."

After the newsagents, they made a quick stop at the butcher's and then set off for home. Karen, excited by her new project, chattered happily about dates and guests and venues while Rosie ambled along beside her, quietly happy just to listen and to give the occasional nod.

On reaching Rosie's gate, Karen took her leave and told Rosie she'd be in touch.

"Oh aye," said Karen as she turned to walk away, "what's your plan for getting your daddy to Liverpool, then?"

"I can't really say," Rosie told her. "I still have to think of a way to break it to Gary."

EIGHT

Hannah was filled with a new sense of optimism. Having been troubled lately by feelings of unease, she was now looking forward to the upcoming festival as a new beginning. It would be, she hoped, an opportunity to consolidate her wavering faith, and a way to bolster and strengthen the beliefs that had shaped her life. She was excited by the prospect.

She had come to view the little doubts that had been clouding her thoughts as a sign she had stumbled onto the wrong path. A path that was leading her away from Jesus Christ, from God and from the one true faith. Sensing a need to get back on track, she felt that the festival had come along at just the right time.

The *Festival of the Light of Jesus Christ* was to be a celebration of Christian faith. Christians from all over the United Kingdom would descend on the cathedral city of Winchester, in the south of England, to share, to discuss, to debate and to pray. The youth group from Hannah's Church had already booked to attend and everyone was making excited preparations for the trip.

For Hannah, it had become a welcome distraction. It had provided her with something else to focus on, something that could occupy her mind and give her some – albeit brief – respite from the constant thoughts of James. She had already made her choice, she believed, but that had not stopped the images of James' face swimming suddenly into view. It had not stopped the feelings, the emotions, the stirrings and the unsettling urges. It had not stopped the longing.

She was walking back from town, swinging a few carrier bags that were filled with purchases for the upcoming trip, and thinking about what she hoped to gain from the festival. She was expecting to have her decision to stop seeing James validated by the experience, which gave her some comfort, but she knew that any sense of optimism would always be tempered by regret. It couldn't be helped, though, she thought. James' beliefs were so wrong, they bordered on blasphemy, and Hannah knew she could never be content with anyone who did not fully accept the truth of Scripture.

Making her way past the Queen's University's Lanyon Building, Hannah felt her pulse quicken as she spied, across the road, a familiar figure heading for the University Bookshop. She smiled to herself. She didn't know anyone other than James who would visit a bookstore so soon after term had ended. Just about every other student from the university would be looking forward to a long, lazy summer, but James, she knew, was made of sterner stuff.

She could still not quite fathom the extent of James' reading habits. For most of her life, reading had been confined to the Bible or to literature related to the Bible which, for Hannah, had always been a limitless source of interest and enquiry. She sensed, though, that James had been exasperated by her adherence to such a narrow literary path.

But what, she wondered, could be more fascinating or more important than Scripture? She knew that she had recently become intrigued by the mysteries of cosmology, but she reconciled this by seeing it as a way of appreciating the full scope of God's Creation. Everything in Hannah's life was in some way connected to understanding the message of God, and she simply could not understand how someone as intelligent as James could throw away their abilities on matters that were – compared to securing your own salvation – inconsequential.

As she continued on her way towards the bus stop, hoping to catch the next bus for her hometown of Saintfield, thoughts began to form in her head and she gradually slowed until she was struck – thunderstruck – by a sudden revelation. She stopped dead.

Could it be that she didn't have to make a choice? Was it possible that she could have both God *and* James? Maybe this was her true calling, she thought excitedly. To bring James into the light. Hannah, standing dead still in the middle of the pavement, was filled with a sudden and overwhelming belief that the approaching festival would grant her the confidence and the zeal she needed to convince James of the truth and, in doing so, save his very soul. And in the process, of course, she would entwine his heart with hers.

Dizzy with a whole new world of possibilities, she strode over to the nearby pedestrian crossing and pushed the little silver button. Then, once the traffic had come to a halt, she hurried eagerly across the road.

Jamesy did not quite have the shop to himself, but he was the only person browsing in the Ancient History section that occupied the far left corner of the ground floor. He frowned at the rather paltry selection of titles on offer concerning the subject on which he was hoping to base his PhD thesis; the ancient style of writing that was known as *cuneiform*.

On the one hand, he was encouraged by the scarcity of literature on the topic. It meant that he would not be entering a crowded field, and he could be sure to find plenty of uncovered ground in a subject that, after all, had spanned three thousand years of human history. On the other hand, though, he was disheartened by the seeming lack of interest in what was one of the most crucial stages in the development of humanity, in a part of the world where western civilisation had been born. Still, he told himself with unwarranted optimism, perhaps his thesis would, in some small way, reinvigorate the field of Assyriology. Maybe his work would even ignite, in the public consciousness, a new-found sense of curious fascination with the extensive collection of cuneiform writings that had made their way down through the millennia to illuminate life in the distant past. Jamesy smiled at such a fanciful notion. The wild fantasies of a history student.

He pulled a slim volume from the shelf in front of him and idly flicked through the pages of glossy photographs. It was a book, he quickly realised, that lacked any real depth, giving only a broad outline of the development of cuneiform and mentioning just two of the languages that used that form of writing. Jamesy was mildly annoyed by this. He knew that the vast majority of cuneiform tablets that had been discovered were written in either Sumerian or Akkadian, but that was no reason to ignore all of the other –

"Anything interesting?" Jamesy, startled, spun around and found himself caught in the full beam of Hannah's smile.

"Hannah?" he stammered. "What are you –?"

"I saw you coming in here," she told him, "so I thought I'd follow you in. Are you after anything in particular?"

"What? Oh, no, not really. I was just looking for something that I could … oh, it doesn't really matter." Jamesy closed the book and placed it back on the shelf. "It's not important," he said, giving Hannah a hesitant smile. "What about *you*? You keeping all right? How did your exams go?"

"Yeah, okay," said Hannah. "At least I think so."

"Mmm, that's … that's good."

"And how have *you* been?"

"Yeah, yeah, okay really." Jamesy gave a little shrug. "Well, you know, as well as can be expected."

"Mmm …" Hannah, Jamesy thought, looked suddenly distracted.

"You okay?"

"What? Oh, yeah, yeah, I'm fine. It's just …" Hannah looked into Jamesy's pale blue eyes. "It's just that … well, I'm going to be going over to England soon, and I was thinking –"

"England? Really?" Jamesy interrupted. "That's funny. So am I."

Hannah stared at him. *Could this be a sign?* she wondered. "You're going to England?"

"Yeah, next week."

"Whereabouts?"

"London."

"London?" Hannah cried excitedly. "I'm going to be in London for a bit as well. I'll be flying back from Heathrow, so we're going to be spending the day in –"

"Why? Where is it you're going?"

"What? Oh, we're going to Hampshire," said Hannah. "To Winchester."

"Winchester?" Jamesy was puzzled. "What for?"

"It's for a national festival of faith. I'm going with my church group."

"Oh. Oh right, okay."

"So, do you think you'll be in London on the sixth?"

"The sixth of July?" Jamesy thought for a moment. "Yeah, actually.

I'll be there on the sixth."

It was a sign, Hannah decided gleefully. It had to be a sign that God was showing His approval of her plan. She thought quickly. "Why don't we meet up?" she said eagerly.

"In London?"

"Why not? I was hoping I'd be able to see you when I got back anyway, but this way I can see you as soon as the festival is finished."

"Um, okay I suppose. What do you suggest?"

"Don't know," said Hannah happily. "I'll have a think about it and let you know."

"Yeah, all right," said Jamesy, unsure of Hannah's motivation. "I'll look forward to it."

They chatted for a few minutes more until Hannah flashed another blazing smile at Jamesy and hurried on her way. Jamesy stood alone and bewildered, staring blankly at the rows of books. He reached out half-heartedly for one of the titles on Mesopotamia, but then let his arm fall limply back to his side. He could no longer concentrate. He just didn't understand women, he thought sadly.

And he walked home confused.

NINE

2,237 years earlier

The Arsehole of Nowhere

The horse stumbled on the loose scree of the narrow path that led toward the high peaks. She turned her head to give her rider a reproving glance, but he was keeping his eyes focused on the way ahead. She turned back to the path and continued to pick her way gingerly up the steep slope.

Pillarchus was well aware of his horse's unhappiness – he'd been with her long enough to know her moods – but he refused to give her the satisfaction of making him feel guilty. He did sympathise with her misery, though. He was miserable himself. His right hand was throbbing – though he could still grip the reins tightly enough with his fingers – but it was more than that that was causing his bleak mood. It had not been long after he had set off on this trek into the mountains that he had started to have doubts. In fact, as soon he had watched the caravan head on without him, he began to have some deep misgivings about the wisdom of his decision. There was safety with the caravan, he thought, not to mention comfort and good company, whereas the mountains, with their hostile tribes and difficult terrain, held any number of hidden dangers.

"Is it much further?" he asked his companion. The little, dark-skinned guide grinned at Pillarchus' discomfort. His own horse moved more easily over the rocky ground than Pillarchus' mare, and even the donkey that followed behind, tethered to the guide's horse, seemed unbothered by the steep track.

"No, not too far," the guide replied. He spoke Greek, though it was stilted and heavily accented, making it difficult for Pillarchus to fully understand him. "We will be there before nightfall."

"Nightfall?" Pillarchus shivered, though the morning sun was climbing high in the sky. He had hoped to be well on his way back to the caravan by nightfall. He was regretting his decision more with every step. Would it be worth it, he wondered, though he suspected he knew the answer to that. How could it possibly be worth it?

Pillarchus had been away from his home for almost three years now. He had been travelling in the company of a scribe, named Glauca, at the behest of his teacher, Valleron, who had once been a pupil of the famous priest, Berossus.

Pillarchus and Glauca had been charged with seeking out and recording the knowledge of the land that lay beyond the eastern mountains, which was due, Pillarchus was sure, to Valleron's envy of the fame that Berossus had achieved with his written account of the history of the land between the great rivers. Berossus had compiled his history for the glory of his patron and his king; Antiochus I, and Pillarchus suspected that Valleron was determined to do the same for the present king; Antiochus II.

Still, Pillarchus decided, it was a worthwhile endeavour, regardless of the motivation, and he and Glauca had gone about their task with enthusiasm and diligence. It was in just the past few weeks that they had finally used up their precious supply of papyrus and had then decided to return to give their final report to Valleron in the city of Seleucia, far to the west.

As they made their way west, they happened to fall in with one of the trade caravans that criss-crossed the plains, following the ancient routes that linked the east to the west. It was a slow but pleasant way to travel and Pillarchus had developed a fondness for those evenings when they stopped to pitch tents, to dine and to drink wine, to play music and to laugh and to dance. And to fall in and out of love.

He had lately caught the eye of a dark beauty, travelling with a merchant who traded in rare silks from the east, and he had spent more than a few joyous occasions in her company. That was where he should be now, he thought unhappily, safe with friends, his belly full of good wine and his face buried deep in soft, dusky skin that smelled of perfume and spice and exotic silk.

He leaned forward to give his horse a reassuring pat on the neck and she whinnied softly in response. As they climbed higher, Pillarchus caught sight of some shy little musk deer, glancing back nervously as they fled at the strangers' approach. An occasional ibex could also be seen, leaping easily over the rocks of the high slopes to their left, but apart from these few sightings, the mountains seemed eerily lifeless. The silence was broken only by the slow clopping of hooves on hard ground, which seemed shockingly loud in the still morning air. It was not yet noon but already Pillarchus was sweating uncomfortably. It was more than just the heat, though, that was making him sweat. He was also keenly aware of the bandits that roamed these hills and, once again, he cursed his own foolishness.

When Pillarchus had first heard the rumour, he had dismissed it as nonsense. It had been in a small town that lay nestled in the main pass through the mountains, where the caravan had paused for a few days to rest and to trade with the townspeople, that he first became aware of the story. At something of a loose end, Pillarchus had filled his time by getting to know the locals; a habit he had acquired from his knowledge-gathering mission of the past few years. He had become reasonably competent in the languages of the Indus valley during his time east of the mountains, but he struggled with the dialects of the mountain tribes, and he had had to employ the help of some of the traders from the caravan. It was then, as he discussed the history of the town with one of the elders, that the tale came out.

The elder had told Pillarchus of a woman who lived in a remote village high above the pass. She was old and blind and was living out her years surrounded by her children and her many grandchildren. The enduring legend of this old woman was that, as a young girl, she had once served in the court of the Golden King.

Pillarchus had immediately scoffed at the idea. The Golden King, he knew, had died many years before Pillarchus had even been born, so even if someone had just been a child at the time they would now have to be almost impossibly ancient. The story, however, persisted.

By the time the caravan had set off once again, Pillarchus had heard the same tale from a variety of different sources and, his curiosity now piqued, he decided to seek the opinion of the local guide, Targa, who had joined the caravan during the approach to the pass.

"Oh yes, it is quite true," Targa told him in clumsy, broken Greek. "Her village lies just north of here, though much higher up in the mountains."

"Have you met her?"

"No," Targa admitted, "but I know where her village is situated, and I have often come across members of her family as they travel throughout the high valleys. Her name is Lianah, and they say she came from far off in the west, many, many years ago."

As Pillarchus thought more on the matter, his curiosity grew. The idea that someone still living may once have been in the presence of the Golden King teased continually at his mind until it was in danger of becoming an obsession. He eventually sought out his old travelling companion, the scribe, Glauca, who was now travelling in the company of a fair-skinned boy that he had purchased soon after he and Pillarchus had joined the caravan.

"I don't know what you expect of me, Pillarchus," Glauca drawled lazily. They were perched comfortably on large cushions, sitting in the glow of a campfire that some of the traders had set up to burn through the night while the caravan stopped to rest. Glauca's young boy was snuggled beside him, dozing happily with his head in Glauca's lap.

"But don't you see?" Pillarchus exclaimed. "It is the chance to look through the eyes of someone who once stood before the living god!"

"According to the stories of primitive tribespeople," Glauca pointed out.

"Well, yes, but the stories must have come from somewhere."

"Even if the stories are true," said Glauca, "I see no reason to deviate from our path just to hear the mutterings of someone who would have been nothing more than a girl at the time. What could she possibly have to say that would be of interest to Valleron?"

"But surely –"

"And besides," Glauca went on, "we have used up all of the papyrus that we had brought with us."

"There are merchants in the caravan who would sell us papyrus," said Pillarchus.

Glauca laughed, disturbing the boy in his lap. He picked up a goblet of wine from a low table by his side and raised it in salute to Pillarchus before taking a gulp. "Yes, my friend," he exclaimed happily, "we could indeed purchase papyrus from the caravan merchants because we are both such wealthy men, are we not?"

Pillarchus stole a quick glance at the boy drowsing by Glauca's side. A boy with such flawless pale skin, he knew, would not have been cheap, but he decided to hold his tongue. He was aware of just how much his own finances had dwindled over the last three years of travelling and he knew that he would baulk at the idea of squandering what was left on expensive papyrus imported from Egypt.

"Most of the traders here use river clay," ventured Pillarchus.

"Ha!" Glauca snorted with disdain. "You expect me to scratch in the dirt like a chicken?"

"I've seen you use clay before," said Pillarchus. "And wax as well, so you're just –"

"It is of no consequence," Glauca insisted. "It does not matter because I have no interest in going looking for this mythical creature." He leaned forward. "Remember, my friend, we are very much in the arsehole of nowhere here, and I, for one, am eager to return to civilisation. I just want to go home."

Pillarchus nodded slowly as he drank his wine. He mostly agreed with Glauca. They had been away from home for long enough now, and he too was looking forward to gazing once more on the rich green land between the great rivers. But, he thought, there was still a part of him that yearned to find this Lianah. Just to see, to touch, to simply be near someone who had once looked upon the god who had walked amongst men would be an experience that he could recount to his children and to his grandchildren.

Such a meeting, however, would have to be recorded. Valleron, Pillarchus knew, would demand nothing less than a written account of Lianah's testimony, but a written account, without Glauca, could prove to be a problem. Pillarchus looked down at his right hand and cursed his own drunken stupidity. It had been about a week earlier when, returning to his tent late at night, he had stumbled and then slid down a steep, rocky bank, clutching at a sharp rock and ripping open his thumb as he tried to save himself. The caravan's physician had done a good job of patching it up, but it was now strapped tightly against Pillarchus' right hand, making it impossible for him to hold a stylus.

"Of course, you're free to go yourself," said Glauca. "I won't try to stop you, but don't expect to take any of the packhorses with you. We can't afford to lose even one in these damned mountains."

"There's no point in just me going, though, is there?" Pillarchus grumbled, holding up his injured hand to the firelight.

"Well, you could always use that little mountain-goat you've got friendly with," said Glauca. He shifted his position to make himself more comfortable, then held his wine towards the waking boy to let him to take a sip. "He was once a scribe, you know."

"Who?" Pillarchus demanded. "You mean Targa?"

"Is that his name?" Glauca asked with little interest. "Yes," he said, "I am led to believe that, in his youth, he trained with the priests along the Indus, and then went on to serve at the courts there for some years."

"Targa can read and write?" asked Pillarchus, dumbfounded.

"Well, up to a point, I suppose."

"How do you know this?"

"By doing what we've both been doing for the last three years," Glauca explained wearily. "By asking questions."

"Oh, yes, of course." Pillarchus now had something to think about. The idea of setting off into the mountains in wild pursuit of something that was little more than a rumour had, up until then, been just that: an idea. It had been an exercise in abstract possibilities that Pillarchus had not seriously entertained, knowing, as he did, that Glauca would never agree to it.

Now, though, Glauca had shown him a way to make the idea become a reality and Pillarchus was not sure how he felt about it. He poured himself some wine and made himself comfortable in the warm glow of the campfire, and, as he watched Glauca drunkenly fondle his little plaything, he let his mind drift away into the distant past. To a sumptuous golden palace, snatched from mighty Persia by the son of Zeus. He pictured a young girl, tiptoeing barefoot across marble floors that shimmered in the glow of a thousand oil-lamps, her shadow flickering across walls richly covered in gold and jade and lapis lazuli, with the heady perfumes of orchids and lilies swimming through the warm night air.

What had she seen? he wondered. *What had she heard?* The thick, sweet wine massaged his imagination and Pillarchus began to picture himself way back then in the old city of Babylon where the God-King had spent his final days. The light of Babylon might now be dimmed, he thought, but it had at one time shone with an intensity that dazzled the world, and Pillarchus could see himself strolling through the streets and broad avenues that had once been witness to the machinations of emperors.

And the greatest of all those emperors, thought Pillarchus, was now within tantalizing reach. A living link to the spirit of the Golden King, the Son of Zeus-Ammon, the King of all Kings was here, he felt, in these wild and desolate mountains, a thousand leagues from Babylon, and all he had to do was reach out and grasp it. The fantasies and the ghosts of gods spun around in his head, faster and faster until, eventually, the empty wine cup slipped from his hand and Pillarchus rolled gently onto his side where he burbled into a happy sleep.

And dreamed of Alexander.

TEN

Rosie could not believe her luck. She had conceived of her plan shortly after speaking to her father on the phone that morning, and had gone over it in her head until she was convinced that it was perfect. Unfortunately, she was not the one that needed to be convinced, and so she had spent her time agonising over the various ways in which she could broach the subject and come up with a convincing method of persuasion. It was a problem that had plagued her throughout the day, but now, as she watched Gary and Seamus stumble around in the garden, she realised it might now be a problem that could easily be resolved. For Gary and Seamus were both now very drunk. And happy. And pliable.

Gary had called in earlier for a late lunch after work. He had already made arrangements to go and watch the football up in the Star, so he had just had time to quickly wolf down a few sandwiches before he headed back out. Rosie hadn't given it much thought, preoccupied, as she was, with her father's problems. She was aware of the significance of that day's match – she had been reminded of it often enough over the past few days – but the consequences that it might bring to bear on her own schemes had yet to occur to her.

It would be, she had been told, the biggest occasion in the history of Irish football. The Republic of Ireland's football team, in their first ever World Cup tournament, was one game away from reaching the quarter-finals, and Northern Ireland's nationalist community – feeling more of an affinity with the Republic than with the unionist-slanted team from Northern Ireland – was determined to cheer them on.

Rosie had been taking only a passing interest in the tournament. She had found the Republic's progress through the group stage – with three draws – to be rather boring, but it had been unavoidable, and she had been forced to sit through most of the tournament, finding genuine enjoyment only through the fearless, free-flowing football of Cameroon.

She could not deny, though, the very real sense of excitement that seemed to be pulsing through the air in Ardoyne ever since Ireland had got through to the knockout stages. It seemed that just about everyone in the district, and throughout Ireland, would be planted in front of a television this afternoon – everyone, that is, apart from the thousands of fans who had made the journey to the stadium in Genoa to watch their team take on Romania, and who now sat singing and chanting in the hot Italian sun.

"How did the match go?" asked Ellie when she got home from work.

"It's still going on," replied Rosie. The television had been left on in the background so that Rosie could be vaguely aware of what was happening. "It was a draw, so I think they're playing an extra half an hour."

"What do you want to do about dinner?"

"Karen brought round a big pot of stew," said Rosie. "She said she'd made far too much."

"Oh, God love her!" cried Ellie. "That's dinner sorted, then. Is Gary up in the Star?"

"Yeah, I think he was meeting Seamus," said Rosie. "You know, I was talking to daddy this morning, and –" The final whistle blew, and Ellie and Rosie turned to the television.

"So, it finished nil-nil?" said Ellie.

"What happens now, then? There has to be a winner today, doesn't there?"

"I think it might be penalties."

The sisters sat quietly and watched as the two teams' penalty-takers were allocated. Each side would take five penalty kicks and if the score was still level after that, then it would go to 'sudden death', where penalties would continue until the deadlock was broken.

Romania would go first and, as the ball was placed on the penalty spot, the stadium became hushed and tense. The first penalty-taker would be Romania's Gheorghe Hagi. He took a short run up and calmly slotted the ball past Packie Bonnar, the Irish goalkeeper.

One-nil to Romania.

"Shit!" hissed Rosie. The TV screen was now filled with crowds of Romanian fans wildly cheering and waving their country's colours in a sudden explosion of relief from the oppressive tension. Ellie and Rosie leaned forward in their seats. They watched as Kevin Sheedy walked up and placed the ball on the spot for Ireland's first kick. Packie Bonnar walked slowly from the goal to be replaced by his Romanian counterpart. The Romanian fans had erupted in joyful celebration of Hagi's goal, but now, once more, the stadium had fallen quiet.

"Jesus, I don't know if I can bear to watch this," said Rosie, staring avidly at the screen. Ellie nodded. The tension of the moment was beginning to take a grip on both sisters.

Big Jack Charlton, the Republic of Ireland's English manager stood by the side of the pitch, his face impassive, pensive, unreadable. And then, as if oblivious to the occasion, Kevin Sheedy simply ran up and scored.

One-one.

"Yes!" Rosie and Ellie screamed as one. The massed ranks of Irish fans behind the goal disappeared beneath a flurry of green, white and orange. Scarves, flags, shirts and even shorts and flip-flops were flung into the air as the tension, if only for a moment, found sudden release. The noisy delirium carried on for a few minutes more until, with the ball back on the penalty spot for Romania's next attempt, another nervy hush descended.

Romania scored.

Two-one.

"Fuck off!" Rosie yelled at the screen.

"Rosie!" Ellie scolded, though she agreed with the sentiment.

Ray Houghton then equalised for Ireland, unleashing another few moments of mayhem.

Two-two.

Romania replied.

Three-two.

"Bastards!"

"Rosie!"

The delicious torture continued with another Irish goal.

Three-three.

"Jesus Christ!" Rosie muttered, unconsciously rubbing her knuckles against her clenched lips. She then put her head in her hands when Romania scored again.

Four-three.

"Come on, Ireland," Ellie whispered. The drama was both compelling and unbearable. A tiny patch of Italian soil was now the sole focus for the entire populations of both Ireland and Romania, as they looked on with equal measures of hope and dread.

Ireland scored.

Four-four.

The two girls were both now shaking with adrenalin, and the relief of the equaliser came almost as a shock. Each team had now just one kick remaining and, with the score level, the match was effectively already down to 'sudden death'.

Daniel Timofte was Romania's fifth penalty-taker. He positioned the ball on the little white spot and then took a few steps back. The air that still hung around inside the stadium was hot and jaded as if worn down by the heavy, unrelenting atmosphere. Timofte seemed almost bored. Without bothering to take any real run-up, he loped lazily up to the ball and swept it contemptuously towards the goal.

And Patrick 'Packie' Bonnar, from County Donegal, with equal contempt, pushed it off to the side. No goal.

Four-four.

Hearts stopped. And then the world erupted. Ellie, without realising, had jumped to her feet, yelling with excitement. Rosie, screaming and with her eyes wide, was punching the air with both fists. Ellie grabbed Rosie's arms and pulled her up from the sofa, and the two sisters jumped and danced with joy as the floorboards shook beneath them.

Taking a look through the windows of the houses across the street, Rosie could see the same unfettered celebrations taking place in every home, with people jumping up and down, arms waving, and with all sorts of objects – including small children – sailing through the air.

But it was not over yet. There was still one kick left to take.

Eventually the celebrations subsided, and Ellie and Rosie, just like every other person in Ireland, sat slowly down and once more gazed entranced at their television screen.

If Ireland could score their fifth penalty, then they would win the match and would progress to the quarter-finals. If not, then the agony would continue.

The pressure, thought Rosie, on the shoulders of David O'Leary, as he positioned the ball, must surely be immense. How could anyone, she wondered, behave normally, knowing that even the slightest move you made was under the most intense scrutiny from every single person in your homeland? How could anyone even *think* straight under such circumstances?

The rich glow of a Mediterranean evening shone from the corner of the little living room in north Belfast and the soft tones of the commentator whispered from the speaker.

A nation holds its breath.

Time slowed. O'Leary seemed to take forever to place the ball on its spot. He would set it down, then, not satisfied, he would pick it up and put it back down again. *That's not a good sign*, thought Rosie. The referee stood beside O'Leary, keen to hurry things along. Finally, the Irish player seemed happy with the ball's position and he stood to prepare himself with some slow, deep breaths and a quick glance towards the Romanian goalkeeper who now loomed impossibly large in the tiny goal.

After what seemed like a silent, frozen eternity, David O'Leary took his penalty kick.

And broke Romanian hearts.

Four-five.

Rosie wasn't quite sure what Gary and Seamus were playing at as she watched them perform some haphazard laps of the garden before they staggered towards the front door. She then heard them tumble into the hallway. After a few moments, the door to the living room was flung open.

"Woman of the house!" Gary shouted as he entered. "Where's me tay?" He then flung an imaginary cap across the room to land on an imaginary hatstand.

Seamus followed Gary into the room and closed the door behind him. He stood to attention, swaying slightly, with his back to the door. "God bless all here!" he exclaimed tearfully in a voice choked with emotion.

"All right there, Seamus?" said Ellie. "We've got plenty of stew, if you fancy it."

"Thank you, ma'am."

"Did you enjoy the match, then?" Rosie asked Gary. Gary stared at her, suspecting he was being accused of something.

"Oh right," he said, remembering that, for once, he was entirely innocent. "Yeah, it was bloody brilliant! Jesus, the Star went mad!"

"I'm sure," said Ellie. "I think the whole district went mad."

"Well, we've set the kitchen table," Rosie said sweetly. "So if you want to come through, we can all sit down to dinner together."

They went through to the kitchen and sat down at the table. Ellie ladled the stew into four bowls and passed them around.

"Your Karen made the stew," Rosie told Gary. "It's lovely. I had some earlier."

"Nice one," said Gary, spooning the food into his mouth. "I'm starving."

"Was it busy up in the Star?" Ellie asked Seamus, who was also hungrily gobbling down the stew.

"Aye, it was packed," he told her in between mouthfuls. "And the drink was flying. They must have made an absolute fortune today."

The stew was soon all gone and Ellie got up to make tea for everyone. Gary lit up a cigarette and leaned forward, resting his elbows on the table.

"Yeah, that was some result," he murmured happily. "I don't think David O'Leary will ever have to buy another drink for the rest of his life."

"Mmm," said Rosie.

"Or Packie Bonnar either, for that matter."

Ellie put down four cups of tea on the table along with a bowl of sugar. "You still off the cigarettes, Seamus?" she asked.

"I'm not really off them," said Seamus. "I'm just trying to cut down a bit."

"Good for you!"

"You know," Rosie ventured, "I actually had a bit of bad news today."

"Really?" asked Gary. "What was that?"

"Well, you know that my daddy was planning to come back home next week, don't you?"

"Yeah, so?"

Rosie shook her head sadly. "Well, it looks like he won't be able to make it. The coach-drivers are going on strike, and he can't afford to get a train all the way up to Liverpool." Rosie sighed and threw up her hands as if the whole situation was completely hopeless.

Gary, filled with drunken concern for the woman he loved, looked affronted on her behalf. In his addled state, he saw himself swooping to the rescue of his fiancée, who was clearly at her wit's end. Poor, sweet, innocent Rosie, he thought. She just wasn't capable of thinking outside the box. She didn't possess the necessary mental agility to overcome such a conundrum.

No, he decided, it would be down to him to step forward and save the day. It would be he, Gary, who would banish the worry from Rosie's eyes and instead fill those eyes with hope. *Cometh the hour, Cometh the man*, he thought. Or rather, he decided, *Cometh the hour, Cometh the hero*.

"Seamus can drive him," he declared heroically.

"What?" asked Seamus. He had been taking little interest in the conversation and had, in fact, been wondering whether he would be able to make it home tonight without falling through someone's garden hedge along the way.

"Drive him?" Rosie asked Gary with wide-eyed innocence. "What do you mean?"

"Seamus is driving over to England around about then, so he could –"

"Oh, that's right!" cried Rosie, putting a hand to her chest. "I'd forgotten all about that!" Ellie gave Rosie an accusing look, which Rosie ignored.

"What was that?" asked Seamus, struggling to keep his thoughts in focus.

"Rosie's da," said Gary to the hazy outline that he guessed was Seamus, "is going to need a lift up to Liverpool. And you'll be coming back from London at the time so you –"

"No, Seamus," Rosie insisted. "It's too far out of your way. You'd have to drive all the way down to the south coast of England, so really, don't worry about it."

Seamus gathered together all of the indignation he could muster and fixed Rosie with a hard stare. Chivalry was not dead, he told himself, not as long as he, Seamus Green, was still drawing a breath. He slammed the palm of his hand on the table, making Gary jump. "I insist!" he exclaimed. "I will absolutely hear no more about it. I will –"

"No really, Seamus, don't worry about it," said Rosie. "For one thing, you don't really know my daddy all that well, and he still suffers from anxiety, so I think there would have to be somebody there that he's comfortable with." Rosie shot Gary a furtive glance, silently urging his barely functioning brain to join up the dots. Eventually, after what seemed like forever, a tiny gleam shone blearily in Gary's eyes.

"Hey," he said, "I've got an idea. Why don't I go as well?"

"What?" asked Rosie, feigning surprise. To her side she could sense Ellie's cold glare, but she carried on regardless. "Jesus, Gary, I never would have thought of that." She suspected that she might be laying it on a bit thick, but she felt that Gary was in no state to appreciate subtlety. "That's actually a really good idea."

Gary sat back with a smug look on his face. He gave a dismissive wave of his hand, as if coming up with good ideas was something that, for him, came naturally. Seamus, however, frowned.

"I'm not sure, actually," he said. "Jamesy wants to come too, you know."

"Jamesy's going?" Gary slurred. "You never told me that!"

"I don't have to tell you everything!" Seamus told him flatly.

"I know, but –"

"All right, all right," said Rosie hastily. She was well aware of how easy it was for these two idiots to become distracted. She needed to keep them focused. "But you've got that lovely big new car, haven't you, Seamus?"

"Well, that's true," said Seamus. He had recently taken possession of a Ford Granada estate, which he was planning to use to ferry stock to and from his newsagent's shop. It was almost brand new, and he had got a good deal on it from someone that he knew in the district. It was still just a five-seater like his previous car, but there was a lot more room in the back. He was pleased with the purchase and was happy to show it off at any opportunity. "I suppose there's room for one more," he said. "And Sean and Bobby will be staying in London, so there would only be four of us coming back."

"Oh, I don't know," sighed Rosie. "It all sounds like an awful lot of trouble for you, Seamus. And, Gary, you'd have to take a bit more holiday, wouldn't you?"

"I don't see why that would be a problem," said Gary expansively. He was feeling rather pleased with himself, believing that his brilliant solution had just fixed everything for Rosie and her father.

"Don't you worry about a thing, Rosie love!" said Seamus sternly as he pointed a finger across the table. "Me and Gary will get your daddy back," he fixed Rosie with a serious stare, "or die trying."

Gary looked quizzically at Seamus. "Well, I don't think –"

"Awk, Seamus love, if you're really sure."

"I insist! I absolutely insist!"

"That would be brilliant!" cried Rosie. "Oh my God, see you two!" she grinned and shook her head in wonder. "You're just the best! You really are!"

Gary pushed himself back in his chair to fully bask in his fiancée's adoration. He could tell she was awestruck by his cleverness, and by his quick, no-nonsense decision-making. He raised his arms in a lazy, nonchalant stretch.

"Well," he said, "now that that's all sorted, I should head off to bed. Early start in the morning."

"Yeah, I should head on too," said Seamus. He took a while to get to his feet and then, after being helped to the door by Ellie, he stumbled off into the night. Rosie helped Gary up from the table and then saw him upstairs and safely into bed. When she came back downstairs, she saw Ellie sitting in one of the armchairs in the living room. Their eyes met, but neither girl spoke. Rosie picked up the TV remote-control from a side-table and sat down on the sofa. She switched on the television and began idly flicking through the channels. After a while she turned to meet Ellie's bemused gaze. Rosie shrugged.

"Like shooting fish in a barrel," she said.

ELEVEN

Harry put down the phone and went back to reading his newspaper. He wasn't sure how he felt about the persistent attention he had been receiving lately and had therefore been deliberately evasive during the call.

On the one hand, he supposed, it was an interesting proposal and it could end up being rather lucrative, but on the other hand, Harry liked to keep his life as simple as possible. He could do without all the extra work that such a new arrangement would bring.

"Was that your man, McClelland, on the phone again?" asked Karen as she came through from the kitchen.

"Aye, for God's sake," Harry replied. "Bloody nuisance!"

"So, what is it that he wants, exactly?"

"He says he wants to invest in the business. Expand it a bit, take on more people, that sort of thing."

"The evil bastard!"

Harry looked at Karen over the top of his paper. "You know he's a hood, don't you?"

"And what are you, the fucking Pope?"

"Look, I just don't know if I want all the hassle at the minute. I've got enough to worry –"

"Aye, all that extra money would be a real pain in the hole, wouldn't it?"

"You know what I mean. Anyway, I didn't turn him down, I said I'd think about it."

"Yeah, well," said Karen, her tone softening, "there's no harm in hearing him out, is there? You could just hear what he has to say, couldn't you? And then make your mind up."

"Aye, don't worry about it, I'll hear him out at some point, so I will. It's just that I've got a load of other stuff to sort out first."

"Like what?"

"Well, the Fleadh's coming up, for one thing, and you know I'm on the committee, don't you?"

"Yeah, but you said it wouldn't be a big deal. You said it would hardly take up any time at all."

"I know, but …" Harry paused and shifted uncomfortably in his seat, "… but the League has said they want to enter the Guider Race this year and I –"

"The Guider Race? What the fuck has that got to do with you?"

"Well, I sort of volunteered to build a guider for them."

"You volunteered? Were you drunk?"

"No!" Harry insisted. "Well, not really. But anyway, who else was going to do it?"

"Anybody can build a guider, Harry!" Karen snapped. "Any one of them lazy fuckers that drink in the League could do it."

"Not properly, though," Harry muttered.

"Oh, is that what this is all about? Nobody else can do it as good as you? Everything has to be fucking perfect, is that it?"

"You want the club to win, don't you?"

"Couldn't give a fuck!"

"Well, I want them to win. The Star thinks they're just going to walk away with it again this year and I just think somebody should give them a run for their money, that's all."

"Hang on a minute," said Karen. "You're not thinking of driving it, are you?"

"No, no," Harry assured her, "I'm just going to build it." Harry's huge size meant that it would be irresponsible and dangerous to have him hurtle at great speed down a steep slope, especially in a densely populated area like Ardoyne. The potential casualties didn't bear thinking about.

"So, what dickhead is going to –?"

"I'm sure we'll find somebody who'll do it," said Harry. "But you see what I mean, don't you? It's going to be taking up a fair bit of my time for a while, and I'm busy at work as well these days, so I'm just going to put McClelland off for the time being."

"Aye all right, but I think it's worth hearing him out." Karen stared thoughtfully out the window, she then walked to the door to the hall before turning back to Harry. "Are you coming upstairs?"

"What for?"

"Well, these knickers aren't going to take themselves off, are they?"

Harry grinned. He and Karen had recently decided to try to start a family and they were both approaching the project with an assiduous enthusiasm. This enthusiasm – given Harry's indelicate bulk and Karen's capacity for screaming – was causing some consternation amongst their immediate neighbours.

Sammy and Maeve were their immediate neighbours on the downward side of the street, and the street's tightly-packed terraced houses – Sammy and Maeve were discovering – had not been built with privacy entirely in mind. This meant that even the most subtle of noises could be picked up through the thin walls, and so, when Harry and Karen succumbed to their procreative urges, Sammy and Maeve were left with the impression that a klaxon-wielding brontosaurus was trampolining on their roof.

"This can't go on!" said Maeve to Sammy one night as they lay together in bed. "You're just going to have to say something."

Sammy lay quietly thinking about this for a while before he realised his wife was being serious. He turned to face her. "Are you being serious?" he asked incredulously. "You want me to go up to Harry, *Harry Hegarty*, and say to him; 'Harry, you wouldn't do us a favour, would you, mate, and stop screwing your wife?'"

"Well, you don't have to put it like that!"

"Can't think of any other way to put it," said Sammy. "Why don't you give it a wee bit more thought, love. I'm sure you can come up with a less messy way for me to commit suicide."

"Well, we can't keep going on like this, can we? We need to get some sleep."

"Oh, I'm sure they'll stop soon enough. And, anyway, you know they're trying for a baby, so I reckon we should just let them get on with it."

"But the whole fucking house is shaking!"

"I know, and that just goes to show how well they built these things," said Sammy, trying to change the subject. "Dead solid, aren't they? You could probably survive an earthquake in these houses."

Maeve didn't reply, she simply lay still and stared quietly at the ceiling. Sammy put his head back on the pillow and they lay side-by-side, motionless and silent as the world around them shuddered and howled. After a while, Sammy cast a tentative glance at Maeve.

"You know," he ventured, "as long as we're both awake, we could always –"

"Fuck off!"

Sammy turned over and tried to get some sleep.

TWELVE

Joker, predictably, was the first to arrive. He was in the Empire, a former church converted into a bar on Botanic Avenue, and after purchasing a pint for himself, he scanned the room and decided upon a large table on a raised section near the front door. He made sure that there would be enough seating for everyone before he sat down and raised the pint to his lips.

Everything was changing, he thought to himself, and he had lately come to realise that he was now a lot more receptive to that change than he had been previously. The thought made him smile with wonder. Carol was to blame, of course – though Joker's brain was keen to point out that 'blame' was probably the wrong word to use. There was still a part of him, he knew, that embraced the cavalier spirit, but that sense of freedom that dismissed the notion of responsibility and the very idea of sensible stability, seemed to become ever more diminished as time passed. A twinge in his right buttock served as a small reminder of his carefree past and he shifted to a more comfortable position as he sipped his beer.

So, Joker asked his brain, *am I growing up?* His brain shrugged unhelpfully. Still, Joker told himself, things were definitely changing. It was not so long ago that a night like this – a Friday night spent drinking with his friends in a lively bar – would have been all that Joker could have wished for, but now he seemed to view the evening as little more than a brief but pleasant distraction from his real life. And his real life was with Carol. Or rather Chiaza.

Joker had suggested to Carol that she should revert to her true Christian name: the *Igbo* name, Chiazacam, from her homeland of Nigeria, and she had said she would give it some consideration.

"Don't be ashamed of where you come from," he had told her.

"It's not about being ashamed," she replied, "it's just that my daddy thought I'd have an easier time growing up if I had a name that people could pronounce. And anyway, Carol was my daddy's mother's name, so that's part of who I am as well."

"Yeah, but Chiaza's such a cool name. It would make you stand out."

"The colour of my skin does that," laughed Carol. Her skin was an intoxicating blend of soft Mediterranean olive and rich African black. "There aren't too many like me knocking about Belfast."

"You know what I mean, though."

"I know, Joseph, and to be honest it's something I've thought about. Everybody still calls me Chiaza when I go back to Nigeria, so it wouldn't really be that big of a jump."

They had left it at that, but Joker still felt that she would better suit the name Chiazacam than the more prosaic *Carol*. Names, he understood, could be significant in defining a person and he sensed the name Chiaza would give a more honest indication of who he believed his girlfriend to be.

It still surprised him how easily he had slipped into the role of boyfriend – though the term *boyfriend* seemed too frivolous a description of how he saw himself. *What should it be, then?* he wondered. *Partner?* Was that what he considered himself to be? *Chiaza's partner?* And would that then bear more weight than *Carol's boyfriend?* His relationship with Carol was still in its infancy, but Joker had already arrived at a point where he could not imagine being without her. How the world turns, he mused.

It had not been all that long ago, he reminisced, that he had gone loping, like a steely-eyed lone-wolf, strong and lithe and hungry, through the dark streets of the city, where he would –

"Hey, wanker! You just getting your own drink these days?"

Joker glowered down at Tone who had just arrived in the main bar area. "There was nobody else here," he protested. "What the fuck was I supposed to do?"

"Excuses! Excuses!" said Tone. He then gestured to Joker's half-full glass. "You okay there?"

"Nah, get us another one, Tone. This one's half-empty."

Tone set off for the bar, and at that moment the front door opened and Jamesy appeared. He nodded to Joker, then followed Tone to the bar.

"*Oooh*," sneered Gary, in a whiny, mocking voice. "I *insist*! I absolutely fucking *insist*!" He took an angry draw from his cigarette and stared at Seamus. "You dumb cunt!"

"Well, what about *you*?" snapped Seamus. "As far as I can remember, it was all your fucking idea!"

"Aye, that's right! Blame me!" said Gary. They were both in Ardoyne, waiting in the queue for a black taxi to take them into town. "I was hardly in any fucking state to be making decisions, was I? Do you really think I want to use up my holiday to go on some wild fucking goose chase over in England with you?" The other people in the queue, embarrassed, were shuffling their feet and looking the other way.

"Who the fuck cares about *you*?" Seamus demanded, pointing his cigarette at Gary's face. "I was supposed to be spending a couple of nights in London, you know! I had it all planned out! Do you really think I want to go driving off to God-knows-where? It's not *my* girlfriend's da, is it?"

"Oh really? Well, what about; *We'll bring your daddy back, Rosie love. Or die trying!*?"

Seamus stared into Gary's eyes. "Did I really say that?"

"Yes!" cried Gary. "You fucking did! And now we're both screwed!"

"Jesus Christ!"

"That's one way to put it." Gary shook his head and flicked his cigarette butt into the road. He was still shaking his head when a taxi pulled up and he and Seamus clambered into the back.

"Well, it's done now," said Seamus. "We're just going to have to deal with it."

"I know, for fuck's sake," Gary sighed. "I've already booked next week off, but I really didn't want to use up the days."

"What's the deal with your paternity leave?"

"The firm's letting me have a week when the kid's born," Gary admitted, "and I was thinking of taking another week after that. But we've got the bloody wedding coming up as well." The taxi bumped and bounced over pot-holed streets until it reached the main Cliftonville Road where it was able to speed up over the smooth tarmac surface.

"Yeah," said Seamus, "you're going to be busy this year, aren't you?"

"I know, and I was thinking of taking Rosie over to Kevin's place in Spain for some sort of honeymoon. It's lucky I haven't told Rosie that yet because it may not happen, but I'm still hoping."

"But what about …?" Seamus began, but then stopped himself.

"What about what?"

"Oh, nothing." The taxi trundled onto the New Lodge Road and Gary turned to gaze thoughtfully out of the window. After a while he turned back to Seamus.

"So, why is Jamesy going, then?"

"I don't know. He just phoned me last week out of the blue. Sounded dead excited, too."

"Well," said Gary, turning back to stare out the window, "we'll find out soon enough, I suppose."

It was only a ten-minute walk from Sean and Bobby's flat to the Empire and, on a warm, sultry evening at the end of June, it was also a pleasant one. Despite running a little late, Sean and Bobby seemed in no great hurry as they strolled through Belfast's university area on their way to Botanic Avenue.

"Did Seamus say why Gary's coming along too?" asked Bobby.

"No," said Sean. "He didn't sound too happy about it, to be honest, so I didn't want to ask."

"Well, with Jamesy going as well, the car's going to be full."

"Yeah, it'll be a bit of a squeeze," agreed Sean, "but it's mostly motorway on the way down from Liverpool so it shouldn't take too long."

"It's meant to be hot next week as well, you know."

"Yeah, but we'll be travelling early in the morning so it shouldn't be too bad. Remember, Seamus is doing us a big favour here. Think of the money we're saving."

"Oh, I know," said Bobby hastily. "I'm not complaining, I'm just saying."

On reaching the entrance to the Empire, they paused, having spotted Seamus and Gary coming from the other direction.

"All right there, lads?" said Gary as he and Seamus approached. "You both all set for next week?"

"Yeah," replied Bobby. They all headed to the entrance which was at the bottom of some stone steps. "I hear you're coming too."

"Aye, I've got to go and sort out some problem with Rosie's da."

"That's good of you."

"Well, you know me, Bobby. Always willing to help out."

Once inside, they made their way to the table and sat down. Tone distributed some cigarettes while Jamesy and Seamus went off to the bar to get a round in.

"So, you're heading off into the big wide world, then?" Tone said to Sean and Bobby.

"Well, London, anyway," said Bobby.

"First steps, Bobby," said Tone. "You've got to start somewhere. Who knows where you'll end up after that."

"Where's everybody going to be watching the match tomorrow night?" asked Gary, referring to Ireland's quarter-final game against Italy. "There's nothing planned, is there?"

"I'm going up to Carol's to watch it," said Joker. "And then we'll be cheering on Cameroon on Sunday."

"Me and Bobby have got to be out of the flat this weekend," Sean said, "so I'll probably end up in Ardoyne tomorrow night."

"Well don't go and watch it up in the Star with that dickhead," Gary told him, pointing to Seamus up at the bar. "You'll just end up in all sorts of shit!"

"What?"

"Never mind."

"I suppose you'll be watching it with Claire?" Bobby asked Tone.

"Yeah, we're going to get some drinks and snacks in, and just watch it in the flat."

"Very cosy."

Seamus and Jamesy got back from the bar with the drinks and were taking their seats just as Kevin arrived.

"That was a shit bit of timing," said Joker. "We've only just got a round in."

"Oh, it's okay, I'll just get myself one," Kevin said, and he set off for the bar.

"All right there, Jamesy?" said Sean. "I hear you're coming to London with us next week. Is that for anything in particular?"

"Yeah, I was just telling Seamus up at the bar there that I've got an idea for a possible PhD thesis and it would be handy if I was able to call into the –"

"Have you seen Hannah lately, Jamesy?" asked Bobby. "I was just wondering if there's been any progress there. I haven't seen her in a while."

"Funny you should say that, Bobby," said Jamesy. "She's going to some festival in England with some people from her church."

"Is she? When's that, then?"

"They actually went today. The thing is, though, they'll be coming back next week, and they're going to be in London at the same time that we'll be there."

"So, what's that mean?"

"That's the weird thing," said Jamesy. "She wants to meet me somewhere in London next Friday. She said she'll give me a ring tomorrow to make the arrangements."

"What did you say she's going to England for?"

"Oh, some religious thing, I think."

Kevin came back from the bar and everyone shuffled around the table to make some room.

"Okay there, Kevin?" Gary called across the table. "How's it going?"

"Oh, not too bad, thanks," said Kevin. He sipped his pint, and Joker, watching from the other side of the table, could not help but think that Kevin seemed to become ever more subdued each time they met.

"I was just wondering," Gary went on, "what the chances would be of me and Rosie getting a lend of your beach-house sometime. Towards the end of the summer, maybe?"

"Of course," said Kevin. "No problem."

"What? Really?"

"Consider it a wedding present."

"Seriously? Fuck me!" Gary raised his glass in thanks. "Cheers, Kevin! You're a mate!"

"That's a good point," said Tone. He looked at Gary. "Have you and Rosie got a wedding list anywhere?"

"Haven't even thought about it," Gary told him. "We're still a bit focused on the kid coming, to be honest. I'll have to see what Rosie wants to do about it."

"I would have thought," Sean said, "that you and Rosie would be happy with just a bit of cash. Especially if you're going to be looking to get your own place at some point. It would be handy to build up a bit of money in the bank, wouldn't it?"

Gary gazed thoughtfully at Sean. Things all now seemed to be getting a little bit too serious for his liking. He hadn't given much thought to a wedding that was now less than eight weeks away. Then again, he hadn't given a lot of consideration to becoming a father, either.

As far as Gary was concerned, his life, with just *him* in it, had been crowded enough, but now he was being forced to accept that he was going to have to squeeze in a few more. He was, of course, an expert in just about everything, but even he was beginning to wonder if adulthood should come with some sort of user's manual.

"Maybe," he said weakly. He took a sip of beer and thought, for the first time in his life, that perhaps he should start to worry.

After a while, the conversation, invariably, came to be dominated by the ongoing World Cup tournament. It had now reached the quarter-final stage, and the four matches that were due to be played over the coming weekend included Ireland vs Italy, and England vs Cameroon.

The Cameroon team had captured the imagination of the world, and most neutral supporters were hoping to see them sweep past England to reach the semi-finals – an unprecedented achievement for any African nation – although for the non-English countries of the UK, it was entirely immaterial who England were playing, as Scotland, Wales and Northern Ireland would be supporting England's opponents, whoever they might be.

Everyone at the table gave their predictions on how the rest of the tournament would play out. The way the draw had been made meant it would be possible for England to meet Ireland in the final, but no one was wishing for this outcome as it was considered to be a match that would be too nail-biting to watch. The best possible final that all could agree upon would be between Ireland and Cameroon; as everyone claimed they would be happy to see either of those teams lift the trophy.

All possible and probable permutations – which included the other four teams in the draw: Argentina, Yugoslavia, West Germany and Czechoslovakia – were discussed and dissected in detail around the table until, eventually, the conversation splintered into localised pools of mumblings and disconnected ramblings.

Joker had been watching Kevin over the course of the evening and sensed that something was troubling him.

"You all right there, Kevin?" he asked. "You're looking very thoughtful over there."

Kevin looked startled. He then cleared his throat and pulled himself closer to the table to rest his elbows on the damp, wooden surface. He glanced at Jamesy, then looked back to Joker.

"Well, there is something that I wanted to talk about," he said. The conversation around the table died down a little. "You're probably all going to rip the piss out of me but, to be honest, I'm past caring." The conversation around the table stopped.

"You sure you want to do this?" said Jamesy quietly. Kevin looked at him, then looked down at the table, nodding determinedly.

"Yes," he muttered. "I have to do *something*!" He glanced up at the quizzical looks around the table and took a deep breath. "I could do with some advice," he said.

"What?" asked Seamus. "From *us*?"

"Yeah, you see, the thing is … well, the thing is, I've never actually been out with a girl, and I was just –"

"*What?*" everyone cried at once.

"I know, it's bit embarrassing, but I –"

"Do you think you might be gay?" asked Gary. "Because that's what –"

"No, no," it's nothing like that!" said Kevin. "It's just that I've never managed to find a girl who wants to go out with me." He shook his head. "It's … it's getting me down a bit, you know?"

"I can imagine," said Bobby. "So, you've never actually …"

"No," said Kevin. "Never."

"Fuck!" said Sean, and everyone nodded in agreement. There was a stunned silence while they all considered Kevin's bombshell.

Tone took a long sip of his beer, his face clouded with thoughts. Joker was the first to comment.

"Well, Kevin," he said, "You've come to the right place. I'm sure that we'll be able to sort something out for you, so don't you worry."

Kevin, still unsure as to whether he'd done the right thing or not, tried to smile. "You think so?"

"Aye, don't you worry about a thing," Joker told him. "Just you leave it to me!"

THIRTEEN

Hannah and her friends had chattered constantly throughout the flight and were chattering still on the train journey from Heathrow to Victoria in central London. Their excitement was palpable, and even the embittered, world-weary commuters of the London Underground felt moved by their infectious happiness.

On arrival at the train station in Victoria, they then had a short walk to the coach station where they would be catching the National Express coach to Winchester. There was talk of a strike by the coach drivers, but it wasn't scheduled to take effect until the following week, when they would be making the return trip, so Hannah's group had looked into taking the train back from Hampshire to London.

By now, the long day's travelling was beginning to take its toll and Hannah and her friends were mostly silent as they dragged their suitcases along the pavement – though their smiles were still evident in the warm light of the smoggy summer evening.

Hannah kept looking around her, searching for a suitable place where she could meet up with James when she came back this way a week from now. It was only when the little group reached the coach station that Hannah spotted what looked to be the very place she had in mind. The Traveller's Tavern was a pub that stood just across the road from the station. It had a dowdy, yet cheerful exterior and seemed like the sort of place where Hannah and James could huddle together in some cosy little corner and where Hannah could begin her mission. It seemed ideal, thought Hannah, but then – as God was smiling warmly on her intentions – why shouldn't it be?

Hannah could hardly wait. She was convinced that what she was doing was all part of God's wonderful plan. It had to be, she decided – for the way in which everything had come together so perfectly could only be divinely inspired. The coming week, she was sure, was God's way of arming her for the battle ahead. She would be recharged, reinvigorated and renewed. She would be filled with the Holy Spirit, and she could picture herself seated across the table from James, putting her hand in his, looking into those astonishing eyes and then confidently leading him towards the truth. She felt thrilled by the prospect.

"Come on, Hannah!" Hannah looked round and saw Becky, one of the members of her group, waving to her. Her friends had carried on into the coach station, leaving her lost in her own thoughts. She could see Greg up ahead, already talking to one of the drivers. She grinned and hurried to catch up.

It was dark when they arrived in Winchester, but the streets were bright and lively with both the usual Friday night revellers and the thousands of Christians who were there for the festival. The festival was not officially due to start until the next morning, but a lot of the attendees had been there for most of the day and were now mingling freely.

Greg led the group to their hotel and everyone chattered excitedly once more as they checked in. It was too late to have dinner at the hotel, but they had all had sandwiches on the coach down from London so, once they had freshened up in their rooms – Hannah and Becky were sharing – they all met up in the hotel bar.

People were often surprised, Hannah knew, that her particular denomination – though strict in other areas – did not demand an abstention from alcohol. She could understand their confusion, though – for many of the other Presbyterian Churches were strictly teetotal, but as James' friend Joseph had once pointed out; *Jesus and his wee mates were always on the sauce*, and that seemed to be the attitude that the elders of her Church were happy to take.

Hannah herself, though, did not drink very often and she could recall only one occasion when she had felt genuinely tipsy. That had been during a Christmas break one year at her parents' home in Saintfield, and the experience had been unsettling enough to make her wary of any subsequent over-indulgence. Her limit seemed to be two small glasses of white wine, and she made a point of sticking to it.

Greg and two other boys from the group went up to the bar while everyone else commandeered a couple of tables near the windows. It soon became clear that many other Christian groups were staying at the same hotel and Hannah was soon aware of a warm sense of camaraderie permeating the room. There was a feeling of love in the air, thought Hannah, as she observed, all around her, happy grins, and eyes that shone wide with excitement. The crowd seemed to pulse with an unspoken, mutual passion. A passion for Christ.

The drinks were ferried back from the bar and Becky teased Hannah when hers was placed in front of her.

"That'll do you for the night, won't it, Hannah?"

"Oh, you never know," said Hannah. "I might just go crazy, seeing that we're on holiday."

"Oh really?" laughed Becky. "I'm going to hold you to that. By the end of the night, I expect to see you up dancing on the table with your pants on your head."

"*Rebecca!*"

Everyone laughed at the expression on Hannah's face. Greg took a seat beside her, smiling at the ludicrous image. He raised his beer to the group of friends. "Cheers, everybody!"

"Cheers!" they all happily toasted.

"Are you here for the festival?" A young man at the table nearest to Greg and Hannah had turned towards them.

"We are," Greg replied. "And you?"

"Yes, we arrived this morning. Is that an Irish accent I hear?"

"*Northern* Irish," Greg stressed.

"Oh yes, of course," said the young man. Hannah, with a guilty start, could not help noting how attractive he was. He held out a hand towards Greg. "I'm Gordon."

"Greg," said Greg, shaking hands. Gordon then reached out to Hannah and their eyes met as they shook hands.

"I'm Hannah," she said, welcoming his calm scrutiny. Gordon then slowly and deliberately, it seemed to Hannah, withdrew his hand and gestured to his companions. Introductions were made between the two groups and Hannah was shocked by the sudden stab of jealousy she felt when Gordon introduced Judith, a pretty girl sitting at his table.

"Judy's my little sister," said Gordon and, again, Hannah was stunned by the irrational wave of relief she experienced. The two groups quickly blended together as they all discussed their expectations for the festival.

"Are you going to be setting up a stall?" Gordon asked. Every group that had booked to attend the festival had been offered the opportunity to organise an information stall for the week in order to explain to the other attendees the basic tenets of their faith. It was seen as a way to quickly open up a discourse between the different denominations and a way to spark lively debate for the week ahead. Greg shook his head.

"No," he said. "We did think about it, but our faith is fairly straightforward, to be honest, and we just thought we'd get more out of the festival if we went around all of the other stalls to see what everybody else has to say."

"I know what you mean," said Gordon, "and I think you'll be in for a few surprises."

Greg gave a quizzical look, and Gordon laughed.

"We've bumped into a few interesting groups already today," he explained. "In particular, you should keep a look out for some guys that call their group *Yeshua the Teacher*."

"Yeshua the Teacher?" asked Hannah.

"Yes," said Gordon grinning. His companions, on hearing the name, began to laugh. "They have some very … um, let's say *interesting* ideas regarding Christianity."

"Like what?"

"Well, they deny the divinity of Jesus, for one thing."

Greg and Hannah stared at Gordon. "What sort of Christians deny Christ's divinity?" asked Greg.

Gordon shrugged. "They refer to themselves as Christian Humanists. Whatever *that* means."

"What would people like that be doing at a festival of faith?" Hannah asked, then shyly dropped her gaze when Gordon smiled at her.

"No idea," said Gordon. He raised his drink. "But here's to some interesting discussions in the days ahead."

As they chatted, it became clear that Gordon and his group shared almost identical beliefs with Greg and Hannah and their friends. They all accepted, without question, the accuracy of Bishop James Ussher's seventeenth-century calculations on the date of Creation, which placed the dawn of the universe in the year 4004BC.

Hannah, still trying to come to terms with the strength of her physical attraction to Gordon, now found herself falling under the spell of his intelligent insights into the early books of the Old Testament. She drank her quota of wine, but felt disappointed when last orders were called and everyone agreed to call it a night.

Becky was merrily inebriated by the time that she and Hannah made it back to their room, but she had been astutely observing Hannah's interactions with Gordon throughout the evening and was now in a mischievous mood.

"That Gordon fella seemed nice," she said.

"He did, didn't he?"

"Good-looking, too."

"You think so?"

"Yeah, I might just drop him a few hints that I'm available. What do you think?"

Hannah was silent for a moment and then gave a nonchalant shrug. "I don't know," she said, trying to sound casual. "Do you really think he's your type?"

Becky burst into sudden laughter. It was a throaty, filthy, suggestive laugh that unnerved Hannah who had often winced at Becky's earthy directness.

"Oh, don't worry yourself," said Becky. "I could tell that you were all over him."

"What?" Hannah was mortified. "What do you mean by that?"

"You couldn't take your eyes off him."

"I don't know what you're talking about."

"Course you don't," laughed Becky, climbing into bed. "Goodnight, Hannah. Try not to dream of Gorgeous Gordon."

Hannah stared speechlessly at Becky. After a while, she could hear Becky's gentle snores and she sighed as she quietly slipped between the covers of her own bed. She lay awake and thought of the coming week. She tried to focus her mind on what she was hoping to achieve at the festival. But focusing her mind, she quickly discovered, proved to be impossible.

The next morning, after breakfast, Hannah and her friends made their way to Winchester Cathedral, which was the festival's central hub. In the grounds to one side of the ancient building, several marquees had been set up to house the information stalls. Tables and chairs had been placed all across the neatly trimmed grass and, by the time Hannah's group arrived, many of these were already occupied by happy, chattering Christians.

Hannah paused to try to fully absorb the atmosphere of the place. There was, it seemed to her, an overall sense of friendliness. A friendliness made clear in the beaming smiles, the easy laughter and the bubbles of unbridled joy that floated on the summer breeze.

Hannah felt instantly at home. These were her people, and she felt a spontaneous urge to hug each and every one of them in a shared understanding of God's truth. She and her friends had decided earlier that they would split up, and she watched Becky peel away with a few of the other group members towards the marquees on the far side of the grounds. Hannah then naturally fell into line alongside Greg and they both strolled happily into the crowd.

A lot of the festival-goers appeared to be Anglicans which, Hannah supposed, made sense, but she was surprised by the broad spectrum of opinions they offered. She and Greg got talking, at one point, to an elderly lady who ranted angrily about the increasingly liberal ideas that were taking hold in the Church of England, and how the Church was constantly conceding ground when it came to women's rights.

"But isn't more rights for women a good thing?" Hannah ventured, and was then greeted with a venomous stare. The old woman pointed a bony finger at her.

"You're not one of those bloody feminists, are you?" she demanded.

"No, of course not," said Hannah, "but don't you think –?"

"If the Church continues down this road," said the woman, "then I, for one, would have to think about joining the Catholics. *That's right!*" she barked. "*The bloody Catholics!*"

Greg and Hannah were both grinning when they managed to slip away, leaving the old woman shaking her head and muttering to herself. They then came across a vicar, small in stature, and with thinning hair and smiling eyes, who admitted to being deeply saddened by the turmoil in Ireland.

"*Northern* Ireland," Greg pointed out.

"Oh yes, of course," said the vicar, who introduced himself as Henry. "A truly ghastly situation. But what's to be done?" he asked rhetorically. "What's to be done?"

Henry turned out to cherish the very views that were so abhorrent to the ranting old woman they had just left, and he extolled to Greg and Hannah the great strides the Anglican Church had been making regarding the roles of women in the clergy.

"Oh yes," he enthused, "I've encountered several lady vicars now, and I must say they've all been marvellous. I can see no reason – no reason at all – why a woman can't do the job as well as any man."

"Well, the disciples that were chosen by Christ were exclusively men," said Greg.

"But He also had many female followers," Henry offered. "And times change, my dear boy, times change. And we must move with the times if we are to progress, don't you think?"

"The Word of God doesn't change."

"Ah, but our interpretation of it does."

"Perhaps that's why the Anglican Church has lost its way," Greg suggested. "Their doctrines have strayed so far from Scripture that what they actually believe now is all muddled and confused."

"Well, that's certainly one way of looking at it," said Henry smiling.

Greg then outlined the core principles of their particular branch of Presbyterianism and how they were based largely on the biblical literalism of James Ussher.

"Good heavens!" cried Henry, genuinely shocked. "I've heard of scriptural literalists before, of course, but I don't believe I've ever come across one."

"We just believe in what Scripture tells us," said Hannah. "Why should that be so shocking?"

"Of course we must follow Scripture, my dear," said Henry placatingly, "but that does not mean we should simply ignore the evidence of our own eyes. I happen to consider myself something of an amateur geologist, you know, and believe me when I say that the history of the Earth can be read quite clearly in the rocks beneath our feet."

"God created those rocks," said Greg, "so they can say whatever He wants them to say."

"You mean God made the rocks to appear older than they are?" asked Henry. "For what possible reason?"

"It is not for us to question God's design."

Henry sighed with exasperation. "That's just the old defence of God works in mysterious ways, isn't it? I've never been entirely satisfied by that reply," he said, "but I suppose it has its uses." He gave both Hannah and Greg a studied look. "Well, I take it that you've been arguing your case for a long time, and nothing that I can say is going to suddenly change your minds, but trust me when I say that I do hope that one day you will discover the truth." With that, he wished them both luck with their time at the festival and went on his way.

"I think we're going to get a lot of that this week," Greg said to Hannah. She nodded thoughtfully.

"Do you never ask yourself why so many Christians have rejected scriptural reality?" she asked.

"Of course I do," replied Greg, "but I've never come up with a satisfactory answer. All we can do is keep on spreading the truth and just hope that more people take notice."

"Well, with God on our side," said Hannah cheerfully, "how can we fail?"

FOURTEEN

After negotiating the Liverpool docks, Seamus drove south towards London, hoping to miss the worst of the early rush-hour traffic around the outskirts of Birmingham. The voyage across the Irish Sea had been reasonably smooth and they had all slept well on the ferry – though the amount of alcohol they had consumed in the ship's bar may have contributed to that.

It was promising to be a hot July day, but with the car's air-conditioning running, everyone was hoping for a relatively comfortable journey. Seamus was expecting to reach London by early afternoon.

"I'm not feeling too great," said Gary as they joined the southbound motorway. He was sitting in the front passenger seat, a combination of carsickness and over-indulgence giving his complexion a greenish tint.

"Well, if you think you're going to be sick," said Seamus, "you know what to do, don't you?"

"What?"

"Undo your seatbelt, open the car door, and jump the fuck out."

"We're on the bloody motorway!"

"What's your point?"

"I should have known I'd get no sympathy from you."

"Seriously," said Seamus turning to face Gary. "And I mean seriously. You are not going to throw up in my new car! Have you fucking got that?"

"I may not have any say in the matter."

"Actually, I agree with Seamus," said Bobby from the back seat. "I don't want to have to sit here smelling your sick the whole way down to London."

"Well, fuck you, Bobby!"

"I think Bobby's got a point," added Jamesy. "That would make the rest of the journey a bit unpleasant, wouldn't it?"

"Fuck you, too!"

"I'm just saying that we should have something to hand, just in case."

"What do you mean?" asked Sean.

"Well, does anybody have an empty carrier bag or something?"

They all gave it some thought, but no one could think of anything suitable.

"There's always the glove box," suggested Gary, then held up his hands when Seamus glared at him. "I'm joking, for fuck's sake!"

"Can't you just open the window?" Sean said.

"What about my fucking paintwork?" demanded Seamus.

"No, I mean the fresh air might stop him feeling sick."

"It's worth a try," said Jamesy.

Gary wound down his window and let his head rest against the door frame. The strong, cool breeze felt good on his face and he soon felt better. He began to rummage around in the box of snacks they had brought along for the journey and Seamus, relaxing a little, could concentrate on the road ahead.

By mid-afternoon, London loomed large, and the traffic got heavier and slower until they got onto London's orbital motorway, the M25, where everything ground to a halt.

"Joker built this road, you know," said Gary.

"That would explain it," Seamus muttered.

The traffic eventually got moving and they made steady progress, arriving at the hotel where Sean and Bobby were staying just before the evening rush hour began. Sean and Bobby unloaded their luggage and the others all shook them by the hand, punched them on the shoulder and wished them the best of luck.

"You'll be back for the wedding, though, won't you?" Gary asked them.

"Wouldn't miss it," they assured him. They then made their way inside the hotel, and Seamus, Gary and Jamesy got back in the car and set off for Clapham, where they had booked a cheap hotel. Jamesy would be staying there for three nights, while Seamus and Gary planned to stay just for the night, before heading on down to the south coast in the morning. They would all meet up again – with Martin in tow – back in London on Saturday for the trip back to Liverpool and the overnight ferry. They would then be back home on Sunday, in plenty of time to watch the final of the World Cup that evening.

They were all ravenous by the time they booked into their hotel in Clapham, so they went in search of a pub that served evening meals.

"This should do," said Seamus, reading a large sign outside a pub called the Queen Charlotte. "It all sounds cheap and cheerful, and they're showing the match as well." They went inside, found a table, and ordered some food. Once they had finished eating, they ordered another round of drinks and sat back contentedly.

"So, are we just going to watch the match in here, then?" asked Gary.

"Why not?" said Seamus. "It's not long till kick-off now anyway."

"Yeah," Jamesy agreed. "There's no point going looking for anything else when we've got a perfectly good bar here."

"Suits me," said Gary. He picked up his beer and relaxed in his seat. "What do you think we should do about Saturday, then? Jamesy has to check out of the hotel by twelve, so if we're running late then he's going to be hanging around waiting for us."

"What do you suggest?" asked Seamus.

"Well, why don't we just meet up in here?" said Gary. "Jamesy could sit with a drink while he's waiting, and we could all have a decent lunch before we head off. It would set us up for the journey."

"Sounds good," said Jamesy.

"Yeah," Seamus conceded, "that's not a bad idea."

"So, in here at lunchtime on Saturday, then? That's that all sorted." They downed their drinks and Seamus went off to get the next round.

"Did Hannah ever get in touch with you about meeting up?" Gary asked Jamesy.

"Yeah, we've arranged to meet at some pub in Victoria on Friday."

"Still no idea why?"

"No," said Jamesy glumly. "None at all."

Gary shook his head. "I just can't figure that girl out," he said.

"Makes two of us."

"I mean, does she want to go out with you or not? She needs to make her mind up."

"Maybe I'll find out on Friday."

"Find out what on Friday?" Seamus had returned with the drinks.

"Jamesy's going to be seeing Hannah on Friday," Gary told him.

"What for?"

"He doesn't know."

"Interesting relationship you've got there, Jamesy."

"That's one way of putting it." Jamesy no longer wished to talk about it. "So, what are you two going to be getting up to for the next couple of days?"

"Well, we're going to drive down to Hastings in the morning," said Seamus. "We'll call in on Martin and just make sure he'll be all ready to go first thing on Saturday. Then we're going to go and stay in Brighton for a couple of nights."

"Brighton?"

"Yeah," said Gary, "Martin said that there's a lot more to do there than in Hastings, so he said we'd be better off staying there till Saturday morning."

"Well, it is a big resort town, isn't it?"

"Exactly, so we might as well try to make a bit of a holiday of it."

"Good idea," said Jamesy. "Hope you have a good time. I'll probably just be having early nights and the odd, lonely drink."

"You want to be careful you don't get a reputation as a hellraiser, you mad fucker," said Gary.

"I'll be careful," Jamesy smiled. He was secretly looking forward to being on his own for a few days, glad that he was no longer expected to accompany Seamus on some exploratory trawl through London's vibrant gay scene. He had been harbouring a nasty suspicion that Seamus had been planning to use him as some sort of bait, but he rejected the thought as being unworthy of him. Seamus, he knew, was a reliable friend who was incapable of resorting to such underhand scheming, and Jamesy felt a little ashamed that he had even entertained the notion. "Be sure and visit the Pavilion when you're in Brighton," he said. "I've never been there myself, but I hear it's well worth a look."

"That sounds like an educational sort of thing," said Gary accusingly.

"Yeah, Jamesy," said Seamus, "you should know that Gary doesn't take too kindly to be being educated."

"Just a suggestion. You know that Queen Charlotte was the mother of George the Fourth?"

Gary and Seamus stared blankly at Jamesy. "You know," Jamesy went on, "George the Fourth, when he was Prince Regent, was the one who –"

"When's this fucking match going to start?" Gary exclaimed, looking at his watch.

"Won't be long now," said Seamus, glancing up at one of the many TV screens that were positioned around the bar.

"I'd better go and get a round in before it starts, then," said Jamesy, getting up. The Queen Charlotte had now got much busier, and Jamesy had to force his way through the football fans who were hoping to watch the England team beat West Germany and make it through to the World Cup final for only the second time in their history. Gary, Seamus and Jamesy would always be supporting the team that England were playing, but they felt, on this occasion, it would be wise to keep that support under wraps.

When they headed back to their hotel later that night, though, they were smiling.

FIFTEEN

It was a thing of beauty. A sleek sculpture of shaped and burnished wood with accents of metal and rubber that sat hunched in the short grass and looked like it wanted to fly.

Harry had used off-cuts of materials from work, so the base was a fine mahogany, varnished and polished until it shone a deep red. This red appeared again in little details of an inlay running around the oak sides that flowed upwards and outwards from the base, attached with special forms of dovetail joints.

The front wheels – a fine pair from a top-quality vintage pram – shone like new and were fixed firmly to the steering bar by a set of custom-made brackets – not for Harry the time-honoured method of simply hammering in a few nails and then bending them over the axle to roughly hold the wheels in place.

The steering bar was attached using a thick bolt and was kept slightly apart from the base by a pair of greased washers. The steering itself was further facilitated by some counter-sunk ball-bearings which made turning the wheels almost effortless.

The rear wheels, though smaller than the front pair, were again of the highest quality with bright white rubber tyres and gleaming chrome spokes, the perfect complement to the wheels at the front. The whole thing seemed perched with folded wings just waiting to break free and hurtle into a hazy blur of speed and madness. Harry's guider.

"I just want to put a couple of rubber pads on the steering bar," Harry told the friends who had called round to check on his progress. "To give a wee bit of grip and all that. And that should be about it." They milled around in Harry's garden with the early evening sun slanting onto the object in question and reflecting a warm glow from the polished surfaces.

Vastly over-engineered and *needlessly ornate* were the predominant thoughts of Harry's visitors, though it appeared that no one wanted to give those thoughts a voice.

"Looks class, Harry," said Terry the Spark. Darren agreed with a thoughtful nod.

"Aye, mate," added Plumber Pete, "a real work of art. I reckon it'll give the *Banshee* a run for its money, that's for sure." The *Banshee* was the guider that had won the race for the Crumlin Star the previous year and the guider that was the hot favourite again for this year. Especially if it was to be paired with the same driver who had steered his way to such an overwhelming victory the year before.

"Is your man, Dessie, going to be driving the *Banshee* again this year?" asked Terry.

"Dashing bloody Desmond," sneered Darren. "Thinks he's God's bloody gift, doesn't he? Thinks all the women are after him, so he does! Dickhead!"

"Well, he's not called Dashing Desmond for nothing," Pete pointed out.

"Yeah, I think he came up with that name himself, though," said Darren.

"Speaking of names," Pete said to Harry, "what are you going to call it?"

"I was thinking of *Dullahan*," said Harry.

"*Dullahan*? Where the hell does that come from?"

"It's an old Irish myth," Harry explained, "about the ghost of a fast horseman. He was said to be more terrifying than any banshee."

"That sounds cool," said Terry. "So, have you tried the *Dullahan* out yet, Harry?"

"No, but then I won't be the one driving it."

"That's where I come in," said Darren cheerfully. "Let me know when you want me to take her for a spin, Harry. I'm ready when you are."

"It'll have to be when the roads are quiet, so I was thinking of Sunday morning. About seven."

"Jesus, Harry! Seven o'clock on Sunday morning?" cried Darren, but he hastily nodded under Harry's blank, intimidating gaze. "Seven it is, Harry! No problem at all, mate."

"I might even come along to cheer you on," said Terry.

"You can count me out," Pete told them. "Sunday's my day of rest."

"You'll be snoring off a hangover, you mean?" said Darren.

"That's exactly what I mean."

"Right then," Harry confirmed. "Just call round here on Sunday morning, and we'll head round to the top of Brompton."

"Aye, I'll look forward to it," said Darren. "Are you coming round the League, Harry?"

"Nah, I can't make it tonight, I've got things to do."

"Right, well we'll see you later." Harry's three friends left the garden and set off for the League. Darren and Pete chatted happily amongst themselves while Terry was thoughtful and quiet. He was wondering to himself whether Harry had deliberately refrained from telling Darren that, in Irish mythology, the *Dullahan* didn't have a head.

SIXTEEN

The man was heavily built, with plump, fleshy lips and an officious, almost arrogant, look in his eyes. He was pointedly ignoring anything that Hannah had to say, and addressed himself only to Gordon and Greg. He was seated at one of the stalls in a large marquee that bustled with people still buzzing with novelty and excitement even after several days of the festival.

Beside the heavy-set man sat a younger man whose smile seemed out of place beneath his hooded eyes. The few glances he shot towards Hannah were heavy with mistrust. Behind the two men, a petite woman sat prissy and prim, staring at the grass between her feet. She wore a headscarf that framed a pleasant but impassive face, and Hannah was trying, unsuccessfully, to catch her eye with a friendly smile.

"*The Way*?" Gordon was saying. "It's an interesting name."

"It was the name used by the original followers of Christ," the heavy-set man told him gravely. "It gives notice of our intent to observe those values that were held at the beginning."

"The beginning?"

"When Scripture was first written," the man explained. "Most of those who call themselves followers of Christ have walked away from those values." He gave Hannah a quick look.

"I'm not sure I follow you," said Greg.

"Too many so-called Christians pay more heed to the book of the Jews than the true Word of God."

"Book of the Jews?" asked Hannah. "You mean the Old Testament?"

"You don't accept the Old Testament as God's Word?" asked Greg.

"Of course not!" the younger of the two men spoke up. "We aren't Jews."

"Well neither are we," Greg told him, "but I don't see how you can have Christianity without the background of the Old Testament. How can you understand Christ's mission without knowing how original sin came about?"

"There is no mention of original sin anywhere in Scripture," said the heavy-set man. "And as far I am aware, it does not appear in any of the Jewish fairy tales."

"Fairy tales?" Greg was aghast.

"How else would you describe a story that involves a talking snake?"

"Most Christians accept that it's the Word of God," Gordon pointed out.

"Calling yourself a Christian is not the same thing as being a true follower of Christ."

"Well, I agree with you there," said Greg.

"You're a perfect example," the younger man said with a sneer. "I suppose you claim to follow Scripture, don't you? And yet you allow your woman out in public with her head uncovered."

"*What?*" Gordon, Greg and Hannah all cried at once.

"Scripture is clear on the matter," said the heavy-set man. "In Corinthians it states that if a woman does not wear a head covering then she should have her cut off."

"But … but …" Greg spluttered.

"Aren't you taking that line out of context?" suggested Gordon.

"How can the Word of God be taken out of context?"

"Is that what *you* believe?" Hannah directed her question to the young woman behind the two men. The woman glanced at Hannah, then quickly looked away.

"Martha is my wife," said the younger man, "and of course she follows Scripture. Especially where it tells us that women should be silent. *If there is anything they desire to know*," he quoted, "*let them ask their husbands at home.*"

"You seem to be focusing fairly heavily on the letters of Paul," said Gordon, "rather than the teachings of Jesus Himself."

"Are you saying that some parts of Scripture should be dismissed?" the heavy-set man demanded.

"Well, if you've already dismissed the Old Testament," Greg began, "then –"

"The book of the Jews has no relevance to Scripture!"

"But surely it foretells the coming of Jesus."

"It tells of a coming messiah," the younger man conceded, "but the Jews have never believed that Christ was that messiah."

"But surely that's just –"

"You have some very interesting views," Gordon hurriedly interrupted. "And you've given us a lot to think about. But we've got a lot to do today, and we really should be moving along." He ushered Greg and Hannah away from the table and out of the marquee. "Well," he said as they made their way across the grass, "I don't think we were going to make much headway there, were we?"

"What did they call themselves?" asked Greg. "*The Way*, was it?"

"That's right," said Gordon. "And *The Way* seems to be to harbour some rather extreme points of view."

"You can say that again!" laughed Greg. Hannah, though, wasn't so sure. She walked along in silence recounting the discussion they had just had. Those men, she realised, were simply following the words they had read in the New Testament. No matter how mistaken or misguided they may have been, it could not be denied that they firmly believed they were simply obeying the Word of God. How could anyone, she wondered, read into God's words something that just wasn't there? How could anyone misinterpret so completely the divine message? And then Hannah's thoughts began to wander off in a somewhat uncomfortable direction. Was it her, she asked herself, who had unconsciously chosen not to see what they had seen?

"Hannah?"

"Um … what? … oh, sorry!" She realised that Gordon had asked her a question, and she blushed. "I'm sorry," she stammered. "What was that?"

"I was just asking if you're going to the lecture tonight."

"What? Oh yes, on Gospel comparison? Yes, I've been looking forward to it."

"Okay, I'll see you there, then," said Gordon. "I'm just going to go and see if I can find Judith."

"Right, I'll see you later."

"See you," said Greg, waving as Gordon left. He turned to Hannah. "Are you all right? You seem a bit distracted."

Hannah smiled. "No, I'm fine," she assured him. "I was just in a wee world of my own there for a minute."

"Well, come on, we're supposed to be meeting up with the rest of them about now."

As they made their way through the crowds, Hannah could not help feeling that the festival no longer seemed as friendly and as welcoming as it had when they first arrived. And far from having her faith reinforced by the experience, Hannah was having to accept that it was being buffeted and shaken from all sides. The festival had just a few more days remaining, and Hannah was not confident that she was ever going to receive the fire of the Holy Spirit that she felt was required for her to carry out her mission.

Still, she told herself, there was still time. Perhaps, in the next few days, the grace and the glory of God's divine light would descend upon her like a thunderbolt from above, giving her the strength and the fervour to spread Christian truth, and to pursue her personal crusade of saving James' soul.

Perhaps.

SEVENTEEN

2,237 years earlier.

A thousand leagues east of Babylon.

The sun had already passed its noontime zenith when Targa led Pillarchus into a sheltered glade a little way off the main path. The glade took up much of a large patch of level ground, and at its centre lay a shallow pool that was filled by a mountain stream flowing in lazy fits and starts over the rocky slopes.

The water in the pool looked almost black in the shadows of the glade's stunted little trees, and around its edge was a thick grey mud. Targa tethered his horse and went to the leather pack that was tied to the back of the donkey. From this he retrieved some wooden frames that he had already made back at the caravan, and then walked to the pool's edge. Pillarchus watched with interest as he himself dismounted and tethered his mare.

"Did you write mostly in clay when you served at the courts," he asked as Targa scooped some of the grey mud into the wooden frames and began smoothing it down with the edge of his sword.

"*Only* clay," said Targa simply, and Pillarchus nodded. He had noted, during his time along the Indus, that papyrus was becoming more prevalent among the wealthier towns, but he suspected it was only a recent development, inspired by increasing influences from both Greece and Egypt. He walked over to the donkey and loosened the bag of feed they had brought for the animals. Once the horses and the donkey had been fed and watered, he spread a woollen blanket on the ground and produced, from his saddlebags, a package wrapped in a light cloth. By now, Targa had filled all the frames and had arranged them on the ground to allow the mud to dry and to stiffen slightly. He took a gourd of wine from his pack and joined Pillarchus on the blanket.

"What made you leave the courts?" Pillarchus asked as he unwrapped the cloth bundle to reveal some bread and goat's cheese and a small jar of spiced oil that he had become partial to during his time east of the mountains. "Surely the life of a scribe is more comfortable than that of a mountain guide."

Targa ripped off a piece of bread and dipped it in the oil. He gave a slight shrug as he chewed. "Some people are born to scratch in the dirt," he said. "Others are not."

Pillarchus gave him a curious glance. "That's not a very satisfactory answer."

Targa looked thoughtfully at Pillarchus and then sighed. "I did not mind the life, I suppose," he said finally. "Like you say, it was comfortable.

But I had not been a scribe for very long when a great *raja* came up from the south. He was wealthy enough to control an army and he soon came to dominate all of the towns in the valley. Eventually I became employed at his court as a chief scribe."

"And this great *raja* disliked you?" Pillarchus suggested.

"Oh no," said Targa. "He liked me very much."

"But then …?"

"He liked me in the same way that your friend likes little boys."

"Oh, I see," said Pillarchus, and gave a little more scrutiny to Targa's appearance. Though Targa's face was now cracked and wind-scorched, Pillarchus decided that at one time, in the distant past, it was a face that would have been attractive in an almost feminine way. "And that made your life a little less comfortable, I suppose."

Targa nodded. "His approaches became difficult for me," he said. "I even began to fear for my life. And so, eventually, I left the valley and went to seek work elsewhere."

"As a scribe?"

"Yes, as a scribe, but I soon came to realise that, outside of the valley, no one wanted to hire a scribe who did not speak Greek."

"And you didn't try to learn back then?"

Targa took a swig of wine and passed the gourd to Pillarchus. "By this time, I had had enough," he said. "The life of a scribe no longer held any appeal for me, and so, over the years, I found many other types of work." He gave Pillarchus a grin. "I was even a sailor for a time."

"A sailor?" Pillarchus raised an eyebrow.

"Yes, I sailed to many places," said Targa, "and learned many languages. I sailed even beyond great Carthage, almost to the end of the world."

"The end of the world? You mean the Pillars of Herakles?"

Targa laughed. "Yes," he cried, "I have always been amused by the way the Greeks must give a name to everything. Even a tiny pebble by the side of the road, the Greeks must stop to give it a name."

Pillarchus smiled. He was feeling happier now that he had eaten. The wine helped too, of course. He gulped some down and passed it back to Targa. "Yes, I know what you mean," he said. "Did you know the Greeks even have a name for these mountains?"

Targa frowned at Pillarchus over the top of the gourd as he drank. He swallowed a mouthful of wine and shook his head. "No, but it does not surprise me," he said, giving a satisfied burp. "So, what name have they given these mountains?"

"Well, the mountains north of here are known as the *Caucasus*, so these have become known as the *Caucasus Indicus*."

Targa frowned. "*Indoo Kush*?"

"No, *Indicus*," corrected Pillarchus. He smiled as he accepted the wine from Targa. "I suppose we should pack up and go soon," he said staring up at the sky, "if we want to get there by nightfall."

They got to their feet and began to pack up. Targa took the mud-filled wooden frames and placed them carefully in their leather pouch, which he then tied to the back of the donkey. Once they were satisfied they were ready, they set off again along the path.

They made good progress and there was still a little light left in the sky when they came upon Lianah's village. As they approached, a youth stepped from the shadow of a hut nearest the path. He was armed with a crude spear, though his manner was more curious than threatening. After a few brief words with Targa – which Pillarchus struggled to follow – the youth grinned and motioned for them to move forward into the centre of the village. Once there, they dismounted and were greeted by a number of villagers who had come from their huts to behold the strange visitors in their midst.

Targa made arrangements for the animals to be stabled and then he and Pillarchus were invited to the hut of the village chieftain to discuss the reason for their visit. Targa did most of the talking, while gesturing from time to time to Pillarchus, and the chief nodded and made occasional replies. After a while Targa turned to Pillarchus. "He believes a meeting with Lianah can be arranged," he said, "but he says that she will expect payment."

For some reason, this had not occurred to Pillarchus, but he nodded with a sigh. "Of course."

They were offered some food and drink, which they both accepted eagerly, and were then led to one of the larger huts of the village where they entered into a torch-lit room that had a wooden table at its centre. Pillarchus and Targa were directed to sit at one side of the table where they waited until, a few moments later, a bent-over figure, draped in a dark cloak, was escorted reverentially into the room and seated at the table opposite them. The figure raised her head to reveal a face that, though lined with age, still shone with a lively curiosity. Her eyes had a dull, opaque sheen to them, though she keenly sniffed the air as if sensing her visitors from smell alone.

The formal introductions were made and as Pillarchus watched the crooked, sightless, old crone nod and smile, he felt his heart sink. Glauca, he suddenly realised, had been right. What could this old woman possibly say that would be of any interest to him? He had studied history and he knew as well as anyone what had happened in the old palace of Nebuchadnezzar in ancient Babylon almost eighty years ago. The King of all Kings, Alexander, had returned to the city after a long campaign, and it was there that he had died. There had been, of course, many rumours surrounding the death but they had all faded over time and it was now generally accepted that Alexander had succumbed to a sickness brought on by his war wounds.

The king's mummified remains were eventually entombed in distant Egypt, far away to the south, where even to this day they still exerted a powerful influence. Pillarchus knew of several people who had travelled in pilgrimage to the Golden King's final resting place, and all had claimed to have been awed by the experience. He would even occasionally propose the idea of making the journey for himself, just to stand in proximity to the god that had once seized the entire world in his fist, but that was an idea that was little more than a vague possibility in some far-off, unknown future.

Here, in this forlorn, humble village that clung to a remote mountain-side, Pillarchus could feel no connection to the glittering God-King. He was simply sitting at a table with a blind, decrepit old woman whose tenuous ties to Alexander, long ago, were of no more than a passing curiosity. He felt suddenly weary and sick for the sight of his homeland but, he decided, now that he was here, he might as well hear what the woman had to say. Beside him, Targa had retrieved the framed slabs of river clay from their leather pouch and was now poised with his stylus which was a reed he had taken from the riverbank and had shaped at one end to a thin wedge shape. Pillarchus briefly speculated as to what language Targa would be writing in, but then he decided that he didn't much care. He just wanted to conclude this business and get back to the caravan as soon as possible.

"So, Lianah," he began, "were you born in Babylon?"

"No," said Lianah, she spoke a passable Greek, but would occasionally break into a language that Targa would have to translate for Pillarchus. "but Babylon is all I knew as a child," Lianah continued. "My mother told me that I was born in Persepolis. My father ranked quite highly, I believe, in the army there."

"Persepolis? So, you're Persian, then?"

"Persian? Yes, I suppose so," said Lianah, "but Alexander came to Persepolis and sent many of the high-born families back to Babylon as hostages."

"I see," Pillarchus nodded, it was a standard tactic. "Are you saying that you were high-born, then?"

"So my mother told me as I grew older. She also told me that we had been enslaved by Alexander, but if that is so, then we were comfortable slaves, for I spent my childhood in the old palace."

"And Alexander, in the meantime, left Persepolis to conquer the lands east of these very mountains, isn't that right?"

"That's right," said Lianah. "It was many years later that he came back to Babylon, but even then I was still very young. I was still waiting for my moon-blood when Alexander returned."

"Did you see him? Were you ever in his presence?"

"Oh yes, many times. I became friendly with a boy called Meklios, who was a servant of Eumenes at that time, and we would often find ourselves mingling with those closest to the king."

"It's said that Eumenes was not popular at court."

Lianah shook her head. "I knew nothing of the politics they played back then, but I liked Eumenes well enough. He was always kind to me. Ptolemy and Perdiccas too for that matter."

"What did you think of Alexander?"

"I was just a child, so to me he seemed old. I know that must sound ridiculous," said Lianah, "for I know now that he was not so very old when he died."

"No, of course not. And did he ever speak to you?" Pillarchus, despite himself, was becoming absorbed.

Lianah smiled. "He did, but naturally he spoke to me as one would speak to a child. I like to believe he was fond of me, though. He would often pat me on the top of my head whenever he saw me."

Pillarchus could not stop himself from staring at the top of the old woman's head, where the hand of a living god had once rested.

"And, of course," Lianah continued, "once he was gone, the whole world was thrown into confusion. We thought the world would end, Meklios and I, but obviously it didn't. The foolishness of children, I suppose." Lianah chuckled at the memory.

Pillarchus nodded silently, then realised that Lianah couldn't see him. "Of course," he said. "And were you still in Babylon when the king's body was taken away to Egypt?"

"Oh, that isn't what happened," said Lianah with a sudden gleam in her sightless eyes. "That isn't what happened at all!"

It was some hours later when Pillarchus stumbled into the amber mist of dawn, shaken by what he had heard. He rushed to the stables, eager to set off as soon as possible.

"We should rest first," said Targa, following behind. He had already carefully stored the written account of Lianah's tale in the leather pouch and was carrying it under his arm.

"We don't have time to rest," Pillarchus told him excitedly. "We need to get going. Help me get these animals ready. The king needs to hear of this!" He paused at the thought. Antiochus himself would demand to see him, he realised. He would be brought before the king to give a full account of what he had learned. He almost wept with anticipation.

"A few hours won't make any difference," Targa protested, though he tied the pouch to the back of the donkey and began to ready his horse for departure. "Not when you consider how far you still have to travel."

"Yes, I know," said Pillarchus, "but how can I sleep after what I just heard? Do you have any idea what this means? This could shift the entire balance of power in the region."

Targa had no interest in the squabbles that went on in the lands far to the west, but he had grown fond of Pillarchus in the time he had known him and was only looking out for his wellbeing.

"Very well," he sighed, "but we must take it easy, and try to rest as much as we can along the way."

"Of course! Of course!" Pillarchus cried delightedly, slapping Targa on the shoulder. "But then I must overtake the caravan and rush towards the west. And there, my clever little friend, is where I will change history."

As they set off, Pillarchus went over in his mind the information that Lianah had divulged to him, and how he could use that information to his best advantage when finally he reached court. He could no longer travel with the slow-moving caravan, he quickly realised, but to travel on alone would be dangerous. He decided that once he had caught up with the caravan, he would try to hire a few men to act as guards for the long journey west. It would cost him the last of his funds, he knew, but that would be a very small price to pay compared to the wealth and the fame that he could expect when he delivered his world-shaking news to the king.

"So, what is this amulet the old woman spoke of?" Targa asked after a while.

"What?" The question pulled Pillarchus out of his fantasies. "Oh, the amulet?" he said. "Well, it is said that it was given to Alexander by the priests at Siwa. The story goes that it contains a message from the gods."

"A message from the gods? What does it say?"

"No one knows," said Pillarchus. "It was written by the gods, you see, so no one could actually understand what it said."

"What's the point of that?"

"I believe that *is* the point."

Targa shook his head in disgust at such foolishness. "And this amulet," he said, "is how your king will know he has found Alexander?"

"Yes!" Pillarchus cried happily. "It is well documented that the King of Kings wore the amulet around his neck at all times and, according to Lianah, it lay against his chest even as his remains were mummified."

"Is it valuable?"

"No, I believe it is more an item of curiosity than of value."

The conversation continued for a while before dwindling to a stop as the sun climbed high in the sky. They continued along the path, and a combination of fatigue and heat and the rhythmic beat of hooves caused their heads to droop with occasional snatched dozes.

Pillarchus was enjoying the sensation of slipping in and out of his dreams as they plodded along to the hypnotic hoofbeats. One moment he was blankly staring at the view of the dusty path between his horse's ears and a moment later he would be surrounded by palatial splendour as he smugly knelt before his astonished king. He was indulging in just such a fantasy when the bridle of his mare was roughly seized and he had to frantically clutch at the horse's mane to stop himself from falling. He then found himself staring into a heavily scarred and bearded face that was yelling at him in a language he didn't understand. He turned instinctively to Targa, only to see two more bandits reach up and pull Targa from his saddle while he desperately tried to free his sword.

Pillarchus stared in horror as Targa was quickly disarmed and then beaten as he lay helpless on the ground. A heartbeat later, the point of Targa's own sword was plunged into his neck and the sudden tang of blood in the air caused Pillarchus' horse to rear in alarm. Pillarchus tumbled to the ground and, with terrified panic, he sensed his attackers swarm around him. Curling into a ball, he then felt their blows on his head and his back. He almost didn't feel the blade when it entered his side, but as it twisted inside him, he screamed in agony. He knew then, as his blood pooled warm and thick beside him, there would be no glorious audience with the king. With the last of his fading vision he saw the bandits rip the packs from the back of the donkey and eagerly pull their contents free.

Pillarchus almost gave a grim smile as he watched the dumb confusion on his killers' faces. They stared with comical disappointment at the worthless grey slabs. The scratches in the thin clay that revealed the true resting place of Alexander the Great were meaningless to these simple hill-bandits, and so, with furious disgust, they hurled the clay-filled frames over the side of the path and watched them tumble down the mountainside. As the bandits then gathered together the captured animals and took whatever they could find of value from the bodies of their two victims, the little slabs of river-mud eventually came to rest on the steep slope of the high mountain.

Where they baked gently in the hot sun.

EIGHTEEN

London, Jamesy mused as he made his way along Bloomsbury Street, was expansive enough to suit all seasons. The narrow, cobbled alleyways of the capital, dimly lit, were perfectly atmospheric in the sad drizzle of winter, while London's leafy avenues would rustle, preen and shiver in the roaring flames of autumn.

In the spring, the heaths and parklands that draped the city like patches of fabric would burst open with all the gaudy colours of joy and hope and life, and then there was the summer when London would tip her crown to a jaunty angle and let shine the sparkling diamonds of her rivers and lakes and waterways, seducing the countless visitors who poured in to gape at the shameless old flirt and to thrill and to be enthralled.

The sun shone on London's pompous glory, and Jamesy, for one, was happy to let himself be seduced. Warmed and cheered by the shimmering grandeur, he strolled with purpose towards what he had often felt was his spiritual home.

Life was good, he decided, realising that if he could forget his misery – even for just a moment – then it might give him some cause for hope. It suggested that there was a chance he would be able to move on. A chance that Hannah would one day be a memory, smeared hazy by time, and he would be happy with a different life in some bright, new future. It was a small chance, he knew, but it was a chance, nonetheless.

Jamesy had no illusions about the upcoming rendezvous in Victoria he had arranged with Hannah. He had resigned himself to the fact that the strict doctrine to which Hannah adhered would allow her no room for manoeuvre. If Hannah had been led to believe that any dalliance with a wicked blasphemer like himself could be an impediment to any chance of eternal life, then what hope did he have? He couldn't compete with the promise of everlasting salvation, bathed in the glory and the light of Almighty God. He wouldn't know where to begin. But strangely enough – and to the puzzled exasperation of Tone – Jamesy placed no blame on either Hannah or her unbending beliefs. He understood that life was complicated. He understood that everyone had to find their own way. Everyone, Jamesy believed, was required to make their own sense of a bewildering world. Everyone had to find a reality that suited them and would enable them to easier negotiate the complexities of existence. Each to their own, in other words.

Jamesy suspected that, because of this, Tone considered him something of a hypocrite, and he could easily understand why. His motto, after all, had long been *Cast a Cold Eye,* meaning he had always been passionate about uncovering truths that could be considered both objective and incontrovertible. So, in that respect, he supposed, he could be accused of hypocrisy for not applying a *cold eye* to the slippery vagaries of faith.

But that, in Jamesy's mind, was different. Facts, for one thing, could be held up to the light. Facts could be examined, tested, held to account and scrutinized. They could be black or they could be white. Any fact that sat on the spectrum between black and white was no longer a fact, but an opinion. But faith was different. Faith defied cold classification. Faith, not being tethered to anything tangible, could be micro-tailored to suit the individual, and Jamesy could appreciate the need for such flexibility. Life could be impossibly confusing, so if it sometimes took a subtle distortion of reality to provide some comfort and hope, then Jamesy had no problem with it. Despite Tone's protestations.

As he turned the corner into Great Russell Street and could make out the entrance just ahead, Jamesy felt a thrill that he would soon be reacquainted with the treasures he had first encountered as a boy. The open space in front of the grand building was wrapped, on three sides, by austere Ionic columns that soared more than forty feet into the air, and Jamesy, as he approached, paused briefly to admire the imposing sight. He then smiled to himself and, with a spring in his step, made his way inside the British Museum.

Once he had entered, he found a little reception office and went up to the middle-aged woman – Brenda, according to her name-tag – who sat behind a desk on the left-hand side just inside the door.

"Hello," he said, "I have an appointment with –"

"Are you James?" Jamesy turned to see a small, neatly dressed man with a full beard and a balding head. He was standing in a corner of the office, flicking through a glossy catalogue.

"Doctor Irving?"

"Yes, yes," said Doctor Irving, grabbing Jamesy's hand and shaking it enthusiastically. "It's good to meet you. I found our phone conversation quite intriguing, and I've been looking forward to seeing you in the flesh." He stood back and looked Jamesy up and down. "Well, you'll do, I suppose," he said, making Jamesy smile. "You'll want to get started right away then, James. Have you had lunch?"

"Oh yes, I'm fine," Jamesy replied. "And like you said, I'm ready to go."

"Good man! Come with me, then!" Doctor Irving led Jamesy out of the office and through the spacious public galleries that swarmed with tourists and students. Jamesy followed Doctor Irving through a door marked *Private*, and then down a flight of stairs. They both chatted happily as they walked, passing through one set of doors after another, moving further away from the crowds in the busy public spaces. They went down a few more flights of stairs and the air became hushed and hallowed as they ventured ever deeper into the very bowels of the museum.

Jamesy had first visited the British Museum as a teenager during a school trip to London and had returned many times since. The exhibits he had seen there had instantly captured his imagination, and he had been transported to the lush, green banks of the Nile in the times of the Pharaohs, to the Athens of Themistocles and Socrates, and to the plains of the ancient Sumerians where western civilisation had begun.

But perhaps what had fascinated Jamesy more than anything was the museum's collection of clay tablets that contained what many historians believed to be mankind's earliest form of writing: *cuneiform*.

The cuneiform style of writing was formed by pressing a stylus – often a simple reed that grew by a river – onto a layer of clay that had been pressed into a wooden frame. The end of the reed-stylus would make tiny, elongated triangular shapes in the soft clay and it was the different arrangement of these triangles that made up the words of the language being written. It was such a simple but effective way of conveying information that it had endured for thousands of years and had been adopted by many languages, until it was superseded by ink on parchment, papyrus, and eventually paper.

These clay slabs would often be subjected to enough heat to make them bake into rock-hard tablets, and it was this durability that allowed them to survive relatively intact right through to the modern age.

Jamesy and Doctor Irving arrived in the first of a series of rooms that were filled with all sorts of cabinets, cupboards and waist-high chests of shallow wooden drawers. Doctor Irving stood in the middle of the first room and waved an arm around him.

"I suppose you're already aware that we don't have anywhere near enough space upstairs to put the entire collection on display," he said.

"Yes, I knew that," said Jamesy, "but … but are you saying that all of these cabinets have cuneiform tablets in them?"

"Oh yes, these rooms contain the bulk of the museum's collection. There are probably other bits and pieces scattered here and there, of course, but you should find enough to keep you busy just here."

Jamesy was silent, feeling suddenly daunted by the task confronting him.

"Yes, there's well over a hundred thousand pieces in these rooms," said Doctor Irving happily. "Should keep you going for a while! Have you thought of a particular topic for your thesis?"

"Well, I had been thinking of charting the geographical spread of cuneiform over the course of its existence, and how the style of it evolved over that period."

Doctor Irving nodded. "That's quite a lot of ground to cover," he said. "Both metaphorically and, indeed, literally."

"Yes," said Jamesy looking around him, "I'm beginning to appreciate that."

"I'm sure you're up to the task. And once you've got your doctorate James, what *then*? Are you planning to specialise in Assyriology?"

"Just general field-archaeology to begin with."

"Ah yes, well I suppose we all have to sow our wild oats while we're still young." Doctor Irving tapped a finger against Jamesy's chest. "But when you tire of that, then just you make sure that you get your head down to some proper study."

"I'll do that," laughed Jamesy.

Doctor Irving then gave Jamesy a quick run-through of each storage section and explained to him just where he could expect to find those items that might prove relevant to his research.

"I think that's everything, James," he said after a while, "but if you have any queries, then just come and find me. I shouldn't have strayed too far away. Good luck, and I'll come and check in on you a little later on."

Doctor Irving then exited the room, leaving Jamesy alone in a heavy silence. He stood in the midst of a hundred thousand clay tablets spanning three thousand years of human history and he felt numb. He didn't have the slightest idea where he should start.

It was almost two hours later when Doctor Irving returned. He was surprised to find Jamesy hunched over a table, staring at a photograph.

"Have you found something interesting, James?" he called out from across the room. Jamesy looked up, then passed the photograph along the table as Doctor Irving approached.

"I'm not sure," he confessed. "I can't decipher it."

"Let's take a look." Doctor Irving picked up the photograph and examined it closely. It was a black and white image of a clay tablet taken at such an angle that the lower half was out of focus. Doctor Irving frowned and turned the picture over to glance at the back. He read out the message that was scribbled there in blue ink. *Hindu Kush, 40.* He looked at Jamesy.

"Where on Earth did you find this?" he asked.

"Over here." Jamesy led Doctor Irving to a cupboard on the other side of the room. "It was in this box with a lot of other photos, right at the back here. It looks like there's more than one box in there too."

"What are the other photographs like?"

"Oh, they're all fairly standard stuff," said Jamesy, "but this one stood out because I just couldn't recognise any of the characters."

Doctor Irving looked again at the image. "Mmm, I see what you mean," he said. "Of course, it doesn't help that half of the writing is blurred out."

"I know, but what *can* be read doesn't seem to make any sense. Do you know where the tablet itself is?"

"That's just what I was wondering," said Doctor Irving. "I don't understand why we would have photographs of tablets, when we already –" He stopped and stared at Jamesy. "Oh, I think I know what these boxes are." He retrieved the box that Jamesy had pointed out and began flicking through the contents. The photographs were of all different sizes and were of varying quality. Some were in colour, and some were monochrome. "Ah yes, I remember now."

"Remember what?" asked Jamesy.

"Well, it was before my time here, you understand," Doctor Irving began. "It must have been more than ten years ago. My predecessor back then, Professor Crummey, had an idea that the museum should attempt to make a comprehensive inventory of all the cuneiform items in the country, and to that end he sent out requests to museums all over the UK for their assistance. Actually, I think he may have been in contact with private collectors as well."

"It sounds ambitious."

"A little too ambitious, I'm afraid. It soon became apparent that it was going to be far too much work even for the dedicated team that we have here at the museum, and the whole project was quietly dropped once Professor Crummey retired about a year later."

"So, you're saying that the tablet in this picture could be anywhere?"

"Anywhere in the UK, James, yes. Presumably *Hindu Kush* refers to where it was discovered, but I don't know what the *40* means"

"A year, maybe?"

"Possibly, though I doubt it. Why not simply write the year in full?"

Jamesy took the photo from Doctor Irving and looked at it again. "I just don't understand why I can't read it," he said. "It isn't Indus Valley, is it?"

"No, it isn't Indus Valley," said Doctor Irving as he stared at the picture in Jamesy's hand. "I must confess that Indus Valley was my first instinct when you said you were struggling, but no, it isn't that. It's very puzzling." Indus Valley was the one language in cuneiform script that experts had yet to translate, but Jamesy's tablet was clearly not Indus Valley which meant that it should have been readable. The fact that it wasn't, however, was causing Doctor Irving some concern.

"I'll need to show this to some of my colleagues," he said, "to see if anyone has any ideas."

"Do you think it would be possible for me to get a photocopy of it?" Jamesy asked.

"What? A photocopy? Oh yes, yes, of course, James, I can organise that for you. But why, though? Do you think you might be able to work it out?"

"Me? No," said Jamesy. "but I just might know someone who can."

NINETEEN

Joker had never been to the new Italian restaurant in University Street, but he had been looking for an opportunity to visit for a while now. This seemed like the perfect excuse.

He had arranged a blind date for Kevin with a girl that Joker's cousin had suggested, and he and Carol, along with Tone and Claire, were planning to accompany them on their date in order to smooth things along and to provide some moral support.

Carol had called to Joker's flat after work and, once she had showered and changed, they took a taxi to the Shore Road to pick up Kevin's date before heading back across town to the restaurant.

At about the same time, Tone and Claire were making their way along University Street.

"You smell good," said Claire, having just caught a whiff of Tone's aftershave.

"Well, if you play your cards right," said Tone, "I'll let you have a really good sniff later."

"Jesus, you really know how to sweep a girl off her feet, don't you?"

"I know. And it all comes naturally, too!"

"Have you ever met this girl that Joseph's bringing?"

"Nope," Tone replied. "And I don't think that Joker has either. It's just some girl that his cousin knows from work."

"Oh, so it's a blind date for everybody, then?"

"Looks that way."

Kevin was already seated at the table when Tone and Claire arrived. He looked nervous.

"All right there, Kevin?" asked Tone as he and Claire sat down.

"Yeah, not too bad. Not sure if I like this whole idea, though."

"Oh, don't worry," said Claire. "I'm sure Joseph knows what he's doing." Tone and Kevin both stared at her, but Tone decided not to pursue the matter and, instead, took a look around him.

"Nice place this, isn't it?" he said. The interior of the restaurant had been designed to give the impression of being outdoors in some sleepy little Italian village. The ground floor dining area was surrounded by artificial trees and by tall Romanesque buildings that had balconies at various levels where diners on the upper floors could sit and look down onto the *piazza*.

"Yeah, it's very clever," said Claire. "It's got a lovely, cosy atmosphere too."

"I wonder if they got much grief when Italy knocked Ireland out of the World Cup," said Tone.

"I wouldn't have thought so," Claire decided. "I mean, the people of Belfast might be idiots, but they're not stupid." Tone grinned at her reply.

"Mmm," Kevin murmured, his mind elsewhere.

"Jesus, Kevin," said Tone, "try to chill out a wee bit."

"I wish I could."

At that moment, Joker, Carol and another girl were led to the table, and they all greeted each other happily.

"This is Ann," said Joker, and he introduced Tone, Claire and Kevin in turn. "You sit there beside Kevin, Ann, and you can get to know each other a wee bit better."

Ann took off her jacket and draped it over the back of her chair before sitting down. Taking occasional glances in her direction, Kevin noted that she had a chiselled profile that could be considered more handsome than pretty. Her medium-length, streaked-blonde hair was blown back in fashionable waves, and she wore a short-sleeved, white, lacy blouse that softened her appearance with a gentle femininity. From the corner of his eye, Kevin then caught a glimpse of part of a tattoo on her upper arm. The top half of the image was obscured by the sleeve of Ann's blouse, but Kevin could recognise it for what it was. It was a depiction of the palm and closed fingers of an open hand. Coloured red.

The *Red Hand of Ulster*. Although it had long been used in the Irish Republic's provincial flag for Ulster, the Red Hand had been seized upon by the Unionists in Northern Ireland as a symbol of their separateness from the rest of the island. The image had become almost a logo for Ulster unionism and was particularly popular with loyalist paramilitaries.

Kevin had already assumed it was likely that anyone being introduced by Joker would be from the unionist community, but to be given such a stark illustration of where her political sympathies lay, brought him up short. He couldn't imagine taking Ann to meet his republican granny up in the Ballymurphy estate. And even his own liberal and open-minded parents, he thought, might baulk at such a candid display of naked sectarianism.

He pushed the thoughts aside, however, and decided he should at least give the girl a chance. She seemed perfectly nice, after all.

Tone ordered some bottles of wine for the table while everyone else studied the menu.

"I'm not all that bothered about starters," said Joker. "What about anybody else?"

"No, just a main's fine for me," said Carol, and they all agreed.

The waiter came back with the wine, which he poured, and then went to fetch a jar of olive oil and a bowl of grated Parmesan for the centre of the table. He was just about to ask if they were ready to order when Ann exclaimed, "Jesus! What's that smell?"

The waiter looked at her and frowned in consternation. She was wrinkling her nose in disgust.

"Um …" said the waiter, "I believe it is the *Parmigiano-Reggiano*."

"The what?"

"The Parmesan," he said, pointing to the bowl on the table. "It is grated cheese. You sprinkle it on your meal." He smiled. "Now," he said looking around, "is everyone ready to order?"

"Just give us a few more minutes," Tone told him. He nodded and walked off.

Kevin could sense that Ann, beside him, was simmering – almost vibrating – with fury.

"Was *he* trying to make a cunt out of me?" Ann demanded as she glared around the table.

"What?" asked Kevin, stupefied.

"He was, wasn't he?" she insisted. "He was trying to make some sort of fucking cunt out of me!"

"No, I … I don't think …"

Ann got to her feet, and, to Kevin's horror, she strode after the poor, unsuspecting waiter.

The attention of all the other diners in the restaurant was then attracted to the scene that followed, as Ann stood and berated the cowering waiter using the most foul-mouthed language imaginable.

Joker watched for a moment, and then turned to Kevin. "So," he asked eagerly, "what do you think of Ann?"

Kevin slowly turned his head towards Joker and could only stare at him in open-mouthed disbelief.

"I've never been thrown out of a restaurant before," observed Claire as she, Tone and Kevin walked down University Street. Joker and Carol had already taken Ann home in a taxi that had been ordered to the restaurant.

"You've led a sheltered life," said Tone casually. "You see, if you stick with me, you'll get to have all sorts of new experiences."

"I never even got to finish my glass of wine."

"Well, the night is young," Tone declared. "I can get you thrown out lots of other places if you want. What about you, Kevin? Are you up for it?"

"What? Um … no, thanks all the same, Tone," said Kevin. "I think I'll just shoot on, if that's okay."

"No problem, and don't you worry. I'm sure I can get you set up with somebody who's a wee bit more … well, demure."

"Right … right, okay," Kevin said distractedly, before disappearing into the night.

"Do you have anybody in mind?" asked Claire when Kevin had gone.

"No," Tone admitted, "but how hard can it be?"

TWENTY

The guesthouse was situated in a residential street, not far from Brighton's busy commercial centre. Once Seamus had parked, he and Gary got out, fetched their bags from the back of the car and walked to the front door.

"So, what made you pick this place, then?" Gary asked as he surveyed the front of the building. It had once been a large nineteenth-century townhouse, possibly a second residence for a prosperous London merchant, but now, like the majority of properties in the street, it had been converted to cater for Brighton's healthy tourist trade.

"Oh, it was just some friend of mine that recommended it," said Seamus evasively. He rang the doorbell and stared ahead, aware of Gary's scrutiny in his peripheral vision.

"Some friend of yours?" asked Gary suspiciously. "One of your wee gay mates, you mean?"

Seamus turned to face Gary with a belligerent look in his eyes. "What if it was?" he challenged. "Why would that make a difference? Do you think it's going be some sort of gay guesthouse?"

"No, that's not what I'm saying!" Gary insisted.

"You're fucking paranoid, you know that?"

"Look, it makes fuck all difference to me. I just want to know where I stand, that's all."

"Where you stand? What the fuck is that supposed to mean?"

"I'm just saying that it's best to know what you're getting –" The front door opened and Seamus and Gary were greeted by a broad smile.

"Good afternoon," said the man with the smile. He was wearing a floral, open-necked shirt, and his tanned face was bright and friendly. Seamus guessed he was in his early forties.

"Oh, right there, mate," said Seamus. "We're booked in for a couple of nights. Name of Green."

"Of course, yes, come in," the man said, still smiling. He led them down a long hallway towards a small reception area. "I'm Alastair, by the way."

Gary gave Seamus a knowing look, but Seamus ignored him. "I'm Seamus," he told Alastair, "and this is Gary."

"Lovely to meet you both," They reached the little desk in reception and Alastair went through the bookings. "Ah yes, here we are. Seamus Green. Two nights, a twin room, wasn't it? That'll be Room 9." Alastair looked beneath the desk for the key. "Is that an Irish accent?" he asked as he handed the key to Seamus.

"It is, yes," Seamus told him. "Belfast."

"Aye," Gary added, "to be honest, we were a wee bit worried about coming here with these accents. You know, with the Grand Hotel and all that?" Six years previously the Irish Republican Army had targeted the Conservative Party Conference with a huge bomb at the Grand Hotel on Brighton's seafront in an attempt to wipe out the British Government. Five people had been killed in an attack that had shaken the nation, though there were those who bemoaned the fact that the widely unpopular Prime Minister at the time, Margaret Thatcher, had survived. Gary and Seamus had both been a little concerned that the scars here would still be raw, and that any Northern Ireland accent would be viewed with suspicion, if not open hostility.

"Yes, that was terrible," said Alastair, "but most people don't really concern themselves with all that political stuff. We've all got our own problems to worry about, haven't we?"

"That's true," agreed Seamus.

Alastair led them up a flight of stairs. "Were you planning to eat here this evening? Or do you want to get something in town?"

"Oh, I didn't realise you did evening meals," said Seamus. He looked at Gary. "I'm happy to eat here, what about you?"

Gary shrugged. "Yeah, suits me." They stopped at the door to their room and Alastair nodded with another smile.

"We start serving dinner at six," he said. "We passed the dining room when we went to get the key, I don't know if you noticed it."

"Yeah, I did," said Gary, "it was on the left, wasn't it? Just before the stairs?"

"That's right. It's actually quite a good menu, if I do say so myself." Alastair's smile was warm and genuine. "Well, I'll leave you to it. If there's anything you need, just give me a shout. I'll be hovering around downstairs somewhere; you can't miss me."

The food was excellent, and Gary expressed surprise that it was just he and Seamus in the dining room.

"I thought the guesthouse was full," he said to Alastair. "There's a *No Vacancy* sign out the front."

"Oh, we *are* full," Alastair told him, "but a lot of our guests prefer to eat out in town. I expect we'll have some people dining with us later, though. We serve dinner right up to eight o'clock."

At that moment another man entered the room, a little older than Alastair, though just as tanned. "How was your meal?" he asked smiling.

"This is Julian," said Alastair. "He does all of the cooking around here."

"And much else besides," Julian sighed. He then shared a fond glance with Alastair. Seamus could sense Gary's amused stare, but again he ignored it and looked at Julian.

"The meal was lovely, thanks," he said.

"Yeah," Gary agreed. "It was absolutely class!"

"Why, thank you!" said Julian, giving a little bow. "You're from Ireland, then?"

Gary and Seamus both nodded. "Yeah, from Belfast."

"I believe I have some family in Ireland," Julian told them. "On my mother's side."

They all chatted amiably for a while until Gary and Seamus said they were planning to go and check out Brighton's nightlife. Alastair and Julian began asking them what sort of places they were interested in and, as they talked, it soon transpired that Seamus, having recently come out as gay, was keen to further explore that side of his nature. Alastair looked at Gary.

"And you're *not* gay, I take it?"

"Most definitely not," said Gary cheerfully, "but I'm happy enough to tag along with Seamus here, to make sure he doesn't get up to any mischief."

"Well, if you're sure you don't mind checking it out," Julian said, "then Brighton has actually developed quite a lively gay scene. We could recommend a few places if you like."

"If you don't mind," said Seamus, "that would be helpful."

"No problem. Now let's see, it's Thursday, isn't it?"

"Oh, what about the Bulldog?" exclaimed Alastair. "Doesn't Sandy play there on a Thursday?"

"Sandy?" asked Gary.

"Yes, Sandy is ..." Alastair looked at Julian. "How do I describe Sandy?"

"I suppose you could call Sandy a drag act," Julian told Gary, "though probably not like any drag act you've ever seen before. He recites poetry on stage." Julian laughed at the look on Gary's face. "Trust me," he said, "Sandy's very funny. He's got a little backing group as well that provides some musical accompaniment. It's one of the most popular acts in Brighton."

"Sounds like we should check it out," said Seamus.

"Aye, why not?" Gary added with a shrug.

Alastair and Julian gave them directions to the Bulldog and wished them luck as they stepped outside. It was still bright out, and the warm salty breeze buoyed their spirits as they walked along.

"You sure you're okay with this?" asked Seamus.

"Yeah, no problem," Gary told him. "I'm curious, if nothing else. Besides," he said, "there might be some lesbians there."

TWENTY ONE

Hannah, Becky and a few other members of their group had just attended a small service in a side chapel inside the cathedral and were now taking a look around at the ornate interior.

"They crowned Richard the Lionheart here, apparently," said Becky, reading from a pamphlet. "Oh, and Jane Austin's buried here as well."

"Have you ever read any Jane Austin?" asked Hannah.

"No, but I've heard of her."

"I suppose that's the same thing."

"And look, see this big window thing?" Becky pointed to an enormous stained-glass window that occupied an entire wall at the cathedral's western end. "Apparently it was destroyed by Oliver Cromwell's men in 1642. And then, years later, the cathedral authorities tried to put it back together again, but they didn't have a clue what they were doing; so, if you look closely, it's all just random bits and pieces stuck here, there and everywhere."

"It's still pretty, I suppose," said Hannah, "but I don't see what it has to do with Christianity."

"I know what you mean," laughed Becky. "Greg says that the Church of England is just Catholicism with a different name."

"Where *is* Greg?" Hannah asked. "I thought he was supposed to be here this morning." She looked inquisitively around the faces in the group, but it seemed that no one had seen him.

"Maybe he fancied doing something different for the last day," someone suggested.

"Yeah, I'm sure he'll show up somewhere," said Becky. "Though I thought you'd be more interested in knowing where Gordon was."

Hannah blushed because Becky was not far from the truth. She had thought of little else since that first night when she and Gordon had met. When he wasn't nearby, she wondered where he was, and when he was nearby, she wondered what it would feel like to have his hands touch her skin, caressing and exploring, and moving slowly towards the places that –.

"What do want to do about lunch?" asked Becky.

"What?"

"Lunch?"

"Um …"

"There's that wee French place in town," said Daniel, the group's tall young farmer.

"Oh yeah," Becky exclaimed. "It's nice in there, isn't it?"

"We'd need to get a move on, though, if we want to get a table."

"Right then, are you up for it, Hannah?"

"What?"

"Lunch! God!" said Becky. "What's up with you today?"

After a lunch of baguettes and *moules marinières*, Hannah and Becky ambled back towards the cathedral while the rest of the group went off to do some sight-seeing. Hannah had all but given up on the idea of becoming inflamed with evangelical fervour, but she still found the festival interesting in an almost detached kind of way.

"Do you think you've got much out of this week, then, Becky?" she asked as they walked.

"Don't know," replied Becky. "Don't know what I was expecting, to be honest."

"I think I was probably expecting too much," said Hannah quietly.

"Still, it's been an experience, hasn't it? And you got to meet Gorgeous Gordon."

"Oh, stop it, you!" Hannah laughed.

"And speaking of Gordon," said Becky excitedly, "wasn't he going on about those guys over there?" She pointed to two men sitting at a table just inside one of the marquees. Attached to the front of the table was a cloth banner with the words *Yeshua the Teacher* printed on it.

"Oh yeah," said Hannah. "I think he did mention them, didn't he?"

"Do you want to have a laugh?" Becky asked while tugging at Hannah's sleeve.

"Yeah, why not?" said Hannah. "It should be a bit of fun."

There were a few empty chairs scattered around inside the marquee, so Hannah and Becky grabbed one each and pulled them over to the table where they sat down facing the two men. The man on the left was large and quite stocky with a greying beard and wire-framed spectacles, while his companion seemed a little younger and had a friendly, easy-going manner.

"Good afternoon," said the bearded man, reaching across to shake their hands. "I'm Bartholomew, and this is my friend, Josh."

"Nice to meet you both," said Hannah and Becky.

"The fact that you're here would suggest that you're curious to know what we're all about, is that right?" asked Josh.

"Well, actually," said Hannah, "we had already heard that you don't accept the divinity of Jesus. Is that true?"

Bartholomew laughed. "Word gets around, doesn't it? Yes, it's true," he said, "but we don't believe that that should devalue what Jesus – or *Yeshua*, to give him his real name – had to say."

"But you don't believe he was the Son of God?" said Becky. "Why not?"

"There's no evidence to suggest he was anything other than a normal man."

"Have you read the Bible?" asked Hannah smiling.

"I've been studying the Bible for over thirty years," Bartholomew told her. "I've read the earliest known texts in the original Hebrew, Aramaic and Greek. I've studied, at some length, the Latin Vulgate of Jerome, as well as the Greek editions of Erasmus and Wettstein. I've also examined many of the English translations, including the King James and some of the more modern versions. So yes," he concluded, "I've read the Bible."

"Oh," said Hannah.

"Don't let him intimidate you," laughed Josh. "He's just showing off."

"I was once a Christian fundamentalist," Bartholomew explained. "I grew up conditioned to believe that every word in the Bible was put there by God, making it perfect and true in every way. And I *did* believe it! I believed it with every fibre of my being. And because of that belief, I wanted to know everything there was to know about this incredible book so that I could strengthen my faith and my understanding of God."

"Let me guess," said Becky. "It didn't go well."

Bartholomew laughed again. "That depends on your point of view, doesn't it?"

"So, you lost your faith because you studied the Bible?" asked Hannah.

"I never lost my faith in the teachings of Yeshua," said Bartholomew. "But understanding that the Bible had, over thousands of years, been chopped and changed and mistranslated and copied incorrectly made me realise that it was a work of man, not God."

"Yes, but even if you acknowledge that Scripture was written down by men," argued Hannah, "you can still agree that they did so under the influence of the Holy Spirit."

"I'm sure a lot of them were under the influence," said Josh, making Becky laugh.

"Why?" demanded Bartholomew. "Why do I have to agree?"

"Well, because …" Hannah hesitated. Saying that the Bible is the Word of God because the Bible says it is the Word of God had always been one of her favourite points to make during debates, but now it just seemed like a weak and circular argument.

"I'm sure you're familiar with the inconsistencies that the Bible contains," Bartholomew went on. "Even the four Gospel stories differ on many points."

"Minor points," said Hannah, though even she thought it sounded hollow.

"Minor points?" Bartholomew scoffed. "Only two of the Gospels mention the nativity story and they hardly agree on any points at all. For one thing, Luke doesn't mention the Massacre of the Innocents or the flight into Egypt, does he? That's hardly a minor point. If the Gospel authors were all writing under divine guidance, as you say they were, then the least you could expect is for them all to agree."

Hannah sighed, feeling that her own nagging doubts were being laid bare and exposed to the world. She refused to accept it, though. She tried to force aside her doubts and embrace the love she knew still existed in her heart for her Lord and Saviour, Jesus Christ.

"How do you justify the Christian paradox?" Josh suddenly asked. He seemed genuinely curious.

"I'm sorry?" said Hannah. "Paradox? I don't know what you mean?"

"Well, I assume that the leaders of your Church like to tell you that if you sin, then you'll go to Hell, right?"

"Of course," said Hannah confidently, feeling now on safer ground. She then experienced a sudden flash of memory from when she was a young teenager. She and Becky had been strolling through their hometown, laughing and happy on a summer's day, when they happened to pass one of the elders from their Church. She could still see the frown of disapproval on his face as he stared at the hemline of her skirt, and she could still feel the tightness in her chest as, gripped by anxiety, she went running home to throw herself sobbing onto her bed.

Hell was real all right. Hannah knew all about Hell.

"And these same people will also tell you that Christ died so that your sins would be forgiven, isn't that right?"

"Yes, but that's …" Hannah paused. Why had that never occurred to her? She had been told her whole life that God was all about forgiveness. It was what her entire faith was based on. Why, then, was she so terrified of sinning when her love for Jesus guaranteed that she'd be forgiven? If wearing a short skirt was a sin, then what did it matter? She'd be forgiven. She felt suddenly relieved, and then angry and then confused. *Is that really how it works?* she wondered. Was she really free to do whatever she liked, knowing that nothing mattered because, ultimately, she would be forgiven? She turned to Becky, but Becky was concentrating on trying to flirt with Josh.

Hannah shook her head. She had never been entirely sure of Becky's true commitment to the faith, but maybe Becky had the right idea.

"You see what I'm getting at, don't you?" Josh smiled, and then leaned back and gave Becky a shameless wink. Becky giggled.

The world's gone mad, thought Hannah. Here she was, having probably the biggest existential crisis of her life, and her oldest friend was sitting beside her, behaving like a giddy schoolgirl.

"Well yes," she said, "I suppose you do make some interesting points, but I think we need to get going. Isn't that right, Becky?" Hannah glared at her friend.

"Do we?"

"Yes, we do! Now come on!"

They got up and left the marquee, with Becky glancing back and smiling.

"Don't you think he's a bit too old for you, Becky?" asked Hannah as they walked across the grass. "Not to mention the fact that he's an atheist."

"His age doesn't bother me," said Becky. "It just makes him more experienced, don't you think?"

"*Rebecca!*"

"Oh, Hannah," Becky sighed, "you really do need to loosen up, you know."

When they got back to their hotel, Becky spotted a few of their friends in the bar and happily joined them while Hannah went upstairs to freshen up. She reached the door to her room and opened her bag to search for the key when she became aware of a commotion coming from just around the corner of the corridor. She was about to open her door and ignore it when she realised that Greg's room was round that way and, remembering that he had been missing all day, she decided to investigate. As she got closer, she could hear a man's voice raised in anger as well as some loud bangs, as if someone were hammering on a door. She turned the corner and was astonished to see the young man she had met a few days earlier. She had never learned his name, but he was a member of the group that called themselves *The Way*. He was the young man that had the submissive wife, who he called … what was it? Martha? Was that it? The man was banging on Greg's door.

"Is there something wrong?" asked Hannah.

He turned to stare at her, then turned back to the door. He was just about to resume his hammering when the door suddenly opened, and Greg's face appeared. He looked terrible, thought Hannah, and he had clearly been drinking. By now, more people had appeared, curious to see what all the noise was about.

"I'm sorry," Greg slurred miserably. "I'm really, really sorry."

The angry young man pushed past Greg and, as the door was flung open, Hannah caught a glimpse of Martha, sitting up in the single bed. She was naked and she was drunk, and she was laughing hysterically at the look on her husband's face.

And even more shocking, Hannah thought wryly; her head was uncovered.

TWENTY TWO

Gary and Seamus stared at the poster by the door of the Bulldog pub. It was a simple text-based design with white lettering set against a pale blue background.

"*Sandy Cove and the Mermaids*." Gary read. "Is that gay enough for you?"

"Mmm … not sure," said Seamus, feeling suddenly nervous. "What do you reckon?"

"I don't see why not. It's a bar, isn't it? We might as well check it out while we're here."

They went inside and found a table beside a small stage area. It was still early so the bar wasn't busy and Gary was quickly served two pints of lager. He went back to the table and sat down beside Seamus who passed him a cigarette. They both lit up.

"Not too bad in here, is it?" Gary said. "Decent size, too."

"Yeah, it seems okay," said Seamus, looking around.

"I think the barman fancies me," said Gary.

"I'm sure he does."

"He was telling me there's always a big crowd in on a Thursday night."

Seamus looked at Gary. "What, because of …?"

"Aye, because of your man, Sandy Cove."

"Well, we've got good seats for it, I suppose."

"That's true."

It wasn't long before the bar began to fill up and Seamus and Gary soon found themselves having to almost shout to be heard.

"Have you been sussing out the talent?" asked Gary.

"What?"

"The talent!"

Seamus leaned forward. "What? The talent? Is that what you said?"

"Aye, is there anybody you fancy?"

"I've noticed a couple of good-looking fellas," Seamus told him. "But it seems to be mostly couples."

"They're probably saying that about us."

Seamus stared at Gary. "I hadn't even thought of that."

By nine o'clock, there was an air of excited expectancy, and when three men wearing shimmering blue and green dresses strolled onto the stage, a huge roar rose from the crowd. The three men stood by microphones on one side of the stage, with one poised by an electronic keyboard.

"Do you think these are the *Mermaids*?" Gary asked Seamus.

"Must be."

One of the *Mermaids* spoke into his mic. "Thank you, everyone!" he shouted to the crowd. The crowd roared back. "And now," he continued, "would you please put your hands together for the phenomenal Sandy Cove!"

Gary and Seamus were both swept up in the excitement as all eyes were drawn to a slight, dark-haired figure who stepped calmly from the shadows and took his place centre-stage. His presence seemed to electrify the crowd, and Seamus, for one, could understand why.

When Seamus and Gary were growing up, the only drag acts they ever got to see were people like Jimmy Young, Dick Emery and Danny LaRue who would often appear on television in brash, over-the top outfits in a grotesque parody of womanhood. They would clearly be men pretending to be women. The three *Mermaids* onstage seemed to be carrying on this tradition with their exaggerated breasts, unrealistic wigs and full-length, figure-hugging dresses that stretched over pot bellies and contrasted absurdly with hairy, manly arms. One of the *Mermaids* even had a beard.

Sandy Cove was different. His clothes were more tasteful – from his immaculate black nylon slacks to the fifties-style, grey woollen cardigan with white piping that elegantly covered his delicate frame. He was both sensual and strangely androgynous, like Dietrich in a suit, or a young Bowie in a dress. The beautifully tailored, understated clothing and his confident, easy grace combined to give an overall effect that was mesmerising.

Seamus was mesmerised.

Gary quietly studied the adoring look on Seamus' face and could tell that his friend was smitten. He had never seen Seamus look at anyone like that before and he knew that his oldest friend's emotions at this time would be in a fragile and precarious state, needing to be handled with tact, understanding and support.

"Wise the fuck up!" he said.

"What?" Seamus was startled. "What the fuck do you mean?"

"You've got no chance!"

"What are you talking about?"

"Your man up there! You've got no fucking chance! Me, on the other hand, I reckon –"

"Seriously!" cried Seamus. "What the fuck –?"

"Shut up! He's starting!"

A hush had fallen over the crowd as Sandy took the microphone from its stand. For the next hour and a half, he regaled the Bulldog with poetry that was accompanied by the keyboard and by the occasional backing vocals of the *Mermaids*. They were poems that were bawdy and clever and funny and touchingly sweet, and Seamus, along with everyone else, hung on every word.

The evening passed too quickly, and the show ended with the audience begging for more. Seamus hoped he might get a chance to meet with Sandy in the bar afterwards, but neither he nor any of his *Mermaids* appeared, and it wasn't long before last orders were called. The crowd seeped away, and Seamus, reluctantly, followed Gary to the street outside.

"I enjoyed that," said Gary as they made their way back to the guest-house. "It was a good laugh."

"It *was* good, wasn't it?" Seamus' words came automatically, for his mind was elsewhere. He was still clinging to the image of Sandy Cove, the slim young man who had stood with poise and elegance beneath the spotlight, and had kept Seamus, and all around him, enthralled and entranced for the entire time he had been on stage.

In the space of a few hours, Seamus felt that his life had been changed forever. He knew that he had never felt this way about anyone before, but his mind told him that Gary had a point. He didn't stand a chance.

His heart, though, was telling him something entirely different.

TWENTY THREE

The atmosphere in the hotel bar that evening was a little subdued. The scandal from earlier in the day had shaken Hannah and her friends, and they sat around their table mostly lost in their own thoughts. Mostly.

"Wouldn't have thought he had it in him," said Becky with that throaty, filthy laugh of hers.

"It's no laughing matter," Hannah scolded.

"Yes it is."

"It's obvious that Greg was led astray."

"It didn't take much for that, though, did it?" laughed Becky. "Greg has always been so high and mighty about the sanctity of marriage, hasn't he? And then it turns out he's just as horny as every other man."

"He's very remorseful," said Hannah. "He says it was a moment of weakness."

"I'm sure God will forgive him," said Becky airily.

At that moment, Gordon and Judith came into the bar and, spotting Hannah's group, they pulled some chairs over to the table.

"How are you all doing?" asked Gordon.

"Well, it hasn't been easy," Hannah told him. "I thought you were going to the choir service at the cathedral tonight."

"We were going to, but we decided we weren't really in the mood."

Hannah nodded. "I know what you mean." She felt a sudden thrill that he was there.

"Is Greg in his room?" asked Judith.

"Yes," said Becky. "I don't think we'll be seeing him again tonight."

Gordon leaned forward. "From what I've been hearing," he began, and everyone around the table leaned in closer, "this wasn't the first time that something like this has happened. I've met a few people who are familiar with *The Way*, and they say that this Martha woman has got a bit of a reputation for this sort of thing."

"*No!*" everyone gasped.

"I don't understand," said Hannah. "If it's happened before then why would her husband put up with it? Why would he still be with her?"

"That's the strange thing," Gordon said, lowering his voice. Everyone leaned in further. "The husband's name is Lucas, apparently, and it's been said that he actually gets some sort of thrill out of it all."

"*What?*" Hannah had never heard of anything so shocking. "He *approves* of it?"

Gordon shrugged and sat back. Becky smiled knowingly. "So, it's all just an act, is it?" she said. "The poor wee downtrodden wife and the strict, forbidding husband? It's one way to get your kicks, I suppose."

Hannah stared at Becky. She couldn't understand why Becky didn't seem to be particularly shocked by such behaviour. If anything, Hannah thought, she seemed quite familiar with the whole idea.

"I do think that *The Way* is a genuine movement," said Gordon, "but maybe some of its members aren't quite as committed to their guidelines as they should be."

"That's an understatement!" laughed Becky, and everyone laughed with her. Hannah, however, was stunned. How could they all treat so casually such appalling deceit? She noticed, then, that Gordon was not laughing, and instead was regarding her closely. She felt herself blush under his scrutiny. She picked up her glass of wine and stared into it as she sipped.

She then shocked herself by wishing that everyone would just go off to their rooms and leave her and Gordon at the table on their own. She wasn't quite sure what would happen in such a scenario, but her desire to find out was almost overwhelming. Gordon wasn't quite James, she knew, but Hannah was beginning to accept that, just maybe, James and her were never meant to be. It was a shame, of course, but, in spite of everything that had happened to her this week, Hannah still clung to her faith, and that faith would always be more compatible with the beliefs of Gordon than with those of James. Unconsciously and almost imperceptibly, she began to physically gravitate towards Gordon and, as if sensing something develop, her group, one-by-one, made their excuses and drifted away until only her and Becky, and Gordon and Judith remained.

Becky watched Hannah carefully. "Well," she said, stretching out her arms, "we've got an early start in the morning, so I think I'll call it a night." She caught Hannah's eye as she got up and gave a furtive wink. Hannah nodded in acknowledgement and sipped her wine.

"How have you enjoyed the week?" Gordon asked Hannah when Becky had gone.

"It's been all right, I suppose," said Hannah, gazing into Gordon's eyes. "Not quite what I'd been expecting, though."

"In what way?"

"Oh, I don't know," she said softly. "Maybe I just wasn't expecting there to be so many conflicting points of view."

"I know what you mean," laughed Gordon. Hannah felt a shiver of excitement when Judith got to her feet. Yawning, she bade both Gordon and Hannah goodnight, and then set off towards the stairs. It was now just the two of them.

Hannah knew that Gordon had a room to himself in the hotel, and she was terrified that she might start shaking with anticipation. To her mild irritation, Gordon kept talking.

"We *are* all Christians, after all," he was saying, "so you would expect a little more harmony in what we believe."

"Well, exactly," Hannah heard herself say. Her mind was racing. It was going to happen, she realised. Tonight! It was going to happen tonight!

She was certain of it. She was now on the brink of experiencing her first true kiss. And maybe even more besides.

"But the sheer variety of opinions on show was really quite breathtaking," said Gordon.

"Mmm …" Hannah murmured. He was prolonging her agony, she thought, but perhaps that was how it was done. The strength of her desire no longer came as a shock to her. She embraced it. There seemed to be no point in trying to contain it or deny it. It was part of her.

"The biggest concern for me, however …"

"Yes, yes," said Hannah, not really listening. She was urging the conversation to end, desperate now for the feel of Gordon's fingertips on her skin. For his tender caresses on those parts of her body that she barely even ...

"… was just how many of the people that were there," Gordon continued, and Hannah, without thinking, loosened the top buttons on her blouse, subconsciously showing off a glimpse of her breasts. She was nodding automatically to the rhythm of his words, wishing they would stop.

"… and these are people who all say they follow Scripture …" said Gordon.

"Oh, I know, I know!"

"… yet they still insist that we all live on some sort of spinning ball!"

"Oh yes, you're so right!" she gasped breathlessly. This was it. This was the moment that she … *wait … what was that*? Hannah frowned. *What did he just say*? She looked at him.

"I don't understand," she said.

"Well, as you know, Scripture tells us that the world we live on is flat. But so many of the people who were –"

"I'm sorry," said Hannah, trying to collect her thoughts. "Are you saying that you think the world is flat?"

"I don't *think* it's flat," Gordon said warily, "I know it is, because the Bible tells me it is."

"Does it?"

"Of course! *He has fixed the earth firm, immovable*," Gordon quoted. "And that phrase occurs several times in Scripture, as I'm sure you know."

"Well, yes, but …"

"I can quote many other passages in both the Old and New Testaments," Gordon went on, "that testify to the world being flat. I thought that you understood this."

"But … but…" Hannah was struggling to think coherently. Did Gordon genuinely believe these things he was saying? Or was it some sort of joke? "But there are photographs of Earth that were taken from space," she said. "I've seen them. The shape of the Earth just isn't in question."

"Don't tell me you've fallen for all of that propaganda!" Gordon cried in disbelief.

"Propaganda?"

"Yes! There's long been a conspiracy to push forward the agenda of the scientists," Gordon told her. "Some say it started with Darwin, but I think it goes back further than that. Back as far as the ancient Greeks, even. And it's been going on for so long now that they have no choice but to keep up the pretence. If the people understood even a fraction of how much they were being lied to, then no government in the world could survive their wrath."

Hannah blinked several times as she buttoned up her blouse. "I see," she said quietly. "Well, it's been nice meeting you, Gordon, but it really is getting late." She stood up and wished him a goodnight before heading for the stairs. She had to make a concerted effort not to run.

With a weary sigh, she stood at the door of her room and searched for her key. As she put the key in the lock and turned it, she realised she was deliberately refusing to acknowledge the new thoughts that were now tumbling around in her mind. She opened the door to her room, got changed and brushed her teeth, and then climbed quietly into bed.

TWENTY FOUR

Gary and Seamus were both up early and, after breakfast, they decided to go out and explore what Brighton had to offer. The day was already starting to warm up, with just a few insignificant clouds wandering aimlessly around an otherwise clear sky and Gary and Seamus naturally gravitated towards the seafront.

"Not a bad wee place," said Gary as they walked.

"What, Brighton?" asked Seamus. "No, it's not bad at all." They ambled along some quaint, shop-filled lanes until they came to a café with several tables outside that offered a decent view of the sea.

"Fancy a coffee?" asked Gary. "I've had enough of this walking lark."

"It's only been ten minutes."

"So? What's your point?"

"Nothing, just saying." They went inside and purchased some drinks and pastries and then managed to acquire the last free table on the pavement outside. They pulled some chairs over and settled down for some light bickering over their morning coffee.

"So, you were just going to use him as bait, then?" Gary was saying as he stirred his drink.

"I wouldn't put it like that," Seamus protested. "I just thought that while –"

"Oh, I just love your accents!"

Gary and Seamus paused for a second and looked up. Seamus felt his heart lurch, for standing by their table was the cool, willowy figure of Sandy Cove.

"I saw you both at the Bulldog last night," said Sandy. "What did you think of the show?"

"Brilliant!" said Seamus eagerly. "We really enjoyed it."

"Aye," Gary agreed, "it was very funny. Do you write all that stuff yourself?"

"Of course," said Sandy. He was cradling a cup of tea in his hands but, as he answered Gary, he pressed one hand to his chest and rolled his eyes with a dramatic sigh. "Just one of the many talents I've been burdened with."

Gary laughed. "Well at least you're not burdened with humility."

"Heaven forbid!" Sandy glanced around at the other tables. They were all crowded with babbling holidaymakers, preparing for another day at the beach. "You don't mind if I squeeze in, do you?" he asked nodding to the table. "I'm only little."

"No, we don't mind at all," said Gary. He gestured to an empty chair. "Go ahead."

"Why, thank you, kind sirs!" Sandy said as he took a seat. He sipped his tea and looked first at Seamus and then at Gary. "Are you here on holiday?" he asked. "You're clearly not local."

"It's not really a holiday," Gary explained. "We're helping somebody move back to Belfast. He's in Hastings at the minute."

"Then how did you end up in the Bulldog?"

Gary shrugged. "We've got a couple of days to kill in Brighton and somebody at our guesthouse recommended it."

"Mm," said Sandy. "And did they explain that it caters mainly to a certain clientele?"

"Oh aye, we knew it was a gay bar."

"So, does that mean that you two are …?" Sandy raised an eyebrow as he lifted the teacup to his lips.

"Oh no," said Gary. He pointed to Seamus. "He's the homo, I was just tagging along."

Sandy gave Gary a bemused grin. "You're a little blunt, aren't you?"

"Is that rhyming slang?" asked Seamus, shooting Gary an angry glance. Sandy laughed.

"No," he said. "In fact, I find such directness rather refreshing."

Gary gave Seamus a smug look as he sipped his coffee. Seamus sat back with an exasperated sigh.

"So, *Sandy Cove,* then?" said Gary. "Where does that come from?"

"Well, I needed a stage name," said Sandy, turning to wave at the sea. "And since I've always lived by the seaside, I thought it should reflect that. It could have been worse, though. *Sandy Crevice* was considered at one point."

"Yeah," Gary agreed, "nobody wants a sandy crevice. I'm Gary, by the way" he said, leaning forward to shake hands. "And your man over there with the grumpy bake is called Seamus."

Sandy shook hands with Seamus. "Nice to meet you both," he said. He gave Seamus a warm smile and a studied appraisal. "What were your impressions of the Bulldog, then?" he asked.

"I thought it had a good atmosphere," said Seamus. "It seemed very friendly."

"I was a wee bit disappointed," Gary remarked.

"Oh really?" said Sandy. "Why was that?"

"He was expecting more lesbians," said Seamus. Sandy glanced at Seamus then turned to Gary with a puzzled look on his face.

"Lesbians?"

"Oh yeah," Gary enthused. "I'm a big fan."

"You're a big fan of lesbians?"

"Yeah, I've seen all their films."

"Well, yes," laughed Sandy, "they do seem to be quite prolific in that respect." He looked thoughtfully at Gary. "You obviously don't mind your friend being a member of the LGB community," he said. "Such understanding, I'm afraid, cannot always be taken for granted."

"LGB?" asked Gary. "What's that?"

"It stands for Lesbian, Gay and Bisexual," Sandy explained. "Though why we all have to be lumped together like that is beyond me. Still, it does convey a sense of solidarity I suppose. That must count for something."

"Especially these days," muttered Seamus. Sandy turned to him and nodded gravely.

"Terrible, isn't it?" he said. "I lost a good friend not that long ago. I don't think there's anyone who hasn't been affected."

"Is this AIDS you're talking about?" asked Gary.

"Mmm," Sandy nodded. "It doesn't hit the headlines as much as it used to, but it hasn't gone away."

"It's been a few years now, though, hasn't it?" said Gary. "You'd have thought they'd have come up with some sort of drug or something by now, wouldn't you?"

"I don't think it's as simple as that," said Seamus.

"No," Sandy agreed. "As Leonard Cohen would say, *There ain't no cure.*"

"Are you a Leonard Cohen fan, then?"

"Yes, I suppose he's been something of an influence on what I do."

"You're much funnier, though," Gary suggested.

"Why, thank you!" laughed Sandy.

Seamus now found himself in a bit of a quandary. Confronted earlier by the sober glare of morning, he had been forced to accept that his heart, the night before, had been egged on by alcohol into an irresponsible pursuit of some unlikely fantasy. Gary, in his own clumsy, brutal, dickhead way, was right. The possibility of someone like Seamus even entering into the orbit of someone with the fluid, stellar elan of Sandy Cove was virtually zero, and so Seamus had decided to soften the blow with a reality of his own. As he showered, he managed to convince himself that, away from the spotlight, Sandy Cove was a monster. He was disdainful. He was remote and aloof. The baying adoration of his fans had seduced him into believing that he was somehow better than everyone else. He looked down on the 'little people' with undisguised disgust as he strolled along with his nose in the air, wrapped tightly in the blanket of his own ego.

Jesus! thought Seamus, towelling himself down in the bathroom. *What an asshole!*

But now the comforting reality that Seamus had nourished was withering away in the harsh white heat of *actual* reality.

For Sandy Cove was adorable. He was funny and humble. He was witty and smart and self-effacing. He laughed freely, and joked, and winked and was just a joy to be around.

Fucking typical! thought Seamus.

Gary threw back his head and laughed loudly at one of Sandy's anecdotes. *Getting on like a bloody house on fire, those two.* Seamus concluded glumly.

"What do you think of this Pavilion place?" Gary asked Sandy. "A mate of ours recommended it."

"I wouldn't have thought it would be your type of thing," said Sandy. "Oh, it's all very lovely and all that – and if you were staying for a week or two, then I'd say; yeah, go for it – but you're leaving tomorrow, didn't you say?"

"Yeah, first thing tomorrow morning."

"Then for the short time you're here, you might prefer a Brighton experience that's a little less sedate."

"What do you suggest?" asked Seamus, trying not to appear too keen.

Sandy thought for a moment and then seemed to make a decision. "I've got a gig on Monday night," he said, "but I'm free till then. I'd be happy to show you around a few places this afternoon, if you'd like."

"Sounds good to me," said Gary.

"Yeah, I suppose." Seamus gave a nonchalant shrug.

"Do you want to meet up somewhere after lunch?"

"What about just here?" Gary suggested.

"Suits me," Sandy replied as he got up. "Say about half-past two?"

"Nice one," said Gary. "Half-past two, it is!" He looked at Seamus.

"Yeah, why not?"

"Right, I'll see you then!" Sandy gave a wave of his hand as he left. Seamus watched him go and gave a casual wave of his own.

He then had to tell his frantic, beating heart to calm the fuck down.

TWENTY FIVE

Hannah felt that Greg was avoiding her gaze as she took leave of her companions at the entrance to the Underground at Victoria train station. She gave Becky a quick hug and then smiled and waved to the others as they made their way down the escalators to catch the tube to Heathrow.

They had caught the early train from Southampton to Waterloo, intending to spend the day sightseeing and shopping in the capital, but, for various reasons, no one really seemed to be up for it and so they had made the decision to make their way to the airport early. Hannah, because of her prior arrangement to meet with James, was planning to catch up with them at the airport later in the day and, as she watched the little group disappear into the London bustle, she stood in the middle of the busy crowd and felt suddenly alone.

The meeting with James was no longer laden with the significance that she had been anticipating just a week before, and she now had to ask herself just what she thought she was going to say. The festival had failed to bolster her faith in the way that she had been expecting it to and now, standing in the middle of the station concourse, as a thousand strangers hurtled by in every direction, she began to feel vaguely foolish.

Was it really just seven days ago, she wondered, when she had walked onto this very concourse, filled with hope and silly fantasies? Had she truly pictured herself, shining with the blazing light of evangelical zeal, striding up to James and leading him by the hand into a glowing future of Christian love? As she stood motionless, she could feel herself being jostled by the crowd.

London, it seemed, had no time for such searching introspection. London was busy. London was loud and fast. London had places to go, things to do, people to see. If what you wanted was quiet and thoughtful self-reflection, then, as far as London was concerned, you could just bugger off and go and sit in a field somewhere. Those who stopped to smell the flowers around here were just getting in the way.

Hannah sighed and turned to make the short walk to the coach station and to the Traveller's Tavern where she expected to find some comfort in James' sober wisdom, and where she hoped to lose herself – if only for a moment – in the gentle calm of those exotic eyes.

Jamesy had found a table for two in a quiet little corner. Though it was out of the way, he could still see, from where he sat, both entrances to the bar, and so could spot Hannah as soon as she came in. He was still unsure as to why Hannah had seemed so keen to meet up, but she had sounded genuinely excited on the phone – and Jamesy was always happy to spend time in her company – so he sat at the table, sipped his beer and simply looked forward to seeing her again.

While he waited, he decided to examine once more the photocopy of the curious image he had uncovered at the museum. The original photograph was of such poor quality that, even though his copy was a faithful reproduction, he still felt exasperated by those parts of the image that were blurred and impossible to make out. As he stared at the sheet, it occurred to him that he should write down *Hindu Kush, 40* on the back in order to further echo the original. The number *40* was still meaningless to him, but it had to refer to something and, as he turned over the paper to write it down, he thought it would at least serve as a reminder that it was on the back of the original photograph that had been buried and forgotten in the bowels of the British Museum. He was still gazing blankly at what he had written, lost in his own thoughts, when he was shaken by a familiar voice.

"What's that you've got?" asked Hannah, her face shining with her usual smile.

"What? Oh … it's nothing," stammered Jamesy. *How does she keep sneaking up on me?* he wondered. He gestured to an empty chair at the table. "Sit down, sit down," he said. "What do you want to drink?"

Hannah took a seat. "Just an orange juice, please, if that's okay?"

"Of course, no problem." Jamesy made his way up to the bar. When he returned with Hannah's drink, he found her staring at the photocopy.

"This looks weird," she said. "What is it?"

Jamesy sat down facing her and took the paper from her hands. He held it up and pointed to the symbols in the image.

"This is an old form of writing," he told her. "It's become known as cuneiform, and it was used for thousands of years in ancient Mesopotamia and beyond. It was made by pressing a piece of reed into a slab of clay to make the letters, you see here and here? The good thing about it – from an archaeologist's point of view – is that once it had baked hard then it would …" Jamesy broke off as he saw the blank look on Hannah's face. There was something else there too, he thought. Something in her eyes that might be described as regret. Jamesy folded the paper and put it back in his pocket. "Still," he said, "I'm sure you don't want to hear about that. You sounded like you had a particular reason to meet up today, so what's on your mind?"

Hannah looked into Jamesy's eyes and gave a weak smile. "It all seems a bit silly now, to be honest." She picked up her drink and took a sip, shaking her head slightly. Jamesy watched her patiently, waiting for her to go on. She glanced at him. "You'll probably laugh," she said, laughing nervously.

"I think you know me better than that."

She sat back in her chair and nodded thoughtfully. After a while she leaned forward. "I had a plan," she said. "I had this big plan where I would go to this festival, and I would become so filled with the Holy Spirit that I'd come back and persuade you to join the true faith. I thought I could make you see the truth and the light, James. I thought I could convert you."

"Is that important to you?" asked Jamesy, slightly shocked by what she had told him.

"I thought it was," she said quietly.

"So, what happened?"

"Well, let's just say that things didn't work out the way I thought they would."

"Do you want to tell me why you thought it was important for me to convert?"

Hannah was suddenly flustered, thrown by the question. "Well, because I … I …" She looked away to try to compose herself. She turned back to find James still gazing at her. She leaned back, folded her arms across her chest and gazed calmly back at him. She then tilted her head and looked curiously into his eyes.

"I don't understand you, James," she said.

"What?"

"How do you do it?"

"How do I do what?"

"How do you reconcile your belief in God with all of those things that you know?"

"Jesus!" Jamesy blurted out. It was his turn to be flustered. "Where the hell did that come from? What sort of festival were you at?"

"Seriously, though," Hannah persisted, "the more I try to learn the truth about God, the further away He seems, but you know about all sorts of things – more than I could ever know – and yet it doesn't seem to have any bearing on your faith at all. I just don't understand how that can be."

"Well, it's just …" Jamesy hesitated, trying to frame an answer that would be satisfactory to both Hannah and himself, when he was suddenly distracted by the door opening. Hannah frowned as she saw James stare over her shoulder, and she turned in her seat to follow his gaze. She gasped with astonishment. Several police officers were filing in through the doors and were beginning to herd people towards the exits.

"What's happening?" she asked, turning back to James.

Jamesy had no time to answer, for a policewoman came over and asked them to make their way outside. She was polite but firm, and Hannah and Jamesy quickly obeyed. When they got outside, they found themselves in the midst of a huge crowd that was slowly being shepherded away from the pub, away from the coach station and away from the road that led to Victoria train station.

"Looks like a bomb-scare," said Jamesy, and Hannah nodded. They were both familiar with bomb-scares from Northern Ireland, but it was only recently that the IRA had realised they could cause a lot more disruption to the British Establishment by targeting London. They didn't even have to plant an actual bomb, for they knew if they just gave a warning using a recognised codeword then the authorities would have no option but to take it seriously and would then have to close off and evacuate any threatened areas accordingly.

If this was done strategically – at certain times and at certain locations – then the capital would, effectively, grind to a halt. This seemed to have all the hallmarks of just such an attack and Hannah was struck with a sudden realisation.

"James!" she cried. "I have to get to the train station! I need to get to Heathrow!"

Jamesy stared at her as they both shuffled further down the pavement along with the rest of the crowd. Traffic in the immediate vicinity was at a standstill, gridlocked with no obvious way forward.

"It looks like they're moving people away from the coach and train stations," he shouted to her over the chaos. He reached out to take a hold of her hand, worried that he might lose her in the press of people. "So, there's a good chance that that's where the bomb-scare is, in one or maybe even both places." Hannah gripped James' hand more tightly as she felt herself being tugged away with the fluctuations of the crowd. "James!" she yelled. Jamesy desperately pushed himself through the mass of bodies towards her and, putting an arm around her shoulder, he pulled her with him into a narrow alleyway. It was dark and quiet in the alley, and they were able to pause for breath as the crowd stumbled past. Jamesy turned to look towards the far end of the alley. He could see another crowd at that end, being hurriedly forced in a similar direction.

"Are you okay?" he asked with a look of concern.

"Yes," replied Hannah. "But …" she looked at all the people rushing past each end of the alley. "… but what am I going to do?"

"I think if we go down that way," Jamesy told her, pointing to the alley's far end, "then at least we'd be closer to the train station. But," he said, looking straight at Hannah, "I would say they've probably closed the station and are trying to get everybody as far away from it as possible." Hannah stared helplessly at him as he tried to think fast. The implications of closing down Victoria on a Friday afternoon in the summer were beginning to dawn on him.

"Jesus!" he hissed.

"Do you think they'll close down the whole of the Underground?"

"It depends," said Jamesy, "on how many other bomb-scares have been called in. This might be happening all over London."

"Oh God!"

"But we shouldn't think about that now. Come on, we need to make a move."

"Where to?" asked Hannah. She allowed herself to be led by the hand back into the crowd.

"Well, I think we need to get as far away from here as we can," said Jamesy, "and the quickest way that I can think of doing that is to get across the river."

"The river? Do you know where it is from here?" London, to Hannah, was one huge, bewildering maze, and she expected that everyone else would feel the same.

"I've got a fair idea," Jamesy told her. They were being pushed and pulled and jostled as they forced their way through the crowd to the other side of the coach station. The crowd had thinned a little here, but they could hear sirens screaming in the distance and Jamesy could see the police putting up cordons across some of the roads up ahead. Jamesy began to hurry now, and they both jogged hand-in-hand down some little side-streets as they angled away from Victoria in an attempt to reach the north bank of the Thames.

Jamesy had always had a good sense of direction, and he knew central London quite well, so they were making good progress until another crowd and another police cordon forced them away from the river and north towards Sloane Square.

Sloane Square, Jamesy knew, would be busy even on a normal afternoon so he made an attempt to skirt around its southern end by using the narrow lanes and alleys that linked the wider streets. Eventually, though, he and Hannah were funnelled further northwards and they could only stare in despair at the thousands of confused people milling around, choking Sloane Square and the roads that led off it.

"Looks like they've closed the tube here as well," Jamesy muttered. Sirens could be heard from every direction now. Jamesy gave Hannah's hand a comforting squeeze as he frantically tried to think. He knew that Hannah had to get to the airport in the next few hours for her flight that evening, but with the Underground closed and the roads cordoned off or effectively blocked with people, that, Jamesy felt, was beginning to look impossible. Jamesy could think of no other option than to follow his original plan of getting across the river, where he hoped the situation would be less chaotic. He was also only too aware of the looming prospect of the Friday rush-hour. Once that began, he thought grimly, then they could forget about going anywhere for the foreseeable future.

"Right," he said, turning to Hannah, "here's the plan. If we can make it to the King's Road," Jamesy pointed off to his left, "then I'm sure we could find some side-streets that'll take us down towards the river. As long as we keep going roughly in that direction then we should get to the river soon enough."

"Do you think it'll be any better over there?" asked Hannah, the concern obvious in her voice.

"Well, it can't be any worse," said Jamesy, attempting to sound confident. They set off towards the beginning of the King's Road and, once there, they inched their way along the pavement, searching for a way out to their left. The road itself was gridlocked with traffic and people, and the air was stifled with exhaust fumes and noise and heat. After a while they came to a turning on the left and Jamesy pulled Hannah with him as he hurried down the street in the general direction of the Thames.

It took another frustrating hour and a half before they finally caught a glimpse of the Chelsea Embankment, but as they arrived, weary and breathless, at the riverbank, Jamesy groaned as he saw the crowds blocking off the roads that led to both the Albert and Chelsea bridges.

He was trying to discern the easiest route they should take when something caught his eye; a large friendly sign that had an arrow pointing down towards the river. Jamesy's eyes followed the arrow and, grinning all of a sudden, he turned back to Hannah.

"Fancy a boat trip?" he asked. Before Hannah could reply, Jamesy led her down a flight of steps and onto a small wooden jetty. "Hello there!" he called to the sprightly, silver-haired figure who sat smoking a pipe and staring at the mayhem on the Albert Bridge. He was clearly the captain of the little pleasure boat, *The Saucy*, that offered river cruises up and down the Thames.

"Hello," said the captain, tamping down his pipe. "Are you after a cruise on the river, then?"

"Actually," said Jamesy, "we just need to get to the other bank. We'll pay full price, of course."

"Come aboard, come aboard!" cried the jovial captain. "I'm Barney, by the way." Barney looked every inch the weather-beaten sailor, with his open-necked, denim shirt and his battered navy cap. His broad, Black Country accent, however, betrayed his former life as an accountant in Wolverhampton.

Once Barney was satisfied that his passengers were familiar with all of the safety protocols, he eased *The Saucy* into the dull, grey waters of the river Thames. They headed upriver first of all, which would take them away from the worst of the disruption in the city, and then Barney steered the little craft towards the middle of the river and the southern bank beyond.

Jamesy and Hannah sat side-by-side on a bench that ran along one side of the boat behind the captain's cockpit. Jamesy had referred to it as the port side of the ship and both Barney and Hannah had been impressed by his nautical knowledge. There was a chill breeze in the middle of the river and Jamesy instinctively put a protective arm around Hannah's shoulders.

"Are you all right?" he asked her. Hannah turned to him and nodded with a smile.

"Yes, I'm fine," she said, though that was only partly true. For as Hannah turned her head to gaze once more over the dark, choppy water – and she felt the breeze tease her hair and splash her face with a cool spray – she had a sudden and stark realisation that she had never felt so exhilarated in her entire life.

TWENTY SIX

The afternoon had flown by, and they seemed to have spent most of their time doubled over with laughter as Sandy gave them a whistle-stop tour of Brighton's lesser-known and quirkier venues. It seemed that everywhere they went, Sandy had been greeted with open affection and now, as they walked along the seafront eating chips and hotdogs, both Gary and Seamus were loath to lose his company.

"You can't leave me alone with this dickhead!" Gary complained.

"No," Seamus agreed, "you can't leave him alone with me!"

Sandy laughed. "Well, I need to go home, anyway," he said. "I'll have to go and get showered and changed if we're going to go out later."

"You sure you don't mind going out with us tonight, then?" asked Gary.

"It's been a while since I've gone clubbing on a Friday night," admitted Sandy, "but you never know, it might do me some good."

When they had finished their food, and arranged a time and a place to meet up later, Sandy headed back to his flat while Gary and Seamus returned to the guesthouse.

Alastair greeted them when they came through the door.

"How are you finding Brighton?" he asked them.

"Class!" said Gary.

"Yeah, it seems like a really fun town," Seamus said. "I'm going to be sad to leave."

"I'm sure it won't be long before you're back again," Alastair told him. "Will you be dining with us again tonight?"

"To be honest with you, Alastair mate," said Gary, "we've just stuffed ourselves with hotdogs and chips."

"Oh."

"So, yeah," Gary went on, "we'll be down shortly."

Alastair laughed. "Right then," he said, "I'll see you soon."

Gary and Seamus hurried upstairs to get ready, both excited for the night ahead.

TWENTY SEVEN

Barney brought *The Saucy* up to a mooring point on the promenade that formed the northern edge of Battersea Park. Hannah and Jamesy gave him their thanks as he waved them off.

"Best of luck to you both," he called after them. They turned to wave as they made their way into the park and Barney smiled. He had formed a fond opinion of the handsome couple in the short time he had known them and, as he slipped his mooring and eased away from the dock, he found himself hoping that they would have a long and happy life together. He then hummed a few bars of the *Spanish Ladies* and, turning *The Saucy's* bows into the wind, he set course for home.

"It doesn't seem so bad here," Hannah ventured.

"No," agreed Jamesy, "but it's hard to tell in the park. We'll have a better idea when we get to the other side." It was pleasant in the park, and they slowed their walk, as if mutually deciding there was no longer a great sense of urgency. The park's trees, shining with new greenery, dappled the grass with sunshine and shade as children ran and played and shrieked, while birds chirped and tweeted in the high branches.

Stopping in a patch of sunlight, Hannah lifted her face to the sky, closed her eyes and bathed in the warmth. Jamesy stood by and quietly watched her. She sighed contentedly and opened her eyes, blushing slightly when she caught Jamesy staring.

"It suits you," he said.

She smiled. "What does?"

James, she thought, looked suddenly serious and sad. "Everything," he said, and Hannah reddened. She gave him an embarrassed slap on the arm, and they walked on, an awkwardness now hanging between them.

"I take it your luggage is at the airport," said Jamesy after a while.

"Yes, I was sharing a suitcase with a friend of mine. We knew we'd be sharing a room, so it made sense to just have the one case."

"Good idea."

They made their way to the park's entrance and Jamesy pulled a map from his pocket. After studying it for a few moments, he looked around him.

"I don't think there are any tube stations nearby," he said, "but, to be honest, I don't really think that that's the way to go. Even if some stations are still open, the whole system is going to be bedlam."

"You've been fairly resourceful up to now," teased Hannah, "so what have you got in mind?"

Jamesy was silent as he scanned the traffic. He then smiled and turned to Hannah. "This," he said, and stretched an arm out into the road. A moment later, a black London taxi pulled into the kerb.

"James!" Hannah protested. "That'll cost a fortune!"

"It's all right," he assured her, though he was dreading what the fare was going to be, "besides, we don't have any choice. This is the only way."

They both climbed into the back and, as they watched the meter in the front of the cab cheerfully climb, the driver confirmed their fears about the travel chaos throughout the capital. The Underground, it seemed, had been completely overwhelmed, while the roads, especially north of the river, were gridlocked.

"Ain't so bad this side of the river, though," the driver told them, "so it should be a clear enough run to the airport." Hannah and James leaned back in the seat and tried to relax.

As it turned out, the fare, though steep, was not as bad as Jamesy had been anticipating and he happily paid the driver – adding a decent tip – when they arrived at Heathrow's Terminal One departure lounge.

"You didn't have to come to the airport with me," said Hannah as they both walked to the entrance.

"I know, but the way that this day's been going I just wanted to make sure you got here okay." Jamesy gave her a smile. "For my own peace of mind, at least."

"Well, I'm glad that you did," said Hannah, almost to herself.

Once inside the terminal, they quickly ascertained that Hannah's flight was on time and would likely be boarding soon.

They stood together staring up at the departure screen and Hannah then turned to Jamesy. "Everybody's probably already gone down to the gate," she said, "though we should still have time for a coffee if you fancy it."

"No, no, we shouldn't tempt fate. I think it's best if you just go and catch up with your friends."

Hannah nodded, then looked into Jamesy's eyes. "I don't know what I would have done without you."

"Well, you'd already be down at the gate, for one thing," Jamesy pointed out, making Hannah laugh.

"You know what I mean," she said. She looked at all the people rushing past. "Well, I suppose I'd better go, then."

"Yeah, have a good flight," said Jamesy. "And I'll … I'll see you about, I suppose."

Hannah did not reply. She stared at James for a brief second and then took a step forward. She intended nothing more than a quick, chaste peck of gratitude before turning and walking away, but her curious lips lingered on his and, as her nostrils flared and softly explored the scent of him, the tip of her tongue, to her alarm, began to nudge insistently forward, forcing her lips apart, probing and testing, searching with determination, pushing eagerly through a second pair of lips, finding the tip of another tongue, finding a moistness; the taste of him, the taste of James. Hannah's eyes began to lose their focus, and her eyelids drooped dreamily as she breathed in James' musky scent and tasted the subtle saltiness of his lips as they pressed against her own and then, as if raging against the exquisite agony of James' restraint, she sucked greedily at his tongue, pulling as much of him inside her as she could, almost trying to …

Hannah jumped back in confusion, her eyes gaping wide with horror and consternation. She could feel a melting softness below her abdomen, and she gasped with shock as her thighs clenched together as if to capture a sensation she wanted to stop but hoped never would. Whatever was happening to her, Hannah did not feel ready.

"I … I …" she stammered, backing away. Jamesy stood rooted to the spot, shocked by his own instantaneous reaction to Hannah's kiss. He could do little more than stand and stare as Hannah twisted away to hurl herself in confused terror towards the departure gate. As she rushed away, throwing occasional worried glances back over her shoulder, her eyes were aflame with panic and fear and wicked, sinful desire.

Jamesy watched Hannah flee towards the gate until she had melted into the crowd that was being funnelled through security and, once he was satisfied that she was gone and he could no longer pick her out, he turned and shuffled stiffly towards the exit.

TWENTY EIGHT

Seamus awoke to the sound of Gary throwing up in the bathroom. He groaned and turned over, trying to avoid, for a while at least, the memories that would soon enough be pushing their way into his consciousness.

He could remember thinking, at one point in the night, that, as he and Gary would have to be up early for a long day's travelling, they should not be drinking too much, and should not be staying out too late. But, judging by the sounds coming from the bathroom and by the rough dryness of his own mouth and tongue, Seamus could only assume that something had gone horribly wrong. The noise from the bathroom stopped and was then replaced by the sound of running water. A short while later, Seamus heard Gary come striding into the bedroom.

"I needed that!" Gary declared happily. He then gave Seamus' mattress a kick. "Come on, you!" he said. "We need to get going!"

Once he had had a quick shower, Seamus began to feel more human and, to his surprise, he and Gary managed to get down to breakfast just after eight o'clock.

"So, you're off soon?" said Julian. He placed a fried breakfast in front of each of them.

"Soon as we finish this," Gary told him. He rubbed his hands in anticipation of the hearty breakfast. "This looks like it'll set us up for the day."

"It looks amazing," Seamus added.

"Thank you! Enjoy!"

After breakfast, they quickly packed, checked out, and were sitting in the car by half-past nine.

"Mad wee fucker, that Sandy fella, wasn't he?" Gary remarked as they set off.

"Mmm," Seamus grunted.

"Good lad, though."

"Do you remember much about last night?"

"Not really. Sandy seemed popular, though."

"Yeah," said Seamus. "Everywhere we went, people were buying us drink."

"Is that what happened?"

"I think so."

Gary looked at Seamus. "Did you get Sandy's phone number?"

"That's none of your fucking business," growled Seamus.

"I know," said Gary, unfazed, "but did you, though?"

Seamus turned towards Gary. The slow grin that spread across his face was answer enough, and Gary nodded with satisfaction as he settled back in his seat. "Good man," he said.

Martin was already waiting outside, enjoying the sunshine, when Seamus and Gary pulled up. His few possessions had been squeezed into two suitcases which were soon loaded into the back of the car next to Seamus and Gary's holdalls and some plastic carrier bags that were filled with snacks and souvenirs.

"Is that everything, Martin?" asked Seamus.

"Yeah, well I've given a couple of things away," Martin replied, "and the rented flat was fully furnished, so this is just about all I own."

"Well, if you're going to be starting a new life, you might as well be starting from scratch."

With the luggage all safely packed away and everyone strapped into their seats, Seamus negotiated the narrow streets of Hastings and then headed north. To London.

They managed to reach Clapham just before noon and Seamus found a place to park in a quiet side street a short distance from the Queen Charlotte.

"I'm sure Rosie and Ellie are looking forward to seeing you again, Martin," Seamus said as they walked to the pub.

"Yeah, I was talking to them last night," said Martin. He turned to Gary. "Rosie was wondering why you hadn't phoned her," he said. "I won't say what she called you."

"Yeah, well I … I was busy!" Gary stammered. He then gave Seamus a slap on the arm. "You should have reminded me!" he exclaimed.

"Me?" Seamus demanded. "What the hell has it got to do with me?"

"You know I've got a lot on my mind!" cried Gary. "You should have known that …"

Martin sighed. He had had to listen to this sort of squabbling the whole way up from the coast and he wasn't relishing the longer trip to Liverpool. He consoled himself by thinking that at least James had struck him as being the quiet, sensible type, the one time he had met him. They reached the pub and Martin held open the door to allow Seamus and Gary, still arguing, to enter before him.

The Queen Charlotte was a light and spacious building with an oval-shaped bar in the centre of a room that had tables spreading out towards walls that were lined with booths.

Like many bars in London, it had a varied clientele. Gary, Seamus and Martin found a table close to the bar and, while Seamus and Martin perused the menu, Gary took a look around. The crowd, for a large part, was made up of well-dressed, middle-aged couples, but Gary's shrewd eye noted a few exceptions. A booth in a corner off to the right contained some young lads who were chattering noisily and flirting with a nearby table crowded with girls who looked like they were taking a break from their Saturday shopping.

Standing by the bar were several men who looked to be in their early thirties. They were all dressed in a similar fashion – with smart, chino-style trousers and pastel-coloured polo shirts. A few of the men also had light, woollen jumpers that were slung over their shoulders and tied loosely by the sleeves across their chests. This last detail identified the men, in Gary's mind at least, as being complete wankers – though in the local vernacular they would be more commonly referred to as *tossers*.

The most striking character in the bar, however, sat at a table over to Gary's left. She was a young girl, possibly in her mid-twenties, and her face, fixed with a seemingly permanent scowl, was heavily made-up with electric blue eyeliner and dark purple lipstick. Her hair was cut savagely short, and a slogan emblazoned across her T-shirt – *Pussy Lover* – gave some hint as to her sexual orientation. The slim redhead that sat opposite her, then, Gary decided, must be her girlfriend.

None of this, however, was what had drawn Gary's attention. What had done that, and what was now causing him to gawp in disbelief, was the girl's size. For she was huge.

This girl, Gary realised, could be compared in size to his brother-in-law, Harry, who was famously enormous. She was both tall and broad and, while not especially overweight, had a certain chubbiness, especially in her arms. She completely dwarfed her partner, who, though probably of average build, looked tiny in comparison.

"That's one scary-looking lesbian," Gary declared in a low voice. Seamus took a quick, surreptitious glance, then looked back at Gary.

"I thought you were a big fan of lesbians," he said.

"Yes, *proper* lesbians," Gary explained, as if speaking to a child. "Not some bloody, quarter-ton, bull dyke."

"I hear she speaks very highly of you," said Seamus drily. He felt some sympathy towards the poor girl. He was keenly aware of the struggles faced by many gay kids growing up in a world filled with prejudices, but to grow up gay while also being a size and a shape that suggested you belonged to a separate species must have been doubly hard.

"I'm not being critical," Gary protested. "I'm just saying it like it is."

"Well, that's good," said Seamus. "I'm glad you cleared that up."

"Anyway, do you know what you want to eat? Martin? You decided yet?"

"What? Oh, yes, yes," said Martin, "I'll just have the burger and chips, if that's okay."

"No problem," said Gary, he turned to Seamus. "What about you?"

"Are we not going to wait for Jamesy before we order?"

"Nah!" Gary exclaimed. "Who knows when he'll come dandering in. We might as well just get our own and let Jamesy look after himself."

Martin was half-expecting another argument to develop so he was surprised when Seamus simply shrugged. "Fair enough," he said. "I'll have the burger and chips too."

"Three burgers and chips, then. I suppose I'm the only one that's having a drink?"

"Well, I'm driving," said Seamus, "so I'll just have a Coke."

"Coke for me too," said Martin. He had struggled with various addictions over the years and was fearful of slipping back into old ways.

"Righty-ho!" said Gary, getting up and edging past the group of tossers as he made for the bar. He waited patiently until the barmaid, a brassy, cockney type, spotted him and came over. He ordered the food and then asked for two Cokes and a pint of lager. One of the tossers, having overheard Gary's order and noting his Irish accent, declared to his friends; "Served in a *trough*!" The other tossers all guffawed loudly at the witticism. The words, Gary knew, were in reference to an infamous comment made by a member of the British royal family that had compared the Irish to pigs, and so, acting as if he hadn't heard, Gary calmly ordered a pint of Guinness.

"And a pint of Guinness," repeated the barmaid. "Coming right up."

As far as Gary was concerned, he could not be held responsible for what was about to happen. How could he be, he asked himself, if he simply had no choice in the matter? Once the Guinness was placed in front of him, Gary gave it a few moments to settle before he picked it up and then, as he pretended to stumble, he poured it all over the tosser who had delivered the humorous aside.

"Oh, sorry about that, mate," said Gary. "I must have tripped."

"You stupid cunt!" shouted the tosser, throwing a punch. Gary avoided the blow with ease, but he was caught off-balance when one of the other tossers pushed into him and sent him flying sideways through the air to land with a crash onto the table where *Pussy Lover* and her friend were seated. Gary's weight and momentum toppled the table onto its side, and he landed heavily amongst the spilt drinks and broken glass. He lay on the floor, winded and dazed, until he felt himself being lifted into the air by a huge pair of hands.

TWENTY NINE

"Have you not heard anything from our Gary yet?" Karen asked Rosie. She had called in on her way back from the shops and was now in the process of making a cup of tea for Rosie and herself.

"No, but I was talking to my daddy last night and he said that Gary and Seamus were going to be picking him up this morning."

"Aye, well," said Karen, bringing two cups of tea in from the kitchen, "if Seamus said he'll be there, then he'll be there." She put the cups down on the coffee table. "Unless our Gary manages to fuck it all up in some way." Karen regarded Rosie sitting on the sofa and looking hot and uncomfortable as she approached the end of her pregnancy. "I got some baps up in O'Hara's," she said, "if you fancy some."

"Oh, I'd love a bit of bap!"

Karen returned to the kitchen and pulled a large, crusty bap from her shopping bag. She cut the bap into thick slices and covered one side of each slice with a slab of butter before arranging the slices on a plate. "I got some gravy rings as well," she said as she brought the plate through to the living room. She sat down on the opposite end of the sofa to Rosie and placed the plate on the cushion between them.

"Jesus, Karen," said Rosie, "you spoil me!" She picked up a piece of bap and then glanced at Karen. "Are the gravy rings not for you and Harry, though?" she asked. "I know Harry loves a gravy ring with his tea."

"Fuck him!" said Karen. "He's been spending all his time with that bloody guider of his. I hardly get to see him at all these days."

"You still trying for a baby?"

"Oh aye!" Karen grinned. "We still make plenty of time for that. But then he just pisses off and goes and starts messing about with wee fucking bits of wood or whatever. I'll be glad when the bloody Fleadh will be over and done with."

Rosie took a bite of her bap and sat quietly as she chewed. She struggled to think as far ahead as the end of the Fleadh. By the time the Fleadh began, she realised with some trepidation, she would already have a child. She would be a mother. And Gary, God forbid, would be a father.

"Have you heard from your Uncle Mark?" asked Karen, interrupting Rosie's train of thought.

"What? Oh, yeah, he's hoping that him and Jack can get down sometime next week."

"And your daddy and our Gary will be back tomorrow? You'll be all set then, won't you?"

"Hope so," Rosie murmured.

Karen caught the anxiety in her friend's reply and smiled supportively.

"You've got nothing to worry about, Rosie love," she said. "Just think, it won't be long before you can leave the baby with that dickhead, Gary, and you can just go out and get pissed with your mates."

Rosie laughed. "So, how are those hen night plans coming along?"

"I'm glad you asked," said Karen, becoming suddenly animated. "I've been talking to Carol about it, and she–"

"Did she say she'd come?"

"Aye, just try and stop her, she said! But she was coming up with a couple of ideas as well."

"Like what?"

"Well, she was talking about us all going out for a meal to start off with. You know, book a nice restaurant somewhere? Carol says there's loads of places up past Queen's, so then I said that, after the meal, we could just pub-crawl our way back into the town. There's plenty of bars all the way down to Great Victoria Street, and then we could finish off the night in some club in town. What do you reckon?"

"We'd need to start early to do all that, though, wouldn't we?"

"Aye, about lunchtime."

Rosie laughed again. "I think going out for a meal's a good plan," she said. "And then, I suppose, we could just play it by ear, couldn't we?"

Yeah, whatever you want. We could even get taxis into town. We'll just see how we feel at the time."

"Have you talked to anybody else?"

"Yeah, so far everybody's said they'll be up for it. I haven't talked to Tony's girlfriend yet, but I can get our Gary to do that."

"What about Hannah?"

"I can't get a hold of her on that number you gave me," said Karen, "but I was thinking of asking Gary to see if James would know of a way to get in touch with her."

"Good idea."

"She probably won't want to come," Karen said, "but at least she'll know she's invited."

"Yeah, I know what you mean," said Rosie thoughtfully. "But she's a good laugh, isn't she? So I really hope she can make it."

THIRTY

Jamesy, strolling through the centre of Clapham with a holdall slung over his right shoulder, was still fixating on the previous day's encounter with Hannah. What had happened, he told himself, had been more than just a simple kiss. It had been more, even, than just passion. It had been a desperation. It had been a hunger. An urgency. It had been a craving that had rattled Jamesy as much as it had aroused him, and it was now clear to him that Hannah wanted *him* as much as he wanted her.

So why the terror that he had glimpsed in her eyes? Why the anguish? What was she so afraid of?

He was aware that Hannah had a deep-rooted fear of sinning, but sins, Jamesy knew, were entirely arbitrary. *One man's mortal sin is another man's bacon sandwich*, Joker had once pithily observed, so Jamesy knew that whatever might have been drummed into Hannah's mind as she was growing up could have been taboos about pretty much anything.

No sex before marriage was the obvious one, he decided, but could there have been others? Had Hannah been conditioned to believe that *kissing* was a sin? Or touching a boy? Touching a Catholic, perhaps? Maybe she had been told that simply having lascivious thoughts would be enough to anger the Almighty. It could be anything, Jamesy realised, and the thought saddened him, for he was now convinced that Hannah was struggling to overcome the ideas that had been implanted in her mind as a child, and, as far as he could tell, it was a struggle that was tearing her apart.

Jamesy, thinking along these lines, reached the Queen Charlotte and then, with a regretful sigh, he pushed open the door.

At first, he was taken aback by the mayhem that greeted him on entering, but, having quickly determined the vortex of the maelstrom, Jamesy inwardly groaned.

Gary was easily conspicuous, Jamesy noted. Or rather, his head was. It was currently being squeezed in a headlock by the left arm of what appeared to be a giant lesbian and – judging by the alarming shade of purple that Gary's face had become – it was being squeezed fairly tightly. A more normal-sized, red-haired woman was tugging at the giant's arm, but to no obvious effect, and Jamesy began to feel some real concern for Gary's immediate prospects.

He glanced to his right and caught sight of Seamus at the centre of a scuffle with a group of angry men, one of whom was damp. A few of the bar's other punters – a bunch of young lads – had decided to intervene on Seamus' behalf, though Jamesy sensed that this came more from a desire to punch some of the angry men – who were clearly tossers – than any belief in the validity of Seamus' cause. Jamesy then spotted Martin, seated at a table by himself with his eyes tightly shut, murmuring and holding his left wrist.

Above the commotion the barmaid could be heard screaming that her customers were a bunch of bloody animals, and that she had called the police, who were now on their way. On catching sight of Jamesy, however, she suddenly calmed herself, smiled girlishly and began smoothing down the front of her blouse in an effort to accentuate her already impressive cleavage.

Having quickly assessed the situation, Jamesy decided that Gary was in the most pressing need of assistance, and so he set down his bag and hurried over to plead for his release. The young lady whose left arm was inflicting increasing amounts of pressure on Gary's head, may have had tastes that were exclusively Sapphic in nature, but she was swayed, nonetheless, by the innate sense of calm that Jamesy exuded, and by the ethereal, misty beauty of his eyes. She begrudgingly relaxed her death-grip and allowed Gary to stand upright. He staggered uncertainly on shaky legs and gulped for breath as his eyeballs bulged hilariously from his brightly coloured face.

"Are you okay?" Jamesy asked him.

"Aye," gasped Gary. "She's fucking lucky you came along, Jamesy!"

They both then turned their attention to Seamus' situation. The tossers, though quite spirited, were proving to be rather ineffectual when it came to bar-brawling and Seamus was largely unharmed. It just meant that his young allies, lacking any real challenge, were being forced to fight amongst themselves.

Several of the well-dressed, middle-aged men had also decided to seize the opportunity to punch a few tossers and were weighing into the fray with unconcealed glee – their partners screaming in the background with either encouragement or disapproval.

Jamesy ducked instinctively as a wooden chair came suddenly flying towards him. He watched, astonished, as it was plucked neatly from the air by Gary's former tormentor, who then hurled it back towards the main fracas. She seemed to be thoroughly enjoying herself, thought Jamesy, as if she'd just found her happy place. And then, with her natural scowl softening a little, she followed the flight of the chair and trundled happily into battle.

Jamesy now realised that Seamus was in real danger of taking some collateral damage, as the lumbering behemoth was likely to lash out in all sorts of random directions. He was just about to turn around and tell Gary that they should just grab Seamus and Martin and get the hell out of there when Gary went hurtling past him to leap onto the back of the monstrous lesbian.

"Jemima!" cried the redhead.

Jemima? thought Jamesy.

The redhead rushed to her companion's aid and managed to grab one of Gary's legs. She pulled hard, trying to drag Gary from her friend's back, but Gary, his arms wrapped tightly around Jemima's neck, was proving difficult to dislodge. Jamesy could only stare after him in dismay as he wondered just what, exactly, Gary thought he was doing. Jemima didn't seem to notice her assailant, and her flailing arms sent middle-aged men, young lads and tossers alike flying in every direction.

Seamus, alert to the danger, ducked just in time as a fist the size of a football sailed over his head. Scrambling around on the wooden floor, he noticed that Martin had been knocked over and was now lying on his side, covering his head with his arms as the chaos swirled around him. Seamus made an attempt to crawl towards him, when a sudden kick to his ribs knocked him painfully onto his side.

One of the young lads, seeing where the real challenge lay, took a short run and launched himself at the she-hulk. A huge arm, raised with perfect timing however, managed to deflect him onto the top of the bar, where he crashed into a pyramid of wine glasses.

"Bastards!" screamed the barmaid. "You fucking bastards!"

Jamesy concluded, once again, that Gary was the one who was most in need of an intervention, and so he rushed forward to grab a hold of Gary's free leg. The red-haired girl who was pulling on his other leg, turned to greet her fellow leg-tugger.

"Hi," she said. "I'm Lorna." She then gave Jamesy a smile that suggested her sexual tastes were not quite as rigid as those of her partner.

"*What*?" Jamesy cried in disbelief. He was so distracted by the inappropriate timing of the introduction, that he felt his grip on Gary's leg loosen just as Jemima quickly spun around. The unexpected centrifugal force sent Jamesy tumbling across the room to collide with one of the tossers who was being assaulted by some of the partners of the middle-aged men. Jamesy paused briefly to wonder just when and why *they* had decided to join in, but then told himself that it didn't really matter. He needed to extricate Gary, Seamus and Martin from this mess and then get them to the car. He could feel himself being jostled in the melee as he tried to figure out the best course of action to take. An idea suddenly occurred to him at exactly the same moment that a fist caught him squarely on the left temple and he dropped, dazed, to the floor.

I may not have thought this through, Gary was being forced to admit. He felt as if he had thrown himself at a tornado and was now having to deal with the repercussions that such a rash decision would entail. It had been pure instinct, though, that had propelled him into his present predicament. An instinct that had been triggered by the impotent rage he had experienced as he felt his brains being squeezed out through his ears, blotting out any thoughts of reason, and compelling him to act in a way that may not have been in his best interests.

The old phrase of *grab a tiger by the tail* occurred to Gary, reminding him that so long as he held onto the tail, he would be safe, which of course implied that the instant he let go, he would be completely fucked, and with that in mind, he tightened his grip and grimly rode the tornado.

Still, Gary always liked to think of himself as someone who lived in the moment, and in this particular moment he was being felt up by an attractive redhead, so … all things considered …

Seamus scurried across the floor with one hand clutching his aching ribs. The drunken promise he had made to Rosie may have been phrased with misplaced melodrama, but the intention behind it, as far as Seamus was concerned, remained the same. He made his way over to where Martin lay curled in a ball, intending to drag him along the floor to a quieter and safer part of the pub. As he straightened up, however, to get a better idea of his surroundings, an elegant woman with a blue-rinse hairstyle, and wearing a pretty floral summer dress, hit him in the face with a barstool.

Jamesy knew that he could not afford to let the situation slip away from him. He knew that if it were left up to Gary and Seamus to settle things, then they could be in all sorts of trouble, so he concentrated on getting his blurred vision back into focus as he struggled to his feet. He leaned heavily on a nearby table to allow his eyesight to clear and was just in time to see several dark figures come rushing through the doors. The Metropolitan Police, it seemed, had arrived in force.

And that's when things started to go wrong.

THIRTY ONE

Harry had added a short length of rope to the steering bar and was now using it to tow the guider behind him. The wheels were turning smooth and whisper-quiet in the still morning, and the three friends were like excited children, released from school to set off into a world of summer adventure.

Brompton Park, the street that formed the western boundary of Ardoyne's Glenard Estate – and where the Guider Race would be taking place in a few weeks' time – sloped in a straight line from north to south for a quarter of a mile. At the top, where the starting line would be, the gradient was suicidally steep – the slope only really levelled off in the street's final third – and Darren could be forgiven for his new-found sense of unease. He glanced at the *Dullahan* and gave an involuntary shudder. It was just a few days ago, he realised, that he had stood admiring Harry's guider as it sat gleaming with cheery flashes of yellows and reds in the evening sunshine, but now, it seemed to him, the beast was prowling under sullen grey skies, smouldering with menace and coloured with the demonic fires of scarlet hell. He shuddered again, which Terry alone, astutely took note of.

"Perfect weather for it," said Harry when they reached the top of the hill. "No wind, no sun, just dead calm."

Terry thought he could detect Darren wince slightly at Harry's use of the word *dead*, but he put the thought out of his mind and stood looking down the long slope. The street was largely deserted – though he could see a few people out and about – and he tried to imagine Darren, clinging tightly to Harry's fearsome contraption, rapidly disappearing into the distance.

Terry had surmised, on first sight of the *Dullahan*, that, for speed, the guider was unlikely to be beaten. He had known Harry for years, and he believed that – despite his profession as a joiner – Harry had the soul of an engineer and the mind of a perfectionist, making it unthinkable for him to approach any project with anything less than total commitment.

But perfection in the details, Terry knew, could lead to imperfection overall, and he had a nagging suspicion that Harry's blinkered desire to have the steering system move as smoothly as possible could prove to be the *Dullahan's* undoing. He hoped he was wrong, of course, but the fact that the racecourse would be nothing more than a straight line suggested that Harry had obsessed needlessly over an irrelevant detail. A strong sense of self-preservation prevented him from pointing this out to Harry, so he watched quietly as his nervous workmate climbed gingerly onto the guider, and he found himself giving a silent prayer that Darren would be up to the challenge of controlling the thing.

"Right, are you all set?" asked Harry. Darren had elected to sit rather than kneel on the guider. His feet were placed on the steering bar in front of him and, for a bit of extra control, he had the rope held tightly between his fingers. Harry was using one hand to hold the *Dullahan* in place while Darren readied himself.

"Aye, I think so, Harry," said Darren uncertainly. Harry, deciding that the answer was good enough, had only to give the slightest of shoves before the *Dullahan*, like a diving falcon, plunged with startling eagerness into the loving arms of gravity's embrace.

Darren was screaming. The sudden shriek filled the empty morning with jarring discordance and made Terry flinch with alarm as he watched with horrified fascination the diminishing figure of Darren perched seemingly atop a flaming arrow that had been shot by the imps of Hades.

The velocity was tugging teardrops from the sides of Darren's eyes, but he was encouraged by the fact that he had made it almost to the halfway point without incident and, because of this, he felt he might even be able to relax and enjoy the ride. He was still screaming, of course, but there was much less of a terrified panic to the sound than before and, as he felt himself relax, the tension in his legs, that had been holding them locked tight to the steering bar, eased a little. At that moment, the *Dullahan's* right front wheel hit a stone on the road and the steering bar spun round, forcing the front wheel into the edge of the guider's wooden base. The whole thing jack-knifed, and Harry and Terry could only watch helplessly as Darren was hurled clear to bounce and roll across the street before coming to a sickening halt, wrapped around the base of a telegraph pole that sprouted from the pavement.

"Steering seems a wee bit twitchy there, Harry," suggested Terry.

"There's nothing wrong with the steering," Harry growled.

"No, no, you're right!" said Terry. "It was that dickhead, Darren, wasn't it? Probably just trying to show off." The two of them stared quietly downhill for a moment before Terry spoke up. "Do you think he's okay?" Darren could be seen, still unmoving, curled around the telegraph pole and Harry strode suddenly forwards, forcing Terry to jog to catch him up.

"Are you all right there, Darren?" Harry asked when he reached the prone figure.

"What? Oh yeah, yeah, I'm dead on, Harry," replied Darren. "No worries, mate."

"Are you going to get up?" asked Terry, arriving behind Harry.

"You know what?" said Darren. "I'm sort of all right where I am for the time being."

"You sure you're okay?"

"Yeah, yeah. You two go on ahead. I'm happy enough just lying here for a minute."

Terry and Harry looked at each other. It later transpired that Darren had broken two of his ribs and was advised by his doctor not to indulge in anything as irresponsibly stupid as *guider-racing* for the foreseeable future.

"Well, that's that, then," said Karen. "You won't find anybody else stupid enough to get on that bloody death-trap."

"It's not a death-trap," Harry quietly insisted.

"Aye, well anyway, all your so-called friends have made themselves scarce, haven't they? Your man, Darren, only agreed to do it because he's so fucking full of himself."

"I think he was a wee bit jealous of Dessie, as well," said Harry.

"Yeah, but Dessie's lovely, isn't he? And Darren's just a dickhead. So I don't see where you're going to find some other dickhead that's so fucking full of himself."

Harry looked thoughtful for a moment and then turned to his wife.

"Didn't your Gary build guiders when he was a kid?"

THIRTY TWO

It was probably nothing, he thought. He walked past the car, then stopped and turned around. He walked past it again and stopped again. It did look suspicious, he told himself, but then, he thought ruefully, in London at the moment, *everything* looked suspicious. He walked past again, trying not to make his interest appear too obvious. It was probably nothing. He walked past again.

"Still," he thought, reaching for his radio, "better safe than sorry."

Due to the campaign of disruption that was currently being waged in London by the IRA, every member of the police in the city was on high alert. Anything that was deemed to be out of the ordinary – especially if it pertained to Northern Ireland – was to be reported immediately, and so, when he radioed through for information on the Northern Irish number plates on a Ford Granada estate not far from Clapham High Street, PC Colin Durham was simply doing his duty.

As he waited for a reply to his query, PC Durham strolled casually along the row of shops on the other side of the street, taking care to keep the car in view in the reflections of the shop windows. He was hoping that the driver of the car would not appear while he was waiting, because that would mean he would have to do something, and Colin Durham was not a man who enjoyed doing things.

It wasn't that he was lazy or anything, it was just that when it came to police work, PC Durham liked to think of himself as more of an observer than a participant. Observation, he would often tell his wife, was just as important – if not more so – than running around bopping people over the head with a truncheon. In his twelve years on the force, Colin Durham could not recall a single occasion when he had had to use his truncheon – or *baton* as he was supposed to call it these days – in anger. In fact, if truth be told, he reckoned that his wife had got more use out of it than he had. He giggled at the thought, then jumped with a guilty start when his radio crackled into life.

PC Durham listened carefully to the message that came over his radio and he struggled to quell a rising urge to flee. From what he was hearing, it seemed that the car sitting just a few feet from where he was standing was registered to a person who – along with three others – was currently being held under the Prevention of Terrorism Act.

The Prevention of Terrorism Act, PC Durham knew, was an Act of Parliament that gave the British police a wide range of special powers that could be employed in the fight against any perceived threats to national security. These powers included the ability to hold in custody, without warrant or charge, anyone that the police might suspect of being engaged in terrorist activity. Any suspects could be held initially for a period of up to 48 hours, though this was subject to review by the Home

Secretary on a case-by-case basis. The four suspects currently under suspicion, had been taken into custody during an altercation the day before and were being held largely because of their nationality, but also because of the heightened state of tension brought on by increased IRA activity in the capital.

PC Durham was told therefore that the suspects' vehicle should be considered a direct and immediate threat to human life, and he was given urgent instructions to secure the area and then await the arrival of the bomb squad and the anti-terrorist officers who were already speeding to his location.

Blimey! thought PC Durham. *Secure the area? What the hell does that mean?*

It didn't take very long for the area to be sealed off and the street was soon swarming with armed police. PC Durham was taken to one side and grilled about what he had seen through the vehicle's windows. He explained that the car seemed empty apart from the back which was filled with a variety of cases and travel bags.

"And could you tell if any of these bags contained anything?" asked a hard-faced officer wielding a machine-gun.

"Well, it was a bit hard to tell with the cases," said PC Durham, "but the soft holdalls were all full. I could make out at least two holdalls in there, plus there were also some plastic carrier bags that seemed to have some items in them."

"Items?"

"I couldn't see anything clearly; the handles were folded over the top."

The hard-faced officer frowned. He stared at PC Durham as if he wanted to throttle him.

"To be honest, though," PC Durham hurriedly explained, "it all looked to me like harmless holiday luggage. I mean if you –"

"Holiday luggage?" sneered the hard-faced officer. "*Who* comes to Clapham for a holiday?"

"Well, I know, but –"

"Thank you!" said the officer. "You've been very helpful. We may require some further information from you, so try not to wander off."

"Mm, okay," mumbled PC Durham, and then, having been dismissed, he wandered off.

Detective Chief Inspector Jason Flint briefed his small squad of experienced anti-terrorist officers as the bomb disposal team began preparing their equipment in the background.

"Right," he said, "the situation is this: we have four individuals currently being held in a secure location. All four were travelling together. One of these individuals is the registered owner of the Ford Granada estate you can see just down the street there. The vehicle is registered to a Belfast address in an area that is known to have strong Irish republican sympathies."

"Are any of these individuals known to us?" asked one of the armed officers who surrounded DCI Flint.

"No, but we haven't dismissed the theory that they could be part of an IRA sleeper cell that has been operating under the radar for some time."

"Are any of the individuals co-operating?"

"Three of them are," said DCI Flint. "But one is being combative and keeps threatening to go on hunger strike."

"Those plates concern me, Chief," said another officer. "They just don't fit the MO."

"Yes, I know what you mean," said Flint. It made no sense for terrorist groups to drive around London in vehicles that so blatantly advertised their origin. "But maybe that's the point," he suggested. "We know that the IRA have stepped up their activity lately, so this could be just another tactic."

"Don't follow."

"Look," Flint said as he pointed down the street. "We've sealed off the entire area and evacuated all of the surrounding buildings. Because of what? Because of some NI plates? We're doing the bloody IRA's job for them!"

"I see what you mean," the officer muttered. "Devious bastards!"

"Exactly," said Flint. "It's likely that the bloody car is entirely harmless, but we can't just ignore it." He glanced over to where the bomb disposal guys were setting up. One of them caught his eye and gave him a thumbs up. "Right!" Flint exclaimed. "Let's crack her open and see what we've got!"

Corporal Jennings of the Royal Engineers was so fond of his Explosive Ordnance Disposal (EOD) robot that he had secretly named it Eddie. Eddie was a tracked vehicle, about the size of a supermarket trolley, that Cpl Jennings could remotely operate as a forward surveillance probe. Eddie could be fitted with a variety of tools and implements to suit any situation and would then be deployed to provide information and reconnaissance from environments deemed potentially too dangerous for humans.

On this occasion, Eddie was fitted with a standard camera for live video feed and a shotgun. Its first task was to gain camera access to the back of the car, and to achieve this it would have to break one of the car windows by firing a shotgun shell at the glass at close range. Cpl Jennings gave his fingertips a little lick before rubbing them with the tips of his thumbs. He then looked down at his control panel and gently pushed the left and right joysticks forward.

Eddie whirred into life and lurched towards the suspect vehicle, the only movement in the otherwise empty street.

DCI Flint and his team quietly observed the robot make its approach. Despite his feelings that the whole exercise would turn out to be a false alarm, Flint had to acknowledge the increased amount of tension in the air. There was always a chance that the threat was real, he told himself grimly. He still felt aggrieved and on edge from the chaos that had been caused in the city just two days before. As he watched the robot arrive at the side of the Ford Granada and position itself to line up the shot against the side window, he could not have known that in one of the holdalls, and directly in the line of fire, was a butane gas canister that one of the suspects – Gary Lingfield – had brought along to refill his cigarette lighter.

DCI Flint prepared himself for the shotgun blast and the shattering of glass. What he hadn't prepared himself for, though, was the subsequent explosion and the orange fireball that engulfed the car.

"*Jesus Christ!*" he screamed as he instinctively ducked.

Corporal Jennings stared down at the control panel. *That wasn't meant to happen,* he thought.

"*Fall back!*" Flint shouted. The car had clearly been booby-trapped, and there was always a chance that there could be some follow-up surprises. He wouldn't put it past those IRA bastards. Everyone retreated to what was considered a safe distance and they then stood and watched as the nearly-new Ford Granada estate went up in flames.

Doctor Irving was a rambler. He liked nothing more, on his days off work, than to go hiking around the countryside with little more than a packet of sandwiches and a flask of tea. He rambled everywhere. In his time, he had rambled up mountains, and along valleys and over hills and dales. He had rambled through sleepy villages, along the sides of rivers and canals and on many of the remote paths and walkways that criss-crossed the nation.

On this particularly fine and warm Sunday afternoon, he was happily rambling along a hilly coastal path in the east of Kent, which, of course, made him fairly tricky to get a hold of.

Not that the police were overly keen to verify their suspects' stories – they were only too happy to let them stew for at least the full 48 hours that the special powers allowed – but even the few half-hearted attempts that they did make on the Sunday proved fruitless.

Bobby and Sean were not at their hotel – having gone on a sightseeing pub-crawl for the day – while Doctor Sedgewick, Martin's mentor, happened to be spending the summer touring Tuscany and could not easily be reached. And so, with no one else to satisfactorily corroborate a reason for them to be in London, the four suspected terrorists were held for the full period allowed by law, and it was therefore Monday afternoon before Gary, Seamus, Martin and Jamesy were, begrudgingly, released back onto the streets of the capital.

"I don't see why you're blaming me," Gary grumbled as they made their way to the address of the impound yard where they had been told Seamus' car was being kept.

"Nobody's blaming you," said Jamesy. Seamus stopped and stared at him.

"What the hell do you mean, nobody's blaming him?" he demanded. "*I'm* blaming him!"

"I'm just saying that it's probably not a good idea to –"

"To be fair," said Martin, "it *was* Gary who started the fight."

"I didn't start anything!" Gary protested. "It was that asshole at the bar who –"

"Look, it doesn't matter who's to blame," said Seamus. "It's done now. We should just go and get the car and head on, and just try to forget it ever happened."

"What about the ferry?" asked Jamesy. "Was the ticket transferable?"

"No," Seamus told him as they walked. "I'll give them a ring later on and see if we can get booked on tonight's crossing."

"What if we can't?" Gary asked.

"Then I don't know," Seamus admitted. "We can have a look at some of the other routes. I'd even be happy to drive to Scotland if it meant we could get home from there."

"Long drive," Gary pointed out.

"Do you have any better ideas?"

"No, I'm just saying."

Seamus shook his head. "I still can't believe we were stuck in that bloody place for two days," he said. "We don't even know who won the World Cup."

"West Germany," said Martin. Everyone stopped.

"How do you know that?" asked Gary.

"One of the cops told me."

"Oh, so you were just chatting to the cops, then?" said Gary. "Very chummy!"

"What's wrong with that?" cried Martin. "There was nobody else to talk to, was there?" They had all been kept in separate cells and this was the first time they had seen each other since Saturday.

"That's not the point, is it? The point is that the fascist enforce–"

"Did you phone Rosie to tell her where you were?" Martin demanded.

"What? No, I thought that you would phone her."

"It's just as well I did."

"Well, there you go," said Gary. "And anyway, I rang my ma, so the whole district probably knows by now."

"We should let Rosie know that we've got out. I'm sure she's worried sick."

"Aye, we'll keep an eye out for a phone box."

When they came across a phone box, Gary, despite his protestations, was made to make the call.

"Why can't *you* phone her?" Gary asked Martin.

"Because I'm sure it's you she wants to talk to."

"I don't know about that."

"She's *your* fiancée," insisted Seamus. "So just bloody phone her!"

Still moaning, Gary eventually entered the phone box while the others waited outside. After a few moments, he reappeared looking ashen-faced.

"How is she?" asked Martin.

"What? Oh, yeah, yeah, she's dead on."

Jamesy stepped past Gary and pulled open the door to the phone box. "I'm just going to give my ma a quick ring," he said, stepping inside and closing the door behind him.

"So, what was Rosie saying?" Martin persisted.

"Oh, just that it's good we got out and all that sort of stuff," Gary replied. He looked a little distracted before glancing at Martin. "Seriously, though, Martin," he said. "You really need to have a word with your daughter about her language."

"*What the fuck?*" Seamus stood by the side of his car with his arms outstretched and his mouth wide open. "*What the actual bloody fuck?*"

"The vehicle is obviously no longer driveable," said the clerk who had accompanied them out to the lot where the remains of Seamus' car had been left. "So you will need to make arrangements to have the vehicle removed."

"*What?*"

"The vehicle is still your responsibility, so you will have to –"

"What happened to it?" asked Martin.

"I don't know all the details," the clerk told him. "It was here when I came in this morning, but I'd hazard a guess that there was some sort of fire."

"You're a sharp one, aren't you?" said Gary. Seamus shot him a look that suggested he should keep his mouth shut.

"So, what do I do now?" Seamus asked the clerk. He was still having trouble fully processing just what, exactly, was going on. "I don't have time to go around trying to organise –"

"We can make all of the necessary arrangements," said the clerk, "but you would be responsible for any expenses that may be incurred."

"Right," sighed Seamus, suddenly deflated, "whatever …" The clerk led him to a nearby office to sort out the paperwork, leaving the others standing bemused at the side of the charred shell.

"Did you have much in your luggage?" Jamesy asked.

"Everything I owned," said Martin with a resigned shrug. "It's lucky I had my wallet in my pocket, though."

"Just some clothes," said Gary. "That's not the problem, though, is it?"

"No, it's not," Jamesy agreed. "The big problem now is how do we get home."

The tense, awkward silence in the back of the London cab that was taking them to Heathrow Airport was beginning to get on Gary's nerves.

"I don't know what you're bloody sulking about," he said to Seamus. "We said we'll pay you back."

Seamus looked at Gary but said nothing. He then turned away to look out the window at the passing cityscape. He felt he no longer had the energy to argue. He just wanted to go home. He wasn't particularly bothered about the huge dent he was making on his credit card for four flights to Belfast – it would be worth it, he decided, if it got them all back home by the end of the day – but he had a lot to think about and he had an almost overwhelming urge to be alone.

He could hardly wait now to get back. He could just picture himself arriving back in his living room. He would close the door and sit down by himself with just a cup of tea and, in the precious silence, he would consider his options.

They had all been offered phone calls while they were in custody. Martin had called his daughter. Gary and Jamesy had both called their mothers.

And Seamus had phoned Sandy.

THIRTY THREE

Push? Rosie wondered. *Push what?* She felt her hand being squeezed and looked up to see someone smiling down at her. He looked familiar. Was it … was it … *D'Artagnan*? Rosie smiled back. She was feeling very content. She liked D'Artagnan, but as she gave him her most flirtatious smile, she realised that he had changed. He was now Officer Dibble from *Top Cat*.

Rosie was mildly surprised by this. What was Officer Dibble doing in her room? Had she done something wrong? Was she going to be … she shrieked with pain and outrage, and her vision blurred with tears as she felt someone … some*thing* try to rip her in half.

The blinding agony threw her back against the bed but then, just as she felt she could bear it no longer, the pain seemed to be sucked from her and she was able to draw a long breath of relief. Her head began to spin with lights and visions. She sensed that some strange woman was trying to show her something. Officer Dibble was shouting at her … no, no it wasn't Officer Dibble anymore … it was Top Cat. Top Cat was giving her the strangest grin and for some reason was shouting *It's a boy!* at her. It was all very confusing.

Rosie, in her muddled state, came to the conclusion that it would probably be in her best interests to simply pass out.

So she did.

Gary shouted for the midwife who hastily handed him the baby before attending to Rosie. A nurse came rushing into the room to assist the midwife while Gary stood aside and stared dumbfounded at the scrunched-up little human he had helped to create.

Rosie, groggily, began to come round and a little while later the midwife seemed satisfied with her condition.

"We'll still need to run some blood tests," she told Rosie, "and we'll be keeping you in for a few more days, but I think you'll be fine." The midwife straightened up and smiled. "Now," she said, "would you like to hold your son?"

Her son? The words almost didn't seem real. Like they didn't belong to her. She sat propped up on the bed, exhausted but with a deep sense of contentment. She watched Gary approach the bed and gently place something into her arms. She looked down.

In the pink, helpless little bundle, Rosie saw her mood-swings. She saw her backache and her varicose veins. She saw her leaky tits and her constant need to pee. She saw the painful little kicks that woke her in the night, and she saw all of her anxious fears and all of her doubts, and she knew with absolute clarity that she would go through it all again, a hundred times over, for just this one single moment.

When her baby's eyes met hers.

A short while later, Martin, Ellie, Jack and Mark all crowded around the bed to fuss over the proud new mother and the infant in her arms. Gary had gone outside for a smoke.

"Are you all right, Rosie love?" asked Martin. "Gary said you had a wee bit of a funny turn."

"Yeah, I'm okay," said Rosie. "The nurse was saying it might have been some sort of allergic reaction to the one of the drugs I was on, but I feel all right now."

"Have they taken a blood sample?" Ellie asked her.

"Yeah, and they're going to keep me in for a couple of days as well."

"I'm sure you could do with the rest," said Mark as Rosie handed over the baby for Ellie to hold.

"Oh, Rosie," said Ellie, "he's gorgeous."

"Takes after his granda," said Martin, looking over Ellie's shoulder.

"Do you know what you're going to call him?" asked Jack.

"Yeah, me and Gary were talking about it and we think we're going to call him Owen."

"Owen?" said Ellie. "Yeah, that's lovely." She handed little Owen over to Martin just as Gary came back.

"I think they're planning to move you out onto one of the wards at some point," Gary told Rosie. "So I think they'll want us all to clear out soon."

"Yeah, no problem," Mark said. "We should be heading back now anyway. Do you need a lift, Gary?"

"No, no, you go on ahead. I've arranged to meet some people later on."

"Right then," said Martin as he handed the baby back to Rosie, "we'll shoot on here. We'll try to get over to see you whenever we can."

"Don't worry about this evening," Rosie told him. "I think all of Gary's ones are planning to come over, so there'll be a bit of a crowd."

"Aye well, I'm sure we can make it over tomorrow, then."

They all headed out, leaving Gary and Rosie alone with their baby for the first time. They gazed down in silence at little Owen, both lost in their own thoughts and both now coming to the understanding that life was about to get interesting.

"You mad bastard!" Joker shouted as Gary came through the doors of Bob Cratchit's bar on the Lisburn Road. "You've only gone and bloody done it!" He grabbed Gary's hand and gave it a hearty shake.

"Well, you know," said Gary casually, "it wasn't that big of a deal really. And Rosie played her part as well. In fact, I don't think I could have done it without her."

"I'm sure it wasn't for want of trying," said Tone as Gary took a seat at the table.

"Is that another way of calling me a wanker?" asked Gary.

"Yes," said Tone, reaching across to shake Gary's hand.

"Thought it was."

"Congratulations!" said Jamesy, taking his turn to shake hands. Seamus, grinning, stood and came around the table. He slapped Gary on the shoulder and grabbed his right hand.

"Congratulations!" he said. "It's good to know you can do *some* things right."

"That's all well and good," said Gary, "but who's getting the round in?"

"I'll get this one," Seamus assured him, and he set off for the bar.

"How's Rosie doing?" asked Jamesy.

"Yeah, she's dead on," Gary said as he accepted a cigarette from Tone. "I mean, I think she's still a wee bit spaced out from the drugs and all, but other than that she's okay."

"And your son?"

"Fighting fit," Gary replied, though the question had stunned him. *Your son!* "They reckon he's got footballer's legs, so I would imagine he'll be signing for United at some point."

"Have you got a name yet?" asked Joker.

"Yeah, we're thinking of maybe Owen."

"Owen? Is that because of Ardoyne?"

"Ardoyne?" Gary looked puzzled. "What do you mean?"

"*Ard Eoin,*" Joker explained, "is Irish for *Owen's Hill.*"

"Is it?"

"Jesus! Do you bloody Fenians know anything?"

"Oh yeah, Joker," said Jamesy, "that reminds me. I've got something that I want you to take a look at."

"Okay, Jamesy," Joker sighed. "Whip it out, and I'll have a look, but I'm not really a doctor you know, so maybe you should –"

"No, I mean I found this thing in –"

"Right! Let's wet this baby's head!" Seamus had returned with a tray of drinks that he placed in the centre of the table. "I got these as well," he said, and passed around cigars to everyone.

"I don't smoke," Jamesy pointed out.

"Don't light it, then," said Tone. "Just stick it in your gob and pretend you're a big lad."

"I can probably manage that."

"Is Kevin coming tonight?" asked Gary.

"No," Tone said. "I got him set up on a date for tonight, so if all goes well, we probably won't be seeing him for a while."

Four out of five cigars were lit, and glasses were raised.

"You just missed the Twelfth, then," said Seamus.

Gary nodded. "Probably just as well."

"Still," Joker exclaimed, "it's *le quatorze juillet.*" Everyone looked at him. "You know," he said, "Bastille Day?"

"So, it's a double celebration, then?" cried Tone. "*Vive la France!*"

"*Vive la France!*" they all toasted.

"And Owen!" said Joker.

"*Owen!*" they toasted once more, and they went on to toast many other things over the course of what would turn out to be a very long night.

And a few days later, Owen Lingfield – with the spirit of *la révolution* coursing through his veins – went home.

To Owen's Hill.

THIRTY FOUR

Martin had gone into town and Ellie was at work, so it was just Gary, Rosie and the baby at home. Rosie lay on the sofa, snoozing to the indistinct murmurings coming from the television, while Gary was pacing gently around the living room, cradling his son in his arms and cooing into the little pink face.

Gary liked to tell himself – and everyone else, for that matter – that he was an excellent father. Parenthood – like everything else in his life, he would say – came naturally to him, and, to the consternation of all who knew him, this just happened to be the one occasion where his boastfulness was justified. He had taken to the role with enthusiasm and with a competence that both surprised and delighted Rosie who had already been resigned to having to look after both Gary and the baby herself.

Owen burbled contentedly, blowing a few inadvertent bubbles of saliva past his lips and Gary was astounded by such a precocious display of talent. Not much more than a week old, he reminded himself with awe, and his boy had already mastered bubbling. He was shaking his head with wonder when he heard the latch on the gate. He looked up and frowned. *What the hell does he want?* he thought.

There was a short rap on the door and then Joker entered. He saw Rosie lift her head from the sofa.

"Oh, sorry, Rosie love," he said. "Did I wake you up?"

"Oh no, it's all right, Joseph. I was only dozing. Just trying to catch up on some sleep." Rosie sat up and stretched. "Do you want a cup of tea?"

"Aye, but you sit there, Rosie," said Joker. "I'll stick the kettle on." He went into the kitchen, and Gary and Rosie exchanged bewildered glances.

"Social call, is it?" asked Gary when Joker returned from the kitchen.

"You may want to sit down," said Joker. Gary looked at him quizzically, but he sat down, still cradling the baby, in the chair by the fireplace. Rosie looked worried.

"They called everybody into the canteen at work today," Joker began, and Gary hissed an expletive. Rosie glanced at him, then turned back to Joker who carried on. "Apparently the new owners are considering fitting their current packaging capacity into three sites instead of four."

"What does that mean?" asked Rosie.

"It means me and Joker are out of a job," Gary told her.

"It's still early days," said Joker. He heard the kettle come to the boil and went back to the kitchen to make the tea. When he returned with three cups, he found Rosie standing in the middle of the floor, nursing the baby, while Gary leaned forward in his seat with his elbows resting on his knees. Joker put the tea on the coffee table and sat down on the sofa.

"What's everybody in work saying?" asked Gary.

"Well," said Joker, sitting back and sipping his tea, "the overall opinion is that they've already made the decision. They wouldn't have told us otherwise."

"Yeah, that's what I was thinking," said Gary.

"And you think it's going to be the Belfast site that goes?" Rosie asked.

Joker shrugged. "It would make the most sense," he said. "Logistically speaking, anyway. Most of our customers are based in England, so I reckon they'll strip us of all those new machines we just got in and put them in their sites across the water."

"Shit!" said Rosie quietly.

"Did anybody mention any sort of timeframe?" asked Gary.

"No," Joker told him, "but I'd say they're going to want to start the whole process sooner rather than later. Some of the guys in work are saying we'll be gone by the end of the year."

"Just in time for Christmas, then?"

"Probably."

Gary got up to stand beside Rosie. He looked down at the baby and gently moved a fold of baby-blue blanket away from his nose and mouth "Nice bit of timing," he said.

Joker nodded. "Yeah, you've got enough going on this year without having to look for another job."

"Thanks for coming up to let us know, Joseph." Rosie said. She put Owen, now asleep, in his cot by the window and picked up her tea. "It was good of you."

"I didn't think it was something you'd want to hear over the phone."

"We won't be due much redundancy," said Gary, taking his cup of tea and sitting down.

"Nah, bugger all," said Joker. "We haven't even been there a year."

Rosie sat down beside Joker. She looked over at Gary who seemed unusually pensive. "What are you thinking?" she asked.

"Well, it's funny," said Gary, "but I was talking to Harry the other night and he was saying he might be looking to take some more people on."

"To do what?" asked Joker.

"All sorts of different things, I suppose."

Rosie tutted. "Is this the same night he talked you into killing yourself?"

Gary rolled his eyes and Joker turned to Rosie. "What?"

"Aye, have you not heard? Gary here is going to be in the Guider Race at the Fleadh!"

Joker looked at Gary who simply shrugged. "Harry's entered a guider for the League," he said, "and he needs a driver. So I said –"

"Tell him why he needs a driver, Gary!" snapped Rosie.

Gary gave a sigh. "His first driver broke a couple of ribs, apparently." He glanced at Rosie. "But that doesn't mean it's going to happen to me, does it?"

"It sounds like a bloody death-trap," Rosie replied.

"Well, anyway, I've already said I'll do it."

Rosie said nothing. She just glared at Gary and sipped her tea.

"Well, I'll be up to cheer you on," said Joker. "I wouldn't want to miss that."

"Have you had a look at that thing of Jamesy's?" asked Gary, changing the subject.

"Yeah," Joker told him. "It's a tricky one, but I think I'm getting there."

"What's this?" asked Rosie.

"When Jamesy was in London," Gary explained, "he found this picture in some museum that had this writing on it that nobody could understand. He brought it back for Joker to take a look at."

Rosie looked at Joker. "And you can understand what it says?"

"I'm still working on it, but I think I'm starting to get the gist of it."

"Well, good for you," said Rosie, impressed. "I wonder if James knows that Hannah came up to see me in the hospital."

"Did she really?" said Joker. "I doubt if he does know. He never said."

"Yeah, she brought me a card and some flowers. It was really nice of her."

"Aye, I've always thought Hannah was dead sound, and she'd suit Jamesy down to the ground, but …" Joker shrugged. "Who knows what's going on?"

"I asked her to come on my hen night," said Rosie.

"Jesus! I can't picture Hannah on a hen night. What did she say?"

"She didn't say *no*," Rosie laughed. "She said she'd let me know."

"It'll probably do her good," said Gary. They chatted on for a while until Joker pushed himself up from the sofa.

"I should head on," he said, "I told my ma I'd call up to see her." He walked across the room, glancing briefly at a black and white photograph on the mantelpiece. He was about to turn the handle on the living room door when he stopped and turned back to stare at the photo.

"Are you okay, Joseph?" asked Rosie.

"I think he might be broken," Gary suggested. Joker stood frozen as he gazed in silence at the group of young men who were grinning and laughing at the camera just before they went off to sail across the sea and bring righteous havoc to the Third Reich.

"Joseph?"

"Is there any chance," said Joker, suddenly spinning round with his eyes gleaming, "that I could get a lend of this picture?"

Rosie frowned. "I don't see why not," she said. "But why?"

"Because *that*," said Joker, pointing to a lanky figure on the left of the photo, "is my granda!"

THIRTY FIVE

"Well, you're just going to have to say something, Davy. He's doing my bloody head in!" Katherine Anderson was in her kitchen, fuming, after another tense altercation with Thomas, her father-in-law. Her husband, Davy, was doing his best to placate her.

"I know, love, I know," he said soothingly, "he's being a bloody nuisance, but you know why he's doing it, don't you?"

Katherine didn't reply. She stood, arms folded, with her back to the kitchen worktop and her head down, glowering at her husband through her eyelashes.

"Just take it easy," Davy went on, "he'll come round in the end, you know he will."

"And I'm sure he's trained that bloody dog of his to piss all over my carpets!"

"Oh, come on," said Davy, though he was harbouring similar suspicions himself. "The dog's just old, he's probably a wee bit incontinent."

"I've never seen him piss on any of your da's carpets."

"Yeah, well, anyway," Davy said hastily. "My da's just worried that he's going to lose his independence. You know what he's like. That's why he's being such a –"

"*Such a crochety old bastard!*" Katherine raised her voice to make sure that Thomas, in the living room, could hear.

"Shush, love," Davy hissed.

"But it's for his own good, Davy!" Katherine insisted.

"I know, love, and I'm sure that he knows it too, but I think he needs this wee fight before he finally has to accept it. It's like his last stand, you know? Look, I know it's not easy, but I really think you should just try and bite your tongue for the time being and let him get it out of his system. Why don't you try one of your meditations? That calms you down, doesn't it?" Katherine had lately been dabbling in Buddhism in an ongoing search for her spiritual side. She looked angrily at Davy.

"I haven't been doing any meditations for ages now," she said. "Not that you would have noticed."

"Oh right," said Davy. "I thought you were getting into it."

Katherine turned to stare out the kitchen window with what she felt was an angry pout.

So, what is it this month? wondered Davy, though he didn't say it out loud.

"Me and Barbara have been getting into *Shaktism*," Katherine said as if reading his thoughts. "We've been going to this wee place in town that tells you all about it."

"Shaktism?" Davy just had to ask, though he knew he'd regret it.

"Yes," said Katherine, "it's the Hindu doctrine of the Eternal Goddess."

Davy stared at his wife, and it took every fibre of his being, every drop of concerted effort and every ounce of self-control to stop his eyes from rolling, but then, fearing that his eyes might just go rolling around his head of their own volition, he turned away.

Thomas Anderson scratched behind the ears of the dog that sat by his chair and smiled to himself at the raised voices coming from the kitchen.

"You're a good boy, Milo," he said. Milo turned his head and gave Thomas a panting, slobbery grin. He knew he was a good boy, of course, but it was always nice to receive some independent affirmation.

Thomas leaned back in his chair and thought about Katherine's accusation. *Crotchety old bastard?* Fair enough, he thought, but hadn't he earned the right to be a crochety old bastard? He'd fought for that right. He felt he'd been fighting his whole life. And he was fighting still.

They wanted to take his home away. They wanted to take away the home where his children had grown up. The home where he and his wife had watched the kids, one-by-one, make their own way into the world, and where he and his wife had stood, uncertain, in the sudden, lingering silence. The home where his wife had once surprised him with a tiny black Labrador puppy who had gone on to turn both of their lives into a wonderful storm of chaos. The home where he had watched his wife weaken and fail. The home where he had played nursemaid for those final years of fear and darkness and sacrifice and love.

It's for your own good, they told him. *You're not getting any younger,* they said. *It makes the most sense for everybody. Just come and live with us. We'll look after you.*

Thomas knew they'd probably win in the end – he couldn't defeat growing old – but he reckoned he had just enough fight left in him to give them a run-around before the final surrender. It was like he always said, he told himself as he felt his eyelids droop heavily in the warm comfort of the armchair; he'd been fighting his whole life.

Montgomery and Eisenhower are at their wits' end. The D-Day landings, after some initial difficulties, have been a success, and the Allies are now loose in France, ready to push on through northern Europe to the heart of Hitler's Reich.

But there's just one problem: Caen.

The picturesque French town of Caen, despite having been pulverised by the RAF, is still in German hands, which means the Allied advance has ground to a halt.

Because German-held Caen is in the way.

'Well, that's that, then,' Eisenhower and Montgomery are saying. 'We might as well just pack up and go home now. Still, we gave it our best shot, and that's the main thing.'

A junior officer, shuffling around at the back of the room, coughs nervously. 'What about those troops who have lately been assigned to the 3rd Infantry?' he asks.

Eisenhower's penetrating stare settles on the officer, who looks quickly down at the floor. 'Are you referring to Tommy Anderson and his boys from Northern Ireland?' he demands in his slow Kansas drawl.

'Yes, General,' the officer quietly replies.

'Good God, man!' cries Montgomery, banging his fist on the map table. 'Don't you think they've been through enough? We can't possibly ask them to take Caen as well!'

Eisenhower is not so sure. He rubs his chin as if deep in thought. 'Maybe we don't have a choice,' he mutters almost imperceptibly.

'But surely you can't expect –?'

Eisenhower cuts off Monty's objections with a raise of his hand. 'This could be our only hope,' he says. 'Otherwise, all of this,' he sweeps an arm through the air, 'will have been in vain. The greatest seaborne invasion in human history will have achieved exactly nothing!'

Montgomery bites his lip and glances at the map. He knows that Eisenhower is right, but that doesn't make the decision any easier. 'They'll need back-up,' he says after a while.

'These guys don't take kindly to any –'

'They'll need back-up!' Montgomery snaps. 'The Canadians will go with them. We'll tell Anderson and his men that they're there as interpreters.'

There are corpses everywhere. French, German, Canadian, British and a host of others all mingling now together in the rubble and the dust. Thomas and his men slip like shadows through the bombed-out suburbs, taking silent blades to the startled Germans who are doggedly defending their lost cause.

Terrified children peek out from dark hiding places, and proud old men wipe tears from their eyes and clench their fists to quietly urge on the stone-faced wraiths who are bringing bloody vengeance to Caen's tormentors.

Thomas pauses. He can sense, rather than hear or see, Billy and Geordie making their way through the upper floors of a hotel on Thomas' right-hand side. He imagines the soft whispering of knives and bayonets sliding across throats and puncturing hearts, and he unconsciously wipes the blood from his own bayonet as he scans the way ahead. From his position, blending invisibly with the wreckage of a townhouse, he sees a shop sitting in tumbled disarray on the apex of a junction fifty yards due north.

Though he can't see it directly, he is aware of a German machine-gun nest perched on the shop's first floor, waiting for any sign of movement in the street below. As he watches, a puff of dust is thrown into view, is sprayed a sudden misty pink, and settles quickly to leave the scene silent and still once more. Thomas remains immobile until he spots a brief signal from the machine-gun nest's position, and he turns his head to his left and motions with his eyes. A shape appears from nowhere and rushes forward to the junction of the street where it once again becomes invisible.

Sounds of gunfire crackle from the rear, and Thomas knows that the Canadians are advancing and are mopping up those pockets of Germans that his men have left for them. He moves ahead and signals to Scotty on the shop's upper floor that they should rendezvous in the courtyard of a grand manor where they have identified the presence of a large number of German defenders. He is keen to move quickly now for he knows he must get to the cathedral where many of the townspeople are sheltering. He suspects that the time for subtlety has passed, and that he and his men must now hit the Germans hard and fast as they make a push for the cathedral to save as many civilian lives as they can.

The Canadian forces, Thomas knows, can be relied upon to swoop in quickly to take advantage of the shock his men will cause by their sudden attack. He reaches the courtyard and steps softly through a gap in the wall, dropping and merging with an overgrown hedge. He watches the unsuspecting German sentries – crouched behind a wall of sandbags in the manor's doorway – as he waits for his squad to assemble around him. They'll split into two groups, he decides. Scotty and Gerry will noisily attack the windows in the rear of the property just a few moments before Thomas and his main force hit the front doors with grenades and rifle-fire. He senses his men, one-by-one, arrive in the courtyard. He turns slowly and motions to Gerry to lie low for the moment. Gerry McCann, cool and professional with a big heart and a generous spirit. Thomas shifts slightly to make a final assessment of the situation before giving the final ... a twig snaps underfoot and alerts the sentries who peer, unseeing, into the bushes. Thomas holds his breath, but he sees one of the sentries get to his feet, nervously holding a rifle at his waist. He seems to look Thomas directly in the eye and Thomas quietly curses as he watches the sentry open his mouth to yell ...

"I've made you a cup of tea."

"What?"

"Here, Thomas," says Katherine. "I've made you a cup of tea." She puts down the cup, along with a plate of biscuits, on the coffee table in front of Thomas' chair. As she turns to go, she gives Milo an evil look, and he lowers his head and slinks down onto his belly. "Joseph said he'll be calling up later," Katherine tells Thomas. "I'm sure he'll be glad to see you."

Thomas sits up and rubs his eyes. Then, yawning, he picks up a chocolate digestive and reaches for his tea.

Joker was, by no means, a cruel man. It could be said that he did not possess a single vindictive bone in his entire body. He was neither petty nor mean. He had never once in his life shown a sadistic side, and he had never once demonstrated any sort of enjoyment when confronted with the suffering of others.

But, at the same time, it could not be denied that he showed no remorse – not one scintilla of regret or hesitation – on the day that he walked into his parents' home with a framed photograph tucked under his arm, and caused his own grandfather to burst into tears.

THIRTY SIX

It was becoming something of a tradition. Friday night with Joker and Carol. Drinks and dinner and loads of craic. Kevin arrived not long after Tone and Claire, and Carol showed him into the music room where everyone was seated. He handed Carol some bottles of wine he had brought.

"Thanks, Kevin," said Carol. "You've never met my daddy, have you?" she gestured to a rather piratical figure in one of the armchairs. Benjamin got up and strode across the room.

"It's nice to meet you, Kevin," he said, shaking hands. "I'm Benjamin."

"Nice to meet you, too," Kevin replied, trying not to stare at Benjamin's black eye-patch.

"Take a seat," said Benjamin. "I've just been hearing all about your Spanish trip. Joseph had already given me his version of events, but it's been interesting hearing what happened from a different point of view."

"It *was* a fairly eventful trip, I suppose."

"Painful too," said Joker.

"Yeah, but you can laugh about it now," said Tone with a grin.

The doorbell rang.

"That's probably James," Carol said, going to the door.

"Well, Kevin," said Tone, "how did your date go?" Tone had set Kevin up with a girl he knew from Divis, and Kevin had booked a romantic meal at a bistro in town.

"It could have gone better."

"Hi, everybody," said Jamesy as he and Carol came in from the hall. "Hope you're all well."

"All right there, Jamesy?"

"Hi, James!"

"Hello, James."

"What was that you were saying, Kevin?" Jamesy asked as he sat down.

"What? Oh, I was just saying that the date I had the other night didn't go as well as I was hoping."

"Sorry to hear it."

"Why? What happened?" asked Tone.

"Well," Kevin began, "she was telling me that she'd not long broken up with some guy called Nick. And then she just started crying."

"Oh, that's not good," said Claire.

"No," Kevin agreed, "it sort of went downhill after that."

While everyone professed sympathy, Benjamin glanced at his watch. "Well, I suppose I'd better get going," he said, getting up and heading for the door. "Have a good evening, everyone."

"Yes, you too!" they all called after him.

"Where's he going?" Jamesy asked Carol when Benjamin had gone.

"He's going out for a meal with some of the faculty members," Carol told him.

"Oh, right," said Jamesy. "So, who else is coming tonight, then?"

"I think this is it," said Joker. "Gary and Rosie are busy, as you can imagine, and Seamus, apparently, is in England."

"England?"

"So Gary says."

Carol turned to Joker. "How's dinner coming along?"

"Oh shit!" Joker exclaimed, jumping to his feet.

"Might be a wee bit well-done," Tone suggested as Joker disappeared into the kitchen.

"Dinner's ready!" Joker shouted from the kitchen, and everyone made their way to the dining room.

After the meal, they all sat around bloated and declared they were too full for pudding. Carol said they could leave it for a while and maybe have some dessert later, so they relaxed at the table and happily sipped their drinks.

"Have you had a look at that cuneiform yet?" Jamesy asked Joker.

"Aye, it was a bit of a mess, to be honest." Joker got up and went out into the hall.

"He used a lot of really bad language," Carol told everyone, "when he was trying to work out what it says."

"What's this?" asked Kevin. Joker came back clutching Jamesy's photocopy in one hand and a small notebook in the other.

"James found this picture in the British Museum," Carol told Kevin, "of some old writing, and Joseph's been trying to translate it for him."

"I've since been in touch with the relevant authorities at the museum," said Jamesy, "and they're still scratching their heads over it. The best answer they could give me is that it's just gobbledegook."

"The problem is," said Joker, sitting down beside Jamesy, "is that it's not all the same language."

Jamesy frowned. "What do you mean?"

"Well, I reckon that some of it's in Greek, but see this bit here?" Joker pointed to a section on the picture, and then opened his notebook. He ran a finger down some of his notes and then tapped the page. "Yeah," he said, "I think this is Old Persian."

Jamesy stared at Joker. "Old Persian?" he exclaimed. "How the hell do you know Old Persian?"

Joker sat back. "I know a lot of things," he said defensively.

"Yeah but, Jesus …"

"So, what does it say?" asked Claire.

"Well, I think it says *shahanshah,*" Joker told her, "which is Persian for –"

"King of Kings," said Jamesy.

"Exactly!"

"King of Kings?" Kevin repeated. "Who would that be, then?"

"It doesn't seem to say," Joker said. "Not on the bits that I can make out, anyway."

Everyone turned to Jamesy. "Well, Jamesy?" said Tone. "Any ideas?"

Jamesy gave a shrug. "Could be anybody."

"Isn't there a poem about a King of Kings?" asked Claire. "Ozzy something."

"*My name is Ozymandias,*" Tone quoted, "*King of Kings. Look on my works, ye mighty, and despair!*" He looked around the table. "Shelley, I believe."

"Would it be him, then?" asked Claire.

"It's possible," said Jamesy. "I think the tablet was found in the mountains of the Hindu Kush, which are a long way from Egypt, but I don't suppose that matters."

"Egypt?"

"Well, yes. Ozymandias is just another name for Ramesses the Second."

"The Pharaoh?" Claire was becoming intrigued. She looked at Joker. "Go on, Joseph. What else does it say?"

"Well, the whole thing seems to be a message from some woman who used to be a slave." Joker showed Jamesy the relevant section on the photocopy. "This looks like a corruption of the Akkadian word, *abdu*, meaning *slave*."

Jamesy nodded. "I think you might be right."

"My God, Joseph!" cried Claire. "You should join the Linguistics Department at Queen's!"

"I've been saying that for years," said Jamesy.

Joker scoffed at the notion, but he couldn't help noticing that his brain was strangely reserved on the matter. "Anyway," he continued, "there's a bit here that's repeated again over here, and the only way I could make any sense of it was to overlay it with the Greek alphabet …"

"But that doesn't make any sense," moaned Jamesy. "Why would anyone write down Greek words using cuneiform script?"

"Well, that's for you to figure out, isn't it Jamesy?" said Joker. "I'm just telling you what it says."

"Okay, so what *does* it say?"

"I think it's a name," Joker held his notebook up to Jamesy and pointed to a word. "*This* name."

"Meklios?"

"Yeah, sounds Greek, doesn't it?"

"So, who was Meklios, then?" Claire demanded.

Jamesy shook his head. "I've never heard the name before."

"Well, it turns out," Joker went on, "that this woman – when she was still just a wee slave girl – and this Meklios character set out one night – at a castle or a palace or something like that – and stole this King of Kings fella. For love, apparently."

"Stole?"

"Yeah," said Joker. "Again, I think it's a Persian word that means *to take* or *to steal*. I'm just assuming from the context that it's *stole*.

"This is getting really interesting!" said Claire beaming. "Do you think that it's somebody talking about robbing a Pharaoh's tomb? Maybe it says pyramid instead of castle."

"Why *for love,* though?" asked Kevin.

"I'm not all that sure that this King of Kings *is* Ramesses the Second," Jamesy told Claire. "A lot of rulers in ancient history would have gone by that title, and the fact that it's in Persian would suggest that it's a Persian emperor."

"It's annoying that the bottom bit's blurred out," said Joker. "It might have given us some more clues."

"But it's a picture of a stone, or a tablet or something, isn't it?" said Kevin. "So, wouldn't it be back at the museum? Couldn't you just get them to –"

"No," said Jamesy miserably, "that's the problem. The museum just has the same photograph that we do. The actual tablet itself could be anywhere in the UK, and the fact that the picture is of such bad quality would suggest to me that it was taken by a private collector."

"So, it might be in a private collection somewhere?" said Tone.

"It's possible," said Jamesy. "The only clue to its whereabouts is this writing that's on the back of the original photo: *Hindu Kush, 40*."

"And it was found in the Hindu Kush?" said Claire. "That's easy enough, but what about the number 40?"

Jamesy held up his hands. "Absolutely no idea!"

"So, it's not a clue at all," Tone pointed out.

"Guess not." Everyone fell silent, contemplating the problem. Carol got up and headed for the kitchen.

"Anybody fancy some dessert now?" she asked, and everyone replied that they did. Carol left, and Claire then turned to Joker.

"Is that all that it says, Joseph?" she pleaded. "That's just so frustrating!"

"Well, I think there's another name here," he said. He put a finger on the image. "You can see the same word is repeated over here as well. "I think it might be Greek too. My best guess is that it's something like *Omenes*, or *Eumenes* maybe, because this wee bit here is …" Joker stopped as he sensed a reaction beside him. He turned to look at Jamesy and then frowned.

Because Jamesy had, all of a sudden, gone very pale.

THIRTY SEVEN

They stumbled, giggling, over the pebbles of Brighton beach. They jostled with the little kids waiting in the queue for the carousel on the promenade, and they angrily chased after seagulls that boldly snatched at food from the bag of chips they were sharing.

They bought candyfloss and hideous seaside souvenirs, and strolled in wide-eyed wonder through the over-the-top splendour of the Royal Pavilion. They leapt, barefoot and shrieking, in and out of the freezing surf of the English Channel, and they marvelled as a petulant sun thrashed with lurid rage against the calm and dusky blues of encroaching night.

They sat with heads together in a quiet little cocktail bar and chatted and gossiped happily over mojitos and margaritas. And they walked back, still chattering, to Sandy's apartment.

"Oh, I wish I could have been there," exclaimed Sandy. "It sounds like an absolute riot!"

"It *was* a bloody riot," said Seamus, "and you agree with me, don't you? It was all Gary's fault."

"I wouldn't say it was *all* his fault," Sandy said carefully. "I've always thought that bigotry should be confronted wherever it is found. I know there have been a lot of times when I've just held my tongue and walked away, but I've always regretted it. I think if you ignore that sort of –"

"But surely you can't be confrontational every time!" Seamus protested. "You have to show some discretion at least some of the time."

"Well, maybe, I suppose. There are times when walking away is the only safe option."

"Exactly. That's always been Gary's problem, you see. He just doesn't stop to think what his options are."

"Maybe fatherhood will calm him down a bit," suggested Sandy as he unlocked his front door and let Seamus into the flat.

"You know, I think you might be right," said Seamus. He looked around the living room that he had only quickly glanced at earlier in the day. He approved of the minimalist – almost stark – décor of the room, with just a few tasteful photographs dotted here and there on the walls. The real feature of the room was the picture window. It afforded Sandy a beautiful view of the sea even though his apartment was set a way back from the seafront.

"Nice view," said Seamus, staring at the calm water glowing dully in the light of a few moonlit clouds. Sandy came and stood beside him.

"I like to remind myself that there's a horizon there," he said. "Even when I can't see it, I still like to know it's there. Like some sort of permanent escape route."

"Escape route?" asked Seamus, and Sandy laughed.

"Perhaps that's a little too dramatic," he said. "But I like to think of it as a room with one wall missing, you know? Knowing that you can step outside anytime you want."

"Only if you have a boat, though."

"Oh, I know the analogy doesn't stand up to scrutiny," laughed Sandy, "but it is how I feel. Maybe it's just some sort of psychological thing."

"If you say so."

"You don't mind being around a bit of a psycho, then?"

"You have met Gary, haven't you?"

Sandy laughed again. "Oh, yes, of course!"

"I reckon everybody's a screw-up in one way or another."

"I suppose you're right," Sandy sighed. "I think if I ever met someone *normal*, I'd run a mile." He watched Seamus walk over to the other side of the room and stop beside a desk that was pushed against the wall. He then saw him idly flick through a notebook that sat on the desktop.

"Is this where you write your poetry?" asked Seamus.

"It is," Sandy told him, "though that particular notebook is for personal stuff."

"Oh, I'm sorry!" said Seamus, hastily letting go of the pages. "I didn't realise."

"Oh no, don't worry," Sandy assured him. "I said it's personal, not private. It's just me fooling around with some ideas, you know? Trying to answer the big questions, that sort of thing."

"The big questions?"

"You know; life, the universe and everything?"

"Isn't the answer 42?"

Sandy clapped his hands delightedly. "I'm so glad you're a fan of Douglas Adams!" he exclaimed. "But I somehow knew you would be."

"Was that a test?"

"What if it was?"

Seamus grinned. "Nothing," he said. Sandy picked up the notebook and went to sit on the sofa. He flicked open the pages as Seamus sat down beside him.

"A lot of this stuff is just random thoughts that happen to come to me," he explained. "Some of them might end up in the performance poems, but not many, to be honest." He got to a certain page and handed the notebook to Seamus. "Stuff like this," he said. "It's all a bit rough and ready, but you get the idea."

Seamus stared at the hand-written lines. *"Circles of fate,"* he read, *"and circles in the universe. And through the spinning realms of air, little circles everywhere."*

"Oh God!" Sandy laughed, burying his face in his hands. "It sounds so embarrassing when it's read back like that!"

"What's it about?"

"Oh, it's just some silly idea I once had about a universal consciousness."

"A consciousness? Like God, you mean?"

"God. Fate. Karma. Call it what you will." Sandy took the notebook and got up to put it back on the desk. "It's still very much a work-in-progress. Do you think *swirling* would sound better than *spinning*? Anyway, it's more than likely it'll end up going nowhere. What can I get you to drink?"

"Whatever you've got."

Sandy went off to the kitchen and came back with two bottles of beer. He handed one to Seamus and then joined him again on the sofa.

"You know," Seamus began as he leaned back cradling his beer, "Gary wants me to invite you to his wedding at the end of August." He could tell that Sandy was genuinely shocked by this by the way he responded.

"I'm genuinely shocked," he said.

"You obviously made quite an impression on him."

"And I got very fond of *him*," said Sandy, "but still …"

"I know, it's a bit much to ask, really."

"So, would I be going as your *plus one,* then?"

"I suppose so. I haven't really thought about it, to be honest," lied Seamus.

"It's something I'll have to think about."

"Oh yeah, absolutely," Seamus stressed. "Don't feel under any pressure about it, I mean I know it's all a bit sudden and all. It's just so you know the offer's there, if you want it."

"Thanks," said Sandy. "I'll let you know." He drained his beer and put the bottle on a side table. He then took Seamus by the hand and led him to the bedroom.

THIRTY EIGHT

"So, who was Eumenes, then?" asked Claire as she finished her pudding. She picked up her glass of wine, sat back, and fixed her gaze on Jamesy.

"Eumenes," said Jamesy after a pause, "was a general and a secretary to King Alexander III of Macedon."

"Alexander III of Macedon?" asked Joker. "You talking about Alexander the Great there, Jamesy?"

"Yes," Jamesy sighed, "I suppose that's how history remembers him."

"You don't sound like a fan," Tone ventured.

"Well, there are those who will tell you that Alexander was the greatest military commander of all time. And there are others who'll tell you that he was just a privileged thug. I suppose I'm somewhere in between."

"But still, though," said Joker, "he did some stuff, didn't he?"

Jamesy gave Joker a look that suggested he was about to say something, but in the end, he simply shook his head and leaned back. "Yes, Joker," he said quietly. "He did some stuff."

"I don't get it," said Carol. "I take it that this King of Kings you were talking about was actually Alexander the Great, but that doesn't explain why anybody would want to steal him, does it? And what does this Eumenes character have to do with anything?"

"I don't know," said Jamesy absent-mindedly. He stared fixedly at the table, thinking furiously, going over in his mind what he knew about Alexander of Macedon, trying to figure out what it all could mean.

"And *stolen for love*," enthused Claire. "It all sounds very mysterious and romantic."

"How do you steal a king, though?" asked Carol.

"Well, obviously," said Joker with some authority, "you wait till it's dark, and then you just sneak up on him."

"Sounds like you're speaking from experience there, Joker," said Tone.

"There's a lot about me you don't know, Tone."

"For which I am deeply thankful."

"Come on, James," prompted Claire. "You're the expert here. Have you got any ideas at all?"

"Not really, no," Jamesy replied. "I would imagine, though, that this person, this slave girl, is referring to Alexander's remains. In no account of Alexander's life that I've ever read is there any mention of him being stolen, or kidnapped, while he was alive."

"So, it was his corpse that was stolen?" Carol suggested.

"That would make the most sense," said Jamesy. "It certainly makes more sense than sneaking up on him in the dark." Everyone turned to Joker.

"Well ... look," Joker spluttered. "That's just Jamesy's theory! I think both ideas are equally valid."

"Still doesn't really help, though, does it?" said Tone, lighting a cigarette. "It still doesn't make any sense. Stolen for love? What the hell is that supposed to mean?"

"I don't know anything about Alexander the Great," said Claire. She looked at Jamesy. "Did he have any famous love in his life? Anybody that would have wanted to steal his corpse?"

Jamesy's mind was still racing, trying to make some sense of Joker's translation. "Well," he said finally, "Alexander had three wives, but they were all matches that were politically motivated. There has never been any suggestion that he ever married for love. The one person that Alexander was closest to for most of his life was a guy called Hephaestion."

"Hephaestion?" asked Carol. "Are you saying that Alexander the Great was gay?"

"It's always been a matter for speculation," said Jamesy. "It just depends on which historian you read. There are no contemporary accounts of Alexander's life – the earliest accounts come from Plutarch, who lived hundreds of years after Alexander – so his sexuality is open to debate."

"What's your take on it, Jamesy?" asked Tone.

Jamesy shrugged. "There's a good enough chance that Alexander was gay," he replied, "or at least bisexual, though in my opinion the greatest love in Alexander's life was Alexander."

"Jesus, you've really got it in for him, haven't you?"

"So, what happened to Hephaestion?" asked Claire.

"He died not long before Alexander did," said Jamesy distractedly.

"There must be a way we can piece all of this together," said Carol, leaning forward. "Tell us the whole story, James. What's supposed to have happened when Alexander died?"

"You shouldn't encourage him, you know, Carol," Tone scolded. "You really don't want to get him started."

"Oh, shut up, you!" said Claire, giving Tone a slap on the leg. "I think it's fascinating."

"Oh, come on!" cried Tone. "Are we really all suggesting that a six-foot-four skinhead from Sandy Row – *Him!* –" he pointed to Joker, "has actually uncovered one of the biggest secrets of ancient history?"

"Stranger things have happened," suggested Kevin.

"Name *one*!" Tone demanded.

"Look, that's not the point," said Carol. "James, did you just say that there are no contemporary accounts from Alexander's own time?"

"Yeah, why?"

"Then what would you call *that*?" Carol pointed to the image on the paper.

"Yes, I know," said Jamesy, "I'd already thought of that. Just this tablet on its own would be a massively significant discovery, but we're stuck with the same problem, aren't we?"

"What's that?" asked Carol.

"Where the hell is it?"

"Oh yeah. That's true."

"Well, anyway, Jamesy," said Joker as he sipped some wine, "tell us the story of what happened to Alexander the Great. Or at least what's supposed to have happened to him."

"Okay then," Jamesy sighed. "Alexander died in the year 323BC, just before his thirty third birthday, in the city of Babylon, which was the capital of the land that the Greeks called *Mesopotamia*."

"That means *Land between the Rivers*," Joker told the rapt faces around the table.

"His body was mummified in the Egyptian manner," Jamesy went on, "in order to keep it preserved, and it then lay at the palace in Babylon that had been built by King Nebuchadnezzar several hundred years before." Everyone was silent as Jamesy continued. "The body stayed in Babylon for more than a year, before it was eventually taken to Egypt by one of Alexander's former generals, Ptolemy, who was, by then, the new ruler of Egypt. The Ptolemies, of course, would go on to rule Egypt for another three centuries, until the dynasty ended with the death of their last monarch, Cleopatra."

"Stick to the point, Jamesy," said Tone, "there's a good lad." He was trying to be flippant, but he was just as captivated by the story as everyone else.

"That's pretty much it," Jamesy said. "An ornate tomb was built in Alexandria – the city that Alexander himself had founded – and it was a bit of a tourist attraction for hundreds of years. Even Julius Caesar went to visit it when he was in Egypt."

"It's not still there, though, is it?" asked Carol.

"No," Jamesy told her. "The tomb of Alexander the Great has been lost for centuries, but it's still assumed to be somewhere in Alexandria. Or, more to the point, *under* it."

"Right," said Claire, "that's the official story, then?" She gestured to the sheet in front of Joker. "But according to that tablet, it may not be what actually happened. Is that right?"

"It seems like it," said Jamesy tentatively.

"Right, then!" Claire leaned forward, the journalist in her coming to the fore. "What do we actually know about this?" she said. "A couple of slaves seem to have abducted the body of Alexander the Great while it lay in state in some palace in the city of Babylon, right?" Everyone nodded. "The only motive that we have is that it was done *for love*, which is sweet, but it doesn't help us much. And then there's this Eumenes character, who may or may not have turned a blind eye." Claire sat back and stared at Jamesy. "What's *his* story, then, James? Is there any reason why he would have looked the other way?"

"There actually is," said Jamesy. "You see, Alexander and his army, and all of his generals, were Macedonian, right? It would have been a very close-knit community, with a sort of *Macedonians against the world* mentality. Eumenes, though, was a Greek, and when Alexander promoted him from his private secretary to a top position in the army then it ruffled a few feathers. Apparently, he was never really accepted by the other top generals and was always regarded as an outsider, only tolerated because of Alexander."

"So he had reason enough to cause a wee bit of mischief, then?" said Joker.

"Yeah, but I doubt he would have been aware of it," Jamesy told him. "Eumenes spent the next few years fighting for his life, so I would imagine he would, at some point, have used the information to help his own cause."

"So," Tone began, "the remains of Alexander the Great may not be buried somewhere in Egypt, like everybody thinks, but could actually be buried somewhere near Babylon, wherever the hell that is. It's an interesting story, I suppose, but I don't see –"

"Yeah, that's a point," said Claire. "Where actually *is* Babylon?"

"Well, most of it is buried under the desert," Jamesy told her, "but the site is in Iraq, not far from Baghdad."

"Why didn't I know that?" Claire frowned.

"Okay," Tone continued, "but even if we could discover the exact resting place, then why would it be a big deal? It's just going to be a pile of old bones in some cave somewhere, isn't it?"

"Discovering the actual final resting place of Alexander the Great," said Jamesy quietly, "would be one of the most important archaeological events of the century. It would rewrite the history books, for one thing."

Tone shrugged. "Yeah, but –"

"And of course," Jamesy smiled, "there's always the Siwan amulet."

"The what?"

"Oh nothing," laughed Jamesy. "It's just a myth."

"Well, you can't just leave it at that, James!" cried Claire. "Tell us the story!"

"No really," Jamesy protested, "it's a legend. It's not actually true."

"Tell us the damn story, Jamesy!" cried Joker, brandishing his dessert spoon like a knife. "Or we'll cut you!"

"All right, fine!" Jamesy sighed. He looked around at all the expectant faces and began. "There's this crackpot theory that's been around for a while amongst Egyptologists," he said. "And I have to stress that it's only within a tiny circle of Egyptologists, it's not something that is even remotely taken seriously by mainstream scholars."

"Well?" Claire prompted.

"Well, the theory claims that a civilisation once existed in Egypt before the time of the pharaohs. The current understanding that we have is that Egyptian civilisation began about five thousand years ago, but this theory would push that date back by several thousand years. The story goes that a civilisation arose along the banks of the Nile and went on to develop incredibly advanced technology thousands of years before the pyramids were built. This civilisation was then somehow lost to history, long before the pharaohs came along." Jamesy shuddered. "I feel dirty just talking about this."

"But wouldn't there be some evidence of an earlier civilisation?" asked Kevin.

"The theory claims that there is," said Jamesy. "The people who believe this stuff say that there are artefacts still being uncovered in the desert that display evidence of advanced stone-working technology that later civilisations tried to copy but never came close to matching."

"So, what's this amulet thing all about, then?" Claire asked.

Jamesy paused before answering. "Well, during the time that Alexander was hacking his way through the Persian Empire, he also took control of Egypt. This was when he founded Alexandria."

"Busy lad," said Tone.

"Is nobody going to mention the fact that he was only thirty-two when he died?" said Kevin.

"He started young," Jamesy told him. "Anyway, when Alexander was in Egypt, he disappeared into the desert for six months to visit the oracle at Siwa. It was there that the priests told him that he was the son of the god, Ammon, which was believed to be the Egyptian version of the Greek god, Zeus."

"They weren't stupid, those priests, were they?" said Tone.

Jamesy smiled. "Yeah, they knew exactly what he wanted to hear."

"And Siwa is where he got the amulet?" asked Carol.

"The amulet is just a myth," Jamesy insisted, "but, yes, the story goes that the priests gave Alexander an amulet of black glass, presumably obsidian, that contained writing that was older than hieroglyphics."

Joker sat up straight. "Older than hieroglyphics?" he demanded. "Why have I never heard of this?"

"It's nice to know you don't know everything," said Jamesy, "but you've probably never heard of it because it isn't real. It doesn't exist."

"Well, what if it did?"

"It doesn't."

"I know, but ..."

"Okay!" Jamesy said, holding up his hands. "If it did exist then it would turn everything that we think we know about human history on its head."

"So, a fairly big deal, then?"

Jamesy said nothing. He sat staring at the grainy, monochromatic image on the table in front of him. "There's a fair chance that the rest of this tablet explains where Alexander's remains are hidden," he said. "Or, at least, gives us some more information to work on."

"So we need to find the tablet," said Claire, "because we can't read any more from the picture."

"No, we can't," Jamesy said sadly. "Why the hell does the bottom half have to be so out of focus?" he moaned.

"It helps to drive the narrative forward," Joker suggested, and Jamesy glared at him.

"Yes, Joker!" he said. "But this isn't some stupid adventure story, is it?"

"It could be."

"What do you mean?"

"Well, Jamesy," Joker began. He poured himself some more wine, then picked up his glass and sat back in the chair, "what are the chances of you ever finding this tablet?"

"Probably about zero," Jamesy muttered.

"Right, then," cried Joker happily. "If you ever do find it, then give me a shout, and the two of us will head off into the desert on a wee adventure to find your stolen king."

Jamesy grinned. "I'll remember you said that. You never know, Joker, one day I might hold you to it."

Joker raised his glass. "Then here's to *one day*!"

Everyone else around the table lifted their drinks. "To *one day*!"

THIRTY NINE

2,312 years earlier

Babylon

It was a part of the city that been abandoned for centuries. The citizens of Babylon tended to build their homes on top of older buildings whose mud bricks had crumbled over the years, but this section had been built upon so many times it was no longer viable to continue.

And so, they had left it to decay. Ancient streets had become blocked as once busy dwellings tumbled down to create a dusty moonscape of hillocks and valleys and caverns. The old quarter slumped in shabby contrast to the dazzling wall and gateway that had been commissioned just two hundred years before by the second Nebuchadnezzar. The huge wall that circled the royal palace and the inner city shone a brilliant blue and was dotted with moulded animal figures that had been coloured gold. The overall effect was striking in the early afternoon sun and provided a perfect frame for the magnificent gate that had been dedicated to the glory of the goddess, Ishtar, who was called the Queen of Heaven.

Lianah could see the wall from where she stood and tried to take comfort from its grandeur.

"You're not scared, are you?" asked Meklios.

"No, I'm not scared!" she exclaimed, though she was terrified. Everyone knew that this place was now inhabited by the *djinns* of the desert, and by the evil spirits who came to feast on the memories of fifteen centuries, and even though Lianah knew that any phantoms would be unlikely to appear during the daytime, the knowledge did little to allay her fears.

"Is it much further?" she asked nervously.

"Just a little bit more," Meklios assured her. "It's within sight of the river, so once we get past that tall building up ahead, we should be able to see it."

They made their way quietly through the ruins, sometimes creeping along twisting, narrow lanes, sometimes clambering over piles of rubble until, at last, Lianah caught a shimmer of white in between the mounds of the tumbled-down buildings, and Meklios pointed excitedly.

"That's it!" he cried. "Do you see the great hill there?"

Lianah frowned. "But it's just a pile of dusty old bricks."

"That shows how much you know," Meklios said haughtily as they walked. "It was once a great palace," he told her, "built by Hammurabi over a thousand years ago."

"How do you know that?"

"My master told me. He knows everything, you see, and he often shares his knowledge with me."

"Just you?"

"Well, no," Meklios admitted. "But he often sits and talks of such things with the comrades of Hephaestion and the emperor, and I am often in the same room."

"As a servant," Lianah pointed out.

"What does that matter?" Meklios demanded. "Have Nikeratos and Laomedon not taken me into their confidence? Have they not shown me where they have hidden the ashes of Hephaestion? And where they intend to place the emperor?"

"Did you know Hephaestion?"

"Of course," said Meklios. He crouched down and pointed to an opening in the sloping side of the old palace. It seemed to descend far into the darkness below. "It's just through here."

"But it's so dark!" cried Lianah.

"You don't have to come if you don't want to," Meklios gently told her.

"No, no," she insisted. "I've … I've come *this* far." She allowed Meklios to lead her by the hand down the narrow pathway until they eventually emerged into a wide chamber. A small amount of sunlight still seeped through from the opening above and, after a while, Lianah's eyes adjusted to the gloom. She looked around in wonder.

The walls were all covered in paintings that still bore evidence of a skilled hand, though their colours were now faded and worn with time.

"We think this must have been the royal dining room," Meklios whispered. "See how many of the figures are eating and drinking?"

Lianah nodded in silent awe. Meklios led her over to a wall directly opposite from where they had entered and gestured to an alcove that had been chiselled out of the soft brick. Lianah gasped at what had been placed inside it.

"The jar that holds Hephaestion's ashes are inside this casket," Meklios told her. She could only stare, transfixed by the ornate box that had been richly decorated with precious stones, and was covered with a fine filigree of gold and silver that had been worked into the shape of a curling grapevine.

"Where did you find it?" asked Lianah.

Meklios shrugged. "I think Nikeratos took it from the palace. The emperor was going to build a great tomb to house it, but then he died and no one cared about Hephaestion anymore."

"Except for … who did you say?"

"Nikeratos and Laomedon," said Meklios. "They believe that the emperor should be with the one that he loved most of all during his life. So that when he goes to join his father on Mount Olympus, he will be accompanied by –"

"Did the king truly love Hephaestion?" asked Lianah, still entranced by the beauty of the casket.

"Of course," Meklios said firmly. "They were inseparable." He grabbed Lianah's arm and turned her towards him. "And that's why you must be sure of what needs to be done. We have already prepared a body to take the place of –"

"I *am* sure," Lianah said petulantly as she twisted from his grasp.

"Tell me again how you're going to lure the guards from their post."

"I'll tell them I saw someone in the courtyard below my window. I'll say that I'm frightened because no one is supposed to be there at night, and I'll ask them to come and chase him away."

"Yes, and you know to wait for my signal, don't you?"

"Yes, I'm not stupid!"

"Very well, then." Meklios gave her a smile. "And you're sure you can do this?"

"Yes," Lianah insisted, though she did feel a little apprehensive.

For, even though the world would soon be ending, it was still no small matter to steal the king who had once held that world together and who had once walked amongst men as a living god.

FORTY

Seamus was first up, and he went into the kitchen to make some tea. He had left Sandy in bed, still sleeping, so he was trying to make as little noise as possible. This meant that even his tiniest movement sounded as if a drum kit and a suit of armour were fighting each other with hammers.

Eventually, he tiptoed with his cup of tea into the living room where he sat down on the sofa and began picking over the events of the night before.

He had agonised over inviting Sandy to Gary's wedding, not wishing to come across as needy and desperate, but now that he had done so, he was agonising over what Sandy must be thinking. *He'll be thinking how needy and desperate I am*, he told himself. Such an assessment, he knew, was not far from the truth, but he would have preferred Sandy to have discovered this much later in their relationship. *Relationship? Ha!* He could forget about any relationship now, he realised. What would someone like Sandy want with such a pathetic loser like *him*?

Seamus sipped his tea and went over all of the painful scenarios of Sandy politely letting him down, and gently but firmly pushing him out of his life. *He's probably only pretending to be asleep,* he decided. *Just lying there, hoping that I'll get dressed quickly and just fuck off. And I don't even blame him.*

Sandy lay awake listening to Seamus shifting around on the living room sofa and wondering just what he was going to do about the wedding invitation. He was still a little unsure about his feelings for Seamus. He had been attracted to him initially just by the ugly music of his Belfast accent, but the more he got to know him, the more he had grown to like him. There was a solid honesty to Seamus, Sandy thought – a solemnity almost – that provided a refreshing contrast to the flighty giddiness of his usual companions.

Seamus, he sensed with utter certainty, would never let him down. He possessed a quiet strength that Sandy was drawn to, and Sandy began to question why that should be. Was he looking for some sort of foundation? Had he tired of all the fun, but empty, encounters of his past? Had the time finally come for him to drop anchor in still and deep waters? Maybe.

But there were other factors at play here as well, he felt. Being drawn to the Belfast accent, he suspected, was an unconscious form of self-punishment; forcing him to look back, forcing him to remember, forcing him to cringe in tortured grief as he acknowledged his own cowardice, standing aside, useless and mute, as he watched his own little sister fade away in pale and pointless agony. The Belfast accent took him back and made him wince as the images blazed, mocking, through his mind. The accusing stare of a man he had once been proud to call friend. The blank, soulless gaze of a man he had once loved. A world shattered and meaningless and a … Sandy blinked away the tears and pushed off the quilt as he got up. He put on a dressing gown and was still doing it up when he walked into the living room.

"Sandy!" Seamus exclaimed a little too eagerly. "Do you want a cup of tea?"

"Oh, yes please!" said Sandy smiling. Seamus hurried to the kitchen, trying not place too much significance on Sandy's smile. "So, how are you this morning?" he asked when he returned with the tea.

"Good, thanks."

"It's looking like a nice day out there," said Seamus, glancing at the bright blue in the frame of the window. He had decided to make no reference to the wedding. With any luck, they would be able to quietly ignore the whole thing and just pretend it had never been mentioned. They could just enjoy the rest of their time together and then maybe build on –

"I've just been thinking about Gary's wedding."

Fuck!

"I'm quite warming to the idea," Sandy went on. "Though I do have some reservations."

Warming to the idea? Holy shit!

Sandy took a sip of tea, cradling the cup in both hands, and looked across at Seamus. "It's probably just a silly prejudice," he said, "but Belfast does get quite a bad press."

"Well, yeah," said Seamus, "but there's a good reason why Belfast gets a bad press."

"What's that, then?"

"It's a violent shithole."

Sandy laughed. "Oh, I see," he said. "That would make sense, then."

"I mean, you can't ignore the Troubles," Seamus told him. "You can't just pretend that nothing's going on, but it's not like everybody's running around with their heads down. Most people just get on with things, and they all try to have a good laugh while they're doing it."

"Still, though …"

"Nobody's going to blame you if you don't want to come, so don't worry about that. If you think you'll feel too uncomfortable in Belfast, then me and Gary will totally understand. But the funny thing is," said Seamus, "the people of Northern Ireland might be trying to kill each other, but as soon as someone from outside comes to visit then some sort of ingrained Irish hospitality seems to kick in. You probably won't even have to buy a drink the whole time you're there. Not in Ardoyne, anyway."

"Mmm," said Sandy, "you're starting to convince me."

"Like I said, there's absolutely no pressure. If you really want to go, then I can pretty much guarantee you'll have a good time, but if you have any doubts at all about going to Belfast, then that's fine too."

Sandy put down his cup and gazed thoughtfully into the middle-distance. "I think if I didn't go," he said finally, "I'd only regret it. And I've already got far too many regrets in my life." He looked at Seamus and smiled. "So, yes!" he exclaimed. "I'd be delighted to accompany you to Gary's wedding!"

"Yes!" cried Seamus, jumping to his feet. Sandy stood as well, and they embraced. And then, as they stood in tearful, happy silence, holding each other and swaying slightly in the middle of the room, Sandy spoke.

"Oh, and Seamus?"

Circles of fate, and circles in the universe,

"What?"

And through the swirling realms of air,

"Call me Matthew."

Little circles everywhere.

FORTY ONE

The prospect of being made redundant had at least solved one of Gary's problems. As he sat on the bus taking him into town, he realised that he no longer had to be concerned about using up all of his holiday entitlement. He still had a week left of the time he had taken for the baby being born, and then he would have just over two weeks of his entitlement remaining. This had bothered him because he had wanted to take at least two weeks off for the wedding and honeymoon, which would have left him just a few days to keep back for the rest of the year.

Now, though, if he was going to be out of work by the end of the year, he could book all the time off he needed without having to worry about having no holiday left to take at Christmas.

It was a small crumb of comfort, but Gary had always been one for seeing the positive side of all things. He stepped off the bus at Peter's Hill and walked the short distance to the factory where Joker would just be finishing his morning shift. They had planned to meet up in order to go into town to look at suits for the wedding, and Joker was already waiting at the gates when Gary arrived.

"Is it okay if we call up to see Carol before we go round the shops?" Joker asked.

"Aye, no problem. Is she at work?"

"Yeah, we should be able to catch her on a break. I think she wants to talk to you about Rosie's hen night."

"And what the fuck would I know about Rosie's hen night?"

"Well, that's what I said, but she was insistent."

"I suppose there's no harm in seeing what she has to say." They set off towards the City Hospital, chatting as they walked.

"Have you had a go on Harry's guider yet?" asked Joker.

"Yeah, yesterday morning," said Gary. "It's bloody fast."

"Isn't that a good thing? For a race, I mean."

"When I say bloody fast, I mean *scary* bloody fast."

"You're still in one piece, though."

"Only just."

"I'm sure a man of your calibre won't have any trouble when it comes down to it."

"Obviously not," said Gary. "I mean, I'm sure the only reason Harry asked me to do it was because he knows I'm probably the only one who can handle it."

"I'm sure you're right," said Joker with a grin. "Is Seamus back yet, do you know?"

"Don't think so. He might be back later today, or maybe tomorrow. He's still sulking about his bloody car, though. I think he blames *me* for what happened in London."

"Do you not think he has a point?"

"Don't *you* fucking start!"

"I'm just saying you could have shown a bit more restraint."

"You weren't there, so you don't know what sort of racist wankers those guys were."

"But do you not think that your actions were a wee bit over-the-top?"

"What? Are you saying I should have just ignored those dickheads?"

"I think it was Kenny Rogers who put it best," said Joker philosophically. "*You gotta know when to hold 'em. Know when to fold 'em. Know when to –*"

"Yeah, very funny," said Gary, "but you would have done the same thing in my position."

"I beg to differ."

"You're a lying bastard! There's absolutely no chance you would have just walked away."

"Well, that might have been the case in my reckless youth," said Joker piously, "but I like to think that I've gone beyond that sort of thing. You see, there's a certain maturity in being able to calmly assess a situation before going on to choose the most suitable course."

"You've matured, have you?"

"I like to think of it as having achieved a certain level of serenity," said Joker. "You just have to accept that not everybody has the same views that you do, and once you do that, then you've taken the first step on the road to inner peace." Joker's brain was listening to all of this with increasing incredulity. "It's sort of like a 'Zen' type of thing."

"It sounds it."

"And now that you've got a kid, you've got even more reason to be responsible. You can't just go around throwing yourself at situations with no thought whatsoever."

"Is this a lecture?"

"Just advice, really. I'm only offering you my humble opinion."

"Well, I must say I'm impressed with this new, mellow Joker," said Gary. "Inner peace, you say? Serenity? That's really quite something. Does Carol know you've become a hippy?"

"It's easy to mock."

"You make it very easy."

"I know you'll come to your senses one day," said Joker serenely. "I just hope, for Rosie and Owen's sake, that it's sooner rather than later."

When they reached the hospital, they made their way to the canteen where Joker had arranged to meet Carol.

"No sign of her," Joker murmured, looking around. "We're probably a bit early. Do you want to go and find a table?"

"Aye, okay," said Gary. "I'll just have a cup of tea." He set off as Joker joined the queue at the counter. A stubby little man appeared and stood behind Joker in the queue. He had short grey hair – in a crew-cut style – and a face that was hard and lined.

"Always bloody busy, this place," he grumbled to Joker.

"Aye, I know," said Joker. "Makes you wonder why, though, because the food's crap."

The man laughed. "Aye, I know what you mean. I suppose we've no choice, though."

"Yeah, bit of a captive audience, really." The queue shuffled along slowly, and Joker and the man chatted amiably until the man glanced at one of the corridors leading off the canteen.

"Not a bad-looking girl, that …" he said.

Joker turned and saw Carol. He smiled. It still surprised him just how much his heart leapt every time he looked at her face. He knew she was the source of his inner peace and he felt grateful to her for it. Being a hippy wasn't so bad, he decided. There was a lot to be said for the tranquillity of tolerance and of universal love for all of mankind.

"No," Joker agreed still smiling. "Not bad at all!"

But the stubby little man, unfortunately, hadn't finished. "… for a nigger," he said.

FORTY TWO

Karen and Harry were on their way to visit Rosie and the baby when they bumped into Dessie, the guider driver for the Star.

"All right there, Dessie love?" said Karen.

"How's it going?" asked Dessie with a handsome smile.

"Yeah, not too bad," said Harry.

"I've been hearing that your guider's a bit of a beast, Harry."

"It'll give *you* a run for your money, anyway."

"I don't doubt it," said Dessie. "How's Darren doing?"

"He's on the mend," said Harry with a shrug.

"He's a stupid fucker," Karen pointed out for no particular reason.

"I hear your Gary's going to be driving on Sunday."

"Aye," said Karen. "He's another stupid –"

"How's the *Banshee* looking this year?" asked Harry.

"She's looking good," Dessie told him. "We've made a few wee improvements here and there, so I'm looking forward to the big day."

"Right, well, we'll see you then."

"Aye, we'll see you, Dessie love," said Karen. "And good luck for Sunday!" Dessie waved as he walked off, leaving Harry staring at his wife.

"What the hell do you mean *good luck for Sunday*?" he demanded.

"I'm just being polite."

"There's a first time for everything, I suppose," Harry muttered under his breath as they set off again.

"What was that?"

"Nothing."

Martin was in the chair by the fireplace, filling in an application form, when Karen and Harry came through the door.

"Where's that wee dote?" called Karen.

"I'm sitting right here," said Martin.

"Aye, you're cute, Martin, so you are, but not like this wee dote here." Karen reached into the cot by the window to rearrange the baby's blanket. Owen, to her disappointment, was fast asleep. "I'm not allowed to wake him up, am I?" she asked.

"No, you're bloody not!" Rosie shouted from the kitchen. "I'm making tea, do you want some?"

"Love some, Rosie, thanks!" Karen yelled back, needlessly loud.

"Stop trying to wake the baby!"

"Oh, all right," Karen grumbled as she took a seat on the sofa beside Harry. "So, how are things with you, then, Martin?" she asked. "I hear you had a wee trip up to Sandy Row."

Martin reached up and took a framed photograph from the mantelpiece. He passed it to Karen.

"Yes, I went to meet *him*," he said, and pointed to the figure on the left of the picture. "He was one of my da's army mates, and it turns out he's Joseph Anderson's granda."

"Aye, Rosie was telling me," said Karen. She shook her head. "Jesus, it's a small world, isn't it?"

Rosie came through from the kitchen with a tray of tea and biscuits. She set it down on the coffee table and looked at the photo in Karen's hands.

"You invited him to the wedding, didn't you, Daddy? she said.

Karen looked over at Martin. "Is he going to come?"

"He said it would be an honour," said Martin.

"Joseph's mummy and daddy were already invited, anyway," said Rosie, "so it looks like the whole family will be there."

"Oh, I love Davy and Katherine," enthused Karen. "They're a good laugh, them two. Aren't they, Harry?"

"They are, aye."

"I just hope that Gary can make it to the wedding," said Rosie pointedly, looking at Harry.

"Look, I don't know what you're so worried about," Harry protested. "He's already had a test run, hasn't he? And there wasn't any hassle at all."

Rosie sat down in the chair beside the cot. "Mmm," she murmured as she sipped her tea.

"You know, Rosie love," said Karen, "you're going to have trouble getting him to sleep tonight if you let him –"

"All right, all right," Rosie sighed. "You can wake him up." And Karen jumped to her feet.

FORTY THREE

They stared intently at the ghostly image glowing eerily against the lightbox. Joker sat in a chair behind them, sheepishly nursing his swollen knuckles. He suspected that Carol was inwardly simmering, and that when the radiographer left the room, she would be outwardly boiling.

"No obvious fractures," said Carol.

"No, it all seems fine to me," the radiographer chirpily agreed. He switched off the lightbox and took down the x-ray of Joker's hand. "Though, going by the state of your fingers," he said to Joker, "your man must have had a really hard head."

"It was like punching a concrete bollard," said Joker, though he dropped his gaze when he caught Carol glaring at him.

"I'm sure!" the radiographer laughed. "Well, I'll just go and file this away," he said to Carol as he headed for the door. Joker was sorry to see him go.

"What the hell were you thinking?" Carol demanded once the radiographer had gone.

"Obviously, I *wasn't* thinking," Joker mumbled.

"What?"

"Nothing."

"You wrecked the whole bloody canteen, Joseph! Seriously, what the hell did you think you were doing?"

"I don't know," said Joker weakly. "It's just that …"

"What?"

"Well, it's just that he …"

"He *what*?" asked Carol. "He called me a nigger, is that it?"

Joker was stunned. He stared at Carol in shock. "How did you –?"

"He calls me a nigger all the time, Joseph, it's just his way."

"But … but ..." Joker's mind was reeling. "And you're just okay with him being a bigot?"

"Oh, for God's sake, Joseph!" cried Carol. "Everybody's a bigot!"

"I'm not," Joker declared loftily.

"Yes you are, Joseph," Carol sighed, rubbing her forehead. "Even if you're just bigoted against bigots, it still makes you a bigot."

"Well, I …" Joker raised a finger. He then requested some assistance from his brain in order to provide an appropriate response, but his brain told him he was on his own with this one.

"You can't just go around attacking people you don't agree with," Carol told him. "You're going to have to grow up at some point, you know."

At that moment, there was knock on the door, and Gary appeared. "Well, what's the damage?" he said with a grin. His right arm was in a sling.

"How's your shoulder?" Carol asked him.

"Oh, it's just a bad sprain," he said. "And what about Mike Tyson here?"

"He'll live," said Carol curtly as she walked to the door. "I'll see you two later."

"So, how's that 'Zen' thing working out for you, then?" asked Gary when Carol had gone.

"Fuck up!"

"Rosie's going to love this," said Gary, pointing to the sling.

"You didn't have to get involved."

"I wasn't getting involved!" cried Gary. "I jumped up to get out of the way, and you two assholes came blundering into me. Knocked me bloody flying!"

"Yeah, well …"

"It buggers up the shopping trip a bit, doesn't it?"

"Just a bit."

"Do you want to go for a drink instead?"

"I suppose so," said Joker, getting to his feet. "I could do with a pint." They walked together along the corridor. "This is going to put an end to your guider racing career, isn't it?"

"Shit! I hadn't thought of that," said Gary. "Harry won't be happy, will he? He won't be happy at all."

FORTY FOUR

Harry wasn't happy at all. Thanks to the antics of his brother-in-law, he was going to have to abandon his plans to beat the Crumlin Star in the Guider Race this weekend. He was walking through the centre of town, heading for the Kitchen Bar, and glumly thinking that he was going to have to put up with the Star's bragging for another year. He had already tried everything he could think of to find someone who was willing to drive the *Dullahan*, but, for some reason, everyone seemed to be busy that day. He'd all but run out of time now, so he simply sighed and walked on to his arranged meeting.

Michael McClelland, despite his best intentions, was finding the trappings of criminality difficult to shed. The recent attempt on his life had spurred his desire for a more conventional and legitimate lifestyle, but, ironically, it had also managed to feed his paranoia. He had, therefore, not only retained the use of his bodyguards – who sat watching from a discreet distance – but had added to their complement with two more men watching the entrance to the bar from a car parked on the road outside.

He told himself that at some point he would have to dispense with his personal security detail, but for now – especially with his treacherous former right-hand man still at large – he felt it was still necessary. Not that it would be much use today, he mused, for if the upcoming meeting were to turn suddenly sour, then Michael was only too aware that nothing short of a tactical air-strike would prevent Hegarty from causing him harm. Even then, he thought grimly, it would probably only serve to irritate the brute who had, in the past, displayed a remorseless determination that put Michael in mind of the cyborg from the movie *The Terminator*.

Michael, however, was unconcerned. He felt that he now had the measure of his man. Harry Hegarty, Michael believed, was not unreasonable. Though quiet and brooding, Hegarty had managed to build up a successful little business that had acquired – according to Michael's sources – a firm and growing reputation for excellence. This was someone that Michael could understand and with whom, he felt, he could do business.

Michael now saw himself as Richard Gere's character in *Pretty Woman*; someone who eventually realises that true fulfilment comes from nurturing an idea, from building up and supporting the dreams of others. From creating, not destroying. There was also some sub-plot involving a character played by Julia Roberts, but that wasn't what Michael had taken from the movie; it was redemption through honest business that had captured his imagination.

He glanced up as the door to the bar opened and the unmistakeable figure of Hegarty entered. Harry scanned the room and then, having nodded his recognition of Michael, he approached the table.

"Just passed your goons in that Corolla outside," said Harry as he sat down opposite Michael. "They don't make it obvious or anything, do they?"

"Yes, well, that's not really important," Michael said dismissively, and made a mental note to get rid of the men and replace them with some people who weren't complete halfwits. "Do you want a drink?"

"No."

"Straight down to business, then? I like your style." Harry made no reply, so Michael carried on. "I just wanted to go over some of the details that we discussed on the phone."

"I haven't said *yes* yet."

"Well, I know, but let me put it this way; I've managed to acquire a certain reputation, you see, and –"

"A reputation?" said Harry. "Of being a hood? Is that what you mean?"

"Okay, Harry," said Michael, holding up his hands. "Fair enough. Let's just be straight with each other. So yes, okay then, a hood, a criminal, a crook. Call it whatever you want, but that's why I'm looking to invest in small businesses like yours. I want to put all of that dodgy stuff behind me."

"You want to be legit?"

"Exactly!"

"Why should I believe you?"

"You don't have to, of course," Michael conceded. "All I can do is ask you to trust me. Look, it isn't just *your* business that I've been looking into. I've got potential opportunities all over the city, so I'm going to be making these investments anyway, Harry. With or without you."

Harry nodded thoughtfully. "I won't pretend I'm not interested," he said. "It's why I'm here, after all. But I just need to make sure that everything's above board."

"Absolutely, Harry. I can hardly blame you for –" Michael almost jumped when a young woman suddenly appeared beside his table. She seemed to have come from nowhere, surprising Michael's bodyguards, who now got to their feet. They moved to approach the woman, but a look from Harry suggested that sitting back down again would be a much better idea.

"Mr McClelland?" the woman asked, looking nervously at the floor.

"Yes," said Michael warily. "What is it?"

"You don't know me," she said. "But my name's Gemma Frazer. I'm Paul Dempsey's girlfriend."

"Paul Dempsey?" said Harry. "You mean Wee Paulie? From Ardoyne? Used to drink in the League?"

Gemma seemed startled by being addressed by Mr McClelland's

monstrous companion, but she nodded shyly and turned back to Michael with a look of desperation. "He's really, really sorry, Mr McClelland," she pleaded. "He just wants to –"

"I don't give a fuck!" snapped Michael, turning away.

"What's this about?" asked Harry.

"Nothing, Harry," Michael hastily assured him. "Don't you worry about it. It's really got nothing to do with you, mate."

Many people tended to form an opinion of Harry based simply on his appearance. They had a tendency to dismiss him as nothing more than a big dumb thug. Those people were idiots. Harry looked shrewdly across the table at Michael.

"What were you doing on that road down south when we picked you up?" he asked. "You were very cagey about it, and Wee Paulie stopped drinking in the League around about the same time. Did he get all the information he needed?"

"Seriously, Harry," cried Michael, "it's really not important. You just –"

Harry ignored him and turned to Gemma. "Is Wee Paulie in hiding?" he asked her. Gemma nodded, glancing nervously at Michael. "Is he in fear of his life?"

"Yes!" cried Gemma. "Mr McClelland here says he's going to –"

"Look, I've fucking said it's not important!" Michael shouted. "Why the fuck is nobody –?"

"I'll make you a deal," Harry told him calmly.

"What?"

"I'll accept any investment offers you want to make," said Harry. "And *you* let Wee Paulie off the hook."

Gemma stared at Harry in disbelief. Was this terrifying giant the answer to her prayers? She could have kissed him. Michael also stared at Harry, but his thoughts were not the same as Gemma's. His face was contorted with fury and indecision. On the one hand, he was struggling to accept the idea of Wee Paulie getting away with attempted murder, but on the other hand, not only did he want in on Harry's business, he also liked the idea of simply having Harry as an acquaintance. In the end, Harry won out. Michael held his hand out over the table.

"Deal," he said, and shook Harry's hand.

"Oh my God!" cried Gemma as the tears poured down her cheeks. "Oh my God! Thank you! Thank you so much!"

Michael regarded Harry with a cool curiosity. "I don't get it, Harry," he said. "Why should you be so concerned about any of this? You don't strike me as the sentimental type."

Harry didn't reply. Instead, he turned to Gemma.

"Can Wee Paulie drive a guider?"

FORTY FIVE

Wee Paulie was on the cusp of greatness. He could sense it. He could feel it in his water. As he stood, silent and still in the early afternoon sun – the crowd hushed in expectation – he gazed at the bottom of the hill, far in the distance, and narrowed his eyes, focusing on the moment. On his time to shine.

The sun beat down, though any uncomfortable heat was snatched away by a cool breeze that rustled the bright green leaves of a sycamore in a garden off to Wee Paulie's right. He barely registered the subtle murmur, as his thoughts, his being, his very soul were all concentrated on the chaos that was to come. The speed, the danger, the excitement, the –

"Get a fucking move on!" The crowd, having found its voice, shook Wee Paulie from his reverie and he hastily pulled on a pair of leather gloves and turned to give Gemma a quick kiss.

"Aaah, that's lovely," sighed the crowd, and also; "That's gay!" said the crowd, somewhat paradoxically.

Wee Paulie climbed onto the *Dullahan* and readied himself for the task ahead. He had elected to kneel, facing forward, on the guider with his hands tightly gripping each side of the steering bar. There was a greater risk of injury from such a position, but Wee Paulie considered it to be worth it for the added control it gave to the jittery steering.

The two racers waited silently in their vehicles. This was the semi-final. It was Wee Paulie in the *Dullahan*, representing the League, versus the independent entry, *My Girlfriend's Box (Cart)*, which had surprised many by its progress; not least of whom were the creators who had only entered on a drunken whim at the very last minute.

The final moments ticked by until, suddenly and shockingly, they were off. Both guiders, trundling at first, soon began to pick up speed. Wee Paulie felt a surge of joy as the adrenalin flooded his veins.

This was his moment, his shot at redemption. This was his chance. This was his one opportunity to become the hero he knew he could be. He would achieve legendary status, he realised, and he would achieve it back in the district that he thought he had left behind. As he hurtled towards his destiny, squinting in the wind, he saw a glorious future laid out before him, and so, his heart elated, he soared onwards. To glory.

Harry slammed down the phone and stared angrily at the wall. He was half-expecting some comment from Karen, but she remained silent, sitting curled up on one end of the sofa, wrapped snugly in a warm bathrobe. Harry glanced over at her.

"That was your woman again," he said after a while.

"Aye, I gathered that."

"I don't know what the hell she expects me to do."

"She expects you to pay for the damage, that's what she expects."

"What bloody damage?" said Harry indignantly. He was fighting to control his temper. "There's not even a scratch on her bloody car!"

"That's not what she says."

"Well, she's a liar," Harry fumed. "I had a look at it, and I even got Mickey from the garage to look at it and we couldn't see anything wrong with it."

"Anyway," said Karen, "nobody seems to be too worried about that wee fella, Paulie."

Harry said nothing. He was still trying to quell the rage and the sense of bitter injustice he was feeling.

"I mean," Karen went on, "the poor wee fucker broke his nose, but you don't seem to be too bothered about that, do you?"

"Well, he shouldn't have …" Harry paused to force down the anger in his voice. "He shouldn't have driven straight into the back of a car, should he? A bloody parked car! What was he thinking? He was well in the lead! He could have won easy! But no! He had to go and …" Harry let his words trail away as he pondered how he was going to have to put up with the crowing of the members of the Star for the next few months.

"There's always next year," Karen suggested.

"That's not the point," he said sullenly.

"Well, anyway …" Karen muttered. She looked at her husband as he glared intensely across the room. "Do you fancy going upstairs?"

He turned towards her, then slowly shook his head. "Sorry, love," he said, "I think I'm just too annoyed, to be honest with you."

It should be pointed out that Karen had never, at any level, studied behavioural psychology. She had never learned the ways in which subtle impulses in the brain can form and develop in order to trigger specific physical reactions. And, incredibly, she had never received any formal scientific training that might have given her some sort of insight into the neurological pathways that are activated under a particular set of chemical stimuli.

But Karen did seem to possess a kind of sixth sense. She seemed to have a certain uncanny knack for understanding how motivational urges can be provoked and manipulated in the psyche of the human species. And, in particular, the male of that species.

She got up and stood in front of Harry. And then, without saying a word, she simply held open her bathrobe. She was naked underneath.

"Well," said Harry, getting up from his chair with a resigned sigh, "it turns out I'm not as annoyed as I thought I was."

They went upstairs.

FORTY SIX

"Hannah!" Karen shrieked. "You crazy wee bitch!" She rushed over and hugged Hannah as she came in through the door. Hannah smiled, bemused, and let Karen lead her over to the table. She felt a little intimidated, as Rosie and Karen were the only ones in the group that she really knew, but once the introductions were made, she happily took her seat and accepted a glass of wine.

"Karen started early," Rosie explained. "But I'm sure you'd already guessed that."

Hannah grinned. "It's a lovely place this," she said, looking around. "I've never been here before."

"Yeah, it was Carol's idea," said Rosie, nodding across the table to Carol. "We'll get something to eat here, and then head on into town."

"I don't know if I'll be able to last the whole night," said Hannah. "I'm a bit of a lightweight."

"Ah, don't worry about it, Hannah love," Rosie told her. "We'll just see how you get on."

"Are you going to be going to the wedding, Hannah?" asked Carol.

"What sort of question's that?" cried Karen. "Of course she's going to the bloody wedding!" She then frowned and turned to Hannah. "You *are*, aren't you?"

"I'm not really sure, to be honest," said Hannah. "I'm not sure if it would be a good idea."

"Why not?" asked Rosie.

"Is it because it's in Ardoyne?" asked Katherine. "I don't blame you, love," she said, making Karen hoot with laughter. "Don't you worry, though. Me and my Davy will make sure you're all right."

"No, it isn't that," insisted Hannah, though it was certainly an issue. "I just think it might be a bit awkward with James being there."

"What's happening with you two, anyway?" asked Karen.

"Well, nothing really," said Hannah. She hadn't seen Jamesy since Heathrow, but that was an encounter that haunted her still.

"But you're both still friends, aren't you?"

"I suppose so."

"Well, then, what's the problem?" said Rosie. "There's nothing to stop two friends from going to the same wedding, is there?"

Hannah took a sip of wine and gave an uncertain smile. "Not really," she said. "Maybe I'll have a think about it."

"You do that," Rosie told her. A waiter came to take the food orders and, after ten minutes of confused shouting and mind-changing, he departed with what he hoped was a coherent list of meals.

After the meal, and after the bill had been settled, Sadie, Rosie's future mother-in-law, approached the bride-to-be. She gestured at some of the women around the table. The older ones. "We're just going to order some taxis to take us into town, Rosie love," she said. "We're not really up to walking it."

"Okay," said Rosie. "We'll just see you in Robinson's, then?"

"Yes, love," said Sadie. She then set off to phone for some taxis, and Rosie looked around the table.

"I could really do with the exercise," she said, "so is everybody else okay to walk it?

"I think so," said Ellie. "It's still a lovely evening out there, isn't it?"

"Right," said Rosie, getting to her feet. "Let's go, then!"

They had all made an effort for their night out. They were all perfumed, and made-up, and were squeezed into all sorts of sequinned and sparkly items of clothing. Karen had poured herself into a shimmering pair of black ski-pants which, on her slender frame, looked stunning. Most of the others had opted for little dresses or skirts that showed off their summer tans. Even Hannah wore a dress, though it was a long-sleeved, sedate affair that came to just below her knees.

Rosie, still carrying a little pregnancy weight, wore a light and lacy number that sat loosely on her, and was more stylish than it was sexy. She looked good, though. They all did.

At the bottom of the Malone Road, several popular bars and nightclubs would, on a warm Friday evening like this one, spill large crowds of revellers out onto the nearby pavements. As the girls sauntered past, it was inevitable they would attract admiring glances from groups of young men on a night out and, sure enough, a host of wolf-whistles arose, along with some good-natured banter and a few salacious smiles.

Rosie and her gang chatted happily amongst themselves, as if oblivious to the stir they were creating. They strolled along, casual and carefree, relishing the attention, but making sure not to acknowledge it, when suddenly, a bunch of grinning, tipsy guys stepped in front of them.

The group's leader – or at least the one who did most of the talking – was very good-looking, with tumbling curly blonde hair and sparkling blue-green eyes. He was dressed in a colourful Hawaiian shirt that enhanced his perfect tan, which, in turn, enhanced his perfect white smile. He flashed that smile at the girls, who were forced to stop or else step out into the road.

"Hello there, ladies," he said. "I shall be your Lover Boy for this evening." He gestured to his friends who stood giggling behind him. "Now if you'll just be so kind as to accompany us, then I can assure you that we shall be able to satisfy all of your needs." He seemed to be the type that was used to getting his own way, and with his friends and several pints of lager backing him up, it was obvious he considered himself to be irresistible.

"Sorry, Lover Boy," said Karen, "but I think we've got all the wankers we need back home."

Lover Boy looked like he'd been slapped, as the girls, roaring with laughter, pushed their way through. He stood aside, looking crestfallen, and Hannah felt quite sorry for him as she walked past, though, she too, was smiling.

"I think you might have hurt his wee feelings there, Karen," said Claire as they walked on.

"Awk, I'm sure he'll get over it!" Karen told her. They made their way past the queue for the disco at the Wellington Park Hotel, and the crowds began to thin out as they approached the entrance to the broad parkland of Botanic Gardens. "How do you think our Gary's getting on, Rosie?" Karen called over her shoulder.

"I'll worry about it tomorrow," said Rosie.

"Is his shoulder okay?" asked Carol, walking alongside Rosie and Hannah.

"Aye, it's not too bad, Carol. Unless I ask him to do something that is, and then it starts giving him jip."

"Why?" said Hannah. "What happened?" Carol began to fill her in on all the details, and Rosie dropped back to chat with Ellie and Sheila who were bringing up the rear. When they reached the gates to the park, Karen and Claire stopped and turned round.

"What way do you think we should go?" Claire asked Rosie. "We could cut through the park and then go down Botanic Avenue, or we could just go straight on past the university."

"Oh, I'm not sure," said Rosie, pausing to look through the open gates.

"What way's the quickest?" asked Karen. "Because I could do with a drink."

They were still standing there, deliberating, when Lover Boy and his friends caught up with them. "All right there, girls?" said Lover Boy through a forced smile. "I think we got off on the wrong foot there."

"Look, we're really not interested," Claire told him.

"Is that right?" he demanded with a slightly menacing tone. He zeroed in on Carol who was easily the most striking of all the girls. "What about you, sweetheart?" he asked. "Are you not interested either?"

"No," Carol said simply. "I'm not."

"Are you sure, love?" Lover Boy snarled. "I mean, I can get you all the fucking bananas you want!"

Hannah gasped in disbelief at Lover Boy's remark. Claire and Rosie stared hatefully at his cocky grin. Ellie and Sheila shook their heads at the sheer malevolence in his eyes. And Karen took a step forward and kicked him in the balls with such enthusiasm he became momentarily taller. He then crumpled, whimpering to the pavement.

"You fucking bitch!" cried one of Lover Boy's companions. He made a lunge for Karen, but Claire reacted quickly and jumped forward to push him in the chest. He teetered off-balance, and then fell backwards over Lover Boy, who still lay curled up on the ground.

"*Run!*" Claire yelled, and the girls bolted into the park, scattering in different directions. Rosie, Claire and Hannah took off to the left, down a tarmac path that led through an archway of tall bushes. Ellie and Sheila headed to the right towards the imposing edifice of the Ulster Museum, and Karen and Carol ran straight ahead towards a large expanse of grass where a crowd of rugby lads could be seen practising their moves.

Lover Boy, having now recovered, got to his feet and urged his mates to catch the vicious little bitch who had assaulted him. They all set off in pursuit of Karen and Carol who had, by this time, shot onto the grass and into the middle of the rugby boys' training session. The burly rugby lads stopped what they were doing, surprised and delighted by the sudden appearance in their midst of a statuesque African goddess. And Karen.

The two girls went hurtling across the pitch, and it was then that Lover Boy's gang burst onto the field, shouting angrily and showing clear intent that they meant to cause harm to the dusky queen and her handmaiden. This did not sit well with the rugby boys, who all liked to believe they possessed a keen, if quaint, sense of gallantry when it came to the fairer sex, and so they leapt to Carol's defence. And Karen's too, of course.

But mostly Carol's.

At the same time, Rosie and Hannah, having run through the archway in the bushes, had discovered that the path then sloped steeply downwards before veering away to the right. It was not long after this discovery that Rosie made a further discovery that she no longer seemed to be in full control of her own momentum.

"*Oh fuck! Oh fuck! Oh fuck!*" she screamed as she clattered like a runaway train down the path towards the sharp, right-hand turn.

"Rosie!" yelled Hannah, trying to catch up. As she sprinted after Rosie, she desperately reached out to try to grasp a handful of Rosie's dress but, just as she was about to grab hold, Rosie was suddenly swallowed by a large rhododendron bush that sat on the corner of the pathway.

"Get the fuck out my way!" Lover Boy arrogantly demanded of the stocky, hairy fella wearing a striped rugby jersey, who stepped in front of him. By way of a reply, the rugby lad rammed a big hairy fist into Lover Boy's perfect white teeth, and Lover Boy dropped, broken and bloodied, onto the grass where he remained, unconscious, in a colourful little pile.

Realising they were no longer being pursued, Carol and Karen slowed, and then stopped and turned round to observe the chaos they had left in their wake. From what they could see, it looked like Lover Boy's friends were having all sorts of shit kicked out of them by a bunch of rough, tough rugby boys. Karen and Carol looked at each other, and then Karen directed Carol's attention to some bushes where she had just spotted Claire jumping up and down and waving both arms in the air in a clear attempt to be noticed.

"What's up?" Karen asked as she and Carol approached.

"I think Rosie might be stuck," Claire told them.

"Stuck?"

"Yes," said Claire. "Through here!" She led them through the bright foliage and across the pathway until they reached a tall, leafy bush. Hannah was holding some branches to one side and was peering into the dark interior. "I think she's caught up on some of the branches in here," she said.

"Hannah?" Rosie's muffled voice could be heard from somewhere inside. "Is that you?"

Karen, crouching down, shouted into the dark undergrowth. "Rosie? Are you okay?"

"I could do with a hand, if it's all the same to you!"

"What's happening?" The question came from behind them, causing Karen to straighten up and turn around. She saw Ellie and Sheila strolling towards them.

"Where the fuck have you two been?" Karen asked them.

"We thought that we could run into the museum," Ellie told her, "but it was closed."

"And then what?"

"Well, then we saw that nobody was chasing us, so we just dandered over here."

"You just dandered over here, did you?"

"Yeah. Why? What's going on?"

"Well, if you'd been paying any –"

"*Are you all just going to fucking stand there?*" yelled Rosie.

"Shit! Sorry, Rosie love!"

Once Rosie had been freed from the branches of the rhododendron, and Carol and Ellie had determined that – apart from a few scratches – she was fine, they headed into town.

It was much later that night, upstairs in Robinson's where they had commandeered an entire corner of the room, that Hannah hoisted her umpteenth glass of wine into the air and called for a toast.

"What are we toasting?" asked Rosie.

"Well," said Hannah, "Lover Boy said that we got off on the wrong foot, didn't he? So, then, here's to Karen for showing him what the right foot looks like!"

And they all raised their glasses and cheered.

FORTY SEVEN

The pale blue morning had assembled some fluffy white clouds and sent them off with a chirpy little breeze to frolic and to play above the twin belltowers of Holy Cross Chapel. The solemn old towers stood solid and square and impassive as they gazed down at the fine-smelling and smartly dressed people who were beginning to swarm around the chapel grounds.

Joker, filled with self-importance in his position as groomsman, was barking orders and pointing officiously at anyone he suspected of being on the verge of shenanigans. No one was paying him any attention. The crowd milled around in the grounds at the base of the chapel steps, smoking, chatting and glancing down the hill towards the quiet little streets of Ardoyne.

"So, how's your induction course going?" Jamesy asked Sean.

"Yeah, it's going well," Sean replied. "I think there's a good chance that I'll be posted to the Far East at the end of it. That's what I've been pushing for, anyway."

"What about Bobby?"

"Oh, he's just planning to come back here," said Sean, "though I think he might have to spend a bit of time in England to begin with."

"All right there?" Karen called out to them as she walked past with Harry. They both smiled back and nodded a greeting.

"Here!" Joker cried, marching over to Sean and Jamesy, "Do you two know where you're sitting?"

"I would imagine that you're about to tell us," Sean suggested.

"Go to the left side when you go in," Joker told them. "Rosie doesn't have that much family, so I'm trying to bulk that side out a bit."

"Fair enough."

"And just watch yourselves," Joker warned them as he walked away. "I'll be keeping an eye on you two."

A short while later, Kevin arrived and joined Jamesy and Sean.

"All right there, Kevin?" asked Sean. "So, how's it all going with you these days?"

"Oh, you know, Sean," said Kevin. "Just the usual, really." He looked around at the crowd. "So, where's the groom, then?"

"He's already inside with Seamus," Jamesy told him.

"Oh yeah," said Sean. "What's this I hear about Seamus bringing some English bloke?"

"Yeah," said Jamesy. "Matt, he's called. He flew over last night, apparently."

"Have you met him?"

"Just briefly this morning. He's inside, as well, with Seamus and Gary."

Bobby then pushed his way through the throng. "Why do I keep hearing jokes about Rosie's bush?" he asked. "Hiya Kevin."

"Rosie's bush?"

"Yeah, I was just talking to Joker's ma and da, and then Carol came over as well and she was laughing about it too."

"No idea," shrugged Sean.

Bobby lit a cigarette and looked at Sean, Jamesy and Kevin. "So, are we just the sad singles, then?" he said smiling. "We should start a gang."

"No luck with Hannah, then?" Sean asked Jamesy.

"Your guess is as good as mine, Sean."

"What's that supposed to mean?"

"Well, she phoned me the other night," Jamesy explained. "And that's the first I've heard from her in ages."

"What did she say?"

"She said that she really wants to come to the wedding today. You know, for Rosie's sake?"

"But?"

"Well, for one thing, she didn't feel comfortable about coming to a Catholic Mass."

"That's understandable," said Bobby. "I'm not happy about it myself."

"And also," Jamesy continued, "she doesn't want to just show up on her own."

"So, what did *you* say?" asked Kevin.

"I said I could come and pick her up after the Mass, and we could just go into the reception together."

"Jesus Christ, Jamesy!" cried Bobby. "I know she's my cousin and all, but it sounds like she's got you wrapped around her finger."

"I'm just helping out a friend," said Jamesy, though he looked miserable.

"I think you're too good for your own bloody good, Jamesy mate," said Sean.

"Where are you picking her up from?" asked Kevin.

"Queen's."

"Are you going to get a taxi over?"

"I was planning to," said Jamesy, "but Seamus has managed to arrange a lift with Rosie's uncle, so that'll be handy enough."

"Even so," said Sean with a shake of his head. At that moment, Tone and Claire appeared.

"Jesus!" said Tone. "Who put Adolf bloody Anderson in charge?"

"Watch what you say," laughed Claire. "He's got your number, you know. He knows *your* sort."

"Bloody hell!" Tone grinned.

"Did he tell you to sit on the left when you go in?" Jamesy asked.

"Yeah, he did," said Tone. "He also said there was to be no funny business."

"I think it's all gone to his head, to be honest."

They stood chatting for a few minutes more until Joker began to usher everyone up the steps and into the chapel.

Gary and Seamus stood side-by-side in front of the altar, watching as all their friends and relations filed in and took their seats. On the right-hand side of the aisle, Matthew sat, smiling happily, a few rows back from the front. Seamus had picked him up from the airport the night before and had taken him to meet Gary and Rosie shortly after they had arrived in Ardoyne. Matthew had been overwhelmed by the welcome he had received and had tearfully declared himself to be in love with Rosie and her family, and they, in turn, admitted to being won over by Matt's easy charm.

Matthew had only known Gary and Seamus for just a few weeks, but he was already beginning to understand just how important they both were to him. He smiled to himself as he realised he saw them as a single entity rather than as two individuals. He believed that one would be utterly lost without the other, regardless of their constant sniping and bickering, and he envied them that bond. He craved such an unspoken attachment, for – ever since he had stumbled away, confused and grief-stricken, from his family home – he had been lost.

Matthew had eventually found acceptance and understanding in Brighton's gay community, but he had never felt that he truly belonged. He accepted his sexuality easily enough – having suffered for so long, suppressing his forbidden urges – but he still felt listless and unconnected to anyone or anything. Always looking to the horizon, he supposed, but perhaps it was now time for him to … The organist struck up *The Wedding March*, and Matthew, along with the rest of the congregation stood up.

Everyone turned to face the doors at the back of the chapel, straining for a first glimpse of the bride.

And then there she was. Rosie.

Rosie had, for the longest time, simply abandoned any notion of ever experiencing a moment such as this. As far as she had been concerned, she was no one. An orphan. Adrift and unwanted. Angry at everything. Angry at life and angry at love. She knew that neither of those four-letter words had ever given her anything except heartbreak, and so she had told herself she would just dispense with love altogether, harden her heart, and snatch from life whatever she could. She smiled inwardly at her own naivety. Because here she was.

She turned her head for a quick glance at her father's face as he led her down the aisle, and she decided that it could not be possible for a man to look any more proud. She turned her head further and smiled at her one single bridesmaid, following behind, and despite the tears that were pouring freely down her sister's face, Rosie believed that Ellie had never looked more beautiful.

Dispense with love? Rosie asked herself mockingly. *I don't bloody think so!*

They reached the altar, and Martin handed her over to Gary, her childhood hero, and it was there, under the mournful gaze of Christ and His saints, that little Rosie McCann with the long black hair– resplendent in an ivory dress that was beautifully simple and simply beautiful – got to marry her musketeer. Her very own D'Artagnan.

And then, to rowdy cheers and rapturous applause, they kissed.

After the ceremony, Jamesy and Rosie's Uncle Mark took off to go and collect Hannah while the other wedding guests spilled once more into the chapel grounds.

"Slept the whole way through," marvelled Sadie as she cradled her grandson. "Not a peep out of him." She was showing off baby Owen to Katherine and Davy. Thomas stood off to the side, staring into the distant past, and quietly assuring his old comrade that his boy and his grandchildren were doing him proud.

Tone and Claire stood with Bobby over by the railings opposite the chapel steps, smoking and chatting, while Sean strolled over to talk to Karen and Harry. Seamus and Matthew came down the steps and Joker guided them towards the bride and groom who were chatting and laughing with well-wishers as they waited, around the side of the chapel, for the photographer to set up.

Martin was beaming as he stood in a little group that included Stephanie and her husband as well as Jack and Tina. Jack was dropping hints that another wedding might be on the horizon, and Martin found himself filled with a sense of wonder at how his life had changed so completely in such a short space of time.

Ellie was struggling with several bouquets of flowers that she had planned to bring round to the cabaret room of the Star, where the reception was due to be held. She was just realising that she had been a little over-optimistic about her ability to carry them all when she heard a voice coming from behind her.

"Do you want a hand with those?"

Ellie turned to see a pleasant, friendly face that held soft, kind eyes and a shy smile. "Oh, yes," she said. "Yes, that would be brilliant, thanks."

Kevin took the bulk of her burden and they walked along side-by-side, occasionally shooting sideways glances at each other before quickly looking away again, and Joker – whose perspicacity was frequently overlooked – smiled.

"Make sure you're back for the photos!" Rosie called after them.

"I take it your Uncle Mark is going to be coming back here as well," said Gary. "Instead of going straight to the Star."

"Yeah, I've already said to him, because I want Hannah to be in the photos too."

"Hey, you! Rosie Lingfield!" Karen shouted over to Rosie. "This better not take too long, because I'm bloody starving!"

"It'll take as long as it takes, Karen Hegarty!" Rosie shouted back, grinning. They then rushed over and embraced each other, laughing excitedly.

"Congratulations, Rosie love," said Karen.

"Thanks!"

Karen then looked across to her brother. "And you'd better make sure you look after her. Do you hear that, Gary?"

Gary held his hands up in protest. "What's that supposed to mean?"

"Just you make … Oh, all right there, Seamus love? I didn't see you there."

"Hiya, Karen," said Seamus. "Have you met Matt?"

"No, I haven't," Karen said as she held a hand out to Matthew, "but I've heard all about you. It's nice to finally meet you, Matt."

"It's nice to meet you, too."

The photographer then asked for the bride and groom to come and pose for their wedding portraits, and the laborious photography session began.

As various different groups were assembled, photographed and dispersed, Kevin and Ellie came strolling up the drive to the chapel grounds, absorbed in conversation, and, a little while later, Mark, Jamesy and Hannah appeared.

The crowd swirled around the grounds, shuffling in and out of position to the direction of the photographer and the stern groomsman. Tone sighed and stubbed out a cigarette as he and Claire were instructed by Joker to move up and get ready for their portrait. As Tone passed behind Seamus, seemingly deep in conversation with someone, he was about to walk on when he suddenly stopped, frowned, and spun around.

"*Matthew?*" he cried.

Matt, startled, turned towards the voice. He stared for a moment in consternation and then, stunned and disbelieving, his eyes widened, and he felt his jaw drop open. "Anthony?" he stammered. "Oh, Anthony, it *is* you!" They both stepped forward and threw their arms around each other, dancing and hugging through their tears, as everyone around them looked on bemused. This was a side to Tone that no one had ever suspected.

Tone, sensing his friends' confusion, broke away and turned to them. "This is Matthew!" he told them excitedly. "*Matthew!* Emily's brother!"

The blank stares slowly gave way to a dawning realisation until, eventually, the overall feeling was best articulated by Seamus, who simply said; "Holy shit!"

The caterers had been busy, and, by the time the first guests began to trickle into the Star's function room, several long tables had been set against one wall and were fully laden with all kinds of food for the buffet lunch.

The photography session had wrapped up quickly after Tone and Matthew's emotional reunion, and it didn't take long for the crowd to make the short walk from the chapel to the reception room. Everyone descended greedily upon the generous spread, and soon the guests were all seated at their tables, eating, drinking and joking amidst the loud murmurings of a host of babbling conversations.

After everyone had eaten their fill, and the dishes were all cleared away, Rosie and Gary went around each table to thank their guests individually for their attendance. They took their time, relishing the joy they encountered wherever they went in the room, and when they eventually made it back to the top table, the DJ was already preparing to set up for the evening.

Rosie was grinning as she sat down and Gary attributed her happiness to her new status as Mrs Lingfield. She leaned towards him, however, and asked a question that threw him.

"Did you notice what your Karen was drinking?"

Gary, already quite tipsy by this stage, looked confused. "Vodka and Coke?" he suggested.

"No," said Rosie. "It looked to me like tomato juice and Worcester sauce. Maybe with a splash of tabasco." Rosie laughed at the look of incomprehension in her husband's eyes. "I'll explain it to you later," she told him.

Hannah sat quietly at a table on her own and watched James make his way back from the bar. Her mind was in turmoil. Everything was suddenly in flux. Her life till now had been a clear and straightforward path, challenging, yes, but entirely worthwhile for the rewards that were promised. Now, though, all of her beliefs, all of her certainties, all of her truths were fading into an indistinct mist she found impossible to clarify. She no longer knew what to believe. What was true? What was real? She had no idea. She had nothing to hold onto that she could trust to be true. Nothing was certain.

No, she thought, that wasn't quite right. There was one thing that was certain. One thing that stood fixed. One thing that remained bright and clear in the haze. One thing that could not be denied and was making her head spin. She saw James, a drink in each hand, stop a few feet from the table to chat to someone Hannah didn't recognise. She watched a smile and an easy laugh light up James' face. The laughter only served to enhance the glittering pearlescence of those strange blue eyes. A loose strand of hair fell across his forehead.

Hannah began to feel unwell, queasy, claustrophobic as the walls around her closed in. She knew with absolute certainty that she had to get away from here. She needed to flee. To escape.

Jamesy broke off from his conversation to place a glass of wine in front of Hannah. She stared at it blankly. As Jamesy moved to sit down, Hannah stopped him with a stare of sudden intensity.

"Could you do me a favour, James?" she said.

"Of course, no problem."

"Could you phone me a taxi?"

Jamesy gave her a concerned look. He then nodded with a sigh. "Had enough, then?" he said. He was standing by the table with a pint in his hand. He put his free hand in his trouser pocket, fishing for some coins for the payphone in the hall. "Can't say I blame you, to be honest," he went on. "It is all a bit much. So, where should I say you're going? Back to your flat, or do you want to go straight on to Saintfield?"

"Neither," Hannah replied. Her voice was soft, like a razor blade. "I'm going back to *your* flat."

"*My* flat?" Jamesy looked puzzled. "But why would you –?" ... *you're a bright lad, Jamesy, but only up to a point* ... "Oh!" he exclaimed. "*Oh right!*" He slammed his drink onto the table, spilling some in his haste, and set off for the hallway. He stumbled over a stray handbag that lay on the floor between the tables and bumped into several people who were standing around chatting.

"Fuck's sake, Jamesy, sober up!" A voice called out.

"Sorry! Sorry!" Jamesy mumbled as he hurried past.

Hannah watched him rush headlong through the crowd before his silhouette disappeared into the bright rectangle of the doorway at the far end of the room. She then turned back to the table, picked up her wine and, raising the glass to her lips, took a long, slow sip.

The taxi-driver was apparently oblivious to the sexual electricity crackling in the back of his cab. He seemed to be more concerned about the fact that the Brits had sealed off the Springfield Road in West Belfast which was causing traffic chaos on the Lower Falls.

"Backed up all the way onto the Westlink," he was saying. "Course, you never see them closing off the bloody Shankill, do you? Oh no, that would never do, would it?"

Jamesy and Hannah nodded appropriately as the angry words washed over their silent urges for a speedy trip across town. Normally it would have taken little more than twenty minutes to reach Jamesy's flat, but the road closures and the Saturday shoppers had combined to make the journey an agonising crawl.

Eventually, after what seemed, for Jamesy and Hannah, an eternity, they arrived outside Jamesy's flat. They both moved quickly. Jamesy rummaged around in his pocket, before flinging a handful of crumpled banknotes at the startled taxi-driver as he and Hannah clambered out of the back seat. Their arms and their tongues were already entwined as they slammed as one into Jamesy's front door. After some frantic fumbling, Jamesy managed to find his key and they fell together through the hall and into the front room, scattering books and papers and clothes, and collapsing onto the sofa as they soared with hungry desperation towards the pinnacle of human experience.

Later, much later, Jamesy would have time to idly reflect on all the different ways we have of killing time. On all the little respites that we cling to along the way. On the stories that we tell and the songs that we sing. Of heroes and angels. Of demons and dragons and unicorns and elves. Of goddesses and gods. All fleeting, all nebulous, all going or gone.

But love – they now understood as they tumbled once more towards the summit – *love endures*.

EPILOGUE

Rough winds do shake the darling buds of May,
and summer's lease hath all too short a date.

William Shakespeare

11 September 2001
New York City

The little girl was entranced by the lilies. She stared up at the explosion of blooms arranged in an enormous spray that sat on top of a great plinth in the centre of the hotel atrium. Impatient that her mother was chatting at the reception desk in the lobby, she had wandered off and now found herself in the marbled hallway that led out, through a set of glass doors, to the noisy bustle of Park Avenue. The girl had enough sense not to venture any further, so she stood and admired the flowers as she waited for her mother to catch her up.

"Well, aren't you just adorable!" An elderly couple had come through the doors and the woman, grey-haired and heavy-set, gushed at the little girl.

"You're just a little cutie," she went on. "Isn't she, Brad?"

"Well, I'd say so," agreed Brad with a friendly smile. "Pretty as a picture!"

The little girl smiled politely as the couple fussed over her and she calmly answered their barrage of questions. What's your name, sweetie? And how old are you? I adore your accent, where is that from? So, where are you off to in such a darling little coat? The little girl replied to each inquiry with an assurance that sat oddly with her youth.

"There you are, you wee minx!" Claire exclaimed as she strolled out from the lobby, a look of mild admonishment on her face. "I've told you before about wandering off like that."

"Oh, she isn't doing any harm," the woman said, giving the little girl a conspiratorial wink. "She was just looking at the lilies, weren't you, honey?" She then turned to Claire. "They're quite something, don't you think?"

"They're gorgeous," Claire agreed. "I don't think I've ever so many lilies in one place before."

"I know," said the woman. "I just love the scent you get when you come through the doors."

"Have you been out already this morning?" Claire asked, looking at her watch. "It's very early."

"Oh yes indeed," the couple told her. "We do enjoy a good walk before breakfast, and it's such a lovely morning. Still a little on the chilly side, but you can tell it's going to be a glorious day. Are you and this little cutie heading out, then?"

"Yes, we're off to Greenwich Village," said Claire. "We're going to meet an old friend for breakfast. Aren't we, sweetheart?"

The little girl nodded enthusiastically. "He's a special envoy," she proudly told the couple.

"Oh my!" said Brad. "A special envoy! He sounds very important."

Claire laughed. "Oh, he's just an old friend we haven't seen for a while, isn't that right, Emily?"

Emily smiled in response and Claire looked back to the elderly couple. "It just turned out that we were going to be in New York at the same time, so it seemed like a good chance to catch up."

They continued chatting for a few moments more, with Emily gently tugging at Claire's hand, until the elderly couple took their leave and headed into the hotel. Claire and Emily stepped out onto Park Avenue and were briefly dazzled by the brightness of the morning. The deep blue of the sky suggested that summer was planning to hang around for a little while longer as Claire helped Emily into the back of a yellow cab and climbed in beside her. She gave instructions to the driver, and they eased into the busy traffic, heading downtown for breakfast in the Village and a reunion with an old friend.

The European Union's Special Envoy to the United Nations, known to his friends as Joker, was seated in a booth of the quaint, retro-styled diner that he had suggested for breakfast. He was sipping a coffee and reading a newspaper when he saw, through the window, Claire and Emily step from the cab and approach the entrance. He stood up to greet them.

"Joseph!" Emily called out when she came through the door. She ran to him and threw her arms around his legs.

"All right there, Trouble?" said Joker, patting her on the back. "What do you think of New York, then?"

"It's really good!" Emily enthused. "We went to the zoo."

"The zoo? And they let you out? I would have thought that –"

"Hiya, Joseph," said Claire, giving Joker a fond embrace and a peck on the cheek. "How have you been keeping?"

"Oh, not too bad, you know? What about yourself? Here, jump on in there," Joker motioned to the booth. "I'll get a couple of menus."

Claire and Emily made themselves comfortable and Joker stepped over to the counter. He came back with some menus and then slipped into the booth, facing mother and daughter across the table.

"So, do you think Tone will be able to make it?" he asked Claire.

"Hopefully," she replied. "Like I said on the phone, he's got an early meeting with his production company, but he doesn't think it'll take too long."

"Should we wait for him before we eat?"

"No, I'm starving."

"Makes two of us," said Joker. "And you're flying back this evening, is that right?"

"Yeah, it's all go at the minute. And what about you?" laughed Claire. "Special Envoy to the UN? Lah-di-dah!"

"Oh, it's just a temporary thing," said Joker. "I think they were just looking for somebody to insult the Zimbabwean delegation in their own language. Stand up to Mugabe, that sort of thing. Anyway, it's not me who's staying at the Waldorf Astoria, is it?"

Claire laughed again. "We got a really good deal on that," she said. "We were supposed to be staying at some place in Queens, but it was overbooked and the travel firm said they could put us up at the Waldorf for an extra twenty dollars."

A waitress, smiling and friendly, came over and took their order. When she'd gone, Joker reached into his briefcase and took out a child's colouring book and a box of crayons. He pushed them across the table towards Emily.

"Here you go, Kiddo," he said. "I thought you'd get bored with me and your auld ma here jabbering away."

Emily accepted the gifts eagerly. "Thank you!" she cried happily. Claire smiled indulgently at her daughter, then turned back to Joker.

"You didn't have to do that, Joseph," she said, "but it was a good idea."

"No problem."

The waitress returned with a pot of coffee. She poured a cup for Claire and refilled the cup that Joker held out. She walked back to the counter, set down the coffee pot and picked up a glass of orange juice which she then placed in front of Emily.

"There you go, Sugar," she said. Emily smiled a thank you.

"How's Chiaza keeping?" Claire asked Joker as the waitress departed.

"To be honest we don't get to see much of each other these days. She spends a lot of time in Nigeria working with that foundation that she's setting up with Benjamin and Zara."

"Oh yeah, how's that going?"

"It's going well, as far as I know. I'll know more about it the next time I see her, whenever that's likely to be."

"You're obviously keeping busy yourself."

"Yeah, well, that may not be –" The waitress returned with their order and began distributing plates of food around the table. When she'd gone, Joker frowned. "What was I saying?" he asked.

"Mmm, not sure," said Claire absent-mindedly, distracted by making sure Emily was settled with her breakfast. "You're keeping busy? Was that it?"

"Oh yeah!" Joker exclaimed. "I was just going to say that I might have to take some leave soon."

"Oh? Why's that, then?"

"Well, I heard from Jamesy the other day."

"Isn't he in Turkey?"

"No, he's back in England, doing some university lecture tour, I think."

"Oh, right. So, what did he have to say?"

"He sent me a text that just said, *It wasn't 40, it was AO*."

"AO?" asked Claire. "What does that mean?"

"Apparently AO," Joker told her, "stands for Ashmolean, Oxford."

"Ashmolean? The museum?"

"Yeah, it sounds like Jamesy's found his wee tablet."

Claire looked blankly at Joker. "And what's that got to do with you?" she asked.

"Don't you remember? I told him that if he ever found his tablet, I'd go with him to see if we could find the final resting place of Alexander the Great. Of course, I never believed in a million years he'd ever find it."

Claire was thoughtful as she chewed a mouthful of bacon. "Oh yeah, that's right," she said. "I remember that. Wasn't it somewhere in Iraq? You can't be thinking of going to Iraq, can you? Surely it's far too dangerous."

Joker shrugged. "I think the Middle East is fairly stable at the minute," he said. "Saddam's been keeping his head down since the war. I mean, he's still a bit of a nuisance as far as his own people are concerned, but he's always been keen to connect himself to Iraq's ancient past. You know, the glory of Babylon, and all that? So I think he'd jump at the chance to have an important archaeological expedition on his doorstep."

"Wouldn't he try to use it for propaganda, though?"

"Of course he would," said Joker, "but that's hardly going to stop Jamesy, is it? Jamesy's never been one for the subtleties of international politics. Well, not contemporary politics, anyway."

"No, I suppose not." Claire began fussing over Emily who had dropped some food in her lap.

"Is James coming?" asked Emily. "And Hannah?"

"No, love," Claire told her, "but they're back in England, so we might be able to see them when we get back to London." Emily scrunched up her face in a manner that suggested a variety of responses.

"Anyway," Joker continued, "it might do me good to take a bit of a break. And I've always been curious to see what Jamesy gets up to on these digs of his."

"Well, good luck with that," said Claire. "Rather you than me."

Tone stood looking out at Manhattan stretching away into the distance. The morning was bright and clear, and from his vantage point high up in the North Tower of the World Trade Center he fancied he could make out the hills of Connecticut, far to the north.

"How did you manage to land an office like this, then?" he asked without taking his gaze from the view.

The woman seated behind the curved mahogany desk did not look up from the pile of papers in front of her. "What the hell do you mean by that, you cheeky so-and-so?" she replied as she read. "I work damn hard at my job!" She turned to face Tone. "As well you know, Buster!"

Tone, grinning, turned away from the window and went to sit in the spacious sofa that sat in the middle of the office. "Just kidding, Stella," he said. "You deserve it, of course."

"And don't you forget it!" Stella took off her glasses and rubbed the bridge of her nose. "Well," she said, "I think that's everything." She placed her glasses on top of the papers and looked over at Tone. "So, you're flying back today, is that right?"

"Yeah, I've arranged to have breakfast in Greenwich Village, but I've got a flight booked for this evening."

"And what about Matt? Is he still in town?"

"No, he flew out to the West Coast on Saturday. Him and Seamus."

"Would that have anything to do with a possible movie deal I keep hearing about?"

"I can't say," said Tone. He then spread his hands in response to Stella's raised eyebrows. "Really, Stella, I can't say. I've heard the same rumours that you have, but Matt hasn't mentioned it. Anyway, a movie deal wouldn't exactly hurt our ticket sales, now would it."

"Of course not," agreed Stella. "And, to be honest, those rumours were probably why I was able to get backing so quickly."

Tone looked thoughtfully at Stella. "Don't you think *The Congregation* would have got backing based on its own merits, then?"

"Oh sure, Tony," said Stella, leaning back in her chair. "It may have just taken a little longer, that's all. Now, you've been lucky these last few years, and –"

"Lucky?"

Stella fixed Tone with a hard stare. "Yes, Tony," she said. "Lucky! Broadway investors can be a conservative bunch. They prefer to stick with a proven formula, something they feel will be a guaranteed success."

"Yeah, but –"

"Oh sure, you had a big hit in London," Stella went on, "but that's a very different crowd. Pitching a musical about religion to a US audience was always going to be a hard sell." Stella folded her arms across her chest. "To be honest, even I had my doubts, and I'm not at all religious."

"You're not?"

"No, I'm Jewish." Stella and Tone both laughed.

"Still," said Tone, "it isn't really critical of Christianity, is it?"

"I wouldn't know. Like I said, I'm Jewish. But for most Americans it's always going to be a touchy subject." Stella leaned forward, putting her elbows on the desk. "How would you describe it, then, Tony? If you say it isn't critical?"

Tone shrugged. "More of an affectionate parody, I'd say."

"Mmm," Stella murmured unconvinced. She moved her glasses onto the desktop and began shuffling the papers into a neat pile. "That's a fine line, isn't it?"

"Not at all," Tone insisted. "In fact, I've had a few arguments with Matt about it. I wanted the script to be a lot more abrasive, you know? More antagonistic, but Matt wouldn't have it."

"Good for Matt." Stella suddenly leaned forward again and gave Tone a curious look. "Yeah, Tony," she said, "I've always thought you've got some anger issues when it comes to religion."

"Anger issues? That's a very American way of –"

"What would *you* call it, then?"

"I'd call it a rational understanding," said Tone.

Stella burst out laughing. "Sure, Tony," she said. "Rational! Yeah, right!"

Tone stared at Stella, then sadly shook his head. "Yeah," he said, "most people don't even bother to think about it."

"I just don't get what your problem is, Tony," said Stella, amused. "What would you do, then? Ban religion?"

"Of course not! It's religions that go around banning stuff."

"What's the problem, then?" asked Stella. "Is it God you have an issue with?"

Tone leaned back and sighed. "Gods are irrelevant," he said. "A god is nothing more than a MacGuffin. A plot device. An easy way for people to endorse their prejudices." He turned to face Stella. "People have played the god card throughout history to justify everything from misogyny and xenophobia to slavery and genocide. Gods are just extensions of personal agenda."

Stella placed her elbows on the desk and rested her chin on her interlocking fingers. She smiled at Tone's sudden passion. "No anger issues there, then," she teased.

Tone simply shrugged and gave her a rueful smile.

"So, what's your answer, then, Tony?" asked Stella. "You've obviously given it some thought."

"Oh, I don't know," Tone said, getting up from the sofa with a weary sigh. "I'd just like to think that one day we'll be able to grow as a species, and then maybe we can put away our childish things."

"Yeah, that's real cute, Tony," said Stella, "but I still think you're making a fuss over nothing."

"Maybe," said Tone. He walked over to the door of the office and put his hand on the handle before turning back to Stella. "But I do think that one day we're going to have to let go of our old superstitions, otherwise we might as well just stop the race altogether."

"What?" Stella barked. "What the hell are you talking about, Tony? What race?"

"Why the human race, my dear!" said Tone as he backed through the doorway with a theatrical bow. "*The human race!*"

AUTHOR'S NOTES

CRAWL

Crawl is set at the end of the 1980s, and all the bars mentioned in the story did exist at that time. Most – like the Crown and Kelly's Cellars – are still around today but, sadly, the Tudor Lounge is long gone. The building, though, still stands, in Fountain Street, and, at the time of writing, in 2022, is called Voodoo, a live music venue providing an outlet for a particular genre, of which Tone, I feel, would have approved.

Kelly's Cellars, built in the early eighteenth century, was indeed, in 1989, huddled within a narrow alley that, due to the tall buildings on either side, received little sunlight. The area has since changed considerably, with Kelly's now sitting proudly on one side of an open public space, and, despite a few precarious moments when it looked like it might have been lost, the 'stubborn little bar' is still going strong.

The Crown Liquor Saloon in Great Victoria Street is justly famous as a perfect example of a Victorian Gin Palace, with ornate interiors created by Italian craftsmen, moonlighting from their day jobs working on some of Belfast's new churches, and is still, I believe, refusing to be seduced by Thomas Edison's new-fangled electric light bulbs.

White's Tavern, dating from 1630, is the oldest bar mentioned in *Crawl*, and, in fact, the oldest bar in Belfast. Situated in one of Belfast's 'entries' – Winecellar Entry – it has been refurbished many times over the years, but still manages to maintain that deep sense of age the centuries have bestowed.

The bars of Belfast are far too numerous to be included here, with many new venues coming and going in a constantly changing environment. The city itself is now unrecognisable from the troubled days of the seventies and eighties, and is now a vibrant, modern metropolis with a growing reputation as something of a party town. History, of course, is still being written, but I would like to think that, whatever the future may bring, Belfast will always be an ideal place for friends to meet for a laugh and a chat. And to go on a pub crawl.

RISE

For anyone wishing to know more about the conflict in Nigeria in the 1960s, then a good place to start would be *The Biafra Story,* by Frederick Forsyth. This is a first-hand account of Forsyth's time working as a journalist in the region, and delivers a detailed, if harrowing, report on the tragedy that was unfolding before him.

Though the novel makes reference to a few historical figures – such as Gowon and Ojukwu – all other characters in the story are fictional. Apart from one.

Louis 'Paddy' Malrooney was an Irishman who fought with the 4th Biafra Commando Brigade under the command of German-born Rolf Steiner. The 4th Commando Brigade seems to have had more than its fair share of colourful characters, including a Welsh major by the name of David 'Taffy' Williams and a Jamaican bartender who went by the unlikely name of Johnny Korea.

I did have some misgivings about throwing yet another stereotypical, drunken Irishman into the mix, but when I learned that Malrooney was often seen heading into battle with a rifle in one hand and a bottle of wine in the other, I felt it was too good an opportunity to waste.

Why Nigeria? you may be asking, and I'm not sure if I can give a satisfactory answer. I can only say that I needed a background for Carol, and, as I was intending to touch lightly on the topic of race in the third book, I wanted that background to be African. The Nigeria/Biafra conflict just happened to fit the timeframe, and, as I had recently finished reading *Half of a Yellow Sun* by Chimamanda Ngozi Adichie, it felt like Biafra would be a natural setting for Carol's early childhood.

Butlin's at Mosney was a popular holiday destination from the late forties onward - becoming simply Mosney Holiday Centre in 1982 - and attracted many families from across the border in Northern Ireland who were happy to escape, if only for a week or two, the tense routine of life back home.

As time passed, however, the concept of the holiday camp fell out of fashion, and the site eventually became a holding centre for migrants seeking asylum in the Irish Republic.

Childhood memories, though, of happy summers spent at Mosney, still make many an old heart in Ireland smile.

RACE

For the record, I never wanted to go to Babylon, but, needing suitable employment for Joker's wayward brain, I was forced to delve into ancient history for a challenge that could be deemed necessarily obscure.

Although it is true that Alexander, during his time in Egypt, visited the oracle at Siwa, there is no record of him ever having received a mysterious amulet that could rewrite history. But, then again, there is no record of him *not* having received it. So, make of that what you will.

The Ishtar Gate, mentioned briefly in the text, can be viewed today. The imposing structure was excavated in the early twentieth century by

German archaeologists, and is on display in the Pergamon Museum in Berlin. There are many in Iraq, however, who would prefer it if the Germans could put it back where they found it.

So the story ends. At least, this particular story ends. The world, of course, still turns and there will always be other stories waiting to emerge.

Whether one such story, though, concerning a bunch of drunken, middle-aged halfwits, bumbling around an ancient desert in search of a stolen king, will ever be told, remains to be seen.

ABOUT THE AUTHOR

John McCormick was born in Belfast in 1966 and lived in that city during the period that became known as The Troubles. He now lives in the south of England with his wife, Mandy.

As soon as John McCormick left Northern Ireland at the end of the 1990s, peace was declared.

Printed in Great Britain
by Amazon

35930004R00360